John Dos Passos was born in Chicago in 1896, thus becoming a member of the extraordinary literary generation that also produced F. Scott Fitzgerald and Ernest Hemingway. His father was a noted lawyer of Portuguese descent, his mother was of distinguished Southern lineage. After graduating from Harvard in 1916, Dos Passos served as an ambulance driver and medical corpsman in Europe in World War I, traveled the world widely, and first won fame with *Three Soldiers* in 1921. *Manhattan Transfer* (1925) marked a further advance, and in 1930 *The 42nd Parallel,* the first volume of his *U.S.A.* trilogy, placed him among the century's major novelists. *Nineteen Nineteen* (1932) and *The Big Money* (1936) completed what was immediately recognized as an American classic. His subsequent novels have included the *District of Columbia* trilogy —*Chosen Country, The Great Days,* and *Midcentury* —as well as several notable works on American history and the recent autobiographical *The Best Times*. When not traveling, Mr. Dos Passos lives and works at his ancestral home in Virginia.

John Dos Passos

THE BIG MONEY

THIRD IN THE TRILOGY *U.S.A.*

Illustrated by REGINALD MARSH
With an Introduction by ALFRED KAZIN

With an Updated Bibliography

A SIGNET CLASSIC

SIGNET CLASSIC
Published by the Penguin Group
Penguin Books USA Inc., 375 Hudson Street,
New York, New York 10014, U.S.A.
Penguin Books Ltd, 27 Wrights Lane,
London W8 5TZ, England
Penguin Books Australia Ltd, Ringwood,
Victoria, Australia
Penguin Books Canada Ltd, 10 Alcorn Avenue,
Toronto, Ontario, Canada M4V 3B2
Penguin Books (N.Z.) Ltd, 182–190 Wairau Road,
Auckland 10, New Zealand

Penguin Books Ltd, Registered Offices:
Harmondsworth, Middlesex, England

Published by Signet Classic, an imprint of Dutton Signet,
a division of Penguin Books USA Inc.

This is an authorized reprint of a hardcover edition published by Houghton Mifflin
Company.

First Signet Classic Printing, March, 1969
20 19 18 17

REGISTERED TRADEMARK—MARCA REGISTRADA

Printed in the United States of America

Introduction

John O'Hara once said that the development of the United States in the first half of the twentieth century is the greatest possible subject for a novelist. He left the implication that anyone lucky enough to have been part of this change, to have made the subject his own, had an advantage over the younger novelists who since 1945 have taken American power for granted and have missed the drama of its emergence.

Whatever else may be said of this proposition, or of the gifted but now "old-fashioned" and resentful novelist who made it, it is a fact that this faith in subject matter as the novelist's secret strength, especially in the "big change" as the greatest of social facts, does characterize the novelists born around the turn of the century—writers otherwise so unlike each other as John O'Hara and John Dos Passos. This faith also distinguishes them from those younger writers like Saul Bellow, Ralph Ellison, Norman Mailer, Flannery O'Connor, who grew up in depression or war, and have never thought the United States to be as unique in world history as Americans used to think it was in 1917. The younger writers have been impressed by America's resemblance to old-world powers, not by the legends of America's special destiny. History, as they see it, sooner or later becomes everywhere the same. And all history is essentially obscure and problematical, in some ways too unreal ever to be fully understood by the individual novelist, who will not feel that *he* can depend on "history" to hold him up, to supply him with material, to infuse him with the vitality that only confidence in one's subject can.

Henry James said that the "novelist succeeds to the sacred office of the historian." The old faith that "history" exists objectively, that it has an ascertainable order, that it is what the novelist most depends on and appeals to, that "history" even supplies the *structure* of the novel—this is what distinguishes the extraordinary invention that is Dos Passos' *U.S.A.* from most novels published since 1940. And it is surely because "history" as order—to say nothing of "history" as something to believe in!—comes so hard to younger writers, and readers, that Dos Passos has been a relatively neglected writer in recent years.

It is often assumed that Dos Passos was a "left-wing" novelist in the thirties who, like other novelists of the period, turned conservative and thus changed and lost his creative identity. *U.S.A.* is certainly the peak of his career and the three novels that make it up were all published in the thirties —*The 42nd Parallel* in 1930, *1919* in 1932, *The Big Money* in 1936. But the trilogy is not simply a "left-wing" novel, and its technical inventiveness and the freshness of its style are typical of the twenties rather than the thirties. In any event, Dos Passos has always been so detached from all group thinking that it is impossible to understand his development as a novelist by identifying him with the radical novelists of the thirties. He began earlier, he has never been a Marxist, and in all periods he has followed his own perky, obstinately independent course. Whatever may be said of Dos Passos' political associations and ideas in recent years, it can be maintained that while some (by no means all) of his values have changed, it is not his values but the loss by many educated people of a belief in "history" that has caused Dos Passos' relative isolation in recent years.

Dos Passos was born in Chicago in 1896, graduated from Harvard in 1916, and served as an ambulance driver in France and Italy before joining the American army. None of the other writers associated with the "lost generation"—not Hemingway or Fitzgerald or Cummings, though they were all close friends—had the passion for history, for retracing history's creative moments, that Dos Passos has shown in his many nonfiction studies of American history as well as in *U. S. A.* Alone among his literary cronies, Dos Passos managed to add this idea of history as the great operative force to their enthusiasm for radical technique, the language of Joyce, and "the religion of the word." Dos Passos shared this cult of art, and *U.S.A.* grew out of it as much as it did out of his sense of American history as the greatest drama of modern times. But neither Fitzgerald, Cummings nor Hemingway ever had Dos Passos' interest in the average man as a subject for fiction.

Most oddly for someone with his "esthetic" concerns, Dos Passos was sympathetic to the long tradition of American radical dissent, and he has always been hostile to political dogma and orthodoxy. *The 42nd Parallel* opens with the story of Mac, a typically rootless Wobbly and "working-class stiff" of the golden age of American socialism before 1917; *The Big Money* ends on the struggles of Mary French (and John Dos Passos) to save Sacco and Vanzetti in 1927. To round out his trilogy when it was finally published in a single volume, Dos Passos added, as preface and epilogue, his sketches of a young man, hungry and alone, walking the highways. "Vag," the American vagrant, is Dos Passos' expression of his life-long fascination with the alienated, the outsider, the beaten, the dissenter: the lost and forgotten in American history. Mac, the American Wobbly and drifter at the beginning of *U.S.A.*, is as much an expression of what has been sacrificed to American progress as Mary French, the middle-class Communist, is at the end of the book. These solitaries, along with the young man endlessly walking America, frame this enormous chronicle of disillusionment with the American promise much as the saints in a medieval painting frame the agony on the cross. The loner in America interested Dos Passos long before he became interested in the American as protester. And despite Dos Passos' disenchantment since the thirties with the radical-as-ideologist, the Communist-as-policeman (at the end of *The Big Money* lonely Mary French identifies herself with a Stalinist orthodoxy to which she will inevitably fall victim), Dos Passos is still fascinated, as witness his books on the Jeffersonian tradition, with the true dissenter, whether he is alone in the White House or on the highway.

It is in his long attraction to figures who somehow illustrate some power for historic perspective (no matter what solitude this may bring) that we can see Dos Passos' particular artistic imperatives. The detachment behind this is very characteristic of those American writers from the upper class, born on the eve of our century—Hemingway, Cummings, Edmund Wilson—whose childhoods were distinctly sheltered and protected, who grew up in stable families where the fathers were ministers (Cummings), lawyers (Wilson), doctors (Hemingway), the mothers the conscious transmitters of the American Puritan tradition in all the old certainty that Americans were more virtuous than other peoples.

To these writers of the "lost generation," brought up in what is now thought of as the last stable period in American history—before America became a world empire—"Mr. Wilson's War," as Dos Passos calls it in his recent book on this central episode in the life of his generation, came as an explosion of the old isolationism and the old provincial self-righteousness. "Mr. Wilson's War" tied America to Europe in a way that was to be stimulating at the time to Dos Passos,

Hemingway and Cummings, but it destroyed their image of America. "Mr. Wilson," the very embodiment of Puritan American high-mindedness and didacticism, managed by "his war" to rob America of its good conscience. From now on the old familiar identification of America with righteousness was a subject for the history books. It was the writers—and some political dissenters—who were the new elect and keepers of the American conscience. "Mr. Wilson's War," from *their* point of view, was a moral cheat and a political catastrophe; as they saw it, it would soon give free rein to the speculators, financiers, and other "rugged individualists" whose unbridled greed was a dangerous American tradition that only men of intellectual principle had ever kept in check. But the writers who went to war (symbolically as ambulance drivers) found in Europe the same detachment from American money-making that they had found in their sheltered childhoods in professional families—plus a passion for the new language of twentieth-century painting and literature. Dos Passos and his friends would yet create something human out of so much destruction.

To these gifts and postures of detachment, natural to creative individualists, Dos Passos brought family circumstances that were certainly distinctive among those members of his social class who also graduated from Choate, Harvard, and the very select Norton-Harjes Volunteer Ambulance Service. The novelist's full name is John Roderigo Dos Passos; his paternal grandfather emigrated to the United States from the Portuguese island of Madeira. The novelist's father, John Randolph Dos Passos, was born in 1844, fought in the Civil War (he was at the Battle of Antietam), and became one of the most famous corporation lawyers of his time, an authority on the law of the stock market (he wrote a famous legal text on the subject). He was a deep-dyed Republican stalwart when this really meant something, in the age of McKinley. He was fifty-two years old when his son was born in Chicago to Lucy Addison Sprigg, who was of an old Maryland and Virginia family. The novelist's complex attitude toward American society may have one source in this complicated heritage. Another source was probably the distant yet flamboyant presence of Dos Passos *père*, who by all accounts was a man of very great abilities and a pillar of Wall Street, but was not a Sunday school type when it came to women. Both the exotic name and the sexual scandal in the background of Dos Passos' family history possibly explain why the autobiographical "Camera Eye" sections of *U.S.A.* dealing with childhood and early youth are deliberately evasive as well as blurred in the style of

Joyce's *A Portrait of the Artist as a Young Man*. The impressionistic style which is Dos Passos' general inspiration enables him to field certain family embarrassments. The perhaps deliberate murkiness of these early "Camera Eye" sections is in striking contrast with the later autobiographical chronicle and the bristlingly clear prose of the "biographies" of famous Americans and the narrative sections proper.

Dos Passos was clearly brought up with the immense reserve of the upper classes in America, and readers encountering him are usually amazed by the contrast between the fluent fast prose he writes and the extraordinarily shy, tight, embarrassed self he shows to strangers. It may be that the concentrated sensitivity of his public personality helps to explain the "streamlined" and even gimmicky side of his famous book; the sensibility that conceived *U.S.A.* is obviously complicated enough to have produced this complicated division into "Camera Eye," "newsreel," "biography," and narrative sections. This structure is surely, among other things, a way of objectifying one vulnerable individual's experience to the uttermost, of turning even the individual life into a facet of history. The hardness behind *U.S.A.* is an idea, not a feeling; it is an esthetic proposition about style in relation to the contemporary world; Dos Passos carries it off brilliantly, but it always remains distinctly *willed*. Malcolm Cowley once pointed out that Dos Passos' college years were those of the "Harvard esthetes." He learned to think of experience as separable into softish dreams and hard realities, of a world coming down on subjectivities of the poet, thus leading him doggedly to train his "camera" on an external world conceived of as a distant *object*—necessarily separable from man's hopes for unity with his surroundings.

The creed behind Dos Passos' first novels—*One Man's Initiation,* (1919),* *Three Soldiers* (1921), *Manhattan Transfer* (1925)—was learned at college and at war, supported by his "esthetic" training and his experiences as an ambulance driver and medical corpsman. The modern world is ugly, hopelessly corrupt, and is to be met not by love or social protest, but by "art." For the writers of the "lost generation," "art" was the highest possible resistance to the "swindle" of the social world and the ultimate proof of one's aristocratic individualism in the modern mass world. Art was the *nuova scienza,* the true science of the new period, the only possible new language—it would capture the discontinuities of the modern world and use for itself the violent motions and radical new energies of the post-war period. The new language was to be modeled on

---

* Republished in 1946 as *First Encounter.*

painting, sculpture, architecture—the arts that alone could do justice to the transformation of space. Dos Passos first went to Europe to study architecture in Spain, and drawing has been his "second" art; he has illustrated some of his early travel books. He saw Europe even in wartime as the unique treasure house of architecture and painting. His obvious imitation of the impressionistic word-ties of Joyce (and perhaps Cummings as well, another painter among writers) was surely motivated by the plastic sense of composition among those writers, like the Futurists, who admired the new technology, the twentieth-century feeling for speed. Dos Passos is actually one of the few American writers of his generation who has been inspired by the industrial landscape and he sought to duplicate some of its forms in *U.S.A.* He has taken from technology the rhythms, images, and above all the headlong energy that would express the complexity of the human environment in the twentieth century.

Dos Passos' first novels no longer have much interest for us today, for they are too moody, self-dramatizingly "sensitive," and marked by the romantic despair that is the individual's conscious sacrifice of his hopes to the world of war, modern plutocracy, the inhuman big city. But with *The 42nd Parallel* (which, coming out in 1930, is of course not a book of the thirties but of the individualistic twenties), one is struck above all by the sharp, confident, radical new *tone* with which Dos Passos gets his singularly new kind of narrative under way. The novel opens with the "newsreel" flashing before us the popular songs, headlines, and the national excitement as the twentieth century opens. Behind his "Camera Eye," Dos Passos first remembers himself as a boy with his mother in Europe, escaping a hostile pro-Boer crowd that thinks them English. The first character in the book is "Mac," Fenian O'Hara McCreary from Middletown, Connecticut, who will devote his restless, baffled life to the "movement." The first biography of an important maker and shaper of the new century is of Eugene V. Debs.

The material from the first is that of labor struggles, imperialism, socialism, war—and the personal sense of futility that expresses itself in whoring, violent drinking, and the aimless moving on of Americans that conveys the prodigality of our continent. With Mac, we start at the bottom of the social pyramid, among the Wobblies, "Reds," militant "working-class stiffs" who will be central to the whole long trilogy because "socialism" has been the great twentieth-century issue, even in America; the radicals in the book seal its meanings like a Greek chorus. These radicals, though they fail like everybody else, are a judgment on the profit system whose business is business, whose most dramatic form of intelligence is money making, and whose violent competitiveness always leads to war. But though Dos Passos' sympathies, at least in *The 42nd Parallel,* are clearly with radicals who are off the main track, he does not particularly respect them. It is inventors, scientists, intellectuals of the highest creative ability, statesmen of rare moral courage who are his heroes. There are no such figures among the characters of the novel; even among the biographies we see the type only in Steinmetz, General Electric's "Socialist" wizard. For the same reason, the tonic edge of the book, its stylistic dash and irony, its gay inventiveness, are the greatest possible homage to art as a new kind of "practicality" in getting down the facts of human existence in our century.

What Dos Passos created with *The 42nd Parallel* was in fact another American invention—an American *thing* peculiar to the opportunity and stress of American life, like the Wright Brothers' airplane, Edison's phonograph, Luther Burbank's hybrids, Thorstein Veblen's social analysis, Frank Lloyd Wright's first office buildings. (All these fellow inventors are celebrated in *U.S.A.*) *The 42nd Parallel* is an artwork. But we soon recognize that Dos Passos' contraption, his new kind of novel, is in fact (reminding us of Frank Lloyd Wright's self-dramatizing Guggenheim Museum) *the greatest character in the book itself.* Our primary pleasure in reading *The 42nd Parallel* is in being surprised, delighted, and provoked by the "scheme," by Dos Passos' shifting "strategy." We recognize that the exciting presence in *The 42nd Parallel* is the book itself, which is always getting us to anticipate some happy new audacity. A mobile by Alexander Calder or a furious mural design by Jackson Pollock makes us dwell on the specific originality of the artist, the most dramatic thing about the work itself. So *The 42nd Parallel* becomes a book about writing *The 42nd Parallel.* That is the tradition of the romantic poet, and reading him we are on every side surrounded by Dos Passos himself: his "idea."

The technical interest of *The 42nd Parallel* was indeed so great for its time that Jean-Paul Sartre, whose restless search for what is "authentic" to our time makes him a prophetic critic, said in 1938: "Dos Passos has invented only one thing, an art of story-telling. But that is enough. . . . I regard Dos Passos as the greatest writer of our time." Thirty years later, that tribute will surprise even the most loyal admirers of *U.S.A.,* for Dos Passos has been more involved in recent years with social and intellectual history than with the art of the novel. Yet he has so absorbed what he invented for

U.S.A. that even his nonfiction books display the flat, clipped, peculiarly rushing style that at his worst is tabloid journalism but at his best a documentary prose with the freshness of free verse. When we look away from his recent books and come back to *The 42nd Parallel*, however, we can see the real ingenuity that went into it. Though the trilogy gets better and stronger as it goes along, this first volume shows what a remarkable tool Dos Passos has invented for evoking the simultaneous actualities of existence.

The 42nd Parallel opens in 1900. It follows Mac the "working-class stiff" as he constantly moves about, recites the biographies of Debs, Luther Burbank, Big Bill Haywood, William Jennings Bryan, Minor Keith of the United Fruit Company, and ends with Charley Anderson the garage mechanic from North Dakota going overseas. (Charley will come back in *The Big Money* an airplane ace and inventor.) The other main characters are Janey Williams, who will become private secretary to J. Ward Moorehouse, the rising man in the rising public relations industry; Eleanor Stoddard, the interior decorator who will become Moorehouse's prime confidante; Eleanor's friend Eveline Hutchins, who is not as frigid and superior as Eleanor (and tired of too many love affairs and too many parties, will commit suicide at the end of *The Big Money*).

The important point about J. Ward Moorehouse's racket, public relations, and Eleanor Stoddard's racket, interior decorating, is that both are new, responsive to big corporations and new money, and are synthetic. J. Ward Moorehouse and Eleanor Stoddard are in fact artificial people, always on stage, who correspondingly suffer from a lack of reality and of human affection. But on the other side of the broad American picture, Mac the professional agitator has no more direction in his life; marriage to a thoroughly conventional girl in San Diego becomes intolerable to him, but as he roams his way across the country, finally ending up in Mexico just as the revolution begins, he is at the mercy of every new "comrade" and every new pickup. The only direction in his life seems to be his symbolic presence wherever the "action" is— he is in Goldfield, Nevada, when the miners go on strike under the leadership of Big Bill Haywood, and he is in Mexico because the Mexican Revolution is taking place.

With the same "representative" quality, J. Ward Moorehouse rises in the public relations "game" in order to show its relation to big business and big government, while Eleanor Stoddard's dabbling in the "little theater" movement represents the artiness of the newly "modern" period just before World War I. History in the most tangible sense—what happened—is obviously more important in Dos Passos' scheme than whom things happened to. The matter of the books is always the representative happening and person, the historical moment illustrated in its catchwords, its songs, its influences; above all, in its speech. What Dos Passos wants to capture more than anything else is the echo of what people were actually saying, exactly in the style in which anyone might have said it. The artistic aim of his book, one may say, is to represent the litany, the tone, the issue of the time in the voice of the time, the banality, the cliche that finally brings home to us the voice in the crowd: the voice of mass opinion. The voice that might be anyone's voice brings home to us, as only so powerful a reduction of the many to the one ever can, the vibrating resemblances that make history. In the flush of Wilson's New Freedom, 1913, Jerry Burnham the professional cynic says to Janey Williams—"I think there's a chance we may get back to being a democracy." Mac and his comrades are always talking about "forming the structure of a new society within the shell of the old." Janey Williams' "Popper" notes—"I don't trust girls nowadays with these here ankle-length skirts and all that." Eveline Hutchins, who will find life too dreary, thinks early in the book, "Maybe she'd been wrong from the start to want everything so justright and beautiful." Charley Anderson, leaving the sticks, thinks—"To hell with all that, I want to see some country."

Yet more important than the sayings, which make *U.S.A.* a compendium of American quotations, is the way in which Dos Passos the objective narrator gets popular rhythms, repetitions, and stock phrases into his running description of people. Terse and external as his narrative style is, it is cunningly made up of all the different speech styles of the people he is writing about. This is the "poetry" behind the book that makes the "history" in it live. The section on J. Ward Moorehouse begins—

He was born in Wilmington, Delaware, on the Fourth of July. Poor Mrs. Moorehouse could hear the firecrackers popping and crackling outside the hospital all through her labor pains. And when she came to a little and they brought the baby to her she asked the nurse in a trembling husky whisper if she thought it could have a bad effect on the baby all that noise, prenatal influence you know.

Moorehouse will always be a parody of the American big shot—all "front"; so this representative figure is born on the Fourth of July. Later in the book, when Eleanor Stoddard's "beautiful friendship" with Moorehouse helps to send Mrs. Moorehouse into a decline, we see all that is chic, proud and angry in Eleanor concentrated into this description.

She got into a taxi and went up to the Pennsylvania Station. It was a premature Spring day. People were walking along the street with their overcoats unbuttoned. The sky was a soft mauve with frail clouds like milkweed floss. In the smell of furs and overcoats and exhausts and bundledup bodies came an unexpected scent of birchbark. Eleanor sat bolt upright in the back of the taxi driving her sharp nails into the palms of her graygloved hands. She hated these treacherous days when winter felt like Spring. They made the lines come out on her face, made everything seem to crumble about her, there seemed to be no firm footing any more.

1919, the second volume of the trilogy, is sharper than *The 42nd Parallel*. The obscenity of *the* war, "Mr. Wilson's War," is Dos Passos' theme, and since this war is the most important political event of the century, he rises to his theme with a brilliance that does not conceal the fury behind it. But it is also clear from the greater assurance of the text that Dos Passos has mastered the special stylistic demands of his experiment, that his contraption is running better with practice. So, apart from the book's unforgettably ironic vibrations as a picture of waste, hypocrisy, debauchery, *1919* shows, as a good poem does, how much more a writer can accomplish by growing into his style. History now is not merely a happening but a bloody farce, is unspeakably wrong, is a complete abandoning of all the hopes associated with the beginning of the century. This is equally true for fictional characters like Joe Williams, Janey's brother, who will be dropped from one ship to another like a piece of cargo, and will eventually be killed in a barroom brawl on Armistice Day; historic personages like the writer and anti-war rebel Randolph Bourne, who died a pariah in 1918, and Paxton Hibben, "A Hoosier Quixote," who sided with the Russian Revolution when he represented the United States abroad. Wesley Everest, whose life is told as a biography under the title "Paul Bunyan," was a Wobbly leader who was castrated and lynched by a mob of businessmen in Centralia, Washington, in 1919. The fictional characters and the historic figures are equally the casualties of war. Just as Dos Passos' own creations are representative Americans, so the historic figures whom he has selected for his biographies become myths in the collective imagination of American history. One of the most brilliant things about Dos

Passos' trilogy is the way in which the fictional and the historic characters come together on the same plane. One character in the book is both "fictional" and "historic": The Unknown Soldier. He is fictional because no one knows who *he* is; yet he was an actual soldier—picked at random from so many other dead soliders. The symbolic corpse has become for Dos Passos the representative American, and his interment in Arlington Cemetery Dos Passos blazingly records in "The Body Of An American," the prose poem that ends *1919* and is the most brilliant single piece of writing in the trilogy:

> they took to Châlons-sur-Marne
> and laid it out neat in a pine coffin
> and took it home to God's Country on a battleship
> and buried it in a sarcophagus in the Memorial
> Amphitheater in the Arlington National Cemetery
> and draped the Old Glory over it
> and the bugler played taps

* * *

Woodrow Wilson brought a bouquet of poppies.

But on the other side of the representative American picture are those who made a good thing of war, like Theodore Roosevelt, "the happy warrior" who loved war and became Governor of New York by riding up San Juan Hill; J. P. Morgan,

> Wars and panics on the stock exchange,
> machinegun fire and arson,
> bankruptcies, warloans,
> starvation, lice, cholera and typhus:
> good growing weather for the House of Morgan;

"Meester Veelson," who despite his premonitions took the country into war; Richard Ellsworth Savage, who went back on his early idealism and profited from the corruption that war had encouraged.

What invests *1919* beyond all else is the contrast of the official and popular idealism with hysterical hedonism of young gentlemen in the ambulance service. Ed Schuyler keeps saying, "Fellers, this ain't a war. It's a goddam whorehouse." The echoes of speech are now our last ties with the doomed. This monument to a whole generation sacrificed is built up out of those mythic quotations and slogans that make up the book in its shattering mimicry. "In Paris they were still haggling over the price of blood, squabbling over toy flags, the river-frontiers on relief maps"; "tarpaper barracks that stank of carbolic"; "the juggling mudspattered faces of the young French soldiers going up for the attack, drunk and desperate, and yelling *à bas la guerre, mort au vaches, à bas la guerre*"; "an establishment where they could *faire rigazig, une maison propre, convenable, et de haute moralité*"; "Did Meester Veelson know that in the peasants' wargrimed houses along the Brenta and the Piave they were burning candles in front of his picture cut out of the illustrated papers."

The Versailles Peace Conference is cut to the style of Dos Passos' generation—"Three old men shuffling the pack, dealing out the cards."

Woodrow Wilson is caught forever when he says in Rome —". . . it is the greatest pride of Americans to have demonstrated the immense love of humanity which they bear in their hearts." But this mimicry is brought to a final pitch of brilliant indignation in the person of the Unknown Soldier, who *is* anybody and everybody. In "The Body Of An American" we see that Dos Passos' book is not so much a novel of a few lives as an epic of democracy. Like other famous American books about democracy—*Representative Men, Leaves of Grass, Moby Dick*—its subject is that dearest of all American myths, the average man. But unlike these great romantic texts of what Whitehead called "the century of hope," *U.S.A.* does not raise the average man to hero. Dos Passos' subject is indeed democracy, but his belief—especially as he goes into the final volume of his trilogy, *The Big Money*—is that the force of circumstances that is twentieth-century life is too strong for the average man, who will probably never rise above mass culture, mass superstition, mass slogans.

The only heroes of *The Big Money* are in the "biographies" —Thorstein Veblen, who drank the "bitter drink" for analyzing predatory American society to its roots; the Wright Brothers, because

the fact remains
that a couple of young bicycle mechanics from Dayton, Ohio
had designed constructed and flown
for the first time ever a practical airplane

and the super-individualist architect, Frank Lloyd Wright, whom Dos Passos thoroughly admires, though Wright never understood that architecture could serve the people and not the architect alone. The other biographies are of celebrities— Henry Ford, Rudolph Valentino, Isadora Duncan, William Randolph Hearst—whose lives ultimately fell victim to the power of the crowd. The mass, the popular idolatries of the time, have become the enemies of "our storybook democracy." (In the forties John Dos Passos will go back to "storybook democracy" in writing about Thomas Jefferson.) Charley Anderson, the garage mechanic who comes back from war a famous ace, gets so caught up in the dizzying profusion of drink, money and girls that his self-destructive ride through New York, Detroit and Miami resembles the mad gyrations of an airplane out of control. Margo Dowling, the movie actress, is a cold, utterly scheming trollop who in Hollywood turns her Cuban ex-husband into her chauffeur. But even she, like the Richard Ellsworth Savage who is now cynically writing advertising copy for "health foods," is just another victim rather than a villain. Society has gone mad with greed. The only fictional character in *The Big Money* who gets our respect is Mary French, the doctor's daughter and earnest social reformer who becomes a fanatical Communist in her rage over Sacco and Vanzetti. The emotions of the Sacco-Vanzetti case provide Dos Passos with his clearest and most powerful "Camera Eye" sections, but Mary French is futilely giving her life to the Communist Party. The chips are down; the only defense against the ravages of our century is personal integrity.

The particular artistic virtue of Dos Passos' book is its clarity, its strong-mindedness, the bold and sharp relief into which it puts all moral issues, all characterizations—indeed, all human destiny. There are no shadows in *U.S.A.*, no approximations, no fuzzy outlines. Everything is focused, set off from what is not itself, with that special clarity of presentation which Americans value above all else in the arts of communication. Yet in these last sections of *The Big Money*, Dos Passos makes it clear that though the subject of his book all along has been democracy itself, democracy can survive only through the superior man, the intellectual aristocrat, the poet who may not value what the crowd does. This is the political lesson of *U.S.A.* and may explain, for young people who come to the trilogy for the first time, why the book did not fertilize other books by Dos Passos equal to it. The philosophy behind *U.S.A.* is finally at variance with its natural interest, its subject matter, its greatest strength—the people and the people's speech. Like so many primary books in the American literary tradition, *U.S.A.* is a book at war with itself. It breathes American confidence and is always so distinct in its effects as to seem simple. But its sense of America is complex, dark, and troubled. Perhaps this gives it the energy of disenchantment.

—Alfred Kazin

U.S.A

The young man walks fast by himself through the crowd that thins into the night streets; feet are tired from hours of walking; eyes greedy for warm curve of faces, answering flicker of eyes, the set of a head, the lift of a shoulder, the way hands spread and clench; blood tingles with wants; mind is a beehive of hopes buzzing and stinging; muscles ache for the knowledge of jobs, for the roadmender's pick and shovel work, the fisherman's knack with a hook when he hauls on the slithery net from the rail of the lurching trawler, the swing of the bridgeman's arm as he slings down the whitehot rivet, the engineer's slow grip wise on the throttle, the dirtfarmer's use of his whole body when, whoaing the mules, he yanks the plow from the furrow. The young man walks by himself searching through the crowd with greedy eyes, greedy ears taut to hear, by himself, alone.

The streets are empty. People have packed into subways, climbed into streetcars and buses; in the stations they've scampered for suburban trains; they've filtered into lodgings and tenements, gone up in elevators into apartmenthouses. In a showwindow two sallow windowdressers in their shirtsleeves are bringing out a dummy girl in a red evening dress, at a corner welders in masks lean into sheets of blue flame repairing a cartrack, a few drunk bums shamble along, a sad streetwalker fidgets under an arclight. From the river comes the deep rumbling whistle of a steamboat leaving dock. A tug hoots far away.

The young man walks by himself, fast but not fast enough, far but not far enough (faces slide out of sight, talk trails into tattered scraps, footsteps tap fainter in alleys); he must catch the last subway, the streetcar, the bus, run up the gangplanks of all the steamboats, register at all the hotels, work in the cities, answer the wantads, learn the trades, take up the jobs, live in all the boardinghouses, sleep in all the beds. One bed is not

xviii

enough, one job is not enough, one life is not enough. At night, head swimming with wants, he walks by himself alone.

No job, no woman, no house, no city.

Only the ears busy to catch the speech are not alone; the ears are caught tight, linked tight by the tendrils of phrased words, the turn of a joke, the singsong fade of a story, the gruff fall of a sentence; linking tendrils of speech twine through the city blocks, spread over pavements, grow out along broad parked avenues, speed with the trucks leaving on their long night runs over roaring highways, whisper down sandy byroads past wornout farms, joining up cities and fillingstations, roundhouses, steamboats, planes groping along airways; words call out on mountain pastures, drift slow down rivers widening to the sea and the hushed beaches.

It was not in the long walks through jostling crowds at night that he was less alone, or in the training camp at Allentown, or in the day on the docks at Seattle, or in the empty reek of Washington City hot boyhood summer nights, or in the meal on Market Street, or in the swim off the red rocks at San Diego, or in the bed full of fleas in New Orleans, or in the cold razorwind off the lake, or in the gray faces trembling in the grind of gears in the street under Michigan Avenue, or in the smokers of limited expresstrains, or walking across country, or riding up the dry mountain canyons, or the night without a sleepingbag among frozen beartracks in the Yellowstone, or canoeing Sundays on the Quinnipiac;

but in his mother's words telling about longago, in his father's telling about when I was a boy, in the kidding stories of uncles, in the lies the kids told at school, the hired man's yarns, the tall tales the doughboys told after taps;

it was the speech that clung to the ears, the link that tingled in the blood; U.S.A.

U.S.A. is the slice of a continent. U.S.A. is a group of holding companies, some aggregations of trade unions, a set of laws bound in calf, a radio network, a chain of moving picture theatres, a column of stockquotations rubbed out and written in by a Western Union boy on a blackboard, a publiclibrary full of old newspapers and dogeared historybooks with protests scrawled on the margins in pencil. U.S.A. is the world's greatest rivervalley fringed with mountains and hills. U.S.A. is a set of bigmouthed officials with too many bankaccounts. U.S.A. is a lot of men buried in their uniforms in Arlington Cemetery. U.S.A. is the letters at the end of an address when you are away from home. But mostly U.S.A. is the speech of the people.

Contents

THE BIG MONEY

The Big Money

Charley Anderson

Charley Anderson lay in his bunk in a glary red buzz. *Oh, Titine,* damn that tune last night. He lay flat with his eyes hot; the tongue in his mouth was thick warm sour felt. He dragged his feet out from under the blanket and hung them over the edge of the bunk, big white feet with pink knobs on the toes; he let them drop to the red carpet and hauled himself shakily to the porthole. He stuck his head out.

Instead of the dock, fog, little graygreen waves slapping against the steamer's scaling side. At anchor. A gull screamed above him hidden in the fog. He shivered and pulled his head in.

At the basin he splashed cold water on his face and neck. Where the cold water hit him his skin flushed pink.

He began to feel cold and sick and got back into his bunk and pulled the stillwarm covers up to his chin. Home. Damn that tune.

He jumped up. His head and stomach throbbed in time now. He pulled out the chamberpot and leaned over it. He gagged; a little green bile came. No, I don't want to puke. He got into his underclothes and the whipcord pants of his uniform and lathered his face to shave. Shaving made him feel blue. What I need's a . . . He rang for the steward. "Bonjour, m'sieur." "Say, Billy, let's have a double cognac tootsuite."

He buttoned his shirt carefully and put on his tunic; looking at himself in the glass, his eyes had red rims and his face looked green under the sunburn. Suddenly he began to feel sick again; a sour gagging was welling up from his stomach to his throat. God, these French boats stink. A knock, the steward's frog smile and "Voilà m'sieur," the white plate slopped with a thin amber spilling out of the glass. "When do we dock?" The steward shrugged and growled, "La brume."

Green spots were still dancing in front of his eyes as he went up the linoleumsmelling companionway. Up on deck

27

the wet fog squeezed wet against his face. He stuck his hands in his pockets and leaned into it. Nobody on deck, a few trunks, steamerchairs folded and stacked. To windward everything was wet. Drops trickled down the brassrimmed windows of the smokingroom. Nothing in any direction but fog.

Next time around he met Joe Askew. Joe looked fine. His little mustache spread neat under his thin nose. His eyes were clear.

"Isn't this the damnedest note, Charley? Fog."

"Rotten."

"Got a head?"

"You look topnotch, Joe."

"Sure, why not? I got the fidgets, been up since six o'clock. Damn this fog, we may be here all day."

"It's fog all right."

They took a couple of turns round the deck.

"Notice how the boat stinks, Joe?"

"It's been at anchor, and the fog stimulates your smellers, I guess. How about breakfast?"

28

Charley didn't say anything for a moment, then he took a deep breath and said, "All right, let's try it."

The diningsaloon smelt of onions and brasspolish. The Johnsons were already at the table. Mrs. Johnson looked pale and cool. She had on a little gray hat Charley hadn't seen before, all ready to land. Paul gave Charley a sickly kind of smile when he said hello. Charley noticed how Paul's hand was shaking when he lifted the glass of orangejuice. His lips were white.

"Anybody seen Ollie Taylor?" asked Charley.

"The Major's feelin' pretty bad, I bet," said Paul, giggling.

"And how are you, Charley?" Mrs. Johnson intoned sweetly.

"Oh, I'm . . . I'm in the pink."

"Liar," said Joe Askew.

"Oh, I can't imagine." Mrs. Johnson was saying, "what kept you boys up so late last night."

"We did some singing," said Joe Askew.

"Somebody I know," said Mrs. Johnson, "went to bed in his clothes." Her eye caught Charley's.

Paul was changing the subject: "Well, we're back in God's country."

"Oh, I can't imagine," cried Mrs. Johnson, "what America's going to be like."

Charley was bolting his wuffs avec du bakin and the coffee that tasted of bilge.

"What I'm looking forward to," Joe Askew was saying, "is a real American breakfast."

"Grapefruit," said Mrs. Johnson.

"Cornflakes and cream," said Joe.

"Hot cornmuffins," said Mrs. Johnson.

"Fresh eggs and real Virginia ham," said Joe.

"Wheatcakes and country sausage," said Mrs. Johnson.

"Scrapple," said Joe.

"Good coffee with real cream," said Mrs. Johnson, laughing.

"You win," said Paul with a sickly grin as he left the table.

Charley took a last gulp of his coffee. Then he said he thought he'd go on deck to see if the immigration officers had come. "Why, what's the matter with Charley?" He could hear Joe and Mrs. Johnson laughing together as he ran up the companionway.

Once on deck he decided he wasn't going to be sick. The fog had lifted a little. Astern of the *Niagara* he could see the shadows of other steamers at anchor, and beyond, a rounded shadow that might be land. Gulls wheeled and screamed overhead. Somewhere across the water a foghorn groaned at intervals. Charley walked up forward and leaned into the wet fog.

Joe Askew came up behind him smoking a cigar and took him by the arm: "Better walk, Charley," he said. "Isn't this a hell of a note? Looks like little cld New York had gotten torpedoed during the late unpleasantness. . . . I can't see a damn thing, can you?"

"I thought I saw some land a minute ago, but it's gone now."

"Musta been Atlantic Highlands; we're anchored off the Hook. . . . Goddam it, I want to get ashore."

"Your wife'll be there, won't she, Joe?"

"She ought to be. . . . Know anybody in New York, Charley?"

Charley shook his head. "I got a long ways to go yet before I go home. . . . I don't know what I'll do when I get there."

"Damn it, we may be here all day," said Joe Askew.

"Joe," said Charley, "suppose we have a drink . . . one final drink."

"They've closed up the damn bar."

They'd packed their bags the night before. There was nothing to do. They spent the morning playing rummy in the smokingroom. Nobody could keep his mind on the game. Paul kept dropping his cards. Nobody ever knew who had taken the last trick. Charley was trying to keep his eyes off Mrs. Johnson's eyes, off the little curve of her neck where it ducked under the gray fur trimming of her dress.

"I can't imagine," she said again, "what you boys found to talk about so late last night. . . . I thought we'd talked about everything under heaven before I went to bed."

"Oh, we found topics, but mostly it came out in the form of singing," said Joe Askew.

"I know I always miss things when I go to bed." Charley noticed Paul beside him staring at her with pale loving eyes. "But," she was saying with her teasing smile, "it's just too boring to sit up."

Paul blushed, he looked as if he were going to cry; Charley wondered if Paul had thought of the same thing he'd thought of.

"Well, let's see; whose deal was it?" said Joe Askew briskly.

Round noon Major Taylor came into the smokingroom. "Good morning, everybody. . . . I know nobody feels worse than I do. Commandant says we may not dock till tomorrow morning."

They put up the cards without finishing the hand.

30

"That's nice," said Joe Askew.

"It's just as well," said Ollie Taylor. "I'm a wreck. The last of the harddrinking hardriding Taylors is a wreck. We could stand the war, but the peace has done us in."

Charley looked up in Ollie Taylor's gray face sagging in the pale glare of the fog through the smokingroom windows and noticed the white streaks in his hair and mustache. Gosh, he thought to himself, I'm going to quit this drinking.

They got through lunch somehow, then scattered to their cabins to sleep.

In the corridor outside his cabin Charley met Mrs. Johnson. "Well, the first ten days'll be the hardest, Mrs. Johnson."

"Why don't you call me Eveline; everybody else does?"

Charley turned red. "What's the use? We won't ever see each other again."

"Why not?" she said.

He looked into her long hazel eyes; the pupils widened till the hazel was all black.

"Jesus, I'd like it if we could," he stammered. "Don't think for a minute I . . ."

She'd already brushed silkily past him and was gone down the corridor. He went into his cabin and slammed the door. His bags were packed. The steward had put away the bedclothes. Charley threw himself face down on the striped mustysmelling ticking of the mattress. "God damn that woman," he said aloud.

The rattle of a steamwinch woke him, then he heard the jingle of the engineroom bell. He looked out the porthole and saw a yellow and white revenuecutter and, beyond, vague pink sunlight on frame houses. The fog was lifting; they were in the Narrows.

By the time he'd splashed the aching sleep out of his eyes and run up on deck, the *Niagara* was nosing her way slowly across the greengray glinting bay. The ruddy fog was looped up like curtains overhead. A red ferryboat crossed their bow. To the right there was a line of four- and five-masted schooners at anchor, beyond them a squarerigger and a huddle of squatty Shipping Board steamers, some of them still striped and mottled with camouflage. Then dead ahead, the up-and-down gleam in the blur of the tall buildings of New York.

Joe Askew came up to him with his trenchcoat on and his German fieldglasses hung over his shoulder. Joe's blue eyes were shining. "Do you see the Statue of Liberty yet, Charley?"

"No . . . yes, there she is. I remembered her lookin' bigger."

"There's Black Tom where the explosion was."

"Things look pretty quiet, Joe."

"It's Sunday, that's why."

"It would be Sunday."

They were opposite the Battery now. The long spans of the bridges to Brooklyn went off into smoky shadow beyond the pale skyscrapers. "Well, Charley, that's where they keep all the money. We got to get some of it away from 'em," said Joe Askew, tugging at his mustache.

"Wish I knew how to start in, Joe."

They were skirting a long row of roofed slips. Joe held out his hand. "Well, Charley, write to me, kid, do you hear? It was a great war while it lasted."

"I sure will, Joe."

Two tugs were shoving the *Niagara* around into the slip against the strong ebbtide. American and French flags flew over the wharfbuilding, in the dark doorways were groups of people waving.

"There's my wife," said Joe Askew suddenly. He squeezed Charley's hand. "Solong, kid. We're home."

First thing Charley knew, too soon, he was walking down the gangplank. The transportofficer barely looked at his papers; the customsman said, "Well, I guess it's good to be home, Lieutenant," as he put the stamps on his grip. He got past the Y man and the two reporters and the member of the mayor's committee; the few people and the scattered trunks looked lost and lonely in the huge yellow gloom of the wharfbuilding. Major Taylor and the Johnsons shook hands like strangers.

Then he was following his small khaki trunk to a taxicab. The Johnsons already had a cab and were waiting for a stray grip. Charley went over to them. He couldn't think of anything to say. Paul said he must be sure to come to see them if he stayed in New York, but he kept standing in the door of the cab, so that it was hard for Charley to talk to Eveline. He could see the muscles relax on Paul's jaw when the porter brought the lost grip. "Be sure and look us up," Paul said and jumped in and slammed the door.

Charley went back to his cab, carrying with him a last glimpse of long hazel eyes and her teasing smile. "Do you know if they still give officers special rates at the McAlpin?" he asked the taximan.

"Sure, they treat you all right if you're an officer. . . . If you're an enlisted man you get your ass kicked," answered the taximan out of the corner of his mouth and slammed the gears.

The taxi turned into a wide empty cobbled street. The cab rode easier than the Paris cabs. The big warehouses and marketbuildings were all closed up.

"Gee, things look pretty quiet here," Charley said, leaning forward to talk to the taximan through the window.

33

"Quiet as hell. . . . You wait till you start to look for a job," said the taximan.

"But, Jesus, I don't ever remember things bein' as quiet as this."

"Well, why shouldn't they be quiet? . . . It's Sunday, ain't it?"

"Oh, sure, I'd forgotten it was Sunday."

"Sure it's Sunday."

"I remember now it's Sunday."

Newsreel XLIV

Yankee Doodle that melodee

COLONEL HOUSE ARRIVES FROM EUROPE

APPARENTLY A VERY SICK MAN

Yankee Doodle that melodee

TO CONQUER SPACE AND SEE DISTANCES

but has not the time come for newspaper proprietors to join in a wholesome movement for the purpose of calming troubled minds, giving all the news but laying less stress on prospective calamities

DEADLOCK UNBROKEN AS FIGHT SPREADS

They permitted the Steel Trust Government to trample underfoot the democratic rights which they had so often been assured were the heritage of the people of this country

SHIPOWNERS DEMAND PROTECTION

Yankee doodle that melodee
Yankee doodle that melodee
Makes me stand right up and cheer

only survivors of crew of schooner *Onato* are put in jail on arrival in Philadelphia

PRESIDENT STRONGER WORKS IN SICKROOM

I'm coming U.S.A.
> *I'll say*

MAY GAG PRESS

There's no land . . . so grand

Charles M. Schwab, who has returned from Europe, was a luncheon guest at the White House. He stated that this country was prosperous but not so prosperous as it should be, because there were so many disturbing investigations on foot

> *. . . as my land*
> *From California to Manhattan Isle*

Charley Anderson

The ratfaced bellboy put down the bags, tried the faucets of the washbowl, opened the window a little, put the key on the inside of the door and then stood at something like attention and said, "Anything else, Lootenant?"

This is the life, thought Charley, and fished a quarter out of his pocket.

"Thank you, sir, Lootenant." The bellboy shuffled his feet and cleared his throat. "It must have been terrible overseas, Lootenant."

Charley laughed. "Oh, it was all right."

"I wish I coulda gone, Lootenant." The boy showed a couple of ratteeth in a grin. "It must be wonderful to be a hero," he said and backed out the door.

Charley stood looking out the window as he unbuttoned his tunic. He was high up. Through a street of grimy square buildings he could see some columns and the roofs of the new Penn Station and beyond, across the trainyards, a blurred sun setting behind high ground the other side of the Hudson. Overhead was purple and pink. An El train clattered raspingly through the empty Sunday evening streets. The wind that streamed through the bottom of the window had a gritty smell of coalashes. Charley put the window down and went to wash his face and hands. The hotel towel felt soft and thick with a little whiff of chloride. He went to the looking-glass and combed his hair. Now what?

He was walking up and down the room fidgeting with a cigarette, watching the sky go dark outside the window, when the jangle of the phone startled him.

It was Ollie Taylor's polite fuddled voice. "I thought maybe you wouldn't know where to get a drink. Do you want to come around to the club?"

"Gee, that's nice of you, Ollie. I was jus' wonderin' what a feller could do with himself in this man's town."

"You know it's quite dreadful here," Ollie's voice went on. "Prohibition and all that, it's worse than the wildest imagination could conceive. I'll come and pick you up with a cab."

"All right, Ollie, I'll be in the lobby."

Charley put on his tunic, remembered to leave off his Sam Browne belt, straightened his scrubby sandy hair again, and went down into the lobby. He sat down in a deep chair facing the revolving doors.

The lobby was crowded. There was music coming from somewhere in back. He sat there listening to the dancetunes, looking at the silk stockings and the high heels and the furcoats and the pretty girls' faces pinched a little by the wind as they came in off the street. There was an expensive jingle and crinkle to everything. Gosh, it was great. The girls left little trails of perfume and a warm smell of furs as they passed him. He started counting up how much jack he had. He had a draft for three hundred bucks he'd saved out of his pay, four yellowbacked twenties in the wallet in his inside pocket he'd won at poker on the boat, a couple of tens, and let's see how much change. The coins made a little jingle in his pants as he fingered them over.

Ollie Taylor's red face was nodding at Charley above a big camel'shair coat. "My dear boy, New York's a wreck. . . . They are pouring icecream sodas in the Knickerbocker bar. . . ." When they got into the cab together he blew a reek of highgrade rye whiskey in Charley's face. "Charley, I've promised to take you along to dinner with me. . . . Just up to ole Nat Benton's. You won't mind . . . he's a good scout. The ladies want to see a real flying aviator with palms."

"You're sure I won't be buttin' in, Ollie?"

"My dear boy, say no more about it."

At the club everybody seemed to know Ollie Taylor. He and Charley stood a long time drinking Manhattans at a darkpaneled bar in a group of whitehaired old gents with a barroom tan on their faces. It was Major this and Major that and Lieutenant every time anybody spoke to Charley. Charley was getting to be afraid Ollie would get too much of a load on to go to dinner at anybody's house.

At last it turned out to be seventhirty, and leaving the finalround of cocktails, they got into a cab again, each of them munching a clove, and started uptown. "I don't know what to say to 'em," Ollie said. "I tell them I've just spent the most delightful two years of my life, and they make funny mouths at me, but I can't help it."

There was a terrible lot of marble, and doormen in green, at the apartmenthouse where they went out to dinner, and the elevator was inlaid in different kinds of wood. Nat Benton, Ollie whispered while they were waiting for the door to open, was a Wall Street broker.

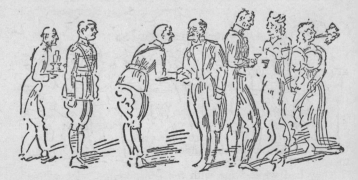

They were all in eveningdress waiting for them for dinner in a pinkishcolored drawingroom. They were evidently old friends of Ollie's because they made a great fuss over him and they were very cordial to Charley and brought out cocktails right away, and Charley felt like the cock of the walk.

There was a girl named Miss Humphries who was as pretty as a picture. The minute Charley set eyes on her Charley decided that was who he was going to talk to. Her eyes and her fluffy palegreen dress and the powder in the little hollow between her shoulderblades made him feel a little dizzy so that he didn't dare stand too close to her.

Ollie saw the two of them together and came up and pinched her ear. "Doris, you've grown up to be a raving beauty." He stood beaming, teetering a little on his short legs. "Hum . . . only the brave deserve the fair. . . . It's not every day we come home from the wars, is it, Charley me boy?"

"Isn't he a darling?" she said when Ollie turned away. "We used to be great sweethearts when I was about six and he was a collegeboy."

When they were all ready to go into dinner Ollie, who'd had a couple more cocktails, spread out his arms and made a speech. "Look at them, lovely, intelligent, lively American women. . . . There was nothing like that on the other side, was there, Charley? Three things you can't get anywhere else in the world, a good cocktail, a decent breakfast, and an American girl, God bless 'em."

"Oh, he's such a darling," whispered Miss Humphries in Charley's ear.

There was silverware in rows and rows on the table and a Chinese bowl with roses in the middle of it, and a group of giltstemmed wineglasses at each plate. Charley was relieved when he found he was sitting next to Miss Humphries. She was smiling up at him.

"Gosh," he said, grinning into her face, "I hardly know how to act."

"It must be a change . . . from over there. But just act natural. That's what I do."

"Oh, no, a feller always gets into trouble when he acts natural."

She laughed. "Maybe you're right. . . . Oh, do tell me what it was really like over there. . . . Nobody'll ever tell me everything." She pointed to the palms on his Croix de Guerre. "Oh, Lieutenant Anderson, you must tell me about those."

They had white wine with the fish and red wine with the roastbeef and a dessert all full of whippedcream. Charley

39

kept telling himself he mustn't drink too much so that he'd be sure to behave right.

Miss Humphries' first name was Doris. Mrs. Benton called her that. She'd spent a year in a convent in Paris before the war and asked him about places she'd known, the Church of the Madeleine and Rumpelmayer's and the pastryshop opposite the Comédie Française. After dinner she and Charley took their coffeecups into a windowbay behind a big pink begonia in a brass pot and she asked him if he didn't think New York was awful. She sat on the windowseat and he stood over her looking past her white shoulder through the window down at the traffic in the street below. It had come on to rain and the lights of the cars made long rippling streaks on the black pavement of Park Avenue. He said something about how he thought home would look pretty good to him all the same. He was wondering if it would be all right if he told her she had beautiful shoulders. He'd just about gotten round to it when he heard Ollie Taylor getting everybody together to go out to a cabaret. "I know it's a chore," Ollie was saying, "but you children must remember it's my first night in New York and humor my weakness."

They stood in a group under the marquee while the door-man called taxicabs. Doris Humphries in her long evening-wrap with fur at the bottom of it stood so close to Charley her shoulder touched his arm. In the lashing rainy wind off the street he could smell the warm perfume she wore and her furs and her hair. They stood back while the older people got into the cabs. For a second her hand was in his, very little and cool as he helped her into the cab. He handed out half a dollar to the doorman who had whispered "Shanley's" to the taxidriver in a serious careful flunkey's voice.

The taxi was purring smoothly downtown between the tall square buildings. Charley was a little dizzy. He didn't dare look at her for a moment, but looked out at faces, cars, traffic-cops, people in raincoats and umbrellas passing against drugstore windows.

"Now tell me how you got the palms."

"Oh, the frogs just threw those in now and then to keep the boys cheerful."

"How many Huns did you bring down?"

"Why bring that up?"

She stamped her foot on the floor of the taxi. "Oh, no-body'll ever tell me anything! . . . I don't believe you were ever at the front, any of you."

Charley laughed. His throat was a little dry. "Well, I was over it a couple of times."

Suddenly she turned to him. There were flecks of light in her eyes in the dark of the cab. "Oh, I understand. . . . Lieutenant Anderson, I think you flyers are the finest people there are."

"Miss Humphries, I think you're a . . . humdinger. . . . I hope this taxi never gets to this dump . . . wherever it is we're goin'."

She leaned her shoulder against his for a second. He found he was holding her hand. "After all, my name is Doris," she said in a tiny babytalk voice.

"Doris," he said. "Mine's Charley."

"Charley, do you like to dance?" she asked in the same tiny voice.

"Sure," Charley said, giving her hand a quick squeeze.

Her voice melted like a little tiny piece of candy. "Me too. . . . Oh, so much."

When they went in, the orchestra was playing *Dardanella*. Charley left his trenchcoat and his hat in the checkroom. The headwaiter's heavy grizzled eyebrows bowed over a white shirtfront. Charley was following Doris's slender back, the hollow between the shoulderblades where his hand would like to be, across the red carpet, between the white tables, the

41

men's starched shirts, the women's shoulders, through the sizzly smell of champagne and welshrabbit and hot chafing-dishes, across a corner of the dancefloor among the swaying couples to the round white table where the rest of them were already settled. The knives and forks shone among the stiff creases of the fresh tablecloth.

Mrs. Benton was pulling off her white kid gloves looking at Ollie Taylor's purple face as he told a funny story. "Let's dance," Charley whispered to Doris. "Let's dance all the time."

Charley was scared of dancing too tough so he held her a little away from him. She had a way of dancing with her eyes closed. "Gee, Doris, you are a wonderful dancer." When the music stopped, the tables and the cigarsmoke and the people went on reeling a little round their heads. Doris was looking up at him out of the corners of her eyes. "I bet you miss the French girls, Charley. How did you like the way the French girls danced, Charley?"

"Terrible."

At the table they were drinking champagne out of breakfast coffeecups. Ollie had had two bottles sent up from the club by a messenger. When the music started again, Charley had to dance with Mrs. Benton, and then with the other lady, the one with the diamonds and the spare tire around her waist. He and Doris only had two more dances together. Charley could see the others wanted to go home because Ollie was getting too tight. He had a flask of rye on his hip and a couple of times had beckoned Charley out to have a swig in the cloakroom with him. Chaley tongued the bottle each time because he was hoping he'd get a chance to take Doris home.

When they got outside, it turned out she lived in the same block as the Bentons did; Charley cruised around on the outside of the group while the ladies were getting their wraps on before going out to the taxicab, but he couldn't get a look from her. It was just, "Goodnight, Ollie dear, goodnight, Lieutenant Anderson," and the doorman slamming the taxi door. He hardly knew which of the hands he had shaken had been hers.

Newsreel XLV

*'Twarn't for powder and for storebought hair
De man I love would not gone nowhere*

if one should seek a simple explanation of his career, it would doubtless be found in that extraordinary decision to forsake the ease of a clerkship for the wearying labor of a section hand. The youth who so early in life had so much of judgment and willpower could not fail to rise above the general run of men. He became the intimate of bankers

*St. Louis woman wid her diamon' rings
Pulls dat man aroun' by her apron strings*

Tired of walking, riding a bicycle or riding in streetcars, he is likely to buy a Ford.

DAYLIGHT HOLDUP SCATTERS CROWD

Just as soon as his wife discovers that every Ford is like every other Ford and that nearly everyone has one, she is likely to influence him to step into the next social group, of which the Dodge is the most conspicuous example.

DESPERATE REVOLVER BATTLE FOLLOWS

The next step comes when daughter comes back from college and the family moves into a new home. Father wants economy. Mother craves opportunity for her children, daughter desires social prestige and son wants travel, speed, get-up-and-go.

43

I hate to see de evenin sun go down
Hate to see de evenin sun go down
'Cause my baby he done lef' dis town

such exploits may indicate a dangerous degree of bravado but they display the qualities that made a boy of highschool age the acknowledged leader of a gang that has been a thorn in the side of the State of

The American Plan

Frederick Winslow Taylor (they called him Speedy Taylor in the shop) was born in Germantown, Pennsylvania, the year of Buchanan's election. His father was a lawyer, his mother came from a family of New Bedford whalers; she was a great reader of Emerson, belonged to the Unitarian Church and the Browning Society. She was a fervent abolitionist and believed in democratic manners; she was a housekeeper of the old school, kept everybody busy from dawn till dark. She laid down the rules of conduct:
selfrespect, selfreliance, selfcontrol
and a cold long head for figures.

But she wanted her children to appreciate the finer things, so she took them abroad for three years on the Continent, showed them cathedrals, grand opera, Roman pediments, the old masters under their brown varnish in their great frames of tarnished gilt.

Later Fred Taylor was impatient of these wasted years, stamped out of the room when people talked about the finer things; he was a testy youngster, fond of practical jokes, and a great hand at rigging up contraptions and devices.

At Exeter he was head of his class and captain of the ballteam, the first man to pitch overhand. (When umpires complained that overhand pitching wasn't in the rules of the game, he answered that it got results.)

As a boy he had nightmares; going to bed was horrible for him; he thought they came from sleeping on his back. He made himself a leather harness with wooden pegs that stuck into his flesh when he turned over. When he was grown he slept in a chair or in bed in a sitting position propped up with pillows. All his life he suffered from sleeplessness.

He was a crackerjack tennisplayer. In 1881, with his friend

Clark, he won the National Doubles Championship. (He used a spoonshaped racket of his own design.)

At school he broke down from overwork, his eyes went back on him. The doctor suggested manual labor. So instead of going to Harvard he went into the machineshop of a small pumpmanufacturing concern, owned by a friend of the family's, to learn the trade of patternmaker and machinist. He learned to handle a lathe and to dress and cuss like a workingman.

Fred Taylor never smoked tobacco or drank liquor or used tea or coffee; he couldn't understand why his fellowmechanics wanted to go on sprees and get drunk and raise cain Saturday nights. He lived at home; when he wasn't reading technical books he'd play parts in amateur theatricals or step up to the piano in the evening and sing a good tenor in *A Warrior Bold* or *A Spanish Cavalier*.

He served his first year's apprenticeship in the machineshop without pay; the next two years he made a dollar and a half a week, the last year two dollars.

Pennsylvania was getting rich off iron and coal. When he was twentytwo, Fred Taylor went to work at the Midvale Iron Works. At first he had to take a clerical job, but he hated that and went to work with a shovel. At last he got them to put him on a lathe. He was a good machinist, he worked ten hours a day and in the evenings followed an engineering course at Stevens. In six years he rose from machinist's helper to keeper of toolcribs to gangboss to foreman to mastermechanic in charge of repairs to chief draftsman and director of research to chief engineer of the Midvale Plant.

The early years he was a machinist with the other machinists in the shop, cussed and joked and worked with the rest of them, soldiered on the job when they did. Mustn't give the boss more than his money's worth. But when he got to be foreman, he was on the management's side of the fence, *gathering in on the part of those on the management's side all the great mass of traditional knowledge which in the past has been in the heads of the workmen and in the physical skill and knack of the workman.* He couldn't stand to see an idle lathe or an idle man.

Production went to his head and thrilled his sleepless nerves like liquor or women on a Saturday night. He never loafed and he'd be damned if anybody else would. Production was an itch under his skin.

He lost his friends in the shop; they called him nigger-driver. He was a stockily built man with a temper and a short tongue.

I was a young man in years, but I give you my word I was a great deal older than I am now, what with the worry, meanness, and contemptibleness of the whole damn thing. It's a horrid life for any man to live, not being able to look any workman in the face without seeing hostility there, and a feeling that every man around you is your virtual enemy.

That was the beginning of the Taylor System of Scientific Management.

He was impatient of explanations, he didn't care whose hide he took off in enforcing the laws he believed inherent in the industrial process.

When starting an experiment in any field, question everything, question the very foundations upon which the art rests, question the simplest, the most selfevident, the most universally accepted facts; prove everything,

except the dominant Quaker Yankee (the New Bedford skippers were the greatest niggerdrivers on the whaling seas) rules of conduct. He boasted he'd never ask a workman to do anything he couldn't do.

He devised an improved steamhammer; he standardized tools and equipment, he filled the shop with college students with stopwatches and diagrams, tabulating, standardizing. *There's the right way of doing a thing and the wrong way of doing it; the right way means increased production, lower costs, higher wages, bigger profits:* the American plan.

He broke up the foreman's job into separate functions, speedbosses, gangbosses, timestudy men, order-of-work men.

The skilled mechanics were too stubborn for him; what he wanted was a plain handyman who'd do what he was told. If he was a firstclass man and did firstclass work, Taylor was willing to let him have firstclass pay; that's where he began to get into trouble with the owners.

At thirtyfour he married and left Midvale and took a flyer for the big money in connection with a pulpmill started in Maine by some admirals and political friends of Grover Cleveland's;

the panic of '93 made hash of that enterprise,

so Taylor invented for himself the job of Consulting Engineer in Management and began to build up a fortune by careful investments.

The first paper he read before the American Society of Mechanical Engineers was anything but a success; they said he was crazy. *I have found,* he wrote in 1909, *that any im-*

provement is not only opposed but aggressively and bitterly opposed by the majority of men.

He was called in by Bethlehem Steel. It was in Bethlehem he made his famous experiments with handling pigiron; he taught a Dutchman named Schmidt to handle fortyseven tons instead of twelve and a half tons of pigiron a day and got Schmidt to admit he was as good as ever at the end of the day.

He was a crank about shovels, every job had to have a shovel of the right weight and size for that job alone; every job had to have a man of the right weight and size for that job alone; but when he began to pay his men in proportion to the increased efficiency of their work,

the owners, who were a lot of greedy smalleyed Dutchmen, began to raise Hail Columbia; when Schwab bought Bethlehem Steel in 1901

Fred Taylor

inventor of efficiency

who had doubled the production of the stampingmill by speeding up the main lines of shafting from ninetysix to twohundred and twentyfive revolutions a minute

was unceremoniously fired.

After that Fred Taylor always said he couldn't afford to work for money.

He took to playing golf (using golfclubs of his own design), doping out methods for transplanting huge boxtrees into the garden of his home.

At Boxly in Germantown he kept open house for engineers, factorymanagers, industrialists;

he wrote papers,

lectured in colleges,

appeared before a congressional committee,

everywhere preached the virtues of scientific management and the Barth slide rule, the cutting-down of waste and idleness, the substitution for skilled mechanics of the plain handyman (like Schmidt the pigiron handler) who'd move as he was told

and work by the piece:

production;

more steel rails more bicycles more spools of thread more armorplate for battleships more bedpans more barbedwire more needles more lightningrods more ballbearings more dollarbills;

(the old Quaker families of Germantown were growing

rich, the Pennsylvania millionaires were breeding billionaires out of iron and coal)

production would make every firstclass American rich who was willing to work at piecework and not drink or raise cain or think or stand mooning at his lathe.

Thrifty Schmidt the pigiron handler can invest his money and get to be an owner like Schwab and the rest of the greedy smalleyed Dutchmen and cultivate a taste for Bach and have hundredyearold boxtrees in his garden at Bethlehem or Germantown or Chestnut Hill,

and lay down the rules of conduct;

the American plan.

But Fred Taylor never saw the working of the American plan;

in 1915 he went to the hospital in Philadelphia suffering from a breakdown.

Pneumonia developed; the nightnurse heard him winding his watch;

on the morning of his fiftyninth birthday, when the nurse went into his room to look at him at fourthirty,

he was dead with his watch in his hand.

Newsreel XLVI

these are the men for whom the rabid lawless, anarchistic element of society in this country has been laboring ever since sentence was imposed, and of late they have been augmented by many good lawabiding citizens who have been misled by the subtle arguments of those propagandists

> *The times are hard and the wages low*
> *Leave her Johnny leave her*
> *The bread is hard and the beef is salt*
> *It's time for us to leave her*

BANKERS HAIL ERA OF EXPANSION

PROSPERITY FOR ALL SEEN ASSURED

Find German Love of Caviar a Danger to Stable Money

EX-SERVICE MEN DEMAND JOBS

> *No one knows*
> *No one cares if I'm weary*
> *Oh how soon they forget Château-Thierry*

WE FEEL VERY FRIENDLY TOWARDS THE TYPEWRITER USERS OF NEW YORK CITY

JOBLESS RIOT AT AGENCY

> *Ships in de oceans*
> *Rocks in de sea*
> *Blond-headed woman*
> *Made a fool outa me*

The Camera Eye (43)

throat tightens when the redstacked steamer churning the faintly heaving slate colored swell swerves slicking in a long greenmarbled curve past the red lightship

spine stiffens with the remembered chill of the offshore Atlantic

and the jag of frame houses in the west above the invisible land and spiderweb rollercoasters and the chewinggum towers of Coney and the freighters with their stacks way aft and the blur beyond Sandy Hook

and the smell of saltmarshes warmclammysweet

remembered bays silvery inlets barred with trestles

the put-put before day of a gasolineboat way up the creek

raked masts of bugeyes against straight tall pines on the shellwhite beach

the limeycold reek of an oysterboat in winter

and creak of rockers on the porch of the scrollsaw cottage and uncles' voices pokerface stories told sideways out of the big mouth (from Missouri who took no rubber nickels) the redskin in the buffalorobe selling snakeroot in the flare of oratorical redfire the sulphury choke and the hookandladder clanging down the redbrick street while the clinging firemen with uncles' faces pull on their rubbercoats

and the crunch of whitecorn muffins and coffee with cream gulped in a hurry before traintime and apartmenthouse mornings stifling with newspapers and the smooth powdery feel of new greenbacks and the whack of a cop's billy cracking a citizen's skull and the faces blurred with newsprint of men in jail

the whine and shriek of the buzzsaw and the tipsy smell of raw lumber and straggling through slagheaps through fireweed through wasted woodlands the shantytowns the shantytowns

what good burying those years in the old graveyard by the brokendown brick church that morning in the spring when the sandy lanes were treated with blue puddles and the air was violets and pineneedles

what good burying those hated years in the latrine-
stench at Brocourt under the starshells

if today the crookedfaced custominspector with the soft
tough talk the burring speech the funnypaper antics of
thick hands jerking thumb

(So you brought home French books didjer?)

is my uncle

Newsreel XLVII

boy seeking future offered opportunity . . . good positions for bright . . . CHANCE FOR ADVANCEMENT . . . boy to learn . . . errand boy . . . office boy

YOUNG MAN WANTED

Oh tell me how long
I'll have to wait

OPPORTUNITY

in bank that chooses its officers from the ranks, for wide-awake ambitious bookkeeper . . . architectural draftsman with experience on factory and industrial buildings in brick, timber, and reinforced concrete . . . bronzefitter . . . letterer . . . patternmaker . . . carriage painter . . . firstclass striper and finisher . . . young man for hosiery, underwear, and notion house . . . assistant in order department . . . firstclass penman accurate at figures . . . energetic hardworker for setting dies in powerpresses for metal parts

canvasser . . . flavor chemist . . . freightelevator man . . . housesalesman . . . insuranceman . . . insuranceman . . . invoice clerk . . . jeweler . . . laborer . . . machinist . . . millingmachine man . . . shipping clerk . . shipping clerk . . . shipping clerk . . . shoe salesman . . . signwriter . . . solicitor for retail fishmarket . . . teacher . . . timekeeper . . . tool and diemaker, tracer, toolroom foreman, translator, typist . . . windowtrimmer . . . wrapper

OPPORTUNITY FOR

52

young man not afraid of hard work
   young man for office
      young man for stockroom
         young man as stenographer
            young man to travel
               young man to learn

OPPORTUNITY

Oh tell me how long

to superintend municipal light, water, and ice plant in beautiful growing, healthful town in Florida's highlands . . . to take charge of underwear department in large wholesale mailhouse . . . to assist in railroad investigation . . . to take charge of about twenty men on tools, dies, gigs, and gauges . . . as bookkeeper in stockroom . . . for light porter work . . . civil engineer . . . machinery and die appraiser . . . building estimator . . . electrical and powerplant engineer

The Camera Eye (44)

the unnamed arrival
(who had hung from the pommel of the unshod white stallion's saddle
a full knapsack
and leaving the embers dying in the hollow of the barren Syrian hills where the Agail had camped when dawn sharpshining cracked night off the ridged desert had ridden towards the dungy villages and the patches of sesame and the apricotgardens)
shaved off his beard in Damascus
and sat drinking hot milk and coffee in front of the hotel in Beirut staring at the white hulk of Lebanon fumbling with letters piled on the table and clipped streamers of newsprint

addressed not to the unspeaker of arabic or the clumsy
scramblerup on camelback so sore in the rump from riding

but to someone

who

(but this evening in the soft nightclimate of the Levan-
tine coast the kind officials are contemplating further improvements

scarcelybathed he finds himself cast for a role provided
with a white tie carefully tied by the viceconsul stuffed
into a boiled shirt a tailcoat too small a pair of dress-
trousers too large which the kind wife of the kind official
gigglingly fastens in the back with safetypins which
immediately burst open when he bows to the High Com-
missioner's lady   faulty costuming makes the role of
eminent explorer impossible to play   and the patent
leather pumps painfully squeezing the toes got lost under
the table during the champagne and speeches)

who arriving in Manhattan finds waiting again the for-
somebodyelsetailored dress suit

the position offered the opportunity presented the col-
larbutton digging into the adamsapple while a wooden
image croaks down a table at two rows of freshlypressed
gentlemen who wear fashionably their tailored names

stuffed into shirts to caption miles lightyears of clipped
streamers of newsprint

Gentlemen I apologize it was the wrong bell it was due
to a misapprehension that I found myself on the stage
when the curtain rose the poem I recited in a foreign language was not mine in fact it was somebody else who was
speaking it's not me in uniform in the snapshot it's a
lamentable error mistaken identity the servicerecord was
lost the gentleman occupying the swivelchair wearing the
red carnation is somebody else than

whoever it was who equipped with false whiskers was
standing outside in the rainy street and has managed un-
detected to make himself scarce down a manhole

the pastyfaced young man wearing somebody else's
readymade business opportunity

is most assuredly not

the holder of any of the positions for which he made
application at the unemployment agency

Charley Anderson

The train was three hours late getting into St. Paul. Charley had his coat on and his bag closed an hour before he got in. He sat fidgeting in the seat, taking off and pulling on a pair of new buckskin gloves. He wished they wouldn't all be down at the station to meet him. Maybe only Jim would be there. Maybe they hadn't got his wire.

The porter came and brushed him off, then took his bags. Charley couldn't see much through the driving steam and snow outside the window. The train slackened speed, stopped in a broad snowswept freightyard, started again with a jerk and a series of snorts from the forced draft in the engine. The bumpers slammed all down the train. Charley's hands were icy inside his gloves. The porter stuck his head in and yelled, "St. Paul." There was nothing to do but get out.

There they all were. Old man Vogel and Aunt Hartmann with their red faces and their long noses looked just the same as ever, but Jim and Hedwig had both of them filled out. Hedwig had on a mink coat and Jim's overcoat looked darn prosperous. Jim snatched Charley's bags away from him and Hedwig and Aunt Hartmann kissed him and old man Vogel thumped him on the back. They all talked at once and asked him all kinds of questions. When he asked about Ma, Jim frowned and said she was in the hospital, they'd go around to see her this afternoon. They piled the bags into a new Ford sedan and squeezed themselves in after with a lot of giggling and squealing from Aunt Hartmann.

"You see I got the Ford agency now," said Jim.

"To tell the truth, things have been pretty good out here."

"Wait till you see the house, it's all been done over," said Hedwig.

"Vell, my poy made de Cherman Kaiser run. Speaking for the Cherman-American commoonity of the Twin Cities, ve are pr'roud of you."

They had a big dinner ready and Jim gave him a drink of whiskey and old man Vogel kept pouring him out beer and saying, "Now tell us all about it." Charley sat there, his face all red, eating the stewed chicken and the dumplings and drinking the beer till he was ready to burst. He couldn't think what to tell them, so he made funny cracks when they asked him questions. After dinner old man Vogel gave him one of his best Havana cigars.

That afternoon Charley and Jim went to the hospital to see Ma. Driving over, Jim said she'd been operated on for a tumor, but that he was afraid it was cancer, but even that hadn't given Charley an idea of how sick she'd be. Her face was shrunken and yellow against the white pillow. When he leaned over to kiss her, her lips felt thin and hot. Her breath was very bad.

"Charley, I'm glad you came," she said in a trembly voice. "It would have been better if you'd come sooner. . . . Not that I'm not comfortable here . . . anyway, I'll be glad having my boys around me when I get well. God has watched over us all, Charley, we mustn't forget Him."

"Now, Ma, we don't want to get tired and excited," said Jim. "We want to keep our strength to get well."

"Oh, but He's been so merciful." She brought her small hand, so thin it was blue, out from under the cover and dabbed at her eyes with a handkerchief. "Jim, hand me my glasses, that's a good boy," she said in a stronger voice. "Let me take a look at the prodigal son."

Charley couldn't help shuffling his feet uneasily as she looked at him.

"You're quite a man now and you've made quite a name for yourself over there. You boys have turned out better than I hoped. . . . Charley, I was afraid you'd turn out a bum like your old man." They all laughed. They didn't know what to say.

She took her glasses off again and tried to reach for the bedside table with them. The glasses dropped out of her hand

56

and broke on the concrete floor. "Oh . . . my . . . never mind, I don't need 'em much here."

Charley picked the pieces up and put them carefully in his vest pocket. "I'll get 'em fixed, Ma."

The nurse was standing in the door beckoning with her head. "Well, goodbye, see you tomorrow," they said.

Once they were out in the corridor, Charley felt that tears were running down his face.

"That's how it is," said Jim, frowning. "They keep her under dope most of the time. I thought she'd be more comfortable in a private room, but they sure do know how to charge in these damn hospitals."

"I'll chip in on it," said Charley. "I got a little money saved up."

"Well, I suppose it's no more than right you should," Jim said.

Charley took a deep breath of the cold afternoon when they paused on the hospital steps, but he couldn't get the smell of ether and drugs and sickness out of his head. It had come fine with an icy wind. The snow on the streets and roofs was bright pink from the flaring sunset.

"We'll go down to the shop and see what's what," said Jim. "I told the guy works for me to call up some of the newspaperboys. I thought it would be a little free advertising if they came down to the salesroom to interview you." Jim slapped Charley on the back. "They eat up this returnedhero stuff. String 'em along a little, won't you?"

Charley didn't answer.

"Jesus Christ, Jim, I don't know what to tell 'em," he said in a low voice when they got back in the car.

Jim was pressing his foot on the selfstarter. "What do you think of comin' in the business, Charley? It's gettin' to be a good 'un, I can tell you that."

"That's nice of you, Jim. Suppose I kinder think about it."

When they got back to the house, they went around to the new salesroom Jim had built out from the garage, that had been a liverystable in the old days, back of old man Vogel's house. The salesroom had a big plateglass window with *Ford* slanting across it in blue letters. Inside stood a new truck all shining and polished. Then there was a green carpet and a veneered mahogany desk and a telephone that pulled out on a nickel accordion bracket and an artificial palm in a fancy jardiniere in the corner.

"Take your weight off your feet, Charley," said Jim, pointing to the swivelchair and bringing out a box of cigars. "Let's sit around and chew the rag a little."

Charley sat down and picked himself out a cigar. Jim

57

stood against the radiator with his thumbs in the armholes of his vest. "What do you think of it, kid; pretty keen, ain't it?"

"Pretty keen, Jim." They lit their cigars and scuffled around with their feet a little.

Jim began again: "But it won't do. I got to get me a big new place downtown. This used to be central. Now it's out to hell and gone."

Charley kinder grunted and puffed on his cigar. Jim took a couple of steps back and forth, looking at Charley all the time. "With your connections in the Legion and aviation and all that kinder stuff, we'll be jake. Every other Ford dealer in the district's got a German name."

"Jim, can that stuff. I can't talk to newspapermen."

Jim flushed and frowned and sat down on the edge of the desk. "But you got to hold up your end. . . . What do you think I'm taking you in on it for? I'm not doin' it for my kid brother's pretty blue eyes."

Charley got to his feet. "Jim, I ain't goin' in on it. I'm already signed up with an aviation proposition with my old C.O."

"Twentyfive years from now you can talk to me about aviation. Ain't practical yet."

"Well, we got a couple of tricks up our sleeve. . . . We're shootin' the moon."

"That's about the size of it." Jim got to his feet. His lips got thin. "Well, you needn't think you can lay around my house all winter just because you're a war hero. If that's your idea you've got another think comin'." Charley burst out

58

laughing. Jim came up and put his hand wheedlingly on Charley's shoulder. "Say, those birds'll be around here in a few minutes. You be a good feller and change into your uniform and put on all the medals. . . . Give us a break."

Charley stood a minute staring at the ash on his cigar. "How about givin' me a break? Haven't been in the house five hours and there you go pickin' on me just like when I was workin' back here. . . ."

Jim was losing control of himself, he was starting to shake. "Well, you know what you can do about that," he said, cutting his words off sharp.

Charley felt like smashing him one in his damn narrow jaw. "If it wasn't for Ma, you wouldn't need to worry about that," he said quietly.

Jim didn't answer for a minute. The wrinkles came out of his forehead. He shook his head and looked grave. "You're right, Charley, you better stick around. If it gives her any pleasure . . ."

Charley threw his cigar halfsmoked into the brass spittoon and walked out the door before Jim could stop him. He went to the house and got his hat and coat and went for a long walk through the soggy snow of the late afternoon.

They were just finishing at the suppertable when Charley got back. His supper had been set out on a plate for him at his place. Nobody spoke but old man Vogel. "Ve been tinking, dese airmen maybe dey live on air too," he said and laughed wheezily. Nobody else laughed. Jim got up and went out of the room. As soon as Charley had swallowed his supper, he said he was sleepy and went up to bed.

Charley stayed on while November dragged on towards Thanksgiving and Christmas. His mother never seemed to be any better. Every afternoon he went over to see her for five or ten minutes. She was always cheerful. It made him feel terrible the way she talked about the goodness of God and how she was going to get better. He'd try to get her talking about Fargo and old Lizzie and the old days in the boardinghouse, but she didn't seem to remember much about that, except about sermons she'd heard in church. He'd leave the hospital feeling weak and groggy. The rest of his time he spent looking up books on internalcombustion motors at the public library, or did odd jobs for Jim in the garage the way he used to when he was a kid.

One evening after Newyear's Charley went over to the Elks Ball in Minneapolis with a couple of fellows he knew. The big hall was full of noise and paper lanterns. He was cruising around threading his way between groups of people waiting for the next dance when he found himself looking into a thin face and blue eyes he knew. It was too late to make out he hadn't seen her. "Hello, Emiscah," he said, keeping his voice as casual as he could.

"Charley . . . my God." He was afraid for a minute that she was going to faint.

"Let's dance," he said.

She felt limp in his arms. They danced awhile without saying anything. She had too much rouge on her cheeks and he didn't like the perfume she had on. After the dance they sat in a corner and talked. She wasn't married yet. She worked in a departmentstore. No, she didn't live at home any more, she lived in a flat with a girlfriend. He must come up. It would be like old times. He must give her his phone number. She supposed things seemed pretty tame to him now after all those French girls. And imagine him getting a commission, the Andersons sure were going up in the world, she guessed they'd be forgetting their old friends. Emiscah's voice had gotten screechy and she had a way he didn't like of putting her hand on his knee.

As soon as he could Charley said he had a headache and had to go home. He wouldn't wait for the guys he'd come with. The evening was ruined for him anyway, he was thinking. He rode back all alone on the interurban trolley. It was cold as blazes. It was about time he got the hell out of this dump. He really did have a splitting headache and chills.

Next morning he was down with the flu and had to stay in bed. It was almost a relief. Hedwig brought him stacks of detective stories and Aunt Hartmann fussed over him and brought him toddies and eggflips, and all he had to do was lie there and read.

First thing he did when he got on his feet was to go over to the hospital. Ma had had another operation and hadn't come out of it very well. The room was darkened and she didn't remember when she'd seen him last. She seemed to think she was home in Fargo and that he'd just come back from his trip south. She held tight to his hand and kept saying, "My son that was lost hath been returned to me . . . thank God for my boy." It took the strength out of him, so he had to sit down for a second in a wicker chair in the corridor when he left her.

A nurse came up to him and stood beside him fidgeting with a paper and pencil. He looked up at her, she had pink cheeks and pretty dark eyelashes. "You mustn't let it get you," she said.

He grinned. "Oh, I'm all right. . . . I just got out of bed from a touch of flu, it sure pulls down your strength."

"I hear you were an aviator," she said. "I had a brother in the Royal Flying Corps. We're Canadians."

"Those were great boys," said Charley. He wondered if he could date her up, but then he thought of Ma. "Tell me honestly what you think, please do."

"Well, it's against the rules, but judging from other cases I've seen her chances are not very good."

"I thought so."

He got to his feet. "You're a peach, do you know it?"

Her face got red from the starched cap to the white collar of her uniform. She wrinkled up her forehead and her voice got very chilly. "In a case like that it's better to have it happen quickly."

Charley felt a lump rise in his throat. "Oh, I know."

"Well, goodbye, Lieutenant, I've got to go about my business."

"Gee, thanks a lot," said Charley.

When he got out in the air he kept remembering her pretty face and her nice lips.

One slushy morning of thaw in early March, Charley was taking a scorched gasket out of a Buick when the garage helper came and said they wanted him on the phone from the hospital. A cold voice said Mrs. Anderson was sinking fast and the family better be notified. Charley got out of his overalls and went to call Hedwig. Jim was out, so they took one of the cars out of the garage. Charley had forgotten to wash his hands and they were black with grease and carbon. Hedwig found him a rag to wipe them off with. "Someday, Hedwig," he said, "I'm going to get me a clean job in a draftin' room."

"Well, Jim wanted you to be his salesman," Hedwig snapped crossly. "I don't see how you're going to get anywheres if you turn down every opportunity."

"Well, maybe there's opportunities I won't turn down."

"I'd like to know where you're going to get 'em except with us," she said.

Charley didn't answer. Neither of them said anything more in the long drive across town. When they got to the hospital, they found that Ma had sunk into a coma. Two days later she died.

At the funeral, about halfway through the service, Charley felt the tears coming. He went out and locked himself in the toilet at the garage and sat down on the seat and cried like a child. When they came back from the cemetery, he was in a

black mood and wouldn't let anybody speak to him. After supper, when he found Jim and Hedwig sitting at the dining-room table figuring out with pencil and paper how much it had cost them, he blew up, and said he'd pay every damn cent of it and they wouldn't have to worry about his staying around the goddam house either. He went out slamming the door after him and ran upstairs and threw himself on his bed. He lay there a long time in his uniform without undressing, staring at the ceiling and hearing mealy voices saying, deceased, bereavement, hereafter.

The day after the funeral Emiscah called up. She said she was so sorry about his mother's death and wouldn't he come around to see her some evening? Before he knew what he was doing, he'd said he'd come. He felt blue and lonely and he had to talk to somebody besides Jim and Hedwig. That evening he drove over to see her. She was alone. He didn't like the cheap gimcracky look her apartment had. He took her out to the movies and she said did he remember the time they went to see *The Birth of a Nation* together. He said he didn't, though he remembered all right. He could see that she wanted to start things up with him again.

Driving back to her place, she let her head drop on his shoulder. When he stopped the car in front of where she lived, he looked down and saw that she was crying. "Charley, won't you give me a little kiss for old times?" she whispered. He kissed her. When she said would he come up, he stammered that he had to be home early. She kept saying, "Oh, come ahead. I won't eat you, Charley," and finally he went up with her, though it was the last thing he'd intended to do.

She made them cocoa on her gasburner and told him how unhappy she was, it was so tiring being on your feet all day behind the counter and the women who came to buy things were so mean to you, and the floorwalkers were always pinching your seat and expecting you to cuddlecooty with them in the fittingbooths. Some day she was going to turn on the gas. It made Charley feel bad having her talk like that and he had to pet her a little to make her stop crying. Then he got hot and had to make love to her. When he left he promised to call her up next week.

Next morning he got a letter that she must have written right after he left, saying that she'd never loved anybody but him. That night after supper he tried to write her that he didn't want to marry anybody and least of all her; he couldn't get it worded right, so he didn't write at all. When she called up next day, he said he was very busy and that he'd have to go up into North Dakota to see about some property his

63

mother had left. He didn't like the way she said, "Of course I understand. I'll call you up when you get back, dear."

Hedwig began to ask who that woman was who was calling him up all the time, and Jim said, "Look out for the women, Charley. If they think you've got anything they'll hold on to you like a leech."

"Yessir," said old man Vogel, "it's not like ven you're in the army yet and can say goodbye, mein schatz, I'm off to the vars; now they can find out vere you live."

"You needn't worry," growled Charley. "I won't stay put."

The day they went over to the lawyer's office to read Ma's will, Jim and Hedwig dressed up fit to kill. It made Charley sore to see them, Hedwig in a new black tailored dress with a little lace at the throat and Jim dressed up like an undertaker in the suit he'd brought for the funeral. The lawyer was a small elderly German Jew with white hair brushed carefully over the big baldspot on the top of his head and goldrimmed pincenez on his thin nose. He was waiting for them when they came into the office. He got up smiling solemnly behind his desk littered with blue bound documents and made a little bow. Then he sat down beaming at them with his elbows among the papers, gently rubbing the tips of his fingers together. Nobody spoke for a moment. Jim coughed behind his hand like in church.

"Now let me see," said Mr. Goldberg in a gentlesweet voice with a slight accent like an actor's. "Oughtn't there to be more of you?"

Jim spoke up. "Esther and Ruth couldn't come. They both live on the coast. . . . I've got their power of attorneys. Ruth had her husband sign hers too, in case there might be any realestate."

Mr. Goldberg made a little clucking noise with his tongue. "Too bad. I'd rather have all parties present. . . . But in this case there will be no difficulty, I trust. Mr. James A. Anderson is named sole executor. Of course you understand that in a case like this the aim of all parties is to avoid taking the will to probate. That saves trouble and expense. There is no need of it when one of the legatees is named executor. . . . I shall proceed to read the will."

Mr. Goldberg must have drafted it himself because he sure seemed to enjoy reading it. Except for a legacy of one thousand dollars to Lizzie Green who had run Ma's boardinghouse up in Fargo, all the estate, real and personal, the lots in Fargo, the Liberty Bonds and the fifteenhundreddollar savingsaccount were left to the children jointly to be administered by James A. Anderson, sole executor, and eventually divided as they should agree among themselves.

"Now are there any questions and suggestions?" asked Mr. Goldberg genially.

Charley couldn't help seeing that Jim felt pretty good about it.

"It has been suggested," went on Mr. Goldberg's even voice that melted blandly among the documents like butter on a hot biscuit, "that Mr. Charles Anderson, who I understand is leaving soon for the East, would be willing to sign a power of attorney similar to those signed by his sisters. . . . The understanding is that the money will be invested in a mortgage on the Anderson Motor Sales Company."

Charley felt himself go cold all over. Jim and Hedwig were looking at him anxiously. "I don't understand the legal talk," he said, "but what I want to do is get mine as soon as possible. . . . I have a proposition in the East I want to put some money in."

Jim's thin lower lip began to tremble. "You'd better not be a damn fool, Charley. I know more about business than you do."

"About your business maybe, but not about mine."

Hedwig, who'd been looking at Charley like she could kill him, began to butt in: "Now, Charley, you let Jim do what he thinks best. He just wants to do what's best for all of us."

"Aw, shut your face," said Charley.

Jim jumped to his feet. "Look here, kid, you can't talk to my wife in that tone of voice."

"My friends, my dear friends," the lawyer crooned, rubbing his fingers together till it looked like they'd smoke, "we mustn't let ourselves be carried away, must we, not on a sol-

65

emn occasion like this. . . . What we want is a quiet fireside chat . . . the friendly atmosphere of the home. . . ."

Charley let out a snorting laugh. "That's what it's always been like in my home," he said halfaloud and turned his back on them to look out of the window over white roofs and iciclehung firescapes. The snow, thawing on the shingle roof of a frame house next door, was steaming in the early afternoon sun. Beyond it he could see blacklots deep in drifts and a piece of clean asphalt street where cars shuttled back and forth.

"Look here, Charley, snap out of it." Jim's voice behind him took on a pleading singsong tone. "You know the proposition Ford has put up to his dealers. . . . It's sink or swim for me. . . . But as an investment it's the chance of a lifetime. . . . The cars are there. . . . You can't lose, even if the company folds up."

Charley turned around. "Jim," he said mildly, "I don't want to argue about it. . . . I want to get my share of what Ma left in cash as soon as you and Mr. Goldberg can fix it up. . . . I got somethin' about airplane motors that'll make any old Ford agency look like thirty cents."

"But I want to put Ma's money in on a sure thing. The Ford car is the safest investment in the world, isn't that so, Mr. Goldberg?"

"You certainly see them everywhere. Perhaps the young man would wait and think things over a little. . . . I can make the preliminary steps . . ."

"Preliminary nothing. I want to get what I can out right now. If you can't do it I'll go and get another lawyer who will."

Charley picked up his hat and coat and walked out.

Next morning Charley turned up at breakfast in his overalls as usual. Jim told him he didn't want him doing any work in his business, seeing the way he felt about it. Charley went back upstairs to his room and lay down on the bed. When Hedwig came in to make it up she said, "Oh, are you still here?" and went out slamming the door after her. He could hear her slamming and banging things around the house as she and Aunt Hartmann did the housework.

About the middle of the morning, Charley went down to where Jim sat worrying over his books at the desk in the office. "Jim, I want to talk to you."

Jim took off his glasses and looked up at him. "Well, what's on your mind?" he asked, cutting off his words the way he had.

Charley said he'd sign a power of attorney for Jim if he'd lend him five hundred dollars right away. Then maybe later,

66

if the airplane proposition looked good, he'd let Jim in on it. Jim made a sour face at that. "All right," said Charley. "Make it four hundred. I got to get out of this dump."

Jim rose to his feet slowly. He was so pale Charley thought he must be sick. "Well, if you can't get it into your head what I'm up against . . . you can't and to hell with you. . . . All right, you and me are through. . . . Hedwig will have to borrow it at the bank in her name. . . . I'm up to my neck."

"Fix it any way you like," said Charley. "I got to get out of here."

It was lucky the phone rang when it did or Charley and Jim would have taken a poke at each other. Charley answered it. It was Emiscah. She said she'd been over in St. Paul and had seen him on the street yesterday and that he'd just said he was going to be out of town to give her the air, and he had to come over tonight or she didn't know what she'd do, he wouldn't want her to kill herself, would he? He got all balled up, what with rowing with Jim and everything and ended by telling her he'd come. By the time he was through talking, Jim had walked into the salesroom and was chinning with a customer, all smiles.

Going over on the trolley he decided he'd tell her he'd got married to a French girl during the war, but when he got up to her flat he didn't know what to say, she looked so thin and pale. He took her out to a dancehall. It made him feel bad how happy she acted, as if everything was fixed up again between them. When he left her he made a date for the next week.

Before that day came, he was off for Chi. He didn't begin to feel really good until he'd transferred acrosstown and was on the New York train. He had a letter in his pocket from Joe Askew telling him Joe would be in town to meet him. He had what was left of the three hundred berries Hedwig coughed up after deducting his board and lodging all winter

at ten dollars a week. But on the New York train he stopped thinking about all that and about Emiscah and the mean time he'd had and let himself think about New York and airplane motors and Doris Humphries.

When he woke up in the morning in the lower berth, he pushed up the shade and looked out; the train was going through the Pennsylvania hills, the fields were freshplowed, some of the trees had a little fuzz of green on them. In a farmyard a flock of yellow chickens were picking around under a peartree in bloom. "By God," he said aloud, "I'm through with the sticks."

Newsreel XLVIII

truly the Steel Corporation stands forth as a corporate colossus both physically and financially

> *Now the folks in Georgia they done gone wild*
> *Over that brand new dancin' style*
> > *Called   Shake   That   Thing*

CARBARNS BLAZE

GYPSY ARRESTED FOR TELLING THE TRUTH

Horsewhipping Hastens Wedding

that strength has long since become almost a truism as steel's expanding career progressed, yet the dimensions thereof need at times to be freshly measured to be caught in proper perspective

DAZED BY MAINE DEMOCRATS CRY FOR MONEY

> *shake that thing*

Woman of Mystery Tries Suicide in Park Lake

shake that thing

OLIVE THOMAS DEAD FROM POISON

LETTER SAID GET OUT OF WALL STREET

BOMB WAGON TRACED TO JERSEY
> *Shake   That   Thing*

Tin Lizzie

"*Mr. Ford the automobileer,*" the featurewriter wrote in 1900,

"*Mr. Ford the automobileer began by giving his steed three or four sharp jerks with the lever at the righthand side of the seat; that is, he pulled the lever up and down sharply in order, as he said, to mix air with gasoline and drive the charge into the exploding cylinder. . . . Mr. Ford slipped a small electric switch handle and there followed a puff, puff, puff. . . . The puffing of the machine assumed a higher key. . . . She was flying along about eight miles an hour. The ruts in the road were deep, but the machine certainly went with a dreamlike smoothness. There was none of the bumping common even to a steamer. . . . By this time the boulevard had been reached, and the automobileer, letting a lever fall a little, let her out. Whiz! She picked up speed with infinite rapidity. As she ran on there was a clattering behind, the new noise of the automobile.*"

For twenty years or more,

ever since he'd left his father's farm when he was sixteen to get a job in a Detroit machineshop, Henry Ford had been nuts about machinery. First it was watches, then he designed a steamtractor, then he built a horseless carriage with an engine adapted from the Otto gasengine he'd read about in *The World of Science*, then a mechanical buggy with a onecylinder fourcycle motor, that would run forward but not back;

at last, in ninetyeight, he felt he was far enough along to risk throwing up his job with the Detroit Edison Company, where he'd worked his way up from night fireman to chief engineer, to put all his time into working on a new gasoline engine,

(in the late eighties he'd met Edison at a meeting of electriclight employees in Atlantic City. He'd gone up to Edison after Edison had delivered an address and asked him if he thought gasoline was practical as a motor fuel. Edison had said yes. If Edison said it, it was true. Edison was the great admiration of Henry Ford's life);

and in driving his mechanical buggy, sitting there at the lever jauntily dressed in a tightbuttoned jacket and a high collar and a derby hat, back and forth over the level illpaved streets of Detroit,

scaring the big brewery horses and the skinny trotting horses and the sleekrumped pacers with the motor's loud explosions,

looking for men scatterbrained enough to invest money in a factory for building automobiles.

He was the eldest son of an Irish immigrant who during the Civil War had married the daughter of a prosperous Pennsylvania Dutch farmer and settled down to farming near Dearborn in Wayne County, Michigan;

like plenty of other Americans, young Henry grew up hating the endless sogging through the mud about the chores, the hauling and pitching manure, the kerosene lamps to clean, the irk and sweat and solitude of the farm.

He was a slender, active youngster, a good skater, clever with his hands; what he liked was to tend the machinery and let the others do the heavy work. His mother had told him not to drink, smoke, gamble, or go into debt, and he never did.

When he was in his early twenties his father tried to get him back from Detroit, where he was working as mechanic and repairman for the Drydock Engine Company that built engines for steamboats, by giving him forty acres of land.

Young Henry built himself an uptodate square white dwellinghouse with a false mansard roof and married and settled down on the farm,

but he let the hired men do the farming;

he bought himself a buzzsaw and rented a stationary engine and cut the timber off the woodlots.

He was a thrifty young man who never drank or smoked or gambled or coveted his neighbor's wife, but he couldn't stand living on the farm.

He moved to Detroit, and in the brick barn behind his house tinkered for years in his spare time with a mechanical buggy that would be light enough to run over the clayey wagonroads of Wayne County, Michigan.

By 1900 he had a practicable car to promote.

He was forty years old before the Ford Motor Company was started and production began to move.

Speed was the first thing the early automobile manufacturers went after. Races advertised the makes of cars.

71

Henry Ford himself hung up several records at the track at Grosse Pointe and on the ice on Lake St. Clair. In his .999 he did the mile in thirtynine and fourfifths seconds.

But it had always been his custom to hire others to do the heavy work. The speed he was busy with was speed in production, the records, records in efficient output. He hired Barney Oldfield, a stunt bicyclerider from Salt Lake City, to do the racing for him.

Henry Ford had ideas about other things than the designing of motors, carburetors, magnetos, jigs and fixtures, punches and dies; he had ideas about sales:

that the big money was in economical quantity production, quick turnover, cheap interchangeable easilyreplaced standardized parts:

it wasn't until 1909, after years of arguing with his partners, that Ford put out the first Model T.

Henry Ford was right.

That season he sold more than ten thousand tin lizzies, ten years later he was selling almost a million a year.

In these years the Taylor Plan was stirring up plantmanagers and manufacturers all over the country. Efficiency was the word. The same ingenuity that went into improving the performance of a machine could go into improving the performance of the workmen producing the machine.

In 1913 they established the assemblyline at Ford's. That season the profits were something like twentyfive million dollars, but they had trouble in keeping the men on the job, machinists didn't seem to like it at Ford's.

Henry Ford had ideas about other things than production.

He was the largest automobile manufacturer in the world; he paid high wages; maybe if the steady workers thought they were getting a cut (a very small cut) in the profits, it would give trained men an inducement to stick to their jobs,

wellpaid workers might save enough money to buy a tin lizzie; the first day Ford's announced that cleancut properlymarried American workers who wanted jobs had a chance to make five bucks a day (of course it turned out that there were strings to it; always there were strings to it)

such an enormous crowd waited outside the Highland Park plant

all through the zero January night

that there was a riot when the gates were opened; cops broke heads, jobhunters threw bricks; property, Henry Ford's

72

own property, was destroyed. The company dicks had to turn on the firehose to beat back the crowd.

The American Plan; automotive prosperity seeping down from above; it turned out there were strings to it.
But that five dollars a day
paid to good, clean American workmen
who didn't drink or smoke cigarettes or read or think,
and who didn't commit adultery
and whose wives didn't take in boarders,
made America once more the Yukon of the sweated workers of the world;
made all the tin lizzies and the automotive age, and incidentally,
made Henry Ford the automobileer, the admirer of Edison, the birdlover,
the great American of his time.

But Henry Ford had ideas about other things besides assemblylines and the living habits of his employees. He was full of ideas. Instead of going to the city to make his fortune, here was a country boy who'd made his fortune by bringing the city out to the farm. The precepts he'd learned out of McGuffey's Reader, his mother's prejudices and preconceptions, he had preserved clean and unworn as freshprinted bills in the safe in a bank.

He wanted people to know about his ideas, so he bought the *Dearborn Independent* and started a campaign against cigarettesmoking.

When war broke out in Europe, he had ideas about that too. (Suspicion of armymen and soldiering were part of the Mid-West farm tradition, like thrift, stickativeness, temperance, and sharp practice in money matters.) Any intelligent American mechanic could see that if the Europeans hadn't been a lot of ignorant underpaid foreigners who drank, smoked, were loose about women, and wasteful in their methods of production, the war could never have happened.

When Rosika Schwimmer broke through the stockade of secretaries and servicemen who surrounded Henry Ford and suggested to him that he could stop the war,
he said sure they'd hire a ship and go over and get the boys out of the trenches by Christmas.

He hired a steamboat, the *Oscar II,* and filled it up with pacifists and socialworkers,
to go over to explain to the princelings of Europe
that what they were doing was vicious and silly.

73

It wasn't his fault that Poor Richard's commonsense no longer rules the world and that most of the pacifists were nuts,

goofy with headlines.

When William Jennings Bryan went over to Hoboken to see him off, somebody handed William Jennings Bryan a squirrel in a cage; William Jennings Bryan made a speech with the squirrel under his arm. Henry Ford threw American Beauty roses to the crowd. The band played *I Didn't Raise My Boy to Be a Soldier.* Practical jokers let loose more squirrels. An eloping couple was married by a platoon of ministers in the saloon, and Mr. Zero, the flophouse humanitarian, who reached the dock too late to sail,

dove into the North River and swam after the boat.

The *Oscar II* was described as a floating Chautauqua; Henry Ford said it felt like a Middle-Western village, but by the time they reached Christiansand in Norway, the reporters had kidded him so that he had gotten cold feet and gone to bed. The world was too crazy outside of Wayne County, Michigan. Mrs. Ford and the management sent an Episcopal dean after him who brought him home under wraps,

and the pacifists had to speechify without him.

Two years later Ford's was manufacturing munitions, Eagle boats; Henry Ford was planning oneman tanks, and oneman submarines like the one tried out in the Revolutionary War. He announced to the press that he'd turn over his war profits to the government,

but there's no record that he ever did.

One thing he brought back from his trip
was the Protocols of the Elders of Zion.

He started a campaign to enlighten the world in the *Dearborn Independent;* the Jews were why the world wasn't like Wayne County, Michigan, in the old horse-and-buggy days;

the Jews had started the war, Bolshevism, Darwinism, Marxism, Nietzsche, short skirts and lipstick. They were behind Wall Street and the international bankers, and the whiteslave traffic and the movies and the Supreme Court and ragtime and the illegal liquor business.

Henry Ford denounced the Jews and ran for Senator and sued the *Chicago Tribune* for libel,

and was the laughingstock of the kept metropolitan press;

but when the metropolitan bankers tried to horn in on his business

he thoroughly outsmarted them.

In 1918 he had borrowed on notes to buy out his minority

stockholders for the picayune sum of seventyfive million dollars.

In Feburary, 1920, he needed cash to pay off some of these notes that were coming due. A banker is supposed to have called on him and offered him every facility if the banker's representative could be made a member of the board of directors. Henry Ford handed the banker his hat,

and went about raising the money in his own way:

he shipped every car and part he had in his plant to his dealers and demanded immediate cash payment. Let the other fellow do the borrowing had always been a cardinal principle. He shut down production and canceled all orders from the supplyfirms. Many dealers were ruined, many supplyfirms failed, but when he reopened his plant,

he owned it absolutely,

the way a man owns an unmortgaged farm with the taxes paid up.

In 1922 there started the Ford boom for President (high wages, waterpower, industry scattered to the small towns) that was skillfully pricked behind the scenes

by another crackerbarrel philosopher,

Calvin Coolidge;

but in 1922 Henry Ford sold one million three hundred and thirty-two thousand two hundred and nine tin lizzies; he was the richest man in the world.

Good roads had followed the narrow ruts made in the mud by the Model T. The great automotive boom was on. At Ford's production was improving all the time; less waste, more spotters, strawbosses, stool-pigeons (fifteen minutes for lunch, three minutes to go to the toilet, the Taylorized speed-up everywhere, reachunder, adjustwasher, screwdown bolt, shove in cotterpin, reachunder, adjustwasher, screwdown bolt, reachunderadjustscrewdownreachunderadjust, until every ounce of life was sucked off into production and at night the workmen went home gray shaking husks).

Ford owned every detail of the process from the ore in the hills until the car rolled off the end of the assemblyline under its own power; the plants were rationalized to the last ten-thousandth of an inch as measured by the Johansen scale:

in 1926 the production cycle was reduced to eightyone hours from the ore in the mine to the finished salable car proceeding under its own power,

but the Model T was obsolete.

New Era prosperity and the American Plan
(there were strings to it, always there were strings to it)
had killed Tin Lizzie.

Ford's was just one of many automobile plants.
When the stockmarket bubble burst,
Mr. Ford the crackerbarrel philosopher said jubilantly,
"I told you so.
Serves you right for gambling and getting in debt.
The country is sound."
But when the country on cracked shoes, in frayed trousers,
belts tightened over hollow bellies,
idle hands cracked and chapped with the cold of that cold-
est March day of 1932,
started marching from Detroit to Dearborn, asking for
work and the American Plan, all they could think of at
Ford's was machineguns.
The country was sound, but they mowed the marchers
down.
They shot four of them dead.

Henry Ford as an old man
is a passionate antiquarian
(lives besieged on his father's farm embedded in an estate
of thousands of millionaire acres, protected by an army of
servicemen, secretaries, secret agents, dicks under orders of
an English exprizefighter,
always afraid of the feet in broken shoes on the roads,
afraid the gangs will kidnap his grandchildren,
that a crank will shoot him,
that Change and the idle hands out of work will break
through the gates and the high fences;
protected by a private army against
the new America of starved children and hollow bellies
and cracked shoes stamping on souplines,
that has swallowed up the old thrifty farmlands
of Wayne County, Michigan,
as if they had never been).
Henry Ford as an old man
is a passionate antiquarian.
He rebuilt his father's farmhouse and put it back exactly in
the state he remembered it in as a boy. He built a village of
museums for buggies, sleighs, coaches, old plows, water-
wheels, obsolete models of motorcars. He scoured the country
for fiddlers to play oldfashioned squaredances.
Even old taverns he bought and put back into their original shape, as well as Thomas Edison's early laboratories.
When he bought the Wayside Inn near Sudbury, Massachusetts, he had the new highway where the newmodel cars
roared and slithered and hissed oilily past (*the new noise of
the automobile*)

moved away from the door,
put back the old bad road,
so that everything might be
the way it used to be,
in the days of horses and buggies.

Newsreel XLIX

Jack o' Diamonds Jack o' Diamonds
You rob my pocket   of silver and gold

WITNESSES OF MYSTERY IN SLUSH PROBE

PHILADELPHIAN BEATEN TO DEATH IN HIS ROOM

the men who the workers had been told a short year
before were fighting their battle for democracy upon the
bloodstained fields of France and whom they had been
urged to support by giving the last of their strength to the
work of production—these men were coming to teach
them democracy and with them came their instruments of
murder, their automatic rifles, their machineguns, their
cannon that could clear a street two miles long in a few
minutes and the helmets that the workers of Gary had
produced

Yes we have no bananas
We have no bananas today

TRACTION RING KILLS BUS BILL

DRUNKEN TROOPS IN SKIRTS DANCE AS HOUSES BURN

GIRL SUICIDE WAS A FRIEND OF OLIVE THOMAS

KILLS SELF DESPITE WIFE WHO GOES MAD

SEEKS FACTS OF HUNT FOR CASH IN THE EAST

the business consists in large part of financing manufacturers and merchants by purchasing evidences of in-

78

debtedness arising from the sale of a large variety of naturally marketed products such as automobiles, electrical appliances, machinery

Charley Anderson

"Misser Andson Misser Andson, telegram for Misser Andson." Charley held out his hand for the telegram, and standing in the swaying aisle read the strips of letters pasted on the paper:

DOWN WITH FLU   WIRE ME ADDRESS   SEE YOU NEXT WEEK   JOE

"A hell of a note," he kept saying to himself as he wormed his way back to his seat past women closing up their bags, a grayhaired man getting into his overcoat, the porter loaded with suitcases. "A hell of a note." The train was already slowing down for the Grand Central.

It was quiet on the gray underground platform when he stepped out of the stuffy Pullman and took his bag from the porter, lonelylooking. He walked up the incline swinging his heavy suitcase. The train had given him a headache. The station was so big it didn't have the crowded look he'd remembered New York had. Through the thick glass of the huge arched windows he could see rain streaking the buildings opposite. Roaming round the station, not knowing which way to go, he found himself looking in the window of a lunchroom.

He went in and sat down. The waitress was a little dark sourfaced girl with rings under her eyes. It was a muggy sort of day, the smell of soap from the dishwashing and of hot grease from the kitchen hung in streaks in the air. When the waitress leaned over to set the place for him, he got a whiff of damp underclothes and armpits and talcumpowder. He looked up at her and tried to get a smile out of her. When she turned to go get him some tomatosoup, he watched her square bottom moving back and forth under her black dress. There was something heavy and lecherous about the rainy eastern day.

He spooned soup into his mouth without tasting it. Before he'd finished, he got up and went to the phonebooth. He didn't have to look up her number. Waiting for the call, he was so nervous the sweat ran down behind his ears. When a woman's voice answered, his voice dried up way down in his throat. Finally he got it out. "I want to speak to Miss Humphries, please. . . . Tell her it's Charley Anderson . . . Lieu-

79

tenant Anderson." He was still trying to clear his throat when her voice came in an intimate caressing singsong. Of course she remembered him, her voice said, too sweet of him to call

her up, of course they must see each other all the time, how thrilling, she'd just love to, but she was going out of town for the weekend, yes, a long weekend. But wouldn't he call her up next week, no, towards the end of the week? She'd just adore to see him.

When he went back to his table the waitress was fussing around it.

"Didn't you like your soup?" she asked him.

"Check. . . . Had to make some phonecalls."

"Oh, phonecalls," she said in a kidding voice. This time it was the waitress who was trying to get a smile out of him.

"Let's have a piece of pie and a cup of coffee," he said, keeping his eyes on the bill-of-fare.

"They got lovely lemonmeringue pie," the waitress said, with a kind of sigh that made him laugh.

He looked up at her laughing feeling horny and outafterit again: "All right, sweetheart, make it lemonmeringue."

When he'd eaten the pie, he paid his check and went back

into the phonebooth. Some woman had been in there leaving a strong reek of perfume. He called up the Century Club to see if Ollie Taylor was in town. They said he was in Europe; then he called up the Johnsons; they were the only people left he knew. Eveline Johnson's voice had a deep muffled sound over the phone. When he told her his name, she laughed and said, "Why, of course we'd love to see you. Come down to dinner tonight; we'll introduce you to the new baby."

When he got out of the subway at Astor Place, it wasn't time to go to dinner yet. He asked the newsvendor which way Fifth Avenue was and walked up and down the quiet redbrick blocks. He felt stuffy from the movie he'd killed the afternoon in. When he looked at his watch, it was only half-past six. He wasn't invited to the Johnsons' till seven. He'd already passed the house three times when he decided to go up the steps. Their names were scrawled out, Paul Johnson—Eveline Hutchins, on a card above the bell. He rang the bell and stood fidgeting with his necktie while he waited. Nobody answered. He was wondering if he ought to ring again when Paul Johnson came briskly down the street from Fifth Avenue with his hat on the back of his head, whistling as he walked.

"Why, hello, Anderson, where did you come from?" he asked in an embarrassed voice. He had several bags of groceries that he had to pile on his left arm before he could shake hands.

"Guess I ought to congratulate you," said Charley.

Paul looked at him blankly for a moment; then he blushed. "Of course . . . the son and heir. . . . Oh, well, it's a hostage to fortune, that's what they say. . . ."

Paul let him into a large bare oldfashioned room with flowing purple curtains in the windows. "Just sit down for a minute. I'll see what Eveline's up to." He pointed to a horsehair sofa and went through the sliding doors into a back room.

He came back immediately, carefully pulling the door to behind him. "Why, that's great. Eveline says you're goin' to have supper with us. She said you just came back from out there. How'd things seem out there? I wouldn't go back if they paid me now. New York's a great life if you don't weaken. . . . Here, I'll show you where you can clean up. . . . Eveline's invited a whole mess of people to supper. I'll have to run around to the butcher's. . . . Want to wash up?"

The bathroom was steamy and smelt of bathsalts. Somebody had just taken a bath there. Babyclothes hung to dry over the tub. A red douchebag hung behind the door and over it a yellow lace négligée of some kind. It made Charley

81

feel funny to be in there. When he'd dried his hands he sniffed them, and the perfume of the soap filled his head.

When he came out of the door, he found Mrs. Johnson leaning against the white marble mantel with a yellowbacked French novel in her hand. She had on a long lacy gown with puff sleeves and wore tortoiseshell readingglasses. She took off the glasses and tucked them into the book and stood holding out her hand.

"I'm so glad you could come. I don't go out much yet, so I don't get to see anybody unless they come to see me."

"Mighty nice of you to ask me. I been out in the sticks. I tell you it makes you feel good to see folks from the other side. . . . This is the nearest thing to Paree I've seen for some time."

She laughed; he remembered her laugh from the boat. The way he felt like kissing her made him fidgety. He lit a cigarette.

"Do you mind not smoking? For some reason tobaccosmoke makes me feel sick ever since before I had the baby, so I don't let anybody smoke. Isn't it horrid of me?"

Charley blushed and threw his cigarette in the grate. He began to walk back and forth in the tall narrow room.

"Hadn't we better sit down?" she said with her slow irritating smile. "What are you up to in New York?"

"Got me a job. I got plans. . . . Say, how's the baby? I'd like to see it."

"All right, when he wakes up I'll introduce you. You can be one of his uncles. I've got to do something about supper now. Doesn't it seem strange us all being in New York?"

"I bet this town's a hard nut to crack."

She went into the back room through the sliding doors and soon a smell of sizzling butter began to seep through them. Charley caught himself just at the point of lighting another cigarette, then roamed round the room, looking at the oldfashioned furniture, the three white lilies in a vase, the shelves of French books, until Paul, red in the face and sweating, passed through with more groceries and told him he'd shake up a drink.

Charley sat down on the couch and stretched out his legs. It was quiet in the highceilinged room. There was something cozy about the light rustle and clatter the Johnsons made moving around behind the sliding doors, the Frenchy smell of supper cooking. Paul came back with a tray piled with plates and glasses and a demijohn of wine. He laid a loaf of frenchbread on the marbletopped table and a plate of tunafish and a cheese. "I'm sorry I haven't got anything to make a cocktail with. . . . I didn't get out of the office till late. . . . All we've got's this dago wine."

"Check. . . . I'm keepin' away from that stuff a little. . . . Too much on my mind."

"Are you round town looking for a job?"

"Feller goin' in on a proposition with me. You remember Joe Askew on the boat? Great boy, wasn't he? The trouble is the damn fool's laid up with the flu and that leaves me high and dry until he gets down here."

"Things are sure tighter than I expected. . . . My old man got me into a grainbroker's office over in Jersey City . . . just to tide me over. But gosh, I don't want to wear out a desk all my life. I wouldn'ta done it if it hadn't been for the little stranger."

"Well, we've got something that'll be worth money if we ever get the kale to put in to develop it."

Eveline opened the sliding doors and brought in a bowl of salad. Paul had started to talk about the grain business, but he shut his mouth and waited for her to speak.

"It's curious," she said. "After the war New York. . . . Nobody can keep away from it."

A baby's thin squalling followed her out of the back room. "That's his messcall," said Paul.

"If you really want to see him," said Eveline, "come along now, but I should think it would be just too boring to look at other people's babies."

"I'd like to," said Charley. "Haven't got any of my own to look at."

"How are you so sure?" said Eveline, with a slow teasing smile. Charley got red and laughed.

They stood round the pink crib with their wineglasses in their hands. Charley found himself looking down into a toothless pink face and two little pudgy hands grabbing the air.

"I suppose I ought to say it looks like Daddy," he said.

"The little darling looks more like our Darwinian ancestor," said Eveline coldly. "When I first saw him I cried and cried. Oh, I hope he grows a chin."

Charley caught himself looking out of the corner of his eye at Paul's chin that wasn't so very prominent either. "He's a cheerful little rascal," he said.

Eveline brought the baby a bottle from the kitchenette next the bathroom, then they went into the other room.

"This layout sure makes me feel envious," Charley was saying when he caught Eveline Johnson's eye. She shrugged her shoulders. "You two and the baby all nicely set with a place to live and a glass of wine and everything. . . . Makes

83

me feel the war's over. . . . What I've got to do is crack down an' get to work."

"Don't worry," said Paul. "It'll happen soon enough."

"Well, I wish people would come. The casserole's all ready," said Eveline. "Charles Edward Holden is coming. . . . He's always late."

"He said maybe he'd come," said Paul. "Here's Al now. That's his knock."

A lanky sallow individual came in the door from the street. Paul introduced him to Charley as his brother Al. The man looked at Charley with a peevish searching gray eye for a moment. "Lieutenant Anderson . . . Say, we've met before someplace."

"Were you over on the other side?"

The lanky man shook his head vigorously. "No. . . . It must have been in New York. . . . I never forget a face." Charley felt his face getting red.

A tall haggardfaced man named Stevens and a plump little girl came in. Charley didn't catch the girl's name. She had straight black bobbed hair. The man named Stevens paid no attention to anybody but Al Johnson. The little girl paid no attention to anybody but Stevens. "Well, Al," he said threateningly, "have recent events changed your ideas any?"

"We've got to go slow, Don, we've got to go slow . . . we

can't affront every decent human instinct. . . . We've got to stick close to the workingclass."

"Oh, if you're all going to start about the workingclass, I think we'd better have supper and not wait for Holden," said Eveline, getting to her feet. "Don'll be so cross if he argues on an empty stomach."

"Who's that? Charles Edward Holden?" asked Al Johnson with a tone of respect in his voice.

"Don't wait for him," said Don Stevens. "He's nothing but a bourgeois muckraker."

Charley and Paul helped Eveline bring in another table that was all set in the bedroom. Charley managed to sit next to her. "Gee, this is wonderful food. It all makes me think of old Paree," he kept saying. "My brother wanted me to go into a Ford agency with him out in the Twin Cities, but how can you keep them down on the farm after they've seen Paree?"

"But New York's the capital now." It was teasing the way she leaned toward him when she spoke, the way her long eyes seemed to be all the time figuring out something about him.

"I hope you'll let me come around sometimes," he said. "It's goin' to be kinder hard sleddin' in New York till I get my feet on the ground."

"Oh, I'm always here," she said, "and shall be till we can afford to get a reliable nurse for Jeremy. Poor Paul has to work late at the office half the time. . . . Oh, I wish we could all make a lot of money right away quick."

Charley smiled grimly. "Give the boys a chance. We ain't properly got the khaki off our skins yet."

Charley couldn't keep up with the conversation very well, so he leaned back on the sofa looking at Eveline Johnson. Paul didn't say much either. After he'd brought in coffee he disappeared altogether. Eveline and the little girl at the head of the table both seemed to think Stevens was pretty wonderful, and Al Johnson, who sat next to Charley on the sofa, kept leaning across him to make a point with Eveline and shake his long forefinger. Part of the time it looked like Al Johnson and Stevens would take a poke at each other. What with not following their talk—after all, he wasn't onto the town yet—and the good food and the wine, Charley began to get sleepy. He finally had to get up to stretch his legs.

Nobody paid any attention to him, so he strolled into the kitchenette where he found Paul washing the dishes. "Lemme help you wipe," he said.

"Naw, I got a system," said Paul. "You see Eveline does all the cooking, so it's only fair for me to wash the dishes."

"Say, won't those birds get in trouble if they talk like that?" Charley jerked his thumb in the direction of the front room.

"Don Stevens is a red, so he's a marked man anyway."

"Mind you, I don't say they're wrong, but, Jesus, we got our livin's to make."

"Al's on the *World*. They're pretty liberal down there."

"Out our way a man can't open his face without stirrin' up a hornet'snest," said Charley, laughing. "They don't know the war's over."

When the dishes were done, they went back to the front room.

Don Stevens strode up to Charley. "Eveline says you are an aviator," he said, frowning. "Tell us what aviators think about. Are they for the exploiting class or the workingclass?"

"That's a pretty big order," drawled Charley. "Most of the fellers I know are tryin' to get into the workin'class."

The doorbell rang. Eveline looked up smiling. "That's probably Charles Edward Holden," said Al.

Paul opened the door.

"Hello, Dick," said Eveline. "Everybody thought you were Charles Edward Holden."

"Well, maybe I am," said a nattilydressed young man with slightly-bulging blue eyes who appeared in the doorway. "I've been feeling a little odd all day."

Eveline introduced the new guy by his military handle: "Captain Savage, Lieutenant Anderson."

"Humph," said Stevens in the back of the room.

Charley noticed that Stevens and the young man who had just come in stared at each other without speaking. It was all getting very confusing. Eveline and the bobbedhaired girl began to make polite remarks to each other in chilly voices. Charley guessed it was about time for him to butt out. "I've got to alley along, Mrs. Johnson," he said.

"Say, Anderson, wait for me a minute. I'll walk along the street with you," Al Johnson called across the room at him.

Charley suddenly found himself looking right in Eveline's eyes. "I sure enjoyed it," he said.

"Come in to tea some afternoon," she said.

"All right, I'll do that." He squeezed her hand hard. While he was saying goodbye to the others, he heard Captain Savage and Eveline giggling together.

"I just came in to see how the other half lives," he was saying. "Eveline, you look too beautiful tonight."

Charley felt good standing on the stoop in the spring evening. The city air had a cool rinsed smell after the rain. He was wondering if she . . . Well, you never can tell till you try.

Al Johnson came out behind him and took his arm. "Say, Paul says you come from out home."

"Sure," said Charley. "Don't you see the hayseed in my ears?"

"Gosh, when Eveline has two or more of her old beaux calling on her at once it's a bit heavy. . . . And she like to froze that poor little girl of Don's to death. . . . Say, how about you and me go have a drink of whiskey to take the taste of that damn red ink out of our mouths?"

"That 'ud be great," said Charley.

They walked across Fifth Avenue and down the street until they got to a narrow black door. Al Johnson rang the bell and a man in shirtsleeves let them into a passage that smelt of toilets. They walked through that into a barroom.

"Well, that's more like it," said Al Johnson. "After all, I have only one night off a week."

"It's like the good old days that never were," said Charley.

They sat down at a small round table opposite the bar and ordered rye. Al Johnson suddenly waved his long forefinger across the table. "I remember when it was I met you. It was the day war was declared. We were all drunk as coots down at Little Hungary." Charley said jeez, he'd met a lot of people that night. "Sure that's when it was," said Al Johnson. "I never forget a face," and he called to the waiter to make it beer chasers.

They had several more ryes with beer chasers on the strength of old times. "Why, New York's like any other dump," Charley was saying, "it's just a village."

"Greenwich Village," said Al Johnson.

They had a flock of whiskies on the strength of the good old times they'd had at Little Hungary. They didn't like it at the table any more, so they stood up at the bar. There were two pallid young men at the bar and a plump girl with stringy hair in a Bulgarian embroidered blouse. They were old friends of Al Johnson's. "An old newspaperman," Al Johnson was saying, "never forgets faces . . . or names." He turned to Charley. "Colonel, meet my very dear friends . . . Colonel . . . er . . ." Charley had put out his hand and was just about to say Anderson when Al Johnson came out with "Charles Edward Holden, meet my artistical friends . . ."

Charley never got a chance to put a word in. The two young men started to explain the play they'd been to at the Washington Square Players. The girl had a turnedup nose and blue eyes with dark rings under them. The eyes looked up at him effusively while she shook his hand.

"Not really. . . . Oh, I've so wanted to meet you, Mr. Holden. I read all your articles."

"But I'm not really . . ." started Charley.

"Not really a colonel," said the girl.

"Just a colonel for a night," said Al with a wave of his hand and ordered some more whiskies.

"Oh, Mr. Holden," said the girl, who put her whiskey away like a trooper, "isn't it wonderful that we should meet like this? . . . I thought you were much older and not so goodlooking. Now, Mr. Holden, I want you to tell me all about everything."

"Better call me Charley."

"My name's Bobbie . . . you call me Bobbie, won't you?"

"Check," said Charley.

She drew him away down the bar a little. "I was having a rotten time. . . . They are dear boys, but they won't talk about anything except how Philip drank iodine because Edward didn't love him any more. I hate personalities, don't you? I like to talk, don't you? Oh, I hate people who don't do things. I mean books and world conditions and things like that, don't you?"

"Sure," said Charley.

They found themselves at the end of the bar. Al Johnson seemed to have found a number of other very dear friends to celebrate old times with.

The girl plucked at Charley's sleeve: "Suppose we go somewhere quiet and talk. I can't hear myself think in here."

"Do you know someplace we can dance?" asked Charley. The girl nodded.

On the street she took his arm. The wind had gone into the north, cold and gusty. "Let's skip," said the girl, "or are you too dignified, Mr. Holden?"

"Better call me Charley."

They walked east and down a street full of tenements and crowded little Italian stores. The girl rang at a basement door. While they were waiting, she put her hand on his arm. "I got some money . . . let this be my party."

"But I wouldn't like that."

"All right, we'll make it fifty-fifty. I believe in sexual equality, don't you?" Charley leaned over and kissed her. "Oh, this is a wonderful evening for me. . . . You are the nicest celebrity I ever met. . . . Most of them are pretty stuffy, don't you think so? No joie de vivre."

"But," stammered Charley, "I'm not . . ."

As he spoke, the door opened. "Hello, Jimmy," said the girl to a slicklooking young man in a brown suit who opened

88

the door. "Meet the boyfriend . . . Mr. Grady . . . Mr. Holden."

The young man's eyes flashed. "Not Charles Edward . . ." The girl nodded her head excitedly, so that a big lock of her hair flopped over one eye. "Well, sir, I'm very happy to meet you. . . . I'm a constant reader, sir."

Bowing and blushing, Jimmy found them a table next to the dancefloor in the stuffy little cabaret hot from the spotlights and the cigarettesmoke and the crowded dancers. They ordered more whiskey and welshrabbits. Then she grabbed Charley's hand and pulled him to his feet. They danced. The girl rubbed close to him till he could feel her little round breasts through the Bulgarian blouse.

"My . . . the boy can dance," she whispered. "Let's forget everything, who we are, the day of the week . . ."

"Me . . . I forgot two hours ago," said Charley, giving her a squeeze.

"You're just a plain farmerlad and I'm a barefoot girl."

"More truth than poetry to that," said Charley through his teeth.

"Poetry . . . I love poetry, don't you?"

They danced until the place closed up. They were staggering when they got out on the black streets. They stumbled past garbagepails. Cats ran out from under their feet. They stopped and talked about free love with a cop. At every corner they stopped and kissed. As she was looking for her latchkey in her purse, she said thoughtfully: "People who really do things make the most beautiful lovers, don't you think so."

Charley woke up first. Sunlight was streaming in through an uncurtained window. The girl was asleep, her face pressed into the pillow. Her mouth was open and she looked considerably older than she had the night before. Her skin was pasty and green and she had stingy hair.

Charley put his clothes on quietly. On big tables inches deep in dust and littered with drawings of funnylooking nudes, he found a piece of charcoal. On the back of a sheet of yellow paper that had a half a poem written on it he wrote: "Had a swell time . . . . Goodbye . . . Goodluck.

Charley." He didn't put his shoes on until he got to the bottom of the creaky stairs.

Out on the street in the cold blowy spring morning he felt wonderful. He kept bursting out laughing. A great little old town. He went into a lunchroom at the corner of Eighth Street and ordered himself a breakfast of scrambled eggs and bacon and hotcakes and coffee. He kept giggling as he ate it. Then he went uptown to Fortysecond Street on the El. Grimy roofs, plateglass windows, grimy bulbs of electriclight signs, fireescapes, watertanks, all looked wonderful in the gusty sunlight.

At the Grand Central Station the clock said eleventhirty. Porters were calling the names of westbound trains. He got his bag from the checkroom and took a taxi to the Chatterton House. That was where Joe Askew had written he ought to stay, a better address than the Y. His suitcase cut into his hand, as it was heavy from blueprints and books on mechanical drawing, so he jumped into a taxi. When the clerk at the desk asked for a reference, he brought out his reserve commission.

The place had an elevator and baths and showers at the ends of the dimlylit halls, and a lot of regulations on the back of the door of the little shoebox of a room they showed him into. He threw himself on the cot with his clothes on. He was sleepy. He lay giggling looking up at the ceiling. A great little old town.

As it turned out, he lived a long time in that stuffy little greenpapered room with its rickety mission furniture. The first few days he went around to see all the aviation concerns he found listed in the phonebook to see if he could pick up some kind of temporary job. He ran into a couple of men he'd known overseas, but nobody could promise him a job; if he'd only come a couple of months sooner. Everybody said things were slack. The politicians had commercial aviation by the short hairs and there you were, that was that. Too damn many flyers around looking for jobs anyway.

At the end of the first week he came back from a trip to a motorbuilding outfit in Long Island City, where they halfpromised him a drafting job later in the summer, that is, if they got the contract their Washington man was laying for, to find a letter from Mrs. Askew: Joe was a very sick man, double pneumonia. It would be a couple of months before he could get to the city. Joe had insisted on her writing, though she didn't think he was well enough to worry about business matters, but she'd done it to ease his mind. He said for Charley to be sure not to let anybody else see his plans until he got a

91

patent, better get a job to tide over until they could get the thing started right.

Tide over, hell; Charley sat on his sagging bed counting his money. Four tens, a two, a one, and fiftythree cents in change. With the room eight dollars a week that didn't make his summer's prospects look so hot.

At last one day he got hold of Doris Humphries on the phone and she asked him to come on up next afternoon. At the Humphries' apartment it was just like it had been at the Bentons' the night he went there with Ollie Taylor, except that there was a maid instead of a butler. He felt pretty uncomfortable because there were only women there. Doris's mother was a haggard dressedup woman who gave him a searching look that he felt went right through him into the wallet in his back pocket.

They had tea and cakes, and Charley wasn't sure if he ought to smoke or not. They said Ollie Taylor had gone abroad again, to the south of France, and as Ollie Taylor was the only thing he had in common with them to talk about, that pretty well dried up the conversation. Dressed in civvies it wasn't so easy talking to rich women as it had been in the uniform. Still Doris smiled at him nicely and talked in a friendly confidential way about how sick she was of this society whirl and everything, that she was going out and get her a job. That's not so easy, thought Charley. She complained she never met any interesting men. She said Charley and Ollie Taylor—of course Ollie was an old dear—were the only men she knew she could stand talking to. "I guess it's the war and going overseas that's done something to you," she said, looking up at him. "When you've seen things like that, you can't take yourself so seriously as these miserable lounge-lizards I have to meet. They are nothing but clotheshangers."

When Charley left the big apartmenthouse, his head was swimming so he was almost bagged by a taxicab crossing the street. He walked down the broad avenue humming with traffic in the early dark. She'd promised to go to a show with him one of these nights.

When he went to get Doris to take her out to dinner one evening in early May, after the engagement had been put off from week to week—she was so terribly busy, she always complained over the phone, she'd love to come but she was so terribly busy—he only had twenty bucks left in his wallet. He waited for her some time alone in the drawingroom of the Humphries' apartment. White covers had been hung on the piano and the chairs and curtains and the big white room smelt of mothballs. It all gave him a feeling he'd come too late. Doris came in at last looking so pale and silky and golden in a lowcut eveningdress it made him catch his breath.

"Hello, Charley, I hope you're not starved," she said in that intimate way that always made him feel he'd known her a long time. "You know I never could keep track of the time."

"Gosh, Doris, you look wonderful." He caught her looking at his gray business suit. "Oh, forgive me," she said. "I'll run and change my clothes." Something chilly came into her voice and left it at once. "It'll take only a minute."

He felt himself getting red. "I guess I oughta have worn eveningclothes," he said. "But I've been so busy. I haven't had my trunk sent out from Minnesota yet."

"Of course not. It's almost summer. I don't know what I was thinking about. Wits woolgathering again."

"Couldn't you go like that, you look lovely."

"But it looks so silly to see a girl dressed up like a plush horse with a man in a business suit. It'll be more fun anyway . . . less the social engagement, you know. . . . Honestly I'll be only five minutes by the clock."

Doris went out and half an hour later came back in a pearlgray streetdress. A maid followed her in with a tray with cocktailshaker and glasses. "I thought we might have a drink before we go out. Then we'll be sure to know what we are getting," she said.

He took her to the McAlpin for supper; he didn't know any place else. It was already eight o'clock. The theatertickets were burning his pocket, but she didn't seem in any hurry. It was halfpast nine when he put her in a taxi to go to the show. The taxi filled up with the light crazy smell of her perfume and her hair.

"Doris, lemme say what I want to say for a minute," he blurted out suddenly. "I don't know whether you like anybody else very much. I kinder don't think you do from what you said about the guys you know."

"Oh, please don't propose," she said. "If you knew how I hated proposals, particularly in a cab caught in a traffic jam."

"No, I don't mean that. You wouldn't want to marry me the way I am now anyway . . . not by a long shot. I gotta get on my hindlegs first. But I'm goin' to pretty soon. . . . You know aviation is the comin' industry. . . . Ten years from now . . . Well, us fellers have a chance to get in on the groundfloor. . . . I want you to give me a break, Doris, hold off the other guys for a little while . . ."

95

"Wait for you ten years, my, that's a romantic notion . . .
my grandmother would have thought it was lovely."

"I mighta known you'd kid about it. Well, here we are."

Charley tried to keep from looking sour when he helped
Doris out. She squeezed his hand just for a second as she
leaned on it. His heart started pounding. As they followed the
usher into the dark theater full of girls and jazz, she put her
small hand very lightly on his arm. Above their heads was
the long powdery funnel of the spotlight spreading to a tin-
selly glitter where a redlipped girl in organdy was dancing.
He squeezed Doris's hand hard against his ribs with his arm.

"All right, you get what I mean," he whispered. "You
think about it . . . I've never had a girl get me this way before, Doris." They dropped into their seats. The people behind started shushing, so Charley had to shut up. He couldn't
pay any attention to the show.

"Charley, don't expect anything, but I think you're a swell
guy," she said when, stuffy from the hot theater and the
lights and the crowd, they got into a taxi as they came out.
She let him kiss her, but terribly soon the taxi stopped at her
apartmenthouse. He said goodnight to her at the elevator.
She shook her head with a smile when he asked if he could
come up.

He walked home weak in the knees through the afterthe-
theater bustle of Park Avenue and Fortysecond Street. He
could still feel her mouth on his mouth, the smell of her pale
frizzy hair, the littleness of her hands on his chest when she
pushed his face away from hers.

The next morning he woke late feeling pooped as if he'd
been on a threeday drunk. He bought the papers and had a
cup of coffee and a doughnut at the coffeebar that stank of
stale swill. This time he didn't look in the Business Opportunities column but under Mechanics and Machinists. That afternoon he got a job in an automobile repairshop on First Avenue. It made him feel bad to go back to the overalls and the
grease under your fingernails and punching the timeclock like
that, but there was no help for it. When he got back to the
house he found a letter from Emiscah that made him feel
worse than ever.

The minute he'd read the letter he tore it up. Nothing
doing, bad enough to go back to grinding valves without
starting that stuff up again. He sat down on the bed with his
eyes full of peeved tears. It was too god-damned hellish to
have everything close in on him like this after getting his
commission and the ambulance service and the Lafayette Es-
cadrille and having a mechanic attend to his plane and do all
the dirty work. Of all the lousy stinking luck. When he felt a

little quieter he got up and wrote Joe for Christ's sake to get well as soon as he could, that he had turned down an offer of a job with Triangle Motors over in Long Island City and was working as a mechanic in order to tide over and that he was darn sick of it and anxious to get going on their little proposition.

He'd worked at the repairshop for two weeks before he found out that the foreman ran a pokergame every payday in a disused office in the back of the building. He got in on it and played pretty carefully. The first couple of weeks he lost half his pay, but then he began to find that he wasn't such a bad pokerplayer at that. He never lost his temper and was pretty good at doping out where the cards were. He was careful not to blow about his winnings either, so he got away with more of their money than the other guys figured. The foreman was a big loudmouthed harp who wasn't any too pleased to have Charley horning in on his winnings; it had been his habit to take the money away from the boys himself. Charley kept him oiled up with a drink now and then, and besides, once he got his hand in he could get through more work than any man there. He always changed into his good clothes before he went home.

He didn't get to see Doris before she went to York Harbor for the summer. The only people he knew were the Johnsons. He went down there a couple of times a week. He built them bookshelves and one Sunday helped them paint the livingroom floor.

Another Sunday he called up early to see if the Johnsons wanted to go down to Long Beach to take a swim. Paul was in bed with a sorethroat but Eveline said she'd go. Well, if she wants it she can have it, he was telling himself as he walked downtown, through the empty grime of the hot Sundaymorning streets. She came to the door in a loose yellow silk and lace négligée that showed where her limp breasts began. Before she could say anything he'd pulled her to him and kissed her. She closed her eyes and let herself go limp in his arms. Then she pushed him away and put her finger on her lips.

He blushed and lit a cigarette. "Do you mind," he said in a shaky voice.

"I'll have to get used to cigarettes again sometime, I suppose," she said, very low.

He walked over to the window to pull himself together. She followed him and reached for his cigarette and took a couple of puffs of it. Then she said aloud in a cool voice, "Come on back and say hello to Paul."

Paul was lying back against the pillows looking pale and sweaty. On a table beside the bed there was a coffeepot and a flowered cup and saucer and a pitcher of hot milk.

"Hi, Paul, you look like you was leadin' the life of Riley," Charley heard himself say in a hearty voice.

"Oh, you have to spoil them a little when they're sick," cooed Eveline.

Charley found himself laughing too loud. "Hope it's nothin' serious, old top."

"Naw, I get these damn throats. You kids have a good time at the beach. I wish I could come too."

"Oh, it may be horrid," said Eveline. "But if we don't like it we can always come back."

"Don't hurry," said Paul. "I got plenty to read. I'll be fine here."

"Well, you and Jeremy keep bachelor hall together."

Eveline had gotten up a luncheonbasket with some sandwiches and a thermos full of cocktails. She looked very stylish, Charley thought, as he walked beside her along the dusty sunny street carrying the basket and the Sunday paper, in her little turnedup white hat and her lightyellow summer dress. "Oh, let's have fun," she said. "It's been so long since I had any fun."

When they got out of the train at Long Beach, a great blue wind was streaming off the sea blurred by little cold patches of mist. There was a big crowd along the boardwalk. The two of them walked a long way up the beach. "Don't you think it would be fun if we could get away from everybody?" she was saying. They walked along, their feet sinking into the sand, their voices drowned in the pound and hiss of the surf. "This is great stuff," he kept saying.

They walked and walked. Charley had his bathingsuit on under his clothes; it had got to feel hot and itchy before they found a place they liked. They set the basket down behind a low dune and Eveline took her clothes off under a big towel she'd brought with her. Charley felt a little shy pulling off his shirt and pants right in front of her, but that seemed to be on the books.

"My, you've got a beautiful body," she said.

Charley tugged uneasily at the end of his bathingsuit. "I'm pretty healthy, I guess," he said. He looked at his hands sticking out red and grimed from the white skin of his forearms that were freckled a little under the light fuzz. "I sure would like to get a job where I could keep my hands clean."

"A man's hands ought to show his work. . . . That's the whole beauty of hands," said Eveline. She had wriggled into her suit and let drop the towel. It was a paleblue onepiece suit very tight.

"Gosh, you've got a pretty figure. That's what I first noticed about you on the boat."

She stepped over and took his arm. "Let's go in," she said. "The surf scares me, but it's terribly beautiful. . . . Oh, I think this is fun, don't you?"

Her arm felt very silky against his. He could feel her bare thigh against his bare thigh. Their feet touched as they walked out of the hot loose sand onto the hard cool sand. A foaming wide tongue of seawater ran up the beach at them and wet their legs to the knees. She let go his arm and took his hand.

He hadn't had much practice with surf and the first thing he knew a wave had knocked him galleywest. He came up spluttering with his mouth and ears full of water. She was on her feet laughing at him holding out her hand to help him to his feet. "Come on out further," she shouted. They ducked through the next wave and swam out. Just outside of the place where the waves broke they bobbed up and down treading water. "Not too far out, on account of the seapussies. . . ."

"What?"

"Currents," she shouted, putting her mouth close to his ear.

He got swamped by another roller and came up spitting and gasping. She was swimming on her back with her eyes closed and her lips pouted. He took two strokes towards her

99

and kissed her cold wet face. He tried to grab her round the body but a wave broke over their heads.

She pushed him off as they came up sputtering. "You made me lose my bathingcap. Look."

"There it is. I'll get it." He fought his way back through the surf and grabbed the cap just as the undertow was sucking it under. "Some surf," he yelled.

She followed him out and stood beside him in the shallow spume with her short hair wet over her eyes. She brushed it back with her hand. "Here we are," she said. Charley looked both ways down the beach. There was nobody to be seen in the earlyafternoon glare. He tried to put his arm around her.

She skipped out of his reach. "Charley . . . aren't you starved?"

"For you, Eveline."

"What I want's lunch."

When they'd eaten up the lunch and drunk all the cocktails, they felt drowsy and a little drunk. They lay side by side in the sun on the big towel. She made him keep his hands to himself. He closed his eyes, but he was too excited to go to sleep. Before he knew it he was talking his head off. "You see Joe's been workin' on the patent end of it, and he knows how to handle the lawyers and the big boys with the big wads. I'm afraid if I try to go into it alone, some bird'll go to work and steal my stuff. That's what usually happens when a guy invents anything."

"Do women ever tell you how attractive you are, Charley?"

"Overseas I didn't have any trouble. . . . You know, Aviat-err, lewtenong, Croix de Guerre, couchay, wee wee. . . . That was all right, but in this man's country no girl you want'll look at a guy unless he's loaded up with jack. . . . Sure, they'll lead you on an' get you halfcrazy." He was a fool to do it, but he went to work and told her all about Doris.

"But they're not all like that," she said, stroking the back of his hand. "Some women are square."

She wouldn't let him do anything but cuddle a little with her under the towel. The sun began to get low. They got up chilly and sandy and with the sunburn starting to tease. As they walked back along the beach, he felt sour and blue. She was talking about the evening and the waves and the seagulls and squeezing his arm as she leaned on it. They went into a hotel on the boardwalk to have a little supper and that just about cleaned his last fivespot.

He couldn't think of much to say going home on the train. He left her at the corner of her street, then walked over to the Third Avenue El and took the train uptown. The train was full of fellows and girls coming home from Sunday excursions. He kept his eye peeled for a pickup, but there was nothing doing. When he got up into his little stuffy greenpapered room, he couldn't stay in it. He went out and roamed up and down Second and Third Avenues. One woman accosted him but she was too fat and old. There was a pretty plump little girl he walked along beside for a long time, but she threatened to call a cop when he spoke to her, so he went back to his room and took a hot shower and a cold shower and piled into bed. He didn't sleep a wink all night.

Eveline called him up so often in the next weeks and left

so many messages for him that the clerk took him aside and warned him that the house was only intended for young men of irreproachable Christian life.

He took to leaving the shop early to go out with her places, and towards the end of July the foreman bounced him. The foreman was getting sore anyway because Charley kept on winning so much money at poker. Charley moved away from the Chatterton House and took a furnished room way east on Fifteenth Street, explaining to the landlady that his wife worked out of town and could only occasionally get in to see him. The landlady added two dollars to the rent and let it go at that. It got so he didn't do anything all day but wait for Eveline and drink lousy gin he bought in an Italian restaurant. He felt bad about Paul, but after all Paul wasn't a particular friend of his and if it wasn't him he reckoned it would be somebody else. Eveline talked so much it made his head spin, but she was certainly a stylishlooking rib and in bed she was swell. It was only when she talked about divorcing Paul and marrying him that he began to feel a little chilly. She was a good sport about paying for dinners and lunches when the money he'd saved up working in the shop gave out, but he couldn't very well let her pay for his rent, so he walked out on the landlady early one morning in September and took his bag up to the Grand Central Station. That same day he went by the Chatterton House to get his mail and found a letter from Emiscah.

He sat on a bench in the park behind the Public Library along with the other bums and read it:

CHARLEY BOY,

You always had such a heart of gold I know if you knew about what awful luck I've been having you would do something to help me. First I lost my job and things have been so slack around here this summer I haven't been able to get another; then I was sick and had to pay the doctor fifty dollars and I haven't been really what you might call well since, and so I had to draw out my savingsaccount and now it's all gone. The family won't do anything because they've been listening to some horrid lying stories too silly to deny. But now I've got to have ten dollars this week or the landlady will put me out and I don't know what will become of me. I know I've never done anything to deserve being so unhappy. Oh, I wish you were here so that you could cuddle me in your strong arms like you used to do. You used to love your poor little Emiscah. For the sake of your poor

102

mother that's dead send me ten dollars right away by special delivery so it wont be too late. Sometimes I think it would be better to turn on the gas. The tears are running down my face so that I can't see the paper any more. God bless you.

EMISCAH

My girlfriend's broke too. You make such big money ten dollars won't mean anything and I promise I won't ask you again.

Charley, if you can't make it ten send five.

Charley scowled and tore up the letter and put the pieces in his pocket. The letter made him feel bad, but what was the use? He walked over to the Hotel Astor and went down to the men's room to wash up. He looked at himself in one of the mirrors. Gray suit still looked pretty good, his straw hat was new and his shirt was clean. The tie had a frayed place, but it didn't show if you kept the coat buttoned. All right if it didn't rain; he'd already hocked his other suit and his trenchcoat and his officers' boots. He still had a couple of dollars in change so he had his shoes shined. Then he went up to the writingroom and wrote to Joe that he was on his uppers and please to send him twentyfive by mail P.D.Q. and for crissake to come to New York. He mailed the letter and walked downtown, walking slowly down Broadway.

The only place he knew where he could bum a meal was the Johnsons', so he turned into their street from Fifth Avenue.

Paul met him at the door and held out his hand. "Hello, Charley," he said. "I haven't seen you for a dog's age."

"I been movin'," stammered Charley, feeling like a louse. "Too many bedbugs in that last dump. . . . Say, I just stopped in to say hello."

"Come on in and I'll shake up a drink. Eveline'll be back in a minute."

Charley was shaking his head. "No, I just stopped to say hello. How's the kid? Give Eveline my best. I got a date."

He walked to a newsstand at the corner of Eighth Street and bought all the papers. Then he went to a blindtiger he knew and had a session with the helpwanted columns over some glasses of needle beer. He drank the beer slowly and noted down the addresses on a piece of paper he'd lifted off the Hotel Astor. One of them was a usedcar dealer, where the manager was a friend of Jim's. Charley had met him out home.

The lights went on and the windows got dark with a stuffy latesummer night. When he'd paid for the beer he only had a

103

quarter left in his pocket. "Damn it, this is the last time I let myself get in a jam like this," he kept muttering as he wandered round the downtown streets. He sat for a long time in Washington Square, thinking about what kind of a salestalk he could give the manager of that usedcar dump.

A light rain began to fall. The streets were empty by this time. He turned up his collar and started to walk. His shoes had holes in them and with each step he could feel the cold water squish between his toes. Under an arclight he took off his straw hat and looked at it. It was already gummy and the rim had a swollen pulpy look. "Now how in Christ's name am I goin' to go around and get me a job tomorrow?"

He turned on his heel and walked straight towards the Johnsons' place. Every minute it rained harder. He rang the bell under the card Paul Johnson—Eveline Hutchins until Paul came to the door in pajamas, looking very sleepy.

"Say, Paul, can I sleep on your couch?"

"It's pretty hard. . . . Come in. . . . I don't know if we've got any clean sheets."

"That's all right . . . just for tonight . . . You see I got cleaned out in a crapgame. I got jack comin' tomorrow. I thought I'd try the benches, but the sonofabitch started to rain on me. I got business to attend to tomorrow an' I got to keep this suit good, see?"

"Sure. . . . Say, you look wet . . . I'll lend you a pair of pajamas and a bathrobe. Better take those things off."

It was dry and comfortable on the Johnsons' couch. After Paul had gone back to bed, Charley lay there in Paul's bathrobe looking up at the ceiling. Through the tall window he could see the rain flickering through the streetlights outside and hear its continuous beat on the pavement. The baby woke up and cried, there was a light in the other room. He could hear Paul's and Eveline's sleepy voices and the rustle of them stirring around. Then the baby quieted down, the light went out. Everything was quiet in the beating rain again. He went off to sleep.

Getting up and having breakfast with them was no picnic nor was borrowing twentyfive dollars from Paul, though Charley knew he could pay it back in a couple of days. He left when Paul left to go to the office without paying attention to Eveline's sidelong kidding glances. Never get in a jam like this again, he kept saying to himself.

First he went to a tailor's and sat there behind a curtain reading the *American* while his suit was pressed. Then he bought himself a new straw hat, went to a barbershop and had a shave, a haircut, a facial massage and a manicure, and went to a cobbler's to get his shoes shined and soled.

By that time it was almost noon. He went uptown on the subway and talked himself into a job as salesman in the secondhand autosales place above Columbus Circle where the manager was a friend of Jim's. When the guy asked Charley about how the folks out in Minneapolis were getting on, he had to make up a lot of stuff. That evening he got his laundry from the Chinaman and his things out of hock and went back to a room, with brown walls this time, at the Chatterton House. He set himself up to a good feed and went to bed early deadtired.

A few days later a letter came from Joe Askew with the twentyfive bucks and the news that he was getting on his feet and would be down soon to get to work. Meanwhile Charley was earning a small amount on commissions, but winning or losing up to a century a night in a pokergame on Sixtythird Street one of the salesmen took him up to. They were mostly automobile salesmen and advertising men in the game and they were free spenders and rolled up some big pots. Charley mailed the twentyfive he owed him down to Paul, and when Eveline called him up on the telephone always said he was terribly busy and would call her soon. No more of that stuff, nosiree. Whenever he won, he put half of his winnings in a savingsbank account he'd opened. He carried the bankbook in his inside pocket. When he noticed it there it always made him feel like a wise guy.

He kept away from Eveline. It was hard for him to get so

far downtown and he didn't need to anyway because one of the other salesmen gave him the phonenumber of an apartment in a kind of hotel on the West Side, where a certain Mrs. Darling would arrange meetings with agreeable young women if she were notified early enough in the day. It cost twentyfive bucks a throw, but the girls were clean and young and there were no followups of any kind. The fact that he could raise twentyfive bucks to blow that way made him feel pretty good, but it ate into his poker winnings. After a session with one of Mrs. Darling's telephone numbers, he'd go back to his room at the Chatterton House feeling blue and disgusted. The girls were all right, but it wasn't fun like it had been with Eveline or even with Emiscah. He'd think of Doris and say to himself goshdarn it, he had to get him a woman of his own.

He took to selling fewer cars and playing more poker as the weeks went on and by the time he got a wire from Joe Askew saying he was coming to town next day, his job had just about petered out. He could tell that it was only because the manager was a friend of Jim's that he hadn't fired him already. He'd hit a losing streak and had to draw all the money out of the savingsaccount. When he went down to the station to meet Joe, he had a terrible head and only a dime in his pocket. The night before they'd cleaned him out at red dog.

Joe looked the same as ever, only he was thinner and his mustache was longer. "Well, how's tricks?"

Charley took Joe's other bag as they walked up the platform.

"Troubled with low ceilin's, air full of holes."

"I bet it is. Say, you look like you'd been hitting it up, Charley. I hope you're ready to get to work."

"Sure. All depends on gettin' the right C.O. . . . Ain't I been to night-school every night?"

"I bet you have."

"How are you feelin' now, Joe?"

"Oh, I'm all right now. I just about fretted myself into a nuthouse. What a lousy summer I've had. . . . What have you been up to, you big bum?"

"Well, I've been gatherin' information about the theory of the straight flush. And women . . . have I learned about women? Say, how's the wife and kids?"

"Fine. . . . You'll meet 'em. I'm goin' to take an apartment here this winter. . . . Well, boy, it's a case of up and at 'em. We are goin' in with Andy Merritt. . . . You'll meet him this noon. Where can I get a room?"

"Well, I'm stayin' at that kind of glorified Y over on Thirty-eighth Street."

"That's all right."

When they got into the taxi, Joe tapped him on the knee and leaned over and asked with a grin, "When are you ready to start to manufacture?"

"Tomorrow mornin' at eight o'clock. Old Bigelow just failed over in Long Island City. I seen his shop. Wouldn't cost much to get it in shape."

"We'll go over there this afternoon. He might take a little stock."

Charley shook his head. "That stock's goin' to be worth money, Joe . . . give him cash or notes or anythin'. He's a halfwit anyway. Last time I went over there it was to try to get a job as a mechanic. . . . Jeez, I hope those days are over. . . . The trouble with me is, Joe, I want to get married, and to get married like I want I got to have beaucoup kale. . . . Believe it nor not, I'm in love."

"With the entire chorus at the Follies, I'll bet. . . . That's a hot one . . . you want to get married." Joe laughed like he'd split. While Joe went up to his room to clean up, Char-

107

ley went round to the corner drugstore to get himself a bromoseltzer.

They had lunch with Merritt, who turned out to be a gray-faced young man with a square jaw, at the Yale Club. Charley still had a pounding headache and felt groggily that he wasn't making much of an impression. He kept his mouth shut and let Joe do the talking. Joe and Merritt talked Washington and War Department and Navy Department and figures that made Charley feel he ought to be pinching himself to see if he was awake.

After lunch Merritt drove them out to Long Island City in an open Pierce Arrow touringcar. When they actually got to

the plant, walking through the long littered rooms looking at lathe and electric motors and stamping and diemaking machines Charley felt he knew his way around better. He took out a piece of paper and started making notes. As that seemed to go big with Merritt, he made a lot more notes. Then Joe started making notes too. When Merritt took out a little book and started making notes himself, Charley knew he'd done the right thing.

They had dinner with Merritt and spent the evening with him. It was heavy sledding because Merritt was one of those people who could size a man up at a glance, and he was trying to size up Charley. They ate at an expensive French speakeasy and sat there a long time afterwards drinking cognac and soda. Merritt was a great one for writing lists of officers and salaries and words like capitalization, depreciation, amortization down on pieces of paper, all of them followed by big figures with plenty of zeroes. The upshot of it seemed to be that Charley Anderson would be earning two hundred and fifty a week (payable in preferred stock), starting last Monday as supervising engineer and that the question of the percentage of capital stock he and Joe would have for their patents would be decided at a meeting of the board of directors next day. The top of Charley's head was floating. His tongue was a little thick from the cognac. All he could think of saying, and he kept saying it, was "Boys, we mustn't go off halfcocked."

When he and Joe finally got Merritt and his Pierce Arrow back to the Yale Club, they heaved a deep breath. "Say, Joe, is that bird a financial wizard or is he a nut? He talks like greenbacks grew on trees."

"He makes 'em grow there. Honestly . . ." Joe Askew took his arm and his voice sunk to a whisper, "that bird is going to be the Durant of aviation financing."

"He don't seem to know a Liberty motor from the hind end of a blimp."

"He knows the Secretary of the Interior, which is a hell of a lot more important."

Charley got to laughing so he couldn't stop. All the way back to the Chatterton House he kept bumping into people walking along the street. His eyes were full of tears. He laughed and laughed. When they went to the desk to ask for their mail and saw the long pale face of the clerk, Charley nudged Joe. "Well, it's our last night in this funeral parlor."

The hallway to their rooms smelt of old sneakers and showers and lockerrooms. Charley got to laughing again. He sat on his bed a long time giggling to himself. "Jesus, this is more like it; this is better than Paree." After Joe had gone to bed, Charley stuck his head in the door still giggling. "Rub me, Joe," he yelled. "I'm lucky."

Next morning they went and ate breakfast at the Belmont. Then Joe made Charley go to Knox's and buy him a derby before they went downtown. Charley's hair was a little too wiry for the derby to set well, but the band had an expensive Englishleathery smell. He kept taking it off and sniffing it on the way downtown in the subway.

"Say, Joe, when my first paycheck comes I want you to take me round and get me outfitted in a soup an' fish. . . . This girl, she likes a feller to dress up."

"You won't be out of overalls, boy," growled Joe Askew, "night or day for six months if I have anything to say about it. We'll have to live in that plant if we expect the product to be halfway decent, don't fool yourself about that."

"Sure, Joe, sure, I was only kiddin'."

They met at the office of a lawyer named Lilienthal. From the minute they gave their names to the elegantlyupholstered blonde at the desk, Charley could feel the excitement of a deal in the air. The blonde smiled and bowed into the receiver. "Oh, yes, of course. . . . Mr. Anderson and Mr. Askew." A scrawny officeboy showed them at once into the library, a dark long room filled with calfbound lawbooks.

They hadn't had time to sit down before Mr. Lilienthal himself appeared through a groundglass door. He was a dark oval neckless man with a jaunty manner. "Well, here's our pair of aces right on time."

When Joe introduced them, he held Charley's hand for a moment in the smooth fat palm of his small hand. "Andy Merritt has just been singing your praises, young fellah, he says you are the coming contactman."

"And here I was just telling him I wouldn't let him out of the factory for six months. He's the bird who's got the feel for the motors."

"Well, maybe he meant you birdmen's kind of contact," said Mr. Lilienthal, lifting one thin black eyebrow.

The lawyer ushered them into a big office with a big empty mahogany desk in the middle of it and a blue Chinese rug on the floor. Merritt and two other men were ahead of them. To Charley they looked like a Kuppenheimer ad standing there amid the blue crinkling cigarettesmoke in their neatly cut dark suits with the bright gray light coming through the window behind them. George Hollis was a pale young man with his hair parted in the middle and the other was a lanky dark-faced Irish lawyer named Burke, who was an old friend of Joe Askew's and would put their patents through Washington for them, Joe explained. They all seemed to think Charley was a great guy, but he was telling himself all the time to keep his mouth shut and let Joe do the talking.

They sat round that lawyer's mahogany desk all morning smoking cigars and cigarettes and spoiling a great deal of yellow scratch paper until the desk looked like the bottom of an uncleaned birdcage and the Luckies tasted sour on Charley's tongue. Mr. Lilienthal was all the time calling in his stenographer, a little mouselike girl with big gray eyes, to take notes and then sending her out again. Occasionally the phone buzzed and each time he answered it in his bored voice, "My dear young lady, hasn't it occurred to you that I might be in conference?"

The concern was going to be called the Askew-Merritt Company. There was a great deal of talk about what state to incorporate in and how the stock was to be sold, how it was going to be listed, how it was going to be divided. When they finally got up to go to lunch, it was already two o'clock and Charley's head was swimming. Several of them went to the men's room on their way to the elevator and Charley managed to get into the urinal beside Joe and to whisper to him, "Say, for crissake, Joe, are we rookin' those guys or are they rookin' us?" Joe wouldn't answer. All he did was to screw his face up and shrug his shoulders.

111

Newsreel L

Don't blame it all on Broadway

with few exceptions the management of our government has been and is in honest and competent hands, that the finances are sound and well managed, and that the business interests of the nation, including the owners, managers, and employees, are representative of honorable and patriotic motives and that the present economic condition warrants a continuation of confidence and prosperity

You have yourself to blame
Don't shame the name of dear old Broadway

GRAND JURY WILL QUIZ BALLPLAYERS

**IMPROVED LUBRICATING SYSTEM THAT INSURES
POSITIVE AND CONSTANT OILING OVER THE
ENTIRE BEARING SURFACES**

I've got a longin' way down in my heart
For that old gang that has drifted apart

the Dooling Shipbuilding Corporation has not paid or agreed to pay and will not pay, directly or indirectly, any bribe of any sort or description to any employee or representative of the U.S. Shipping Board, the Emergency Fleet Corporation, or any other government agency

SLAIN RICH MAN BURIED IN CELLAR

I can't forget that old quartette
That sang Sweet Adeline

Goodbye forever old fellows and gals
Goodbye forever old sweethearts and pals

NEWLY DESIGNED GEARS AFFORDING NOT
ONLY GREATER STRENGTH AND LONGER
LIFE BUT INCREASED SMOOTHNESS

NEW CLUTCH—AN ENGINEERING ACHIEVEMENT
THAT ADDS WONDERFUL POSITIVENESS TO
POWER TRANSMISSION THAT MAKES
GEARSHIFTING EASY AND NOISELESS

NEW AND LARGER BULLET LAMPS AFFORD THE
MOST PERFECT ILLUMINATION EVER
DEVELOPED FOR MOTOR USE

GARY CALLS ROMANTIC PUBLIC RESPONSIBLE
FOR EIGHTHOUR DAY

the prices obtained for packinghouse products were the
results of purely economic laws. Official figures prove that
if wheat prices are to respond to the law of supply and
demand

PIGIRON OUTPUT SHARPLY CURBED

And if you should be dining with a little stranger
Red lights seem to warn you of a danger
Don't blame it all on Broadway

The Bitter Drink

Veblen,
a grayfaced shambling man lolling resentful at his desk
with his cheek on his hand, in a low sarcastic mumble of in-
tricate phrases subtly paying out the logical inescapable rope
of matter-of-fact for a society to hang itself by,
dissecting out the century with a scalpel so keen, so comical, so exact that the professors and students ninetenths of
the time didn't know it was there, and the magnates and the
respected windbags and the applauded loudspeakers never
knew it was there.

113

Veblen

asked too many questions, suffered from a constitutional inability to say yes.

Socrates asked questions, drank down the bitter drink one night when the first cock crowed,

but Veblen

drank it in little sips through a long life in the stuffiness of classrooms, the dust of libraries, the staleness of cheap flats such as a poor instructor can afford. He fought the bogy all right, pedantry, routine, timesavers at office desks, trustees, collegepresidents, the plump flunkies of the ruling businessmen, all the good jobs kept for yesmen, never enough money, every broadening hope thwarted. Veblen drank the bitter drink all right.

The Veblens were a family of freeholding farmers.

The freeholders of the narrow Norwegian valleys were a stubborn hardworking people, farmers, dairymen, fishermen, rooted in their fathers' stony fields, in their old timbered farmsteads with carved gables they took their names from, in the upland pastures where they grazed the stock in summer.

During the early nineteenth century the towns grew; Norway filled up with landless men, storekeepers, sheriffs, moneylenders, bailiffs, notaries in black with stiff collars and briefcases full of foreclosures under their arms. Industries were coming in. The townsmen were beginning to get profits out of the country and to finagle the farmers out of the freedom of their narrow farms.

The meanspirited submitted as tenants, daylaborers; but the strong men went out of the country

as their fathers had gone out of the country centuries before when Harald the Fairhaired and Saint Olaf hacked to pieces the liberties of the Northern men, who had been each man lord of his own creek, to make Christians and serfs of them,

only in the old days it was Iceland, Greenland, Vineland the Northmen had sailed west to; now it was America.

Both Thorstein Veblen's father's people and his mother's people had lost their farmsteads and with them the names that denoted them free men.

Thomas Anderson for a while tried to make his living as a traveling carpenter and cabinetmaker, but in 1847 he and his wife, Kari Thorsteinsdatter, crossed in a whalingship from Bremen and went out to join friends in the Scandihoovian colonies round Milwaukee.

Next year his brother Haldor joined him.

114

They were hard workers; in another year they had saved up money to pre-empt a claim on a hundred and sixty acres of uncleared land in Sheboygan County, Wisconsin; when they'd gotten that land part cleared they sold it and moved to an all-Norway colony in Manitowoc County, near Cato, and a place named Valders after the valley they had all come from in the old country;

there in the house Thomas Anderson built with his own tools, the sixth of twelve children, Thorstein Veblen was born.

When Thorstein was eight years old, Thomas Anderson moved west again into the blacksoil prairies of Minnesota that the Sioux and the buffalo had only been driven off from a few years before. In the deed to the new farm Thomas Anderson took back the old farmstead name of Veblen.

He was a solid farmer, builder, a clever carpenter, the first man to import merino sheep and a mechanical reaper and binder; he was a man of standing in the group of Norway people farming the edge of the prairie, who kept their dialects, the manner of life of their narrow Norway valleys, their Lutheran pastors, their homemade clothes and cheese and bread, their suspicion and stubborn dislike of townsmen's ways.

The townspeople were Yankees mostly, smart to make two dollars grow where a dollar grew before, storekeepers, middlemen, speculators, moneylenders, with long heads for politics and mortgages; they despised the Scandihoovian dirtfarmers they lived off, whose daughters did their wives' kitchenwork.

The Norway people believed as their fathers had believed that there were only two callings for an honest man, farming or preaching.

Thorstein grew up a hulking lad with a reputation for laziness and wit. He hated the irk of everrepeated backbreaking chores round the farm. Reading he was happy. Carpentering he liked or running farmmachinery. The Lutheran pastors who came to the house noticed that his supple mind slid easily round the corners of their theology. It was hard to get farmwork out of him; he had a stinging tongue and was famous for the funny names he called people; his father decided to make a preacher out of him.

When he was seventeen he was sent for out of the field where he was working. His bag was already packed. The

115

horses were hitched up. He was being sent to Carleton Academy in Northfield, to prepare for Carleton College.

As there were several young Veblens to be educated, their father built them a house on a lot near the campus. Their food and clothes were sent to them from the farm. Cash money was something they never saw.

Thorstein spoke English with an accent. He had a constitutional inability to say yes. His mind was formed on the Norse sagas and on the matter-of-fact sense of his father's farming and the exact needs of carpenterwork and threshingmachines.

He could never take much interest in the theology, sociology, economics of Carleton College where they were busy trimming down the jagged dogmas of the old New England Bibletaught traders to make stencils to hang on the walls of commissionmerchants' offices.

Veblen's collegeyears were the years when Darwin's assertions of growth and becoming were breaking the set molds of the Noah's Ark world,

when Ibsen's women were tearing down the portières of the Victorian parlors,

and Marx's mighty machine was rigging the countinghouse's own logic to destroy the countinghouse.

When Veblen went home to the farm, he talked about these things with his father, following him up and down at his plowing, starting an argument while they were waiting for a new load for the wheatthresher. Thomas Anderson had seen Norway and America; he had the squarebuilt mind of a carpenter and builder, and an understanding of tools and the treasured elaborated builtupseasonbyseason knowledge of a careful farmer.

a tough whetstone for the sharpening steel of young Thorstein's wits.

At Carleton College young Veblen was considered a brilliant unsound eccentric; nobody could understand why a boy of such attainments wouldn't settle down to the business of the day, which was to buttress property and profits with anything usable in the débris of Christian ethics and eighteenth-century economics that cluttered the minds of college professors, and to reinforce the sacred, already shaky edifice with the new strong girderwork of science Herbert Spencer was throwing up for the benefit of the bosses.

People complained they never knew whether Veblen was joking or serious.

In 1880 Thorstein Veblen started to try to make his living by teaching. A year in an academy at Madison, Wisconsin, wasn't much of a success. Next year he and his brother Andrew started graduate work at Johns Hopkins. Johns Hopkins didn't suit, but boarding in an old Baltimore house with some ruined gentlewomen gave him a disdaining glimpse of an etiquette motheaten now but handed down through the lavish leisure of the slaveowning planters' mansions straight from the merrie England of the landlord cavaliers.

(The valleyfarmers had always been scornful of outlanders' ways.)

He was more at home at Yale, where in Noah Porter he found a New England roundhead granite against which his Norway granite rang in clear dissent. He took his Ph.D. there. But there was still some question as to what department of the academic world he could best make a living in.

He read Kant and wrote prize essays. But he couldn't get a job. Try as he would he couldn't get his mouth round the essential yes.

He went back to Minnesota with a certain intolerant knowledge of the amenities of the higher learning. To his slight Norwegian accent he'd added the broad "a."

At home he loafed about the farm and tinkered with inventions of new machinery and read and talked theology and philosophy with his father. In the Scandihoovian colonies the price of wheat and the belief in God and Saint Olaf were going down together. The farmers of the Northwest were starting their long losing fight against the parasite businessmen who were sucking them dry. There was a mortgage on the farm, interest on debts to pay, always fertilizer, new machines to buy to speed production to pump in a halfcentury the wealth out of the soil laid down in a million years of buffalograss. His brothers kept grumbling about this sardonic loafer who wouldn't earn his keep.

Back home he met again his college sweetheart, Ellen Rolfe, the niece of the president of Carleton College, a girl who had railroadmagnates and money in the family. People in Northfield were shocked when it came out that she was going to marry the drawling pernickety bookish badly-dressed young Norwegian ne'erdowell.

Her family hatched a plan to get him a job as economist for the Santa Fe Railroad, but at the wrong moment Ellen Rolfe's uncle lost control of the line. The young couple went to live at Stacyville where they did everything but earn a living. They read Latin and Greek and botanized in the woods and along the fences and in the roadside scrub. They boated on the river and Veblen started his translation of the *Laxdae-*

117

lasaga. They read *Looking Backward* and articles by Henry George. They looked at their world from the outside.

In '91 Veblen got together some money to go to Cornell to do postgraduate work. He turned up there in the office of the head of the economics department wearing a coonskin cap and gray corduroy trousers and said in his low sarcastic drawl, "I am Thorstein Veblen,"

but it was not until several years later, after he was established at the new University of Chicago that had grown up next to the World's Fair, and had published *The Theory of the Leisure Class,* put on the map by Howells's famous review, that the world of the higher learning knew who Thorstein Veblen was.

Even in Chicago as the brilliant young economist he lived pioneer-fashion. (The valleyfarmers had always been scornful of outlanders' ways.) He kept his books in packingcases laid on their sides along the walls. His only extravagances were the Russian cigarettes he smoked and the red sash he sometimes sported. He was a man without smalltalk. When he lectured he put his cheek on his hand and mumbled out his long spiral sentences, reiterative like the eddas. His language was a mixture of mechanics' terms, scientific latinity, slang, and Roget's *Thesaurus.* The other profs couldn't imagine why the girls fell for him so.

The girls fell for him so that Ellen Rolfe kept leaving him. He'd take summer trips abroad without his wife. There was a scandal about a girl on an ocean liner.

Tongues wagged so (Veblen was a man who never explained, who never could get his tongue around the essential yes; the valleyfarmers had always been scornful of the outlanders' ways, and their opinions) that his wife left him and went off to live alone on a timberclaim in Idaho and the president asked for his resignation.

Veblen went out to Idaho to get Ellen Rolfe to go with him to California when he succeeded in getting a job at a better salary at Leland Stanford, but in Palo Alto it was the same story as in Chicago. He suffered from woman trouble and the constitutional inability to say yes and an unnatural tendency to feel with the workingclass instead of with the profittakers. There were the same complaints that his courses were not constructive or attractive to bigmoney bequests and didn't help his students to butter their bread, make Phi Beta Kappa, pick plums off the hierarchies of the academic grove. His wife left him for good. He wrote to a friend: "The president doesn't approve of my domestic arrangements; nor do I."

Talking about it he once said, "What is one to do if the woman moves in on you?"

He went back up to the shack in the Idaho woods.

Friends tried to get him an appointment to make studies in Crete, a chair at the University of Pekin, but always the bogy, routine, businessmen's flunkies in all the university offices . . . for the questioner the bitter drink.

His friend Davenport got him an appointment at the University of Missouri. At Columbia he lived like a hermit in the basement of the Davenports' house, helped with the work round the place, carpentered himself a table and chairs. He was already a bitter elderly man with a gray face covered with a net of fine wrinkles, a Vandyke beard and yellow teeth. Few students could follow his courses. The college authorities were often surprised and somewhat chagrined that when visitors came from Europe, it was always Veblen they wanted to meet.

These were the years he did most of his writing, trying out his ideas on his students, writing slowly at night in violet ink with a pen of his own designing. Whenever he published a book, he had to put up a guarantee with the publishers. In *The Theory of Business Enterprise, The Instinct of Workmanship, The Vested Interests and the Common Man,*

he established a new diagram of a society dominated by monopoly capital,

etched in irony

the sabotage of production by business,

the sabotage of life by blind need for money profits,

pointed out the alternatives: a warlike society strangled by the bureaucracies of the monopolies forced by the law of diminishing returns to grind down more and more the common man for profits,

or a new matter-of-fact commonsense society dominated by the needs of the men and women who did the work and the incredibly vast possibilities for peace and plenty offered by the progress of technology.

These were the years of Debs' speeches, growing laborunions, the I.W.W. talk about industrial democracy: these years Veblen still held to the hope that the workingclass would take over the machine of production before monopoly had pushed the western nations down into the dark again.

War cut across all that: under the cover of the bunting of Woodrow Wilson's phrases the monopolies cracked down. American democracy was crushed.

The war at least offered Veblen an opportunity to break out of the airless greenhouse of academic life. He was offered a job with the Food Administration, he sent the Navy Department a device for catching submarines by trailing lengths of stout bindingwire. (Meanwhile the government found his books somewhat confusing. The postoffice was forbidding the mails to *Imperial Germany and the Industrial Revolution* while propaganda agencies were sending it out to make people hate the Huns. Educators were denouncing *The Nature of Peace* while Washington experts were clipping phrases out of it to add to the Wilsonian smokescreen.)

For the Food Administration Thorstein Veblen wrote two reports: in one he advocated granting the demands of the I.W.W. as a wartime measure and conciliating the workingclass instead of beating up and jailing all the honest leaders; in the other he pointed out that the Food Administration was a businessman's racket and was not aiming for the most efficient organization of the country as a producing machine. He suggested that, in the interests of the efficient prosecution of the war, the government step into the place of the middleman and furnish necessities to the farmers direct in return for raw materials;

but cutting out business was not at all the Administration's idea of making the world safe for democracy,

so Veblen had to resign from the Food Administration.

He signed the protests against the trial of the hundred and one wobblies in Chicago.

After the armistice he went to New York. In spite of all the oppression of the war years, the air was freshening. In Russia the great storm of revolt had broken, seemed to be sweeping west; in the strong gusts from the new world in the east the warshodden multitudes began to see again. At Versailles allies and enemies, magnates, generals, flunkey politicians were slamming the shutters against the storm, against the new, against hope. It was suddenly clear for a second in the thundering glare what war was about, what peace was about.

In America, in Europe, the old men won. The bankers in their offices took a deep breath, the bediamonded old ladies of the leisure class went back to clipping their coupons in the refined quiet of their safe-deposit vaults.

the last puffs of the ozone of revolt went stale

in the whisper of speakeasy arguments.

Veblen wrote for the *Dial,*

lectured at the New School for Social Research.

He still had a hope that the engineers, the technicians, the nonprofiteers whose hands were on the switchboard might take up the fight where the workingclass had failed. He helped form the Technical Alliance. His last hope was the British general strike.

Was there no group of men bold enough to take charge of the magnificent machine before the pigeyed speculators and the yesmen at office desks irrevocably ruined it

and with it the thopes of four hundred years?

No one went to Veblen's lectures at the New School. With every article he wrote in the *Dial* the circulation dropped.

Harding's normalcy, the new era was beginning;

even Veblen made a small killing on the stockmarket.

He was an old man and lonely.

His second wife had gone to a sanitarium suffering from delusions of persecution.

There seemed no place for a masterless man.

Veblen went back out to Palo Alto

to live in his shack in the tawny hills and observe from outside the last grabbing urges of the profit system taking on, as he put it, the systematized delusions of dementia praecox.

There he finished his translation of the *Laxdaelasaga.*

He was an old man. He was much alone. He let the woodrats take what they wanted from his larder. A skunk that hung round the shack was so tame he'd rub up against Veblen's leg like a cat.

He told a friend he'd sometimes hear in the stillness about him the voices of his boyhood talking Norwegian as clear as on the farm in Minnesota where he was raised. His friends found him harder than ever to talk to, harder than ever to interest in anything. He was running down. The last sips of the bitter drink.

He died on August 3, 1929.

Among his papers a penciled note was found:

It is also my wish, in case of death, to be cremated if it can conveniently be done, as expeditiously and inexpensively as may be, without ritual or ceremony of any kind; that my ashes be thrown loose into the sea or into some sizable stream running into the sea; that no tombstone, slab, epitaph, effigy, tablet, inscription or monument of any name or nature, be set up to my memory or name in any place or at any time; that no obituary, memorial, portrait or biography of

me, nor any letters written to or by me be printed or pub-
lished, or in any way reproduced, copied or circulated;
   but his memorial remains
   riveted into the languages:
   the sharp clear prism of his mind.

Newsreel LI

The sunshine drifted from our alley

HELP WANTED: ADVANCEMENT

positions that offer quick, accurate, experienced, well-recommended young girls and young women . . . good chance for advancement

Ever since the day
Sally went away

GIRLS   GIRLS   GIRLS

canvassers . . . caretakers . . . cashiers . . . chambermaids . . . waitresses . . . cleaners . . . file clerks . . . companions . . . comptometer operators . . . collection correspondents . . . cooks . . . dictaphone operators . . . gentlewomen . . . multigraph operators . . . Elliott Fisher operators . . . bill and entry clerks . . . gummers . . . glove buyers . . . governesses . . . hairdressers . . . models . . . good opportunity for stylish young ladies . . . intelligent young women

Went down to St. James Infirmary
Saw my baby there
All stretched out on a table
So pale, so cold, so fair

Went up to see the doctor

WE HAVE HUNDREDS OF POSITIONS OPEN

we are anxious to fill vacancies, we offer good salaries,

commissions, bonuses, prizes, business opportunities, training, advancement, educational opportunities, hospital service . . . restroom and lunchroom where excellent lunch is served at less than cost

> *Let her go let her go God bless her*
> *Wherever she may be*
> *She may roam this wide world over*
> *She'll never find a sweet man like me*

Mary French

Poor Daddy never did get tucked away in bed right after supper the way he liked with his readinglight over his left shoulder and his glasses on and the paper in his hand and a fresh cigar in his mouth that the phone didn't ring, or else it would be a knocking at the back door and Mother would send little Mary to open it and she'd find a miner standing there whitefaced with his eyelashes and eyebrows very black from the coaldust saying, "Doc French, pliz . . . heem coma queek," and poor Daddy would get up out of bed yawning in his pajamas and bathrobe and push his untidy gray hair off his forehead and tell Mary to go get his instrumentcase out of the office for him, and be off tying his necktie as he went, and half the time he'd be gone all night.

Mealtimes it was worse. They never seemed to get settled at the table for a meal, the three of them, without that awful phone ringing. Daddy would go and Mary and Mother would sit there finishing the meal alone, sitting there without saying anything, little Mary with her legs wrapped around the chairlegs staring at the picture of two dead wild ducks in the middle of the gingercolored wallpaper above Mother's trim black head. Then Mother would put away the dishes and clatter around the house muttering to herself that if poor Daddy ever took half the trouble with his paying patients that he did with those miserable foreigners and miners he would be a rich man today and she wouldn't be killing herself with housework. Mary hated to hear Mother talk against Daddy the way she did.

Poor Daddy and Mother didn't get along. Mary barely remembered a time when she was very very small when it had been different and they'd lived in Denver in a sunny house with flowering bushes in the yard. That was before Brother was taken and Daddy lost that money in the investment.

Whenever anybody said Denver it made her think of sunny. Now they lived in Trinidad where everything was black like coal, the scrawny hills tall, darkening the valley full of rows of sooty shanties, the minetipples, the miners most of them greasers and hunkies and the awful saloons and the choky smeltersmoke and the little black trains. In Denver it was sunny, and white people lived there, real clean American children like Brother who was taken, and Mother said if poor Daddy cared for his own flesh and blood the way he cared for those miserable foreigners and miners Brother's life might have been saved. Mother had made her go into the parlor, she was so scared, but Mother held her hand so tight it hurt terribly, but nobody paid any attention, they all thought it was on account of Brother she was crying, and Mother made her look at him in the coffin under the glass.

After the funeral Mother was very sick and had a night and a day nurse and they wouldn't let Mary see her and Mary had to play by herself all alone in the yard. When Mother got well, she and poor Daddy didn't get along and always slept in separate rooms and Mary slept in the little hallroom between them. Poor Daddy got gray and worried and never laughed round the house any more after that and then it was all about the investment and they moved to Trinidad and Mother wouldn't let her play with the minechildren and when she came back from school she had nits in her hair.

Mary had to wear glasses and was good at her studies and was ready to go to highschool at twelve. When she wasn't

studying she read all the books in the house. "The child will ruin her eyes," Mother would say to poor Daddy across the breakfasttable when he would come down with his eyes puffy from lack of sleep and would have to hurry through his breakfast to be off in time to make his calls. The spring Mary finished the eighth grade and won the prizes in French and American history and English, Miss Parsons came around specially to call on Mrs. French to tell her what a good student little Mary French was and such a comfort to the teachers after all the miserable ignorant foreigners she had to put up with.

"My dear," Mother said, "don't think I don't know how it is." Then suddenly she said, "Miss Parsons, don't tell anybody, but we're going to move to Colorado Springs next fall."

Miss Parsons sighed. "Well, Mrs. French, we'll hate to lose you, but it certainly is best for the child. There's a better element in the schools there." Miss Parsons lifted her teacup with her little finger crooked and let it down again with a dry click in the saucer.

Mary sat watching them from the little tapestry stool by the fireplace. "I hate to admit it," Miss Parsons went on, "because I was born and bred here, but Trinidad's no place to bring up a sweet clean little American girl."

Granpa Wilkins had died that spring in Denver and Mother was beneficiary of his life insurance, so she carried off things with a high hand. Poor Daddy hated to leave Trinidad and they hardly even spoke without making Mary go and read in the library while they quarreled over the dirty dishes in the kitchen. Mary would sit with an old red embossedleather *Ivanhoe* in her hand and listen to their bitter wrangling voices coming through the board partition. "You've ruined my life and now I'm not going to let you ruin the child's," Mother would yell in that mean voice that made Mary feel so awful and Mary would sit there crying over the book until she got started reading again and after a couple of pages had forgotten everything except the yeomen in Lincoln Green and the knights on horseback and the castles. That summer, instead of going camping in Yellowstone like Daddy had planned, they moved to Colorado Springs.

At Colorado Springs they stayed first in a boardinghouse and then when the furniture came they moved to the green shingled bungalow where they were going to live that was set way back from the red gravel road in a scrawny lawn among tall poplartrees.

In the long grass Mary found the scaled remains of a croquetset. While Daddy and Mother were fussing about the furnishings that the men were moving in from a wagon, she ran around with a broken mallet slamming at the old cracked balls that hardly had any paint left on their red and green and yellow and blue bands. When Daddy came out of the house looking tired and gray with his hair untidy over his forehead, she ran up to him waving the mallet and wanted him to play croquet. "No time for games now," he said.

Mary burst out crying and he lifted her on his shoulder and carried her round the back porch and showed her how by climbing on the roof of the little toolhouse behind the kitchen door you could see the mesa and beyond, behind a tattered fringe of racing cheesecloth clouds, the blue sawtooth ranges piling up to the towering smooth mass of mountains where Pike's Peak was. "We'll go up there some day on the cogwheel railroad," he said in his warm cozy voice close to her ear. The mountains looked so far away and the speed of the clouds made her feel dizzy. "Just you and me," he said; "but you mustn't ever cry . . . it'll make the children tease you in school, Mary."

In September she had to go to highschool. It was awful going to a new school where she didn't have any friends. The girls seemed so well-dressed and stuckup in the firstyear high. Going through the corridors hearing the other girls talk about parties and the Country Club and sets of tennis and summer hotels and automobiles and friends in finishing-schools in the East, Mary, with her glasses and the band to straighten her teeth Mother had had the dentist put on, that made her lisp a little, and her freckles and her hair that wasn't red or blond but just sandy, felt a miserable foreigner like the smelly bawling miners' kids back in Trinidad.

She liked the boys better. A redheaded boy grinned at her sometimes. At least they let her alone. She did well in her classes and thought the teachers were lovely. In English they read *Ramona,* and one day Mary, scared to death all alone, went to the cemetery to see the grave of Helen Hunt Jackson. It was beautifully sad that spring afternoon in Evergreen Cemetery. When she grew up, she decided, she was going to be like Helen Hunt Jackson.

They had a Swedish girl named Anna to do the housework and Mother and Daddy were hardly ever home when she came back from school. Daddy had an office downtown in a new officebuilding and Mother was always busy with churchwork or at the library reading up for papers she delivered at the women's clubs. Half the time Mary had her supper all alone reading a book or doing her homework. Then she would go out in the kitchen and help Anna tidy up and try to keep her from going home and leaving her alone in the house. When she heard the front door opening, she would

127

run out breathless. Usually it was only Mother, but sometimes it was Daddy with his cigar and his tired look and his clothes smelling of tobacco and iodoform and carbolic, and maybe she could get him to sit on her bed before she went to sleep to tell her stories about the old days and miners and prospectors and the war between the sheepherders and the ranchers.

At highschool Mary's best friend was Ada Cohn whose father was a prominent Chicago lawyer who had had to come out for his health. Mother did everything she could to keep her from going to the Cohns' and used to have mean arguments with Daddy about how it was only on account of his being so shiftless that her only daughter was reduced to going around with Jews and every Tom Dick and Harry, and why didn't he join the Country Club and what was the use of her struggling to get a position for him among the better element by church activities and women's clubs and communitychest work if he went on being just a poor man's doctor and was seen loafing around with all the scum in poolrooms and worse places for all she knew instead of working up a handsome practice in a city where there were so many wealthy sick people; wasn't it to get away from all that sort of thing they'd left Trinidad?

"But, Hilda," Daddy would say, "be reasonable. It's on account of Mary's being a friend of the Cohns' that they've given me their practice. They are very nice kindly people."

Mother would stare straight at him and hiss through her teeth: "Oh, if you only had a tiny bit of ambition."

Mary would run away from the table in tears and throw herself on her bed with a book and lie there listening to their voices raised and then Daddy's heavy slow step and the slam of the door and the sound of him cranking the car to start off on his calls again. Often she lay there with her teeth clenched wishing if Mother would only die and leave her and Daddy living alone quietly together. A cold shudder would go through her at the thought of how awful it was to have thoughts like that, and she'd start reading, hardly able to see the printed page through her tears at first, but gradually forgetting herself in the story in the book.

One thing that Mother and Daddy agreed about was that they wanted Mary to go to a really good Eastern college. The year before she graduated from highschool Mary had passed all the College Board exams except solid geometry. She was crazy to go.

Except for a few days camping every summer with Daddy and one summer month she spent answering the phone and making out the cards of the patients and keeping his accounts and sending out his bills at his office, she hated it in Colorado Springs. Her only boyfriend was a young fellow with a clubfoot named Joe Denny, the son of a saloonkeeper in Colorado City. He was working his way through Colorado College. He was a bitter slowspoken towheaded boy with a sharp jaw, a wizard in math. He hated liquor and John D. Rockefeller more than anything in the world. She and Joe and Ada would go out on picnics Sunday to the Garden of the Gods or Austin Bluffs or one of the canyons and read poetry together. Their favorites were *The Hound of Heaven* and *The City of Dreadful Night*. Joe thrilled the girls one day standing on a flat rock above the little fire they were frying their bacon over and reciting *The Man with the Hoe*. At first they thought he'd written it himself.

When they got in, feeling sunburned and happy after a day in the open, Mary would so wish she could take her friends home the way Ada did. The Cohns were kind and jolly and always asked everybody to stay to dinner in spite of the fact that poor Mr. Cohn was a very sick man. But Mary didn't dare take anybody home to her house for fear Mother would be rude to them, or that there'd be one of those yelling matches that started up all the time between Mother and Daddy. The summer before she went to Vassar, Mother and Daddy weren't speaking at all after a terrible argument when Daddy said one day at supper that he was going to vote for Eugene V. Debs in November.

At Vassar the girls she knew were better dressed than she was and had uppity finishingschool manner, but for the first time in her life she was popular. The instructors liked her because she was neat and serious and downright about everything and the girls said she was as homely as a mud fence but a darling.

It was all spoiled the second year when Ada came to Vassar. Ada was her oldest friend and Mary loved her dearly, so she was horrified to catch herself wishing Ada hadn't come. Ada had gotten so lush and Jewish and noisy, and her clothes were too expensive and never just right. They roomed together and Ada bought most of Mary's clothes and books for her because her allowance was so tiny. After Ada came, Mary wasn't popular the way she'd been, and the most successful girls shied off from her. Mary and Ada majored in sociology and said they were going to be socialworkers.

When Mary was a junior Mother went to Reno and got a divorce from Daddy, giving intemperance and mental cruelty as the cause. It had never occurred to Mary that poor Daddy drank. She cried and cried when she read about it in a newspaper clipping marked in red pencil some nameless well-

wisher sent her from Colorado Springs. She burned the clipping in the fireplace so that Ada shouldn't see it, and when
Ada asked her why her eyes were so red said it was because
it had made her cry to read about all those poor soldiers
being killed in the war in Europe. It made her feel awful
having told Ada a lie and she lay awake all night worrying
about it.

The next summer the two of them got jobs doing settlementwork at Hull House in Chicago. Chicago was scary and
poor Ada Cohn couldn't keep on with the work and went up
to Michigan to have a nervous breakdown; it was so awful
the way poor people lived and the cracked red knuckles of
the women who took in washing and the scabby heads of the
little children and the clatter and the gritty wind on South
Halstead Street and the stench of the stockyards; but it made
Mary feel like years back in Trinidad when she was a little
girl, the way she'd felt the summer she worked in Daddy's
office.

When she went back to Colorado Springs for two weeks
before Vassar opened, she found Mother staying in style in a
small suite at the Broadmoor. Mother had inherited a block
of stocks in American Smelting and Refining when Uncle
Henry was killed in a streetcar accident in Denver, and had
an income of twenty thousand a year. She had become a
great bridgeplayer and was going round the country speaking
at women's clubs against votes for women. She spoke of
Daddy in a sweet cold acid voice as "your poor dear father,"
and told Mary she must dress better and stop wearing those
awful spectacles. Mary wouldn't take any money from her
mother because she said nobody had a right to money they
hadn't earned, but she did let her fit her out with a new tailored tweed suit and a plain afternoondress, with a lace collar
and cuffs. She got along better with her mother now, but
there was always a cold feeling of strain between them.

Mother said she didn't know where Daddy was living, so
Mary had to go down to the office to see him. The office was
dingier than she remembered it, and full of patients, down-
andoutlooking people mostly, and it was an hour before he
could get away to take her to lunch.

They ate perched on stools at the counter of the little
lunchroom next door. Daddy's hair was almost white now
and his face was terribly lined and there were big gray
pouches under his eyes. Mary got a lump in her throat every
time she looked at him.

"Oh, Daddy, you ought to take a rest."

"I know . . . I ought to get out of the altitude for a while.
The old pump isn't so good as it was."

"Daddy, why don't you come East at Christmas?"

"Maybe I will if I can raise the kale and get somebody to take over my practice for a month."

She loved the deep bass of his voice so. "It would do you so much good. . . . It's so long since we had a trip together."

It was late. There was nobody in the lunchroom except the frozen-mouthed waitress who was eating her own lunch at a table in the back. The big tiredfaced clock over the coffeeurn was ticking loud in the pauses of Daddy's slow talk.

"I never expected to neglect my own little girl . . . you know how it is . . . that's what I've done. . . . How's your mother?"

"Oh, Mother's on top of the world," she said, with a laugh that sounded tinny in her ears. She was working to put Daddy at his ease, like a charity case.

"Oh, well, that's all over now. . . . I was never the proper husband for her," said Daddy.

Mary felt her eyes fill with tears. "Daddy, after I've graduated will you let me take over your office? That awful Miss Hyland is so slipshod. . . ."

"Oh, you'll have better things to do. It's always a surprise to me how many people pay their bills anyway . . . I don't pay mine."

"Daddy, I'm going to have to take you in hand."

"I reckon you will, daughter . . . your settlementwork is just trainin' for the reform of the old man, eh?" She felt herself blushing.

She'd hardly settled down to being with him when he had to rush off to see a woman who had been in labor five days and hadn't had her baby yet. She hated going back to the Broadmoor and the bellhops in monkeyjackets and the overdressed old hens sitting in the lobby. That evening Joe Denny called up to see if he could take her out for a drive. Mother was busy at bridge, so she slipped out without saying anything to her and met him on the hotel porch. She had on her new dress and had taken off her glasses and put them in her little bag. Joe was all a blur to her, but she could make out that he looked well and prosperous and was driving a new little Ford roadster.

"Why, Mary French," he said, "why, if you haven't gone and got goodlooking on me. . . . I guess there's no chance now for a guy like me."

They drove slowly round the park for a while and then he parked the car in a spot of moonlight over a culvert. Down the little gully beyond the quakingaspens you could see the plains dark and shimmery stretching way off to the moonlit horizons. "How lovely," she said.

131

He turned his serious face with its pointed chin to hers and said, stammering a little: "Mary, I've got to spit it out. . . . I want you and me to be engaged. . . . I'm going to Cornell to take an engineering course . . . scholarship. . . . When I get out I ought to be able to make fair money inside of a couple of years and be able to support a wife. . . . It would make me awful happy . . . if you'd say maybe . . . if by that time . . . there wasn't anybody else. . . ." His voice dwindled away.

Mary had a glimpse of the sharp serious lines of his face in the moonlight. She couldn't look at him.

"Joe, I always felt we were friends like Ada and me. It spoils everything to talk like that . . . When I get out of college I want to do socialservice work and I've got to take care of Daddy. . . . Please don't . . . anything like that makes me feel awful."

He held his square hand out and they shook hands solemnly over the dashboard. "All right, sister, what you say goes," he said and drove her back to the hotel without another word. She sat a long time on the porch looking out at the September moonlight, feeling awful.

A few days later when she left to go back to school it was Joe who drove her to the station to take the train East because Mother had an important committeemeeting and Daddy had to be at the hospital. When they said goodbye and shook hands, he tapped her nervously on the shoulder a couple of times and acted like his throat was dry, but he didn't say anything more about getting engaged. Mary was so relieved.

On the train she read Ernest Poole's *The Harbor* and reread *The Jungle* and lay in the Pullman berth that night too excited to sleep, listening to the rumble of the wheels over the rails, the clatter of crossings, the faraway spooky wails of the locomotive, remembering the overdressed women putting on airs in the ladies' dressingroom who'd elbowed her away from the mirror and the heavyfaced businessmen snoring in their berths, thinking of the work there was to be done to make the country what it ought to be, the social conditions, the slums, the shanties with filthy tottering backhouses, the miners' children in grimy coats too big for them, the overworked women stooping over stoves, the youngsters struggling for an education in nightschools, hunger and unemployment and drink, and the police and the lawyers and the judges always ready to take it out on the weak; if the people in the Pullman cars could only be made to understand how it was; if she sacrificed her life, like Daddy taking care of his patients night and day, maybe she, like Miss Addams . . .

She couldn't wait to begin. She couldn't stay in her berth. She got up and went and sat tingling in the empty dressingroom trying to read *The Promise of American Life*. She read a few pages, but she couldn't take in the meaning of the words; thoughts were racing across her mind like the tatters of cloud pouring through the pass and across the dark bulk of the mountains at home. She got cold and shivery and went back to her berth.

Crossing Chicago she suddenly told the taximan to drive her to Hull House. She had to tell Miss Addams how she felt. But when the taxi drew up to the curb in the midst of the familiar squalor of South Halstead Street and she saw two girls she knew standing under the stone porch talking, she

133

suddenly lost her nerve and told the driver to go on to the station.

Back at Vassar that winter everything seemed awful. Ada had taken up music and was studying the violin and could think of nothing but getting down to New York for concerts. She said she was in love with Doctor Muck of the Boston Symphony and wouldn't talk about the war or pacifism or social work or anything like that. The world outside—the submarine campaign, the war, the election—was so vivid Mary couldn't keep her mind on her courses or on Ada's gabble about musical celebrities. She went to all the lectures about current events and social conditions.

The lecture that excited her most that winter was G. H. Barrow's lecture on "The Promise of Peace." He was a tall thin man with bushy gray hair and a red face and a prominent adam'sapple and luminous eyes that tended to start out of his head a little. He had a little stutter and a warm confidential manner when he talked. He seemed so nice somehow Mary felt sure he had been a workingman. He had red gnarled hands with long fingers and walked up and down the room with a sinewy stride, taking off and putting on a pair of tortoiseshell glasses. After the lecture he was at Mr. Hardwick's house and Mrs. Hardwick served lemonade and cocoa and sandwiches and the girls all gathered round and asked questions. He was shyer than on the platform, but he talked

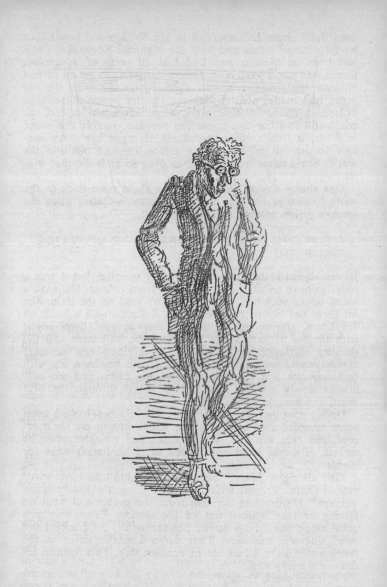

beautifully about Labor's faith in Mr. Wilson and how Labor would demand peace and how the Mexican Revolution (he'd just been to Mexico and had had all sorts of adventures there) was just a beginning. Labor was going to get on its feet all over the world and start cleaning up the mess the old order had made, not by violence but by peaceful methods, Wilsonian methods. That night when Mary got to bed she could still feel the taut appealing nervous tremble that came into Mr. Barrow's voice sometimes. It made her crazy anxious to get out of this choky collegelife and out into the world. She'd never known time to drag so as it did that winter.

One slushy day of February thaw she'd gone back to the room to change her wet overshoes between classes when she found a yellow telegram under the door:

BETTER COME HOME FOR A WHILE   YOUR MOTHER NOT VERY WELL.

It was signed DADDY. She was terribly worried, but it was a relief to have an excuse to get away from college. She took a lot of books with her, but she couldn't read on the train. She sat there too hot in the greenplush Pullman with a book on her knees, staring out at the flat snowcovered fields edged with tangles of bare violet trees and the billboards and the shanties and redbrick falsefront stores along new concrete highways and towns of ramshackle frame houses sooty with factorysmoke and the shanties and the barns and the outhouses slowly turning as the train bored through the Mid West, and thought of nothing.

Daddy met her at the station. His clothes looked even more rumpled than usual and he had a button off his overcoat. His face was full of new small fine wrinkles when he smiled. His eyes were redrimmed as if he hadn't slept for nights.

"It's all right, Mary," he said. "I oughtn't to have wired you to come . . . just selfindulgence . . . gettin' lonely in my old age." He grabbed her bag from the porter and went on talking as they walked out of the station. "Your mother's goin' along fine . . . I pulled her through. . . . Lucky I got wind that she was sick. That damn housephysician at the hotel would have killed her in another day. This Spanish influenza is tricky stuff."

"Is it bad there, Daddy?"

"Very. . . . I want you to be very careful to avoid infection. . . . Hop in, I'll drive you out there." He cranked the rusty touringcar and motioned her into the front. "You know

136

how your poor mother feels about liquor? . . . Well, I kept her drunk for four days."

He got in beside her and started, talking as he drove. The iron cold made her feel better after the dusty choking plush-smell of the sleeper. "She was nicer than I've ever known her. By God, I almost fell in love with her all over again. . . . You must be very careful not to let her do too much when she gets up . . . you know how she is. . . . It's the relapses that kill in this business."

Mary felt suddenly happy. The bare twigs of the trees rosy and yellow and purple spread against the blue over the broad quiet streets. There were patches of frozen snow on the lawns. The sky was tremendously tall and full of yellow sunlight. The cold made the little hairs in her nose crisp.

Out at the Broadmoor Mother was lying in her bed in her neat sunny room with a pink bedjacket on over her night-

gown and a lace boudoircap on her neatly combed black hair. She looked pale but so young and pretty and sort of foolish that for a second Mary felt that she and Daddy were the grownup people and Mother was their daughter. Right away Mother started talking happily about the war and the Huns and the submarine campaign and what could Mr. Wilson be thinking of not teaching those Mexicans a lesson. She was sure it wouldn't have been like that if Mr. Hughes had been elected; in fact she was sure that he had been elected legally and that the Democrats had stolen the election by some skul-duggery or other. And that dreadful Bryan was making the country a laughingstock. "My dear, Bryan is a traitor and ought to be shot."

Daddy grinned at Mary, shrugged his shoulders, and went

off saying, "Now, Hilda, just stay in bed, and please, no alcoholic excess."

When Daddy had gone, Mother suddenly started to cry. When Mary asked her what was the matter she wouldn't say. "I guess it's the influenza makes me weak in the head," she said. "My dear, it's only by the mercy of God that I was spared."

Mary couldn't sit all day listening to her mother go on about preparedness, it made her feel too miserable; so she went down to Daddy's office next morning to see if she could catch a glimpse of him. The waiting room was crowded. When she peeped into his consultingroom, she could see at a glance that he hadn't been to bed all night. It turned out that Miss Hylan had gone home sick the day before. Mary said she'd take her place, but Daddy didn't want to let her. "Nonsense," said Mary, "I can say doctor's office over the phone as well as that awful Miss Hylan can." He finally gave her a gauze mask and let her stay.

When they'd finished up the last patient, they went over to the lunchroom for something to eat. It was three o'clock. "You'd better go out and see your mother," he said. "I've got to start on my rounds. They die awful easy from this thing. I've never seen anything like it."

"I'll go back and tidy up the desk first," said Mary firmly.

"If anybody calls up, tell them that if they think it's the flu, the patient must be put right to bed, keep their feet warm with a hotwaterbottle and plenty of stimulants. No use trying to go to the hospital because there's not a bed in a radius of a hundred miles."

Mary went back to the office and sat down at the desk. There seemed to be an awful lot of new patients; on the last day Miss Hylan had run out of indexcards and had written their names on a scratchpad. They were all flu cases. While she sat there the phone rang constantly. Mary's fingers were cold and she felt trembly all over when she heard the anxious voices, men's, women's, asking for Doc French. It was five before she got away from the office. She took the streetcar out to the Broadmoor.

It gave her quite a turn to hear the band playing in the casino for the teadance and to see the colored lights and feel the quiet warmth of the hotel halls and the air of neat luxury in her mother's room. Mother was pretty peevish and said what was the use of her daughter's coming home if she neglected her like this. "I had to do some things for Daddy," was all Mary said. Mother started talking a blue streak about her campaign to put German women out of the Women's Tuesday Lunch Club. It went on all through supper. After supper they played cribbage until Mother began to feel sleepy.

The next day Mother said she felt fine and would sit up in a chair. Mary tried to get Daddy on the phone to see if she ought to, but there was no answer from the office. Then she remembered that she'd said she'd be there at nine and rushed downtown. It was eleven o'clock and the waitingroom was full before Daddy came in. He'd evidently just been to a barbershop to get shaved, but he looked deadtired.

"Oh, Daddy, I bet you haven't been to bed."

"Sure, I got a couple of hours in one of the interne's rooms at the hospital. We lost a couple of cases last night."

All that week Mary sat at the desk in the waitingroom of Daddy's office, answering the phone through the gauze mask, telling frightened flushed men and women who sat there feeling the aches beginning in their backs, feeling the rising fever flush their cheeks, not to worry, that Doc French would be right back. At five she'd knock off and go to the hotel to eat supper and listen to her mother talk, but Daddy's work would be just beginning. She tried hard to get him to take a night off for sleep every other night.

"But how can I? McGuthrie's laid up and I've got all his practice to handle as well as my own. . . . This damn epidemic can't last indefinitely. . . . When it lets up a little we'll go out to the Coast for a couple of weeks. How about it?" He had a hacking cough and looked gray under the eyes, but he insisted he was tough and felt fine.

Sunday morning she got downtown late because she'd had to go to church with Mother and found Daddy dozing hunched up in a chair. When she came into the office he jumped up with a guilty look and she noticed that his face was very flushed.

"Been to church, eh, you and your mother?" he said in a curious rasping voice. "Well, I've got to be gettin' about my business." As he went out the door with his soft felt hat pushed far down over his eyes, it crossed Mary's mind that perhaps he'd been drinking.

There didn't seem to be many calls that Sunday so she went back home in time to take a drive with her mother in the afternoon. Mrs. French was feeling fine and talking about how Mary ought to make her début next fall. "After all, you owe it to your parents to keep up their position, dear." Talk like that made Mary feel sick in the pit of her stomach. When they got back to the hotel, she said she felt tired and went to her room and lay on the bed and read *The Theory of the Leisure Class*.

Before she went out next morning she wrote a letter to Miss Addams telling her about the flu epidemic and saying that she just couldn't go back to college, with so much misery going on in the world, and couldn't they get her something to do at Hull House? She had to feel she was doing something real. Going downtown in the streetcar she felt rested and happy at having made up her mind; at the ends of streets she could see the range of mountains white as lumps of sugar in the brilliant winter sunshine. She wished she was going out for a hike with Joe Denny. When she put her key in the office door the carbolic iodoform alcohol reek of the doctor's office caught her throat. Daddy's hat and coat were hanging on the rack. Funny, she hadn't noticed his car at the curb. The groundglass door to the consultingroom was closed. She tapped on it. "Daddy," she called. There was no answer. She pushed the door open. Oh, he was asleep. He was lying on the couch with the laprobe from the car over his knees. The thought crossed her mind, how awful if he was deaddrunk. She tiptoed across the room. His head was jammed back between the pillow and the wall. His mouth had fallen open. His face, rough with the gray stubble, was twisted and strangled, eyes open. He was dead.

Mary found herself going quietly to the telephone and calling up the emergency hospital to say Doctor French had collapsed. She was still sitting at the telephone when she heard the ambulance bell outside. An interne in a white coat came in. She must have fainted because she next remembered being taken in a big car out to the Broadmoor. She went right to her room and locked herself in. She lay down on her bed and began to cry. Some time in the night she called up her mother's room on the phone. "Please, Mother, I don't want to see anybody. I don't want to go to the funeral. I want to go right back to college."

Mother made an awful rumpus, but Mary didn't listen to what she said and at last next morning Mother gave her a hundred dollars and let her go. She didn't remember whether she'd kissed her mother when she left or not. She went down to the depot alone and sat two hours in the waitingroom because the train East was late. She didn't feel anything. She seemed to be seeing things unusually vividly, the brilliant winter day, the etched faces of people sitting in the waitingroom, the colors on the magazines on the newsstand. The porter came to get her for the train. She sat in the Pullman looking out at the snow, the yellow grass, the red badlands, the wire fences, the stockcorrals along the track standing up gray and yellowish out of the snow, the watertanks, the little stations, the grain elevators, the redfaced trainmen with their earflaps and gauntlets. Early in the morning going through the industrial district before Chicago she looked out at the men, young men old men with tin dinnerpails, faces ruddy and screwed up with the early cold, crowding the platforms waiting to go to work. She looked in their faces carefully, studying their faces; they were people she expected to get to know, because she was going to stay in Chicago instead of going back to college.

The Camera Eye (45)

the narrow yellow room teems with talk under the low ceiling and crinkling tendrils of cigarettesmoke twine blue and fade round noses behind ears under the rims of women's hats in arch looks changing arrangements of lips the toss of a bang the wise I-know-it wrinkles round the eyes all scrubbed stroked clipped scraped with the help of lipstick rouge shavingcream razorblades into a certain pattern that implies

this warmvoiced woman who moves back and forth

141

with a throaty laugh head tossed a little back distributing
with teasing looks the parts in the fiveoclock drama

every man his pigeonhole

the personality must be kept carefully adjusted over the
face

to facilitate recognition she pins on each of us a badge
today entails tomorrow

Thank you but why me? Inhibited? Indeed goodby

the old brown hat flopped faithful on the chair beside
the door successfully snatched

outside the clinking cocktail voices fade

even in this elderly brick dwellinghouse made over
with green paint orange candles a little tinted calcimine
into

Greenwich Village

the stairs go up and down

lead through a hallway ranked with bells names evoking lives tangles unclassified

into the rainy twoway street where cabs slither slushing
footsteps plunk slant lights shimmer on the curve of a wet
cheek a pair of freshcolored lips a weatherlined neck a
gnarled grimed hand an old man's bloodshot eye

street twoway to the corner of the roaring avenue
where in the lilt of the rain and the din the four directions

(the salty in all of us ocean the protoplasm throbbing
through cells growing dividing sprouting into the billion
diverse not yet labeled not yet named

always they slip through the fingers

the changeable the multitudinous lives)

box dizzyingly the compass

Mary French

For several weeks the announcement of a lecture had
caught Mary French's eye as she hurried past the bulletinboard of Hull House: "May 15 G. H. Barrow, Europe: Problems of Postwar Reconstruction." The name teased her memory, but it wasn't until she actually saw him come into the
lecturehall that she remembered that he was the nice skinny
redfaced lecturer who talked about how it was the workingclass that would keep the country out of war at Vassar that
winter. It was the same sincere hesitant voice with a little

stutter in the beginning of the sentences sometimes, the same informal way of stalking up and down the lecturehall and sitting on the table beside the waterpitcher with his legs crossed. At the reception afterwards she didn't let on that she'd met him before. When they were introduced she was happy to be able to give him some information he wanted about the chances exsoldiers had of finding jobs in the Chicago area. Next morning Mary French was all of a fluster when she was called to the phone and there was Mr. Barrow's voice asking her if she could spare him an hour that afternoon as he'd been asked by Washington to get some unofficial information for a certain bureau. "You see, I thought you would be able to give me the real truth because you are in daily contact with the actual people." She said she'd be delighted and he said would she meet him in the lobby of the Auditorium at five.

At four she was up in her room curling her hair, wondering what dress to wear, trying to decide whether she'd go without her glasses or not. Mr. Barrow was so nice.

They had such an interesting talk about the employment situation which was not at all a bright picture and when Mr. Barrow asked her to go to supper with him at a little Italian place he knew in the Loop, she found herself saying yes without a quiver in spite of the fact that she hadn't been out to dinner with a man since she left Colorado Springs after her father's death three years ago. She felt somehow that she'd known Mr. Barrow for years.

Still she was a bit surprised at the toughlooking place with sawdust on the floor he took her to, and that they sold liquor there and that he seemed to expect her to drink a cocktail. He drank several cocktails himself and ordered red wine. She turned down the cocktails, but did sip a little of the red wine not to seem too oldfashioned. "I admit," he said, "that I'm reaching the age where I have to have a drink to clear the work out of my head and let me relax. . . . That was the great thing about the other side . . . having wine with your meals. . . . They really understand the art of life over there."

After they'd had their spumoni Mr. Barrow ordered himself brandy and she drank the bitter black coffee and they sat in the stuffy noisy restaurant, smelly of garlic and sour wine and tomatosauce and sawdust, and forgot the time and talked. She said she'd taken up socialservice work to be in touch with something real, but now she was beginning to feel coopedup and so institutional that she often wondered if she wouldn't have done better to join the Red Cross overseas or the Friends Reconstruction Unit as so many of the girls had

143

but she so hated war that she didn't want to do anything to help even in the most peaceful way. If she'd been a man she would have been a C.O., she knew that.

Mr. Barrow frowned and cleared his throat: "Of course I suppose they were sincere, but they were very much mistaken and probably deserved what they got."

"Do you still think so?"

"Yes, dear girl, I do. . . . Now we can ask for anything; nobody can refuse us, wages, the closed shop, the eighthour day. But it was hard differing with old friends . . . my attitude was much misunderstood in certain quarters. . . ."

"But you can't think it's right to give them these dreadful jail sentences."

"That's just to scare the others. . . . You'll see they'll be getting out as soon as the excitement quiets down . . . Debs's pardon is expected any day."

"I should hope so," said Mary.

"Poor Debs," said Mr. Barrow, "one mistake has destroyed the work of a lifetime, but he has a great heart, the greatest

144

heart in the world." Then he went on to tell her about how he'd been a railroadman himself in the old days, a freight agent in South Chicago; they'd made him the business agent of his local and he had worked for the Brotherhood, he'd had a hard time getting an education and suddenly he'd wake up, when he was more than thirty, in New York City writing a set of articles for the *Evening Globe,* to the fact that there was no woman in his life and that he knew nothing of the art of life and the sort of thing that seemed to come natural to them over there and to the Mexicans now. He'd married unwisely and gotten into trouble with a chorusgirl, and a woman had made his life a hell for five years, but now that he'd broken away from all that, he found himself lonely getting old wanting something more substantial than the little pickups a man traveling on missions to Mexico and Italy and France and England, little international incidents, he called them with a thinlipped grin, that were nice affairs enough at the time but were just dust and ashes. Of course he didn't believe in bourgeois morality, but he wanted understanding and passionate friendship in a woman.

When he talked he showed the tip of his tongue sometimes through the broad gap in the middle of his upper teeth. She could see in his eyes how much he had suffered, "Of course I don't believe in conventional marriage either," said Mary. Then Mr. Barrow broke out that she was so fresh so young so eager so lovely so what he needed in his life and his speech began to get a little thick and she guessed it was time she was getting back to Hull House because she had to get up so early. When he took her home in a taxi, she sat in the furthest corner of the seat, but he was very gentlemanly, although he did seem to stagger a little when they said goodnight.

After that supper the work at Hull House got to be more and more of a chore, particularly as George Barrow, who was making a lecturetour all over the country in defense of the President's policies, wrote her several times a week. She wrote him funny letters back, kidding about the oldmaids at Hull House and saying that she felt it in her bones that she was going to graduate from there soon, the way she had from Vassar. Her friends at Hull House began to say how pretty she was getting to look now that she was curling her hair.

For her vacation that June Mary French had been planning to go up to Michigan with the Cohns, but when the time came she decided she really must make a break; so instead she took the *Northland* around to Cleveland and got herself a job as countergirl in the Eureka Cafeteria on Lakeside Avenue near the depot.

It was pretty tough. The manager was a fat Greek who pinched the girls' bottoms when he passed behind them along the counter. The girls used rouge and lipstick and were mean to Mary, giggling in corners about their dates or making dirty jokes with the busboys. At night she had shooting pains in her insteps from being so long on her feet and her head spun from the faces the asking mouths the probing eyes jerking along in the rush hours in front of her like beads on a string. Back in the rattly brass bed in the big yellowbrick roominghouse a girl she talked to on her boat had sent her to, she couldn't sleep or get the smell of cold grease and dishwashing out of her nose; she lay there scared and lonely listening to the other roomers stirring behind the thin partitions, tramping to the bathroom, slamming doors in the hall.

After she'd worked two weeks at the cafeteria, she decided she couldn't stand it another minute, so she gave up the job and went and got herself a room at the uptown Y.W.C.A. where they were very nice to her when they heard she'd come from Hull House and showed her a list of socialservice jobs she might want to try for, but she said No, she had to do real work in industry for once, and took the train to Pittsburgh where she knew a girl who was an assistant librarian at Carnegie Institute.

She got into Pittsburgh late on a summer afternoon. Crossing the bridge she had a glimpse of the level sunlight blooming pink and orange on a confusion of metalcolored smokes that jetted from a wilderness of chimneys ranked about the huge corrugated iron and girderwork structures along the riverbank. Then right away she was getting out of the daycoach into the brownish dark gloom of the station with her suitcase cutting into her hand. She called up her friend from a dirty phonebooth that smelled of cigarsmoke.

"Mary French, how lovely!" came Lois Speyer's comical burbling voice. "I'll get you a room right here at Mrs. Gansemeyer's, come on out to supper. It's a boardinghouse. Just wait till you see it. . . . But I just can't imagine anybody coming to Pittsburgh for their vacation."

Mary found herself getting red and nervous right there in

the phonebooth. "I wanted to see something different from the socialworker angle."

"Well, it's so nice the idea of having somebody to talk to that I hope it doesn't mean you've lost your mind . . . you know they don't employ Vassar graduates in the openhearth furnaces."

"I'm not a Vassar graduate," Mary French shouted into the receiver, feeling the near tears stinging her eyes. "I'm just like any other workinggirl. . . . You ought to have seen me working in that cafeteria in Cleveland."

"Well, come on out, Mary darling. I'll save some supper for you."

It was a long ride out in the streetcar. Pittsburgh was grim all right.

Next day she went around to the employment offices of several of the steelcompanies. When she said she'd been a socialworker, they looked at her awful funny. Nothing doing; not taking on clerical or secretarial workers now. She spent days with the newspapers answering helpwanted ads.

Lois Speyer certainly laughed in that longfaced sarcastic way she had when Mary had to take a reporting job that Lois had gotten her because Lois knew the girl who wrote the society column on the *Times Sentinel*.

As the Pittsburgh summer dragged into August, hot and choky with coalgas and the strangling fumes from blastfurnaces, bloomingmills, rollingmills that clogged the smoky Y where the narrow rivervalleys came together, there began to be talk around the office about how red agitators had gotten into the mills. A certain Mr. Gorman, said to be one of the head operatives for the Sherman Service, was often seen smoking a cigar in the managingeditor's office. The paper began to fill up with news of alien riots and Russian Bolshevists and the nationalization of women and the defeat of Lenin and Trotsky.

Then one afternoon in early September Mr. Healy called Mary French into his private office and asked her to sit down. When he went over and closed the door tight, Mary thought for a second he was going to make indecent proposals to her, but instead he said in his most tired fatherly manner: "Now, Miss French, I have an assignment for you that I don't want you to take unless you really want to. I've got a daughter myself, and I hope when she grows up she'll be a nice simple wellbroughtup girl like you are. So honestly if I thought it was demeaning I wouldn't ask you to do it . . .

148

you know that. We're strictly the family newspaper . . . we let the other fellers pull the rough stuff. . . . You know an item never goes through my desk that I don't think of my own wife and daughters; how would I like to have them read it."

Ted Healy was a large round blackhaired man with a rolling gray eye like a codfish's eye.

"What's the story, Mr. Healy?" asked Mary briskly; she'd made up her mind it must be something about the whiteslave traffic.

"Well, these damned agitators, you know they're trying to start a strike. . . . Well, they've opened a publicity office downtown. I'm scared to send one of the boys down . . . might get into some trouble with those gorillas . . . I don't want a dead reporter on my front page. . . . But sending you down . . . You know you're not working for a paper, you're a socialservice worker, want to get both sides of the story. . . . A sweet innocentlooking girl can't possibly come to any harm. . . . Well, I want to get the lowdown on the people working there . . . what part of Russia they were born in, how they got into this country in the first place . . . where the money comes from . . . prisonrecords, you know. . . . Get all the dope you can. It'll make a magnificent Sunday feature."

"I'm very much interested in industrial relations . . . it's a wonderful assignment. . . . But, Mr. Healy, aren't conditions pretty bad in the mills?"

Mr. Healy jumped to his feet and began striding up and down the office. "I've got all the dope on that. . . . Those damn guineas are making more money than they ever made in their lives, they buy stocks, they buy washingmachines and silk stockings for their women and they send money back to the old folks. While our boys were risking their lives in the trenches, they held down all the good jobs and most of 'em are enemy aliens at that. Those guineas are welloff, don't you forget it. The one thing they can't buy is brains. That's how those agitators get at 'em. They talk their language and fill 'em up with a lot of notions about how all they need to do is stop working and they can take possession of this country that we've built up into the greatest country in the world. . . . I don't hold it against the poor devils of guineas, they're just ignorant; but those reds who accept the hospitality of our country and then go around spreading their devilish propaganda . . . My God, if they were sincere I could forgive 'em, but they're just in it for the money like anybody else. We have absolute proof that they're paid by Russian reds with money and jewels they've stole over there; and they're not content with that, they go around shaking down those poor ignorant guineas . . . Well, all I can say is shooting's too good for 'em." Ted Healy was red in the face. A boy in a green eyeshade burst in with a big bunch of flimsy.

Mary French got to her feet. "I'll get right after it, Mr. Healy," she said.

She got off the car at the wrong corner and stumbled up the uneven pavement of a steep broad cobbled street of little gimcrack stores poolrooms barbershops and Italian spaghetti-parlors. A gusty wind whirled dust and excelsior and old papers. Outside an unpainted doorway foreignlooking men stood talking in low voices in knots of three or four. Before she could get up her nerve to go up the long steep dirty narrow stairs, she looked for a minute into the photographer's window below at the tinted enlargements of babies with too-pink cheeks and the family groups and the ramrodstiff bridal couples. Upstairs she paused in the littered hall. From offices on both sides came a sound of typing and arguing voices.

In the dark she ran into a young man. "Hello," he said in a gruff voice she liked, "are you the lady from New York?"

"Not exactly. I'm from Colorado."

"There was a lady from New York comin' to help us with some publicity. I thought maybe you was her."

"That's just what I came for."

"Come in, I'm just Gus Moscowski. I'm kinder the office-boy." He opened one of the closed doors for her into a small dusty office piled with stackedup papers and filled up with a large table covered with clippings at which two young men in glasses sat in their shirtsleeves. "Here are the regular guys." All the time she was talking to the others she couldn't keep her eyes off him. He had blond closecropped hair and very blue eyes and a big bearcub look in his cheap serge suit shiny at the elbows and knees. The young men answered her questions so politely that she couldn't help telling them she was trying to do a feature story for the *Times-Sentinel*. They laughed their heads off.

"But Mr. Healy said he wanted a fair wellrounded picture. He just thinks the men are being misled." Mary found herself laughing too.

"Gus," said the older man, "you take this young lady around and show her some of the sights. . . . After all, Ted Healy may have lost his mind. First here's what Ted Healy's friends did to Fanny Sellers."

She couldn't look at the photograph that he poked under her nose. "What had she done?"

"Tried to organize the workingclass; that's the worst crime you can commit in this man's country."

It was a relief to be out on the street again, hurrying along while Gus Moscowski shambled grinning beside her. "Well, I guess I'd better take you first to see how folks live on fortytwo cents an hour. Too bad you can't talk Polish. I'm a Polack myself."

"You must have been born in this country."

"Sure, highschool graduate. If I can get the dough I want to take engineering at Carnegie Tech. . . . I dunno why I string along with these damn Polacks." He looked her straight in the face and grinned when he said that.

She smiled back at him. "I understand why," she said.

He made a gesture with his elbow as they turned a corner past a group of ragged kids making mudpies; they were pale flabby filthy little kids with pouches under their eyes. Mary turned her eyes away, but she'd seen them, as she'd seen the photograph of the dead woman with her head caved in.

"Git an eyeful of cesspool alley the land of opportunity," Gus Moscowski said way down in his throat.

That night when she got off the streetcar at the corner nearest Mrs. Gansemeyer's, her legs were trembling and the small of her back ached. She went right up to her room and hurried into bed. She was too tired to eat or sit up listening to Lois Speyer's line of sarcastic gossip. She couldn't sleep. She lay in her sagging bed listening to the voices of the boarders rocking on the porch below and to the hooting of engines and the clank of shunted freightcars down in the valley, seeing again the shapeless broken shoes and the worn

hands folded over dirty aprons and the sharp anxious headiness of women's eyes, feeling the quake underfoot of the crazy stairways zigzagging up and down the hills black and bare as slagpiles where the steelworkers lived in jumbled shanties and big black rows of smokegnawed clapboarded houses, in her nose the stench of cranky backhouses and kitchens with cabbage cooking and clothes boiling and unwashed children and drying diapers. She slept by fits and starts and would wake up with Gus Moscowski's warm tough voice in her head, and her whole body tingling with the hard fuzzy bearcub feel of him when his arm brushed against her arm or he put out his big hand to steady her at a place where the boardwalk had broken through and she'd started to slip on the loose shaly slide underneath. When she fell solidly asleep she went on dreaming about him. She woke up early feeling happy because she was going to meet him again right after breakfast.

That afternoon she went back to the office to write the piece. Just the way Ted Healy had said, she put in all she could find out about the boys running the publicity bureau. The nearest to Russia any of them came from was Canarsie, Long Island. She tried to get in both sides of the question, even called them "possibly misguided."

About a minute after she'd sent it in to the Sunday editor, she was called to the city desk. Ted Healy had on a green eyeshade and was bent over a swirl of galleys. Mary could see her copy on top of the pile of papers under his elbow. Somebody had scrawled across the top of it in red pencil: "Why wish this on me?"

"Well, young lady," he said, without looking up, "you've written a firstrate propaganda piece for the *Nation* or some other parlorpink sheet in New York, but what the devil do you think we can do with it? This is Pittsburgh." He got to his feet and held out his hand. "Goodbye, Miss French, I wish I had some way of using you because you're a mighty smart girl . . . and smart girl reporters are rare. . . . I've

sent your slip to the cashier. . . ." Before Mary French could get her breath, she was out on the pavement with an extra week's salary in her pocketbook, which after all was pretty white of old Ted Healy.

That night Lois Speyer looked aghast when Mary told her she'd been fired, but when Mary told Lois that she'd gone down and gotten a job doing publicity for Amalgamated, Lois burst into tears. "I said you'd lost your mind and it's true. . . . Either I'll have to move out of this boardinghouse or you will . . . and I won't be able to go around with you like I've been doing."

"How ridiculous, Lois."

"Darling you don't know Pittsburgh. I don't care about those miserable strikers, but I absolutely have got to hold on to my job. . . . You know I just have to send money home. . . . Oh, we were just beginning to have such fun and now you have to go and spoil everything."

"If you'd seen what I've seen you'd talk differently," said Mary French coldly. They were never very good friends again after that.

Gus Moscowski found her a room with heavy lace curtains in the windows in the house of a Polish storekeeper who was a cousin of his father's. He escorted her solemnly back there from the office nights when they worked late, and they always did work late.

Mary French had never worked so hard in her life. She wrote releases, got up statistics on t.b., undernourishment of children, sanitary conditions, crime, took trips on interurban trolleys and slow locals to Rankin and Braddock and Homestead and Bessemer and as far as Youngstown and Steubenville and Gary, took notes on speeches of Foster and Fitzpatrick, saw meetings broken up and the troopers in their dark-gray uniforms moving in a line down the unpaved alleys of company patches, beating up men and women with their clubs, kicking children out of their way, chasing old men off their front stoops. "And to think," said Gus of the troopers, "that the sonsabitches are lousy Polacks themselves most of 'em. Now ain't that just like a Polack?"

She interviewed metropolitan newspapermen, spent hours trying to wheedle A.P. and U.P. men into sending straight stories, smoothed out the grammar in the Englishlanguage leaflets. The fall flew by before she knew it. The Amalgamated could only pay the barest expenses, her clothes were in awful shape, there was no curl in her hair, at night she couldn't sleep for the memory of the things she'd seen, the jailings, the bloody heads, the wreck of some family's parlor, sofa cut open, chairs smashed, chinacloset hacked to pieces

with an axe, after the troopers had been through looking for
"literature." She hardly knew herself when she looked at her
face in the greenspotted giltframed mirror over the washstand
as she hurriedly dressed in the morning. She had a haggard
desperate look. She was beginning to look like a striker herself.

She hardly knew herself either when Gus's voice gave her cold shivers or when whether she felt good or not that day depended on how often he smiled when he spoke to her; it didn't seem like herself at all the way that, whenever her mind was free for a moment, she began to imagine him coming close to her, putting his arms around her, his lips, his big hard hands. When that feeling came on, she would have to close her eyes and would feel herself dizzily reeling. Then she'd force her eyes open and fly at her typing and after a while would feel cool and clear again.

The day Mary French admitted to herself for the first time that the highpaid workers weren't coming out and that the lowpaid workers were going to lose their strike, she hardly

dared look Gus in the face when he called for her to take her home. It was a muggy drizzly outofseason November night. As they walked along the street without saying anything, the fog suddenly glowed red in the direction of the mills.

"There they go," said Gus. The glow grew and grew, first pink then orange. Mary nodded and said nothing. "What can you do when the woikin'class won't stick together! Every kind of damn foreigner thinks the others is bums and the 'Mericans they think everybody's a bum 'cept you an' me. Wasn't so long ago we was all foreigners in this man's country. Christ, I dunno why I string along wid 'em."

"Gus, what would you do if we lost the strike? I mean you personally."

"I'll be on the black books all right. Means I couldn't get me another job in the metaltrades, not if I was the last guy on earth. . . . Hell, I dunno. Take a false name an' join the Navy, I guess. They say a guy kin get a real good eddication in the Navy."

"I guess we oughtn't to talk about it. . . . Me, I don't know what I'll do."

"You kin go anywheres and git a job on a paper like you had. . . . I wish I had your schoolin'. . . . I bet you'll be glad to be quit of this bunch of hunkies."

"They are the workingclass, Gus."

"Sure, if we could only git more sense into our damn heads. . . . You know I've got an own brother scabbin' right to this day."

"He's probably worried about his wife and family."

"I'd worry him if I could get my hands on him. . . . A woikin'man ain't got no right to have a wife and family."

"He can have a girl . . ." Her voice failed. She felt her heart beating so hard as she walked along beside him over the uneven pavement she was afraid he'd hear it.

"Girls aplenty," Gus laughed. "They're free and easy, Polish girls are. That's one good thing."

"I wish . . ." Mary heard her voice saying.

"Well, goodnight. Rest good, you look all in." He'd given her a pat on the shoulder and he'd turned and gone off with his long shambling stride. She was at the door of her house. When she got in her room she threw herself on the bed and cried.

It was several weeks later that Gus Moscowski was arrested distributing leaflets in Braddock. She saw him brought up before the squire, in the dirty courtroom packed close with the gray uniforms of statetroopers, and sentenced to five years. His arm was in a sling and there was a scab of clotted blood on the towy stubble on the back of his head. His blue

157

eyes caught hers in the crowd and he grinned and gave her a jaunty wave of a big hand.

"So that's how it is, is it?" snarled a voice beside her. "Well, you've had the last piece of c—k you get outa dat baby."

There was a hulking gray trooper on either side of her. They hustled her out of court and marched her down to the interurban trolleystop. She didn't say anything, but she couldn't keep back the tears. She hadn't known men could talk to women like that. "Come on now, loosen up, me an' Steve here we're twice the men . . . You ought to have better sense than to be spreadin' your legs for that punk."

At last the Pittsburgh trolley came and they put her on it with a warning that if they ever saw her around again they'd have her up for soliciting. As the car pulled out she saw them turn away slapping each other on the back and laughing. She sat there hunched up in the seat in the back of the car with her stomach churning and her face set. Back at the office all she said was that the cossacks had run her out of the courthouse.

When she heard that George Barrow was in town with the Senatorial Investigating Commission, she went to him at

once. She waited for him in the lobby of the Schenley. The still winter evening was one block of black iron cold. She was shivering in her thin coat. She was deadtired. It seemed weeks since she'd slept. It was warm in the big quiet hotel lobby, through her thin paper soles she could feel the thick nap of the carpet. There must have been a bridgeparty somewhere in the hotel because groups of welldressed middleaged women that reminded her of her mother kept going through the lobby. She let herself drop into a deep chair by a radiator and started at once to drowse off.

"You poor little girl, I can see you've been working. . . . This is different from socialservice work, I'll bet." She opened her eyes. George had on a furlined coat with a furcollar out of which his thin neck and long knobby face stuck out comically like the head of a marabou stork.

159

She got up. "Oh, Mr. Barrow . . . I mean George." He took her hand in his left hand and patted it gently with his right. "Now I know what the frontline trenches are like," she said, laughing at his kind comical look.

"You're laughing at my furcoat. . . . Wouldn't help the Amalgamated if I got pneumonia, would it? Why haven't you got a warm coat? . . . Sweet little Mary French. . . . Just exactly the person I wanted to see. . . . Do you mind if we go up to the room? I don't like to talk here, too many eavesdroppers."

Upstairs in his square warm room with pink hangings and pink lights he helped her off with her coat. He stood there frowning and weighing it in his hand. "You've got to get a warm coat," he said. After he'd ordered tea for her from the waiter, he rather ostentatiously left the door into the hall open. They settled down on either side of a little table at the foot of the bed that was littered with newspapers and typewritten sheets. "Well, well well," he said. "This is a great pleasure for a lonely old codger like me. What would you think of having dinner with the Senator? . . . To see how the other half lives."

They talked and talked. Now and then he slipped a little whiskey in her tea. He was very kind, said he was sure all the boys could be gotten out of jail as soon as the strike was settled and that it virtually was settled. He'd just been over in Youngstown talking to Fitzpatrick. He thought he'd just about convinced him that the only thing to do was to get the men back to work. He had Judge Gary's own private assurance that nobody would be discriminated against and that experts were working on the problem of an eighthour day. As soon as the technical difficulties could be overcome, the whole picture of the steelworker's life would change radically for the better. Then and there he offered to put Mary French on the payroll as his secretary. He said her actual experience with conditions would be invaluable in influencing legislation. If the great effort of the underpaid steelworkers wasn't to be lost, it would have to be incorporated in legislation. The center of the fight was moving to Washington. He felt the time was ripe in the Senate. She said her first obligation was to the strike committee. "But, my dear sweet child," George Barrow said, gently patting the back of her hand, "in a few days there won't be any strikecommittee."

The Senator was a Southerner with irongray hair and white spats who looked at Mary French when he first came in the room as if he thought she was going to plant a bomb under the big bulge of his creamcolored vest, but his fatherly respectful delicate flowerofwomanhood manner was soothing.

They ordered dinner brought up to George's room. The Senator kidded George in a heavy rotund way about his dangerous Bolsheviki friends. They'd been putting away a good deal of rye and the smoky air of George's room was rich with whiskey. When she left them to go down to the office again, they were talking about taking in a burlesque show.

The bunch down at the office looked haggard and sour. When she told them about G. H. Barrow's offer, they told her to jump at it; of course it would be wonderful to have her working for them in Washington and besides they wouldn't be able to pay even her expenses any more. She finished her release and glumly said goodnight. That night she slept better than she had for weeks, though all the way home she was haunted by Gus Moscowski's blue eyes and his fair head with the blood clotted on it and his jaunty grin when his eyes met hers in the courtroom. She had decided that the best way to get the boys out of jail was to go to Washington with George.

Next morning George called her up at the office first thing and asked her what about the job. She said she'd take it. He said would fifty a week be all right; maybe he could raise it to seventyfive later. She said it was more than she'd ever made in her life. He said he wanted her to come right around to the Schenley; he had something important for her to do. When she got there he met her in the lobby with a hundreddollar bill in his hand. "The first thing I want you to do, sweet girl, is to go buy yourself a warm overcoat. Here's two weeks' salary in advance. . . . You won't be any good to me as a secretary if you catch your death of pneumonia the first day."

On the parlorcar going to Washington he handed over to her two big square black suitcases full of testimony.

"Don't think for a moment there's no work concerned with this job," he said, fishing out manila envelope after manila envelope full of closely typed stenographers' notes on onionskin paper. "The other stuff was more romantic," he said, sharpening a pencil, "but this in the longrange view is more useful."

"I wonder," said Mary.

"Mary dear, you are very young . . . and very sweet." He sat back in his greenplush armchair looking at her a long time with his bulging eyes while the snowy hills streaked with green of lichened rocks and laced black with bare branches of trees filed by outside. Then he blurted out, Wouldn't it be fun if they got married when they got to Washington. She shook her head and went back to the problem of strikers' defense, but she couldn't help smiling at him when she said she didn't want to get married just yet; he'd been so kind. She felt he was a real friend.

In Washington she fixed herself up a little apartment in a house on H Street that was being sublet cheap by Democratic officeholders who were moving out. She often cooked supper for George there. She'd never done any cooking before except camp cooking, but George was quite an expert and knew how to make Italian spaghetti and chiliconcarne and oysterstew and real French bouillabaisse. He'd get wine from the Rumanian Embassy and they'd have very cozy meals together after long days working in the office. He talked and talked about love and the importance of a healthy sexlife for men and women, so that at last she let him. He was so tender and gentle that for a while she thought maybe she really loved him. He knew all about contraceptives and was very nice and humorous about them. Sleeping with a man didn't make as much difference in her life as she'd expected it would.

The day after Harding's inauguration two seedylooking men in shapeless gray caps shuffled up to her in the lobby of the little building on G Street where George's office was. One of them was Gus Moscowski. His cheeks were hollow and he looked tired and dirty.

"Hello, Miss French," he said. "Meet the kid brother . . . not the one that scabbed, this one's on the up and up. . . . You sure do look well."

"Oh, Gus, they let you out."

He nodded. "New trial, cases dismissed. . . . But I tell you it's no fun in that cooler."

She took them up to George's office. "I'm sure Mr. Barrow'll want to get firsthand news of the steelworkers."

Gus made a gesture of pushing something away with his hand. "We ain't steelworkers, we're bums. . . . Your friends the Senators sure sold us out pretty. Every sonofabitch ever walked across the street with a striker's blacklisted. The old man got his job back, way back at fifty cents instead of a dollar-ten after the priest made him kiss the book and promise not to join the union. . . . Lots of people goin' back to the old country. Me an' the kid we pulled out, went down to Baltimore to git a job on a boat somewheres, but the seamen are piled up ten deep on the wharf. . . . So we thought we might as well take in the 'nauguration and see how the fat boys looked."

Mary tried to get them to take some money, but they shook their heads and said, "We don't need a handout, we can woik."

They were just going when George came in. He didn't seem any too pleased to see them, and began to lecture them

163

on violence; if the strikers hadn't threatened violence and allowed themselves to be misled by a lot of Bolshevik agitators, the men who were really negotiating a settlement from the inside would have been able to get them much better terms.

"I won't argue with you, Mr. Barrow. I suppose you think Father Kazinski was a red and that it was Fanny Sellers that bashed in the head of a statetrooper. An' then you say you're on the side of the workin'man."

"And, George, even the Senate committee admitted that the violence was by the deputies and statetroopers. . . . I saw it myself after all," put in Mary.

"Of course, boys . . . I know what you're up against. . . . I hold no brief for the Steel Trust. . . . But, Mary, what I want to impress on these boys is that the workingman is often his own worst enemy in these things."

"The woikin'man gets f'rooked whatever way you look at it," said Gus, "and I don't know whether it's his friends or his enemies does the worst rookin'. . . . Well, we got to git a move on."

"Boys, I'm sorry I've got so much pressing business to do. I'd like to hear about your experiences. Maybe some other time," said George, settling down at his desk.

As they left, Mary French followed them to the door and whispered to Gus, "And what about Carnegie Tech?"

His eyes didn't seem so blue as they'd seemed before he went to jail. "Well, what about it?" said Gus, without looking at her and gently closed the groundglass door behind him.

That night while they were eating supper Mary suddenly got to her feet and said, "George, we're as responsible as anybody for selling out the steelworkers."

"Nonsense, Mary, it's the fault of the leaders who picked the wrong minute for the strike and then let the bosses hang a lot of crazy revolutionary notions on them. Organized Labor gets stung every time it mixes in politics. Gompers knows that. We all did our best for 'em."

Mary French started to walk back and forth in the room. She was suddenly bitterly uncontrollably angry. "That's the way they used to talk back in Colorado Springs. I might better go back and live with Mother and do charitywork. It would be better than making a living off the workingclass."

She walked back and forth. He went on sitting there at the table she'd fixed so carefully with flowers and a white cloth, drinking little sips of wine and putting first a little butter on the corner of a cracker and then a piece of Roquefort cheese and then biting it off and then another bit of butter and another piece of cheese, munching slowly all the time. She could feel his bulging eyes traveling over her body. "We're just laborfakers," she yelled in his face, and ran into the bedroom.

He stood over her still chewing on the cheese and crackers as he nervously patted the back of her shoulder. "What a spiteful thing to say. . . . My child, you mustn't be so hysterical. . . . This isn't the first strike that's ever come out badly. . . . Even this time there's a gain. Fairminded people all over the country have been horrified by the ruthless violence of the steelbarons. It will influence legislation. . . . Sit up and have a glass of wine. . . . Now, Mary, why don't we get married? It's too silly living like this. I have some small investments. I saw a nice little house for sale in Georgetown just the other day. This is just the time now to buy a house when prices are dropping . . . personnel being cut out of all the departments. . . . After all I've reached an age when I have a right to settle down and have a wife and kids. . . . I don't want to wait till it's too late."

Mary sat up sniveling. "Oh, George, you've got plenty of time. . . . I don't know why I've got a horror of getting married. . . . Everything gives me the horrors tonight."

"Poor little girl, it's probably the curse coming on," said George and kissed her on the forehead. After he'd gone home to his hotel, she decided she'd go back to Colorado Springs to visit her mother for a while. Then she'd try to get some kind of newspaper job.

Before she could get off for the West, she found that a month had gone by. Fear of having a baby began to obsess her. She didn't want to tell George about it because she knew he'd insist on their getting married. She couldn't wait. She didn't know any doctor she could go to. Late one night she went into the kitchenette to stick her head in the oven and tried to turn on the gas, but it seemed so inconvenient somehow and her feet felt so cold on the linoleum that she went back to bed.

Next day she got a letter from Ada Cohn all about what a wonderful time Ada was having in New York where she had the loveliest apartment and was working so hard on her violin and hoped to give a concert in Carnegie Hall next season. Without finishing reading the letter, Mary French started packing her things. She got to the station in time to get the teno'clock to New York. From the station she sent George a wire:

FRIEND SICK   CALLED TO NEW YORK   WRITING

She'd wired Ada and Ada met her at the Pennsylvania Station in New York looking very handsome and rich. In the taxicab Mary told her that she had to lend her the money to have an abortion. Ada had a crying fit and said of course she'd lend her the money, but who on earth could she go to? Honestly she wouldn't dare ask Doctor Kirstein about it because he was such a friend of her father's and mother's that he'd be dreadfully upset. "I won't have a baby. I won't have a baby," Mary was muttering.

Ada had a fine threeroom apartment in the back of a building on Madison Avenue with a light tancolored carpet and a huge grandpiano and lots of plants in pots and flowers in vases. They ate their supper there and strode up and down the livingroom all evening trying to think. Ada sat at the piano and played Bach preludes to calm her nerves, she said,

but she was so upset she couldn't follow her music. At last Mary wrote George a specialdelivery letter asking him what to do. Next evening she got a reply. George was brokenhearted, but he enclosed the address of a doctor.

Mary gave the letter to Ada to read. "What a lovely letter! I don't blame him at all. He sounds like a fine sensitive beautiful nature."

"I hate him," said Mary, driving her nails into the palms of her hands. "I hate him."

Next morning she went down all alone to the doctor's and had the operation. After it she went home in a taxicab and Ada put her to bed. Ada got on her nerves terribly tiptoeing in and out of the bedroom with her face wrinkled up. After about a week Mary French got up. She seemed to be all right, and started to go around New York looking for a job.

The Camera Eye (46)

walk the streets and walk the streets inquiring of Coca-Cola signs Lucky Strike ads pricetags in storewindows scraps of overheard conversations stray tatters of newsprint yesterday's headlines sticking out of ashcans

for a set of figures a formula of action an address you don't quite know you've forgotten the number the street may be in Brooklyn a train leaving for somewhere a steamboat whistle stabbing your ears a job chalked up in front of an agency

to do to make there are more lives than walking desperate the streets hurry underdog do   make

a speech urging action in the crowded hall after handclapping the pats and smiles of others on the platform the scrape of chairs the expectant hush the few coughs during the first stuttering attempt to talk straight tough going the snatch for a slogan they are listening and then the easy climb slogan by slogan to applause (if somebody in your head didn't say liar to you and on Union Square

that time you leant from a soapbox over faces   avid young opinionated old the middleaged numb with overwork eyes bleared with newspaperreading   trying to tell them the straight dope   make them laugh tell them what they want to hear wave a flag whispers the internal agitator crazy to succeed)

you suddenly falter ashamed flush red break out in sweat   why not tell these men stamping in the wind that we stand on a quicksand?   that doubt is the whetstone of understanding is too hard hurts instead of urging   picket John D. Rockefeller the bastard if the cops knock your blocks off it's all for the advancement of the human race   while I go home after a drink and a hot meal and read (with some difficulty in the Loeb Library trot) the epigrams of Martial and ponder the course of history and what leverage might pry the owners loose from power and bring back (I too Walt Whitman) our storybook democracy

and all the time in my pocket that letter from that collegeboy asking me to explain why being right which he admits   the radicals are in their private lives such shits

lie abed underdog (peeling the onion of doubt) with the book unread in your hand and swing on the seesaw maybe after all maybe topdog   make

money   you understand what he meant the old party with the white beard beside the crystal inkpot at the cleared varnished desk in the walnut office in whose voice boomed all the clergymen of childhood and shrilled the hosannahs of the offkey female choirs. All you say is very true but there's such a thing as sales   And I have daughters   I'm sure you too will end by thinking differently   make

money in New York (lipstick kissed off the lips of a girl fashionablydressed fragrant at five o'clock in a taxicab careening down Park Avenue when at the end of each crosstown street the west is flaming with gold and white smoke billows from the smokestacks of steamboats leaving port and the sky is lined with greenbacks

the riveters are quiet the trucks of the producers are shoved off onto the marginal avenues

winnings sing from every streetcorner

crackle in the ignitions of the cars swish smooth in ballbearings sparkle in the lights going on in the showwindows croak in the klaxons tootle in the horns of imported millionaire shining towncars

dollars are silky in her hair soft in her dress sprout in the elaborately contrived rosepetals that you kiss become pungent and crunchy in the speakeasy dinner sting shrill in the drinks

make loud the girlandmusic show set off the laughing jag in the cabaret swing in the shufflingshuffling orchestra click sharp in the hatcheck girl's goodnight)

if not why not?   walking the streets rolling on your bed eyes sting from peeling the speculative onion of doubt if somebody in your head   topdog?   underdog?   didn't   (and on Union Square)   say liar to you

168

Newsreel LII

assembled to a service for the dear departed, the last half hour of devotion and remembrance of deeds done and work undone; the remembrance of friendship and love; of what was and what could have been. Why not use well that last half hour, why not make that last service as beautiful as Frank E. Campbell can make it at the funeral church (nonsectarian)

BODY TIED IN BAG IS FOUND FLOATING

*Chinatown my Chinatown where the lights are low
Hearts that know no other land
Drifting to and fro*

APOPLEXY BRINGS END WHILE WIFE READS TO HIM

Mrs. Harding was reading to him in a low soothing voice. It had been hoped that he would go to sleep under that influence

DAUGHERTY IN CHARGE

*All alone
By the telephone
Waiting for a ring*

TWO WOMEN'S BODIES IN SLAYER'S BAGGAGE

WORKERS MARCH ON REICHSTAG CITY IN DARKNESS

RACE IN TAXI TO PREVENT SUICIDE ENDS IN FAILURE AT THE BELMONT

PERSHING DANCES TANGO IN THE ARGENTINE

HARDING TRAIN CRAWLS FIFTY MILES THROUGH
MASSED CHICAGO CROWDS

GIRL OUT OF WORK DIES FROM POISON

MANY SEE COOLIDGE BUT FEW HEAR HIM

> *If you knew Susie*
> *Like I know Susie*
> *Oh oh oh what a girl*

Art and Isadora

In San Francisco in eighteen-seventyeight Mrs. Isadora
O'Gorman Duncan, a highspirited lady with a taste for the
piano, set about divorcing her husband, the prominent Mr.
Duncan, whose behavior we are led to believe had been
grossly indelicate; the whole thing made her so nervous that
she declared to her children that she couldn't keep anything
on her stomach but a little champagne and oysters; in the
middle of the bitterness and recriminations of the family row,

into a world of gaslit boardinghouses kept by ruined
Southern belles and railroadmagnates and swinging doors and
whiskery men nibbling cloves to hide the whiskey on their
breaths and brass spittoons and four-wheel cabs and basques
and bustles and long ruffled trailing skirts (in which lecturehall and concertroom, under the domination of ladies of culture, were the centers of aspiring life)

she bore a daughter whom she named after herself Isadora.

The break with Mr. Duncan and the discovery of his du-
plicity turned Mrs. Duncan into a bigoted feminist and an
atheist, a passionate follower of Bob Ingersoll's lectures and
writings; for God read Nature; for duty beauty, *and only
man is vile*.

Mrs. Duncan had a hard struggle to raise her children in
the love of beauty and the hatred of corsets and conventions
and manmade laws. She gave pianolessons, she did embroidery and knitted scarves and mittens.

The Duncans were always in debt.

The rent was always due.

Isadora's earliest memories were of wheedling grocers and

butchers and landlords and selling little things her mother had made from door to door,

helping handvalises out of back windows when they had to jump their bills at one shabbygenteel boardinghouse after another in the outskirts of Oakland and San Francisco.

The little Duncans and their mother were a clan; it was the Duncans against a rude and sordid world. The Duncans weren't Catholics any more or Presbyterians or Quakers or Baptists; they were Artists.

When the children were quite young they managed to stir up interest among their neighbors by giving theatrical performances in a barn; the older girl Elizabeth gave lessons in society dancing; they were Westerners, the world was a goldrush; they weren't ashamed of being in the public eye. Isadora had green eyes and reddish hair and a beautiful neck and arms. She couldn't afford lessons in conventional dancing, so she made up dances of her own.

They moved to Chicago. Isadora got a job dancing to *The Washington Post* at the Masonic Temple Roof Garden for fifty a week. She danced at clubs. She went to see Augustin Daly and told him she'd discovered

the Dance

and went on in New York as a fairy in cheesecloth in a production of *Midsummer Night's Dream* with Ada Rehan.

The family followed her to New York. They rented a big room in Carnegie Hall, put mattresses in the corners, hung drapes on the wall and invented the first Greenwich Village studio.

They were never more than one jump ahead of the sheriff, they were always wheedling the tradespeople out of bills, standing the landlady up for the rent, coaxing handouts out of rich philistines.

Isadora arranged recitals with Ethelbert Nevin

danced to readings of Omar Khayyáam for society women at Newport. When the Hotel Windsor burned they lost all their trunks and the very long bill they owed and sailed for London on a cattleboat

to escape the materialism of their native America.

In London at the British Museum
they discovered the Greeks;
the Dance was Greek.

Under the smoky chimneypots of London, in the sootcoated squares, they danced in muslin tunics, they copied poses from Greek vases, went to lectures, artgalleries, concerts, plays, sopped up in a winter fifty years of Victorian culture.

Back to the Greeks.

Whenever they were put out of their lodgings for nonpayment of rent, Isadora led them to the best hotel and engaged a suite and sent the waiters scurrying for lobster and champagne and fruits outofseason; nothing was too good for Artists, Duncans, Greeks;

and the nineties London liked her gall.

In Kensington and even in Mayfair she danced at parties in private houses,

the Britishers, Prince Edward down,

were carried away by her preraphaelite beauty

her lusty American innocence

her California accent.

After London, Paris during the great exposition of nineteenhundred. She danced with Loïe Fuller. She was still a virgin too shy to return the advances of Rodin the great master, completely baffled by the extraordinary behavior of Loïe Fuller's circle of crackbrained invert beauties. The Duncans were vegetarians, suspicious of vulgarity and men and materialism. Raymond made them all sandals.

Isadora and her mother and her brother Raymond went about Europe in sandals and fillets and Greek tunics

staying at the best hotels leading the Greek life of nature in a flutter of unpaid bills.

Isadora's first solo recital was at a theater in Budapest;

after that she was the diva, had a loveaffair with the leading actor; in Munich the students took the horses out of her carriage. Everything was flowers and handclapping and champagne suppers. In Berlin she was the rage.

With the money she made on her German tour she took the Duncans all to Greece. They arrived on a fishingboat from Ithaca. They posed in the Parthenon for photographs and danced in the Theater of Dionysus and trained a crowd of urchins to sing the ancient chorus from the *Suppliants* and built a temple to live in on a hill overlooking the ruins of ancient Athens, but there was no water on the hill and their money ran out before the temple was finished

so they had to stay at the Hôtel d'Angleterre and run up a bill there. When credit gave out, they took their chorus back to Berlin and put on the *Suppliants* in ancient Greek. Meeting Isadora in her peplum marching through the Tiergarten at the head of her Greek boys marching in order, all in Greek tunics, the Kaiserin's horse shied,

and Her Highness was thrown.

Isadora was the vogue.

She arrived in St. Petersburg in time to see the night funeral of the marchers shot down in front of the Winter Palace in 1905. It hurt her. She was an American like Walt Whitman; the murdering rulers of the world were not her people; the marchers were her people; artists were not on the side of the machineguns; she was an American in a Greek tunic; she was for the people.

In St. Petersburg, still under the spell of the eighteenthcentury ballet of the court of the Sunking,

her dancing was considered dangerous by the authorities.

In Germany she founded a school with the help of her sister Elizabeth who did the organizing, and she had a baby by Gordon Craig.

She went to America in triumph as she'd always planned and harried the home philistines with a tour; her followers were all the time getting pinched for wearing Greek tunics; she found no freedom for Art in America.

Back in Paris it was the top of the world; Art meant Isadora. At the funeral of the Prince de Polignac she met the mythical millionaire (sewingmachine king) who was to be her backer and to finance her school. She went off with him in his yacht (whatever Isadora did was Art)

to dance in the Temple at Paestum

only for him,

but it rained and the musicians all got drenched. So they all got drunk instead.

Art was the millionaire life. Art was whatever Isadora did. She was carrying the millionaire's child to the great scandal of the oldlady clubwomen and spinster artlovers when she danced on her second American tour;

she took to drinking too much and stepping to the footlights and bawling out the boxholders.

Isadora was at the height of glory and scandal and power and wealth, her school going, her millionaire was about to build her a theater in Paris, the Duncans were the priests of a cult (Art was whatever Isadora did),

when the car that was bringing her two children home from the other side of Paris stalled on a bridge across the Seine. Forgetting that he'd left the car in gear the chauffeur got out to crank the motor. The car started, knocked down the chauffeur, plunged off the bridge into the Seine.

The children and their nurse were drowned.

The rest of her life moved desperately on
in the clatter of scandalized tongues, among the kidding faces of reporters, the threatening of bailiffs, the expostulations of hotelmanagers bringing overdue bills.

Isadora drank too much, she couldn't keep her hands off goodlooking young men, she dyed her hair various shades of brightred, she never took the trouble to make up her face properly, was careless about her dress, couldn't bother to keep her figure in shape, never could keep track of her money
but a great sense of health
filled the hall
when the pearshaped figure with the beautiful great arms tramped forward slowly from the back of the stage.

She was afraid of nothing; she was a great dancer.

In her own city of San Francisco the politicians wouldn't let her dance in the Greek Theater they'd built under her influence. Wherever she went she gave offense to the philistines. When the war broke out she danced the *Marseillaise,* but it didn't seem quite respectable and she gave offense by refusing to give up Wagner or to show the proper respectable feelings
of satisfaction at the butchery.

On her South American tour
she picked up men everywhere,
a Spanish painter, a couple of prizefighters, a stoker on the boat, a Brazilian poet,
brawled in tangohalls, bawled out the Argentines for niggers from the footlights, lushly triumphed in Montevideo and Brazil; but if she had money she couldn't help scandalously spending it on tangodancers, handouts, aftertheater suppers, the generous gesture, no, all on my bill. The managers gypped her. She was afraid of nothing, never ashamed in the public eye of the clatter of scandalized tongues, the headlines in the afternoon papers.

When October split the husk off the old world, she remembered St. Petersburg, the coffins lurching through the silent streets, the white faces, the clenched fists that night in St. Petersburg, and danced the *Marche Slave,*
and waved red cheesecloth under the noses of the Boston old ladies in Symphony Hall;
but when she went to Russia full of hope of a school and
174

work and a new life in freedom, it was too enormous, it was too difficult: cold, vodka, lice, no service in the hotels, new and old still piled pellmell together, seedbed and scrapheap, she hadn't the patience, her life had been too easy;

she picked up a yellowhaired poet
and brought him back
to Europe and the grand hotels.

Yessenin smashed up a whole floor of the Adlon in Berlin in one drunken party, he ruined a suite at the Continental in Paris. When he went back to Russia he killed himself. It was too enormous, it was too difficult.

When it was impossible to raise any more money for Art, for the crowds eating and drinking in the hotel suites and the rent of Rolls Royces and the board of her pupils and disciples,

Isadora went down to the Riviera to write her memoirs to scrape up some cash out of the American public that had awakened after the war to the crassness of materialism and the Greeks and scandal and Art, and still had dollars to spend.

She hired a studio in Nice, but she could never pay the rent. She'd quarreled with her millionaire. Her jewels, the famous emerald, the ermine cloak, the works of art presented by the artists, had all gone into the pawnshops or been seized by hotelkeepers. All she had was the old blue drapes that had seen her great triumphs, a redleather handbag, and an old furcoat that was split down the back.

She couldn't stop drinking or putting her arms round the neck of the nearest young man; if she got any cash she threw a party or gave it away.

She tried to drown herself, but an English naval officer pulled her out of the moonlit Mediterranean.

One day at a little restaurant at Golfe Juan she picked up a goodlooking young wop who kept a garage and drove a little Bugatti racer.

Saying that she might want to buy the car, she made him go to her studio to take her out for a ride;

her friends didn't want her to go, said he was nothing but a mechanic; she insisted, she'd had a few drinks (there was nothing left she cared for in the world but a few drinks and a goodlooking young man);

she got in beside him and

she threw her heavilyfringed scarf round her neck with a big sweep she had and

turned back and said,

with the strong California accent her French never lost:

175

Adieu, mes amis, je vais à la gloire.

The mechanic put his car in gear and started.

The heavy trailing scarf caught in a wheel, wound tight. Her head was wrenched against the side of the car. The car stopped instantly; her neck was broken, her nose crushed, Isadora was dead.

Newsreel LIII

Bye bye blackbird

ARE YOU NEW YORK'S MOST BEAUTIFUL
GIRL STENOGRAPHER?

*No one here can love and understand me
Oh what hard luck stories they all hand me*

BRITAIN DECIDES TO GO IT ALONE

you too can quickly learn dancing at home without
music and without a partner . . . produces the same results as an experienced masseur only quicker, easier, and
less expensive. Remember only marriageable men in the
full possession of unusual physical strength will be accepted as the Graphic Apollos

*Make my bed and light the light
I'll arrive late tonight*

WOMAN IN HOME SHOT AS BURGLAR

GRAND DUKE HERE TO ENJOY HIMSELF

ECLIPSE FOUR SECONDS LATE

DOWNTOWN GAZERS SEE CORONA

others are more dressy being made of rich ottoman
silks, heavy satins, silk crêpe or côte de cheval with orna-
mentation of ostrich perhaps

MAD DOG PANIC IN PENN STATION

the richly blended beauty of the finish, both interior and exterior, can come only from the hand of an artist working towards an idea. *Substitutes good normal solid tissue for that disfiguring fat.* He touches every point in the entire compass of human need. It may look a little foolish in print, but he can show you how to grow brains. If you are a victim of physical ill-being he can liberate you from pain. He can show you how to dissolve marital or conjugal problems. He is an expert in matters of sex.

Blackbird bye bye

SKYSCRAPERS BLINK ON EMPTY STREETS.

it was a very languid, a very pink and white Peggy Joyce in a very pink and white boudoir who held out a small white hand

Margo Dowling

When Margie got big enough she used to go across to the station to meet Fred with a lantern dark winter nights when he was expected to be getting home from the city on the nine-fourteen. Margie was very little for her age, Agnes used to say, but her red broadcloth coat with the fleece collar tickly

round her ears was too small for her all the same, and left her chapped wrists out nights when the sleety wind whipped round the corner of the station and the wire handle of the heavy lantern cut cold into her hand. Always she went with a chill creeping down her spine and in her hands and feet for fear Fred wouldn't be himself and would lurch and stumble the way he sometimes did and be so red in the face and talk so awful. Mr. Bemis the stoopshouldered station agent used to kid about it with big Joe Hines the sectionhand who was often puttering around in the station at traintime, and Margie would stand outside in order not to listen to them saying, "Well, here's bettin' Fred Dowlin' comes in stinkin' again tonight." It was when he was that way that he needed Margie and the lantern on account of the plankwalk over to the house being so narrow and slippery. When she was a very little girl she used to think that it was because he was so tired from the terrible hard work in the city that he walked so funny when he got off the train, but by the time she was eight or nine Agnes had told her all about how getting drunk was something men did and that they hadn't ought to. So every night she felt the same awful feeling when she saw the lights of the train coming towards her across the long trestle from Ozone Park.

Sometimes he didn't come at all and she'd go back home crying; but the good times he would jump springily off the train, square in his big overcoat that smelt of pipes, and swoop down on her and pick her up lantern and all: "How's Daddy's good little girl?" He would kiss her and she would feel so proudhappy riding along there and looking at mean old Mr. Bemis from up there, and Fred's voice deep in his chest would go rumbling through his muffler, "Goodnight, chief," and the yellowlighted windows of the train would be moving and the red caterpillar's eyes in its tail would get little and draw together as the train went out of sight across the trestle towards Hammels. She would bounce up and down on his shoulder and feel the muscles of his arm hard like oars tighten against her when he'd run with her down the plankwalk shouting to Agnes, "Any supper left, girlie?" and Agnes would come to the door grinning and wiping her hands on her apron and the big pan of hot soup would be steaming on the stove, and it would be so cozywarm and neat in the kitchen, and they'd let Margie sit up till she was nodding and her eyes were sandy and there was the sandman coming in the door, listening to Fred tell about pocket billiards and sweepstakes and racehorses and terrible fights in the city. Then Agnes would carry her into bed in the cold room and Fred would stand over her smoking his pipe and tell her about shipwrecks at Fire Island when he was in the Coast Guard, till the chinks of light coming in through the door from the kitchen got more and more blurred, and in spite of Margie's trying all the time to keep awake because she was so happy listening to Fred's burring voice, the sandman she'd tried to pretend had lost the train would come in behind Fred, and she'd drop off.

As she got older and along in gradeschool at Rockaway Park, it got to be less often than that. More and more Fred was drunk when he got off the train or else he didn't come at all. Then it was Agnes who would tell her stories about the old days and what fun it had been, and Agnes would sometimes stop in the middle of a story to cry, about how Agnes and Margie's mother had been such friends and both of them had been salesladies at Siegel Cooper's at the artificialflower counter and used to go to Manhattan Beach, so much more refined than Coney, Sundays, not to the Oriental Hotel of course, that was too expensive, but to a little beach near there, and how Fred was lifeguard there.

"You should have seen him in those days, with his strong tanned limbs he was the handsomest man . . ."

"But he's handsome now, isn't he, Agnes?" Margie would put in anxiously.

"Of course, dearie, but you ought to have seen him in those days."

And Agnes would go on about how lucky he was at the races and how many people he'd saved from drowning and how all the people who owned the concessions chipped in to give him a bonus every year and how much money he always had in his pocket and a wonderful laugh and was such a cheery fellow. "That was the ruination of him," Agnes would say. "He never could say no." And Agnes would tell about the wedding and the orangeblossoms and the cake and how Margie's mother Margery died when she was born. "She gave her life for yours, never forget that"; it made Margie feel dreadful, like she wasn't her own self, when Agnes said that.

And then one day when Agnes came out of work, there he'd been standing on the sidewalk wearing a derby hat and all dressed in black and asking her to marry him because she'd been Margery Ryan's best friend, and so they were married, but Fred never got over it and never could say no and that was why Fred took to drinking and lost his job at Holland's and nobody would hire him on any of the beaches on account of his fighting and drinking and so they'd moved to Broad Channel, but they didn't make enough with bait and rowboats and an occasional shoredinner so Fred had gotten a job in Jamaica in a saloon keeping bar because he had such a fine laugh and was so goodlooking and everybody liked him so. But that was the ruination of him worse than ever.

"But there's not a finer man in the world than Fred Dowling when he's himself. . . . Never forget that, Margie." And they'd both begin to cry, and Agnes would ask Margie if she loved her as much as if she'd been her own mother and Margie would cry and say, "Yes, Agnes darling." "You must always love me," Agnes would say, "because God doesn't seem to want me to have any little babies of my own."

Margie had to go over on the train every day to go to school at Rockaway Park. She got along well in the gradeschool and liked the teachers and the books and the singing, but the children teased her because her clothes were all homemade and funnylooking and because she was a mick and a Catholic and lived in a house on stilts. After she'd been Goldilocks in the school play one Christmas, that was all changed and she began to have a better time at school than at home.

At home there was always so much housework to do,

Agnes was always washing and ironing and scrubbing because Fred hardly ever brought in any money any more. He'd lurch into the house drunk and dirty and smelling of stale beer and whiskey and curse and grumble about the food and why didn't Agnes ever have a nice piece of steak any more for him like she used to when he got home from the city and Agnes would break down, blubbering, "What am I going to use for money?" Then he would call her dirty names, and Margie would run into her bedroom and slam the door and sometimes even pull the bureau across it and get into bed and lie there shaking. Sometimes when Agnes was putting breakfast on the table, always in a fluster for fear Margie would miss the train to school, Agnes would have a black eye and her face would be swollen and puffy where he'd hit her and she'd have a meek sorryforherself look Margie hated. And Agnes would be muttering all the time she watched the cocoa and condensed milk heating on the stove, "God knows I've done my best and worked my fingers to the bone for him.

182

. . . Holy saints of God, things can't go like this." All Margie's dreams were about running away.

In summer they would sometimes have had fun if it hadn't been for always dreading that Fred would take a bit too much. Fred would get the rowboats out of the boathouse for the first sunny day of spring and work like a demon calking and painting them a fresh green and whistle as he worked, or he would be up before day digging clams or catching shiners for bait with a castingnet, and there was money around and big pans of chowder Long Island style and New England style simmering on the back of the stove, and Agnes was happy and singing and always in a bustle fixing shoredinners and sandwiches for fishermen, and Margie would go out sometimes with fishingparties, and Fred taught her to swim in the clear channel up under the railroad bridge and took her with him barefoot over the muddy flats clamming and after softshell crabs, and sportsmen with fancy vests who came down to rent a boat would often give her a quarter. When Fred was in a sober spell it was lovely in summer, the warm smell of the marshgrass, the freshness of the tide coming in through the inlet, the itch of saltwater and sunburn, but then as soon as he'd gotten a little money together Fred would get to drinking and Agnes's eyes would be red all the time and the business would go to pot. Margie hated the way Agnes's face got ugly and red when she cried; she'd tell herself that she'd never cry no matter what happened when she grew up.

Once in a while during the good times Fred would say he was going to give the family a treat and they'd get all dressed-up and leave the place with old man Hines, Joe Hines's father, who had a wooden leg and big bushy white whiskers, and go over on the train to the beach and walk along the boardwalk to the amusementpark at Holland's.

It was too crowded and Margie would be scared of getting something on her pretty dress and there was such a glare and men and women with sunburned arms and legs and untidy hair lying out in the staring sun with sand over them, and Fred and Agnes would romp around in their bathingsuits like the others. Margie was scared of the big spuming surf crashing over her head; even when Fred held her in his arms she was scared and then it was terrible he'd swim so far out.

Afterwards they'd get back itchy into their clothes and walk along the boardwalk shrilling with peanutwagons and reeking with the smell of popcorn and saltwater taffy and hotdogs and mustard and beer all mixed up with the surf and the clanking roar of the rollercoaster and the steamcalliope

184

from the merrygoround and so many horrid people pushing and shoving, stepping on your toes. She was too little to see over them. It was better when Fred hoisted her on his shoulder, though she was too old to ride on her father's shoulder in spite of being so small for her age and kept pulling at her pretty paleblue frock to keep it from getting above her knees.

What she liked at the beach was playing the game where you rolled a little ball over the clean narrow varnished boards into holes with numbers, and there was a Jap there in a clean starched white coat and shelves and shelves of the cutest things for prizes: teapots, little china men that nodded their heads, vases for flowers, rows and rows of the prettiest Japanese dolls with real eyelashes some of them, and jars and jugs and pitchers. One time Margie won a little teapot shaped like an elephant that she kept for years. Fred and Agnes didn't seem to think much of the little Jap who gave the prizes, but Margie thought he was lovely, his face was so smooth and he had such a funny little voice and his lips and eyelids were so clearly marked just like the dolls' and he had long black eyelashes too.

Margie used to think she'd like to have him to take to bed with her like a doll. She said that and Agnes and Fred laughed and laughed at her so that she felt awful ashamed.

But what she liked best at Holland's Beach was the vaudeville theater. They'd go in there and the crowds and laughs and racket would die away as the big padded doors closed behind them. There'd be a movingpicture going on when they went in. She didn't like that much, but what she liked best in all the world were the illustrated songs that came next, the pictures of lovely ladies and gentlemen in colors like tinted flowers and such lovely dresses and big hats and the words with pansies and forgetmenots around them and the lady or gentleman singing them to the dark theater. There were always boats on ripply streams and ladies in lovely dresses being helped out of them, but not like at Broad Channel where it was so glary and there was nothing but mudflats and the slimysmelly piles and the boatlanding lying on the ooze when the tide went out, but lovely blue ripply rivers with lovely green banks and weepingwillowtrees hanging over them. After that it was vaudeville. There were acrobats and trained seals and men in straw hats who told funny jokes and ladies that danced. The Merry Widow Girls it was once, in their big black hats tipped up so wonderfully on one side and their sheathdresses and trains in blue and green and purple and yellow and orange and red, and a handsome young man in a cutaway coat waltzing with each in turn.

The trouble with going to Holland's Beach was that Fred would meet friends there and keep going in through swinging doors and coming back with his eyes bright and a smell of whiskey and pickled onions on his breath, and halfway through the good time, Margie would see that worried meek look coming over Agnes's face, and then she'd know that there would be no more fun that day. The last time they all went over together to the beach they lost Fred, although they looked everywhere for him, and had to go home without him. Agnes sobbed so loud that everybody stared at her on the train and Ed Otis the conductor, who was a friend of Fred's, came over and tried to tell her not to take on so, but that only made Agnes sob the worse. Margie was so ashamed she decided to run away or kill herself as soon as she got home so that she wouldn't have to face the people on the train ever again.

That time Fred didn't turn up the next day the way he usually did. Joe Hines came in to say that a guy had told him he'd seen Fred on a bat over in Brooklyn and that he didn't think he'd come home for a while. Agnes made Margie go to bed and she could hear her voice and Joe Hines's in the kitchen talking low for hours. Margie woke up with a start to find Agnes in her nightgown getting into bed with her.

Her cheeks were fiery hot and she kept saying, "Imagine his nerve and him a miserable trackwalker. . . . Margie. . . . We can't stand this life any more, can we, little girl?"

"I bet he'd come here fussing, the dreadful old thing," said Margie.

"Something like that. . . . Oh, it's too awful, I can't stand it any more. God knows I've worked my fingers to the bone."

Margie suddenly came out with, "Well, when the cat's away the mice will play," and was surprised at how long Agnes laughed, though she was crying too.

In September, just when Agnes was fixing up Margie's dresses for the opening of school, the rentman came round for the quarter's rent. All they'd heard from Fred was a letter with a fivedollar bill in it. He said he'd gotten into a fight and gotten arrested and spent two weeks in jail, but that he had a job now and would be home as soon as he'd straightened things out a little. But Margie knew they owed the five dollars and twelve dollars more for groceries. When Agnes came back into the kitchen from talking to the rentman with her face streaky and horrid with crying, she told Margie that they were going into the city to live. "I always told Fred Dowling the day would come when I couldn't stand it any more. Now he can make his own home after this."

187

It was a dreadful day when they got their two bags and the awful old dampeaten trunk up to the station with the help of Joe Hines, who was always doing odd jobs for Agnes when Fred was away, and got on the train that took them into Brooklyn. They went to Agnes's father's and mother's, who lived in the back of a small paperhanger's store on Fulton Street under the El. Old Mr. Fisher was a paperhanger and plasterer and the whole house smelt of paste and turpentine and plaster. He was a small little gray man and Mrs. Fisher was just like him except that he had drooping gray mustaches and she didn't. They fixed up a cot for Margie in the parlor, but she could see that they thought she was a nuisance. She didn't like them either and hated it in Brooklyn.

It was a relief when Agnes said one evening when she came home before supper looking quite stylish, Margie thought, in her city clothes, that she'd taken a position as cook with a family on Brooklyn Heights and that she was going to send Margie to the Sisters' this winter.

Margie was a little scared all the time she was at the convent, from the minute she went in the door of the graystone vestibule with a whitemarble figure standing up in the middle of it. Margie hadn't ever had much religion, and the Sisters

188

were scary in their dripping black with their faces and hands looking so pale always edged with white starched stuff, and the big dark church full of candles and the catechismclass and confession, and the way the little bell rang at Mass for everybody to close their eyes when the Saviour came down among angels and doves in a glare of amber light onto the altar. It was funny, after the way Agnes had let her run round the house without any clothes on, that when she took her bath once a week the Sister made her wear a sheet right in the tub and even soap herself under it.

The winter was a long slow climb to Christmas, and after all the girls had talked about what they'd do at Christmas so much Margie's Christmas was awful, a late gloomy dinner with Agnes and the old people and only one or two presents. Agnes looked pale, she was deadtired from getting the Christmas dinner for the people she worked for. She did bring a net stocking full of candy and a pretty goldenhaired dolly with eyes that opened and closed, but Margie felt like crying. Not even a tree. Already sitting at the table she was busy making up things to tell the other girls anyway.

Agnes was just kissing her goodnight and getting ready putting on her little worn furpiece to go back to Brooklyn Heights when Fred came in very much under the influence and wanted to take them all out on a party. Of course they wouldn't go and he went away mad and Agnes went away crying, and Margie lay awake half the night on the cot made up for her in the old people's parlor thinking how awful it was to be poor and have a father like that.

It was dreary, too, hanging round the old people's house while the vacation lasted. There was no place to play and they scolded her for the least little thing. It was bully to get back to the convent where there was a gym and she could play basketball and giggle with the other girls at recess. The winter term began to speed up towards Easter. Just before, she took her first communion. Agnes made the white dress for her and all the Sisters rolled up their eyes and said how pretty and pure she looked with her golden curls and blue eyes like an angel, and Minette Hardy, an older girl with a snubnose, got a crush on her and used to pass her chocolate-peppermints in the playground wrapped in bits of paper with little messages scrawled on them: "To Goldilocks with love from her darling Minette," and things like that.

She hated it when commencement came, and there was nothing about summer plans she could tell the other girls. She grew fast that summer and got gawky and her breasts began to show. The stuffy gritty hot weather dragged on endlessly at the Fishers'. It was awful there cooped up with the old people. Old Mrs. Fisher never let her forget that she wasn't really Agnes's little girl and that she thought it was silly of her daughter to support the child of a noaccount like Fred. They tried to get her to do enough housework to pay for her keep and every day there were scoldings and tears and tantrums.

Margie was certainly happy when Agnes came in one day and said that she had a new job and that she and Margie would go over to New York to live. She jumped up and down yelling, "Goody goody. . . . Oh, Agnes, we're going to get rich."

"A fat chance," said Agnes, "but anyway it'll be better than being a servant."

They gave their trunks and bags to an expressman and went over to New York on the El and then uptown on the subway. The streets of the uptown West Side looked amazingly big and wide and sunny to Margie. They were going to live with the Francinis in a little apartment on the corner on the same block with the bakery they ran on Amsterdam Avenue where Agnes was going to work. They had a small room for the two of them, but it had a canarybird in a cage and a lot of plants in the window and the Francinis were both of them fat and jolly and they had cakes with icing on them at every meal. Mrs. Francini was Grandma Fisher's sister.

They didn't let Margie play with the other children on the block; the Francinis said it wasn't a safe block for little girls. She only got out once a week and that was Sunday evening; everybody always had to go over to the Drive and walk up to Grant's Tomb and back. It made her legs ache to walk so slowly along the crowded streets the way the Francinis did. All summer she wished for a pair of rollerskates, but the way the Francinis talked and the way the nuns talked about dangers made her scared to go out on the streets alone. What she was so scared of she didn't quite know. She liked it, though, helping Agnes and the Francinis in the bakery.

That fall she went back to the convent. One afternoon soon after she'd gone back from the Christmas holidays Agnes came over to see her; the minute Margie went in the door of the visitors' parlor she saw that Agnes's eyes were red and asked what was the matter. Things had changed dreadfully at the bakery. Poor Mr. Francini had fallen dead in the middle of his baking from a stroke and Mrs. Francini was going out to the country to live with Uncle Joe Fisher.

"And then there's something else," Agnes said and smiled and blushed. "But I can't tell you about it now. You mustn't think that poor Agnes is bad and wicked, but I couldn't stand it being so lonely."

Margie jumped up and down. "Oh, goody, Fred's come back."

"No, darling, it's not that," Agnes said and kissed her and went away.

That Easter Margie had to stay at the convent all through the vacation. Agnes wrote she didn't have any place to take her just then. There were other girls there and it was rather fun. Then one day Agnes came over to get her to go out, bringing in a box right from the store a new darkblue dress and a little straw hat with pink flowers on it. It was lovely the way the tissuepaper rustled when she unpacked them. Margie ran up to the dormitory and put on the dress with her heart pounding, it was the prettiest and grownupest dress she'd ever had. She was only twelve, but from what little she could see of herself in the tiny mirrors they were allowed it made her look quite grownup. She ran down the empty graystone stairs, tripped and fell into the arms of Sister Elizabeth.

"Why such hurry?"

"My mother's come to take me out on a party with my father and this is my new dress."

"How nice," said Sister Elizabeth, "but you mustn't . . ."

Margie was already off down the passage to the parlor and was jumping up and down in front of Agnes hugging and kissing her. "It's the prettiest dress I ever had." Going over to New York on the Elevated Margie couldn't talk about anything else but the dress.

Agnes said they were going to lunch at a restaurant where theatrical people went. "How wonderful! I've never had lunch in a real restaurant. . . . He must have made a lot of money and gotten rich."

"He makes lots of money," said Agnes in a funny stammering way as they were walking west along Thirtyeighth Street from the El station.

Instead of Fred it was a tall dark man with a dignified manner and a long straight nose who got up from the table to meet them. "Margie," said Agnes, "this is Frank Mandeville." Margie never let on she hadn't thought all the time that that was how it would be.

The actor shook hands with her and bowed as if she was a grownup young lady. "Aggie never told me she was such a beauty . . . what eyes . . . what hair!" he said in his solemn voice.

They had a wonderful lunch and afterwards they went to Keith's and sat in orchestra seats. Margie was breathless and excited at being with a real actor. He'd said that the next day he was leaving for a twelveweeks tour with a singing and piano act and that Agnes was going with him. "And after

191

that we'll come back and make a home for my little girl," said Agnes. Margie was so excited that it wasn't till she was back in bed in the empty dormitory at the convent that she doped out that what it would mean for her was she'd have to stay at the Sisters' all summer.

The next fall she left the convent for good and went to live with Mr. and Mrs. Mandeville, as they called themselves, in two front rooms they sublet from a chiropractor. It was a big old brownstone house with a high stoop and steps way west on Seventyninth Street. Margie loved it there and got on fine with the theater people, all so welldressed and citifiedlooking, who lived in the apartments upstairs. Agnes said she must be careful not to get spoiled, because everybody called attention to her blue eyes and her curls like Mary Pickford's and her pert frozenface way of saying funny things.

Frank Mandeville always slept till twelve o'clock and Agnes and Margie would have breakfast alone quite early, talking in whispers so as not to wake him and looking out of the window at the trucks and cabs and movingvans passing in the street outside and Agnes would tell Margie about vaudeville houses and onenight stands and all about how happy she was and what a free-and-easy life it was and so different from the daily grind at Broad Channel and how she'd first met Frank Mandeville when he was broke and blue and almost ready to turn on the gas. He used to come into the bakery every day for his breakfast at two in the afternoon just when all the other customers had gone. He lived around the corner on Onehundredandfourth Street. When he was completely flat, Agnes had let him charge his meals and had felt so sorry for him on account of his being so gentlemanly about it and out of a job, and then he got pleurisy and was threatened with t.b. and she was so lonely and miserable that she didn't care what anybody thought, she'd just moved in with him to

nurse him and had stayed ever since, and now they were Mr. and Mrs. Mandeville to everybody and he was making big money with his act The Musical Mandevilles. And Margie would ask about Frank Mandeville's partners, Florida Schwartz, a big hardvoiced woman with titian hair, "Of course she dyes it," Agnes said, "henna," and her son, a horrid waspwaisted young man of eighteen who paid no attention to Margie at all. The chiropractor downstairs whom everybody called Indian was Florida's affinity and that was why they'd all come to live in his house. "Stagepeople are odd, but I think they have hearts of gold," Agnes would say.

The Musical Mandevilles used to practice afternoons in the front room where there was a piano. They played all sorts of instruments and sang songs and Mannie whose stage name was Eddy Keller did an eccentric dance and an imitation of Hazel Dawn. It all seemed wonderful to Margie, and she was so excited she thought she'd die when Mr. Mandeville said suddenly one day when they were all eating supper brought in from a delicatessen that the child must take singing and dancing lessons.

"You'll be wasting your money, Frank," said Mannie through a chickenbone he was gnawing.

"Mannie, you're talking out of turn," snapped Florida.

"Her father was a great one for singing and dancing in the old days," put in Agnes in her breathless timid manner.

A career was something everybody had in New York and Margie decided she had one too. She walked down Broadway every day to her lesson in a studio in the same building as the Lincoln Square Theater. In October The Musical Mandevilles played there two weeks. Almost every day Agnes would come for her after the lesson and they'd have a sandwich and a glass of milk in a dairy lunch and then go to see the show.

Agnes could never get over how pretty and young Mrs. Schwartz looked behind the footlights and how sad and dignified Frank looked when he came in in his operacloak.

During the winter Agnes got a job too, running an artistic tearoom just off Broadway and Seventysecond Street, with a Miss Franklyn, a redhaired lady who was a theosophist and was putting in the capital. They all worked so hard they only met in the evenings when Frank and Florida and Mannie would be eating a bite in a hurry before going off to their theater.

The Musical Mandevilles were playing Newark the night Margie first went on. She was to come out in the middle of an *Everybody's Doing It* number rolling a hoop, in a blue muslin dress she didn't like because it made her look about six and she thought she ought to look grownup to go on the stage, and do a few steps of a ragtime dance and then curtsy like they had taught her at the convent and run off with her hoop. Frank had made her rehearse it again and again. She'd often burst out crying in the rehearsals on account of the mean remarks Mannie made.

She was dreadfully scared and her heart pounded waiting for the cue, but it was over before she knew what had happened. She had run on from the grimy wings into the warm glittery glare of the stage. They'd told her not to look out into the audience. Just once she peeped out into the blurry lightpowdered cave of ranked white faces. She forgot part of her song and skimped her business and cried in the dressing-room after the act was over, but Agnes came round back saying she'd been lovely and Frank was smiling, and even Mannie couldn't seem to think of anything mean to say; so the next time she went on her heart wasn't pounding so hard. Every littlest thing she did got an answer from the vague cave of faces. By the end of the week she was getting such a hand that Frank decided to run the *Everybody's Doing It* number just before the finale.

Florida Schwartz had said that Margery was too vulgar a given name for the stage, so she was billed as Little Margo.

All winter and the next summer they toured on the Keith circuit, sleeping in Pullmans and in all kinds of hotels and going to Chicago and Milwaukee and Kansas City and so many towns that Margie couldn't remember their names. Agnes came along as wardrobemistress and attended to the transportation and fetched and carried for everybody. She was always washing and ironing and heating up canned soup on an alcohol stove. Margie got to be ashamed of how shabby Agnes looked on the street beside Florida Schwartz. Whenever she met other stagechildren and they asked her who she thought the best matinee idol was, she'd answer Frank Mandeville.

When the war broke out The Musical Mandevilles were back in New York looking for new bookings. One evening

Frank was explaining his plan to make the act a real head-liner by turning it into a vestpocket operetta, when he and the Schwartzes got to quarreling about the war. Frank said the Mandevilles were descended from a long line of French nobility and that the Germans were barbarian swine and had no idea of art. The Schwartzes blew up and said that the French were degenerates and not to be trusted in money matters and that Frank was holding out receipts on them. They made such a racket that the other boarders banged on the wall and a camelfaced lady came up from the basement wearing a dressinggown spattered with red and blue poppies and with her hair in curlpapers to tell them to keep quiet. Agnes cried and Frank in a ringing voice ordered the Schwartzes to leave the room and not to darken his door again, and Margie got an awful fit of giggling. The more Agnes scolded at her the more she giggled. It wasn't until Frank took her in the arms of his rakishlytailored checked suit and stroked her hair and her forehead that she was able to quiet down. She went to bed that night still feeling funny and breathless inside with the whiff of bay rum and energine and Egyptian ciga-rettes that had teased her nose when she leaned against his chest.

That fall it was hard times again, vaudeville bookings were hard to get and Frank didn't have a partner for his act. Agnes went back to Miss Franklyn's teashop and Margie had to give up her singing and dancing lessons. They moved into one room, with a curtained cubicle for Margie to sleep in.

October was very warm that year. Margie was miserable hanging round the house all day, the steamheat wouldn't turn off altogether and it was too hot even with the window open. She felt tired all the time. The house smelled of frizzing hair and beautycreams and shavingsoap. The rooms were all rented to theater people and there was no time of the day that you could go up to the bathroom without meeting heavy-eyed people in bathrobes or kimonos on the stairs. There was something hot and sticky in the way the men looked at Margie when she brushed past them in the hall that made her feel awful funny.

She loved Frank best of anybody. Agnes was always pee-vish, in a hurry to go to work or else deadtired just back from work, but Frank always spoke to her seriously as if she were a grownup young lady. The rare afternoons when he was in, he coached her on elocution and told her stories about the time he'd toured with Richard Mansfield. He'd give her bits of parts to learn and she had to recite them to him when he came home. When she didn't know them, he'd get very cold and stride up and down and say, "Well, it's up to you, my dear, if you want a career you must work for it. . . . You have the godgiven gifts . . . but without hard work they are nothing. . . . I suppose you want to work in a tearoom like poor Agnes all your life."

Then she'd run up to him and throw her arms round his neck and kiss him and say, "Honest, Frank, I'll work terrible hard." He'd be all flustered when she did that or mussed his hair and would say, "Now, child, no liberties," and suggest they go out for a walk up Broadway. Sometimes when he had a little money they'd go skating at the St. Nicholas rink. When they spoke of Agnes they always called her poor Agnes as if she were a little halfwitted. There was something a little hick about Agnes.

But most of the time Margie just loafed or read magazines in the room or lay on the bed and felt the hours dribble away so horribly slowly. She'd dream about boys taking her out to the theater and to restaurants and what kind of a house she would live in when she became a great actress, and the jewelry she'd have, or else she'd remember how Indian the chiropractor had kneaded her back the time she had the sick headache. He was strong and brown and wiry in his shirtsleeves working on her back with his bigknuckled hands. It was only his eyes made her feel funny; eyes like Indian's would suddenly be looking at her when she was walking along Broadway, she'd hurry and wouldn't dare turn back to see if they were still looking, and get home all breathless and scared.

One warm afternoon in the late fall, Margie was lying on the bed reading a copy of the *Smart Set* Frank had bought that Agnes had made her promise not to read. She heard a shoe creak and jumped up popping the magazine under the pillow.

Frank was standing in the doorway looking at her. She didn't need to look at him twice to know that he'd been drinking. His eyes had that look and there was a flush on his usually white face. "Haha, caught you that time, Little Margo," he said.

"I bet you think I don't know my part," said Margie.

"I wish I didn't know mine," he said. "I've just signed the lousiest contract I ever signed in my life. . . . The world will soon see Frank Mandeville on the filthy stage of a burlesque house." He sat down on the bed with his felt hat still on his head and put a hand over his eyes. "God, I'm tired. . . ." Then he looked up at her with his eyes red and staring. "Little Margo, you don't know what it is yet to buck the world."

Margie said with a little giggle that she knew plenty and sat down beside him on the bed and took his hat off and

198

smoothed his sweaty hair back from his forehead. Something inside of her was scared of doing it, but she couldn't help it.

"Let's go skating, Frank, it's so awful to be in the house all day."

"Everything's horrible," he said. Suddenly he pulled her to him and kissed her lips. She felt dizzy with the smell of bay rum and cigarettes and whiskey and cloves and armpits that came from him. She pulled away from him. "Frank, don't, don't." He had tight hold of her. She could feel his hands trembling, his heart thumping under his vest. He had grabbed her to him with one arm and was pulling at her clothes with the other. His voice wasn't like Frank's voice at all. "I won't hurt you. I won't hurt you, child. Just forget. It's nothing. I can't stand it any more." The voice went on and on whining in her ears. "Please. Please."

She didn't dare yell for fear the people in the house might come. She clenched her teeth and punched and scratched at the big wetlipped face pressing down hers. She felt weak like in a dream. His knee was pushing her legs apart.

When it was over, she wasn't crying. She didn't dare. He was walking up and down the room sobbing. She got up and straightened her dress.

He came over to her and shook her by the shoulders. "If you ever tell anybody I'll kill you, you damn little brat. . . . Are you bleeding?" She shook her head.

He went over to the washstand and washed his face.

"I couldn't help it. I'm not a saint. . . . I've been under a terrible strain."

Margie heard Agnes coming, the creak of her steps on the stairs. Agnes was puffing as she fumbled with the doorknob.

"Why, what on earth's the matter?" she said, coming in all out of breath.

"Agnes, I've had to scold your child," Frank was saying in his tragedy voice. "I come in deadtired and find the child reading that filthy magazine. . . . I won't have it. . . . not while you are under my protection."

"Oh, Margie, you promised you wouldn't. . . . But what did you do to your face?"

Frank came forward into the center of the room, patting his face all over with the towel. "Agnes, I have a confession to make. . . . I got into an altercation downtown. I've had a very trying day downtown. My nerves have all gone to pieces. What will you think of me when I tell you I've signed a contract with a burlesque house?"

"Why, that's fine," said Agnes. "We certainly need the money. . . . How much will you be making?"

"It's shameful . . . twenty a week."

"Oh, I'm so relieved . . . I thought something terrible had happened. Maybe Margie can start her lessons again."

"If she's a good girl and doesn't waste her time reading trashy magazines."

Margie was trembly like jelly inside. She felt herself breaking out in a cold sweat. She ran upstairs to the bathroom and doublelocked the door and stumbled to the toilet and threw up. Then she sat a long time on the edge of the bathtub. All she could think of was to run away.

But she couldn't seem to get to run away. At Christmas some friends of Frank's got her a job in a children's play. She made twentyfive dollars a performance and was the pet of all the society ladies. It made her feel quite stuckup. She almost got caught with the boy who played the Knight doing it behind some old flats when the theater was dark during a rehearsal.

It was awful living in the same room with Frank and Agnes. She hated them now. At night she'd lie awake with her eyes hot in the stuffy cubicle and listen to them. She knew that they were trying to be quiet, that they didn't want her to hear, but she couldn't help straining her ears and holding her breath when the faint rattle of springs from the rickety old iron bed they slept in began. She slept late after those nights in a horrible deep sleep she never wanted to wake up from. She began to be saucy and spiteful with Agnes and would never do anything she said. It was easy to make Agnes cry. "Drat the child," she'd say, wiping her eyes. "I can't do anything with her. It's that little bit of success that went to her head."

That winter she began to find Indian in the door of his consultationroom when she went past, standing there brown and sinewy in his white coat, always wanting to chat or show her a picture or something. He'd even offer her treatments free, but she'd look right into those funny blueblack eyes of his and kid him along. Then one day she went into the office when there were no patients and sat down on his knee without saying a word.

But the boy she liked best in the house was a Cuban named Tony Garrido, who played the guitar for two South Americans who danced the maxixe in a Broadway cabaret. She used to pass him on the stairs and knew all about it and decided she had a crush on him long before they ever spoke. He looked so young with his big brown eyes and his smooth oval face a very light coffeecolor with a little flush on the cheeks under his high long cheekbones. She used to wonder if he was the same color all over. He had polite bashful manners and a low grownup voice. The first time he spoke to her, one spring evening when she was standing on the stoop wondering desperately what she could do to keep from going up to the room, she knew he was going to fall for her. She kidded him and asked him what he put on his eyelashes to make them so black. He said it was the same thing that made her hair so pretty and golden and asked her to have an icecream soda with him.

Afterwards they walked on the Drive. He talked English fine with a little accent that Margie thought was very distinguished. Right away they'd stopped kidding and he was telling her how homesick he was for Havana and how crazy he was to get out of New York, and she was telling him what an awful life she led and how all the men in the house were always pinching her and jostling her on the stairs, and how she'd throw herself in the river if she had to go on living in one room with Agnes and Frank Mandeville. And as for that Indian, she wouldn't let him touch her not if he was the last man in the world.

She didn't get home until it was time for Tony to go downtown to his cabaret. Instead of supper they ate some more icecream sodas. Margie went back happy as a lark. Coming out of the drugstore, she'd heard a woman say to her friend, "My, what a handsome young couple."

Of course Frank and Agnes raised cain. Agnes cried and Frank lashed himself up into a passion and said he'd punch the damn greaser's head in if he so much as laid a finger on a pretty, pure American girl. Margie yelled out that she'd do what she damn pleased and said everything mean she could think of. She'd decided that the thing for her to do was to marry Tony and run away to Cuba with him.

Tony didn't seem to like the idea of getting married much, but she'd go up to his little hall bedroom as soon as Frank was out of the house at noon and wake Tony up and tease him and pet him. He'd want to make love to her but she wouldn't let him. The first time she fought him off he broke down and cried and said it was an insult and that in Cuba men didn't allow women to act like that. "It's the first time in my life a woman has refused my love."

Margie said she didn't care, not till they were married and had gotten out of this awful place. At last one afternoon she teased him till he said all right. She put her hair up on top of her head and put on her most grownuplooking dress and they went down to the marriagebureau on the subway. They were both of them scared to death when they had to go up to the clerk he was twentyone and she said she was nineteen and got away with it. She'd stolen the money out of Agnes's purse to pay for the license.

She almost went crazy the weeks she had to wait for Tony
to finish out his contract. Then one day in May, when she
tapped on his bedroom door he showed her two hundred dollars in bills he'd saved up and said, "Today we get married.
. . . Tomorrow we sail for La 'Avana. We can make very
much money there. You will dance and I will sing and play
the guitar." He made the gesture of playing the guitar with
the thinpointed fingers of one of his small hands. Her heart
started beating hard. She ran downstairs. Frank had already
gone out. She scribbled a note to Agnes on the piece of cardboard that had come back from the laundry in one of Frank's
boiled shirts:

AGNES DARLING:
    Don't be mad. Tony and I got married today and
we're going to Havana, Cuba, to live. Tell Father if he
comes around. I'll write lots. Love to Frank.
Your grateful daughter,
MARGERY

Then she threw her clothes into an English pigskin suitcase
of Frank's that he'd just got back from the hockshop and ran

down the stairs three at a time. Tony was waiting for her on the stoop, pale and trembling with his guitarcase and his suitcase beside him. "I do not care for the money. Let's take a taxi," he said.

In the taxi she grabbed his hand, it was icy cold. At City Hall he was so fussed he forgot all his English and she had to do everything. They borrowed a ring from the justice of the peace. It was all over in a minute, and they were back in the

taxi again going uptown to a hotel. Margie never could remember afterwards what hotel it was, only that they'd looked oo fussed that the clerk wouldn't believe they were married until she showed him the marriagelicense, a big sheet of paper all bordered with forgetmenots. When they got up to the room they kissed each other in a hurry and washed up to go out to a show. First they went to Shanley's to dinner. Tony ordered expensive champagne and they both got to giggling on it.

He kept telling her what a rich city La 'Avana was and how the artists were really appreciated there and rich men would pay him fifty, one hundred dollars a night to play at their parties, "And with you, darling Margo, it will be two three six time that much. . . . And we shall rent a fine house in the Vedado, very exclusive section, and servants very cheap there, and you will be like a queen. You will see I have many friends there, many rich men like me very much." Margie sat back in her chair, looking at the restaurant and the welldressed ladies and gentlemen and the waiters so deferential and the silver dishes everything came in and at Tony's long eyelashes brushing his pink cheek as he talked about how warm it was and the cool breeze off the sea, and the palms and the roses, and parrots and singing birds in cages, and how everybody spent money in La 'Avana. It seemed the only happy day she'd ever had in her life.

When they took the boat the next day, Tony had only enough money to buy secondclass passages. They went over to Brooklyn on the El to save taxifare. Margie had to carry both bags up the steps because Tony said he had a headache and was afraid of dropping his guitarcase.

Newsreel LIV

there was nothing significant about the morning's trading. The first hour consisted of general buying and selling to even up accounts, but soon after eleven o'clock prices did less fluctuating and gradually firmed

TIMES SQUARE PATRONS LEFT HALF-SHAVED

Will Let Crop Rot in Producers' Hands Unless Prices Drop

RUSSIAN BARONESS SUICIDE AT MIAMI

> *. . . the kind of a girl that men forget*
> *Just a toy to enjoy for a while*

Coolidge Pictures Nation Prosperous Under His Policies

HUNT JERSEY WOODS FOR ROVING LEOPARD

PIGWOMAN SAW SLAYING

It had to be done and I did it, says Miss Ederle

FORTY-TWO INDICTED IN FLORIDA DEALS

Saw a Woman Resembling Mrs. Hall Berating Couple Near Murder Scene, New Witness Says

several hundred tents and other light shelters put up by campers on a hill south of Front Street, which overlooks Hempstead Harbor, were laid in rows before the tornado as grass falls before a scythe

> *When they play   Here   comes   the   bride*
> *You'll stand outside*

THREE THOUSAND AMERICANS FOUND PENNILESS IN PARIS

> *I am a poor girl*
> *My fortune's been sad*
> *I always was courted*
> *By the wagoner's lad*

NINE DROWNED IN UPSTATE FLOODS

SHEIK SINKING

Rudolph Valentino, noted screen star, collapsed suddenly yesterday in his apartment at the Hotel Ambassador. Several hours later he underwent

Adagio Dancer

The nineteenyearold son of a veterinary in Castellaneta in the south of Italy was shipped off to America like a lot of other unmanageable young Italians when his parents gave up trying to handle him, to sink or swim and maybe send a few lire home by international postal moneyorder. The family was through with him. But Rodolfo Guglielmi wanted to make good.

He got a job as assistant gardener in Central Park, but that kind of work was the last thing he wanted to do; he wanted to make good in the brightlights; money burned his pockets.

He hung around cabarets doing odd jobs, sweeping out for the waiters, washing cars; he was lazy handsome wellbuilt slender goodtempered and vain; he was a born tangodancer.

Lovehungry women thought he was a darling. He began to get engagements dancing the tango in ballrooms and cabarets; he teamed up with a girl named Jean Acker on a vaudeville tour and took the name of Rudolph Valentino.

Stranded on the Coast he headed for Hollywood, worked for a long time as an extra for five dollars a day; directors began to notice he photographed well.

He got his chance in *The Four Horsemen*
and became the gigolo of every woman's dreams.

206

Valentino spent his life in the colorless glare of klieg lights, in stucco villas obstructed with bricabrac, Oriental rugs, tigerskins, in the bridalsuites of hotels, in silk bathrobes in private cars.

He was always getting into limousines or getting out of limousines,

or patting the necks of fine horses.

Wherever he went the sirens of the motorcyclecops screeched ahead of him.

flashlights flared,

the streets were jumbled with hysterical faces, waving hands, crazy eyes; they stuck out their autographbooks, yanked his buttons off, cut a tail off his admirablytailored dress-suit; they stole his hat and pulled at his necktie; his valets removed young women from under his bed; all night in nightclubs and cabarets actresses leching for stardom made sheepseyes at him under their mascaraed lashes

He wanted to make good under the glare of the milliondollar searchlights

of El Dorado:

the Sheik, the Son of the Sheik;

personal appearances.

He married his old vaudeville partner, divorced her, married the adopted daughter of a millionaire, went into lawsuits with the producers who were debasing the art of the screen, spent a million dollars on one European trip:

he wanted to make good in the brightlights.

When the Chicago *Tribune* called him a pink powderpuff and everybody started wagging their heads over a slavebracelet he wore that he said his wife had given him and his taste for mushy verse of which he published a small volume called *Daydreams* and the whispers grew about the testimony in his divorce case that he and his first wife had never slept together,

it broke his heart.

He tried to challenge the Chicago *Tribune* to a duel;

he wanted to make good

in heman twofisted broncobusting pokerplaying stockjuggling America. (He was a fair boxer and had a good seat on a horse; he loved the desert like the sheik and was tanned from the sun of Palm Springs.) He broke down in his suite in the Hotel Ambassador in New York: gastric ulcer.

When the doctors cut into his elegantlymolded body, they found that peritonitis had begun; the abdominal cavity contained a large amount of fluid and food particles; the viscera were coated with a greenishgray film; a round hole a centimeter in diameter was seen in the anterior wall of the stomach; the tissue of the stomach for one and one half centimeters immediately surrounding the perforation was necrotic. The appendix was inflamed and twisted against the small intestine.

When he came to from the ether, the first thing he said was, "Well, did I behave like a pink powderpuff?"

His expensivelymassaged actor's body fought peritonitis for six days.

The switchboard at the hospital was swamped with calls, all the corridors were piled with flowers, crowds filled the street outside, filmstars who claimed they were his bethrothed entrained for New York.

Late in the afternoon a limousine drew up at the hospital door (where the grimyfingered newspapermen and photographers stood around bored tired hoteyed smoking too many cigarettes making trips to the nearest speak exchanging wisecracks and deep dope waiting for him to die in time to make the evening papers), *and a woman, who said she was a maid employed by a dancer who was Valentino's first wife, alighted. She delivered to an attendant an envelope addressed to the filmstar and inscribed "From Jean," and a package. The package contained a white counterpane with lace ruffles and the word "Rudy" embroidered in the four corners. This was accompanied by a pillowcover to match over a blue silk scented cushion.*

Rudolph Valentino was only thirtyone when he died.

His managers planned to make a big thing of his highlypublicized funeral, but the people in the streets were too crazy.

While he lay in state in a casket covered with a cloth of gold, tens of thousands of men, women, and children packed the streets outside. Hundreds were trampled, had their feet hurt by policehorses. In the muggy rain the cops lost control. Jammed masses stampeded under the clubs and the rearing hoofs of the horses. The funeral chapel was gutted, men and women fought over a flower, a piece of wallpaper, a piece of the broken plateglass window. Showwindows were burst in. Parked cars were overturned and smashed. When finally the mounted police after repeated charges beat the crowd off Broadway, where traffic was tied up for two hours, they picked up twentyeight separate shoes, a truckload of umbrellas, papers, hats, tornoff sleeves. All the ambulances in that part of the city were busy carting off women who'd fainted, girls who'd been stepped on. Epileptics threw fits. Cops collected little groups of abandoned children.

The fascisti sent a guard of honor and the antifascists drove them off. More rioting, cracked skulls, trampled feet. When the public was barred from the undertaking parlors, hundreds of women groggy with headlines got in to view the poor body.

claiming to be exdancingpartners, old playmates, relatives from the old country, filmstars; every few minutes a girl fainted in front of the bier and was revived by the newspapermen who put down her name and address and claim to notice in the public prints. Frank E. Campbell's undertakers and pallbearers, dignified women of black broadcloth and tackersup of crape, were on the verge of a nervous breakdown. Even the boss had his fill of publicity that time.

It was two days before the cops could clear the streets enough to let the flowerpieces from Hollywood be brought in and described in the evening papers.

The church service was more of a success. The policecommissioner barred the public for four blocks round.

Many notables attended.

America's Sweetheart, sobbing bitterly in a small black straw with a black band and a black bow behind, in black georgette over black with a white lace collar and white lace cuffs, followed the coffin that was

covered by a blanket of pink roses

sent by a filmstar who appeared at the funeral heavily veiled, and swooned and had to be taken back to her suite at the Hotel Ambassador after she had shown the reporters a message allegedly written by one of the doctors alleging that Rudolph Valentino had spoken of her at the end

as his bridetobe.

A young woman committed suicide in London.

Relatives arriving from Europe were met by police reserves and Italian flags draped with crape. Exchamp Jim Jeffries said, "Well, he made good." The champion allowed himself to be quoted that the boy was fond of boxing and a great admirer of the champion.

The funeral train left for Hollywood.

In Chicago a few more people were hurt trying to see the coffin, but only made the inside pages.

The funeral train arrived in Hollywood on page 23 of the *New York Times*.

Newsreel LV

THRONGS IN STREETS

LUNATIC BLOWS UP PITTSBURGH BANK

**KRISHNAMURTI HERE SAYS HIS MESSAGE IS
WORLD HAPPINESS**

*Close the doors
They are coming
Through the windows*

**AMERICAN MARINES LAND IN NICARAGUA TO
PROTECT ALIENS**

PANGALOS CAUGHT; PRISONER IN ATHENS

*Close the windows
They are coming through the doors*

**SAW PIGWOMAN, THE OTHER SAYS, BUT NEITHER
CAN IDENTIFY ACCUSED**

FUNDS ACCUMULATE IN NEW YORK

the desire for profits and more profits kept on increasing and the quest for easy money became well nigh universal. All of this meant an attempt to appropriate the belongings of others without rendering a corresponding service

**"PHYSICIAN" WHO TOOK PROMINENT PART IN VALENTINO
FUNERAL EXPOSED AS FORMER CONVICT**

Close the doors they are coming through the windows
My God they're coming through the floor

The Camera Eye (47)

sirens bloom in the fog over the harbor   horns of all colors everyshaped whistles reach up from the river and the churn of screws the throb of engines   bells

the steady broken swish of waves cut by prows   out of the unseen stirring tumblingly through the window tentacles stretch tingling

to release the spring

tonight start out ships somewhere join up sign on the dotted line enlist become one of

hock the old raincoat of incertitude (in which you hunch alone from the upsidedown image on the retina painstakingly out of color shape words remembered light and dark straining

to rebuild yesterday   to clip out paper figures to stimulate growth   warp newsprint into faces smoothing and wrinkling in the various barleyfelt velocities of time)

tonight now   the room fills with the throb and hubbub of departure   the explorer gets a few necessities together coaches himself on a beginning

better the streets   first a stroll   uptown downtown along the wharves under the el peering into faces in taxicabs at the drivers of trucks at old men chewing in lunchrooms at drunk bums drooling puke in alleys what's the newsvendor reading?   what did the elderly wop selling chestnuts whisper to the fat woman behind the picklejars? where is she going the plain girl in a red hat running up the subway steps and the cop joking the other cop across the street? and the smack of a kiss from two shadows under the stoop of the brownstone house and the grouchy faces at the streetcorner suddenly gaping black with yells   at the thud of a blow a whistle scampering feet   the event?

tonight now

but instead you find yourself (if self is the bellyaching malingerer so often the companion of aimless walks) the

jobhunt forgotten   neglected the bulletinboard where the
futures are scrawled in chalk

among nibbling chinamen at the Thalia

ears dazed by the crash of alien gongs the chuckle of
rattles the piping of incomprehensible flutes the swing and
squawk of ununderstandable talk   otherworld music antics postures costumes

an unidentified stranger

destination unknown

hat pulled down over the   has he any?   face

Charley Anderson

It was a bright metalcolored January day when Charley
went downtown to lunch with Nat Benton. He got to the broker's office a little early, and sat waiting in an empty office
looking out through the broad steelframed windows at the
North River and the Statue of Liberty and the bay beyond all
shiny ruffled green in the northwest wind, spotted with white

dabs of smoke from tugboats, streaked with catspaws in the churny wakes of freighters bucking the wind, checkered with lighters and flatboats, carferries, barges, and the red sawedoff passengerferries. A schooner with gray sails was running out before the wind.

Charley sat at Nat Benton's desk smoking a cigarette and being careful to get all his ashes in the polished brass ashreceiver that stood beside the desk. The phone buzzed. It was the switchboard girl. "Mr. Anderson . . . Mr. Benton asked me to beg you to excuse him for a few more minutes. He's out on the floor. He'll be over right away." A little later Benton stuck in the crook of the door his thin pale face on a long neck like a chicken's. "Hullo, Charley . . . be right there." Charley had time to smoke one more cigarette before Benton came back. "I bet you're starved."

"That's all right, Nat, I been enjoyin' the view."

"View? . . . Sure . . . Why, I don't believe I look out of that window from one week's end to the other. . . . Still it was on one of those darned red ferries that old Vanderbilt got his start . . . I guess if I took my nose out of the ticker now and then I'd be better off. . . . Come along, let's get something to eat." Going down in the elevator Nat Benton went on talking. "Why, you are certainly a difficult customer to get hold of."

"The first time I've had my overalls off in a year," said Charley, laughing.

The cold stung when they stepped out of the revolving doors. "You know, Charley, there's been quite a little talk about you fellers on the street. . . . Askew-Merritt went up five points yesterday. The other day there was a feller from Detroit, a crackerjack feller . . . you know the Tern outfit . . . looking all over for you. We'll have lunch together next time he's in town."

When they got to the corner under the El, an icy blast of wind lashed their faces and brought tears to their eyes. The street was crowded; men, errandboys, pretty girl stenographers, all had the same worried look and pursed lips Nat Benton had. "Plenty cold today." Benton was gasping, tugging at his coatcollar. "These steamheated offices soften a feller up." They ducked into a building and went down into the warm hotrolls smell of a basement restaurant. Their faces were still tingling from the cold when they had sat down and were studying the menucards.

"Do you know," Benton said, "I've got an idea you boys stand in the way of making a little money out there."

"It's sure been a job gettin' her started," said Charley as he put his spoon into a plate of peasoup. He was hungry. "Every

213

time you turn your back somethin' breaks down and everythin' goes cockeyed. But now I've got a wonderful guy for a foreman. He's a Heinie, used to work for the Fokker outfit."

Nat Benton was eating rawroastbeef sandwiches and buttermilk. "I've got no more digestion than . . ."

"Than John D. Rockefeller," put in Charley. They laughed.

Benton started talking again. "But as I was saying, I don't know anything about manufacturing, but it's always been my idea that the secret of moneymaking in that line of business was discovering proper people to work for you. They work for you or you work for them. That's about the size of it. After all, you fellers turn out the product there in Long Island City, but if you want to make the money you've got to come down here to make it. . . . Isn't that true?"

Charley looked up from the juicy sirloin he was just about to cut. He burst out laughing. "I guess," he said. "A man 'ud be a damn fool to keep his nose on his draftin'board all his life."

They talked about golf for a while, then, when they were having their coffee, Nat Benton said, "Charley, I just wanted to pass the word along, on account of you being a friend of old Ollie's and the Humphries and all that sort of thing . . . don't you boys sell any of your stock. If I were you, I'd scrape up all the cash you could get ahold of for a margin and buy up any that's around loose. You'll have the chance soon."

"You think she'll keep on risin'?"

"Now keep this under your hat . . . Merritt and that crowd are worried. They're selling, so you can expect a drop. That's what these Tern people in Detroit are waiting for to get in cheap, see, they like the looks of your little concern. . . . They think your engine is a whiz. . . . If it's agreeable to you, I'd like to handle your brokerage account, just for old times' sake, you understand."

Charley laughed. "Gosh, I hadn't pictured myself with a brokerage account . . . but, by heck, you may be right."

"I wouldn't like to see you wake up one morning and find yourself out on the cold cold pavement, see, Charley?"

After they'd eaten, Nat Benton asked Charley if he'd ever seen the stock exchange operating. "It's interesting to see if a feller's never seen it," he said, and led Charley across Broadway where the lashing wind cut their faces and down a narrow street shaded by tall buildings into a crowded vestibule.

"My, that cold nips your ears," he said.

"You ought to see it out where I come from," said Charley.

They went up in an elevator and came out in a little room where some elderly parties in uniform greeted Mr. Benton with considerable respect. Nat signed in a book and they were let out through a small door into the visitors' gallery and stood a minute looking down into a great greenish hall like a railroadstation onto the heads of a crowd of men, some in uniform, some with white badges, slowly churning around the tradingposts. Sometimes the crowd knotted and thickened at one booth and sometimes at another. The air was full of shuffle and low clicking machinesounds in which voices were lost.

"Don't look like much," said Nat, "but that's where it all changes hands." Nat pointed out the booths where different classes of stocks were traded.

"I guess they don't think much about aviation stocks," said Charley.

"No, it's all steel and oil and the automotive industries," said Nat.

"We'll give 'em a few years . . . what do you say, Nat?" said Charley boisterously.

Charley went uptown on the Second Avenue El and out across the Queensboro Bridge. At Queens Plaza he got off and walked over to the garage where he kept his car, a Stutz roadster he'd bought secondhand. The traffic was heavy and he was tired and peevish before he got out to the plant. The sky had become overcast and dry snow drove on the wind. He turned in and jammed on his brakes in the crunching ash of the yard in front of the office, then he pulled off his padded aviator's helmet and sat there a minute in the car after he'd switched off the motor listening to the hum and whirr and clatter of the plant. "The sonsabitches are slakenin' up," he muttered under his breath.

He stuck his head in Joe's office for a moment, but Joe was busy talking to a guy in a coonskin coat who looked like a bond salesman. So he ran down the hall to his own office, said, "Hello, Ella, get me Mr. Stauch," and sat down at his desk which was covered with notes on blue and yellow sheets. "A hell of a note," he was thinking, "for a guy to be glued to a desk all his life."

Stauch's serious square pale face topped by a brush of colorless hair sprouting from a green eyeshade was leaning over him.

"Sit down, Julius," he said "How's tricks? . . . Burnishin' room all right?"

"Ach, yes, but we haf two stampingmachines broken in one day."

"The hell you say. Let's go look at them."

When Charley got back to the office, he had a streak of grease on his nose. He still had an oily micrometer in his hand. It was six o'clock. He called up Joe. "Hello, Joe, goin' home?"

"Sure, I was waiting for you; what was the trouble?"

"I was crawlin' around on my belly in the grease as usual." Charley washed his hands and face in the lavatory and ran down the rubbertreaded steps.

Joe was waiting for him in the entry. "My wife's got my car, Charley, let's take yours," said Joe.

"It'll be a bit drafty, Joe."

"We can stand it."

"Goodnight, Mr. Askew, goodnight, Mr. Anderson," said the old watchman in his blue cap with earflaps, who was closing up behind them.

"Say, Charley," Joe said when they'd turned into the stream of traffic at the end of the alley, "why don't you let Strauch do more of the routine work? He seems pretty efficient."

"Knows a hell of a lot more than I do," said Charley, squinting through the frosted windshield.

The headlights coming the other way made big sparkling blooms of light in the driving snow. On the bridge the girders were already marked out with neat streaks of white. All you could see of the river and the city was a shadowy swirl, now dark, now glowing. Charley had all he could do to keep the car from skidding on the icy places on the bridge.

"Attaboy, Charley," said Joe as they slewed down the ramp into the crosstown street full of golden light.

Across Fiftyninth they had to go at a snail's pace. They were stiff with cold and it was seven-thirty before they drove up to the door of the apartmenthouse on Riverside Drive where Charley had been living all winter with the Askews. Mrs. Askew and two yellowhaired little girls met them at their door.

Grace Askew was a bleachedlooking woman with pale hair and faint crowsfeet back of her eyes and on the sides of her neck that gave her a sweet crumpled complaining look. "I was worried," she said, "about your not having the car in this blizzard."

Jean, the oldest girl, was jumping up and down singing, "Snowy snowy snowy, it's going to be snowy."

"And, Charles," said Grace in a teasing voice as they went into the parlor, that smelt warm of dinner cooking, to spread their hands before the gaslogs, "if she called up once she called up twenty times. She must think I'm trying to keep you away from her."

216

"Who . . . Doris?"

Grace pursed up her lips and nodded. "But, Charles, you'd better stay home to dinner. I've got a wonderful leg of lamb and sweetpotatoes. You know you like our dinners better here than all those fancy fixin's over there . . ."

Charley was already at the phone. "Oh, Charley," came Doris's sweet lisping voice, "I was afraid you'd been snowed in over on Long Island. I called there but nobody answered. . . . I've got an extra place . . . I've got some people to dinner you'd love to meet. . . . He was an engineer under the Czar. We're all waiting for you."

"But honestly, Doris, I'm all in "

"This'll be a change. Mother's gone south and we'll have the house to ourselves. We'll wait . . ."

"It's those lousy Russians again," muttered Charley as he ran to his room and hopped into his dinnerclothes.

"Why, look at the loungelizard," kidded Joe from the easychair where he was reading the evening paper with his legs stretched out towards the gaslogs.

"Daddy, what's a loungelizard?" intoned Jean.

"Grace, would you mind?" Charley went up to Mrs. Askew blushing with the two ends of his black tie hanging from his collar.

"Well, it's certainly devotion," Grace said, getting up out of her chair—to tie the bow she had to stick the tip of her tongue out of the corner of her mouth—"on a night like this."

"I'd call it dementia if you asked me," said Joe.

"Daddy, what's dementia?" echoed Jean, but Charley was already putting on his overcoat as he waited for the elevator in the fakemarble hall full of sample whiffs of all the dinners in all the apartments on the floor.

He pulled on his woolly gloves as the got into the car. In the park the snow hissed under his wheels. Turning out of the driveway at Fiftyninth, he went into a skid, out of it, into it again. His wheels gripped the pavement just beside a cop who stood at the corner beating his arms against his chest. The cop glared. Charley brought his hand up to his forehead in a snappy salute. The cop laughed. "Naughty, naughty," he said and went on thrashing his arms.

When the door of the Humphries' apartment opened, Charley's feet sank right away into the deep nap of a Baluchistan rug. Doris came out to meet him. "Oh, you were a darling to come in this dreadful weather," she cooed. He kissed her. He wished she didn't have so much greasy lipstick on. He hugged her to him so slender in the palegreen eveninggown. "You're the darling," he whispered.

217

From the drawingroom he could hear voices, foreign accents, and the clink of ice in a shaker. "I wish we were goin' to be alone," he said huskily.

"Oh, I know, Charley, but they were some people I just had to have. Maybe they'll go home early." She straightened his necktie and patted down his hair and pushed him before her into the drawingroom.

When the last of Doris's dinnerguests had gone, the two of them stood in the hall facing each other. Charley drew a deep breath. He had drunk a lot of cocktails and champagne. He was crazy for her. "Jesus, Doris, they were pretty hard to take."

"It was sweet of you to come, Charley."

Charley felt bitter smoldering anger swelling inside him. "Look here, Doris, let's have a talk . . ."

"Oh, now we're going to be serious." She made a face as she let herself drop on the settee.

"Now look here, Doris . . . I'm crazy about you, you know that . . ."

"Oh, but, Charley, we've had such fun together . . . we don't want to spoil it yet. . . . You know marriage isn't always so funny. . . . Most of my friends who've gotten married have had a horrid time."

"If it's a question of jack, don't worry. The concern's goin' to go big. . . . I wouldn't lie to you. Ask Nat Benton. Just this after' he was explainin' to me how I could start gettin' in the money right away."

Doris got up and went over to him and kissed him. "Yes, he was a poor old silly. . . . You must think I'm a horrid mercenary little bitch. I don't see why you'd want to marry me if you thought I was like that. Honestly, Charley, what I'd love more than anything in the world would be to get out and make my own living. I hate this plushhorse existence."

He grabbed her to him. She pushed him away. "It's my dress, darling, yes, that costs money, not me. . . . Now you go home and go to bed like a good boy. You look all tired-out."

When he got down to the street, he found the snow had drifted in over the seat of the car. The motor would barely turn over. No way of getting her to start. He called his ga-

rage to send somebody to start the car. Since he was in the phonebooth he might as well call up Mrs. Darling. "What a dreadful night, dearie. Well, since it's Mr. Charley, maybe we can fix something up, but it's dreadfully short notice and the end of the week too. Well . . . in about an hour."

Charley walked up and down in the snow in front of the apartmenthouse waiting for them to come round from the garage. The black angry bile was still rising in him. When they finally came and got her started, he let the mechanic take her back to the garage. Then he walked around to a speak he knew.

The streets were empty. Dry snow swished in his face as he went down the steps to the basement door. The bar was full of men and girls halftight and bellowing and tittering. Charley felt like wringing their goddam necks. He drank off four whiskies one after another and went around to Mrs. Darling's. Going up in the elevator he began to feel tight. He gave the elevatorboy a dollar and caught out of the corner of his eye the black boy's happy surprised grin when he shoved the bill into his pocket. Once inside he let out a whoop. "Now, Mr. Charley," said the colored girl in starched cap and apron who had opened the door, "you know the missis don't like no noise . . . and you're such a civilspoken young gentleman."

"Hello, dearie." He hardly looked at the girl. "Put out the light," he said. "Remember your name's Doris. Go in the bathroom and take your clothes off and don't forget to put on lipstick, plenty lipstick." He switched off the light and tore off his clothes. In the dark it was hard to get the studs out of his boiled shirt. He grabbed the boiled shirt with both hands and ripped out the buttonholes. "Now come in here, goddamn you. I love you, you bitch Doris." The girl was trembling. When he grabbed her to him she burst out crying.

He had to get some liquor for the girl to cheer her up and that started him off again. Next day he woke up late feeling

too lousy to go out to the plant, he didn't want to go out, all he wanted to do was drink, so he hung around all day drinking gin and bitters in Mrs. Darling's draperychoked parlor. In the afternoon Mrs. Darling came in and played Russian bank with him and told him about how an operasinger had ruined her life, and wanted to get him to taper off on beer. That evening he got her to call up the same girl again. When she came he tried to explain to her that he wasn't crazy. He woke up alone in the bed feeling sober and disgusted.

The Askews were at breakfast when he got home Sunday morning. The little girls were lying on the floor reading the funny papers. There were Sunday papers on all the chairs. Joe was sitting in his bathrobe smoking a cigar over his last cup of coffee. "Just in time for a nice cup of fresh coffee," he said.

"That must have been quite a dinnerparty," said Grace, giggling.

"I got in on a little pokergame," growled Charley.

When he sat down his overcoat opened and they saw his torn shirtfront. "I'd say it was quite a pokergame," said Joe.

"Everything was lousy," said Charley. "I'll go and wash my face."

When he came back in his bathrobe and slippers he began to feel better.

Grace got him some country sausage and hot cornbread.

"Well, I've heard about these Park Avenue parties before, but never one that lasted two days."

"Oh, lay off, Grace."

"Say, Charley, did you read that article in the financial section of the *Evening Post* last night tipping off about a boom in airplane stocks?"

"No . . . but I had a talk with Nat Benton, you know he's a broker I told you about, a friend of Ollie Taylor's . . . Well, he said . . ."

Grace got to her feet. "Now you know if you boys talk shop on Sundays I leave the room." Joe took his wife's arm and gently pulled her back into her chair. "Just let me say one thing and then we'll shut up. . . . I hope we keep out of the hands of the operators for at least five years. I'm sorry the damned stuff's listed. I wish I trusted Merritt and them as much as I do you and me."

"We'll talk about that," said Charley.

Joe handed him a cigar. "All right, Gracie," he said. "How about a selection on the victrola?"

Charley had been planning all winter to take Doris with him to Washington when he flew down one of the sample planes to show off some of his patents to the experts at the

War Department, but she and her mother sailed for Europe the week before. That left him with nothing to do one springy Saturday night, so he called up the Johnsons. He'd met Paul in the subway during the winter and Paul had asked him in a hurt way why he never came down any more. Charley had answered honestly he hadn't stuck his nose out of the plant in months. Now it made him feel funny calling up, listening to the phone ring and then Eveline's teasing voice that always seemed to have a little jeer in it: What fun, he must come down at once and stay to supper, she had a lot of funny people there, she said.

Paul opened the door for him. Paul's face had a tallowy look Charley hadn't noticed before. "Welcome, stranger," he said in a forced boisterous tone and gave him a couple of pats on the back as he went into the crowded room. There were some very pretty girls, and young men of different shapes and sizes, cocktailglasses, trays of little things to eat on crackers, cigarettesmoke. Everybody was talking and screeching like a lot of lathes in a turningplant.

At the back of the room Eveline, looking tall and pale and beautiful, sat on a marbletopped table beside a small man with a long yellow nose and pouches under his eyes. "Oh, Charley, how prosperous you look. . . . Meet Charles Edward Holden . . . Holdy, this is Charley Anderson; he's in flyingmachines. . . . Why, Charley, you look filthy rich."

"Not yet," said Charley. He was trying to keep from laughing.

"Well, what are you looking so pleased about? Everybody is just too dreary about everything this afternoon."

"I'm not dreary," said Holden. "Now don't tell me I'm dreary."

"Of course, Holdy, you're never dreary, but your remarks tend toward murder and suicide."

Everybody laughed a great deal. Charley found himself pushed away from Eveline by people trying to listen to what Charles Edward Holden was saying. He found himself talking to a plain young woman in a shiny gray hat that had a big buckle set in it like a headlight.

"Do tell me what you do," she said.

"How do you mean?"

"Oh, I mean almost everybody here does something, writes or paints or something."

"Me? No, I don't do anything like that . . . I'm in airplane motors."

"A flyer, oh my, how thrilling. . . . I always love to come to Eveline's, you never can tell who you'll meet. . . . Why, last time I was here Houdini had just left. She's wonderful on celebrities. But I think it's hard on Paul, don't you? . . . Paul's such a sweet boy. She and Mr. Holden . . . It's all so public. He writes about her all the time in his column. . . . Of course I'm very oldfashioned. Most people don't seem to think anything of it. . . . Of course it's grand to be honest. . . . Of course he's such a celebrity too. . . . I certainly think people ought to be honest about their sexlife, don't you? It avoids all those dreadful complexes and things. . . . But it's too bad about Paul, such a nice cleancut young fellow. . . ."

When the guests had thinned out a little, a Frenchspeaking colored maid served a dinner of curry and rice with lots of little fixings. Mr. Holden and Eveline did all the talking. It was all about people Charley hadn't ever heard of. He tried to break it up by telling about how he'd been taken for Charles Edward Holden in that saloon that time, but nobody listened, and he guessed it was just as well anyway. They had just come to the salad when Holden got up and said, "My dear, my only morals consist in never being late to the theater, we must run." He and Eveline went out in a hurry leaving Charley and Paul to talk to a quarrelsome middleaged man and his wife that Charley had never been introduced to. It wasn't much use trying to talk to them because the man was too tight to listen to anything anybody said and the woman was set on some kind of a private row with him and

223

couldn't be got off it. When they staggered out, Charley and Paul were left alone. They went out to a moving picture house for a while, but the film was lousy, so Charley went uptown glum and tumbled into bed.

Next day Charley went by early for Andy Merritt and sat with him in the big antisepticlooking diningroom at the Yale Club while he ate his breakfast.

"Will it be bumpy?" was the first thing he asked.

"Weather report was fine yesterday."

"What does Joe say?"

"He said for us to keep our goddam traps shut an' let the other guys do the talkin'."

Merritt was drinking his last cup of coffee in little sips. "You know Joe's a little overcautious sometimes. . . . He wants to have a jerkwater plant to run himself and hand down to his grandchildren. Now that was all very well in upstate New York in the old days . . . but now if a business isn't expanding it's on the shelf."

"Oh, we're expandin' all right," said Charley, getting to his feet to follow Merritt's broadshouldered tweed suit to the door of the diningroom. "If we weren't expandin', we wouldn't be at all."

While they were washing their hands in the lavatory Merritt asked Charley what he was taking along for clothes. Charley laughed and said he probably had a clean shirt and a toothbrush somewhere.

Merritt turned a square serious face to him: "But we might have to go out. . . . I've engaged a small suite for us at the Waldman Park. You know in Washington those things count a great deal."

"Well, if the worst comes to the worst, I can rent me a soup an' fish."

As the porter was putting Merritt's big pigskin suitcase and his hatbox into the rumbleseat of the car, Merritt asked with a worried frown if Charley thought it would be too much weight. "Hell, no, we could carry a dozen like that," said Charley, putting his foot on the starter. They drove fast through the empty streets and out across the bridge and along the wide avenues bordered by low gimcrack houses out toward Jamaica. Bill Cermak had the ship out of the hangar and all tuned up.

Charley put his hand on the back of Bill's greasy leather jerkin. "Always on the dot, Bill," he said. "Meet Mr. Merritt. . . . Say, Andy . . . Bill's comin' with us, if you don't mind . . . he can rebuild this motor out of old hairpins and chewin'gum if anythin' goes wrong."

Bill was already hoisting Merritt's suitcase into the tail.

Merritt was putting on a big leather coat and goggles like Charley had seen in the windows of Abercrombie and Fitch.

"Do you think it will be bumpy?" Merritt was asking again.

Charley gave him a boost. "Maybe a little bumpy over Pennsylvania . . . but we ought to be there in time for a good lunch. . . . Well, gents, this is the first time I've ever been in the Nation's Capital."

"Me neither," said Bill.

"Bill ain't never been outside of Brooklyn," said Charley, laughing.

He felt good as he climbed up to the controls. He put on his goggles and yelled back at Merritt, "You're in the observer's seat, Andy."

The Askew-Merritt starter worked like a dream. The motor sounded smooth and quiet as a sewingmachine. "What do you think of that, Bill?" Charley kept yelling at the mechanic behind him. She taxied smoothly across the soft field in the early spring sunshine, bounced a couple of times, took the air and banked as he turned out across the slatecolored squares of Brooklyn. The light northwest wind made a million furrows on the opaque green bay. Then they were crossing the gutted factory districts of Bayonne and Elizabeth. Beyond the russet saltmeadows, Jersey stretched in great flat squares, some yellow, some red, some of them misted with the green of new crops.

There were ranks of big white cumulus clouds catching the sunlight beyond the Delaware. It got to be a little bumpy and Charley rose to seven thousand feet where it was cold and clear with a fiftymile wind blowing from the northwest.

225

When he came down again it was noon and the Susquehanna shone bright blue in a rift in the clouds. Even at two thousand feet he could feel the warm steam of spring from the plowed land. Flying low over the farms he could see the white fluff of orchards in bloom. He got too far south, avoiding a heavy squall over the head of the Chesapeake, and had to follow the Potomac north up toward the glinting white dome of the Capitol and the shining sliver of the Washington Monument. There was no smoke over Washington. He circled around for half an hour before he found the flyingfield. There was so much green it all looked like flyingfield.

"Well, Andy," said Charley when they were stretching their legs on the turf, "when those experts see that starter their eyes'll pop out of their heads."

Merritt's face looked pale and he tottered a little as he walked. "Can't hear," he shouted. "I got to take a leak."

Charley followed him to the hangar, leaving Bill to go over the motor. Merritt was phoning for a taxi. "Christamighty, am I hungry?" roared Charley.

Merritt winced. "I got to get a drink to settle my stomach first."

When they got into the taxi with their feet on Merritt's enormous pigskin suitcase, "I'll tell you one thing, Charley," Merritt said, "we've got to have a separate corporation for that starter . . . might need a separate productionplant and everything. Standard Airparts would list well."

They had two rooms and a large parlor with pink easychairs in it at the huge new hotel. From the windows you could look down into the fresh green of Rock Creek Park. Merritt looked around with considerable satisfaction. "I like to get into a place on Sunday," he said. "It gives you a chance to get settled before beginning work." He added that he didn't think there'd be anybody in the diningroom he knew, not on a Sunday, but as it turned out it took them quite a while to get to their table. Charley was introduced on the way to a senator, a corporation lawyer, the youngest member of the House of Representatives and a nephew of the Secretary of the Navy. "You see," explained Merritt, "my old man was a senator once."

After lunch Charley went out to the field again to take a look at the ship. Bill Cermak had everything bright as a jeweler's window. Charley brought Bill back to the hotel to give him a drink. There were waiters in the hall outside the suite and cigarsmoke and a great sound of social voices pouring out the open door. Bill laid a thick finger against his crooked nose and said maybe he'd better blow.

"Gee, it does sound like the socialregister. Here, I'll let you in my bedroom an' I'll bring you a drink if you don't mind waiting a sec."

"Sure, it's all right by me, boss."

Charley washed his hands and straightened his necktie and went into the sittingroom all in a rush like a man diving into a cold pool.

Andy Merritt was giving a cocktailparty with dry martinis, chickensalad, sandwiches, a bowl of caviar, strips of smoked fish, two old silverhaired gentlemen, three huskyvoiced Southern belles with too much makeup on, a fat senator and a very thin senator in a high collar, a sprinkling of pale young men with Harvard accents and a sallow man with a gold tooth who wrote a syndicated column called *Capitol Small Talk*. There was a young publicityman named Savage he'd met at Eveline's. Charley was introduced all around and stood first on one foot and then on the other until he got a chance to sneak into the bedroom with two halftumblers of rye and a plate of sandwiches. "Gosh, it's terrible in there. I don't dare opon my mouth for fear of puttin' my foot in it."

Charley and Bill sat on the bed eating the sandwiches and listening to the jingly babble that came in from the other room. When he'd drunk his whiskey Bill got to his feet, wiped his mouth on the back of his hand and asked what time Charley wanted him to report in the morning.

"Nine o'clock will do. You sure you don't want to stick around? . . . I don't know what to say to those birds . . . we might fix you up with a Southern belle."

Bill said he was a quiet family man and would get him a flop and go to bed. When he left, it meant Charley had to go back to the cocktailparty.

When Charley went back into Merritt's room, he found the black eyes of the fat senator fixed on him from between the two cute bobbing hats of two pretty girls. Charley found himself saying goodbye to them. The browneyed one was a blonde and the blueeyed one had very black hair. A little tang of perfume and kid gloves lingered after them when they left.

"Now which would you say was the prettiest, young man?" The fat senator was standing beside him looking up at him with a tooconfidential smile.

Charley felt his throat stiffen, he didn't know why. "They're a couple of beauties," he said.

"They leave you like the ass between two bundles of hay," said the fat senator with a soft chuckle that played smoothly in and out of the folds of his chin.

"Buridan's ass died of longing, Senator," said the thin senator putting the envelope back in his pocket on which he and Andy Merritt had been doping out figures of some kind.

"And so do I, Senator," said the fat one, pushing back the streak of black hair from his forehead, his loose jowls shaking. "I die daily. . . . Senator, will you dine with me and these young men? I believe old Horace is getting us up a little terrapin." He put a small plump hand on the thin senator's shoulder and another on Charley's.

"Sorry, Senator, the missis is having some friends out at the Chevy Chase Club."

"Then I'm afraid these youngsters will have to put up with eating dinner with a pair of old fogies. I'd hoped you'd bridge the gap between the generations. . . . General Hicks is coming."

Charley saw a faint pleased look come over Andy Merritt's serious wellbred face. The fat senator went on with his smooth ponderous courtroom voice. "Perhaps we had better be on our way. . . . He's coming at seven and those old warhorses tend to be punctual."

A great black Lincoln was just coming to a soundless stop at the hotel entry when the four of them, Charley and Andy Merritt and Savage and the fat senator, came out into the Washington night that smelt of oil on asphalt and the exhausts of cars and of young leaves and of wistariablossoms The senator's house was a continuation of his car, big and dark and faintly gleaming and soundless. They sprawled in big blackleather chairs and an old whitehaired mulatto brought around manhattans on an engraved silver tray.

The senator took each of the men separately to show them where to wash up. Charley didn't much like the little pats on the back he got from the senator's small padded hands as he was ushered into a big oldfashioned bathroom with a setin marble tub. When he came back from washing his hands the folding doors were open to the diningroom and a halelooking old gentleman with a white mustache and a slight limp was walking up and down in front of them impatiently. "I can smell that terrapin, Bowie," he was saying. "Ole Horace is still up to his tricks."

With the soup and the sherry the general began to talk from the head of the table. "Of course all this work with flyin'machines is very interestin' for the advancement of sci-

229

ence . . . I tell you, Bowie, you're one of the last people in this town who sets a decent table . . . perhaps it points to vast possibilities in the distant future. . . . But speakin' as a military man, gentlemen, you know some of us don't feel they have proved their worth. . . . The terrapin is remarkable, Bowie. . . . I mean we don't put the confidence in the flyin'machine that they seem to have over at the Navy Department. . . . A good glass of burgundy, Bowie, nothin' I like so much. . . . Experiment is a great thing, gentlemen, and I don't deny that perhaps in the distant future . . ."

"In the distant future," echoed Savage, laughing, as he followed Merritt and Charley out from under the stone portico of Senator Planet's house. A taxi was waiting for him. "Where can I drop you, gentlemen? . . . The trouble with us is we are in the distant future and don't know it."

"They certainly don't know it in Washington," said Merritt as they got into the cab.

Savage giggled. "The senator and the general were pricelessly archaic . . . like something dug up. . . . But don't worry about the general . . . once he knows he's dealing with . . . you know . . . presentable people, he's gentle as Santa Claus . . . He believes in a government of gentlemen, for gentlemen and by gentlemen."

"Well, don't we all?" said Merritt sternly.

Savage let out a hooting laugh. "Nature's gentlemen . . . been looking for one for years." Then he turned his bulging alcoholic eyes and his laughing pugface to Charley. "The senator thinks you're the whiteheaded boy. . . . He asked me to bring you around to see him . . . the senator is very susceptible, you know." He let out another laugh.

The guy must be pretty tight, thought Charley. He was a little woozy himself from the Napoleon brandy drunk out of balloonshaped glasses they'd finished off the dinner with. Savage let them out at the Waldman Park and his taxi went on. "Say, who is that guy, Andy?"

"He's a wild man," said Merritt. "He is one of Moorehouse's bright young men. He's bright enough, but I don't like the stories I hear about him. He wants the Askew-Merritt contract, but we're not in that class yet. Those publicrelations people will eat you out of house and home."

As they were going up in the elevator, Charley said, yawning, "Gee, I hoped those pretty girls were comin' to dinner."

"Senator Planet never has women to dinner. . . . He's got a funny reputation. . . . There are some funny people in this town."

"I guess there are," said Charley. He was all in; he'd hardly got his clothes off before he was asleep.

At the end of the week Charley and Bill flew back to New York leaving Andy Merritt to negotiate contracts with the government experts. When they'd run the ship into the hangar, Charley said he'd wheel Bill home to Jamaica in his car. They stopped off in a kind of hofbrau for a beer. They were hungry and Bill thought his wife would be through supper, so they ate noodlesoup and schnitzels. Charley found they had some fake Rhinewine and ordered it. They drank the wine and ordered another set of schnitzels. Charley was telling Bill how Andy Merritt said the government contracts were going through and Andy Merritt was always right and he'd said it was a patriotic duty to capitalize production on a broad base. "Bill, goddam it, we'll be in the money. How about another bottle? . . . Good old Bill, the pilot's nothin' without his mechanic, the promoter's nothin' without production. . . . You and me, Bill, we're in production, and by God I'm goin' to see we don't lose out. If they try to rook us we'll fight, already I've had offers, big offers from Detroit . . . in five years now we'll be in the money and I'll see you're in the big money too."

They ate applecake and then the proprietor brought out a bottle of kümmel. Charley bought the bottle. "Cheaper than payin' for it drink by drink, don't you think so, Bill?" Bill began to start saying he was a family man and had better be getting along home. "Me," said Charley, pouring out some kümmel into a tumbler, "I haven't got no home to go to. . . . If she wanted she could have a home. I'd make her a wonderful home."

Charley discovered that Bill Cermak had gone and that he was telling all this to a stout blond lady of uncertain age with a rich German accent. He was calling her Aunt Hartmann and telling her that if he ever had a home she'd be his housekeeper. They finished up the kümmel and started drinking beer. She stroked his head and called him her vandering yunge. There was an orchestra in Bavarian costume and a thicknecked man that sang. Charley wanted to yodel for the company, but she pulled him back to the table. She was very strong and pushed him away with big red arms when he tried to get friendly, but when he pinched her seat she looked down into her beer and giggled. It was all like back home in the old days, he kept telling her, only louder and funnier. It was dreadfully funny until they were sitting in the car and she had her head on his shoulder and was calling him schatz and her long coils of hair had come undone and hung down over the wheel. Somehow he managed to drive.

He woke up next morning in a rattletrap hotel in Coney Island. It was nine o'clock; he had a frightful head and Aunt

Hartmann was sitting up in bed looking pink, broad, and beefy and asking for kaffee und schlagsahne. He took her out to breakfast at a Vienna bakery. She ate a great deal and cried a great deal and said he mustn't think she was a bad woman, because she was just a poor girl out of work and she'd felt so badly on account of his being a poor homeless boy. He said he'd be a poor homeless boy for fair if he didn't get back to the office. He gave her all the change he had in his pocket and a fake address and left her crying over a third cup of coffee in the Vienna bakery and headed for Long Island City. About Ozone Park he had to stop to upchuck on the side of the road. He just managed to get into the yard of the plant with his last drop of gas. He slipped into his office. It was ten minutes of twelve.

His desk was full of notes and letters held together with clips and blue papers marked IMMEDIATE ATTENTION. He was scared Miss Robinson or Joe Askew would find out he was back. Then he remembered he had a silver flask of old bourbon in his desk drawer that Doris had given him the night before she sailed, to forget her by she'd said, kidding him. He'd just tipped his head back to take a swig when he saw Joe Askew standing in front of his desk.

Joe stood up with his legs apart with a worn frowning look on his face. "Well, for Pete's sake, where have you been? We been worried as hell about you. . . . Grace waited dinner an hour."

"Why didn't you call up the hangar?"

"Everybody had gone home. . . . Stauch's sick. Everything's tied up."

"Haven't you heard from Merritt?"

"Sure . . . but that means we've got to reorganize production. . . . And frankly, Charley, that's a hell of an example to set the employees . . . boozing around the office. Last time I kept my mouth shut, but my god . . ."

Charley walked over to the cooler and drew himself a couple of papercupfuls of water. "I got to celebratin' that trip to Washington last night. . . . After all, Joe, these contracts will put us on the map. . . . How about havin' a little drink?"

Joe frowned. "You look like you'd been having plenty . . . and how about shaving before you come into the office? We expect our employees to do it, we ought to do it too. . . . For craps' sake, Charley, remember that the war's over." Joe turned on his heel and went back to his own office.

Charley took another long pull on the flask. He was mad. "I won't take it," he muttered, "not from him or anybody else." Then the phone rang. The foreman of the assembly-room was standing in the door. "Please, Mr. Anderson," he said.

That was the beginning of it. From then everything seemed to go haywire. At eight o'clock that night Charley hadn't yet had a shave. He was eating a sandwich and drinking coffee out of a carton with the mechanics of the repair crew over a busted machine. It was midnight and he was all in before he got home to the apartment. He was all ready to give Joe a piece of his mind, but there wasn't an Askew in sight.

Next morning at breakfast Grace's eyebrows were raised when she poured out the coffee. "Well, if it isn't the lost battalion," she said.

Joe Askew cleared his throat. "Charley," he said nervously, "I didn't have any call to bawl you out like that . . . I guess I'm getting cranky in my old age. The plant's been hell on wheels all week."

The two little girls began to giggle.

"Aw, let it ride," said Charley.

"Little pitchers, Joe," said Grace, rapping on the table for order. "I guess we all need a rest. Now this summer, Joe, you'll take a vacation. I need a vacation in the worst way myself, especially from entertaining Joe's dead cats. He hasn't had anybody to talk to since you've been away, Charley, and the house has been full of dead cats."

"That's just a couple of guys I've been trying to fix up with jobs. Grace thinks they're no good because they haven't much social smalltalk."

"I don't think, I know they are dead cats," said Grace. The little girls started to giggle some more.

Charley got to his feet and pushed back his chair.

"Comin', Joe?" he said. "I've got to get back to my wreckin'crew."

It was a couple of weeks before Charley got away from the plant except to sleep. At the end of that time Stauch was back with his quiet regretful manner like the manner of an assisting physician in a hospital operatingroom, and things began to straighten out. The day Stauch finally came to Charley's office door saying, "Production is now again smooth, Mr. Anderson," Charley decided he'd knock off at noon. He called up Nat Benton to wait for him for lunch and slipped out by the employees' entrances so that he wouldn't meet Joe in the entry.

In Nat's office they had a couple of drinks before going

out to lunch. At the restaurant after they'd ordered, he said, "Well, Nat, how's the intelligence service going?"

"How many shares have you got?"

"Five hundred."

"Any other stock, anything you could put up for margin?"

"A little. . . . I got a couple of grand in cash."

"Cash," said Nat scornfully. "For a rainy day . . . stuff and nonsense. . . . Why not put it to work?"

"That's what I'm talkin' about."

"Suppose you try a little flyer in Auburn just to get your hand in."

"But how about Merritt?"

"Hold your horses. . . . What I want to do is get you a little capital so you can fight those birds on an equal basis. . . . If you don't they'll freeze you out sure as fate."

"Joe wouldn't," said Charley.

"I don't know the man personally, but I do know men, and there are darn few who won't look out for number one first."

"I guess they'll all rook you if they can."

"I wouldn't put it just that way, Charley. There are some magnificent specimens of American manhood in the business world."

That night Charley got drunk all by himself at a speak in the fifties.

By the time Doris landed from Europe in the fall, Charley had made two killings in Auburn and was buying up all the Askew-Merritt stock he could lay his hands on. At the same time he discovered he had credit, for a new car, for suits at Brooks Brothers, for meals at speakeasies. The car was a Packard sports phaeton with a long low custombody upholstered in red leather. He drove down to the dock to meet Doris and Mrs. Humphries when they came in on the *Leviathan*. The ship had already docked when Charley got to Hoboken. Charley parked his car and hurried through the shabby groups at the thirdclass to the big swirl of welldressed people chattering round piles of pigskin suitcases, patentleather hatboxes, wardrobetrunks with the labels of Ritz hotels on them, in the central part of the wharfbuilding. Under the H he caught sight of old Mrs. Humphries. Above the big furcollar her face looked like a faded edition of Doris's, he had never before noticed how much.

She didn't recognize him for a moment. "Why, Charles Anderson, how very nice." She held her hand out to him without smiling. "This is most trying. Doris, of course, had to leave her jewelcase in the cabin. . . . You are meeting someone, I presume."

Charley blushed. "I thought I might give you a lift . . . I got a big car now. I thought it would take your bags better than a taxi."

Mrs. Humphries wasn't paying much attention. "There she is. . . ." She waved a gloved hand with an alligatorskin bag in it. "Here I am."

Doris came running through the crowd. She was flushed and her lips were very red. Her little hat and her fur were just the color of her hair. "I've got it, Mother . . . what a silly girl."

"Every time I go through this," sighed Mrs. Humphries, "I decide I'll never go abroad again."

Doris leaned over to tuck a piece of yellow something into a handbag that had been opened.

"Here's Mr. Anderson, Doris," said Mrs. Humphries.

Doris turned with a jump and ran up to him and threw her arms round his neck and kissed him on the cheek. "You darling to come down." Then she introduced him to a redfaced

young Englishman in an English plaid overcoat who was carrying a big bag of golfclubs. "I know you'll like each other."

"Is this your first visit to this country?" asked Charley.

"Quite the contrary," said the Englishman, showing his yellow teeth in a smile. "I was born in Wyoming."

It was chilly on the wharf. Mrs. Humphries went to sit in the heated waitingroom.

When the young man with the golfsticks went off to attend to his own bags, Doris said: "How do you like George Duquesne? He was born here and brought up in England. His mother comes from people in the Doomsday Book. I went to stay with them at the most beautiful old abbey. . . . I had the time of my life in England. I think George is a duck. The Duquesnes have copper interests. They are almost like the Guggenheims except, of course, they are not Jewish. . . . Why, Charley, I believe you're jealous. . . . Silly . . . George and I are just like brother and sister, really . . . It's not like you and me at all, but he's such fun."

It took the Humphries family a couple of hours to get through the customs. They had a great many bags and Doris had to pay duty on some dresses. When Mrs. Humphries found she was to drive uptown in an open car with the top down, she looked black indeed, the fact that it was a snakylooking Packard didn't seem to help.

"Why, it's a regular rubberneck wagon," said Doris. "Mother, this is fun . . . Charley'll point out all the tall buildings."

Mrs. Humphries was grumbling as, surrounded by handbaggage, she settled into the back seat, "Your dear father, Doris, never liked to see a lady riding in an open cab, much less in an open machine."

When he'd taken them uptown, Charley didn't go back to the plant. He spent the rest of the day till closing at the Askews' apartment on the telephone talking to Benton's office. Since the listing of Standard Airparts there'd been a big drop in Askew-Merritt. He was hocking everything and waiting for it to hit bottom before buying. Every now and then he'd call up Benton and say, "What do you think, Nat?"

Nat still had no tips late that afternoon, so Charley spun a coin to decide; it came heads. He called up the office and told them to start buying at the opening figure next day. Then he changed his clothes and cleared out before Grace brought the little girls home from school; he hardly spoke to the Askews these days. He was fed up out at the plant and he knew Joe thought he was a slacker.

When he changed his wallet from one jacket to the other, he opened it and counted his cash. He had four centuries and some chickenfeed. The bills were crisp and new, straight from the bank. He brought them up to his nose to sniff the new sweet sharp smell of the ink. Before he knew what he'd done he'd kissed them. He laughed out loud and put the bills back in his wallet. Jesus, he was feeling good. His new blue suit fitted nicely. His shoes were shined. He had clean socks on. His belly felt hard under his belt. He was whistling as he waited for the elevator.

Over at Doris's there was George Duquesne saying how ripping the new buildings looked on Fifth Avenue.

"Oh, Charley, wait till you taste one of George's alexanders, they're ripping," said Doris. "He learned to make them out in Constant after the war. . . . You see he was in the British army. . . . Charley was one of our star aces, George."

Charley took George and Doris to dinner at the Plaza and to a show and to a nightclub. All the time he was feeding

239

highpower liquor into George in the hope he'd pass out, but all George did was get redder and redder in the face and quieter and quieter, and he hadn't had much to say right at the beginning. It was three o'clock and Charley was sleepy and pretty tight himself before he could deliver George at the Saint Regis where he was staying.

"Now what shall we do?"

"But, darling, I've got to go home."

"I haven't had a chance to talk to you. . . . Jeez, I haven't even had a chance to give you a proper hug since you landed." They ended by going to the Columbus Circle Childs and eating scrambled eggs and bacon.

Doris was saying there ought to be beautiful places where people in love could go where they could find privacy and bed in beautiful surroundings. Charley said he knew plenty of places, but they weren't so beautiful.

"I'd go, Charley, honestly, if I wasn't afraid it would be sordid and spoil everything."

Charley squeezed her hand hard. "I wouldn't have the right to ask you, kid, not till we was married."

As they walked up the street to where he'd parked his car, she let her head drop on his shoulder. "Do you want me, Charley?" she said in a little tiny voice. "I want you too . . . but I've got to go home or Mother'll be making a scene in the morning."

Next Saturday afternoon Charley spent looking for a walkup furnished apartment. He rented a livingroom, kitchenette, and bath, all done in gray, from a hennahaired artist lady in flowing batiks who said she was going to Capri for six months of sheer beauty, and called up an agency for a Japanese houseboy to take care of it. Next day at breakfast he told the Askews he was moving.

Joe didn't say anything at first, but after he'd drunk the last of his cup of coffee, he got up frowning and walked a couple of times across the livingroom. Then he went to the window, saying quietly, "Come here, Charley, I've got something to show you." He put a hand on Charley's arm. . . . "Look here, kid, it isn't on account of me being so sour all the time, is it? You know I'm worried about the damn business . . . seems to me we're getting in over our heads . . . but you know Grace and I both think the world of you. . . . I've just felt that you were putting in too much time on the stockmarket. . . . I don't suppose it's any of my damn business. . . . Anyway, us fellows from the old outfit, we've got to stick together."

"Sure, Joe, sure. . . . Honestly, the reason I want this damn apartment has nothin' to do with that. . . . You're a married man with kids and don't need to worry about that sort of thing . . . but me, I got woman trouble."

Joe burst out laughing. "The old Continental sonofagun, but for crying out loud, why don't you get married?"

"God damn it, that's what I want to do," said Charley. He laughed and so did Joe.

"Well, what's the big joke?" said Grace from behind the coffee-urn.

Charley nodded his head toward the little girls. "Smokin'-room stories," he said.

"Oh, I think you're mean," said Grace.

One snowy afternoon before Christmas, a couple of weeks after Charley had moved into his apartment, he got back to town early and met Doris at the Biltmore. She said, "Let's go somewhere for a drink," and he said he had drinks all laid out and she ought to come up to see the funny little sandwiches Taki made, all in different colors. She asked if the Jap was there now. He grinned and shook his head. It only took the taxi a couple of minutes to get them around to the converted brownstone house.

"Why, isn't this cozy?" Doris panted a little breathless from the stairs, as she threw open her furcoat. "Now I feel really wicked."

"But it's not like it was some guy you didn't know," said Charley, "or weren't fond of." She let him kiss her. Then she took off her coat and hat and dropped down beside him on the windowseat warm from the steamheat.

"Nobody knows the address, nobody knows the phonenumber," said Charley. When he put his arm around her thin shoulders and pulled her to him, she gave in to him with a little funny shudder and let him pull her on his knee. They kissed for a long time and then she wriggled loose and said, "Charley, darling, you invited me here for a drink."

He had the fixings for oldfashioneds in the kitchenette and a plate of sandwiches. He brought them in and set them out on the round wicker table.

Doris bit into several sandwiches before she decided which she liked best. "Why, your Jap must be quite an artist, Charley," she said.

"They're a clever little people," said Charley.

"Everything's lovely, Charley, except this light hurts my eyes."

When he switched off the lights the window was brightblue. The lights and shadows of the taxis moving up and down the snowy street and the glare from the stores opposite made shifting orange oblongs on the ceiling.

"Oh, it's wonderful here," said Doris. "Look how oldtimy the streets look with all the ruts in the snow."

Charley kept refilling the oldfashioneds with whiskey. He got her to take her dress off. "You know you told me about how dresses cost money."

"Oh, you big silly. . . . Charley, do you like me a little bit?"

"What's the use of talking . . . I'm absolutely cuckoo about you . . . you know I want us to be always together. I want us to get mar——"

"Don't spoil everything, this is so lovely, I never thought anything could be like this. . . . Charley, you're taking precautions, aren't you?"

"Sure thing," said Charley through clenched teeth and went to his bureau for a condom.

At seven o'clock she got dressed in a hurry, said she had a dinner engagement and would be horribly late. Charley took her down and put her in a taxi. "Now, darling," he said, "we won't talk about what I said. We'll just do it." Walking back up the steep creaky stairs, he could taste her mouth, her hair, his head was bursting with the perfume she used. A chilly bitter feeling was getting hold of him, like the feeling of seasickness. "Oh, Christ," he said aloud and threw himself face down on the windowseat.

The apartment and Taki and the bootlegger and the payments on his car and the flowers he sent Doris every day all ran into more money than he expected every month. As soon as he made a deposit in the bank, he drew it out again. He owned a lot of stock, but it wasn't paying dividends. At Christmas he had to borrow five hundred bucks from Joe Askew to buy Doris a present. She'd told him he mustn't give her jewelry, so he asked Taki what he thought would be a suitable present for a very rich and beautiful young lady and Taki had said a silk kimono was very suitable, so Charley went out and bought her a mandarincoat. Doris made a funny face when she saw it, but she kissed him with a little quick peck in the corner of the mouth, because they were at her mother's, and said in a singsongy tone, "Oh, what a sweet boy."

Mrs. Humphries had asked him for Christmas dinner. The house smelt of tinsel and greens, there was a lot of tissuepaper and litter on the chairs. The cocktails were weak and everybody stood around. Nat and Sally Benton, and some nephews and nieces of Mrs. Humphries, and her sister Eliza who was very deaf, and George Duquesne who would talk of nothing but wintersports, waiting for the midafternoon dinner to be announced. People seemed sour and embarrassed, except Ollie Taylor who was just home from Italy full of the Christmas spirit. He spent most of the time out in the pantry with his coat off manufacturing what he called an oldtime Christmas punch. He was so busy at it that it was hard to get him to the table for dinner. Charley had to spend all his time taking care of him and never got a word with Doris all day. After dinner and the Christmas punch he had to take Ollie back to his club. Ollie was absolutely blotto and huddled fat and whitefaced in the taxi, bubbling "Damn good Christmas" over and over again.

When he'd put Ollie in the hands of the doorman, Charley couldn't decide whether to go back to the Humphries' where he'd be sure to find Doris and George with their heads together over some damnfool game or other or to go up to the Askews' as he'd promised to. Bill Cermak had asked him out to take a look at the bohunks in Jamaica, but he guessed it wouldn't be the thing, he'd said. Charley said sure he'd come, anyplace to get away from the stuffedshirts. From the Penn Station he sent a wire wishing the Askews a Merry Christmas. Sure the Askews would understand he had to spend his Christmas with Doris. On the empty train to Jamaica, he got to worrying about Doris, maybe he oughtn't to have left her with that guy.

Out in Jamaica, Bill Cermak and his wife and their elderly inlaws and friends were all tickled and a little bit fussed by Charley's turning up. It was a small frame house with a green papertile roof in a block of identical little houses with every other roof red and every other roof green. Mrs. Cermak was a stout blonde, a little fuddled from the big dinner and the wine that had brought brightened spots to her cheeks. She made Charley eat some of the turkey and the plumpudding they'd just taken off the table. Then they made hot wine with cloves in it and Bill played tunes on the piano accordion while everybody danced and the kids yelled and beat on drums and got underfoot.

When Charley said he had to go, Bill walked to the station with him. "Say, boss, we sure do appreciate your comin' out," began Bill.

"Hell, I ain't no boss," said Charley. "I belong with the mechanics . . . don't I, Bill? You and me, Bill, the mechanics against the world . . . and when I get married you're comin' to play that damned accordeen of yours at the weddin' . . . get me, Bill . . . it may not be so long."

Bill screwed up his face and rubbed his long crooked nose. "Women is fine once you got 'em pinned down, boss, but when they ain't pinned down they're hell."

"I got her pinned down, I got her pinned down all right so she's got to marry me to make an honest man of me."

"Thataboy," said Bill Cermak. They stood laughing and shaking hands on the drafty station platform till the Manhattan train came in.

During the automobile show Nat called up one day to say Farrell who ran the Tern outfit was in town and wanted to see Charley and Charley told Nat to bring him around for a cocktail in the afternoon. This time he got Taki to stay.

James Yardly Farrell was a roundfaced man with sandygray hair and a round bald head. When he came in the door, he began shouting, "Where is he? Where is he?"

"Here he is," said Nat Benton, laughing.

Farrell pumped Charley's hand. "So this is the guy with the knowhow, is it? I've been trying to get hold of you for months . . . ask Nat if I haven't made his life miserable. . . . Look here, how about coming out to Detroit . . . Long Island City's no place for a guy like you. We need your knowhow out there . . . and what we need we're ready to pay for."

Charley turned red. "I'm pretty well off where I am, Mr. Farrell."

"How much do you make?"

"Oh, enough for a young feller."

"We'll talk about that . . . but don't forget that in a new industry like ours the setup changes fast. . . . We got to keep our eyes open or we'll get left. . . . Well, we'll let it drop for the time being. . . . But I can tell you one thing, Anderson, I'm not going to stand by and see this industry ruined by being broken up in a lot of little onehorse units all cutting each other's throats. Don't you think it's better for us to sit around the table and cut the cake in a spirit of friendship and mutual service, and I tell you, young man, it's going to be a whale of a big cake." He let his voice drop to a whisper.

Taki, with his yellow face drawn into a thin diplomatic smile, came around with a tray of bacardi cocktails.

"No, thanks, I don't drink," said Farrell. "Are you a bachelor, Mr. Anderson?"

"Well, something like that. . . . I don't guess I'll stay that way long."

"You'd like it out in Detroit, honestly. . . . Benton tells me you're from Minnesota."

"Well, I was born in North Dakota." Charley talked over his shoulder to the Jap. "Taki, Mr. Benton wants another drink."

"We got a nice sociable crowd out there," said Farrell.

After they'd gone, Charley called up Doris and asked her right out if she'd like to live in Detroit after they were married. She gave a thin shriek at the other end of the line. "What a dreadful idea! . . . and who said anything about that dreadful . . . you know, state . . . I don't like even to mention the horrid word. . . . Don't you think we've had fun in New York this winter?"

"Sure," answered Charley. "I guess I'd be all right here if . . . things were different. . . . I thought maybe you'd like a change, that's all. . . . I had an offer from a concern out there, see."

"Now, Charley, you must promise not to mention anything so silly again."

"Sure . . . if you'll have dinner with me tomorrow night."

"Darling, tomorrow I couldn't."

"How about Saturday then?"

"All right, I'll break an engagement. Maybe you can come by for me at Carnegie Hall after the concert."

"I'll even go to the damn concert if you like."

"Oh, no, Mother's asked a lot of old ladies." She was talking fast, her voice twanging in the receiver. "There won't be any room in the box. You wait for me at the little tearoom, the Russian place where you waited and got so cross the time before."

"All right, any place. . . . Say, you don't know how I miss you when you're not with me."

"Do you? Oh, Charley, you're a dear." She rang off.

Charley put the receiver down and let himself slump back in his chair. He couldn't help feeling all of a tremble when he talked to her on the telephone. "Hey, Taki, bring me that bottle of Scotch. . . . Say, tell me, Taki," Charley went on, pouring himself a stiff drink, "in your country . . . is it so damn difficult for a guy to get married?"

The Jap smiled and made a little bow. "In my country everything much more difficult."

Next day when Charley got back from the plant he found a wire from Doris saying Saturday absolutely impossible. "Damn the bitch," he said aloud. All evening he kept calling up on the phone and leaving messages, but she was never in. He got to hate the feel of the damn mouthpiece against his lips. Saturday he couldn't get any word to her either. Sunday morning he got Mrs. Humphries on the phone. The cold creaky old-woman's voice shrieked that Doris had suddenly gone to Southampton for the weekend. "I know she'll come back with a dreadful cold," Mrs. Humphries added. "Weekends in this weather."

"Well, goodbye, Mrs. Humphries," said Charley and rang off.

Monday morning when Taki brought him a letter in Doris's hand, a big blue envelope that smelt of her perfume, the minute he opened it he knew before he read it what it would say.

CHARLEY DEAR,

You are such a dear and I'm so fond of you and do so want you for a friend [underlined]. You know the silly life I lead, right now I'm on the most preposterous weekend and I've told everybody I have a splitting headache and have gone to bed just to write to you. But, Charley, please forget all about weddings and things like that. The very idea makes me physically sick and besides I've promised George I'd marry him in June and the Duquesnes have a public-relations counsel—isn't it just too silly—but his business is to keep the Duquesnes popular with the public and he's given the whole story to the press, how I was courted among the Scotch moors and in the old medieval abbey and everything. And that's why I'm in such a hurry to write to you, Charley

246

darling, because you're the best friend [twice underlined] I've got and the only one who lives in the real world of business and production and labor and everything like that, which I'd so love to belong to, and I wanted you to know first thing. Oh, Charley darling, please don't think horrid things about me.

Your loving friend [three times underlined]

D

Be a good boy and burn up this letter, won't you?

The buzzer was rattling. It was the boy from the garage with his car. Charley got on his hat and coat and went downstairs. He got in and drove out to Long Island City, walked up the rubbertreaded steps to his office, sat down at his desk, rustled papers, talked to Stauch over the phone, lunched in the employees' lunchroom with Joe Askew, dictated letters to the new towhaired stenographer, and suddenly it was six o'clock and he was jockeying his way through the traffic home.

Crossing the bridge he had an impulse to give a wrench to

247

the wheel and step on the gas, but the damn car wouldn't clear the rail anyway, it would just make a nasty scrapheap of piledup traffic and trucks.

He didn't want to go home or to the speakeasy he and Doris had been having dinner in several times a week all winter, so he turned down Third Avenue. Maybe he'd run into somebody at Julius's. He stood up at the bar. He didn't want to drink any more than he wanted to do anything else. A few raw shots of rye made him feel better. To hell with her. Nothing like a few drinks. He was alone, he had money on him, he could do any goddam thing in the world.

Next to Charley at the bar stood a couple of fattish dowdylooking women. They were with a redfaced man who was pretty drunk already. The women were talking about clothes and the man was telling about Belleau Wood. Right away he and Charley were old buddies from the A.E.F. "The name is De Vries. Profession . . . bonvivant," said the man and tugged at the two women until they faced around toward Charley. He put his arms around them with a flourish and shouted, "Meet the wife."

They had drinks on Belleau Wood, the Argonne, the St. Mihiel salient, and the battle of Paree. The women said goodness, how they wanted to go to Hoboken to the hofbrau. Charley said he'd take them all in his car. They sobered up a little and were pretty quiet crossing on the ferry. At the restaurant in the chilly dark Hoboken street they couldn't get anything but beer. After they'd finished supper De Vries said he knew a place where they could get real liquor. They circled round blocks and blocks and ended in a dump in Union City. When they'd drunk enough to start them doing squaredances, the women said wouldn't it be wonderful to go to Harlem. This time the ferry didn't sober them up so much because they had a bottle of Scotch with them. In Harlem they were thrown out of a dancehall and at last landed in a nightclub. The bonvivant fell down the redcarpeted stairs and Charley had a time laughing that off with the management. They ate fried chicken and drank some terrible gin the colored waiter sent out for, and danced. Charley kept thinking how beautifully he was dancing. He couldn't make out why he didn't have any luck picking up any of the highyallers.

Next morning he woke up in a room in a hotel. He looked around. No, there wasn't any woman in the bed. Except that his head ached and his ears were burning, he felt good. Stomach all right. For a moment he thought he'd just landed from France. Then he thought of the Packard, where the hell had he left it? He reached for the phone. "Say, what hotel is this?" It was the McAlpin, goodmorning. He remembered Joe

Turbino's number and phoned him to ask what the best thing for a hangover was. When he was through phoning, he didn't feel so good. His mouth tasted like the floor of a chickencoop. He went back to sleep. The phone woke him. "A gentleman to see you." Then he remembered all about Doris. The guy from Turbino's brought a bottle of Scotch. Charley took a drink of it straight, drank a lot of icewater, took a bath, ordered up some breakfast. But it was time to go out to lunch. He put the bottle of Scotch in his overcoat pocket and went round to Frank and Joe's for a cocktail.

That night he took a taxi up to Harlem. He went from joint to joint dancing with the highyallers. He got in a fight in a breakfastclub. It was day when he found himself in another taxi going downtown to Mrs. Darling's. He didn't have any money to pay the taximan and the man insisted on going up in the elevator while he got the money. There was nobody in the apartment but the colored maid and she shelled out five dollars. She tried to get Charley to lie down, but he wanted to write her out a check. He could sign his name all right, but he couldn't sign it on the check. The maid tried to get him to take a bath and go to bed. She said he had blood all over his shirt.

He felt fine and was all cleaned up, had been asleep in a barberchair while the barber shaved him and put an icebag on his black eye, and he had gone back to Frank and Joe's for a pickup when there was Nat Benton. Good old Nat was worried asking him about his black eye and he was showing Nat where he'd skinned his knuckles on the guy, but Nat kept talking about the business and Askew-Merritt and Standard Airparts and said Charley'd be out on the sidewalk if it wasn't for him. They had some drinks, but Nat kept talking about buttermilk and wanted Charley to come around to the hotel and meet Farrell. Farrell thought Charley was about the best guy in the world, and Farrell was the coming man in the industry, you could bet your bottom dollar on Farrell. And right away there was Farrell and Charley was showing him his knuckle and telling him he'd socked the guy in that lousy pokergame and how he'd have cleaned 'em all up if somebody hadn't batted him back of the ear with a stocking full of sand. Detroit, sure. He was ready to go to Detroit any time, Detroit or anywhere else. Goddam it, a guy don't like to stay in a town where he'd just been rolled. And that damn highyaller had his pocketbook with all his addresses in it. Papers? Sure. Sign anythin' you like, anythin' Nat says. Stock, sure. Swap every last share. What the hell would a guy want stock for in a plant in a town where he'd been rolled in a clipjoint. Detroit, sure, right away. Nat, call a taxi, we're goin' to Detroit.

Then they were back at the apartment and Taki was chattering and Nat attended to everything and Farrell was saying, "I'd hate to see the other guy's eye," and Charley could sign his name all right this time. First time he signed it on the table, but then he got it on the contract, and Nat fixed it all up about swapping his Askew-Merritt stock for Tern stock and then Nat and Farrell said Charley must be sleepy and Taki kept squeaking about how he had to take right away a hot bath.

Charley woke up the next morning feeling sober and dead like a stiff laid out for the undertaker. Taki brought him orangejuice, but he threw it right up again. He dropped back on the pillow. He'd told Taki not to let anybody in, but there was Joe Askew standing at the foot of the bed. Joe looked paler than usual and had a worried frown like at the office, and was pulling at his thin blond mustache. He didn't smile. "How are you coming?" he said.

"Soso," said Charley.

"So it's the Tern outfit, is it?"

"Joe, I can't stay in New York now. I'm through with this burg."

"Through with a lot of other things, it looks like to me."

"Joe, honest I wouldn'ta done it if I hadn't had to get out of this town . . . and I put as much into this as you did, some people think a little more."

Joe's thin lips were clamped firmly together. He started to say something, stopped himself, and walked stiffly out of the room.

"Taki," called Charley, "try squeezin' out half a grapefruit, will you?"

Newsreel LVI

his first move was to board a fast train for Miami to
see whether the builders engaged in construction financed
by his corporation were speeding up the work as much as
they might and to take a look at things in general

Pearly early in the mornin'

LUTHERANS DROP HELL FOR HADES

Oh joy
Feel that boat arockin'
Oh boy
See those darkies flockin'
What's that whistle sayin'
All aboard toot toot

AIR REJECTION BLAMED FOR WARSHIP DISASTER

You're in Ken-tucky just as sure as you're born

LINER AFIRE

POSSE CLOSING IN ON AIRMAIL BANDITS

Down beside the summer sea
Along Miami Shore
Some one waits alone for me
Along Miami Shore

SINCE THIS TIME YESTERDAY NEARLY TWO
THOUSAND MEN HAVE CHANGED TO
CHESTERFIELDS

> *Saw a rosebud in a store*
> *So I'm goin' where there's more*
> *Good-bye blues*

the three whites he has with him appear to be of primitive Nordic stock. Physically they are splendid creatures. They have fine flaxen hair, blue-green eyes and white skins. The males are covered with a downlike hair

> *Let me lay down to sleep in Carolina*
> *With a peaceful pillow 'neath my weary head*
> *For a rolling stone like me there's nothing finer*
> *Oh Lordy what a thrill*
> *To hear that whip-poor-will*
> *In Carolina*

The Camera Eye (48)

westbound to Havana Puerto-Mexico Galveston out of Santander (the glassy estuary the feeling of hills hemming the moist night an occasional star drips chilly out of the rainy sky a row of lights spills off the muffled shore) the twinscrews rumble

at last westbound away from pension spinsters tasty about watercolors the old men with crocodile eyes hiding their bloody claws under the neat lisle gloves the landscapes corroded with literature   westbound

> *for an old man he is old*
> *for an old man he is gray*
> *but a young man's heart is full of love*
> *get away old man get away*

at the dinnertable westbound in the broadlit saloon the amplybosomed broadbeamed   la bella cubana in a yellow lowcut dress archly with the sharp rosy nail of her littlest finger points

the curlyhaired young bucks from Bilbao (louder and funnier) in such tightwaisted icecreamcolored suits silk

shirts striped ties (westbound to Havana for the sugar-
boom) the rich one has a diamond ring   tooshiny eyes
look the way her little finger jabs

but a young man's heart is full of love

she whispers   He came out of her cabin when I was
on the way to the bath   Why was she giggling in number
sixtysix? the rich one from Bilbao orders champagne

to echo the corks that pop in an artillery salute from
the long table where the Mexican general tall solemnfaced with a black mustache and five tall solemnfaced
bluejowled sons a fat majordomo and a sprinkling of
blank henshaped ladies who rustle out hurriedly in black
silk with their handkerchiefs to their mouths as soon as
we round the cape where the lighthouse is

westbound (out of old into new inordinate new undeci-
phered new) southerly summertime crossing (towards
events) the roar in the ears the deep blue heaving the sun
hot on the back of your hand the feel of wet salt on the
handrails the smell of brasspolish and highpressure steam
the multitudinous flickering dazzle of light

and every noon we overeat hors d'oeuvres drink too
much wine while gigglingly with rolling eyes la bella to
indicate who slept with who sharply jabs with littlest pin-
sharpened finger

la juerga

alas the young buck from Bilbao the one with the dia
mond ring suffers amidships (westbound the ancient fu-
ries follow in our wake) a kick from Venus's dangerous
toe   retires to bed   we take our coffee in his cabin
instead of the fumoir   the ladies interest themselves in
his plight

two gallegos loosemouthed frognecked itinerant are invited up from the steerage to sing to the guitar (Vichy
water and deep song argyrol rhymes with rusiñol)

si quieres qu'el carro cante
mójele y déjele en rio
que después de buen moja'o
canta com' un silbí'o

and funny stories a thousand and one Havana nights

the dance of the millions   the fair cubanas a ellas les gustan los negros

but stepping out on deck to get a breath of briny afternoon there's more to be seen than that rusty freighter wallowing in indigo   el rubio   the buck from Bilbao who has no diamond ring beset with yelling cubans   la bella leads with heaving breast a small man with gray sideburns is pushed out at el rubio they shove at him from behind

escándalo

alternately the contestants argue with their friends who hold them back   break loose   fly at each other with threshing arms   are recaptured   pulled apart

ships officers intervene

pale and trembling the champions are led away   he of the sideburns to the ladies' drawingroom   el rubio aft to fumoir

there we masticate the insults   what was it all about?   no señor no   el rubio grabs a sheet of the notepaper of the Compagnie Générale Transatlantique but fingers refuse to hold the pen   while he twined them in his long curly hair an unauthorized observer who had become involved in the broil misspelled glibly to his dictation

a challenge

and carried it frozenfaced to the parties in the ladies' drawingroom   coño

then we walk el rubio back and forth across the palpitating stern discuss rapiers pistols fencingpractice

now only the westbound observer appears at meals   el rubio mopes at the end of the bunk of his beclapped friend and prepares for doom   the ship's agog with dueltalk until mon commandant a redfaced Breton visits all parties and explains that this kind of nonsense is expressly forbidden in the regulations of the Compagnie Générale Transatlantique and that the musical gallegos must go back to the steerage from whence they sprang

despair

enter with martial tread mi general expert he says in affairs of honor un militar   coño   vamos may he try to conciliate the parties

all to the fumoir where already four champagnebottles

are ranked cozily iced in their whitemetal pails   coño
    sandwiches are served   mi general clears up
the misunderstanding something about los negros and las
cubans overhead in the cabin of the bucks from Bilbao by
listening   vamos   down the ventilator many things
were that better were unsaid but in any case honor in-
sulated by the ventilator was intact gingerly the champions
take each others hands coño palmas sombreros música
mi general is awarded the ear

    in the steerage the gallegos sing and strum

    el rubio at the bar confides to me   that it was from la
bella of the pink jabbing finger and the dainty ear at ven-
tilators that he with the diamond ring received the   and
that he himself has fears   coño una puta indecente

    arrival in Havana   an opulentlydressed husband in a
panama hat receives la bella   the young bucks from Bilbao go to the Sevilla-Biltmore and I

    dance of the millions or not lackofmoney has raised its
customary head inevitable as visas

    in the whirl of sugarboom prices in the Augustblis-
tering sun yours truly tours the town and the sugary nights
with twenty smackers fifteen eightfifty dwindling in the
jeans in search of lucrative

    and how to get to Mexico
    or anywhere

Margo Dowling

Margo Dowling was sixteen when she married Tony. She
loved the trip down to Havana on the boat. It was very
rough, but she wasn't sick a minute; Tony was. He turned
very yellow and lay in his bunk all the time and only groaned
when she tried to make him come out on deck to breathe some
air. The island was in sight before she could get him into his
clothes. He was so weak she had to dress him like a baby. He
lay on his bunk with his eyes closed and his cheeks hollow
while she buttoned his shoes for him. Then she ran up on
deck to see Havana, Cuba. The sea was still rough. The
waves were shooting columns of spray up the great rocks
under the lighthouse. The young thinfaced third officer who'd
been so nice all the trip showed her Morro Castle back of the
lighthouse and the little fishingboats with tiny black or brown

figures in them swinging up and down on the huge swells outside it. The other side the pale caramelcolored houses looked as if they were standing up right out of the breakers. She asked him where Vedado was and he pointed up beyond into the haze above the surf. "That's the fine residential section," he said. It was very sunny and the sky was full of big white clouds.

By that time they were in the calm water of the harbor passing a row of big schooners anchored against the steep hill under the sunny forts and castles, and she had to go down into the bilgy closeness of their cabin to get Tony up and close their bags. He was still weak and kept saying his head was spinning. She had to help him down the gangplank.

The ramshackle dock was full of beadyeyed people in white and tan clothes bustling and jabbering. They all seemed to have come to meet Tony. There were old ladies in shawls and pimplylooking young men in straw hats and an old gentleman with big bushy white whiskers wearing a panama hat. Children with dark circles under their eyes got under everybody's feet. Everybody was yellow or coffeecolored and had black eyes, and there was one grayhaired old niggerwoman in a pink dress. Everybody cried and threw up their arms and hugged and kissed Tony and it was a long time before anybody noticed Margo at all. Then all the old women crowded around kissing her and staring at her and making exclamations in Spanish about her hair and her eyes and she felt awful silly not understanding a word and kept asking Tony which his mother was, but Tony had forgotten his English. When he finally pointed to a stout old lady in a shawl and said la mamá she was very much relieved it wasn't the colored one.

If this is the fine residential section, Margo said to herself when they all piled out of the streetcar, after a long ride

through yammering streets of stone houses full of dust and oily smells and wagons and mulecarts, into the blisteringhot sun of a cobbled lane, I'm a milliondollar heiress.

They went through a tall doorway in a scabby peeling pinkstucco wall cut with narrow barred windows that went right down to the ground, into a cool rankishsmelling vestibule set with wicker chairs and plants. A parrot in a cage squawked and a fat piggy little white dog barked at Margo and the old lady who Tony had said was la mamá came forward and put her arm around her shoulders and said a lot of things in Spanish. Margo stood there standing first on one foot and then on the other. The doorway was crowded with the neighbors staring at her with their monkeyeyes.

"Say, Tony, you might at least tell me what she's saying," Margo whined peevishly.

"Mother says this is your house and you are welcome, things like that. Now you must say muchas gracias, mamá."

Margo couldn't say anything. A lump rose in her throat and she burst out crying.

She cried some more when she saw her room, a big dark alcove hung with torn lace curtains mostly filled up by a big iron bed with a yellow quilt on it that was all spotted with a brown stain. She quit crying and began to giggle when she saw the big cracked chamberpot with roses on it peeping out from under.

Tony was sore. "Now you must behave very nice," he said. "My people they say you are very pretty but not wellbred."

"Aw, you kiss my foot," she said.

All the time she was in Havana she lived in that alcove with only a screen in front of the glass door to the court. Tony and the boys were always out. They'd never take her anywhere. The worst of it was when she found she was going to have a baby. Day after day she lay there all alone staring up at the cracked white plaster of the ceiling, listening to the shrill jabber of the women in the court and the vestibule and the parrot and the yapping of the little white dog that was named Kiki. Roaches ran up and down the wall and ate holes in any clothes that weren't put away in chests.

Every afternoon a hot square of sunlight pressed in through the glass roof of the court and ran along the edge of the bed and across the tiled floor and made the alcove glary and stifling.

Tony's family never let her go out unless one of the old women went along, and then it was usually just to market or to church. She hated going to the market that was so filthy and rancidsmelling and jammed with sweaty jostling Negroes and Chinamen yelling over coops of chickens and slimy stalls of fish. La mamá and Tia Feliciana and Carná the old niggerwoman seemed to love it. Church was better; at least people wore better clothes there and the tinsel altars were often full of flowers, so she went to confession regularly, though the priest didn't understand the few Spanish words she was beginning to piece together, and she couldn't understand his replies. Anyway, church was better than sitting all day in the heat and the rancid smells of the vestibule trying to talk to the old women who never did anything but fan and chatter, while the little white dog slept on a dirty cushion on a busted gilt chair and occasionally snapped at a fly.

Tony never paid any attention to her any more; she could hardly blame him, her face looked so redeyed and swollen from crying. Tony was always around with a middleaged babyfaced fat man in a white suit with an enormous double gold watchchain looped across his baywindow whom everybody spoke of very respectfully as el señor Manfredo. He was a sugarbroker and was going to send Tony to Paris to study music. Sometimes he'd come and sit in the vestibule on a wicker chair with his gold-headed cane between his fat knees. Margo always felt there was something funny about Señor Manfredo, but she was as nice to him as she could be. He paid no attention to her either. He never took his eyes off Tony's long black lashes.

Once she got desperate and ran out alone to Central Park to an American drugstore she'd noticed there one evening when the old women had taken her to hear the military band play. Every man she passed stared at her. She got to the drugstore on a dead run and bought all the castoroil and quinine she had money for. Going home she couldn't seem to go a block without some man following her and trying to take her arm. "You go to hell," she'd say to them in English and walk all the faster. She lost her way, was almost run over by a car, and at last got to the house breathless. The old women were back and raised cain.

When Tony got home they told him and he made a big scene and tried to beat her up, but she was stronger than he was and blacked his eye for him. Then he threw himself on the bed sobbing and she put cold compresses on his eye to get the swelling down and petted him and they were happy and cozy together for the first time since they'd come to Havana. The trouble was the old women found out about how she'd blacked his eye and everybody teased him about it. The whole street seemed to know and everybody said Tony was a sissy. La mamá never forgave Margo and was mean and spiteful to her after that.

If she only wasn't going to have the baby, Margo would have run away. All the castoroil did was to give her terrible colic and the quinine just made her ears ring. She stole a sharppointed knife from the kitchen and thought she'd kill herself with it, but she didn't have the nerve to stick it in. She thought of hanging herself by the bedsheet, but she couldn't seem to do that either. She kept the knife under the mattress and lay all day on the bed dreaming about what she'd do if she ever got back to the States and thinking about Agnes and Frank and vaudeville shows and the Keith Circuit and the Saint Nicholas Rink. Sometimes she'd get herself to believe that this was all a long nightmare and that she'd wake up in bed at home at Indian's.

She wrote Agnes every week and Agnes would sometimes send her a couple of dollars in a letter. She'd saved fifteen dollars in a little alligatorskin purse Tony had given her when they first got to Havana, when he happened to look into it one day and pocketed the money and went out on a party. She was so sunk that she didn't even bawl him out about it when he came back after a night at a rumbajoint with dark circles under his eyes. Those days she was feeling too sick to bawl anybody out.

When her pains began, nobody had any idea of taking her to the hospital. The old women said they knew just what to do, and two Sisters of Mercy with big white butterfly headdresses began to bustle in and out with basins and pitchers of hot water. It lasted all day and all night and some of the next day. She was sure she was going to die. At last she yelled so loud for a doctor that they went out and fetched an old man with yellow hands all knobbed with rheumatism and a tobaccostained beard they said was a doctor. He had goldtrimmed eyeglasses on a ribbon that kept falling off his long twisted nose. He examined her and said everything was fine and the old women grinning and nodding stood around behind him. Then the pains grabbed her again; she didn't know anything but the pain.

After it was all over, she lay back so weak she thought she must be dead. They brought it to her to look at, but she wouldn't look. Next day when she woke up she heard a thin cry beside her and couldn't imagine what it was. She was too sick to turn her head to look at it. The old women were shaking their heads over something, but she didn't care. When they told her she wasn't well enough to nurse it and that it would have to be raised on a bottle, she didn't care either.

A couple of days passed in blank weakness. Then she was able to drink a little orangejuice and hot milk and could raise her head on her elbow and look at the baby when they brought it to her. It looked dreadfully little. It was a little girl. Its poor little face looked wrinkled and old like a monkey's. There was something the matter with its eyes.

She made them send for the old doctor and he sat on the edge of her bed looking very solemn and wiping and wiping his eyeglasses with his big clean silk handkerchief. He kept calling her a poor little niña and finally made her understand that the baby was blind and that her husband had a secret disease and that as soon as she was well enough she must go to a clinic for treatments. She didn't cry or say anything, but just lay there staring at him with her eyes hot and her hands and feet icy. She didn't want him to go, that was all she could think of. She made him tell her all about the disease and the treatment and made out to understand less Spanish than she did, just so that he wouldn't go away.

A couple of days later the old women put on their best black silk shawls and took the baby to the church to be christened. Its little face looked awful blue in the middle of all the lace they dressed it in. That night it turned almost black. In the morning it was dead. Tony cried and the old women all

carried on and they spent a lot of money on a little white casket with silver handles and a hearse and a priest for the funeral. Afterwards the Sisters of Mercy came and prayed beside her bed and the priest came and talked to the old women in a beautiful tragedy voice like Frank's voice when he wore his morningcoat, but Margo just lay there in the bed hoping she'd die too, with her eyes closed and her lips pressed tight together. No matter what anybody said to her, she wouldn't answer or open her eyes.

When she got well enough to sit up, she wouldn't go to the clinic the way Tony was going. She wouldn't speak to him or to the old women, She pretended not to understand what they said. La mamá would look into her face in a spiteful way she had and shake her head and say, "Loca." That meant crazy.

Margo wrote desperate letters to Agnes: for God's sake she must sell something and send her fifty dollars so that she could get home. Just to get to Florida would be enough. She'd get a job. She didn't care what she did if she could only get back to God's Country. She just said that Tony was a bum and that she didn't like it in Havana. She never said a word about the baby or being sick.

Then one day she got an idea; she was an American citizen, wasn't she? She'd go to the consul and see if they wouldn't send her home. It was weeks before she could get out without one of the old women. The first time she got down to the consulate all dressed up in her one good dress only to find it closed. The next time she went in the morning when the old women were out marketing and got to see a clerk who was a towheaded American collegeboy. My, she felt good talking American again.

She could see he thought she was a knockout. She liked him, too, but she didn't let him see it. She told him she was sick and had to go back to the States and that she'd been gotten down there on false pretenses on the promise of an engagement at the Alhambra.

"The Alhambra," said the clerk. "Gosh, you don't look like that kind of a girl."

"I'm not," she said.

His name was George. He said that if she'd married a Cuban there was nothing he could do, as you lost your citizenship if you married a foreigner. She said suppose they weren't really married. He said he thought she'd said she wasn't that kind of a girl. She began to blubber and said she didn't care what kind of a girl she was, she had to get home. He said to come back next day and he'd see what the consulate could do, anyway wouldn't she have tea with him at the Miami that afternoon.

She said it was a date and hurried back to the house feeling better than she had for a long time. The minute she was by herself in the alcove, she took the marriagelicense out of her bag and tore it up into little tiny bits and dropped it into the filthy yellow bowl of the old watercloset in the back of the court. For once the chain worked and every last bit of forgetmenotspotted paper went down into the sewer.

That afternoon she got a letter from Agnes with a fiftydollar draft on the National City Bank in it. She was so excited her heart almost stopped beating. Tony was out gallivanting around somewhere with the sugar-broker. She wrote him a note saying it was no use looking for her, she'd gone home, and pinned it on the underpart of the pillow on the bed. Then she waited until the old women had drowsed off for their siesta, and ran out.

She wasn't coming back. She just had the clothes she had on, and a few little pieces of cheap jewelry Tony had given her when they were first married, in her handbag. She went to the Miami and ordered an icecreamsoda in English so that everybody would know she was an American girl, and waited for George.

She was so scared every minute she thought she'd keel over. Suppose George didn't come. But he did come and he certainly was tickled when he saw the draft, because he said the consulate didn't have any funds for a case like hers. He said he'd get the draft cashed in the morning and help her buy her ticket and everything. She said he was a dandy and then suddenly leaned over and put her hand in its white kid glove on his arm and looked right into his eyes that were blue like hers were and whispered, "George, you've got to help me some more. You've got to help me hide. . . . I'm so scared of that Cuban. You know they are terrible when they're jealous."

George turned red and began to hem and haw a little, but Margo told him the story of what happened on her street just the other day, how a man, an armyofficer, had come home and found, well, his sweetheart, with another man, well, she might as well tell the story the way it happened, she guessed George wasn't easily shocked anyway, they were in bed to-

gether and the armyofficer emptied all the chambers of his revolver into the other man and then chased the woman up the street with a carvingknife and stabbed her five times in the public square. She began to giggle when she got that far, and George began to laugh. "I know it sounds funny to you . . . but it wasn't so funny for her. She died right there without any clothes on in front of everybody."

"Well, I guess we'll have to see what we can do," said George, "to keep you away from that carvingknife."

What they did was to go over to Matanzas on the Hershey electriccar and get a room at a hotel. They had supper there and a lot of ginfizzes and George, who'd told her he'd leave her to come over the next day just in time for the boat, got romantic over the ginfizzes and the moonlight and dogs barking and the roosters crowing. They went walking with their arms round each other down the quiet chalkycolored moon-

263

struck streets, and he missed the last car back to Havana. Margo didn't care about anything except not to be alone in that creepy empty whitewalled hotel with the moon so bright and everything. She liked George anyway.

The next morning at breakfast he said she'd have to let him lend her another fifty so that she could go back firstclass and she said honestly she'd pay it back as soon as she got a job in New York and that he must write to her every day.

He went over on the early car because he had to be at the office and she went over later all alone through the glary green countryside shrilling with insects, and went in a cab right from the ferry to the boat. George met her there at the dock with her ticket and a little bunch of orchids, the first she'd ever had, and a roll of bills that she tucked into her purse without counting. The stewards seemed awful surprised that she didn't have any baggage, so she made George tell them that she'd had to leave home at five minutes' notice because her father, who was a very wealthy man, was sick in New York. She and George went right down to her room, and he was very sad about her going away and said she was the loveliest girl he'd ever seen and that he'd write her every day too, but she couldn't follow what he was saying she was so scared Tony would come down to the boat looking for her.

At last the gong rang and George kissed her desperate hard and went ashore. She didn't dare go up on deck until she heard the engineroom bells and felt the shaking of the boat as it began to back out of the dock. Out of the porthole, as the boat pulled out, she got a glimpse of a dapper dark man in a white suit, that might have been Tony, who broke away from the cops and ran yelling and waving his arms down to the end of the wharf.

Maybe it was the orchids or her looks or the story about her father's illness, but the captain asked her to his table and all the officers rushed her, and she had the time of her life on the trip up. The only trouble was that she could only come on the deck in the afternoon because she had only that one dress.

She'd given George a cable to send, so when they got to New York Agnes met her at the dock. It was late fall and Margo had nothing on but a light summer dress, so she said she'd set Agnes up to a taxi to go home. It was only when they got into the cab that she noticed Agnes was wearing black. When she asked her why, Agnes said Fred had died in Bellevue two weeks before. He'd been picked up on Twenty-third Street deaddrunk and died there without coming to.

"Oh, Agnes, I knew it . . . I had a premonition on the boat," sobbed Margo.

When she'd wiped her eyes, she turned and looked at Agnes. "Why, Agnes dear, how well you look," she said. "What a pretty suit. Has Frank got a job?"

"Oh, no," said Agnes. "You see Miss Franklyn's teashops are doing quite well. She's branching out and she's made me manageress of the new branch on Thirtyfourth Street at seventyfive dollars a week. Wait till you see our new apartment just off the Drive. . . . Oh, Margie, you must have had an awful time."

"Well," said Margo, "it was pretty bad. His people are pretty well off and prominent and all that, but it's hard to get on to their ways. Tony's a bum and I hate him more than anything in the world. But after all it was quite an experience . . . I wouldn't have missed it."

Frank met them at the door of the apartment. He looked fatter than when Margo had last seen him and had patches of silvery hair on either side of his forehead that gave him a distinguished look like a minister or an ambassador. "Little Margo. . . . Welcome home, my child. . . . What a beautiful young woman you have become." When he took her in his arms and kissed her on the brow, she smelt again the smell of bayrum and energine she'd remembered on him. "Did Agnes tell you that I'm going on the road with Mrs.

Fiske? . . . Dear Minnie Maddern and I were children together."

The apartment was a little dark, but it had a parlor, a diningroom and two bedrooms, and a beautiful big bathroom and kitchen. "First thing I'm goin' to do," said Margo, "is take a hot bath. . . . I don't believe I've had a hot bath since I left New York."

While Agnes, who had taken the afternoon off from the tearoom, went out to do some marketing for supper, Margo went into her neat little bedroom with chintz curtains on the walls and took off her chilly rumpled summer dress and got into Agnes's padded dressinggown. Then she sat back in the morrischair in the parlor and strung Frank along when he asked her questions about her life in Havana.

Little by little he sidled over to the arm of her chair, telling her how attractivelooking she'd become. Then suddenly he made a grab for her. She'd been expecting it and gave him

a ringing slap on the face as she got to her feet. She felt herself getting hysterical as he came toward her across the room panting.

"Get away from me, you old buzzard," she yelled; "get away from me or I'll tell Agnes all about you and Agnes and me we'll throw you out on your ear." She wanted to shut up, but she couldn't stop yelling. "Get away from me. I caught a disease down there; if you don't keep away from me you'll catch it too."

Frank was so shocked he started to tremble all over. He let himself drop into the morrischair and ran his long fingers through his slick silverandblack hair. She slammed her bedroom door on him and locked it. Sitting in there alone on the bed, she began to think how she would never see Fred again, and could it have been a premonition when she'd told them on the boat that her father was sick. Tears came to her eyes. Certainly she'd had a premonition. The steamheat hissed cozily. She lay back on the bed that was so comfortable with its clean pillows and silky comforter, and still crying fell asleep.

Newsreel LVII

the psychic removed all clothing before séances at Harvard. Electric torches, bells, large megaphones, baskets, all illuminated by phosphorescent paint, formed the psychic's equipment

> *My brother's coming*
> > *with pineapples*
> *Watch the circus begin*

IS WILLING TO FACE PROBERS

the psychic's feet were not near the professor's feet when his trouser leg was pulled. An electric bulb on the ceiling flashed on and off. Buzzers rang. A teleplasmic arm grasped objects on the table and pulled Doctor B.'s hair. Doctor B. placed his nose in the doughnut and encouraged Walter to pull as hard as possible. His nose was pulled.

> *Altho' we both agreed to part*
> *It left a sadness in my heart*

UNHAPPY WIFE TRIES TO DIE

SHEIK DENTIST RECONCILED

FINANCING ONLY PROBLEM

> *I though that I'd get along*
> > *and now*
> *I find that I was wrong*
> > *somehow*

SOCIETY WOMEN SEEK JOBS IN VAIN AS
MAIDS TO QUEEN

NUN WILL WED GOB

I'm brokenhearted

QUEEN HONORS UNKNOWN SOLDIER

POLICE GUARD QUEEN IN MOB

Beneath a dreamy Chinese moon
Where love is like a haunting tune

PROFESSOR TORTURES RIVAL

QUEEN SLEEPS AS HER TRAIN DEPARTS

SOCIAL STRIFE BREWS

COOLIDGE URGES ADVERTISING

I found her beneath the setting sun
When the day was done

COP FEEDS CANARY ON FIVE HUNDRED DOLLARS
RICH BRIDE LEFT

While the twilight deepened
The sky above
I told my love
In o-o-old Ma-an-ila-a-a

ABANDONED APOLLO STILL HOPES FOR RETURN
OF WEALTHY BRIDE

Margo Dowling

Agnes was a darling. She managed to raise money through
the Morris Plan for Margo's operation when Doctor Dennison
said it was absolutely necessary if her health wasn't to be se-

riously impaired, and nursed her the way she'd nursed her when she'd had measles when she was a little girl. When they told Margo she never could have a baby, Margo didn't care so much, but Agnes cried and cried.

By the time Margo began to get well again and think of getting a job, she felt as if she and Agnes had just been living together always. The Old Southern Waffle Shop was doing very well and Agnes was making seventyfive dollars a week; it was lucky that she did because Frank Mandeville hardly ever seemed able to get an engagement any more, there's no demand for real entertainment since the war he'd say. He'd become very sad and respectable since he and Agnes had been married at the Little Church Around the Corner, and spent most of his time playing bridge at the Lambs Club and telling about the old days when he'd toured with Richard Mansfield. After Margo got on her feet, she spent a whole dreary winter of hanging around the agencies and in the casting offices of musical shows, before Flo Ziegfeld happened to see her one afternoon sitting in the outside office in a row of other girls. By chance she caught his eye and made a faint

ghost of a funny face when he passed; he stopped and gave her a onceover; next day Mr. Herman picked her for the first row in the new show. Rehearsals were the hardest work she'd ever done in her life.

Right from the start Agnes said she was going to see to it that Margo didn't throw herself away with a trashy crowd of chorusgirls; so, although Agnes had to be at work by nine o'clock sharp every morning, she always came by the theater every night after late rehearsals or evening performances to take Margo home. It was only after Margo met Tad Whittlesea, a Yale halfback who spent his weekends in New York once the football season was over, that Agnes missed a single night. The nights Tad met her, Agnes stayed home. She'd looked Tad over carefully and had him to Sunday dinner at the apartment and decided that for a millionaire's son he was pretty steady and that it was good for him to feel some responsibility about Margo.

Those nights Margo would be in a hurry to give a last pat to the blond curls under the blue velvet toque and to slip into the furcape that wasn't silver fox but looked a little like it at a distance, and to leave the dusty stuffy dressingroom and the smells of curling irons and cocoabutter and girls' armpits and stagescenery and to run down the flight of drafty cement stairs and past old grayfaced Luke who was in his little glass box pulling on his overcoat getting ready to go home himself. She'd take a deep breath when she got out into the cold wind of the street. She never would let Tad meet her at the theater with the other stagedoor Johnnies. She liked to find him standing with his wellpolished tan shoes wide apart and his coonskin coat thrown open so that you could see his striped tie and soft rumpled shirt, among people in evening dress in the lobby of the Astor.

Tad was a simple kind of redfaced boy who never had much to say. Margo did all the talking from the minute he handed her into the taxi to go to the nightclub. She'd keep him laughing with stories about the other girls and the wardrobewomen and the chorusmen. Sometimes he'd ask her to tell him a story over again so that he could remember it to tell his friends at college. The story about how the chorusmen, who were most of them fairies, had put the bitches' curse on a young fellow who was Maisie De Mar's boyfriend, so that he'd turned into a fairy too, scared Tad half to death.

"A lot of things sure do go on that people don't know about," he said.

Margo wrinkled up her nose. "You don't know the half of it, dearie."

"But it must be just a story."

"No, honestly, Tad, that's how it happened . . . we could hear them yelling and oohooing like they do down in their dressingroom. They all stood around in a circle and put the bitches' curse on him. I tell you we were scared."

That night they went to the Columbus Circle Childs for some ham and eggs.

"Gee, Margo," said Tad with his mouth full as he was finishing his second order of buttercakes. "I don't think this is the right life for you. . . . You're the smartest girl I ever met and damn refined too."

"Don't worry, Tad, little Margo isn't going to stay in the chorus all her life."

On the way home in the taxi Tad started to make passes at her. It surprised Margo because he wasn't a fresh kind of a boy. He wasn't drunk either, he'd only had one bottle of Canadian ale.

"Gosh, Margo, you're wonderful. . . . You won't drink and you won't cuddlecooty."

She gave him a little pecking kiss on the cheek.

"You ought to understand, Tad," she said, "I've got to keep my mind on my work."

"I guess you think I'm just a dumb cluck."

"You're a nice boy, Tad, but I like you best when you keep your hands in your pockets."

"Oh, you're marvelous," sighed Tad, looking at her with round eyes from out of his turnedup fuzzy collar from his own side of the cab.

"Just a woman men forget," she said.

Having Tad to Sunday dinner got to be a regular thing. He'd come early to help Agnes lay the table, and take off his coat and roll up his shirtsleeves afterwards to help with the dishes, and then all four of them would play hearts and each drink a glass of beefironandwine tonic from the drugstore. Margo hated those Sunday afternoons, but Frank and Agnes seemed to love them, and Tad would stay till the last minute before he had to rush off to meet his father at the Metropolitan Club, saying he'd never had such a good time in his life.

One snowy Sunday afternoon, when Margo had slipped away from the cardtable saying she had a headache, and had lain on the bed all afternoon listening to the hissing of the steamheat, almost crying from restlessness and boredom, Agnes said with her eyes shining when she came in in her négligée after Tad was gone: "Margo, you've got to marry him. He's the sweetest boy. He was telling us how this place is the first time in his life he's ever had any feeling of home. He's been brought up by servants and ridingmasters and people like that. . . . I never thought a millionaire could be such a dear. I just think he's a darling."

"He's no millionaire," said Margo, pouting.

"His old man has a seat on the stockexchange," called Frank from the other room. "You don't buy them with cigarstore coupons, do you, dear child?"

"Well," said Margo, stretching and yawning, "I certainly wouldn't be getting a spendthrift for a husband . . ." Then she sat up and shook her finger at Agnes. "I can tell you right now why he likes to come here Sundays. He gets a free meal and it don't cost him a cent."

Jerry Herman, the yellowfaced bald shriveledup little castingdirector, was a man all the girls were scared to death of. When Regina Riggs said she'd seen Margo having a meal with him at Keene's Chophouse between performances, one Saturday, the girls never quit talking about it. It made Margo sore and gave her a sick feeling in the pit of her stomach to

273

hear them giggling and whispering behind her back in the dressingroom.

Regina Riggs, a broadfaced girl from Oklahoma whose real name was Queenie and who'd been in the Ziegfeld choruses since the days when they had horsecars on Broadway, took Margo's arm when they were going down the stairs side by side after a morning rehearsal. "Look here, kiddo," she said, "I just want to tip you off about that guy, see? You know me, I been through the mill an' I don't give a hoot in hell for any of 'em . . . but let me tell you somethin'. There never been a girl got a spoken word by givin' that fourflusher a lay. Plenty of 'em have tried it. Maybe I've tried it myself. You can't beat the game with that guy an' a beautiful white body's about the cheapest thing there is in this town. . . . You got a kinda peart innocent look and I thought I'd put you wise."

Margo opened her blue eyes wide. "Why, the idea. . . . What made you think I'd . . ." She began to titter like a schoolgirl.

"All right, baby, let it ride. . . . I guess you'll hold out for the weddin'bells." They both laughed. They were always good friends after that.

But not even Queenie knew about it when, after a long wearing rehearsal late one Saturday night of a new number that was coming in the next Monday, Margo found herself stepping into Jerry Herman's roadster. He said he'd drive her home, but when they reached Columbus Circle, he said wouldn't she drive out to his farm in Connecticut with him and have a real rest. Margo went into a drugstore and phoned Agnes that there'd be rehearsals all day Sunday and that she'd stay down at Queenie Riggs's flat that was nearer the theater.

Driving out, Jerry kept asking Margo about herself. "There's something different about you, little girl," he said. "I bet you don't tell all you know. . . . You've got mystery."

All the way out, Margo was telling about her early life on a Cuban sugarplantation and her father's great townhouse in the Vedado and Cuban music and dances, and how her father had been ruined by the sugartrust and she'd supported the family as a child actress in Christmas pantomimes in England and about her early unfortunate marriage with a Spanish nobleman, and how all that life was over now and all she cared about was her work.

"Well, that story would make great publicity," was what Jerry Herman said about it.

When they drew up at a lighted farmhouse under a lot of tall trees, they sat in the car a moment, shivering a little in the chilly mist that came from a brook somewhere. He turned to her in the dark and seemed to be trying to look in her face. "You know about the three monkeys, dear?"

"Sure," said Margo. "See no evil, hear no evil, speak no evil."

"Correct," he said. Then she let him kiss her.

Inside it was the prettiest farmhouse with a roaring fire and two men in checked lumberman's shirts and a couple of funnylooking women in Paris clothes with Park Avenue voices who turned out to be in the decorating business. The two men were scenic artists. Jerry cooked up ham and eggs in the kitchen for everybody and they drank hard cider and had quite a time, though Margo didn't quite know how to behave. To have something to do she got hold of a guitar that was hanging on the wall and picked out *Siboney* and some other Cuban songs Tony had taught her.

When one of the women said something about how she ought to do a Cuban specialty, her heart almost stopped beating. Blue daylight was coming through the mist outside of the windows before they got to bed. They all had a fine country breakfast giggling and kidding in their dressinggowns and Sunday afternoon Jerry drove her in to town and let her out on the Drive near Seventyninth Street.

Frank and Agnes were in a great stew when she got home. Tad had been calling all day. He'd been to the theater and found out that there weren't any rehearsals called. Margo said spitefully that she had been rehearsing a little specialty and that if any young collegeboy thought he could interfere with her career he had another think coming. The next weekend when he called up she wouldn't see him.

But a week later, when she came out of her room about two o'clock on Sunday afternoon just in time for Agnes's big Sunday dinner, Tad was sitting there hanging his head, with his hick hands dangling between his knees. On the chair beside him was a green florist's box that she knew when she looked at it was American Beauty roses.

He jumped up. "Oh, Margo . . . don't be sore . . . I just can't seem to have a good time going around without you."

"I'm not sore, Tad," she said. "I just want everybody to understand that I won't let my life interfere with my work."

"Sure, I get you," said Tad.

Agnes came forward, all smiles, and put the roses in water.

"Gosh, I forgot," said Tad, and pulled a redleather case out of his pocket. He was stuttering. "You see D-d-dad g-g-

gave me some s-s-stocks to play around with an' I made a killing last week and I bought these, only we can't wear them except when we both go out together, can we?" It was a string of pearls, small and not very well matched, but pearls all right.

"Who else would take me anyplace where I could wear them, you mut?" said Margo. Margo felt herself blushing. "And they're not Teclas?" Tad shook his head. She threw her arms around his neck and kissed him.

"Gosh, you honestly like them," said Tad, talking fast. "Well, there's one other thing . . . Dad's letting me have the *Antoinette*—that's his boat, you know—for a two weeks' cruise this summer with my own crowd. I want you and Mrs. Mandeville to come. I'd ask Mr. Mandeville, too, but . . ."

"Nonsense," said Agnes. "I'm pretty sure the party will be properly chaperoned without me. . . . I'd just get seasick. . . . It used to be terrible when poor Fred used to take me out fishing."

"That was my father," said Margo. "He loved being out on the water . . . yachting . . . that kind of thing. . . . I guess that's why I'm such a good sailor."

"That's great," said Tad.

At that minute Frank Mandeville came in from his Sunday walk, dressed in his morningcoat and carrying a silverheaded cane, and Agnes ran into the kitchenette to dish up the roast stuffed veal and vegetables and the strawberrypie from which warm spicy smells had been seeping through the air of the small apartment for some time.

"Gosh, I like it here," said Tad, leaning back in his chair after they'd sat down to dinner.

The rest of that spring Margo had quite a time keeping Tad and Jerry from bumping into each other. She and Jerry never saw each other at the theater; early in the game she'd told him she had no intention of letting her life interfere with her work and he'd looked sharply at her with his shrewd boiledlooking eyes and said, "Humph . . . I wish more of our young ladies felt like you do. . . . I spend most of my time combing them out of my hair."

"Too bad about you," said Margo. "The Valentino of the castingoffice."

She liked Jerry Herman well enough. He was full of dope about the theater business. The only trouble was that when they got confidential he began making Margo pay her share of the check at restaurants and showed her pictures of his wife and children in New Rochelle. She worked hard on the Cuban songs, but nothing ever came of the specialty.

In May the show went on the road. For a long time she couldn't decide whether to go or not. Queenie Riggs said absolutely not. It was all right for her, who didn't have any ambition any more except to pick her off a travelingman in a onehorse town and marry him before he sobered up, but for Margo Dowling, who had a career ahead of her, nothing doing. Better be at liberty all summer than a chorine on the road.

Jerry Herman was sore as a crab when she wouldn't sign the roadcontract. He blew up right in front of the officeforce and all the girls waiting in line and everything.

"All right, I seen it coming . . . now she's got a swelled head and thinks she's Peggy Joyce. . . . All right, I'm through."

Margo looked him straight in the eye. "You must have me confused with somebody else, Mr. Herman. I'm sure I never started anything for you to be through with."

278

All the girls were tittering when she walked out, and Jerry Herman looked at her like he wanted to choke her. It meant no more jobs in any company where he did the casting.

She spent the summer in the hot city hanging round Agnes's apartment with nothing to do. And there was Frank always waiting to make a pass at her, so that she had to lock her door when she went to bed. She'd lie around all day in the horrid stuffy little room with furry green wallpaper and an unwashed window that looked out on cindery backyards and a couple of ailanthus trees and always washing hung out. Tad had gone to Canada as soon as college was over. She spent the days reading magazines and monkeying with her hair and manicuring her fingernails and dreaming about how she could get out of this miserable sordid life. Sordid was a word she'd just picked up. It was in her mind all the time, sordid, sordid, sordid. She decided she was crazy about Tad Whittlesea.

When August came, Tad wrote from Newport that his mother was sick and the yachting trip was off till next winter. Agnes cried when Margo showed her the letter. "Well, there are other fish in the sea," said Margo.

She and Queenie, who had resigned from the road tour when she had a runin with the stagemanager, started making the rounds of the castingoffices again. They rehearsed four weeks for a show that flopped the opening night. Then they got jobs in the Greenwich Village Follies. The director gave Margo a chance to do her Cuban number and Margo got a special costume made and everything, only to be cut out before the dressrehearsal because the show was too long.

She would have felt terrible if Tad hadn't turned up after Thanksgiving to take her out every Saturday night. He talked a lot about the yachting trip they were going to take during his midwinter vacation. It all depended on when his exams came.

After Christmas she was at liberty again. Frank was sick in bed with kidney trouble and Margo was crazy to get away from the stuffy apartment and nursing Frank and doing the housekeeping for Agnes, who often didn't get home from her job till ten or eleven o'clock at night. Frank lay in bed, his face looking drawn and yellow and pettish, and needed attention all the time. Agnes never complained, but Margo was so fed up with hanging around New York she signed a contract for a job as entertainer in a Miami cabaret, though Queenie and Agnes carried on terrible and said it would ruin her career.

She hadn't yet settled her wrangle with the agent about

279

who was going to pay her transportation South when one morning in February Agnes came in to wake her up.

Margo could see that it was something because Agnes was beaming all over her face. It was Tad calling her on the phone. He'd had bronchitis and was going to take a month off from college with a tutor on his father's boat in the West Indies. The boat was in Jacksonville. Before the tutor got there, he'd be able to take anybody he liked for a little cruise. Wouldn't Margo come and bring a friend? Somebody not too gay. He wished Agnes could go, he said, if that was impossible on account of Mr. Mandeville's being sick, who else could she take? Margo was so excited she could hardly breathe.

"Tad, how wonderful," she said. "I was planning to go South this week, anyway. You must be a mindreader."

Queenie Riggs arranged to go with her, though she said she'd never been on a yacht before and was scared she wouldn't act right.

"Well, I spent a lot of time in rowboats when I was a kid. . . . It's the same sort of thing," said Margo.

When they got out of the taxicab at the Penn Station there was Tad and a skinny little sleekhaired boy with him waiting to meet them. They were all very much excited and the boys' breaths smelled pretty strong of gin.

"You girls buy your own tickets," said Tad, taking Margo by the arm and pushing some bills down into the pocket of her furcoat. "The reservations are in your name, you'll have a drawingroom and we'll have one."

"A couple of wise guys," whispered Queenie in her ear as they stood in line at the ticketwindow.

The other boy's name was Dick Rogers. Margo could see right away that he thought Queenie was too old and not refined enough. Margo was worried about their baggage too. The bags looked awful cheap beside the boys' pigskin suitcases. She felt pretty down in the mouth when the train pulled out of the station. Here I am pulling a boner the first thing, she thought. And Queenie was throwing her head back and showing her gold tooth and yelling and shrieking already like she was at a fireman's picnic.

The four of them settled down in the girls' stateroom with the little table between them to drink a snifter of gin and began to feel more relaxed. When the train came out of the tunnel and lights began flashing by in the blackness outside, Queenie pulled down the shade. "My, this is real cozy," she said.

"Now the first thing I got to worry about is how to get you girls out on the boat. Dad won't care if he thinks we met you

in Jacksonville, but if he knew we'd brought you down from New York he'd raise Hail Columbia."

"I think we've got a chaperon all lined up in Jacksonville," said young Rogers, "She's a wonder. She's deaf and blind and she can't speak English."

"I wish we had Agnes along," said Tad. "That's Margo's stepmother. My, she's a good sport."

"Well, girls," said young Rogers, taking a noisy swig from the ginbottle, "when does the necking start?"

After they'd had dinner in the diningcar, they went lurching back to the drawingroom and had some more gin and young Rogers wanted them to play strip poker, but Margo said no.

"Aw, be a sport," Queenie giggled. Queenie was pretty tight already.

Margo put on her furcoat. "I want Tad to turn in soon," she said. "He's just out of a sickbed."

She grabbed Tad's hand and pulled him out into the passage. "Come on, let's give the kids a break. . . . The trouble with you collegeboys is that the minute a girl's unconventional you think she's an easy mark."

"Oh, Margo . . ." Tad hugged her through her furcoat as they stepped out into the cold clanging air of the observation platform. "You're grand."

That night after they'd gotten undressed, young Rogers came in the girls' room in his bathrobe and said there was somebody asking for Margo in the other stateroom.

She slept in the same stateroom with Tad, but she wouldn't let him get into the bunk with her. "Honest, Tad, I like you fine," she said, peeking from under the covers in the upper berth, "but you know . . . Heaven won't protect a workinggirl unless she protects herself. . . . And in my family we get married before the loving instead of after."

Tad sighed and rolled over with his face to the wall on the berth below. "Oh, heck . . . I'd been thinking about that."

She switched off the light. "But, Tad, aren't you even going to kiss me goodnight?"

In the middle of the night there was a knock on the door. Young Rogers came in, looking pretty rumpled. "Time to switch," he said. "I'm scared the conductor'll catch us."

"The conductor'll mind his own damn business," said Tad grumpily, but Margo had already slipped out and gone back to her own stateroom.

Next morning at breakfast in the diningcar, Margo wouldn't stop kidding the other two about the dark circles under their eyes. Young Rogers ordered a plate of oysters and they thought they'd never get over the giggles. By the time they got to Jacksonville, Tad had taken Margo back to the observation platform and asked her why the hell they didn't get married anyway, he was free white and twentyone, wasn't he? Margo began to cry and grinned at him through her tears and said she guessed there were plenty of reasons why not.

"By gum," said Tad when they got off the train into the sunshine of the station, "we'll buy us an engagement ring anyway."

First thing on the way to a hotel in a taxi they went to a jeweler's and Tad bought her a solitaire diamond set in platinum and paid for it with a check. "My, his old man must be some millionaire," whispered Queenie into Margo's ear in a voice like in church.

After they'd been to the jeweler's, the boys drove the girls to the Mayflower Hotel. They got a room there and went upstairs to fix up a little. The girls washed their underclothes and took hot baths and laid out their dresses on the beds.

"If you want my opinion," Queenie was saying while she was helping Margo wash her hair, "those two livewires are gettin' cold feet. . . . All my life I've wanted to go on a yachtin' trip an' now we're not gettin' to go any more than a rabbit. . . . Oh, Margo, I hope it wasn't me gummed the game."

"Tad'll do anything I say," said Margo crossly.

"You wait and see," said Queenie. "But here we are squabblin' when we ought to be enjoyin' ourselves. . . . Isn't this the swellest room in the swellest hotel in Jacksonville, Florida?"

Margo couldn't help laughing. "Well, whose fault is it?"

"That's right," said Queenie, flouncing out of the shampoosteaming bathroom where they were washing their hair, and slamming the door on Margo. "Have the last word."

At one o'clock the boys came by for them, and made them get all packed up and check out of the hotel. They went down to the dock in a Lincoln car Tad had hired. It was a beautiful sunny day. The *Antoinette* was anchored out in the St. John's River, so they had to go out in a little speedboat.

The sailor was a goodlooking young fellow all in white; he touched his cap and held out his arm to help the girls in. When Margo put her hand in his arm to step into the boat, she felt the hard muscles under the white duck sleeve and noticed how the sun shone on the golden hairs on his brown hand. Sitting on the darkblue soft cushion she looked up at Tad handing the bags down to the sailor. Tad looked pale from being sick and had that funny simple broadfaced look, but he was a husky wellbuilt boy too. Suddenly she wanted to hug him.

Tad steered and the speedboat went through the water so fast it took the girls' breath away and they were scared for fear the spray would spoil the new sportdresses they were wearing for the first time. "Oh, what a beauty," they both sighed when they saw the *Antoinette* so big and white with a mahogany deckhouse and a broad yellow chimney.

"Oh, I didn't know it was a steamyacht," crooned Queenie. "Why, my lands, you could cross the ocean in it."

"It's a diesel," said Tad.

"Aren't we all?" said Margo.

Tad was going so fast they crashed right in the little mahogany stairway they had for getting on the boat, and for a second it cracked and creaked like it would break right off, but the sailors managed to hold on somehow.

"Hold her, Newt," cried young Rogers, giggling.

"Damn," said Tad, and he looked very sore as they went on board.

The girls were glad to get up onto the beautiful yacht and out of the tippy little speedboat where they were afraid of getting their dresses splashed.

The yacht had goodlooking officers in white uniforms and a table was all ready for lunch out under an awning on deck and a Filipino butler was standing beside it with a tray of cocktails and all kinds of little sandwiches cut into fancy shapes. They settled down to lunch in a hurry, because the

boys said they were starved. They had broiled Florida lobster in a pink sauce and cold chicken and salad and they drank champagne. Margo had never been so happy in her life.

While they were eating, the yacht started to move slowly down the river, away from the ramshackle wharves and the dirtylooking old steamboats into the broad reaches of brown river that was splotched with green floating patches of water-hyacinths. A funny damp marshy smell came on the wind off the tangled trees that hid the banks. Once they saw a dozen big white birds with long necks fly up that Tad said were egrets. "I bet they're expensive," said Queenie. "They're protected by the federal government," said young Rogers.

They drank little glasses of brandy with their coffee. By the time they got up from the table, they were all pretty well spiffed. Margo had decided that Tad was the swellest boy she'd ever known and that she wouldn't hold out on him any longer, no matter what happened.

After lunch Tad showed them all over the boat. The diningroom was wonderful, all mirrors paneled in white and gold, and the cabins were the coziest things. The girls' cabin was just like an oldfashioned drawingroom. Their things had been all hung out for them while they'd been eating lunch.

While they were looking at the boat, young Rogers and Queenie disappeared somewhere, and the first thing Margo knew she and Tad were alone in a cabin looking at a photograph of a sailboat his father had won the Bermuda race with. Looking at the picture his cheek brushed against hers and there they were kissing.

"Gee, you're great," said Tad. "I'm kind of clumsy at this . . . no experience, you know."

She pressed against him. "I bet you've had plenty." With

his free hand he was bolting the door. "Will you do like the ring said, Tad?"

When they went up on deck afterwards, Tad was acting kind of funny; he wouldn't look her in the eye and talked all the time to young Rogers. Queenie looked flushed and all rumpledup like she'd been through a wringer, and staggered when she walked. Margo made her fix herself up and do her hair. She sure was wishing she hadn't brought Queenie. Margo looked fresh as a daisy herself, she decided, when she looked in the big mirror in the upstairs saloon.

The boat had stopped. Tad's face looked like a thundercloud when he came back from talking to the captain.

"We've got to go back to Jacksonville, burned out a bearing on the oilpump," he said. "A hell of a note."

"That's great," said young Rogers. "We can look into the local nightlife."

"And what I want to know is," said Queenie, "where's that chaperon you boys were talkin' about?"

"By gum," said Tad, "we forgot Mrs. Vinton. . . . I bet she's been waiting down at the dock all day."

"Too late for herbicide," said Margo, and they all laughed except Tad who looked sourer than ever.

It was dark when they got to Jacksonville. They'd had to pack their bags up again and they'd changed into different dresses.

While they were changing their clothes, Queenie had talked awful silly. "You mark my words, Margo, that boy wants to marry you."

"Let's not talk about it," Margo said several times.

"You treat him like he was dirt."

Margo heard her own voice whining and mean: "And whose business is it?"

Queenie flushed and went on with her packing. Margo could see she was sore.

They ate supper grumpily at the hotel. After supper young Rogers made them go out to a speakeasy he'd found. Margo didn't want to go and said she had a headache, but everybody said now be a sport and she went. It was a tough kind of a place with oilcloth on the tables and sawdust on the floor. There were some foreigners, wops or Cubans or something, standing against a bar in another room. Queenie said she didn't think it was the kind of place Mother's little girl ought to be seen in.

"Who the hell's going to see us?" said Tad still in his grouch.

"Don't we want to see life?" Rogers said, trying to cheer everybody up.

Margo lost track of what they were saying. She was staring through the door into the barroom. One of the foreigners standing at the bar was Tony. He looked older and his face was kind of puffy, but there was no doubt that it was Tony. He looked awful. He wore a rumpled white suit frayed at the cuffs of the trousers and he wiggled his hips like a woman as he talked. The first thing Margo thought was how on earth she could ever have liked that fagot. Out of the corner of her eye she could see Tad's sullen face and his nice light untidy hair and the cleancut collegeboy way he wore his clothes. She had to work fast. She was just opening her mouth to say honestly she had to go back to the hotel, when she caught sight of Tony's big black eyes and dark lashes. He was coming toward the table with his mincing walk, holding out both hands. "Querida mía. . . . Why are you here?"

She introduced him as Antonio de Garrido, her partner in a Cuban dance number on the Keith Circuit, but he let the cat out of the bag right away by calling her his dear wife. She could feel the start Tad gave when he heard that. Then suddenly Tad began to make a great fuss over Tony and to order up drinks for him. He and Rogers kept whispering and laughing together about something. Then Tad was asking Tony to come on the cruise with them.

She could see Tad was acting drunker than he really was. She was ready for it when the boys got up to go. Tad's face was red as a beet.

"We got to see the skipper about that engine trouble," he said. "Maybe Señor de Garrido will see you girls back to the hotel. . . . Now don't do anything I wouldn't do."

"See you in the morning, cuties," chimed in young Rogers.

After they'd gone, Margo got to her feet. "Well, no use waiting around this dump. . . . You sure put your foot in it, Tony."

Tony had tears in his eyes. "Everything is very bad with me," he said. "I thought maybe my little Margo remembered . . . you know we used to be very fond. Don Manfredo, you remember my patron, Margo, had to leave Havana very suddenly. I hoped he would take me to Paris, but he brought me to Miami with him. Now we are no more friends. We have been unlucky at roulette. . . . He has only enough money for himself."

"Why don't you get a job?"

"In these clothes . . . I am ashamed to show my face . . . maybe your friends . . ."

"You lay off them, do you hear?" Margo burst out.

Queenie was blubbering, "You should have bought us return tickets to New York. Another time you remember that. Never leave the homeplate without a return ticket."

Tony took them home to the hotel in a taxi and insisted on paying for it. He made a big scene saying goodnight. "Little Margo, if you never see me again, remember I loved you. . . . I shall keel myself." As they went up in the elevator, they could see him still standing on the sidewalk where they had left him.

In the morning they were waked up by a bellboy bringing an envelope on a silver tray. It was a letter to Margo from Tad. The handwriting was an awful scrawl. All it said was that the trip was off because the tutor had come and they were going to have to pick up Dad in Palm Beach. Enclosed there were five twenties.

"Oh, goody goody," cried Queenie, sitting up in bed when she saw them. "It sure would have been a long walk home. . . . Honest, that boy's a prince."

"A damn hick," said Margo. "You take fifty and I take fifty. . . . Lucky I have an engagement fixed up in Miami."

It was a relief when Queenie said she'd take the first train back to little old New York. Margo didn't want ever to see any of that bunch again.

They hadn't finished packing their bags when there was Tony at the door. He sure looked sick. Margo was so nervous she yelled at him, "Who the hell let you in?"

Tony let himself drop into a chair and threw back his head with his eyes closed. Queenie closed up her travelingbag and came over and looked at him. "Say, that bozo looks half-starved. Better let me order up some coffee or something. . . . Was he really your husband like he said?"

Margo nodded.

"Well, you've got to do something about him. Poor boy, he sure does look down on his uppers."

"I guess you're right," said Margo, staring at them both with hot dry eyes.

She didn't go down to Miami that day. Tony was sick and threw up everything he ate. It turned out he hadn't had anything to eat for a week and had been drinking hard. "I bet you that boy dopes," Queenie whispered in Margo's ear.

They both cried when it was time for Queenie to go to her train. "I've got to thank you for a wonderful time while it lasted," she said.

Margo put Tony to bed after Queenie had gone off to her train. When they objected down at the desk, she said he was her husband. They had to register again. It made her feel awful to have to write down in the book Mr. and Mrs. Antonio de Garrido. Once it was written it didn't look so bad, though.

It was three days before Tony could get up. She had to have a doctor for him. The doctor gave him bromides and hot milk. The room was seven-fifty a day and the meals sent up and the doctor and medicine and everything ran into money. It began to look like she'd have to hock the ring Tad had given her.

It made her feel like she was acting in a play living with Tony again. She was kind of fond of him after all, but it sure wasn't what she'd planned. As he began to feel better, he began to talk confidently about the magnificent act they could put on together. Maybe they could sell it to the cabaret she'd signed an engagement with in Miami. After all, Tony was a sweettempered kind of a boy.

The trouble was that whenever she went out to get her hair curled or something, she'd always find one of the bellhops, a greasylooking black-haired boy who was some kind of a spick himself, in the room with Tony. When she asked Tony what about it, he'd laugh and say, "It is nothing. We talk Spanish together. That is all. He has been very attentive."

"Yes, yes," said Margo. She felt so damn lousy about everything she didn't give a damn anyway.

One morning when she woke up, Tony was gone. The roll of bills in her pocketbook was gone and all her jewelry except the solitaire diamond she wore on her finger was gone, too. When she called up the desk to ask if he'd paid the bill, they said that he had left word for her to be called at twelve and that was all. Nobody had seen him go out. The spick bellhop had gone, too.

All that Margo had left was her furcoat and fifteen cents. She didn't ask for the bill, but she knew it must be about fifty or sixty bucks. She dressed thoughtfully and carefully and decided to go out to a lunchroom for a cup of coffee. That was all the breakfast she had the price of.

Outside it was a warm spring day. The sunshine glinted on the rows of parked cars. The streets and the stores and the newsstands had a fresh sunny airy look. Margo walked up and down the main street of Jacksonville with an awful hollow feeling in the pit of her stomach. She looked in haberdashery store windows and in the windows of cheap jewelers and hockshops and read over carefully all the coming attractions listed at the moving picture houses. She found herself in front of a busstation. She read the fares and the times buses left for Miami and New Orleans and Tallahassee and Orlando and Tampa and Atlanta, Georgia, and Houston, Texas, and Los Angeles, California. In the busstation there was a lunchcounter. She went in to spend her fifteen cents. She'd get more for the ring at a hockshop if she didn't barge in on an empty stomach, was what she was thinking as she sat down at the counter and ordered a cup of coffee and a sandwich.

Newsreel LVIII

In my dreams it always seems
I hear you softly call to me
Valencia!
Where the orange trees forever scent the
Breeze beside the sea

which in itself typifies the great drama of the Miami we have today. At the time only twenty years ago when the site of the Bay of Biscayne Bank was a farmer's hitching-yard and that of the First National Bank a public barbe-cueground, the ground here where this ultramodern hotel and club stands was isolated primeval forest. My father and myself were clearing little vegetable patches round it and I was peddling vegetables at the hotel Royal Palm, then a magnificent hotel set in a wild frontier. Even eight years ago I was growing tomatoes

Valencia!

SEEK MISSING LOOT

WOMAN DIRECTS HIGHWAY ROBBERY

Lazy River flowing to the southland
Down where I long to be

RADIUM VICTIMS TIPPED BRUSHES IN MOUTHS

this peninsula has been white every month though there have been some months when West Florida was represented as only fair

When the red red robin
Comes bob bob bobbin' along along

We Want You to Use Our Credit System to Your Utmost Advantage. Only a Small Down Payment and the Balance in Small Amounts to Suit Your Convenience.

There'll be no more sobbin'
When he starts throbbin'

URGES STRIKES BE TERMED FELONIES

When he starts throbbin'
His old sweet song
When the red red robin

bright and early he showed no signs of fatigue or any of the usual evidences of a long journey just finished. There was not a wrinkle on his handsome suit of silken material, the weave and texture and color of which were so suitable for tropic summer days. His tie with its jeweled stickpin and his finger ring were details in perfect accord with his immaculate attire. Though small in stature and unassuming in manner, he disposed of twenty million dollars worth of building operations with as little fuss or flurry as ordinarily accompanies the act of a passenger on a trolley car in handing a nickel to the conductor.

The Campers at Kitty Hawk

On December seventeenth, nineteen hundred and three, Bishop Wright, of the United Brethren, onetime editor of the *Religious Telescope,* received in his first frame on Hawthorn Street in Dayton, Ohio, a telegram from his boys Wilbur and Orville who'd gotten it into their heads to spend their vacations in a little camp out on the dunes of the North Carolina coast tinkering with a homemade glider they'd knocked together themselves. The telegram read:

SUCCESS   FOUR FLIGHTS THURSDAY MORNING ALL
AGAINST   TWENTYONE-MILE   WIND   STARTED   FROM
LEVEL WITH ENGINEPOWER ALONE   AVERAGE SPEED
THROUGH AIR THIRTYONE MILES   LONGEST FIFTY-
SEVEN SECONDS   INFORM PRESS   HOME CHRISTMAS

The figures were a little wrong because the telegraph operator misread Orville's hasty penciled scrawl.

but the fact remains

that a couple of young bicycle mechanics from Dayton, Ohio,

had designed, constructed, and flown

for the first time ever a practical airplane.

After running the motor a few minutes to heat it up, I released the wire that held the machine to the track and the machine started forward into the wind. Wilbur ran at the side of the machine holding the wing to balance it on the track. Unlike the start on the fourteenth, made in a calm, the machine facing a twentyseven-mile wind started very slowly. . . . Wilbur was able to stay with it until it lifted from the track after a forty-foot run. One of the lifesaving men snapped the camera for us, taking a picture just as it reached the end of the track and the machine had risen to a height of about two feet. . . . The course of the flight up and down was extremely erratic, partly due to the irregularities of the air, partly to lack of experience in handling this machine. A sudden dart when a little over a hundred and twenty feet from the point at which it rose in the air ended the flight. . . . This flight lasted only twelve seconds, but it was nevertheless the first in the history of the world in which a machine carrying a man had raised itself by its own power into the air in full flight, had sailed forward without reduction of speed, and had finally landed at a point as high as that from which it started.

A little later in the day the machine was caught in a gust of wind and turned over and smashed, almost killing the coastguardsman who tried to hold it down;

it was too bad,

but the Wright brothers were too happy to care;

they'd proved that the damn thing flew.

When these points had been definitely established, we at once packed our goods and returned home, knowing that the age of the flying machine had come at last.

They were home for Christmas in Dayton, Ohio, where they'd been born in the seventies of a family who had been settled west of the Alleghenies since eighteen-fourteen; in Dayton, Ohio, where they'd been to grammarschool and highschool and joined their father's church and played baseball and hockey and worked out on the parallel bars and the flying swing and sold newspapers and built themselves a printingpress out of odds and ends from the junkheap and flown kites and tinkered with mechanical contraptions and gone around town as boys doing odd jobs to turn an honest penny.

The folks claimed it was the Bishop's bringing home a helicopter, a fiftycent mechanical toy made of two fans worked by elastic bands that was supposed to hover in the air, that had got his two youngest boys hipped on the subject of flight.

so that they stayed home instead of marrying the way the other boys did, and puttered all day about the house picking up a living with jobprinting.

bicyclerepair work,

sitting up late nights reading books on aerodynamics,

Still they were sincere churchmembers, their bicycle business was prosperous, a man could rely on their word. They were popular in Dayton.

In those days flyingmachines were the big laugh of all the crackerbarrel philosophers. Langley's and Chanute's unsuccessful experiments had been jeered down with an I-told-you-so that rang from coast to coast. The Wrights' big problem was to find a place secluded enough to carry on their experiments without being the horselaugh of the countryside. Then they had no money to spend;

they were practical mechanics; when they needed anything they built it themselves.

They hit on Kitty Hawk,

on the great dunes and sandy banks that stretch south toward Hatteras seaward of Albemarle Sound,

a vast stretch of seabeach,

empty except for a coastguard station, a few fishermen's shacks, and the swarms of mosquitoes and the ticks and chiggers in the crabgrass behind the dunes,

and overhead the gulls and swooping terns, in the evening fishhawks and cranes flapping across the saltmarshes, occasionally eagles

that the Wright brothers followed soaring with their eyes
as Leonardo watched them centuries before,
straining his sharp eyes to apprehend
the laws of flight.

Four miles across the loose sand from the scattering of shacks, the Wright brothers built themselves a camp and a shed for their gliders. It was a long way to pack their groceries, their tools, anything they happened to need; in summer it was hot as blazes, the mosquitoes were hell;

but they were alone there,

and they'd figured out that the loose sand was as soft as anything they could find to fall in.

There with a glider made of two planes and a tail in which they lay flat on their bellies and controlled the warp of the planes by shimmying their hips, taking off again and again all day from a big dune named Kill Devil Hill,

they learned to fly.

Once they'd managed to hover for a few seconds
and soar ever so slightly on a rising aircurrent,
they decided the time had come
to put a motor in their biplane.

Back in the shop in Dayton, Ohio, they built an airtunnel, which is their first great contribution to the science of flying, and tried out model planes in it.

They couldn't interest any builders of gasoline engines, so they had to build their own motor.

It worked; after that Christmas of nineteen-three the Wright brothers weren't doing it for fun any more; they gave up their bicycle business, got the use of a big old cowpasture belonging to the local banker for practice flights, spent all the time when they weren't working on their machine in promotion, worrying about patents, infringements, spies, trying to interest government officials, to make sense out of the smooth involved heartbreaking remarks of lawyers.

In two years they had a plane that would cover twentyfour miles at a stretch round and round the cowpasture.

People on the interurban car used to crane their necks out of the windows when they passed along the edge of the field, startled by the clattering pop-pop of the old Wright motor and the sight of the white biplane like a pair of ironingboards one on top of the other chugging along a good fifty feet in the air. The cows soon got used to it.

As the flights got longer,
the Wright brothers got backers,
engaged in lawsuits,
lay in their beds at night sleepless with the whine of phantom millions, worse than the mosquitoes at Kitty Hawk.

In nineteen-seven they went to Paris,
allowed themselves to be togged out in dress suits and silk hats,
learned to tip waiters,
talked with government experts, got used to gold braid and

postponements and Vandyke beards and the outspread palms of politicos. For amusement
    they played diabolo in the Tuileries Gardens.

They gave publicized flights at Fort Myers, where they had their first fatal crackup, St. Petersburg, Paris, Berlin; at Pau they were all the rage,
    such an attraction that the hotelkeeper
    wouldn't charge them for their room.
Alfonso of Spain shook hands with them and was photographed sitting in the machine.
    King Edward watched a flight,
    the Crown Prince insisted on being taken up,
    the rain of medals began.

They were congratulated by the Czar
    and the King of Italy and the amateurs of sport, and the society climbers and the papal titles,
    and decorated by a society for universal peace.

Aeronautics became the sport of the day.
The Wrights don't seem to have been very much impressed by the upholstery and the braid and the gold medals and the parades of plush horses;
    they remained practical mechanics
    and insisted on doing all their own work themselves, even to filling the gasolinetank.

In nineteen-eleven they were back on the dunes
    at Kitty Hawk with a new glider.
Orville stayed up in the air for nine and a half minutes, which remained a long time the record for motorless flight.
The same year Wilbur died of typhoidfever in Dayton.
In the rush of new names: Farman, Blériot, Curtiss, Ferber, Esnault-Peltrie, Delagrange;
    in the snorting impact of bombs and the whine and rattle of shrapnel and the sudden stutter of machineguns after the motor's been shut off overhead,
    and we flatten into the mud
    and make ourselves small cowering in the corners of ruined walls,
    the Wright brothers passed out of the headlines;
    but not even headlines or the bitter smear of newsprint or the choke of smokescreen and gas or chatter of brokers on the stockmarket or barking of phantom millions or oratory of brasshats laying wreaths on new monuments
    can blur the memory

of the chilly December day
two shivering bicycle mechanics from Dayton, Ohio,
first felt their homemade contraption,
whittled out of hickory sticks,
gummed together with Arnstein's bicycle cement,
stretched with muslin they'd sewn on their sister's sewingmachine in their own backyard on Hawthorn Street in Dayton, Ohio,
  soar into the air
  above the dunes and the wide beach
  at Kitty Hawk.

Newsreel LIX

the stranger first coming to Detroit, if he be interested in the busy economic side of modern life, will find a marvelous industrial beehive; if he be a lover of nature, he will take notice of a site made forever remarkable by the waters of that noble strait that gives the city its name; if he be a student of romance and history, he will discover legends and records as entertaining and as instructive as the continent can supply

> *I've a longing for my Omaha town*
> *I long to go there and settle down*

DETROIT LEADS THE WORLD IN THE
MANUFACTURE OF AUTOMOBILES

> *I want to see my pa*
> *I want to see my ma*
> *I want to go to dear old Omaha*

DETROIT IS FIRST
IN PHARMACEUTICALS
STOVES RANGES FURNACES
ADDING MACHINES
PAINTS AND VARNISHES
MARINE MOTORS
OVERALLS
SODA AND SALT PRODUCTS
SPORT SHOES
TWIST DRILLS
SHOWCASES
CORSETS
GASOLINE TORCHES
TRUCKS

Mr. Radio Man won't you do what you can
'Cause I'm so lonely
Tell my Mammy to come back home
Mr. Radio Man

DETROIT THE DYNAMIC RANKS HIGH

IN FOUNDRY AND MACHINE SHOP PRODUCTS
IN BRASS AND BRASS PRODUCTS
IN TOBACCO AND CIGARS
IN ALUMINUM CASTINGS
IN IRON AND STEEL
IN LUBRICATOR TOOLS
MALLEABLE IRON
METAL BEDS

Back to the land that gave me birth
The grandest place on God's green earth
California! That's where I belong.

"DETROIT THE CITY WHERE LIFE IS WORTH
LIVING"

Charley Anderson

First thing Charley heard when he climbed down from the controls was Farrell's voice shouting, "Charley Anderson, the boy with the knowhow. Welcome to little old Detroit"; and then he saw Farrell's round face coming across the green grass of the field and his big mouth wide open. "Kind of bumpy, wasn't it?"

"It was cold as hell," said Charley. "Call this a field?"

"We're getting the Chamber of Commerce het up about it. You can give 'em an earful about it, maybe."

"I sure did slew around in that mud. Gosh, I pulled out in such a hurry I didn't even bring a toothbrush."

Charley pulled off his gloves that were dripping with oil from a leak he'd had trouble with in the bumpy going over the hills. His back ached. It was a relief that Bill Cermak was there to get the boat into the hangar.

"All right, let's go," he said.

"Thataboy," roared Farrell and put his hand on Charley's

shoulder. "We'll stop by the house and see if I can fit you into a change of clothes."

At that moment a taxi rolled out onto the field and out of it stepped Taki. He came running over with Charley's suitcase. He reached the car breathless. "I hope you have a nice journey, sir."

"Check," said Charley. "Did you get me a walkup?"

"Very nice inexpensive elevator apartment opposed to the Museum of Municipal Art," panted Taki in his squeaky voice.

"Well, that's service," Farrell said, and put his foot on the starter of his puttycolored Lincoln towncar. The motor purred silkily.

Taki put the suitcase in back and Charley hopped in beside Farrell. "Taki thinks we lack culture," said Charley, laughing. Farrell winked.

It was pleasant sitting slumped in the seat beside Farrell's welldressed figure behind the big softpurring motor, letting a little drowsiness come over him as they drove down broad straight boulevards with here and there a construction job that gave them a whiff of new bricks and raw firboards and fresh cement as they passed. A smell of early spring came off the fields and backlots on a raw wind that had little streaks of swampy warmth in it.

"Here's our little shanty," said Farrell and swerved into a curving graded driveway and jammed on the brakes at the end of a long graystone house with narrow pointed windows and Gothic pinnacles like a cathedral. They got out and Charley followed Farrell across a terrace down an avenue of boxtrees in pots and through a frenchwindow into a billiardroom with a heavilycarved ceiling.

"This is my playroom," said Farrell. "After all, a man's got to have someplace to play. . . . Here's a bathroom you can change in. I'll be back for you in ten minutes."

It was a big bathroom all in jadegreen with a couch, an easychair, a floorlamp, and a set of chestweights and indianclubs in the corner. Charley stripped and took a hot shower and changed his clothes.

He was just putting on his bestlooking striped tie when Farrell called through the door. "Everything O.K.?"

301

"Check," said Charley as he came out. "I feel like a million dollars."

Farrell looked him in the eye in a funny way and laughed. "Why not?" he said.

The office was in an unfinished officebuilding in a ring of unfinished officebuildings round Grand Circus Park.

"You won't mind if I run you through the publicity department first, Charley," said Farrell. "Eddy Sawyer's a great boy. Then we'll all get together in my office and have some food."

"Check," said Charley.

"Say, Eddy, here's your birdman," shouted Farrell, pushing Charley into a big bright office with orange hangings. "Mr. Sawyer, meet Mr. Anderson . . . the Charley Anderson, our new consulting engineer. . . . Give us a buzz when you've put him through a course of sprouts."

Farrell hurried off, leaving Charley alone with a small yellowfaced man with a large towhead who had the talk and manners of a highschool boy with the cigarette habit. Eddy Sawyer gave Charley's hand a tremendous squeeze, asked him how he liked the new offices, explained that orange stood for optimism, asked him if he ever got airsick, explained that he did terribly, wasn't it the damnedest luck seeing the business he was in, brought out from under his desk a bottle of whiskey. "I bet J. Y. didn't give you a drink. . . . That man lives on air, a regular salamander."

Charley said he would take a small shot and Eddy Sawyer produced two glasses that already had the ice in them and a siphon. "Say when." Charley took a gulp, then Eddy leaned back in his swivelchair having drained off his drink and said, "Now Mr. Anderson, if you don't mind let's have the old lifehistory, or whatever part of it is fit to print. . . . Mind you, we won't use anything right away, but we like to have the dope so that we can sort of feed it out as occasion demands."

Charley blushed. "Well," he said, "there's not very much to tell."

"Thataboy," said Eddy Sawyer, pouring out two more drinks and putting away the whiskeybottle. "That's how all the best stories begin." He pressed a buzzer and a curlyhaired stenographer with a pretty pink dollface came in and sat down with her notebook at the other side of the desk.

While he was fumbling through his story, Charley kept repeating to himself in the back of his head, "Now, bo, don't make an ass of yourself the first day." Before they were through, Farrell stuck his head in the door and said to come along, the crowd was waiting.

"Well, did you get all fixed up? . . . Charley, I want you

302

to meet our salesmanager . . . Joe Stone, Charley Anderson. And Mr. Frank and Mr. O'Brien, our battery of legal talent, and Mr. Bledsoe, he's in charge of output . . . that's your department."

Charley shook a number of hands; there was a slick black head with hair parted in the middle, a pair of bald heads and a steelgray head with hair bristling up like a shoebrush, noseglasses, tortoiseshell glasses, one small mustache. "Sure, Mike," Eddy Sawyer was stuttering away nervously. "I've got enough on him to retire on the blackmail any time now."

"That's a very good starter, young man," said Cyrus Bledsoe, the grayhaired man, gruffly. "I hope you've got some more notions left in the back of your head."

"Check," said Charley.

They all, except Bledsoe who growled that he never ate lunch, went out with him to the Athletic Club where they had a private diningroom and cocktails set out. Going up in the elevator a voice behind him said, "How's the boy, Charley?" and Charley turned round to find himself face to face with Andy Merritt. Andy Merritt's darkgray suit seemed to fit him even better than usual. His sour smile was unusually thin.

"Why, what are you doing here?" Charley blurted out.

"Detroit," said Andy Merritt, "is a town that has always interested me extremely."

"Say, how's Joe making out?"

Andy Merritt looked pained and Charley felt he ought to have kept his mouth shut. "Joe was in excellent health when I last saw him," said Andy. It turned out that Andy was lunching with them too.

When they were working on the filetmignon, Farrell got up and made a speech about how this luncheon was a beginning of a new spirit in the business of manufacturing airplane parts and motors and that the time had come for the airplane to quit hanging on the apronstrings of the automotive business because airplanes were going to turn the automobilemen into a lot of bicycle manufacturers before you could say Jack Robinson. A milliondollar business had to be handled in a milliondollar way. Then everybody yelled and clapped and Farrell held up his hand and described Charley Anderson's career as a war ace and an inventor and said it was a very happy day, a day he'd been waiting for a long time, when he could welcome him into the Tern flock. Then Eddy Sawyer led a cheer for Anderson and Charley had to get up and say how he was glad to get out there and be back in the great open spaces and the real manufacturing center of this country, and when you said manufacturing center of this country what you meant was manufacturing center of the whole bloody world. Eddy Sawyer led another cheer and then they all settled down to eat their peachmelba.

When they were getting their hats from the checkroom downstairs, Andy Merritt tapped Charley on the shoulder and said, "A very good speech. . . . You know I'd felt for some time we ought to make a break. . . . You can't run a bigtime business with smalltown ideas. That's the trouble with poor old Joe, who's a prince, by the way . . . smalltown ideas . . ."

Charley went around to see the apartment. Taki had everything fixed up in great shape, flowers in the vases and all that sort of thing.

"Well, this is slick," said Charley. "How do you like it in Detroit?"

"Very interesting," said Taki. "Mr. Ford permits to visit Highland Park."

"Gosh, you don't lose any time. . . . Nothing like that assemblyline in your country, is there?"

Taki grinned and nodded. "Very interesting," he said with more emphasis.

Charley took off his coat and shoes and lay down on the couch in the sittingroom to take a nap, but it seemed he'd just closed his eyes when Taki was grinning and bowing from the door.

"Very sorry, sir, Mr. Benton, longdistance."

"Check," said Charley.

Taki had his slippers there for him to stick his feet into and had discreetly laid his bathrobe on a chair beside the couch. At the phone Charley noticed that it was already dusk and that the streetlights were just coming on.

"Hello, Nat."

"Hey, Charley, how are you making out?"

"Great," said Charley.

"Say, I just called up to let you know you and Andy Merritt were going to be elected vicepresidents at the next meeting of Tern stockholders."

"How do you know?" Nat laughed into the phone. "Some intelligence service," said Charley.

"Well, service is what we're here for," said Nat. "And Charley, there's a little pool down here. . . . I'm taking a dip myself and I thought you might like to come in. . . . I can't tell you the details over the phone, but I wrote you this afternoon."

"I haven't got any cash."

"You could put up about ten grand of stock to cover. The stock won't be tied up long."

"Check," said Charley. "Shoot the moon . . . this is my lucky year."

The plant was great. Charley drove out there is a new Buick sedan he bought himself right off the dealer's floor the next morning. The dealer seemed to know all about him and wouldn't even take a downpayment. "It'll be a pleasure to have your account, Mr. Anderson," he said.

Old Bledsoe seemed to be on the lookout for him and showed him around. Everything was lit with skylights. There wasn't a belt in the place. Every machine had its own motor. "Farrell thinks I'm an old stickinthemud because I don't talk high finance all the time, but goddamn it, if there's a more uptodate plant than this anywhere, I'll eat a goddamned dynamo."

"Gee, I thought we were in pretty good shape out at Long Island City. . . . But this beats the Dutch."

"That's exactly what it's intended to do," growled Bledsoe.

Last Bledsoe introduced Charley to the engineering force and then showed him into the office off the draftingroom that was to be his. They closed the groundglass door and sat down facing each other in the silvery light from the skylight. Bledsoe pulled out a stogie and offered one to Charley. "Ever smoke these? . . . They clear the head."

Charley said he'd try anything once. They lit the stogies and Bledsoe began to talk between savage puffs of stinging

305

blue smoke. "Now look here, Anderson, I hope you've come out here to work with us and not to juggle your damned stock. . . . I know you're a war hero and all that and are slated for windowdressing, but it looks to me like you might have somep'n in your head too. . . . I'm saying this once and I'll never say it again. . . . If you're workin' with us, you're workin' with us, and if you're not, you'd better stick around your broker's office where you belong."

"But, Mr. Bledsoe, this is the chance I've been lookin' for," stammered Charley. "Hell, I'm a mechanic, that's all. I know that."

"Well, I hope so. . . . If you are, and not a goddamned bondsalesman, you know that our motor's lousy and the ships they put it in are lousy. We're ten years behind the rest of the world in flyin' and we've got to catch up. Once we get the designs, we've got the production apparatus to flatten 'em all out. Now I want you to go home and get drunk or go wenchin' or whatever you do when you're worried and think about this damn business."

"I'm through with that stuff," said Charley. "I had enough of that in New York."

Bledsoe got to his feet with a jerk, letting the ash from his stogie fall on his alpaca vest. "Well, you better get married then."

"I been thinkin' of that. . . . But I can't find the other name to put on the license," said Charley, laughing.

Bledsoe smiled. "You design me a decent light dependable sixteencylinder aircooled motor and I'll get my little girl to introduce you to all the bestlookin' gals in Detroit. She knows 'em all. . . . And if it's money you're lookin' for, they sweat money."

The phone buzzed. Bledsoe answered it, muttered under his breath, and stamped out of the office.

At noon Farrell came by to take Charley out to lunch. "Did old Bledsoe give you an earful?" he asked. Charley nodded. "Well, don't let him get under your skin. His bark is worse than his bite. He wouldn't be in the outfit if he wasn't the best plantmanager in the country."

It was at the Country Club dance that Farrell and his wife, who was a thin oldish blonde, haggard and peevish under a festoon of diamonds, took him out to, that Charley met old Bledsoe's daughter Anne. She was a squareshouldered girl in pink with a large pleasantlysmiling mouth and a firm handshake. Charley cottoned to her first thing. They danced to *Just a Girl That Men Forget,* and she talked about how crazy she was about flying and had five hours toward her pilot's license. Charley said he'd take her up any time if she wasn't too proud to fly a Curtiss-Robin. She said he'd better not make a promise if he didn't intend to keep it because she always did what she said she'd do. Then she talked about golf and he didn't let on that he'd never had a golfclub in his hand in his life.

At supper when he came back from getting a couple of plates of chickensalad, he found her sitting at a round table under a Japanese lantern with a pale young guy, who turned out to be her brother Harry, and a girl with beautiful ashenblond hair and a touch of Alabama in her talk whose name was Gladys Wheatley. She seemed to be engaged or something to Harry Bledsoe, who had a silver flask and kept pouring gin into the fruitpunch and held her hand and called her Glad. They were all younger than Charley, but they made quite a fuss over him and kept saying what a godawful town Detroit was. When Charley got a little gin inside of him, he started telling war yarns for the first time in his life.

He drove Anne home and old Bledsoe came out with a copy of the *Engineering Journal* in his hand and said, "So you've got acquainted, have you?"

"Oh, yes, we're old friends, Dad," she said. "Charley's going to teach me to fly."

"Humph," said Bledsoe and closed the door in Charley's face with a growling: "You go home and worry about that motor."

All that summer everybody thought that Charley and Anne were engaged. He'd get away from the plant for an hour or two on quiet afternoons and take a ship up at the flyingfield to give her a chance to pile up flying hours and on Sundays they'd play golf. Charley would get up early Sunday mornings to take a lesson with the golf pro out at the Sunnyside Club where he didn't know anybody. Saturday nights they'd often have dinner at the Bledsoes' house and go out to the Country Club to dance. Gladys Wheatley and Harry were usually along and they were known as a foursome by all the younger crowd. Old Bledsoe seemed pleased that Charley had taken up with his youngsters and began to treat him as a member of the family. Charley was happy, he enjoyed his work; after the years in New York being in Detroit was like being home. He and Nat made some killings in the market. As vicepresident and consulting engineer of the Tern Company he was making twenty-five thousand dollars a year.

Old Bledsoe grumbled that it was too damn much money for a young engineer, but it pleased him that Charley spent most of it on a small experimental shop where he and Bill Cermak were building a new motor on their own. Bill Cermak had moved his family out from Long Island and was

full of hunches for mechanical improvements. Charley was so busy he didn't have time to think of women or take anything but an occasional drink in a social way. He thought Anne was a peach and enjoyed her company, but he never thought of her as a girl he might someday go to bed with.

Over the Labor Day weekend the Farrells invited the young Bledsoes and Gladys Wheatley out for a cruise. When he was asked, Charley felt that this was highlife at last and suggested he bring Taki along to mix drinks and act as steward. He drove the Bledsoes down to the yachtclub in his Buick.

Anne couldn't make out why he was feeling so good. "Nothing to do for three days but sit around on a stuffy old boat and let the mosquitoes bite you," she was grumbling in a gruff tone like her father's. "Dad's right when he says he doesn't mind working over his work but he's darned if he'll work over his play."

"But look at the company we'll have to suffer in, Annie." Charley put his arm around her shoulders for a moment as she sat beside him on the front seat.

Harry, who was alone in the back, let out a giggle. "Well, you needn't act so smart, Mister," said Anne, without turning back. "You and Gladys certainly do enough public petting to make a cat sick."

"The stern birdman's weakening," said Harry.

Charley blushed. "Check," he said.

They were already at the yachtclub and two young fellows in sailorsuits were taking the bags out of the back of the car.

Farrell's boat was a fast fiftyfoot cruiser with a diningroom on deck and wicker chairs and a lot of freshvarnished mahogany and polished brass. Farrell wore a yachtingcap and walked up and down the narrow deck with a worried look as the boat nosed out into the little muggy breeze. The river in the late afternoon had a smell of docks and weedy swamps.

"It makes me feel good to get out on the water, don't it you, Charley? . . . The one place they can't get at you."

Meanwhile Mrs. Farrell was apologizing to the ladies for the cramped accommodations. "I keep trying to get Yardly to get a boat with some room in it, but it seems to me every one he gets is more cramped up than the last one."

Charley had been listening to a light clinking sound from the pantry. When Taki appeared with a tray of manhattan cocktails, everybody cheered up. As he watched Taki bobbing with the tray in front of Gladys, Charley thought how wonderful she looked all in white with her pale abundant hair tied up in a white silk handkerchief.

Smiling beside him was Anne with her brown hair blowing in her eyes from the wind of the boat's speed. The engine made so much noise and the twinscrews churned up so much water that he could talk to her without the others' hearing.

"Annie," he said suddenly, "I been thinking it's about time I got married."

"Why, Charley, a mere boy like you."

Charley felt warm all over. All at once he wanted a woman terribly bad. It was hard to control his voice.

"Well, I suppose we're both old enough to know better, but what would you think of the proposition? I've been pretty lucky this year as far as dough goes."

Anne sipped her cocktail, looking at him and laughing with her hair blowing across her face. "What do you want me to do, ask for a statement of your bankdeposit?"

"But I mean you."

"Check," she said.

Farrell was yelling at them, "How about a little game of penny ante before supper? . . . It's gettin' windy out here. We'd be better off in the saloon."

"Aye, aye, cap," said Anne.

Before supper they played penny ante and drank manhattans and after supper the Farrells and the Bledsoes settled down to a game of auction. Gladys said she had a headache and Charley, after watching the game for a while, went out on deck to get the reek of the cigar he'd been smoking out of his lungs.

The boat was anchored in a little bay, near a lighted wharf that jutted out from shore. A halfmoon was setting behind a rocky point where one tall pine reached out of a dark snarl of branches above a crowd of shivering whitebirches. At the end of the wharf there was some sort of clubhouse that spilt ripples of light from its big windows; dancemusic throbbed and faded from it over the water. Charley sat in the bow. The boys who ran the boat for Farrell had turned in. He could hear their low voices and catch a smell of cigarette-smoke from the tiny hatch forward of the pilothouse. He leaned over to watch the small gray waves slapping against the bow. "Bo, this is the bigtime stuff," he was telling himself.

When he turned around, there was Gladys beside him. "I thought you'd gone to bed, young lady," he said.

"Thought you'd gotten rid of me for one night?" She wasn't smiling.

"Don't you think it's a pretty night, Glad?"

He took her hand; it was trembling and icecold. "You don't want to catch cold, Glad," he said.

She dug her long nails into his hand. "Are you going to marry Anne?"

"Maybe. . . . Why? You're goin' to marry Harry, aren't you?"

"Nothing in this world would make me marry him."

310

Charley put his arms round her. "You poor little girl, you're cold. You ought to be in bed." She put her head on his chest and began to sob. He could feel the tears warm through his shirt. He didn't know what to say. He stood there hugging her with the smell of her hair giddy, like the smell of Doris's hair used to be, in his nostrils.

"I wish we were off this damn boat," he whispered. Her face was turned up to his, very round and white. When he kissed her lips, she kissed him too. He pressed her to him hard. Now it was her little breasts he could feel against his chest. For just a second she let him put his tongue between her lips, then she pushed him away.

"Charley, we oughtn't to be acting like this, but I suddenly felt so lonely."

Charley's voice was gruff in his throat. "I'll never let you feel like that again. . . . Never, honestly . . . never. . . ."

"Oh, you darling Charley." She kissed him again very quickly and deliberately and ran away from him down the deck.

311

He walked up and down alone. He didn't know what to do. He was crazy for Gladys now. He couldn't go back and talk to the others. He couldn't go to bed. He slipped down the forward hatch and through the galley, where Taki sat cool as a cucumber in his white coat reading some thick book, into the cabin where his berth was and changed into his bathingsuit and ran up and dove over the side. The water wasn't as cold as he'd expected. He swam around for a while in the moonlight. Pulling himself up the ladder aft, he felt cold and goosefleshy. Farrell with a cigar in his teeth leaned over, grabbed his hand and hauled him on deck.

"Ha, ha, the iron man," he shouted. "The girls beat us two rubbers and went to bed with their winnings. Suppose you get into your bathrobe and have a drink and half an hour of red dog or something silly before we turn in."

"Check," said Charley, who was jumping up and down on the deck to shake off the water.

While Charley was rubbing himself down with a towel below, he could hear the girls chattering and giggling in their stateroom. He was so embarrassed when he sat down next to Harry, who was a little drunk and silly that he drank off half a tumbler of rye and lost eighty dollars. He was glad to see that it was Harry who won. "Lucky at cards, unlucky in love," he kept saying to himself after he'd turned in.

A week later, Gladys took Charley to see her parents after they'd had tea together at his flat chaperoned by Taki's grin and his bobbing black head. Horton B. Wheatley was a power, so Farrell said, in the Security Trust Company, a red-faced man with grizzled hair and a small silvery mustache. Mrs. Wheatley was a droopy woman with a pretty Alabama voice and a face faded and pouchy and withered as a spent toyballoon.

Mr. Wheatley started talking before Gladys had finished the introductions: "Well, sir, we'd been expectin' somethin' like that to happen. Of course, it's too soon for us all to make up our minds, but I don't see how I kin help tellin' you, ma boy, that I'd rather see ma daughter wedded to a boy like you that's worked his way up in the world, even though we don't know much about you yet, than to a boy like Harry who's a nice enough kid in his way, but who's never done a thing in his life but take the schoolin' his father provided for him. Ma boy, we are mighty proud, my wife and me, to know you and to have you and our little girl . . . she's all we've got in this world, so she's mighty precious to us . . ."

"Your parents are . . . have been called away, I believe, Mr. Anderson," put in Mrs. Wheatley. Charley nodded. "Oh,

I'm so sorry. . . . They were from St. Paul, Gladys says . . ."

Mr. Wheatley was talking again. "Mr. Anderson, Mother, was one of our most prominent war aces; he won his spurs fightin' for the flag, Mother, an' his whole career seems to me to be an example . . . now I'm goin' to make you blush, ma boy . . . of how American democracy works at its very best pushin' forward to success the most intelligent and bestfitted and weedin' out the weaklin's. . . . Mr. Anderson, there's one thing I'm goin' to ask you to do right now. I'm goin' to ask you to come to church with us next Sunday an' address ma Sundayschool class. I'm sure you won't mind sayin' a few words of inspiration and guidance to the youngsters there."

Charley blushed and nodded. "Aw, Daddy," sang Gladys, putting her arms around both their necks, "don't make him do that. Sunday's the only day the poor boy gets any golf. . . . You know I always said I never would marry a Sundayschool teacher."

Mr. Wheatley laughed and Mrs. Wheatley cast down her eyes and sighed. "Once won't hurt him, will it, Charley?"

"Of course not," Charley found himself saying. "It would be an inspiration."

Next day Charley and Mr. Wheatley had lunch alone at the University Club. "Well, son, I guess the die is cast," said Mr. Wheatley when they met in the lobby. "The Wheatley women have made up their minds, there's nothin' for us to do but bow to the decision. I certainly wish you children every happiness, son. . . ." As they ate, Mr. Wheatley talked about the bank and the Tern interests and the merger with Askew-Merritt that would a little more than double the capitalization of the new Tern Aviation Company. "You're surprised that I know all about this, Charley . . . that's what I'd been thinkin', that boy's a mechanical genius, but he don't keep track of the financial end . . . he don't realize what his holdin's in that concern mean to him and the financial world."

"Well, I know some pretty good guys who give me the lowdown," said Charley.

"Fair enough, fair enough," said Mr. Wheatley, "but now that it's in the family maybe some of ma advice, the result of twenty years of bankin' experience at home in Birmingham and here in this great new dazzlin' city of Detroit . . ."

"Well, I sure will be glad to take it, Mr. Wheatley," stammered Charley.

Mr. Wheatley went on to talk about a lot on the waterfront with riparian rights at Grosse Pointe he was planning to turn over to the children for a weddingpresent and how they ought to build on it right away if only as an investment in the most restricted residential area in the entire United States of America. "And, son, if you come around to ma office after lunch, you'll see the plans for the prettiest little old English house to set on that lot you ever did see. I've been havin' 'em drawn up as a surprise for Mother and Gladys, by Ordway and Ordway. . . . Half-timbered Tudor they call it. I thought I'd turn the whole thing over to you children, as it'll be too big for Mother and me now that Gladys is gettin' married. I'll chip in the lot and you chip in the house and we'll settle the whole thing on Gladys for any children."

They finished their lunch. As they got up, Mr. Wheatley took Charley's hand and shook it. "And I sincerely hope and pray that there'll be children, son."

Just after Thanksgiving the society pages of all the Detroit papers were full of a dinnerdance given by Mr. and Mrs. Horton B. Wheatley to announce the approaching marriage of their daughter Gladys to Mr. Charles Anderson, inventor war ace and head of the research department at the great Tern Airplane Plant.

Old Bledsoe never spoke to Charley after the day the engagement was announced, but Anne came over to Charley and Gladys the night of the Halloween dance at the Country Club and said she thoroughly understood and wished them every happiness.

A few days before the wedding, Taki gave notice. "But I thought you would stay on. . . . I'm sure my wife would like it, too. Maybe we can give you a raise."

Taki grinned and bowed. "It is regrettable," he said, "that I experience only bachelor establishments . . . but I wish you hereafter every contentment."

What hurt Charley most was that when he wrote Joe Askew asking him to be his bestman, he wired back only one word: "No."

The wedding was at the Emmanuel Baptist Church. Charley wore a cutaway and new black shoes that pinched his toes. He kept trying to remember not to put his hand up to his tie. Nat Benton came on from New York to be bestman and was a great help. While they were waiting in the vestry, Nat pulled a flask out of his pants pocket and tried to get Charley to take a drink. "You look kinda green around the gills, Charley." Charley shook his head and made a gesture with his thumb in the direction from which the organ music was coming. "Are you sure you got the ring?" Nat grinned and took a drink himself. He cleared his throat. "Well, Charley, you ought to congratulate me for picking a winner. . . . If I could spot the market like I can spot a likely youngster, I'd be in the money right now."

Charley was so nervous he stammered. "Did . . . don't worry, Nat, I'll take care of you." They both laughed and felt better. An usher was already beckoning wildly at them from the vestry door.

Gladys in so many satinwhite frills and the lace veil and the orange-blossoms, with a little boy in white satin holding up her train, looked like somebody Charley had never seen before. They both said, "I will" rather loud without looking at each other. At the reception afterwards there was no liquor in the punch on account of the Wheatleys. Charley felt halfchoked with the smell of the flowers and of women's furs and with trying to say something to all the overdressed old ladies he was introduced to, who all said the same thing about what a beautiful wedding. He'd just broken away to go upstairs to change his clothes when he saw Ollie Taylor, very tight, trip on a Persian rug in the hall and measure his length at the feet of Mrs. Wheatley who'd just come out of the receptionroom looking very pale and weepy in lavender and orchids. Charley kept right on upstairs.

In spite of the wedding's being dry, Nat and Farrell had

certainly had something, because their eyes were shining and there was a moist look round their mouths when they came into the room where Charley was changing into a brown suit for traveling.

"Lucky bastards," he said. "Where did you get it? . . . Gosh, you might have kept Ollie Taylor out."

"He's gone," said Nat. They added in chorus, "We attend to everything."

"Gosh," said Charley, "I was just thinkin' it's a good thing I sent my brother in Minneapolis and his gang invitations too late for 'em to get here. I can just see my old Uncle Vogel runnin' around pinchin' the dowagers in the seat and cryin' hochheit."

"It's too bad about Ollie," said Nat. "He's one of the best-hearted fellers in the world."

"Poor old Ollie," echoed Charley. "He's lost his grip."

There was a knock on the door. It was Gladys, her little face pale and goldenhaired and wonderful-looking in the middle of an enormous chinchilla collar. "Charley, we've got to go. You naughty boy, I don't believe you've looked at the presents yet."

She led them into an upstairs sittingroom stacked with glassware and silver table articles and flowers and smokingsets and toiletsets and cocktailshakers until it looked like a department store. "Aren't they sweet?" she said.

"Never saw anythin' like it in my life," said Charley. They saw more guests coming in at the other end and ran out into the back hall again.

"How many detectives have they got?" asked Charley.

"Four," said Gladys.

"Well, now," said Charley, "we vamoose."

"Well, it's time for us to retire," chorused Farrell, and Nat suddenly doubled up laughing. "Or may we kiss the bride?"

"Check," said Charley. "Thank all the ushers for me."

Gladys fluttered her hand. "You are dears . . . go away now."

Charley tried to hug her to him, but she pushed him away. "Daddy's got all the bags out the kitchen door. . . . Oh, let's hurry. . . . Oh, I'm almost crazy."

They ran down the backstairs and got into a taxi with their baggage. His was pigskin; hers was shiny black. The bags had a new expensive smell. Charley saw Farrell and Nat come out from under the columns of the big colonial porch, but before they could throw the confetti the taxidriver had stepped on the gas and they were off.

At the depot there was nobody but the Wheatleys, Mrs. Wheatley crying in her baggy mink coat, Mr. Wheatley orating about the American home whether anybody listened or not. By the time the train pulled out, Gladys was crying too and Charley was sitting opposite her feeling miserable and not knowing how the hell to begin.

"I wish we'd flown."

"You know it wouldn't have been possible in this weather," said Gladys, and then burst out crying again.

To have something to do, Charley ordered some dinner from the diningcar and sent the colored porter to get a pail of ice for the champagne.

"Oh, my nerves," moaned Gladys, pressing her gloved hands over her eyes.

"After all, kid, it isn't as if it was somebody else. . . . It's just you and me," said Charley gently.

She began to titter. "Well, I guess I'm a little silly."

When the porter, grinning and respectfully sympathetic,

317

opened the champagne, she just wet her lips with it. Charlie drank off his glass and filled it up again. "Here's how, Glad, this is the life." When the porter had gone, Charley asked her why she wouldn't drink. "You used to be quite a rummy out at the countryclub, Glad."

"I don't want you to drink either."

"Why?"

She turned very red. "Mother says that if the parents get drunk, they have idiot children."

"Oh, you poor baby," said Charley, his eyes filling with tears. They sat for a long time looking at each other while the fizz went out of the champagne in the glasses and the champagne slopped out onto the table with the jolting of the train. When the broiled chicken came, Gladys couldn't eat a bite of it. Charley ate both portions and drank up the champagne and felt he was acting like a hog.

The train clanked and roared in their ears through the snowy night. After the porter had taken away the supper-dishes, Charley took off his coat and sat beside her and tried to make love to her. She'd only let him kiss her and hug her like they'd done before they were married. When he tried to undo her dress, she pushed him away. "Wait, wait."

She went into the lavatory to get into her nightdress. He thought he'd go crazy she took so long. He sat in his pajamas in the icy gritty flaw of wind that came in through the crack of the window until his teeth were chattering. At last he started to bang on the door of the toilet. "Anything wrong, Glad? What's the matter, darlin'?"

She came out in a fluffy lace négligée. She'd put on too much makeup. Her lips were trembling under the greasy lipstick. "Oh, Charley, don't let's tonight on the train, it's so awful like this."

Charley felt suddenly uncontrollably angry. "But you're my wife. I'm your husband, goddam it." He switched off the light. Her hands were icy in his. As he grabbed her to him, he felt the muscles of his arms swelling strong behind her slender back. It felt good the way the lace and silk tore under his hands.

Afterwards she made him get out of bed and lie on the couch wrapped in a blanket. She bled a great deal. Neither of them slept. Next day she looked so pale and the bleeding hadn't stopped and they were afraid they'd have to stop somewhere to get a doctor. By evening she felt better, but still she couldn't eat anything. All afternoon she lay halfasleep on the couch while Charley sat beside her holding her hand with a pile of unread magazines on his knees.

It was like getting out of jail when they got off the train at Palm Beach and saw the green grass and the palmtrees and the hedges of hibiscus in flower. When she saw the big rooms of their corner suite at the Royal Poinciana, where she'd wanted to go because that was where her father and mother had gone on their weddingtrip, and the flowers friends had sent that filled up the parlor, Gladys threw her arms around his neck and kissed him even before the last bellboy had got out of the room. "Oh, Charley, forgive me for being so horrid." Next morning they lay happy in bed side by side after they'd had their breakfast and looked out of the window at the sea beyond the palmtrees, and smelt the freshness of the surf and listened to it pounding along the beach. "Oh, Charley," Gladys said, "let's have everything always just like this."

Their first child was born in December. It was a boy. They named him Wheatley. When Gladys came back from the hospital, instead of coming back to the apartment she went into the new house out at Grosse Pointe that still smelt of paint and raw plaster. What with the hospital expenses and the furniture bills and Christmas, Charley had to borrow twenty thousand from the bank. He spent more time than ever talking over the phone to Nat Benton's office in New York. Gladys bought a lot of new clothes and kept tiffanyglass bowls full of freezias and narcissus all over the house. Even on the dressingtable in her bathroom she always had flowers. Mrs. Wheatley said she got her love of flowers from her grandmother Randolph, because the Wheatleys had never been able to tell one flower from another. When the next child turned out to be a girl, Gladys said, as she lay in the hospital, her face looking drawn and yellow against the white pillows, beside the great bunch of glittering white orchids Charley had ordered from the florist at five dollars a bloom, she wished she could name her Orchid. They ended by naming her Marguerite after Gladys's grandmother Randolph.

Gladys didn't recover very well after the little girl's birth and had to have several small operations that kept her in bed three months. When she got on her feet, she had the big room next to the nursery and the children's nurse's room redecorated in white and gold for her own bedroom. Charley groused about it a good deal because it was in the other wing of the house from his room. When he'd come over in his bathrobe before turning in and try to get into bed with her, she would keep him off with a cool smile, and when he insisted, she would give him a few pecking kisses and tell him not to make a noise or he would wake the babies. Sometimes tears of irritation would start into his eyes. "Jesus, Glad, don't you love me at all?" She would answer that if he really loved her he'd have come home the night she had the Smyth Perkinses to dinner instead of phoning at the last minute that he'd have to stay at the office.

"But, Jesus, Glad, if I didn't make the money how would I pay the bills?"

"If you loved me you'd be more considerate, that's all," she would say, and two curving lines would come on her face from her nostrils to the corners of her mouth like the lines on her mother's face and Charley would kiss her gently and say poor little girl and go back to his room feeling like a louse. Times she did let him stay she lay so cold and still and talked about how he hurt her, so that he would go back to the tester bed in his big bedroom feeling so nervous and jumpy it would take several stiff whiskies to get him in shape to go to sleep.

One night when he'd taken Bill Cermak, who was now a foreman at the Flint plant, over to a roadhouse the other side of Windsor to talk to him about the trouble they were having with molders and diemakers, after they'd had a couple of whiskies, Charley found himself instead asking Bill about married life. "Say, Bill, do you ever have trouble with your wife?"

"Sure, boss," said Bill, laughing. "I got plenty trouble. But the old lady's all right, you know her, nice kids good cook, all time want me to go to church."

"Say, Bill, when did you get the idea of callin' me boss? Cut it out."

"Too goddam rich," said Bill.

"Hell, have another whiskey." Charley drank his down. "And beer chasers like in the old days. . . . Remember that Christmas party out in Long Island City and that blonde at the beerparlor. . . . Jesus, I used to think I was a little devil with the women. . . . But my wife she don't seem to get the idea."

"You have two nice kids already; what the hell, maybe you're too ambitious."

"You wouldn't believe it . . . only once since little Peaches was born."

"Most women gets hotter when they're married awhile. . . . That's why the boys are sore at your damned efficiency expert."

"Stauch? Stauch's a genius at production."

"Maybe, but he don't give the boys any chance for reproduction." Bill laughed and wiped the beer off his mouth.

"Good old Bill," said Charley. "By god, I'll get you on the board of directors yet."

Bill wasn't laughing any more. "Honestly, no kiddin'. That damn squarehead make the boys work so hard they can't get a hardon when they go to bed, an' their wives raise hell with 'em. I'm strawboss and they all think sonofabitch too, but they're right."

Charley was laughing. "You're a squarehead yourself, Bill, and I don't know what I can do about it, I'm just an employee of the company myself. . . . We got to have efficient production or they'll wipe us out of business. Ford's buildin' planes now."

"You'll lose all your best guys. . . . Slavedrivin' may be all right in the automobile business, but buildin' an airplane motor's skilled labor."

"Aw, Christ, I wish I was still tinkerin' with that damn motor and didn't have to worry about money all the time. . . . Bill, I'm broke. . . . Let's have another whiskey."

"Better eat."

"Sure, order up a steak . . . anythin' you like. Let's go take a piss. That's one thing they don't charge for. . . . Say, Bill, does it seem to you that I'm gettin' a potbelly? . . . Broke, a potbelly, an' my wife won't sleep with me. . . . Do you think I'm a rummy, Bill. I sometimes think I better lay off for keeps. I never used to pull a blank when I drank."

"Hell, no, you smart young feller, one of the smartest, a fool for a threepoint landing and a pokerplayer . . . my God."

"What's the use if your wife won't sleep with you?"

Charley wouldn't eat anything. Bill ate up both their

321

steaks. Charley kept on drinking whiskey out of a bottle he had under the table and beer for chasers. "But tell me . . . your wife, does she let you have it anytime you want it? . . . The guys in the shop, their wives won't let 'em alone, eh?"

Bill was a little drunk too. "My wife she do what I say."

It ended by Bill's having to drive Charley's new Packard back to the ferry. In Detroit, Bill made Charley drink a lot of sodawater in a drugstore, but when he got back in the car he just slumped down at the wheel. He let Bill drive him home to Grosse Pointe. Charley could hear Bill arguing with the guards along the road, each one really had to see Mr. Anderson passed out in the back of the car before he'd let Bill through, but he didn't give a hoot, struck him so funny he began to giggle. The big joke was when the houseman had to help Bill get him up to his bedroom. "The boss a little sick, see, overwork," Bill said each time, then he'd tap his head solemnly. "Too much brainwork."

Charley came to up in his bedroom and was able to articulate muzzily: "Bill, you're a prince. . . . George, call a taxi to take Mr. Cermak home . . . lucky bastard go home to his wife." Then he stretched out on the bed with one shoe on and one shoe off and went quietly to sleep.

When he came back from his next trip to New York and Washington, he called up Bill at the plant. "Hey, Bill, how's the boy? Your wife still do what you say, ha ha? Me, I'm terrible, very exhaustin' business trip, understand . . . never drank so much in my life or with so many goddam crooks. Say, Bill, don't worry if you get fired, you're on my private payroll, understand. . . . We're goin' to fire the whole outfit. . . . Hell, if they don't like it workin' for us, let 'em try to like it workin' for somebody else. . . . This is a free country. I wouldn't want to keep a man against his will. . . . Look, how long will it take you to tune up that little Moth type, you know, number 16 . . . yours truly's Mosquito? . . . Check. . . . Well, if we can get her in shape soon enough so they can use her as a model, see, for their specifications . . . Jesus, Bill, if we can do that . . . we're on easystreet . . . You won't have to worry about if the kids can go to college or not . . . goddam it, you an' the missis can go to college yourselves. . . . Check."

Charley put the receiver back on the desk. His secretary, Miss Finnegan, was standing in the door. She had red hair and a beautiful complexion with a few freckles round her little sharp nose. She was a snappy dresser. She was looking at Charley with her lightbrown eyes all moist and wide as he was laying down the law over the phone. Charley felt his chest puff out a little. He pulled in his belly as hard as he could. "Gosh," he was saying at the back of his head, "maybe I could lay Elsie Finnegan." Somebody had put a pot of blue hyacinths on his desk: a smell of spring came from them that all at once made him remember Bar-le-Duc, and troutfishing up the Red River.

It was a flowerysmelling spring morning again when Charley drove out to the plant from the office to give the Anderson Mosquito its trial spin. He had managed to give Elsie Finnegan a kiss for the first time and had left her crumpled and trembling at her desk. Bill Cermak had said over the phone that the tiny ship was tuned up and in fine shape. It was a relief to get out of the office where he'd been fidgeting for a couple of hours trying to get through a call to Nat Benton's office about some stock he'd wired them to take a profit on. After he'd kissed her, he'd told Elsie Finnegan to switch the call out to the trial field for him. It made him feel good to be driving out through the half-built town, through the avenue jammed with trucks full of construction materials, jockeying his car among the trucks with a feeling of shine and strength at the perfect action of his clutch and the smooth response of the gears. The gatekeeper had the New York call for him. The connection was perfect. Nat had banked thirteen grand for him. As he hung up the receiver, he thought, Poor little Elsie, he'd have to buy her something real nice. "It's a great day, Joe, ain't it?" he said to the gatekeeper.

Bill was waiting for him beside the new ship at the entrance to the hangar, wiping grease off his thick fingers with a bunch of waste.

Charley slapped him on the back. "Good old Bill, . . . isn't this a great day for the race?" Bill fell for it. "What race, boss?"

"The human race, you fathead. . . . Say, Bill," he went on as he took off his gloves and his welltailored spring overcoat, "I don't mind tellin' you I feel wonderful today . . . made thirteen grand on the market yesterday . . . easy as rollin' off a log."

While Charley pulled a suit of overalls on, the mechanics pushed the new ship out onto the grass for Bill to make his general inspection. "Jesus, she's pretty." The tiny aluminum ship glistened in the sun out on the green grass like something in a jeweler's window. There were dandelions and clover on the grass and a swirling flight of little white butterflies went up right from under his black clodhoppers when Bill came back to Charley and stood beside him.

Charley winked at Bill Cermak standing beside him in his

blue denims stolidly looking at his feet. "Smile, you sonofabitch," he said. "Don't this weather make you feel good?"

Bill turned a square bohunk face toward Charley. "Now look here, Mr. Anderson, you always treat me good . . . from way back Long Island days. You know me, do work, go home, keep my face shut."

"What's on your mind, Bill? . . . Want me to try to wangle another raise for you? Check."

Bill shook his heavy square face and rubbed his nose with a black forefinger. "Tern Company used to be good place to work—good work, good pay. You know me, Mr. Anderson, I'm no bolshayvik . . . but no stoolpigeon either."

"But damn it, Bill, why can't you tell those guys to have a little patience . . . we're workin' out a profitsharin' scheme. I've worked on a lathe myself. . . . I've worked as a mechanic all over this goddam country. . . . I know what the boys are up against, but I know what the management's up against too. . . . Gosh, this thing's in its infancy; we're pouring more capital into the business all the time. . . . We've got a responsibility toward our investors. Where do you think that jack I made yesterday's goin' but the business of course? The oldtime shop was a great thing, everybody kidded and smoked and told smutty stories, but the pressure's too great now. If every department don't click like a machine, we're rooked. If the boys want a union, we'll give 'em a union. You get up a meeting and tell 'em how we feel about it, but tell 'em we've got to have some patriotism. Tell 'em the industry's the first line of national defense. We'll send Eddy Sawyer down to talk to 'em . . . make 'em understand our problems."

Bill Cermak shook his head. "Plenty other guys do that."

Charley frowned. "Well, let's see how she goes," he snapped impatiently. "Gosh, she's a honey."

The roar of the motor kept them from saying any more. The mechanic stepped from the controls and Charley climbed in. Bill Cermak got in behind. She started taxiing fast across the green field. Charley turned her into the wind and let her have the gas. At the first soaring bounce there was a jerk. As he pitched forward, Charley switched off the ignition.

They were carrying him across the field on a stretcher. Each step of the men carrying the stretcher made two jagged things grind together in his leg. He tried to tell 'em that he had a piece of something in his side, but his voice was very small and hoarse. In the shadow of the hangar he was trying to raise himself on his elbow. "What the devil happened? Is Bill all right?" The men shook their heads. Then he passed out again like the juice failing in a car.

In the ambulance he tried to ask the man in the white jacket about Bill Cermak and to remember back exactly what had happened, but the leg kept him too busy trying not to yell. "Hey, doc," he managed to croak, "can't you get these aluminum splinters out of my side?" The damn ship must have turned turtle on them. Wings couldn't take it, maybe, but it's time they got the motor lifted off me. "Hey, doc, why can't they get a move on?"

When he got the first whiff of the hospital, there were a lot of men in white jackets moving and whispering round him. The hospital smelt strong of ether. The trouble was he couldn't breathe. Somebody must have spilt that damned ether. No, not on my face. The motor roared. He must have been seeing things. The motor's roar swung into an easy singsong. Sure, she was taking it fine, steady as one of those big old bombers. When he woke up, a nurse was helping him puke into a bowl.

When he woke up again, for chrissake no more ether, no, it was flowers, and Gladys was standing beside the bed with a big bunch of sweetpeas in her hand. Her face had a pinched look.

"Hello, Glad, how's the girl?"

"Oh, I've been so worried, Charley. How do you feel? Oh, Charley, for a man of your standing to risk his life in practice flights . . . Why don't you let the people whose business it is do it, I declare."

There was something Charley wanted to ask. He was scared about something. "Say, are the kids all right?"

"Wheatley skinned his knee and I'm afraid the baby has a little temperature. I've phoned Doctor Thompson. I don't think it's anything, though."

"Is Bill Cermak all right?"

Gladys's mouth trembled. "Oh, yes," she said, cutting the words off sharply. "Well, I suppose this means our dinner-dance is off. . . . The Edsel Fords were coming."

"Hell, no, why not have it, anyway? Yours truly can attend in a wheelchair. Say, they sure have got me in a straitjacket. . . . I guess I busted some ribs."

Gladys nodded; her mouth was getting very small and thin. Then she suddenly began to cry.

The nurse came in and said reproachfully, "Oh, Mrs. Anderson."

Charley was just as glad when Gladys went out and left him alone with the nurse. "Say, nurse, get hold of the doctor, will you? Tell him I'm feeling fine and want to look over the extent of the damage."

"Mr. Anderson, you mustn't have anything on your mind."

"I know, tell Mrs. Anderson I want her to get in touch with the office."

"But it's Sunday, Mr. Anderson. A great many people have been downstairs, but I don't think the doctor is letting them up yet." The nurse was a freshfaced girl with a slightly Scotch way of talking.

"I bet you're a Canadian," said Charley.

"Right, that time," said the nurse.

"I knew a wonderful nurse who was a Canadian once. If I'd had any sense, I'd have married her."

The housephysician was a roundfaced man with a jovial smooth manner almost like a headwaiter at a big hotel.

"Say, doc, ought my leg to hurt so damn much?"

"You see we haven't set it yet. You tried to puncture a lung, but didn't quite get away with it. We had to remove a few little splinters of rib."

"Not from the lung . . ."

"Luckily not."

"But why the hell didn't you set the leg at the same time?"

"Well, we're waiting for Doctor Roberts to come on from New York. . . . Mrs. Anderson insisted on him. Of course, we are all very pleased as he's one of the most eminent men in his profession. . . . It'll be another little operation."

It wasn't until he'd come to from the second operation that they told him that Bill Cermak had died of a fractured skull.

Charley was in the hospital three months with his leg in a Balkan frame. The fractured ribs healed up fast, but he kept on having trouble with his breathing. Gladys handled all the house bills and came every afternoon for a minute. She was always in a hurry and always terribly worried. He had to turn over a power of attorney to Moe Frank, his lawyer, who used to come to see him a couple of times a week to talk things over. Charley couldn't say much, he couldn't say much to anybody he was in so much pain.

He liked it best when Gladys sent Wheatley to see him. Wheatley was three years old now and thought it was great in the hospital. He liked to see the nurse working all the little weights and pulleys of the frame the leg hung in. "Daddy's living in a airplane," was what he always said about it. He had tow hair and his nose was beginning to stick up and Charley thought he took after him.

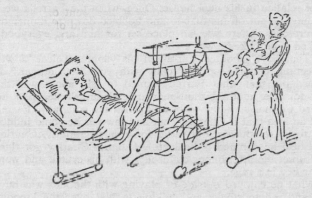

Marguerite was still too little to be much fun. The one time Gladys had the governess bring her, she bawled so at the look of the scarylooking frame she had to be taken home. Gladys wouldn't let her come again. Gladys and Charley had a bitter row about letting Wheatley come, as she said she didn't want the child to remember his father in the hospital.

"But, Glad, he'll have plenty of time to get over it, get over it a damn sight sooner than I will."

Gladys pursed her lips together and said nothing. When she'd gone, Charley lay there hating her and wondering how they could ever have had children together.

Just about the time he began to see clearly that they all expected him to be a cripple the rest of his life, he began to mend, but it was winter before he was able to go home on crutches. He still suffered sometimes from a sort of nervous difficulty in breathing. The house seemed strange as he

327

dragged himself around in it. Gladys had had every room re-decorated while he was away and all the servants were different. Charley didn't feel it was his house at all. What he enjoyed best was the massage he had three times a week. He spent his days playing with the kids and talking to Miss Jarvis, their stiff and elderly English governess. After they'd go to bed, he'd sit in his sittingroom drinking Scotch-and-soda and feeling puffy and nervous. Goddam it, he was getting too fat. Gladys was always cool as a cucumber these days; even when he went into fits of temper and cursed at her, she'd stand there looking at him with a cold look of disgust on her carefully madeup face. She entertained a great deal, but made the servants understand that Mr. Anderson wasn't well enough to come down. He began to feel like a poor relation in his own house. Once, when the Farrells were coming, he put on his tuxedo and hobbled down to dinner on his crutches. There was no place set for him and everybody looked at him like he was a ghost.

"Thataboy!" shouted Farrell in his yapping voice. "I was expecting to come up and chin with you after dinner." It turned out that what Farrell wanted to talk about was the suit for five hundred thousand some damn shyster had induced Cermak's widow to bring against the company. Farrell had an idea that if Charley went and saw her he could induce her to be reasonable and settle for a small annuity. Charley said he'd be damned if he'd go. At dinner Charley got tight and upset the afterdinner coffeecups with his crutch and went off to bed in a rage.

What he enjoyed outside of playing with the kids was buying and selling stocks and talking to Nat over the longdistance. Nat kept telling him he was getting the feel of the market. Nat warned him and Charley knew damn well that he was slipping at Tern and that if he didn't do something he'd be frozen out, but he felt too rotten to go to directors' meetings; what he did do was to sell out about half his stocks in small parcels. Nat kept telling him if he'd only get a move on, he could get control of the whole business before Andy Merritt pulled off his new reorganization, but he felt too damn nervous and miserable to make the effort. All he could seem to do was to grumble and call Julius Stauch and raise hell about details. Stauch had taken over his work on the new monoplane and turned out a little ship that had gone through all tests with flying colors. When he'd put down the receiver, Charley would pour himself a little Scotch and settle back on the couch in his window and mutter to himself, "Well, you're dished this time."

One evening Farrell came around and had a long talk and

said what Charley needed was a fishing trip; he'd never get well if he kept on this way. He said he'd been talking to Doc Thompson and that he recommended three months off and plenty of exercise if he ever expected to throw away his crutches.

Gladys couldn't go because old Mrs. Wheatley was sick, so Charley got into the back of his Lincoln towncar alone with the chauffeur to drive him, and a lot of blankets to keep him warm, and a flask of whiskey and a thermosbottle of hot coffee, to go down all alone to Miami.

At Cincinnati he felt so bum he spent a whole day in bed in the hotel there. He got the chauffeur to get him booklets about Florida from a travel agency, and finally sent a wire to Nat Benton asking him to spend a week with him down at the Key Largo fishingcamp. Next morning he started off again early. He'd had a good night's sleep and he felt better and began to enjoy the trip. But he felt a damn fool sitting there being driven like an old woman all bundled up in rugs.

He was lonely, too, because the chauffeur wasn't the kind of bird you could talk to. He was a sourlooking Canuck Gladys had hired because she thought it was classy to give her orders in French through the speakingtube; Charley was sure the bastard gypped him on the price of gas and oil and repairs along the road; that damn Lincoln was turning out a bottomless pit for gas and oil.

In Jacksonville the sun was shining. Charley gave himself the satisfaction of firing the chauffeur as soon as they'd driven up to the door of the hotel. Then he went to bed with a pint of bum corn the bellboy sold him and slept like a log.

In the morning he woke up late feeling thirsty but cheerful. After breakfast he checked out of the hotel and drove around the town a little. It made him feel good to pack his own bag and get into the front seat and drive his own car.

The town had a cheerful rattletrap look in the sunlight

under the big white clouds and the blue sky. At the lunchroom next to the busstation he stopped to have a drink. He felt so good that he got out of the car without his crutches and hobbled across the warm pavement. The wind was fluttering the leaves of the magazines and the pink and palegreen sheets of the papers outside the lunchroom window. Charley was out of breath from the effort when he slid onto a stool at the counter. "Give me a limeade and no sweetnin' in it, please," he said to the ratfaced boy at the fountain.

The sodajerker didn't pay any attention, he was looking down the other way. Charley felt his face get red. His first idea was, I'll get him fired. Then he looked where the boy was looking. There was a blonde eating a sandwich at the other end of the counter. She certainly was pretty. She wore a little black hat and a neat bluegray suit and a little white lace around her neck and at her wrists. She had an amazed look on her face like she'd just heard something extraordinarily funny. Forgetting to favor his game leg Charley slipped up several seats toward her.

"Say, bo, how about that limeade?" he shouted cheerfully at the sodajerker.

The girl was looking at Charley. Her eyes really were a perfectly pure blue. She was speaking to him. "Maybe you know how long the bus takes to Miami, Mister. This boy thinks he's a wit, so I can't get any data."

"Suppose we try it out and see," said Charley.

"They surely come funny in Florida. . . . Another humorist."

"No, I mean it. If you let me drive you down, you'll be doing a sick man a great favor."

"Sure it won't mean a fate worse than death?"

"You'll be perfectly safe with me, young lady. I'm almost a cripple. I'll show you my crutches in the car."

"What's the trouble?"

"Cracked up in a plane."

"You a pilot?"

Charlie nodded.

"Not quite skinny enough for Lindbergh," she said, looking him up and down.

Charley turned red. "I am a little overweight. It's being cooped up with this lousy leg."

"Well, I guess I'll try it. If I step into your car and wake up in Buenos Aires, it'll be my bad luck."

Charley tried to pay for her coffee and sandwich, but she wouldn't let him. Something about her manner kept him laughing all the time.

When he got up and she saw how he limped, she pursed

330

her mouth up. "Gee, that's too bad." When she saw the car, she stopped in her tracks. "Zowie," she said, "we're bloomin' millionaires."

They were laughing as they got into the car. There was something about the way she said things that made him laugh. She wouldn't say what her name was. "Call me Madame X," she said.

"Then you'll have to call me Mr. A," said Charley.

They laughed and giggled all the way to Daytona Beach where they stopped off and went into the surf for a dip. Charley felt ashamed of his pot and his pale skin and his limp as he walked across the beach with her looking brown and trim in her blue bathingsuit. She had a pretty figure, although her hips were a little big.

331

"Anyway, it's not as if I'd come out of it with one leg shorter than the other. The doc says I'll be absolutely O.K. if I exercise it right."

"Sure, you'll be great in no time. And me thinkin' you was an elderly sugardaddy in the drugstore there."

"I think you're a humdinger, Madame X."

"Be sure you don't put anything in writing, Mr. A."

Charley's leg ached like blazes when he came out of the water, but it didn't keep him from having a whale of a good appetite for the first time in months. After a big fishdinner they started off again. She went to sleep in the car with her neat little head on his shoulder. He felt very happy driving down the straight smooth concrete highway, although he felt tired already. When they got into Miami that night, she made him take her to a small hotel back near the railroad tracks and wouldn't let him come in with her. "But gosh, couldn't we see each other again?"

"Sure, you can see me any night at the Palms. I'm an entertainer there."

"Honest . . . I knew you were an entertainer, but I didn't know you were a professional."

"You sure did me a good turn, Mr. A. Now it can be told . . . I was flat broke with exactly the price of that ham sandwich and if you hadn't brought me down I'd a lost the chance of working here. . . . I'll tell you about it sometime."

"Tell me your name. I'd like to call you up."

"You tell me yours."

"Charles Anderson. I'll be staying bored to death at the Miami-Biltmore."

"So you really are Mr. A. . . . Well, goodbye, Mr. A, and thanks a million times." She ran into the hotel.

Charley was crazy about her already. He was so tired he just barely made his hotel. He went up to his room and tumbled into bed and for the first time in months went to sleep without getting drunk first.

A week later, when Nat Benton turned up, he was surprised to find Charley in such good shape. "Nothin' like a change," said Charley, laughing. They drove on down toward the Keys together. Charley had Margo Dowling's photograph in his pocket, a professional photograph of her dressed in Spanish costume for her act. He'd been to the Palms every night, but he hadn't managed to get her to go out with him yet. When he'd suggest anything, she'd shake her head and make a face and say, "I'll tell you all about it sometime." But the last night she had given him a number where he could call her up.

Nat kept trying to talk about the market and the big reorganization of Tern and Askew-Merritt that Merritt was engineering, but Charley would shut him up with, "Aw, hell, let's talk about somethin' else."

The camp was all right, but the mosquitoes were fierce. They spent a good day on the reef fishing for barracuda and grouper. They took a jug of bacardi out in the motorboat and fished and drank and ate sandwiches. Charley told Nat all about the crackup. "Honestly, I don't think it was my fault. It was one of those damn things you can't help. . . . Now I feel as if I'd lost the last friend I had on earth. Honest, I'd a given anythin' I had in the world if that hadn't happened to Bill."

"After all," said Nat, "he was only a mechanic."

One day when they got in from fishing, drunk and with their hands and pants fishy, and their faces burned by the sun and glare, and dizzy from the sound and smell of the motor and the choppy motion of the boat, they found waiting for them a wire from Benton's office.

UNKNOWN UNLOADING TERN STOP DROPS FOUR AND
A HALF POINTS STOP WIRE INSTRUCTIONS

"Instructions hell," said Benton, jamming his stuff into his suitcase. "We'll go up and see. Suppose we charter a plane at Miami."

"You take the plane," said Charley coolly. "I'm going to ride on the train."

In New York he sat all day in the back room of Nat Benton's office smoking too many cigars, watching the ticker, fretting and fuming, riding up and down town in taxicabs, getting the lowdown from various sallow-faced friends of Nat's and Moe Frank's. By the end of the week he'd lost four hundred thousand dollars and had let go every airplane stock he had in the world.

All the time he was sitting there putting on a big show of business he was counting the minutes, the way he had when he was a kid in school, for the market to close so that he could go uptown to a speakeasy on Fiftysecond Street to meet a hennahaired girl named Sally Hogan he'd met when he was out with Nat at the Club Dover. She was the first girl he'd picked up when he got to New York. He didn't give a damn about her, but he had to have some kind of a girl. They were registered at the hotel as Mr. and Mrs. Smith.

One morning when they were having breakfast in bed there was a light knock on the door. "Come in," yelled Charley, thinking it was the waiter. Two shabbylooking men rushed into the room, followed by O'Higgins, a shyster lawyer he'd met a couple of times back in Detroit. Sally let out a shriek and covered her head with the pillow.

"Howdy, Charley," said O'Higgins. "I'm sorry to do this, but it's all in the line of duty. You don't deny that you are Charles Anderson, do you? Well, I thought you'd rather hear it from me than just read the legal terms. Mrs. Anderson is suing you for divorce in Michigan. . . . That's all right, boys."

The shabby men bowed meekly and backed out the door. "Of all the lousy stinkin' tricks . . ."

"Mrs. Anderson's had the detectives on your trail ever since you fired her chauffeur in Jacksonville."

Charley had such a splitting headache and felt so weak from a hangover that he couldn't lift his head. He wanted to get up and sock that sonofabitch O'Higgins, but all he could do was lie there and take it. "But she never said anything about it in her letters. She'd been writin' me right along. There's never been any trouble between us."

O'Higgins shook his curly head. "Too bad," he said.

335

"Maybe if you can see her you can arrange it between you. You know my advice about these things is always keep 'em out of court. Well, I'm heartily sorry, old boy, to have caused you and your charming friend any embarrassment . . . no hard feelings I hope, Charley, old man. . . . I thought it would be pleasanter, more open and aboveboard, if I came along, if you saw a friendly face, as you might say. I'm sure this can all be amicably settled." He stood there awhile rubbing his hands and nodding and then tiptoed to the door. Standing there with one hand on the doorknob he waved the other big flipper toward the bed. "Well, so long, Sally. . . . Guess I'll be seein' you down at the office."

Then he closed the door softly after him. Sally had jumped out of bed and was running toward the door with a terrified look on her face. Charley began to laugh in spite of his splitting headache. "Aw, never mind, girlie," he said. "Serves me right for bein' a sucker. . . . I know we all got our livin's to make. . . . Come on back to bed."

Newsreel LX

Was Céline to blame? To young Scotty marriage seemed just a lark, a wild time in good standing. But when she began to demand money and the extravagant things he couldn't afford, did Céline meet him halfway? Or did she blind herself to the very meaning of the sacred word: wife?

CROOK FROZEN OUT OF SHARE IN BONDS TELLS MURDER PLOT

TO REPEAL DECISION ON CASTIRON PIPE

In a little Spanish town
'Twas on a night like this

speculative sentiment was encouraged at the opening of the week by the clearer outlook. Favorable weather was doing much to eliminate the signs of hesitation lately evinced by several trades

I'm in love again
And the Spring
Is comin'
I'm in love again
Hear my heart strings
Strummin'

ITCHING GONE IN ONE NIGHT

thousands of prosperous happy women began to earn double and treble their former wages and sometimes even more immediately

Yes sir that's my baby
That's my baby na-ow!

APE TRIAL GOAT TO CONFER WITH ATTORNEYS

MYSTERIOUS MR. Y TO TESTIFY

an exquisite replica in miniature of a sunlit French country home on the banks of the Rhone boldly built on the crest of Sunset Ridge overlooking the most beautiful lakeland in New Jersey where every window frames a picture of surprising beauty

And the tune I'm hummin'
I'll not go roamin' like a kid again
I'll stay home and be a kid again

NEIGHBORS ENJOIN NOCTURNAL SHOUTS IN
TURKISH BATH

ALL CITY POLICE TURN OUT IN BANDIT HUNT

CONGOLEUM BREAK FEATURES OPENING

for the sixth week freightcar loadings have passed the million mark in this country, indicating that prosperity is general and that records are being established and broken everywhere

Good-bye east and good-bye west
Good-bye north and all the rest
Hello Swan-ee Hello

Margo Dowling

When Margo got back to the city after her spring in Miami, everybody cried out how handsome she looked with her tan and her blue eyes and her hair bleached out light by the Florida sun. But she sure found her work cut out for her. The Mandevilles were in a bad way. Frank had spent three months in the hospital and had had one kidney removed in an operation. When he got home he was still so sick that Agnes gave up her position to stay home and nurse him; she and Frank had taken up Science and wouldn't have the doctor any more. They talked all the time about having proper thoughts and about how Frank's life had been saved by Miss Jenkins, a practitioner Agnes had met at her tearoom. They owed five hundred dollars in doctor's bills and hospital expenses, and talked about God all the time. It was lucky that Mr. Anderson the new boyfriend was a very rich man.

Mr. A, as she called him, kept offering to set Margo up in an apartment on Park Avenue, but she always said nothing doing, what did he think she was, a kept woman? She did let him play the stockmarket a little for her, and buy her clothes and jewelry and take her to Atlantic City and Long Beach weekends. He'd been an airplane pilot and decorated in the war and had big investments in airplane companies. He drank more than was good for him; he was a beefy florid guy who looked older than he was, a big talker, and hard to handle when he'd been drinking, but he was openhanded and liked laughing and jokes when he was feeling good. Margo thought that he was a pretty good egg.

"Anyway, what can you do when a guy picks up a telephone and turns over a thousand dollars for you?" was what she'd tell Agnes when she wanted to tease her.

"Margie, dear, you mustn't talk like that," Agnes would say. "It sounds so mercenary."

Agnes talked an awful lot about Love and right thoughts and being true and good these days. Margo liked better to hear Mr. Anderson blowing about his killings on the stockmarket and the planes he'd designed, and how he was going to organize a net of airways that would make the Pennsylvania Railroad look like a suburban busline.

Evening after evening she'd have to sit with him in speakeasies in the Fifties drinking whiskey and listening to him talk about this business and that and big deals in stocks down on the Street, and about how he was out to get that Detroit crowd that was trying to ease him out of Standard Airparts and about his divorce and how much it was costing him. One night at the Stork Club, when he was showing her pictures of his kids, he broke down and started to blubber. The court had just awarded the custody of the children to his wife.

Mr. A had his troubles all right. One of the worst was a readheaded girl he'd been caught with in a hotel by his wife's detectives who was all the time blackmailing him, and threatening to sue for breach of promise and give the whole story to the Hearst papers.

"Oh, how awful," Agnes would keep saying, when Margo would tell her about it over a cup of coffee at noon. "If he only had the right thoughts. . . . You must talk to him and make him try and see. . . . If he only understood I know everything would be different. . . . A successful man like that should be full of right thoughts."

"Full of Canadian Club, that's what's the matter with him. . . . You ought to see the trouble I have getting him home nights." "You're the only friend he has," Agnes would say, rolling up her eyes. "I think it's noble of you to stick by him."

Margo was paying all the back bills up at the apartment and had started a small account at the Bowery Savings Bank, just to be on the safe side. She felt she was getting the hang of the stockmarket a little. Still it made her feel trashy not working and it gave her the creeps sitting around in the apartment summer afternoons while Agnes read Frank *Science and Health* in a singsong voice, so she started going around the dress shops to see if she could get herself a job as a model.

"I want to learn some more about clothes . . . mine always look like they were made of old floursacks," she explained to Agnes.

"Are you sure Mr. Anderson won't mind?"

"If he don't like it he can lump it," said Margo, tossing her head.

In the fall they finally took her on at Piquot's new French gownshop on Fiftyseventh Street. It was tiresome work, but it left her evenings free. She confided to Agnes that if she ever let Mr. A out of her sight in the evening some little floosey or other would get hold of him sure as fate.

Agnes was delighted that Margo was out of the show business. "I never felt it was right for you to do that sort of thing and now I feel you can be a real power for good with poor Mr. Anderson," Agnes said. Whenever Margo told them about a new plunger he had taken on the market, Agnes and Frank would hold the thought for Mr. Anderson.

Jules Piquot was a middleaged roundfaced Frenchman with a funny waddle like a duck who thought all the girls were crazy about him. He took a great fancy to Margo, or maybe it was that he'd found out somewhere that her protector, as he called it, was a millionaire. He said she must always keep that beautiful golden tan and made her wear her hair smooth on her head instead of in the curls she'd worn it

in since she had been a Follies girl. "Vat is te use to make beautiful clothes for American women if tey look so healty like from milkin' a cow?" he said. "Vat you need to make interestin' a dress is 'ere," and he struck himself with a pudgy ringed fist on the bosom of his silk pleated shirt. "It is drama. . . . In America all you care about is te perfect tirty-six."

"Oh, I guess you think we're very unrefined," said Margo.

"If I only 'ad some capital," groaned Piquot, shaking his head as he went back to his office on the mezzanine that was all glass and eggshellwhite with aluminum fittings. "I could make New York te most stylish city in te vorld."

Margo liked it parading around in the Paris models and in Piquot's own slinky contraptions over the deep puttycolored rugs. It was better than shaking her fanny in the chorus all right. She didn't have to get down to the showrooms till late. The showrooms were warm and spotless, with a faint bitter smell on the air of new materials and dyes and mothballs, shot through with a whiff of scented Egyptian cigarettes. The models had a little room in the back where they could sit and read magazines and talk about beauty treatments and the theaters and the football season, when there were no customers. There were only two other girls who came regularly and there weren't too many customers either. The girls said that Piquot was going broke.

When he had his sale after Christmas, Margo got Agnes to go down one Monday morning and buy her three stunning gowns for thirty dollars each; she tipped Agnes off on just what to buy and made out not to know her when she pranced out to show the new spring models off.

There wasn't any doubt any more that Piquot was going broke. Bill-collectors stormed in the little office on the mezzanine and everybody's pay was three weeks in arrears, and Piquot's moonshaped face drooped in tiny sagging wrinkles. Margo decided she'd better start looking around for another job, especially as Mr. A's drinking was getting harder and harder to handle. Every morning she studied the stockmarket reports. She didn't have the faith she had at first in Mr. A's tips after she'd bought Sinclair one day and had had to cover her margin and had come out three hundred dollars in the hole.

One Saturday there was a great stir around Piquot's. Piquot himself kept charging out of his office waving his short arms, sometimes peevish and sometimes cackling and giggling, driving the salesladies and models before him like a new rooster in a henyard. Somebody was coming to take photographs for *Vogue*. The photographer when he finally came was a thinfaced young Jewish boy with a pasty skin and dark circles under his eyes. He had a regular big photographer's camera and a great many flashbulbs all silvercrinkly inside that Piquot kept picking up and handling in a gingerly kind of way and exclaiming over. "A vonderful invention. . . . I vould never 'ave photographs taken before because I detest explosions and ten te danger of fire."

It was a warm day in February and the steamheated showrooms were stifling hot. The young man who came to take the pictures was drenched in sweat when he came out from under the black cloth. Piquot wouldn't leave him alone for a second. He had to take Piquot in his office, Piquot at the draftingboard, Piquot among the models. The girls thought their turn would never come. The photographer kept saying, "You let me alone, Mr. Piquot. . . . I want to plan something artistic." The girls all got to giggling. At last Piquot went off and locked himself in his office in a pet. They could see him in there through the glass partition, sitting at his desk with his head in his hands. After that things quieted down. Margo and the photographer got along very well. He kept whispering to her to see what she could do to keep the old gent out of the pictures. When he left to go up to the loft upstairs where the dresses were made, the photographer handed her his card and asked her if she wouldn't let him take her picture at his studio some Sunday. It would mean a great deal to him and it wouldn't cost her anything. He was sure he could get something distinctively artistic. She took his card and said she'd be around the next afternoon. On the card it said Margolies, Art Photographer.

That Sunday Mr. A took her out to lunch at the Hotel Pennsylvania and afterwards she managed to get him to drive her over to Margolies' studio. She guessed the young Jewish boy wasn't so well off and thought Mr. A might just as well pay for a set of photographs. Mr. A was sore about going because he'd gotten his big car out and wanted to take her for a drive up the Hudson. Anyway he went. It was funny in Margolies' studio. Everything was hung with black velvet and there were screens of different sizes in black and white and yellow and green and silver standing all over the big dusty room under the grimy skylights. The young man acted funny, too, as if he hadn't expected them.

"All this is over," he said. "This is my brother Lee's studio. I'm attending to his clientèle while he's abroad. . . . My interests are in the real art of the future."

"What's that?" asked Mr. A, grumpily clipping the end off a cigar as he looked around for a place to sit down.

"Motionpictures. You see I'm Sam Margolies. . . . You'll hear of me if you haven't yet."

Mr. A sat down grouchily on a dusty velvet modelstand. "Well, make it snappy. . . . We want to go driving."

Sam Margolies seemed sore because Margo had just come in her streetclothes. He looked her over with his petulant gray eyes for a long time. "I may not be able to do anything . . . I can't create if I'm hurried. . . . I had seen you stately in Spanish black."

Margo laughed. "I'm not exactly the type."

"The type for a small infanta by Velasquez." He had a definite foreign accent when he spoke earnestly.

"Well, I was married to a Spaniard once. . . . That was enough of Spanish grandees and all that kind of thing to last me a lifetime."

"Wait, wait," said Sam Margolies, walking all round her. "I see it, first in streetclothes and then . . ." He ran out of the room and came back with a black lace shawl. "An infanta in the court of old Spain."

"You don't know what it's like to be married to one," said Margo. "And to live in a house full of noble spick relatives."

While Sam Margolies was posing her in her streetclothes Mr. A was walking up and down fidgeting with his cigar. It must have been getting cloudy out because the overhead skylight grew darker and darker. When Sam Margolies turned the floodlights on her, the skylight went blue, like on the

stage. Then, when he got to posing her in the Spanish shawl and made her take her things off and let her undies down so that she had nothing on but the shawl above the waist, she noticed that Mr. A had let his cigar go out and was watching intently. The reflection from the floodlight made his eyes glint.

After the photographer was through, when they were walking down the gritty wooden stairs from the studio, Mr. A said, "I don't like that guy . . . makes me think of a pimp."

"Oh, no, it's just that he's very artistic," said Margo. "How much did he say the photographs were?"

"Plenty," said Mr. A.

In the unlighted hall that smelt of cabbage cooking somewhere, he grabbed her to him and kissed her. Through the glass front door she could see a flutter of snow in the street that was empty under the lamps.

"Aw, to hell with him," he said, stretching his fingers out across the small of her back. "You're a great little girl, do you know it? Gosh. I like this house. It makes me think of the old days."

Margo shook her head and blinked. "Too bad about our drive," she said. "It's snowing."

"Drive, hell," said Mr. A. "Let's you and me act like we was fond of each other for tonight at least. . . . First we'll go to the Meadowbrook and have a little bite to drink. . . . Jesus, I wish I'd met you before I got in on the dough, when I was livin' in bedbug alley and all that sort of thing."

She let her head drop on his chest for a moment. "Charley, you're number one," she whispered.

That night he got Margo to say that when Agnes took Frank out to his sister's house in New Jersey like she was planning, to try if a little country air wouldn't do him good, she'd go and live with him.

"If you knew how I was sick of this hellraisin' kind of life," he told her.

She looked straight up in his boiled blue eyes. "Do you think I like it, Mr. A?" She was fond of Charley Anderson that night.

After that Sunday, Sam Margolies called up Margo about every day, at the apartment and at Piquot's, and sent her photographs of herself all framed for hanging, but she would never see him. She had enough to think of, what with being alone in the apartment now, because Agnes had finally got Frank away to the country with the help of a practitioner and a great deal of reading of *Science and Health,* and all the bills to pay and daily letters from Tony who'd found out her address, saying he was sick and begging for money and to be allowed to come around to see her.

Then one Monday morning she got down to Piquot's late and found the door locked and a crowd of girls milling shrilly around in front of it. Poor Piquot had been found dead in his bathtub from a dose of cyanide of potassium and there was nobody to pay their back wages.

Piquot's being dead gave Margo the creeps so that she didn't dare go home. She went down to Altman's and did some shopping and at noon called up Mr. A's office to tell him about Piquot and to see if he wouldn't have lunch with her. With poor old Piquot dead and her job gone, there was nothing to do but to strike Mr. A for a lump sum. About two grand would fix her up, and she could get her solitaire diamond Tad had given her out of hock. Maybe if she teased him he would put her up to something good on the market. When she called up, they said Mr. Anderson wouldn't be in his office until three. She went to Schrafft's and had chickenpatties for lunch all by herself in the middle of the crowd of cackling women shoppers.

She already had a date to meet Mr. A that evening at a French speakeasy on Fiftysecond Street where they often ate dinner. When she got back from having her hair washed and waved, it was too early to get dressed, but she started fiddling around with her clothes anyway because she didn't know what else to do, and it was so quiet and lonely in the empty apartment. She took a long time doing her nails and then started trying on one dress after another. Her bed got all piled with rumpled dresses. Everything seemed to have spots on it. She was almost crying when she at last slipped her furcoat over a paleyellow eveningdress that had come from Piquot's, but that she wasn't sure about, and went down in the shabby elevator into the smelly hallway of the apartmenthouse. The elevatorboy fetched her a taxi.

There were white columns in the hall of the oldfashioned

wealthy family residence converted into a restaurant, and a warm expensive pinkish glow of shaded lights. She felt cozier than she'd felt all day as she stepped in on the thick carpet. The headwaiter bowed her to a table and she sat there sipping an oldfashioned, feeling the men in the room looking at her and grinning a little to herself when she thought what the girls at Piquot's would have said about a dame who got to a date with the boyfriend ahead of time. She wished he'd hurry up and come, so that she could tell him the story and stop imagining how poor old Piquot must have looked slumped down in his bathtub, dead from cyanide. It was all on the tip of her tongue ready to tell.

Instead of Mr. A a freshlooking youngster with a long sandy head and a lantern jaw was leaning over her table. She straightened herself in her chair to give him a dirty look, but smiled up at him when he leaned over and said in a Brooklyn confidential kind of voice, "Miss Dowlin' . . . excuse it . . . I'm Mr. Anderson's secretary. He had to hop the plane to Detroit on important business. He knew you were crazy to go to the Music Box opening, so he sent me out to get tickets. Here they are, I pretty near had to blackjack a guy to get 'em for you. The boss said maybe you'd like to take Mrs. Mandeville." He had been talking fast, like he was afraid she'd shut him up; he drew a deep breath and smiled.

Margo took the two green tickets and tapped them peevishly on the tablecloth. "What a shame . . . I don't know who I could get to go now, it's so late. She's in the country."

"My, that's too bad. . . . I don't suppose I could pinchhit for the boss?"

"Of all the gall . . ." she began; then suddenly she found herself laughing. "But you're not dressed."

"Leave it to me, Miss Dowlin'. . . . You eat your supper and I'll come back in a soup an' fish and take you to the show."

Promptly at eight there he was back with his hair slicked, wearing a rustylooking dinnerjacket that was too short in the sleeves. When they got in the taxi, she asked him if he'd hijacked a waiter and he put his hand over his mouth and said, "Don't say a woid, Miss Dowlin' . . . it's hired."

Between the acts, he pointed out all the celebrities to her, including himself. He told her that his name was Clifton Wegman and that everybody called him Cliff and that he was twentythree years old and could play the mandolin and was a little demon with pocket billiards.

"Well, Cliff, you're a likely lad," she said.

"Likely to succeed?"

"I'll tell the world."

347

"A popular graduate of the New York School of Business . . . opportunities wanted."

They had the time of their lives together. After the show Cliff said he was starved, because he hadn't had his supper, what with chasing the theatertickets and the tuck and all, and she took him to the Club Dover to have a bite to eat. He surely had an appetite. It was a pleasure to see him put away a beefsteak with mushrooms. They had some drinks there

and laughed their heads off at the floorshow, and, when he tried to get fresh in the taxicab, she slapped his face, but not very hard. That kid could talk himself out of anything.

When they got to her door, he said could he come up, and before she could stop herself she'd said yes, if he acted like a gentleman. He said that wasn't so easy with a girl like her, but he'd try, and they were laughing and scuffling so in front of her door she dropped her key. They both stooped to pick it up. When she got to her feet flushing from the kiss he'd given her, she noticed that the man sitting all hunched up on the stairs beside the elevator was Tony.

"Well, goodnight, Cliff, thanks for seeing a poor little workinggirl home," Margo said cheerily.

Tony got to his feet and staggered over toward the open

door of the apartment. His face had a green pallor and his clothes looked like he'd lain in the gutter all night.

"This is Tony," said Margo. "He's a . . . a relative of mine . . . not in very good repair."

Cliff looked from one to the other, let out a low whistle and walked down the stairs.

"Well, now you can tell me what you mean by hanging around my place. . . . I've a great mind to have you arrested for a burglar."

Tony could hardly talk. His lip was bloody and all puffed up. "No place to go," he said. "A gang beat me up." He was teetering so she had to grab the sleeve of his filthy overcoat to keep him from falling.

"Oh, Tony," she said, "you sure are a mess. Come on in, but if you pull any tricks like you did last time . . . I swear to God I'll break every bone in your body."

She put him to bed. Next morning he was so jittery she had to send for a doctor. The sawbones said he was suffering from dope and exposure and suggested a cure in a sanatorium. Tony lay in bed white and trembling. He cried a great deal, but he was as meek as a lamb and said yes, he'd do anything the doctor said. Once he grabbed her hand and kissed it and begged her to forgive him for having stolen her money so that he could die happy.

"You won't die, not you," said Margo, smoothing the stiff black hair off his forehead with her free hand. "No such luck." She went out for a little walk on the Drive to try to decide what to do. The dizzysweet clinging smell of the paraldehyde the doctor had given Tony for a sedative had made her feel sick.

At the end of the week when Charley Anderson came back from Detroit and met her at the place on Fiftysecond Street for dinner, he looked worried and haggard. She came out with her sad story and he didn't take it so well. He said he was hard up for cash, that his wife had everything tied up on him, that he'd had severe losses on the market; he could raise five hundred dollars for her, but he'd have to pledge some securities to do that. Then she said she guessed she'd have to go back to her old engagement as entertainer at the Palms at Miami and he said, swell, if she didn't look out he'd come down there and let her support him.

"I don't know why everybody's got to thinkin' I'm a lousy millionaire. All I want is get out of the whole business with enough jack to let me settle down to work on motors. If it hadn't been for this sonofabitchin' divorce I'd been out long ago. This winter I expect to clean up and get out. I'm only a dumb mechanic anyway."

"You want to get out and I want to get in," said Margo, looking him straight in the eye. They both laughed together.

"Aw, let's go up to your place, since the folks are away. I'm tired of these lousy speakeasies."

She shook her head, still laughing. "It's swarming with Spanish relatives," she said. "We can't go there."

They got a bag at his hotel and went over to Brooklyn in a taxi, to a hotel where they were wellknown as Mr. and Mrs. Dowling. On the way over in the taxi she managed to get the ante raised to a thousand.

Next day she took Tony to a sanatorium up in the Catskills. He did everything she said like a good little boy and talked about getting a job when he got out and about honor and manhood. When she got back to town, she called up the office and found that Mr. A was back in Detroit, but he'd left instructions with his secretary to get her her ticket and a drawingroom and fix up everything about the trip to Miami. She closed up her apartment and the office attended to storing the furniture and the packing and everything.

When she went down to the train there was Cliff waiting to meet her with his wiseguy grin and his hat on the back of his long thin head.

"Why, this certainly is sweet of him," said Margo, pinning some liliesofthevalley Cliff had brought her to her furcoat as two redcaps rushed forward to get her bags.

"Sweet of who?" Cliff whispered. "Of the boss or of me?"

There were roses in the drawingroom, and Cliff had bought her *Theatre* and *Variety* and *Zit's Weekly* and *Town Topics* and *Shadowland*. "My, this is grand," she said.

He winked. "The boss said to send you off in the best possible style." He brought a bottle out of his overcoat pocket. "That's Teacher's Highland Cream. . . . Well, so long." He made a little bow and went off down the corridor.

Margo settled herself in the drawingroom and almost wished Cliff hadn't gone so soon. He might at least have taken longer to say goodbye. My, that boy was fresh. The train had no sooner started when there he was back, with his hands in his pants pockets, looking anxious and chewing gum at a great rate.

"Well," she said, frowning, "now what?"

"I bought me a ticket to Richmond. . . . I don't travel enough . . . freedom from office cares."

"You'll get fired."

"Nope . . . this is Saturday. I'll be back bright and early Monday morning."

"But he'll find out."

Cliff took his coat off, folded it carefully and laid it on the

350

rack, then he sat down opposite her and pulled the door of the drawingroom to. "Not unless you tell him."

She started to get to her feet. "Well, of all the fresh kids."

He went on in the same tone of voice. "And you won't tell him and I won't tell him about . . . er . . ."

"But, you damn fool, that's just my exhusband."

"Well, I'm lookin' forward to bein' the exboyfriend. . . . No, honestly, I know you'll like me . . . they all like me." He leaned over to take her hand. His hand was icycold. "No, honest, Margo, why's it any different from the other night? Nobody'll know. You just leave it to me."

Margo began to giggle. "Say, Cliff, you ought to have a sign on you."

"Sayin' what?"

"Fresh paint."

She went over and sat beside him. Through the shaking rumble of the train she could feel him shaking. "Why, you funny kid," she said. "You were scared to death all the time."

Newsreel LXI

*High high high
  Up in the hills
    Watching the clouds roll by*

genius, hard work, vast resources, and the power and will to achieve something distinctive, something more beautiful, something more appealing to the taste and wise judgment of the better people than are the things which have made the Coral Gables of today, and that tomorrow may be better, bigger, more compellingly beautiful

High high high up in the hills

GIANT AIRSHIP BREAKS IN TWO IN MIDFLIGHT

here young and old will gather to disport themselves in fresh invigorating salt water, or to exchange idle gossip in the loggias which overlook the gleaming pool, and at night the tinkle of music will tempt you to dance the hours away.

Shaking hands with the sky

It is the early investor who will share to the fullest extent in the large and rapid enhancement of values that will follow such characterful development

*Who's the big man with gold in his mouth?
  Where does he come from? he comes from the south*

TOWN SITE OF JUPITER SOLD FOR TEN MILLION DOLLARS

like Aladdin with his magic lamp, the Capitalist, the Investor, and the Builder converted what was once a desolate swamp into a wonderful city linked with a network of glistening boulevards

> *Sleepy head sleepy head*
> *Open your eyes*
> *Sun's in the skies*
> *Stop yawnin'*
> *It's mornin'*

ACRES OF GOLD NEAR TAMPA

like a magnificent shawl of sapphire and jade, studded with a myriad of multicolored gems, the colorful waters of the lower Atlantic weave a spell of lasting enchantment. The spot where your future joy, contentment, and happiness is so sure that to deviate is to pass up the outstanding opportunity of your lifetime

MATE FOLLOWS WIFE IN LEAP FROM WINDOW

BATTLE DRUG-CRAZED KILLERS

> *Lulu always wants to do*
> *What we boys don't want her to*

A detachment of motorcycle police led the line of march and cleared the way for the whiteclad columns. Behind the police rose A. P. Schneider, grand marshal. He was followed by Mr. Sparrow's band and members of the painters' union. The motionpicture operators were next in line and the cigarworkers, the glaziers, the musicians, the signpainters and the Brotherhood of Railway Trainmen followed in the order named. The meatcutters brought up the rear of the first division.

The second division was composed of more than thirty-five hundred carpenters. The third division was led by the Clown Band and consisted of electricians, blacksmiths, plasterers, printers, pressmen, elevator constructors, post-office clerks, and plumbers and steamfitters.

The fourth division was led by ironworkers, brickmasons,

the Brotherhood of Locomotive Engineers, steam and operating engineers, the Typographical Union, lathers, composition roofers, sheetmetal workers, tailors and machinists

Don't bring Lulu
I'll bring her myself

Charley Anderson

"You watch, Cliff. . . . We'll knock 'em higher than a kite," Charley said to his secretary, as they came out of the crowded elevator into the humming lobby of the Woolworth Building. "Yessiree," said Cliff, nodding wisely. He had a long face with a thin parchment skin drawn tightly from under his brown felt hat over high cheekbones and thin nose. The lipless mouth never opened very wide above the thin jaw. He repeated out of the corner of his mouth, "Yessiree, bobby . . . higher than a kite."

They went through the revolving doors into the fiveo'clock crowd that packed the lower Broadway sidewalks to the curbs in the drizzly dust of a raw February day.

Charley pulled a lot of fat envelopes out of the pockets of his English waterproof and handed them to Cliff. "Take these up to the office and be sure they get into Nat Benton's personal safe. They can go over to the bank in the mornin' . . . then you're through. Call me at nine, see? You were a little late yesterday. . . . I'm not goin' to worry about anythin' till then."

"Yessir, get a good night's sleep, sir," said Cliff and slid out of sight in the crowd.

Charley stopped a cruising taxicab and let himself drop into the seat. Weather like this his leg still ached. He swallowed a sigh; what the hell was the number? "Go on uptown up Park Avenue," he yelled at the driver. He couldn't think of the number of the damn place. . . . "To East Fiftysecond Street. I'll show you the house." He settled back against the cushions. Christ, I'm tired, he whispered to himself. As he sat slumped back jolted by the stopping and starting of the taxi in the traffic, his belt cut into his belly. He loosened the belt a notch, felt better, brought a cigar out of his breastpocket and bit the end off.

It took him some time to light the cigar. Each time he had the match ready the taxi started or stopped. When he did light it, it didn't taste good. "Hell, I've smoked too much today . . . what I need's a drink," he muttered aloud.

The taxi moved jerkily uptown. Now and then out of the corner of his eye he caught gray outlines of men in other taxis and private cars. As soon as he'd made out one group of figures, another took its place. On Lafayette Street the traffic was smoother. The whole stream of metal, glass, upholstery, overcoats, haberdashery, flesh and blood was moving uptown. Cars stopped, started, shifted gears in unison as if they were run by one set of bells. Charley sat slumped in the seat feeling the layer of fat on his belly against his trousers, feeling the fat of his jowl against his stiff collar. Why the hell couldn't he remember that number? He'd been there every night for a month. A vein in his left eyelid kept throbbing.

"Bonjour, monsieur," said the plainclothes doorman. "How do you do, mon capitaine," said Freddy the rattoothed proprietor, nodding a sleek black head. "Monsieur dining with Mademoiselle tonight?"

Charley shook his head. "I have a feller coming to dinner with me at seven."

"Bien, monsieur."

"Let's have a Scotch-and-soda while I'm waitin' and be sure it ain't that rotgut you tried to palm off on me yesterday."

Freddy smiled wanly. "It was a mistake, Mr. Anderson. We have the veritable pinchbottle. You see the wrappings. It is still wet from the saltwater." Charley grunted and dropped into an easy chair in the corner of the bar.

He drank the whiskey off straight and sipped the soda afterwards. "Hey, Maurice, bring me another," he called to the grayhaired old wrinkefaced Swiss waiter. "Bring me another. Make it double, see? . . . in a regular highball glass. I'm tired this evenin'."

The shot of whiskey warmed his gut. He sat up straighter. He grinned up at the waiter. "Well, Maurice, you haven't told me what you thought about the market today."

"I'm not sure, sir. . . . But you know, Mr. Anderson. . . . If you only wanted to you could tell me."

Charley stretched his legs out and laughed. "Flyin' higher than a kite, eh. . . . Oh, hell, it's a bloody chore. I want to forget it."

By the time he saw Eddy Sawyer threading his way toward him through the faces, the business suits, the hands holding glasses in front of the cocktailbar, he felt good.

He got to his feet. "How's the boy, Eddy? How's things in little old Deetroit? They all think I'm pretty much of a sonofabitch, don't they? Give us the dirt, Eddy."

Eddy sighed and sank into the deep chair beside him. "Well, it's a long story, Charley."

"What would you say to a bacardi with a touch of absinthe in it? . . . All right, make it two, Maurice."

Eddy's face was yellow and wrinkled as a summer apple that's hung too long on the tree. When he smiled, the deepening wrinkles shot out from his mouth and eyes over his cheeks. "Well, Charley, old man, it's good to see you. . . . You know they're calling you the boy wizard of aviation financing?"

"Is that all they're callin' me?" Charley tapped his dead cigar against the brass rim of the ashtray. "I've heard worse things than that."

By the time they'd had their third cocktail, Charley got so he couldn't stop talking. "Well, you can just tell J. Y. from me that there was one day I could have put him out on his ass and I didn't do it. Why didn't I do it? Because I didn't give a goddam. I really owned my stock. They'd hocked everythin' they had an' still they couldn't cover, see. . . . I thought, hell, they're friends of mine. Good old J. Y. Hell, I said to Nat Benton when he wanted me to clean up while the cleanin' was good . . . they're friends of mine. Let 'em ride along with us. An' now look at 'em gangin' up on me with Gladys. Do you know how much alimony Gladys got awarded her? Four thousand dollars a month. Judge is a friend of her old man . . . probably gets a rakeoff. Stripped me of my children . . . every damn thing I've got they've tied up on me. . . . Pretty, ain't it, to take a man's children away from him? Well, Eddy, I know you had nothin' to do with it, but when you get back to Detroit and see those yellow bastards who had to get behind a woman's skirts because they couldn't outsmart me any other way . . . you tell 'em from me that I'm out to strip 'em to their shirts every last one of 'em. . . . I'm just beginnin' to get the hang of this game. I've made some dust fly . . . the boy wizard, eh? . . . Well, you just tell 'em they ain't seen nothin' yet. They think I'm just a dumb cluck of an inventor . . . just a mechanic like poor old Bill Cermak. . . . Hell, let's eat."

They were sitting at the table and the waiter was putting differentcolored horsd'oeuvres on Charley's plate. "Take it away . . . I'll eat a piece of steak, nothing else."

Eddy was eating busily. He looked up at Charley and his face began to wrinkle into a wisecrack. "I guess it's another case of the woman always pays."

Charley didn't laugh. "Gladys never paid for anythin' in her life. You know just as well as I do what Gladys was like. All of those Wheatleys are skinflints. She takes after the old

356

man. . . . Well, I've learned my lesson. . . . No more rich bitches. . . . Why, a goddam whore wouldn't have acted the way that bitch has acted . . . Well, you can just tell 'em, when you get back to your employers in Detroit . . . I know what they sent you for. . . . To see if the old boy could still take his liquor. . . . Drinkin' himself to death, so that's the story, is it? Well, I can still drink you under the table, good old Eddy, ain't that so? You just tell 'em, Eddy, that the old boy's as good as ever, a hell of a lot wiser. . . . They thought they had him out on his can after the divorce, did they? Well, you tell 'em to wait an' see. An' you tell Gladys the first time she makes a misstep . . . just once, she needn't think I haven't got my operatives watchin' her . . . Tell her I'm out to get the kids back, an' strip her of every goddam thing she's got. . . . Let her go out on the streets, I don't give a damn."

Eddy was slapping him on the back. "Well, oldtimer, I've got to run along. . . . Sure good to see you still riding high, wide, and handsome."

"Higher than a kite," shouted Charley, bursting out laughing. Eddy had gone. Old Maurice was trying to make him eat the piece of steak he'd taken out to heat up. Charley couldn't eat. "Take it home to the wife and kiddies," he told Maurice. The speak had cleared for the theatertime lull. "Bring me a bottle of champagne, Maurice, old man, and then maybe I can get the steak down. That's how they do it in the old country, eh? Don't tell me I been drinkin' too much . . . I know it. . . . When everybody you had any confidence in has rooked you all down the line, you don't give a damn, do you, Maurice?"

A man with closecropped black hair and a closecropped black mustache was looking at Charley, leaning over a cocktailglass on the bar. "I say you don't give a damn," Charley shouted at the man when he caught his eye. "Do you?"

"Hell, no, got anything to say about it?" said the man, squaring off toward the table.

"Maurice, bring this gentleman a glass." Charley got to his feet and swayed back and forth bowing politely across the table. The bouncer, who'd come out from a little door in back wiping his red hands on his apron, backed out of the room again. "Anderson my name is. . . . Glad to meet you, Mr. . . ."

"Budkiewitz," said the blackhaired man, who advanced scowling and swaying a little to the other side of the table.

Charley pointed to a chair. "I'm drunk . . . beaucoup champagny water . . . have a glass."

"With pleasure if you put it that way. . . . Always rather

357

drink than fight. . . . Here's to the old days of the Rainbow Division."

"Was you over there?"

"Sure. Put it there, buddy."

"Those were the days."

"And now you come back and over here there's nothin' but a lot of doublecrossin' bastards."

"Businessmen . . . to hell wid 'em . . . doublecrossin' bastards I call 'em."

Mr. Budkiewitz got to his feet, scowling again. "To what kind of business do you refer?"

"Nobody's business. Take it easy, buddy." Mr. Budkiewitz sat down again. "Oh, hell, bring out another bottle, Maurice, and have it cold. Ever drunk that wine in Saumur, Mr. Budkiebbitzer?"

"Have I drunk Saumur? Why shouldn't I drink it? Trained there for three months."

"That's what I said to myself. That boy was overseas," said Charley.

"I'll tell the cockeyed world."

"What's your business, Mr. Buchanan?"

"I'm an inventor."

"Just up my street. Ever heard of the Askew-Merritt starter?"

He'd never heard of the Askew-Merritt starter and Charley had never heard of the Autorinse washingmachine, but soon

they were calling each other Charley and Paul. Paul had had trouble with his wife too, said he was going to jail before he'd pay her any more alimony. Charley said he'd go to jail too.

Instead they went to a nightclub where they met two charming girls. Charley was telling the charming girls how he was going to set Paul, good old Paul, up in business, in the washingmachine business. They went places in taxicabs under the El with the girls. They went to a place in the Village. Charley was going to get all the girls, the sweet pretty little girls, jobs in the chorus. Charley was explaining how he was going to take the shirts off those bastards in Detroit. He'd get the girls jobs in the chorus so that they could take their shirts off. It was all very funny.

In the morning light he was sitting alone in a place with torn windowshades. Good old Paul had gone and the girls had gone and he was sitting at a table covered with cigarette-stubs and spilt dago red looking at the stinging brightness coming through the worn places in the windowshade. It wasn't a hotel or a callhouse, it was some kind of a dump with tables, and it stank of old cigarsmoke and last night's spaghetti and tomatosauce and dago red.

Somebody was shaking him. "What time is it?"

A fat wop and a young slickhaired wop in their dirty shirt-sleeves were shaking him. "Time to pay up and get out. Here's your bill."

A lot of things were scrawled on a card. Charley could only read it with one eye at a time. The total was seventyfive dollars. The wops looked threatening.

"You tell us give them girls twentyfive dollars each on account."

Charley reached for his billroll. Only a dollar. Where the hell had his wallet gone? The young wop was playing with a small leather blackjack he'd taken out of his back pocket.

"A century ain't high for what you spent an' the girls an' all. . . . If you f—k around it'll cost you more. . . . You got your watch, ain't you? This ain't no clipjoint."

"What time is it?"

"What time is it, Joe?"

"Let me call up the office. I'll get my secretary to come up."

"What's the number? What's his name?" The young wop tossed up the blackjack and caught it. "I'll talk to him. We're lettin' you out of this cheap. We don't want no hard feelin's."

After they'd called up the office and left word that Mr. Anderson was sick and to come at once, they gave him coffee with rum in it that made him feel sicker than ever. At last Cliff was standing over him looking neat and wellshaved. "Well, Cliff, I'm not the drinker I used to be."

In the taxicab he passed out cold.

He opened his eyes in his bed at the hotel "There must have been knockout drops in the coffee," he said to Cliff who sat by the window reading the paper.

"Well, Mr. Anderson, you sure had us worried. A damn lucky thing it was they didn't know who they'd bagged in that clipjoint. If they had, it would have cost us ten grand to get out of there."

"Cliff, you're a good boy. After this you get a raise."

"Seems to me I've heard that story before, Mr. Anderson."

"Benton know?"

"I had to tell him some. I said you'd eaten some bad fish and had ptomaine poisoning."

"Not so bad for a young feller. God, I wonder if I'm gettin' to be a rummy. . . . How are things downtown?"

"Lousy. Mr. Benton almost went crazy trying to get in touch with you yesterday."

"Christ, I got a head. . . . Say, Cliff, you don't think I'm gettin' to be a rummy, do you?"

"Here's some dope the sawbones left."

"What day of the week is it?"

"Saturday."

"Jesus Christ, I thought it was Friday."

The phone rang. Cliff went over to answer it. "It's the massageman."

"Tell him to come up. . . . Say, is Benton stayin' in town?"

"Sure he's in town, Mr. Anderson, he's trying to get hold of Merritt and see if he can stop the slaughter. . . . Merritt . . ."

"Oh, hell, I'll hear about it soon enough. Tell this masseur to come in."

After the massage, that was agony, especially the cheerful German-accent remarks about the weather and the hockey season made by the big curlyhaired Swede who looked like a doorman, Charley felt well enough to go to the toilet and throw up some green bile. Then he took a cold shower and went back to bed and shouted for Cliff, who was typing letters in the drawingroom, to ring for the bellhop to get cracked ice for a rubber icepad to put on his head.

He lay back on the pillows and began to feel a little better.

"Hey, Cliff, how about lettin' in the light of day? What time is it?"

"About noon."

"Christ. . . . Say, Cliff, did any women call up?" Cliff shook his head. "Thank God."

"A guy called up, said he was a taxidriver, said you'd told him you'd get him a job in an airplane factory. . . . I told him you'd left for Miami."

Charley was beginning to feel a little better. He lay back in the soft comfortable bed on the crisplylaundered pillows and looked around the big clean hotel bedroom. The room was high up. Silvery light poured in through the broad window. Through the A between the curtains in the window he could see a piece of sky bright and fleecy as milkweed silk. Charley began to feel a vague sense of accomplishment, like a man getting over the fatigue of a long journey or a dangerous mountainclimb.

"Say, Cliff, how about a small gin and bitters with a lot of ice in it? . . . I think that 'ud probably be the makin' of me."

"Mr. Anderson, the doc said to swear off and to take some of that dope whenever you felt like taking a drink."

"Every time I take it, that stuff makes me puke. What does he think I am, a hophead?"

"All right, Mr. Anderson, you're the boss," said Cliff, screwing up his thin mouth.

"Thataboy, Cliff. . . . Then I'll try some grapefruitjuice

and if that stays down I'll take a good breakfast and to hell wid 'em. . . . Why aren't the papers here?"

"Here they are, Mr. Anderson. . . . I've got 'em all turned to the financial section."

Charley looked over the reports of trading. His eyes wouldn't focus very well yet. He still did better by closing one eye. A paragraph in *News and Comment* made him sit up.

"Hey, Cliff," he yelled, "did you see this?"

"Sure," said Cliff. "I said things were bad."

"But if they're goin' ahead, it means Merritt and Farrell have got their proxies sure."

Cliff nodded wisely with his head a little to one side.

"Where the hell's Benton?"

"He just phoned, Mr. Anderson, he's on his way uptown now."

"Hey, give me that drink before he comes and then put all the stuff away and order up a breakfast."

Benton came in the bedroom behind the breakfasttray. He

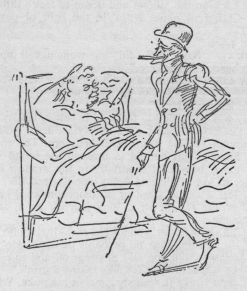

wore a brown suit and a derby. His face looked like an old dishcloth in spite of his snappy clothes.

Charley spoke first, "Say, Benton, am I out on my fanny?"

Benton carefully and slowly took off his gloves and hat and overcoat and set them on the mahogany table by the window.

"The sidewalk is fairly well padded," he said.

"All right, Cliff. . . . Will you finish up that correspondence?" Cliff closed the door behind him gently. "Merritt outsmarted us?"

"He and Farrell are playing ball together. All you can do is take a licking and train up for another bout."

"But damn it, Benton . . . ."

Benton got to his feet and walked up and down the room at the foot of the bed. . . . "No use cussing at me. I'm going to do the cussing today. What do you think of a guy who goes on a bender at a critical moment like this? Yellow, that's what I call it. . . . You deserved what you got . . . and I had a hell of a time saving my own hide, I can tell you. Well, I picked you for a winner, Anderson, and I still think that if you cut out the funny business you could be in the real money in ten years. Now let me tell you something, young man, you've gone exactly as far as you can go on your record overseas, and that was certainly a hell of a lot further than most. As for this invention racket . . . you know as well as I do there's no money in it unless you have the genius for promotion needed to go with it. You had a big initial success and thought you were the boy wizard and could put over any damn thing you had a mind to."

"Hey, Nat, for Pete's sake don't you think I've got brains enough to know that? . . . This darn divorce and bein' in hospital so long kinder got me, that's all."

"Alibis."

"What do you think I ought to do?"

"You ought to pull out of this town for a while. . . . How about your brother's business out in Minnesota?"

"Go back to the sticks and sell tin lizzies . . . that's a swell future."

"Where do you think Henry Ford made his money?"

"I know. But he keeps his dealers broke. . . . What I need's to get in good physical shape. I always have a good time in Florida. I might go down there and lay around in the sun for a month."

"O.K. if you keep out of that landboom."

"Sure, Nat, I won't even play poker . . . I'm goin' down there for a rest. Get my leg in real good shape. Then when I come back we'll see the fur fly. After all, there's still that Standard Airparts stock."

"No longer listed."

"Check."

"Well, optimist, my wife's expecting me for lunch. . . . Have a good trip."

Benton went out. "Hey, Cliff," Charley called through the door. "Tell 'em to come and get this damn breakfasttray. It didn't turn out so well. And phone Parker to get the car in shape. Be sure the tires are all O.K. I'm pullin' out for Florida Monday."

In a moment Cliff stuck his head in the door. His face was red. "Are you . . . will you be needing me down there, sir?"

"No, I'll be needin' you here to keep an eye on the boys downtown. . . . I got to have somebody here I can trust. . . . I'll tell you what I will have you do, though . . . go down to Trenton and accompany Miss Dowlin' down to Norfolk. I'll pick her up there. She's in Trenton visitin' her folks. Her old man just died or somethin'. You'd just as soon do that, wouldn't you? It'll give you a little trip."

Charley was watching Cliff's face. He screwed his mouth further to one side and bowed like a butler. "Very good, sir," he said.

Charley lay back on the pillows again. His head was throbbing, his stomach was still tied up in knots. When he closed his eyes dizzy red lights bloomed in front of them. He began to think about Jim and how Jim had never paid over his share of the old lady's money he'd put into the business. Anyway, he ain't got a plane, two cars, a suite at the Biltmore, and a secretary that'll do any goddam thing in the world for you, and a girl like Margo. He tried to remember how her face looked, the funny amazed way she opened her eyes wide when she was going to make a funny crack. He couldn't remember a damn thing, only the sick feeling he had all over and the red globes blooming before his eyes. In a little while he fell asleep.

He was still feeling so shaky when he started South that he took Parker along to drive the car. He sat glumly in his new camel'shair coat with his hands hanging between his knees staring ahead through the roaring blank of the Holland Tunnel, thinking of Margo and Bill Edwards, the patent lawyer he had to see in Washington about a suit, and remembering the bills in Cliff's deskdrawer and wondering where the money was coming from to fight this patent suit against Askew-Merritt. He had a grand in bills in his pocket and that made him feel good, anyway. Gosh, money's a great thing, he said to himself.

They came out of the tunnel into a rainygray morning and the roar and slambanging of trucks through Jersey City. Then the traffic gradually thinned and they were going across the flat farmlands of New Jersey strawcolored and ruddy with winter. At Philadelphia Charley made Parker drive him to Broad Street. "I haven't got the patience to drive, I'll take the afternoon train. Come to the Waldman Park when you get in."

He hired a drawingroom in the parlorcar and went and lay down to try to sleep. The train clattered and roared so and the gray sky and the lavender fields and yellow pastures and the twigs of the trees beginning to glow red and green and paleyellow with a foretaste of spring made him feel so blue, so like howling like a dog, that he got fed up with being shutup in the damn drawingroom and went back to the clubcar to smoke a cigar.

He was slumped in the leather chair fumbling for the cigarclipper in his vest pocket when the portly man in the next chair looked up from a bluecovered sheaf of lawpapers he was poring over. Charley looked into the black eyes and the smooth bluejowled face and at the bald head still neatly plastered with a patch of black hair shaped like a bird's wing, without immediately recognizing it.

"Why, Charley, ma boy, I reckon you must be in love."

Charley straightened up and put out his hand. "Hello, senator," he said, stammering a little like he used to in the old days. "Goin' to the nation's capital?"

"Such is my unfortunate fate." Senator Planet's eyes went searching all over him. "Charley, I hear you had an accident."

"I've had a series of them," said Charley, turning red.

Senator Planet nodded his head understandingly and made a clucking noise with his tongue. "Too bad . . . too bad . . . Well, sir, a good deal of water has run under the bridge since you and young Merritt had dinner with me that night in Washington. . . . Well, we're none of us gettin' any younger."

Charley got the feeling that the senator's black eyes got considerable pleasure from exploring the flabby lines where his neck met his collar and the bulge of his belly against his vest. "Well, we're none of us getting any younger," the senator repeated.

"You are, senator. I swear you look younger than you did the last time I saw you."

The senator smiled. "Well, I hope you'll forgive me for makin' the remark . . . but it's been one of the most sensational careers I have had the luck to witness in many years of public life."

"Well, it's a new industry. Things happen fast."

"Unparalleled," said the senator. "We live in an age of unparalleled progress . . . everywhere except in Washington. . . . You should come down to our quiet little village more often. . . . You have many friends there. I see by the papers, as Mr. Dooley used to say, that there's been considerable reorganization out with you folks in Detroit. Need a broader capital base, I suppose."

"A good many have been thrown out on their broad capital bases," said Charley.

He thought the senator would never quit laughing. The senator pulled out a large initialed silk handkerchief to wipe the tears from his eyes and brought his small pudgy hand down on Charley's knee. "Godalmighty, we ought to have a drink on that."

The senator ordered whiterock from the porter and mysteriously wafted a couple of slugs of good rye whiskey into it from a bottle he had in his Gladstone bag. Charley began to feel better. The senator was saying that some interesting developments were to be expected from the development of airroutes. The need for subsidies was pretty generally admitted if this great nation was to catch up on its lag in air transportation. The question would be of course which of a number of competing concerns enjoyed the confidence of the Administration. There was more in this airroute business than there ever had been in supplying ships and equipment. "A question of the confidence of the Administration, ma boy." At the word confidence, Senator Planet's black eyes shone. "That's why, ma boy, I'm glad to see you up here. Stick close to our little village on the Potomac, ma boy."

"Check," said Charley.

"When you're in Miami, look up my old friend Homer Cassidy. . . . He's got a nice boat . . . he'll take you fishin' . . . I'll write him, Charley. If I could get away I might spend a week down there myself next month. There's a world of money bein' made down there right now."

"I sure will, senator, that's mighty nice of you, senator."

By the time they got into the Union Station Charley and the senator were riding high. They were talking trunklines and connecting lines, airports and realestate. Charley couldn't make out whether he was hiring Senator Planet for the lobbying or whether Senator Planet was hiring him. They parted almost affectionately at the taxistand.

Next afternoon he drove down through Virginia. It was a pretty, sunny afternoon. The judastrees were beginning to come out red on the sheltered hillsides. He had two bottles of that good rye whiskey Senator Planet had sent up to the hotel for him. As he drove, he began to get sore at Parker the chauffeur. All the bastard did was get rakeoffs on the spare parts and gas and oil. Here he'd charged up eight new tires in the last month; what did he do with tires, anyway, eat them? By the time they were crossing the tollbridge into Norfolk, Charley was sore as a crab. He had to hold himself in to keep from hauling off and giving the bastard a crack on the sallow jaw of his smooth flunkey's face. In front of the hotel he blew up.

"Parker, you're fired. Here's your month's wages and your trip back to New York. If I see your face around this town tomorrow, I'll have you run in for theft. You know what I'm referrin' to just as well as I do. You damn chauffeurs think you're too damn smart. I know the whole racket, see. . . . I have to work for my dough just as hard as you do. Just to prove it I'm goin' to drive myself from now on." He hated the man's smooth unmoving face.

"Very well, sir," Parker said coolly. "Shall I return you the uniform?"

"You can take the uniform and shove it up your . . ." Charley paused. He was stamping up and down red in the face on the pavement at the hotel entrance in a circle of giggling colored bellboys. "Here, boy, take those bags in and have my car taken around to the garage. . . . All right, Parker, you have your instructions."

He strode into the hotel and ordered the biggest double suite they had. He registered in his own name. "Mrs. Anderson will be here directly." Then he called up the other hotels

367

to find out where the hell Margo was. "Hello, kid," he said when at last it was her voice at the end of the wire. "Come on over. You're Mrs. Anderson and no questions asked. Aw, to hell with 'em; nobody's goin' to dictate to me what I'll do or who I'll see or what I'm goin' to do with my money. I'm through with all that. Come right around. I'm crazy to see you . . ."

When she came in, followed by the bellhop with the bags, she certainly looked prettier than ever.

"Well, Charley," she said, when the bellhop had gone out, "this sure is the cream de la cream. . . . You must have hit oil." After she'd run all around the rooms, she came back and snuggled up to him. "I bet you been giving 'em hell on the market."

"They tried to put somethin' over on me, but it can't be done. Take it from me. . . . Have a drink, Margo. . . . Let's get a little bit cockeyed, you and me, Margo. . . . Christ, I was afraid you wouldn't come."

She was doing her face in the mirror. "Me? Why, I'm only a pushover," she said in that gruff low tone that made him shiver all up his spine.

"Say, where's Cliff?"

"Our hatchetfaced young friend who was kind enough to accompany me to the meeting with the lord and master? He pulled out on the sixo'clock train."

"The hell he did. I had some instructions for him."

"He said you said to be in the office Tuesday morning and he'd do it if he had to fly. Say, Charley, if he's a sample of your employees, they must worship the ground you walk on. He couldn't stop talking about what a great guy you were."

"Well, they know I'm regular, been through the mill . . . understand their point of view. It wasn't so long ago I was workin' at a lathe myself."

Charley felt good. He poured them each another drink. Margo took his and poured half of the rye back into the bottle. "Don't want to get too cockeyed, Mr. A," she said in that new low caressing voice.

Charley grabbed her to him and kissed her hard on the mouth. "Christ, if you only knew how I've wanted to have a really swell woman all to myself. I'd had some awful bitches . . . Gladys, God, what a bitch she was! She pretty near ruined me . . . tried to strip me of every cent I had in the world . . . ganged up on me with guys I thought were my friends. . . . But you just watch, little girl. I'm goin' to show 'em. In five years they'll come crawlin' to me on their bellies. I don't know what it is, but I got a kind of feel for the big money . . . Nat Benton says I got it . . . I know I got it. I can travel on a hunch, see. Those bastards all had money to begin with."

After they'd ordered their supper and while they were having just one little drink waiting for it, Margo brought out some bills she had in her handbag.

"Sure, I'll handle 'em right away." Charley shoved them into his pocket without looking at them.

"You know, Mr. A, I wouldn't have to worry you about things like that if I had an account in my own name."

"How about ten grand in the First National Bank when we get to Miami?"

"Suit yourself, Charley . . . I never did understand more money than my week's salary, you know that. That's all any real trouper understands. I got cleaned out fixing the folks up in Trenton. It certainly costs money to die in this man's country."

Charley's eyes filled with tears. "Was it your dad, Margery?"

She made a funny face. "Oh, no. The old man bumped off from too much Keeley cure when I was a little twirp with my hair down my back. . . . This was my stepmother's second husband. I'm fond of my stepmother, believe it or not. . . . She's been the only friend I had in this world. I'll tell you about her someday. It's quite a story."

"How much did it cost? I'll take care of it."

Margo shook her head. "I never loaded my relations on any man's back," she said.

When the waiter came in with a tray full of big silver dishes followed by a second waiter pushing in a table already set, Margo pulled apart from Charley. "Well, this is the life," she whispered in a way that made him laugh.

Driving down was a circus. The weather was good. As they went further south there began to be a green fuzz of spring on the woods. There were flowers in the pinebarrens. Birds were singing. The car ran like a dream. Charley kept her at sixty on the concrete roads, driving carefully, enjoying the driving, the good fourwheel brakes, the easy whir of the motor under the hood. Margo was a smart girl and crazy about him and kept making funny cracks. They drank just enough to keep them feeling good. They made Savannah late that night and felt so good they got so tight there the manager threatened to run them out of the big old hotel. That was when Margo threw an ashtray through the transom.

They'd been too drunk to have much fun in bed that night and woke up with a taste of copper in their mouths and horrible heads. Margo looked haggard and green and saggy under the eyes before she went in to take her bath. Charley made her a prairie oyster for breakfast like he said the English aviators used to make over on the other side, and she threw it right up without breaking the eggyolk. She made him come and look at it in the toilet before she pulled the chain. There was the raw eggyolk looking up at them like it had just come out of the shell. They couldn't help laughing about it in spite of their heads.

It was eleven o'clock when they pulled out. Charley drove kind of easy along the winding road through the wooded section of southern Georgia, cut with inlets and saltmarshes from which cranes flew up and once a white flock of egrets. They felt pretty pooped by the time they got to Jacksonville. Neither of them could eat anything but a lambchop washed down with some lousy gin they paid eight dollars a quart for to the colored bellboy who claimed it was the best English gin imported from Nassau the night before. They drank the gin with bitters and went to bed.

Driving down from Jax to Miami, the sun was real hot. Charley wanted to have the top down to get plenty of air, but Margo wouldn't hear of it. She made him laugh about it. "A girl'll sacrifice anything for a man except for her complexion." They couldn't eat on the way down, though Charley kept tanking up on the gin. When they got into Miami they went right to the old Palms where Margo used to work and got a big ovation from Joe Kantor and Eddy Palermo and the boys of the band. They all said it looked like a honeymoon and kidded about seeing the marriagelicense. "Merely a chance acquaintance . . . something I picked up at the busstation in Jax," Margo kept saying. Charley ordered the best meal they had in the house and drinks all around and champagne. They danced all evening in spite of his game leg. When he passed out, they took him upstairs to Joe and Mrs. Kantor's own room. When he began to wake up, Margo was sitting fully dressed looking fresh as a daisy on the edge of the bed. It was late in the morning. She brought him up breakfast on a tray herself.

"Look here, Mr. A," she said. "You came down here for a rest. No more nightclubs for a while. I've rented us a little bungalow down on the beach and we'll put you up at the hotel to avoid the breath of scandal and you'll like it. What we need's the influence of the home. . . . And you and me, Mr. A, we're on the wagon."

The bungalow was in Spanishmission style, and cost a lot, but they sure had a good time at Miami Beach. They played the dograces and the roulettewheels and Charley got in with a bunch of allnight pokerplayers through Homer Cassidy, Senator Planet's friend, a big smiling cultured whitehaired South-

erner in a baggy linen suit, who came round to the hotel to look him up. After a lot of talking about one thing and another, Cassidy got around to the fact that he was buying up options on property for the new airport and would let Charley in on it for the sake of his connections, but he had to have cash right away. At poker Charley's luck was great, he always won enough to have a big roll of bills on him, but his bankaccount was a dog of a different stripe. He began burning up the wires to Nat Benton's office in New York.

Margo tried to keep him from drinking; the only times he could really get a snootful were when he went out fishing with Cassidy. Margo wouldn't go fishing; she said she didn't like the way the fish looked at her when they came up out of the water. One day he'd gone down to the dock to go fishing with Cassidy, but found that the norther that had come up that morning was blowing too hard. It was damn lucky because just as Charley was leaving the dock a Western Union messengerboy came up on his bike. The wind was getting sharper every minute and blew the chilly dust in Charley's face as he read the telegram. It was from the senator:

As soon as he got back to the beach, Charley talked to Benton over longdistance. Next day airplane stocks bounced when the news came over the wires of a bill introduced to subsidize airlines. Charley sold everything he had at the top, covered his margins, and was sitting pretty when the afternoon papers killed the story.

A week later he started to rebuy at twenty points lower. Anyway, he'd have the cash to refinance his loans and go in with Cassidy on the options. When he told Cassidy he was ready to go in with him, they went out on the boat to talk things over. A colored boy made them mintjuleps. They sat in the stern with their rods and big straw hats to keep the sun out of their eyes, and the juleps on a table behind them. When they got to the edge of the blue water they began to troll for sailfish.

It was a day of blue sky with big soft pinkishwhite clouds lavender underneath drifting in the sun. There was enough wind blowing against the current out in the Gulf Stream to make sharp choppy waves green where they broke and blue and purple in the trough. They followed the long streaks of mustardcolored weed, but they didn't see any sailfish. Cassidy caught a dolphin and Charley lost one. The boat pitched so that Charley had to keep working on the juleps to keep his stomach straight.

Most of the morning they cruised back and forth in front of the mouth of the Miami River. Beyond the steep dark waves they could see the still sunny brown water of the bay and against the horizon the new buildings sparkling white among a red web of girder construction.

"Buildin', that's what I like to see," said Homer Cassidy, waving a veined hand that had a big old gold sealring on it toward the city. "And it's just beginnin'. . . . Why, boy, I kin remember when Miamah was the jumpin'off place, a little collection of broken-down shacks between the railroad and the river, and I tell you the mosquitoes were fierce. There were a few crackers down here growin' early tomatoes and layin' abed half the time with chills and fever . . . and now look at it . . . an' up in New York they try to tell you the boom ain't sound." Charley nodded without speaking. He was having a tussle with a fish on his line. His face was getting red and his hand was cramped from reeling. "Nothin' but a small bonito," said Cassidy. ". . . The way they try to tell you the fishin' ain't any good . . . that's all propaganda for the West Coast. . . . Boy, I must admit that I saw it comin' years ago when I was workin' with old Flagler. There was a man with vision. . . . I went down with him on the first train that went over the overseas extension into Key West . . . I was one of the attorneys for the road at the time. Schoolchildren threw roses under his feet all the way from his private car to the carriage. . . . We had nearly a thousand men carried away in hurricanes before the line was completed . . . and now the new Miamah . . . an' Miamah Beach, what do you think of Miamah Beach? It's Flagler's dream come true."

"Well, what I'd like to do . . ." Charley began, and stopped to take a big swig of the new julep the colored boy had just handed him. He was beginning to feel wonderful now that the little touch of seasickness had gone. Cassidy's fishing guide had taken Charley's rod up forward to put a new hook on it, so Charley was sitting there in the stern of the motorboat feeling the sun eat into his back and little flecks of salt spray drying on his face with nothing to do but sip the julep, with nothing to worry about. "Cassidy, this sure is the life . . . why can't a guy do what he wants to with his life? I was just goin' to say what I want to do is get out of this whole racket . . . investments, all that crap. . . . I'd like to get out with a small pile and get a house and settle down to monkeyin' around with motors and designin' planes and stuff like that. . . . I always thought if I could pull out with enough jack I'd like to build me a windtunnel all my own . . . you know that's what they test out model planes in."

"Of course," said Cassidy, "it's aviation that's goin' to make Miamah. . . . Think of it, eighteen, fourteen, ten hours from New York. . . . I don't need to tell you . . . and you and me and the senator . . . we're right in among the foundin' fathers with that airport. . . . Well, boy, I've waited all ma life to make a real killin'. All ma life I been servin' others . . . on the bench, railroad lawyer, all that sort of thing. . . . Seems to me about time to make a pile of ma own."

"Suppose they pick some other place, then we'll be holdin' the bag. After all, it's happened before," said Charley.

"Boy, they can't do it. You know yourself that that's the ideal location, and then . . . I oughtn't to be tellin' you this, but you'll find it out soon anyway . . . well, you know our Washington friend, well, he's one of the forwardestlookin' men in this country. . . . That money I put up don't come out of Homer Cassidy's account because Homer Cassidy's broke. That's what's worryin' me right this minute. I'm merely his agent. And in all the years I've been associated with Senator Planet, upon ma soul and body I've never seen him put up a cent unless it was a sure thing."

Charley began to grin. "Well, the old sonofabitch."

Cassidy laughed. "You know the one about a nod's as good as a wink to a blind mule. How about a nice Virginia ham sandwich?"

They had another drink with the sandwiches. Charley got to feeling like talking. It was a swell day. Cassidy was a prince. He was having a swell time. "Funny," Charley said, "when I first saw Miami it was from out at sea like this. I never would have thought I'd be down here shovelin' in the dough. . . . There weren't all those tall buildin's then either. I was goin' up to New York on a coastin' boat. I was just a kid and I'd been down to New Orleans for the Mardi Gras and I tell you I was broke. I got on the boat to come up to New York and got to pallin' with a Florida cracker . . . he was a funny guy. . . . We went up to New York together. He said the thing to do was get over an' see the war, so him and me like a pair of damn fools we enlisted in one of those volunteer ambulance services. After that I switched to aviation. That's how I got started in my line of business. Miami didn't mean a thing to me then."

"Well, Flagler gave me ma start," said Cassidy. "And I'm not ashamed to admit it . . . buyin' up rightofway for the Florida East Coast. . . . Flagler started me and he started Miamah."

That night, when they got in sunburned and a little drunk from the day on the Gulf Stream, they tucked all the options away in the safe of Judge Cassidy's office and went over to the Palms to relax from business cares. Margo wore her silver dress and she certainly looked stunning. There was a thin dark Irishlooking girl there named Eileen who seemed to know Cassidy from way back. The four of them had dinner together, Cassidy got good and tight and opened his mouth wide as a grouper's talking about the big airport and saying how he was going to let the girls in on some lots on the deal. Charley was drunk, but he wasn't too drunk to know Cassidy ought to keep his trap shut. When he danced with Eileen, he talked earnestly in her ear telling her she ought to make the boyfriend keep his trap shut until the thing was made public from the proper quarters. Margo saw them with their heads together and acted the jealous bitch and started making over Cassidy to beat the cars. When Charley got her to dance with him, she played dumb and wouldn't answer when he spoke to her.

He left her at the table and went over to have some drinks at the bar. There he got into an argument with a skinny guy who looked like a cracker. Eddy Palermo, with an oily smile on his face the shape and color of an olive, ran over and got between them. "You can't fight this gentleman, Mr. Ander-

375

son, he's our county attorney. . . . I know you gentlemen would like each other . . . Mr. Pappy, Mr. Anderson was one of our leading war aces."

They dropped their fists and stood glaring at each other with the little wop nodding and grinning between them. Charley put out his hand. "All right, put it there, pal," he said. The county attorney gave him a mean look and put his hands in his pockets. "County attorney, s—t," said Charley. He was reeling. He had to put his hand against the wall to steady himself. And he turned and walked out the door. Outside he found Eileen who'd just come out of the ladies' room and was patting back her sleek hair in front of the mirror by the hatchecking stand. He felt choked with the whiskey and the cigarsmoke and the throbbing hum of the band and the shuffle of feet. He had to get outdoors. "Come on, girlie, we're goin' for a ride, get some air." Before the girl could open her mouth, he'd dragged her out to the parking lot.

"Oh, but I don't think we ought to leave the others," she kept saying.

"They're too goddam drunk to know. I'll bring you back in five minutes. A little air does a little girl good, especially a pretty little girl like you."

The gears shrieked because he didn't have the clutch shoved out. The car stalled; he started the motor again and immediately went into high. The motor knocked for a minute, but began to gather speed. "See," he said, "not a bad little bus." As he drove, he talked out of the corner of his mouth to Eileen. "That's the last time I go into that dump. . . . Those little cracker politicians fresh out of the turpentine camps can't get fresh with me. I can buy and sell 'em too easy like buyin' a bag of peanuts. Like that bastard Farrell. I'll buy and sell him yet. You don't know who he is, but all you need to know is he's a crook, one of the biggest crooks in the country, an' he thought, the whole damn lot of 'em thought, they'd put me out like they did poor old Joe Askew. But the man with the knowhow, the boy who thinks up the gadgets, they can't put him out. I can outsmart 'em at their own game too. We got somethin' bigger down here than they ever dreamed of. And the Administration all fixed up. This is goin' to be big, little girl, the biggest thing you ever saw and I'm goin' to let you in on it. We'll be on easystreet from now on. And when you're on easystreet you'll all forget poor old Charley Anderson the boy that put you wise."

"Oh, it's so cold," moaned Eileen. "Let's go back. I'm shivering." Charley leaned over and put his arm round her shoulders. As he turned, the car swerved. He wrenched it back onto the concrete road again. "Oh, please do be careful, Mr.

Anderson. . . . You're doing eightyfive now. . . . Oh, don't scare me, please."

Charley laughed. "My, what a sweet little girl! Look, we're down to forty, just bowlin' pleasantly along at forty. Now we'll turn and go back, it's time little chickens were in bed. But you must never be scared in a car when I'm driving. If there's one thing I can do, it's drive a car. But I don't like to drive a car. Now if I had my own ship here. How would you like to take a nice trip in a plane? I'da had it down here before this, but it was in hock for the repair bills. Had to put a new motor in. But now I'm on easystreet. I'll get one of the boys to fly it down to me. Then we'll have a real time. You an' me an' Margo. Old Margo's a swell girl, got an awful temper, though. That's one thing I can do, I know how to pick the women."

When they turned to run back toward Miami, they saw the long streak of the dawn behind the broad barrens dotted with dead pines and half-built stucco houses and closed servicestations and dogstands.

"Now the wind's behind us. We'll have you back before you can say Jack Robinson." They were running along beside a railroad track. They were catching up on two red lights. "I

wonder if that's the New York train." They were catching up on it, past the lighted observation car, past the sleepers with no light except through the groundglass windows of the dressingrooms at the ends of the cars. They were creeping up on the baggagecar and mailcars and the engine, very huge and tall and black with a little curling shine from Charley's headlights in the dark. The train had cut off the red streak of the dawn. "Hell, they don't make no speed." As they passed the cab, the whistle blew. "Hell, I can beat him to the crossin'." The lights of the crossing were ahead of them and the long beam of the engine's headlight, that made the red and yellow streak of the dawn edging the clouds very pale and far away. The bar was down at the crossing. Charley stepped on the gas. They crashed through the bar, shattering their headlights. The car swerved around sideways. Their eyes were full of the glare of the locomotive headlight and the shriek of the whistle. "Don't be scared, we're through!" Charley yelled at the girl. The car swerved around on the tracks and stalled.

He was jabbing at the starter with his foot. The crash wasn't anything. When he came to, he knew right away he was in a hospital. First thing he began wondering if he was going to have a hangover. He couldn't move. Everything was dark. From way down in a pit he could see the ceiling. Then he could see the peak of a nurse's cap and a nurse leaning over him. All the time he was talking. He couldn't stop talking.

"Well, I thought we were done for. Say, nurse, where did we crack up? Was it at the airport? I'd feel better if I could remember. It was this way, nurse . . . I'd taken that little girl up to let her get the feel of that new Boeing ship . . . you know the goldarned thing. . . . I was sore as hell at somebody, must have been my wife, poor old Gladys, did she give me a dirty deal? But now after this airport deal I'll be buyin' an' sellin' the whole bunch of them. Say, nurse, what happened? Was it at the airport?"

The nurse's face and her hair were yellow under the white cap. She had a thin face without lips and thin hands that went past his eyes to smooth the sheet under his chin.

"You must try and rest," she said. "Or else I'll have to give you another hypodermic."

"Say, nurse, are you a Canadian? I bet you're a Canadian."

"No, I'm from Tennessee . . . Why?"

"My mistake. You see always when I've been in a hospital before the nurses have been Canadians. Isn't it kinder dark in here? I wish I could tell you how it happened. Have they called the office? I guess maybe I drink too much. After this I attend strictly to business. I tell you a man has to keep his eyes open in this game. . . . Say, can't you get me some water?"

"I'm the night nurse. It isn't day yet. You try and get some sleep."

"I guess they've called up the office. I'd like Stauch to take

378

a look at the ship before anything's touched. Funny, nurse. I don't feel much pain, but I feel so terrible."

"That's just the hypodermics," said the nurse's brisk low voice. "Now you rest quietly and in the morning you'll wake up feeling a whole lot better. You can only rinse out your mouth with this."

"Check."

He couldn't stop talking. "You see it was this way. I had some sort of a wrangle with a guy. Are you listenin', nurse? I guess I've got a kind of a chip on my shoulder since they've been gangin' up on me so. In the old days I used to think everybody was a friend of mine, see. Now I know they're all crooks . . . even Gladys, she turned out the worst crook of the lot. . . . I guess it's the hangover makes me so terribly thirsty."

The nurse was standing over him again. "I'm afraid we'll have to give you a little of the sleepy stuff, brother. . . . Now just relax. Think of somethin' nice. That's a good boy."

He felt her dabbing at his arm with something cold and wet. He felt the prick of the needle. The hard bed where he lay awake crumbled gradually under him. He was sinking, without any sweetness of sleep coming on, he was sinking into dark.

This time it was a stout starched woman standing over him. It was day. The shadows were different. She was poking some papers under his nose. She had a hard cheerful voice. "Good morning, Mr. Anderson, is there anything I can do for you?"

Charley was still down in a deep well. The room, the stout starched woman, the papers were far away above him somewhere. All around his eyes was stinging hot.

"Say, I don't feel as if I was all there, nurse."

"I'm the superintendent. There are a few formalities if you don't mind . . . if you feel well enough."

"Did you ever feel like it had all happened before? . . . Say, where, I mean what town . . . ? Never mind, don't tell me, I remember it all now."

"I'm the superintendent. If you don't mind, the office would like a check for your first week in advance and then there are some other fees."

"Don't worry. I've got money. . . . For God's sake, get me a drink."

"It's just the regulations."

"There must be a checkbook in my coat somewhere. . . . Or get hold of Cliff . . . Mr. Wegman, my secretary. . . . He can make out a check for you."

"Now don't you bother about anything, Mr. Anderson.

. . . The office has made out a blank check. I'll fill in the name of the bank. You sign it. That will be two hundred and fifty dollars on account."

"Bankers' Trust, New York. . . . Gosh, I can just about sign my name."

"The questionnaire we'll get the nurse to fill out later . . . for our records. . . . Well, goodbye, Mr. Anderson, I hope you have a very pleasant stay with us and wishing you a quick recovery." The stout starched woman had gone.

"Hey, nurse," called Charley. He suddenly felt scared. "What is this dump, anyway? Where am I? Say, nurse, nurse." He shouted as loud as he could. The sweat broke out all over his face and neck and ran into his ears and eyes. He could move his head and his arms, but the pit of his stomach was gone. He had no feeling in his legs. His mouth was dry with thirst.

A new pretty pink nurse was leaning over him. "What can I do for you, Mister?" She wiped his face and showed him where the bell was hanging just by his hand.

"Nurse, I'm terribly thirsty," he said in a weak voice.

"Now you must just rinse out your mouth. The doctor doesn't want you to eat or drink anything until he's established the drainage."

"Where is this doctor? . . . Why isn't he here now? . . . Why hasn't he been here right along? If he isn't careful I'll fire him and get another."

"Here's Doctor Snyder right now," said the nurse in an awed whisper.

"Well, Anderson, you surely had a narrow squeak. You probably thought you were in a plane all the time. . . . Funny, I've never known an airplane pilot yet who could drive a car. My name's Snyder. Doctor Ridgely Snyder of New York. Doctor Booth the housephysician here has called me in as a consultant. It's possible we may have to patch up your inside a little. You see when they picked you up, as I understand it, a good deal of the car was lying across your middle . . . a very lucky break that it didn't finish you right there. . . . You understand me, don't you?"

Doctor Snyder was a big man with flat closeshaven cheeks and square hands ending in square nails. A song old man Vogel used to sing ran across Charley's faint mind as he looked at the doctor standing there big and square and paunchy in his white clothes: he looked like William Kaiser the butcher, but they don't know each other.

"I guess it's the dope, but my mind don't work very good. . . . You do the best you can, doc . . . and don't spare any expense. I just fixed up a little deal that'll make their ears ring. . . . Say, doctor, what about that little girl? Wasn't there a little girl in the car?"

"Oh, don't worry about her. She's fine. She was thrown absolutely clear. A slight concussion, a few contusions, she's coming along splendidly."

"I was scared to ask."

"We've got to do a little operating . . . suture of the intestine, a very interesting problem. Now I don't want you to have anything on your mind, Mr. Anderson. . . . It'll just be a stitch here and a stitch there . . . we'll see what we can do. This was supposed to be my vacation, but of course I'm always glad to step in in an emergency."

"Well, thank you, doc, for whatever you can do. . . . I guess I ought not to drink so much. . . . Say, why won't they let me drink some water? . . . It's funny, when I first came to in here I thought I was in another of them clipjoints. Now Doris, she wouldn'ta liked me to talk like that, you know, bad grammar, conduct unbecoming an officer and a gentleman. But you know, doc, when you get so you can buy 'em and sell 'em like an old bag of peanuts, a bag of stale goobers, you don't care what they think. You know, doc, it may be a great thing for me bein' laid up, give me a chance to lay off the liquor, think about things. . . . Ever thought about things, doc?"

"What I'm thinking right now, Mr. Anderson, is that I'd like you to be absolutely quiet."

"All right, you do your stuff, doc . . . you send that pretty nurse in an' lemme talk to her. I want to talk about old Bill Cermak. . . . He was the only straight guy I ever knew, him an' Joe Askew. . . . I wonder how he felt when he died. . . . You see the last time I was—well, call it constitutionally damaged . . . him and me smashed up in a plane . . . the new Mosquito . . . there's millions in it now, but the bastards got the stock away from me. . . . Say, doc, I don't suppose you ever died, did you?"

There was nothing but the white ceiling above him, brighter where the light came from the window. Charley remembered the bell by his hand. He rang and rang it. Nobody came. Then he yanked at it until he felt the cord pull out somewhere. The pretty pink nurse's face bloomed above him like a closeup in a movie. Her young rarelykissed mouth was moving. He could see it making clucking noises, but a noise like longdistance in his ears kept him from hearing what she said. It was only when he was talking he didn't feel scared. "Look here, young woman . . ." he could hear himself talking. He was enjoying hearing himself talking. "I'm payin' the bills in this hospital and I'm goin' to have everythin' just how

381

I want it. . . . I want you to sit here an' listen while I talk, see. Let's see, what was I tellin' that bird about? He may be a doctor, but he looks like William Kaiser the butcher to me. You're too young to know that song."

"There's somebody to see you, Mr. Anderson. Would you like me to freshen your face up a little?"

Charley turned his eyes. The screen had been pushed open. In the gray oblong of the door there was Margo. She was in yellow. She was looking at him with eyes round as a bird's.

"You're not mad, Margery, are you?"

"I'm worse than mad, I'm worried."

"Everythin's goin' to be oke, Margo. I got a swell sawbones from New York. He'll patch me up. He looks like William Kaiser the butcher all except the mustaches . . . what do you know about that, I forgot the mustaches. . . . Don't look at me funny like that. I'm all right, see. I just feel better if I talk, see. I bet I'm the talkin'est patient they ever had in this hospital. . . . Margo, you know I mighta gotten to be a rummy if I'd kept on drinkin' like that. It's just as well to be caught up short."

"Say, Charley, are you well enough to write out a check? I've got to have some jack. You know you were goin' to give me a commission on that airport deal. And I've got to hire a lawyer for you. Eileen's folks are going to sue. That county attorney's sworn out a warrant. I brought your New York checkbook."

"Jesus, Margo, I've made a certain amount of jack, but I'm not the Bank of England."

"But, Charley, you said you'd open an account for me."

"Gimme a chance to get out of the hospital."

"Charley, you poor unfortunate Mr. A . . . you don't think it's any fun for me to worry you at a time like this . . . but I've got to eat like other people . . . an' if I had some jack I could fix that county attorney up . . . and keep the stuff out of the papers and everything. You know the kind of story they'll make out of it . . . but I got to have money quick."

"All right, make out a check for five thousand. . . . Damn lucky for you I didn't break my arm."

The pretty pink nurse had come back. Her voice was cold and sharp and icy. "I'm afraid it's time," she said.

Margo leaned over and kissed him on the forehead. Charley felt like he was in a glass case. There was the touch of her lips, the smell of her dress, her hair, the perfume she used, but he couldn't feel them. Like a scene in a movie he watched her walk out, the sway of her hips under the tight

382

dress, the little nervous way she was fluttering the check under her chin to dry the ink on it.

"Say, nurse, it's like a run on a bank . . . I guess they think the old institution's not so sound as it might be. . . . I'm givin' orders now, see, tell 'em down at the desk, no more visitors, see? You and me an' Doctor Kaiser William there, that's enough, see."

"Anyway, now it's time for a little trip across the hall," said the pretty pink nurse, in a cheerful voice like it was a show or a baseball game they were going to.

An orderly came in. The room started moving away from the cot, a gray corridor was moving along, but the moving made blind spasms of pain rush up through his legs. He sank into sour puking blackness again. When it was light again, it was very far away. His tongue was dry in his mouth he was so thirsty. Reddish mist was over everything. He was talking, but way off somewhere. He could feel the talk coming out of his throat, but he couldn't hear it. What he heard was the doctor's voice saying peritonitis like it was the finest party in the world, like you'd say Merry Christmas. There were other voices. His eyes were open, there were other voices. He must be delirious. There was Jim sitting there with a puzzled sour gloomy look on his face like he used to see him when he was a kid on Sunday afternoons going over his books.

"That you, Jim? How did you get here?"

"We flew," answered Jim. It was a surprise to Charley that people could hear him, his voice was so far away. "Everything's all right, Charley . . . you mustn't exert yourself in the least way. I'll attend to everything."

"Can you hear me, Jim? It's like a bum longdistance phone connection."

"That's all right, Charley. . . . We'll take charge of everything. You just rest quiet. Say, Charley, just as a precaution I want to ask you, did you make a will?"

"Say, was it peritonitis I heard somebody say? That's bad, ain't it?"

Jim's face was white and long. "It's . . . it's just a little operation. I thought maybe you'd better give me power of attorney superseding all others, so that you won't have anything on your mind, see. I have it all made out, and I have Judge Grey here as a witness and Hedwig'll come in a minute. . . . Tell me, are you married to this woman?"

"Me married? Never again. . . . Good old Jim, always wantin' people to sign things. Too bad I didn't break my arm. Well, what do you think about planes now, Jim? Not practical yet . . . eh? But practical enough to make more money than you ever made sellin' tin lizzies. . . . Don't get sore, Jim. . . . Say, Jim, be sure to get plenty of good doctors . . . I'm pretty sick, do you know it? . . . It makes you so hoarse . . . make 'em let me have some water to drink, Jim. Don't do to save on the doctors. . . . I want to talk like we used to when, you know, up the Red River fishin' when there wasn't any. We'll try the fishin' out here . . . swell fishin' right outside of Miami here. . . . I feel like I was passin' out again. Make that doctor give me somethin'. That was a shot. Thank you, nurse, made me feel fine, clears everythin' up. I tell you, Jim, things are hummin' in the air . . . mail subsidies . . . airports . . . all these new airlines . . . we'll be the foundin' fathers on all that. . . . They thought they had me out on my ass, but I fooled 'em. . . . Jesus, Jim, I wish I could stop talkin' and go to sleep. But this passin' out's not like sleep, it's like a . . . somethin' phony."

He had to keep on talking, but it wasn't any use. He was too hoarse. His voice was a faint croak, he was so thirsty. They couldn't hear him. He had to make them hear him. He was too weak. He was dropping spinning being sucked down into

Newsreel LXII

STARS PORTEND EVIL FOR COOLIDGE

If you can't tell the world
She's a good little girl
Then just say nothing at all

the elder Way had been attempting for several years to get a certain kind of celery spray on the market. The investigation of the charges that he had been beaten revealed that Way had been warned to cease writing letters, but it also brought to light the statement that the leading celery growers were using a spray containing deadly poison

As long as she's sorree
She needs sympathee

MINERS RETAIL HORRORS OF DEATH PIT

inasmuch as banks are having trouble in Florida at this time, checks are not going through as fast as they should. To prevent delay please send us express money order instead of certified check

Just like a butterfly that's caught in the rain
Longing for flowers
Dreaming of hours
Back in that sun-kissed lane

TOURISTS ROB GAS STATION

PROFIT TAKING FAILS TO CHECK STOCK RISE

the climate breeds optimism and it is hard for pessimism to survive the bright sunshine and balmy breezes that blow from the Gulf and the Atlantic

Oh it ain't gonna rain no more

HURRICANE SWEEPS SOUTH FLORIDA

SOUTH FLORIDA DEVASTATED
ONE THOUSAND DEAD, THIRTY-EIGHT THOUSAND DESTITUTE

BROADWAY BEAUTY BEATEN

Fox he got a bushy tail
Possum's tail is bare
Rabbit got no tail at all
But only a tuft o' hair

FLORIDA RELIEF FUND FAR SHORT

MARTIAL LAW LOOMS

It ain't gonna rain no more

according to the police the group spent Saturday evening at Hillside Park, a Belleville amusement resort, and about midnight went to the bungalow. The Bagley girls retired, they told the police, and when the men entered their room one of the girls jumped from a window

But how in hell kin the old folks tell
It ain't gonna rain no more?

Margo Dowling

Agnes got off the sleeper dressed from head to foot in black crape. She had put on weight and her face had a gray rumpled look Margo hadn't noticed on it before. Margo put her head on Agnes's shoulder and burst out crying right there in the sunny crowded Miami station. They got into the

Buick to go out to the beach. Agnes didn't even notice the car or the uniformed chauffeur or anything. She took Margo's hand and they sat looking away from each other out into the sunny streets full of slowlymoving people in light clothes. Margo was patting her eyes with her lace handkerchief.

"Oughtn't you to wear black?" Agnes said. "Wouldn't you feel better if you were wearing black?"

It wasn't until the blue Buick drew up at the door of the bungalow on the beach and Raymond, the thinfaced mulatto chauffeur, hopped out smiling respectfully to take the bags, that Agnes began to notice anything. She cried out, "Oh, what a lovely car."

Margo showed her through the house and out on the screened porch under the palms facing the purpleblue sea and the green water along the shore and the white breakers. "Oh, it's too lovely," Agnes said and let herself drop into a Gloucester hammock, sighing. "Oh, I'm so tired." Then she began to cry again. Margo went to do her face at the long mirror in the hall. "Well," she said when she came back looking freshpowdered and rosy, "how do you like the house? Some little shack, isn't it?"

"Oh, we won't be able to stay here now. . . . What'll we do now?" Agnes was blubbering. "I know it's all the wicked unreality of matter. . . . Oh, if he'd only had proper thoughts."

"Anyway, the rent's paid for another month," said Margo.

"Oh, but the expense," sobbed Agnes.

Margo was looking out through the screendoor at a big black tanker on the horizon. She turned her head and talked peevishly over her shoulder. "Well, there's nothing to keep me from turning over a few options, is there? I tell you what they are having down here's a boom. Maybe we can make some money. I know everybody who is anybody in this town. You just wait and see, Agnes."

Eliza, the black maid, brought in a silver coffeeservice and cups and a plate of toast on a silver tray covered by a lace doily. Agnes pushed back her veil, drank some coffee in little gulps and began to nibble at a piece of toast.

"Have some preserves on it," said Margo, lighting herself a cigarette. "I didn't think you and Frank believed in mourning."

"I couldn't help it. It made me feel better. Oh, Margo, have you ever thought that if it wasn't for our dreadful unbelief they might be with us this day." She dried her eyes and went back to the coffee and toast. "When's the funeral?"

"It's going to be in Minnesota. His folks have taken charge of everything. They think I'm ratpoison."

"Poor Mr. Anderson. . . . You must be prostrated, you poor child."

"You ought to see 'em. His brother Jim would take the pennies off a dead man's eyes. He's threatening to sue to get back some securities he claims were Charley's. Well, let him sue. Homer Cassidy's my lawyer and what he says goes in this town. . . . Agnes, you've got to take off those widow's weeds and act human. What would Frank think if he was here?"

"He is here," Agnes shrieked and went all to pieces and started sobbing again. "He's watching over us right now. I know that!" She dried her eyes and sniffed. "Oh, Margie, coming down on the train I'd been thinking that maybe you and Mr. Anderson had been secretly married. He must have left an enormous estate."

"Most of it is tied up. . . . But Charley was all right, he fixed me up as we went along."

"But just think of it, two such dreadful things happening in one winter."

"Agnes," said Margo, getting to her feet, "if you talk like that I'm going to send you right back to New York. . . . Haven't I been depressed enough? Your nose is all red. It's awful. . . . Look, you make yourself at home. I'm going out to attend to some business."

"Oh, I can't stay here. I feel too strange," sobbed Agnes.

"Well, you can come along if you take off that dreadful veil. Hurry up, I've got to meet somebody."

She made Agnes fix her hair and put on a white blouse. The black dress really was quite becoming to her. Margo made her put on a little makeup. "There, dearie. Now you look lovely," she said and kissed her.

"Is this really your car?" sighed Agnes as she sank back on the seat of the blue Buick sedan. "I can't believe it."

"Want to see the registration papers?" said Margo. "All right, Raymond, you know where the broker's office is."

"I sure do, Miss," said Raymond, touching the shiny visor of his cap as the motor started to hum under the unscratched paint of the hood.

At the broker's office there was the usual welldressed elderly crowd in sportclothes filling up the benches, men with panamahats held on knees of palmbeach suits and linen plusfours, women in pinks and greens and light tan and white crisp dresses. It always affected Margo a little like church, the whispers, the deferential manners, the boys quick and attentive at the long blackboards marked with columns of symbols, the click of the telegraph, the firm voice reading the quotations off the ticker at a desk in the back of the room. As they went in, Agnes in an awed voice whispered in Margo's ear hadn't she better go and sit in the car until Margo had finished her business. "No, stick around," said Margo. "You see those boys are chalking up the stockmarket play by play on those blackboards. . . . I'm just beginning to get on to this business." Two elderly gentlemen with white hair and broadflanged Jewish noses smilingly made room for them on a bench in the back of the room. Several people turned and stared at Margo. She heard a woman's voice hissing something about Anderson to the man beside her. There was a little stir of whispering and nudging. Margo felt welldressed and didn't care.

"Well, ma dear young lady," Judge Cassidy's voice purred behind her, "buyin' or sellin' today?"

Margo turned her head. There was the glint of a gold tooth in the smile on the broad red face under the thatch of silvery hair the same color as the gray linen suit which was crossed by another glint of gold in the watchchain looped double across the ample bulge of the judge's vest. Margo shook her head. "Nothing much doing today," she said. Judge Cassidy jerked his head and started for the door. Margo got up and followed, pulling Agnes after her. When they got out in the breezy sunshine of the short street that ran to the bathingbeach, Margo introduced Agnes as her guardian angel.

"I hope you won't disappoint us today the way you did yesterday, ma dear young lady," began Judge Cassidy. "Perhaps we can induce Mrs. Mandeville . . ."

"I'm afraid not," broke in Margo. "You see the poor darling's so tired. . . . She's just gotten in from New York. . . . You see, Agnes dear, we are going to look at some lots. Raymond will take you home, and lunch is all ordered for you and everything. . . . You just take a nice rest."

"Oh, of course I do need a rest," said Agnes, flushing. Margo helped her into the Buick that Raymond had just brought around from the parkingplace, kissed her, and then walked down the block with the judge to where his Pierce Arrow touringcar stood shiny and glittery in the hot noon sunlight.

The judge drove his own car. Margo sat with him in the front seat. As soon as he'd started the car, she said, "Well, what about that check?"

"Why, ma dear young lady, I'm very much afraid that no funds means no funds. . . . I presume we can recover from the estate."

"Just in time to make a first payment on a cemetery lot."

"Well, those things do take time . . . the poor boy seems to have left his affairs in considerable confusion."

"Poor guy," said Margo, looking away through the rows of palms at the brown reaches of Biscayne Bay. Here and there on the green islands new stucco construction stuck out raw, like stagescenery out on the sidewalk in the daytime. "Honestly I did the best I could to straighten him out."

"Of course. . . . Of course he had very considerable holdings. . . . It was that crazy New York life. Down here we take things easily, we know how to let the fruit ripen on the tree."

"Oranges," said Margo, "and lemons." She started to laugh, but the judge didn't join in.

Neither of them said anything for a while. They'd reached the end of the causeway and turned past yellow frame wharfbuildings into the dense traffic of the Miami waterfront. Everywhere new tall buildings iced like layercake were standing up out of scaffolding and builder's rubbish.

Rumbling over the temporary wooden bridge across the Miami River in a roar of concretemixers and a drive of dust from the construction work, Margo said, turning a roundeyed pokerface at the judge, "Well, I guess I'll have to hock the old sparklers."

The judge laughed and said, "I can assure you the bank will afford you ever facility. . . . Don't bother your pretty little head about it. You hold some very considerable options right now if I'm not mistaken."

"I don't suppose you could lend me a couple of grand to run on on the strength of them, judge."

They were running on a broad new concrete road through dense tropical scrub. "Ma dear young lady," said Judge Cassidy in his genial drawl, "I couldn't do that for your own sake . . . think of the false interpretations . . . the idle gossip. We're a little oldfashioned down here. We're easygoin', but once the breath of scandal . . . Why, even drivin' with such a charmin' passenger through the streets of Miamah is a folly, a very pleasant folly. But you must realize, ma dear young lady . . . A man in ma position can't afford . . . Don't misunderstand ma motive, ma dear young lady. I never turned down a friend in ma life. . . . But ma position would unfortunately not be understood that way. Only a husband or a . . ."

"Is this a proposal, judge?" she broke in sharply. Her eyes were stinging. It was hard keeping back the tears.

"Just a little advice to a client. . . ." The judge sighed. "Unfortunately I'm a family man."

"How long is this boom going to last?"

"I don't need to remind you what type of animal is born every minute."

"No need at all," said Margo gruffly.

They were driving into the parkinglot behind the great new caramelcolored hotel.

As she got out of the car, Margo said, "Well, I guess some of them can afford to lose their money, but we can't, can we, judge?"

"Ma dear young lady, there's no such word in the bright lexicon of youth." The judge was ushering her into the diningroom in his fatherly way. "Ah, there are the boys now."

At a round table in the center of the crowded diningroom sat two fatfaced young men with big mouths wearing pinkstriped shirts and nilegreen wash neckties and white suits. They got up still chewing and pumped Margo's hand when the judge presented them. They were twins. As they sat down again, one of them winked and shook a fat forefinger. "We used to see you at the Palms, girlie, naughty, naughty."

"Well, boys," said the judge, "how's tricks?"

"Couldn't be better," one of them said with his mouth full.

"You see, boys," said the judge, "this young lady wants to make a few small investments with a quick turnover. . . ." The twins grunted and went on chewing.

After lunch the judge drove them all down to the Venetian Pool where William Jennings Bryan sitting in an armchair on the float under a striped awning was talking to the crowd. From where they were they couldn't hear what he was saying, only the laughter and handclapping of the crowd in the pauses. "Do you know, judge," said one of the twins, as they worked their way through the fringes of the crowd around the pool, "if the old boy hadn't wasted his time with politics, he'da made a great auctioneer."

391

Margo began to feel tired and wilted. She followed the twins into the realestateoffice full of perspiring men in shirt-sleeves. The judge got her a chair. She sat there tapping with her white kid foot on the tiled floor with her lap full of blue-prints. The prices were all so high. She felt out of her depth and missed Mr. A to buy for her, he'd have known what to buy sure. Outside, the benches on the lawn were crowded. Bawling voices came from everywhere. The auction was beginning. The twins on the stand were waving their arms and banging with their hammers. The judge was striding around behind Margo's chair talking boom to anybody who would listen.

When he paused for breath, she looked up at him and said, "Judge Cassidy, could you get me a taxi?"

"Ma dear young lady, I'll drive you home myself. It'll be a pleasure."

"O.K.," said Margo.

"You are very wise," whispered Judge Cassidy in her ear.

As they were walking along the edge of the crowd, one of the twins they'd had lunch with left the auctioneer's stand and dove through the crowd after them. "Miss Dowlin'," he said, "kin me an' Al come to call?"

"Sure," said Margo, smiling. "Name's in the phonebook under Dowling."

"We'll be around." And he ran back to the stand where his brother was pounding with his hammer. She'd been afraid she hadn't made a hit with the twins. Now she felt the tired lines smoothing out of her face.

"Well, what do you think of the great development of Coral Gables?" said the judge as he helped her into the car.

"Somebody must be making money," said Margo dryly.

Once in the house she pulled off her hat and told Raymond, who acted as butler in the afternoons, to make some martini cocktails, found the judge a cigar, and then excused herself for a moment. Upstairs she found Agnes sitting in her room in a lavender négligée manicuring her nails at the dress-ingtable. Without saying a word Margo dropped on the bed and began to cry.

Agnes got up looking big and flabby and gentle and came over to the bed. "Why, Margie, you never cry. . . ."

"I know I don't," sobbed Margo, "but it's all so awful. . . . Judge Cassidy's down there, you go and talk to him. . . ."

"Poor little girl. Surely I will, but it's you he'll be wanting to see. . . . You've been through too much."

"I won't go back to the chorus . . . I won't," Margo sobbed.

"Oh, no, I wouldn't like that. . . . But I'll go down now. . . . I feel really rested for the first time in months," said Agnes.

When Margo was alone, she stopped bawling at once. "Why, I'm as bad as Agnes," she muttered to herself as she got to her feet. She turned on the water for a bath. It was late by the time she'd gotten into an afternoondress and come downstairs. The judge looked pretty glum. He sat puffing at the butt of a cigar and sipping at a cocktail while Agnes talked to him about Faith.

He perked up when he saw Margo coming down the stairs. She put some dancemusic on the phonograph.

"When I'm in your house I'm like that famed Grecian sage in the house of the sirens . . . I forget hometies, engagements, everything," said the judge, coming toward her onestepping.

They danced. Agnes went upstairs again. Margo could see that the judge was just on the edge of making a pass at her.

She was wondering what to do about it when Cliff Wegman was suddenly ushered into the room. The judge gave the young man a scared suspicious look. Margo could see he thought he was going to be framed.

"Why, Mr. Wegman, I didn't know you were in Miami." She took the needle off the record ánd stopped the phonograph. "Judge Cassidy, meet Mr. Wegman."

"Glad to meet you, judge. Mr. Anderson used to talk about you. I was his personal secretary." Cliff looked haggard and nervous. "I just pulled into this little old town," he said. "I hope I'm not intruding." He grinned at Margo. "Well, I'm woiking for the Charles Anderson estate now."

"Poor fellow," said Judge Cassidy, getting to his feet. "I had the honor of bein' quite a friend of Lieutenant Anderson's. . . ." Shaking his head he walked across the soft plumcolored carpet to Margo. "Well, ma dear young lady, you must excuse me. But duty calls. This was indeed delightful."

Margo went out with him to his car. The rosy evening was fading into dusk. A mockingbird was singing in a peppertree beside the house. "When can I bring the jewelry?" Margo said, leaning toward the judge over the front seat of the car.

"Perhaps you better come to my office tomorrow noon. We'll go over to the bank together. Of course, the appraisal will have to be at the expense of the borrower."

"O.K. and by that time I hope you'll have thought of some way I can turn it over quick. What's the use of having a boom if you don't take advantage of it?" The judge leaned over to kiss her. His wet lips brushed against her ear as she pulled her head away. "Be yourself, judge," she said.

In the livingroom Cliff was striding up and down fit to be tied. He stopped in his tracks and came toward her with his fists clenched as if he were going to hit her. He was chewing gum; the thin jaw moving from side to side gave him a face like a sheep. "Well, the boss soitenly done right by little Orphan Annie."

"Well, if that's all you came down here to tell me you can just get on the train and go back home."

"Look here, Margo, I've come on business."

"On business?" Margo let herself drop into a pink overstuffed chair. "Sit down, Cliff . . . but you didn't need to come barging in here like a process-server. Is it about Charley's estate?"

"Estate, hell . . . I want you to marry me. The pickin's are slim right now, but I've got a big career ahead."

Margo let out a shriek and let her head drop on the back of the chair. She got to laughing and couldn't stop laughing. "No, honestly, Cliff," she spluttered. "But I don't want to marry anybody just now. . . . Why, Cliff, you sweet kid. I could kiss you." He came over and tried to hug her. She got to her feet and pushed him away. "I'm not going to let things like that interfere with my career either."

Cliff frowned. "I won't marry an actress. . . . You'd have to can that stuff."

Margo got to laughing again. "Not even a movingpicture actress?"

"Aw, hell, all you do is kid and I'm nuts about you." He sat down on the davenport and wrung his head between his hands.

She moved over and sat down beside him. "Forget it, Cliff."

Cliff jumped up again. "I can tell you one thing, you won't get anywheres fooling around with that old buzzard Cassidy. He's a married man and so crooked he has to go through a door edgeways. He gypped hell out of the boss in that airport deal. Hell. . . . That's probably no news to you. You probably were in on it and got your cut first thing. . . . And then you think it's a whale of a joke when a guy comes all the way down to the jumpingoff place to offer you the protection of his name. All right, I'm through. Good . . . night." He went out slamming the glass doors into the hall so hard that a pane of glass broke and tinkled down to the floor.

Agnes rushed in from the diningroom. "Oh, how dreadful," she said. "I was listening. I thought maybe poor Mr. Anderson had left a trustfund for you."

"That boy's got bats in his belfry," said Margo.

A minute later the phone rang. It was Cliff with tears in his voice, apologizing, asking if he couldn't come back to talk it over. "Not on your tintype," said Margo and hung up. "Well, Agnes," said Margo as she came from the telephone, "that's that. . . . We've got to figure these things out. . . . Cliff's right about that old fool Cassidy. He never was in the picture anyways."

"Such a dignified man," said Agnes, making clucking noises with her tongue.

Raymond announced dinner. Margo and Agnes ate alone, each at one end of the long mahogany table covered with doilies and silverware. The soup was cold and too salty. "I've told that damn girl a hundred times not to do anything to the soup but take it out of the can and heat it," Margo said peevishly. "Oh, Agnes, please do the housekeeping. . . I can't get 'em to do anything right."

"Oh, I'd love to," said Agnes. "Of course I've never kept house on a scale like this."

"We're not going to, either," said Margo. "We've got to cut down."

"I guess I'd better write Miss Franklyn to see if she's got another job for me."

"You just wait a little while," said Margo. "We can stay on here for a coupla months. I've got an idea it would do Tony good down here. Suppose we send him his ticket to come down? Do you think he'd sell it on me and hit the dope again?"

"But he's cured. He told me himself he'd straightened out

completely." Agnes began to blubber over her plate. "Oh, Margo, what an openhanded girl you are . . . just like your poor mother . . . always thinking of others."

When Tony got to Miami, he looked pale as a mealyworm, but lying on the beach in the sun and dips in the breakers soon got him into fine shape. He was good as gold and seemed very grateful and helped Agnes with the housework, as they'd let the maids go; Agnes declared she couldn't do anything with them and would rather do the work herself. When men Margo knew came around, she introduced him as a Cuban relative. But he and Agnes mostly kept out of sight when she had company. Tony was tickled to death when Margo suggested he learn to drive the car. He drove fine right away, so they could let Raymond go. One day when he was getting ready to drive her over to meet some big realtors at Cocoanut Grove, Margo suggested, just as a joke, that Tony try to see if Raymond's old uniform wouldn't fit him. He looked fine in it. When she suggested he wear it when he drove her, he went into a tantrum, and talked about honor and manhood. She cooled him down saying that the whole thing was a joke and he said, well, if it was a joke, and wore it. Margo could tell he kinder liked the uniform because she saw him looking at himself in it in the pierglass in the hall.

Miami realestate was on the skids, but Margo managed to make a hundred thousand dollars profit on the options she held; on paper. The trouble was that she couldn't get any cash out of her profits.

The twins she'd met at Coral Gables gave her plenty of advice, but she was leery, and advice was all they did give her. They were always around in the evenings and Sundays, eating up everything Agnes had in the icebox and drinking all the liquor and talking big about the good things they were going to put youall onto. Agnes said she never shook the sand out of her beachslippers without expecting to find one of the twins in it. And they never came across with any parties either, didn't even bring around a bottle of Scotch once in a while. Agnes was kinder soft on them because Al made a fuss over her while Ed was trying to make Margo. One Sunday when they'd all been lying in the sun on the beach and sopping up cocktails all afternoon Ed broke into Margo's room when she was dressing after they'd come in to change out of their bathingsuits and started tearing her wrapper off her. She gave him a poke, but he was drunk as a fool and came at her worse than ever. She had to yell for Tony to come in and play the heavy husband. Tony was white as a sheet and trembled all over, but he managed to pick up a chair and was going to crown Ed with it when Al and Agnes came in to see

what the racket was about. Al stuck by Ed and gave Tony a poke and yelled that he was a pimp and that they were a couple of goddam whores. Margo was scared. They never would have got them out of the house if Agnes hadn't gone to the phone and threatened to call the police. The twins said nothing doing, the police were there to run women like them out of town, but they got into their clothes and left and that was the last Margo saw of them.

After they'd gone, Tony had a crying fit and said that he wasn't a pimp and that this life was impossible and that he'd kill himself if she didn't give him money to go back to Havana. To get Tony to stay, they had to promise to get out of Miami as soon as they could. "Now, Tony, you know you want to go to California," Agnes kept saying and petting him like a baby. "Sandflies are getting too bad on the beach, anyway," said Margo. She went down in the livingroom and shook up another cocktail for them all. "The bottom's dropped out of this dump. Time to pull out," she said. "I'm through."

It was a sizzling hot day when they piled the things in the

398

Buick and drove off up U.S. 1 with Tony, not in his uniform, but in a new waspwaisted white linen suit, at the wheel. The Buick was so piled with bags and household junk there was hardly room for Agnes in the back seat. Tony's guitar was slung from the ceiling. Margo's wardrobetrunk was strapped on behind. "My goodness," said Agnes when she came back from the restroom of the fillingstation in West Palm Beach where they'd stopped for gas, "we look like a traveling tentshow."

Between them they had about a hundred dollars in cash that Margo had turned over to Agnes to keep in her black handbag. The first day Tony would talk about nothing but the hit he'd make in the movies. "If Valentino can do it, it will be easy for me," he'd say, craning his neck to see his clear brown profile in the narrow drivingmirror at the top of the windshield.

399

At night they stopped in touristcamps, all sleeping in one cabin to save money, and ate out of cans. Agnes loved it. She said it was like the old days when they were on the Keith Circuit and Margo was a child actress. Margo said child actress, hell, it made her feel like an old crone. Toward afternoon Tony would complain of shooting pains in his wrists and Margo would have to drive.

Along the gulf coast of Alabama, Mississippi, and Louisiana the roads were terrible. It was a relief when they got into Texas, though the weather there was showery. They thought they never would get across the State of Texas, though. Agnes said she didn't know there was so much alfalfa in the world. In El Paso they had to buy two new tires and get the brakes fixed. Agnes began to look worried when she counted over the roll of bills in her purse. The last couple of days across the desert to Yuma they had nothing to eat but one can of baked beans and a bunch of frankfurters. It was frightfully hot, but Agnes wouldn't even let them get Coca-Cola at the dustylooking drugstores in the farbetween little towns because she said they had to save every cent if they weren't going to hit Los Angeles deadbroke. As they were wallowing along in the dust of the unfinished highway outside of Yuma, a shinylooking S.P. expresstrain passed them, big

new highshouldered locomotive, Pullmancars, diner, clubcar with girls and men in light suits lolling around on the observation platform. The train passed slowly and the colored porters leaning out from the Pullmans grinned and waved. Margo remembered her trips to Florida in a drawingroom and sighed.

"Don't worry, Margie," chanted Agnes from the back seat. "We're almost there."

"But where? Where? That's what I want to know," said Margo, with tears starting into her eyes. The car went over a bump that almost broke the springs.

"Never mind," said Tony, "when I make the orientations I shall be making thousands a week and we shall travel in a private car."

In Yuma they had to stop in the hotel because the camps were all full and that set them back plenty. They were all in, the three of them, and Margo woke up in the night in a high fever from the heat and dust and fatigue. In the morning the fever was gone, but her eyes were puffed up and red and she looked a sight. Her hair needed washing and was stringy and dry as a handful of tow.

The next day they were too tired to enjoy it when they went across the high fragrant mountains and came out into the San Bernardino Valley full of wellkept fruittrees, orangegroves that still had a few flowers on them, and coolsmelling irrigation ditches. In San Bernardino Margo said she'd have to have her hair washed if it was the last thing she did on this earth. They still had twentyfive dollars that Agnes had saved out of the housekeeping money in Miami, that she hadn't said anything about. While Margo and Agnes went to a beautyparlor, they gave Tony a couple of dollars to go around and get the car washed. That night they had a regular fiftycent dinner in a restaurant and went to a movingpicture show. They slept in a nice roomy cabin on the road to Pasadena in a camp the woman at the beautyparlor had told them about, and the next morning they set out early before the white clammy fog had lifted.

The road was good and went between miles and miles of orangegroves. By the time they got to Pasadena the sun had come out and Agnes and Margo declared it was the loveliest place they'd ever seen in their lives. Whenever they passed a particularly beautiful residence Tony would point at it with his finger and say that was where they'd live as soon as he had made the orientations.

They saw signs pointing to Hollywood, but somehow they got through the town without noticing it, and drew up in front of a small rentingoffice in Santa Monica. All the furnished bungalows the man had listed were too expensive and the man insisted on a month's rent in advance, so they drove on. They ended up in a dusty stucco bungalow court in the outskirts of Venice where the man seemed impressed by the blue Buick and the wardrobe trunk and let them take a place with only a week paid in advance. Margo thought it was horrid, but Agnes was in the highest spirits. She said Venice reminded her of Holland's in the old days. "That's what gives me the sick," said Margo. Tony went in and collapsed on the couch and Margo had to get the neighbors to help carry in the bags and wardrobetrunk. They lived in that bungalow court for more months than Margo ever liked to admit even at the time.

Margo registered at the agency as Margo de Garrido. She got taken on in society scenes as extra right away on account of her good clothes and a kind of a way of wearing them she had that she'd picked up at old Piquot's. Tony sat in the agency and loafed around outside the gate of any studio where there was a Spanish or South American picture being cast, wearing a broadbrimmed Cordoba hat he'd bought at a costumer's and tightwaisted trousers and sometimes cowboy boots and spurs, but the one thing there always seemed to be enough of was Latin types. He turned morose and peevish and took to driving the car around filled up with simpering young men he'd picked up, until Margo put her foot down and said it was her car and nobody else's, and not to bring his fagots around the house either. He got sore at that and walked out, but Agnes, who did the housekeeping and handled all the money Margo brought home, wouldn't let him have any pocketmoney until he'd apologized. Tony was away two days and came back looking hungry and hangdog.

After that Margo made him wear the old chauffeur's uniform when he drove her to the lot. She knew that if he wore that he wouldn't go anywhere after he'd left her except right home to change and then Agnes could take the car key. Margo would come home tired from a long day on the lot to find that he'd been hanging round the house all day strumming *It Ain't Gonna Rain No More* on his guitar, and sleeping and yawning on all the beds and dropping cigaretteashes everywhere. He said Margo had ruined his career. What she hated most about him was the way he yawned.

One Sunday, after they had been three years in the outskirts of L.A., moving from one bungalow to another, Margo getting on the lots fairly consistently as an extra, but never getting noticed by a director, managing to put aside a little money to pay the interest, but never getting together enough in a lump sum to bail out her jewelry at the bank in Miami, they had driven up to Altadena in the afternoon; on the way back they stopped at a garage to get a flat fixed; out in front of the garage there were some secondhand cars for sale. Margo walked up and down looking at them to have something to do while they were waiting.

"You wouldn't like a Rolls-Royce, would you, lady?" said the garage attendant kind of kidding as he pulled the jack out from under the car. Margo climbed into the big black limousine with a red coatofarms on the door and tried the seat. It certainly was comfortable. She leaned out and said, "How much is it?"

"One thousand dollars . . . it's a gift at the price."

"Cheap at half the price," said Margo.

Agnes had gotten out of the Buick and come over. "Are you crazy, Margie?"

"Maybe," said Margo and asked how much they'd allow her if she traded in the Buick. The attendant called the boss, a toadfaced young man with a monogram on his silk shirt.

He and Margo argued back and forth for an hour about the price. Tony tried driving the car and said it ran like a dream. He was all pepped up at the idea of driving a Rolls, even an old one. In the end the man took the Buick and five hundred dollars in tendollar weekly payments. They signed the contract then and there, Margo gave Judge Cassidy's and Tad Whittlesea's names as references; they changed the plates and drove home that night in the Rolls-Royce to Santa Monica where they were living at the time. As they turned into Santa Monica Boulevard at Beverly Hills, Margo said carelessly, "Tony, isn't that mailed hand holding a sword very much like the coatofarms of the Counts de Garrido?"

"These people out here are so ignorant they wouldn't know the difference," said Tony.

"We'll just leave it there," said Margo.

"Sure," said Tony, "it looks good."

The other extras surely stared when Tony in his trim gray uniform drove her down to the lot next day, but Margo kept her pokerface. "It's just the old family bus," she said when a girl asked her about it. "It's been in hock."

"Is that your mother?" the girl asked again, pointing with her thumb at Agnes who was driving away sitting up dressed in her best black in the back of the huge shiny car with her nose in the air.

"Oh, no," said Margo coldly. "That's my companion."

Plenty of men tried to date Margo up, but they were mostly extras or cameramen or propertymen or carpenters and she and Agnes didn't see that it would do her any good to mix up with them. It was a lonely life after all the friends and the guys crazy about her and the business deals and everything in Miami. Most nights she and Agnes just played Russian bank or threehanded bridge if Tony was in and not too illtempered to accommodate. Sometimes they went to the movies or to the beach if it was warm enough. They drove out through the crowds on Hollywood Boulevard nights when there was an opening at Grauman's Chinese Theater. The Rolls looked so fancy and Margo still had a good eveningdress not too far out of style so that everybody thought they were filmstars.

One dusty Saturday afternoon in midwinter Margo was feeling particularly desperate because styles had changed so she couldn't wear her old dresses any more and didn't have any money for new; she jumped up from her seat knocking the pack of solitaire cards onto the floor and shouted to Agnes that she had to have a little blowout or she'd go crazy. Agnes said why didn't they drive to Palm Springs to see the new resort hotel. They'd eat dinner there if it wouldn't set them back too much and then spend the night at a tourist-camp down near the Salton Sea. Give them a chance to get the chill of the Los Angeles fog out of their bones.

When they got to Palm Springs, Agnes thought everything looked too expensive and wanted to drive right on, but Margo felt in her element right away. Tony was in his uniform and had to wait for them in the car. He looked so black in the face Margo thought he'd burst when she told him to go and get himself some supper at a dogwagon, but he didn't dare answer back because the doorman was right there.

They'd been to the ladies' room to freshen their faces up and were walking up and down under the big datepalms looking at the people to see if they could recognize any movie actors, when Margo heard a voice that was familiar. A dark thinfaced man in white serge who was chatting with an importantlooking baldheaded Jewish gentleman was staring at her. He left his friend and came up. He had a stiff walk like an officer reviewing a company drawn up at attention.

"Miss Dowling," he said, "how very lucky for both of us."

Margo looked smiling into the twitching sallow face with dark puffs under the eyes. "You're the photographer," she said.

He stared at her hard. "Sam Margolies," he said. "Well, I've searched all over America and Europe for you. . . . Please be in my office for a screentest at ten o'clock tomorrow. . . . Irwin will give you the details." He waved his hand lackadaisically toward the fat man. "Meet Mr. Harris . . . Miss Dowling . . . forgive me, I never take upon myself the responsibility of introducing people . . . But I want Irwin to see you . . . this is one of the most beautiful women in America, Irwin." He drew his hand down in front of Margo a couple of inches from her face working the fingers as if he were modeling something out of clay. "Ordinarily it would be impossible to photograph her. Only I can put that face on the screen. . . ."

Margo felt cold all up her spine. She heard Agnes's mouth come open with a gasp behind her. She let a slow kidding smile start in the corners of her mouth.

"Look, Irwin," cried Margolies, grabbing the fat man by the shoulder. "It is the spirit of comedy. . . . But why didn't you come to see me?" He spoke a strong foreign accent of some kind. "What have I done that you should neglect me?"

Margo looked bored. "This is Mrs. Mandeville, my . . . companion. . . . We are taking a little look at California."

"What's there here except the studios?"

"Perhaps you'd show Mrs. Mandeville around a moving-

405

picture studio. She's so anxious to see one, and I don't know a soul in this part of the world . . . not a soul."

"Of course, I'll have someone take you to all you care to see tomorrow. Nothing to see but dullness and vulgarity. . . . Irwin, that's the face I've been looking for for the little blond girl . . . you remember. . . . You talk to me of agencies, extras, nonsense, I don't want actors . . . But, Miss Dowling, where have you been? I halfexpected to meet you at Baden-Baden last summer. . . . You are the type for Baden-Baden. It's a ridiculous place, but one has to go somewhere. . . . Where have you been?"

"Florida . . . Havana . . . that sort of thing." Margo was thinking to herself that the last time she met him he hadn't been using the broad "a."

"And you've given up the stage?"

Margo gave a little shrug. "The family were so horrid about it."

"Oh, I never liked her being on the stage," cried Agnes who'd been waiting for a chance to put a word in.

"You'll like working in pictures," said the fat man soothingly.

"My dear Margo," said Margolies, "it is not a very large part, but you are perfect for it, perfect. I can bring out in you the latent mystery. . . . Didn't I tell you, Irwin, that the thing to do was to go out of the studio and see the world . . . open the book of life? . . . In this ridiculous caravanserai we find the face, the spirit of comedy, the smile of the Mona Lisa. . . . That's a famous painting in Paris said to be worth five million dollars. . . . Don't ask me how I knew she would be here. . . . But I knew. Of course we cannot tell definitely until after the screentest . . . I never commit myself . . ."

"But, Mr. Margolies, I don't know if I can do it," Margo said, her heart pounding. "We're in a rush . . . We have important business to attend to in Miami . . . family matters, you understand."

"That's of no importance. I'll find you an agent . . . we'll send somebody. . . . Petty details are of no importance to me. Realestate, I suppose."

Margo nodded vaguely.

"A couple of years ago the house where we'd been living, it was so lovely, was washed clear out to sea," said Agnes breathlessly.

"You'll get a better house . . . Malibu Beach, Beverly Hills. . . . I hate houses. . . . But I have been rude, I have detained you. . . . But you will forget Miami. We have everything out here. . . . You remember, Margo dearest, I told you that day that pictures had a great future . . . you and . . . you know, the great automobile magnate, I have forgotten his name . . . I told you you would hear of me in the pictures. . . . I rarely make predictions, but I am never wrong. They are based on belief in a sixth sense."

"Oh, yes," interrupted Agnes, "it's so true, if you believe you're going to succeed you can't fail, that's what I tell Margie . . ."

"Very beautifully said, dear lady. . . . Miss Dowling darling, Continental Attractions at ten. . . . I'll have somebody stationed at the gate so that they'll let your chauffeur drive right to my office. It is impossible to reach me by phone. Even Irwin can't get at me when I am working on a picture. It will be an experience for you to see me at work."

"Well, if I can manage it and my chauffeur can find the way."

"You'll come," said Margolies and dragged Irwin Harris away by one short white flannel arm into the diningroom.

Welldressed people stared after them as they went. Then they were staring at Margo and Agnes.

"Let's go to the dogwagon and tell Tony. They'll just think we are eccentric," whispered Margo in Agnes's ear. "I declare I never imagined the Margolies was him."

"Oh, isn't it wonderful!" said Agnes.

They were so excited they couldn't eat. They drove back to Santa Monica that night and Margo went straight to bed so as to be rested for the next morning.

Next morning when they got to the lot at a quarter of ten Mr. Margolies hadn't sent word. Nobody had heard of an appointment. They waited half an hour. Agnes was having trouble keeping back the tears. Margo was laughing. "I bet that bozo was full of hop or something and forgot all about it." But she felt sick inside.

Tony had just started the motor and was about to pull away because Margo didn't like being seen waiting at the gate like that when a white Pierce Arrow custombuilt towncar with Margolies all in white flannel with a white béret sitting alone in the back drove up alongside. He was peering into the Rolls-Royce and she could see him start with surprise when he recognized her. He tapped on the window of his car with a porcelainheaded cane. Then he got out of his car and reached in and took Margo by the hand. "I never apologize. . . . It is often necessary for me to keep people waiting. You will come with me. Perhaps your friend will call for you at five o'clock. . . . I have much to tell you and to show you."

They went upstairs in the elevator in a long plainfaced building. He ushered her through several offices where young men in their shirtsleeves were working at draftingboards, stenographers were typing, actors were waiting on benches. "Frieda, a screentest for Miss Dowling right away, please," he said, as he passed a secretary at a big desk in the last room. Then he ushered her into his own office hung with Chinese paintings and a single big carved Gothic chair set in the glare of a babyspot opposite a huge carved Gothic desk. "Sit there, please. . . . Margo darling, how can I explain to you the pleasure of a face unsmirched by the camera? I can see that there is no strain. . . . You do not care. Celtic freshness combined with insouciance of noble Spain. . . . I can see that you've never been before a camera before. . . . Excuse me." He sank in the deep chair behind his desk and started telephoning. Every now and then a stenographer came and took notes that he recited to her in a low voice. Margo sat and sat. She thought Margolies had forgotten her. The room was warm and stuffy and began to make her feel sleepy. She was fighting to keep her eyes open when Margolies jumped up from his desk and said, "Come, darling, we'll go down now."

Margo stood around for a while in front of some cameras in a plasterysmelling room in the basement and then Margolies took her to lunch at the crowded restaurant on the lot. She could feel that everybody was looking up from their plates to see who the new girl was that Margolies was taking to lunch. While they ate, he asked her questions about her life on a great sugarplantation in Cuba, and her débutante girlhood in New York. Then he talked about Carlsbad and

Baden-Baden and Marienbad and how Southern California was getting over its early ridiculous vulgarity: "We have everything here that you can find anywhere," he said.

After lunch they went to see the rushes in the projection-room. Mr. Harris turned up, too, smoking a cigar. Nobody said anything as they looked at Margo's big gray and white face, grinning, turning, smirking, mouth opening and closing, head tossing, eyes rolling. It made Margo feel quite sick looking at it, though she loved still photographs of herself. She couldn't get used to its being so big. Now and then Mr. Harris would grunt and the end of his cigar would glow red. Margo felt relieved when the film was over and they were in the dark again. Then the lights were on and they were filing out of the projectionroom past a redfaced operator in shirtsleeves who had thrown open the door to the little black box where the machine was and gave Margo a look as she passed. Margo couldn't make out whether he thought she was good or not.

On the landing of the outside staircase, Margolies put out his hand coldly and said, "Goodbye, dearest Margo. . . . There are a hundred people waiting for me." Margo thought it was all off. Then he went on: "You and Irwin will make

410

the business arrangements . . . I have no understanding of those matters. . . . I'm sure you'll have a very pleasant afternoon."

He turned back into the projectionroom swinging his cane as he went. Mr. Harris explained that Mr. Margolies would let her know when he wanted her and that meanwhile they would work out the contract. Did she have an agent? If she didn't he would recommend that they call in his friend Mr. Hardbein to protect her interests.

When she got into the office with Mr. Harris sitting across the desk from her and Mr. Hardbein, a hollowfaced man with a tough kidding manner, sitting beside her, she found herself reading a threeyear contract at three hundred a week. "Oh, dear," she said, "I'm afraid I'd be awfully tired of it after that length of time. . . . Do you mind if I ask my companion Mrs. Mandeville to come around? . . . I'm so ignorant about these things." Then she called up Agnes and they fiddled around talking about the weather until Agnes got there.

Agnes was wonderful. She talked about commitments and important business to be transacted and an estate to care for, and said that at that figure it would not be worth Miss Dowling's while to give up her world cruise, would it, darling, if she appeared in the picture, anyway, it was only to accommodate an old friend Mr. Margolies, and of course Miss Dowling had always made sacrifices for her work, and that she herself made sacrifices for it, and if necessary would work her fingers to the bone to give her a chance to have the kind of success she believed in and that she knew she would have because if you believed with an unsullied heart God would bring things about the way they ought to be. Agnes went on to talk about how awful unbelief was and at five o'clock just as the office was closing they went out to the car with a contract for three months at five hundred a week in Agnes's handbag. "I hope the stores are still open," Margo was saying. "I've got to have some clothes."

A toughlooking grayfaced man in ridingclothes with light tow hair was sitting in the front seat beside Tony. Margo and Agnes glared at the flat back of his head as they got into the car.

"Take us down to Tasker and Harding's on Hollywood Boulevard . . . the Paris Gown Shop," Agnes said. "Oh, goody, it'll be lovely to have you have some new clothes," she whispered in Margo's ear.

When Tony let the stranger off at the corner of Hollywood and Sunset, he bowed stiffly and started off up the broad sidewalk. "Tony, I don't know how many times I've told you you couldn't pick up your friends in my car," began Margo.

She and Agnes nagged at him so that when he got home he was in a passion and said that he was moving out next day. "You have done nothing but exploit me and interfere with

my career. That was Max Hirsch. He's an Austrian count and a famous poloplayer." Next day, sure enough, Tony packed his things and left the house.

The five hundred a week didn't go as far as Agnes and Margo thought it would. Mr. Hardbein the agent took ten per cent of it first thing, then Agnes insisted on depositing fifty to pay off the loan in Miami so that Margo could get her jewelry back. Then moving into a new house in the nice part of Santa Monica cost a lot. There was a cook and a housemaid's wages to pay and they had to have a chauffeur now that Tony had gone. And there were clothes and a publicityman and all kinds of charities and handouts around the studio that you couldn't refuse. Agnes was wonderful. She attended to everything. Whenever any business matter came up, Margo would press her fingers to the two sides of her forehead and let her eyes close for a minute and groan. "It's too bad, but I just haven't got a head for business."

It was Agnes who picked out the new house, a Puerto Rican cottage with the cutest balconies, jampacked with antique Spanish furniture. In the evening Margo sat in an easychair in the big livingroom in front of an open fire playing Russian bank with Agnes. They got a few invitations from actors and people Margo met on the lot, but Margo said she wasn't going out until she found out what was what in this town.

"First thing you know we'll be going around with a bunch of bums who'll do us more harm than good."

"How true that is," sighed Agnes. "Like those awful twins in Miami."

They didn't see anything of Tony until, one Sunday night that Sam Margolies was coming to the house for the first time, he turned up drunk at about six o'clock and said that he and Max Hirsch wanted to start a polo school and that he had to have a thousand dollars right away.

"But Tony," said Agnes, "where's Margie going to get it? . . . You know just as well as I do how heavy our expenses are."

Tony made a big scene, stormed and cried and said Agnes and Margo had ruined his stage career and that now they were out to ruin his career in pictures. "I have been too patient," he yelled, tapping himself on the chest. "I have let myself be ruined by women."

Margo kept looking at the clock on the mantel. It was nearly seven. She finally shelled out twentyfive bucks and told him to come back during the week. "He's hitting the hop again," she said after he'd gone. "He'll go crazy one of these days."

"Poor boy," sighed Agnes, "he's not a bad boy, only weak."

"What I'm scared of is that that Heinie'll get hold of him and make us a lot of trouble. . . . That bird had a face like state's prison . . . guess the best thing to do is get a lawyer and start a divorce."

"But think of the publicity," wailed Agnes.

"Anyway," said Margo, "Tony's got to pass out of the picture. I've taken all I'm going to take from that greaser."

Sam Margolies came an hour late. "How peaceful," he was saying. "How can you do it in delirious Hollywood?"

"Why, Margie's just a quiet little workinggirl," said Agnes, picking up her sewingbasket and starting to sidle out.

He sat down in the easychair without taking off his white béret and stretched out his bowlegs toward the fire. "I hate the artificiality of it."

"Don't you now?" said Agnes from the door.

Margo offered him a cocktail, but he said he didn't drink. When the maid brought out the dinner that Agnes had worked on all day, he wouldn't eat anything but toast and lettuce. "I never eat or drink at mealtimes. I come only to look and to talk."

"That's why you've gotten so thin," kidded Margo.

"Do you remember the way I used to be in those old days? My New York period. Let's not talk about it. I have no memory. I live only in the present. Now I am thinking of the picture you are going to star in. I never go to parties, but you must come with me to Irwin Harris's tonight. There will be people there you'll have to know. Let me see your dresses. I'll pick out what you ought to wear. After this you must always let me come when you buy a dress." Following her up the creaking stairs to her bedroom, he said, "We must have a different setting for you. This won't do. This is suburban."

Margo felt funny driving out through the avenues of palms of Beverly Hills sitting beside Sam Margolies. He'd made her put on the old yellow eveningdress she'd bought at Piquot's years ago that Agnes had recently had done over and lengthened by a little French dressmaker she'd found in Los Angeles. Her hands were cold and she was afraid Margolies would hear her heart knocking against her ribs. She tried to think of something funny to say, but what was the use, Margolies never laughed. She wondered what he was thinking. She could see his face, the narrow forehead under his black bang, the pouting lips, the beaklike profile very dark against the streetlights as he sat stiffly beside her with his hands on his knees. He still had on his white flannels and a white stock with a diamond pin in it in the shape of a golf club. As the car turned into a drive toward a row of bright tall frenchwindows through the trees, he turned to her and said, "You are afraid you will be bored. . . . You'll be surprised. You'll find we have something here that matches the foreign and New York society you are accustomed to." As he turned his face toward her the light glinted on the whites of his eyes and sagging pouches under them and the wet broad lips. He went on whispering, squeezing her hand as he helped her out of the car. "You will be the most elegant woman there, but only as one star is brighter than the other stars."

Going into the door past the butler, Margo caught herself starting to giggle. "How you do go on," she said. "You talk like a . . . like a genius."

"That's what they call me," said Margolies in a loud voice, drawing his shoulders back and standing stiffly at attention to let her go past through the large glass doors into the vestibule.

The worst of it was going into the dressingroom to take off her wraps. The women who were doing their faces and giving a last pat to their hair all turned and gave her a quick once-over that started at her slippers, ran up her stockings, picked out every hook and eye of her dress, ran round her neck to see if it was wrinkled and up into her hair to see if it was dyed. At once she knew that she ought to have an er-mine wrap. There was one old dame standing smoking a ciga-rette by the lavatory door in a dress all made of cracked ice who had X-ray eyes; Margo felt her reading the pricetag on her stepins. The colored maid gave Margo a nice toothy grin as she laid Margo's coat over her arm that made her feel bet-ter. When she went out, she felt the stares clash together on her back and hang there like a tin can on a dog's tail. Keep a

stiff upper lip, they can't eat you, she was telling herself as the door of the ladies' room closed behind her. She wished Agnes was there to tell her how lovely everybody was.

Margolies was waiting for her in the vestibule full of sparkly chandeliers. There was an orchestra playing and they were dancing in a big room. He took her to the fireplace at the end. Irwin Harris and Mr. Hardbein, who looked as alike as a pair of eggs in their tight dress suits, came up and said goodevening. Margolies gave them each a hand without looking at them and sat down by the fireplace with his back to the crowd in a big carved chair like the one he had in his office. Mr. Harris asked her to dance with him. After that it was like any other collection of dressedup people. At least until she found herself dancing with Rodney Cathcart.

She recognized him at once from the pictures, but it was a shock to find that his face had color in it and that there was warm blood and muscle under his rakish eveningdress. He was a tall tanned young man with goldfishyellow hair and an

417

English way of mumbling his words. She'd felt cold and shivery until she started to dance with him. After he'd danced with her once, he asked her to dance with him again. Between dances he led her to the buffet at the end of the room and tried to get her to drink. She held a Scotch-and-soda in a big blue glass each time and just sipped it while he drank down a couple of Scotches straight and ate a large plate of chicken salad. He seemed a little drunk, but he didn't seem to be getting any drunker. He didn't say anything, so she didn't say anything either. She loved dancing with him.

Every now and then when they danced round the end of the room, she caught sight of the whole room in the huge mirror over the fireplace. Once when she got just the right angle she thought she saw Margolies' face staring at her from out of the carved highbacked chair that faced the burning logs. He seemed to be staring at her attentively. The firelight playing on his face gave it a warm lively look she hadn't noticed on it before. Immediately blond heads, curly heads, bald heads, bare shoulders, black shoulders got in her way and she lost sight of that corner of the room.

It must have been about twelve o'clock when she found him standing beside the table where the Scotch was.

"Hello, Sam," said Rodney Cathcart. "How's every little thing?"

"We must go now, the poor child is tired in all this noise. . . . Rodney, you must let Miss Dowling go now."

"O.K., pal," said Rodney Cathcart and turned his back to pour himself another glass of Scotch.

When Margo came back from getting her wraps, she found Mr. Hardbein waiting for her in the vestibule. He bowed as he squeezed her hand. "Well, I don't mind telling you, Miss Dowling, that you made a sensation. The girls are all asking what you used to dye your hair with." A laugh rumbled down into his broad vest. "Would you come by my office? We might have a bit of lunch and talk things over a bit."

Margo gave a little shudder. "It's sweet of you, Mr. Hardbein, but I never go to offices . . . I don't understand business. . . . You call us up, won't you?"

When she got out to the colonial porch there was Rodney Cathcart sitting beside Margolies in the long white car. Margo grinned and got in between them as cool as if she'd expected to find Rodney Cathcart there all the while. The car drove off. Nobody said anything. She couldn't tell where they were going, the avenues of palms and the strings of streetlamps all looked alike. They stopped at a big restaurant.

"I thought we'd better have a little snack. . . . You didn't

418

eat anything all evening," Margolies said, giving her hand a squeeze as he helped her out of the car.

"That's the berries," said Rodney Cathcart who'd hopped out first. "This dawncing makes a guy beastly 'ungry."

The headwaiter bowed almost to the ground and led them through the restaurant full of eyes to a table that had been reserved for them on the edge of the dancefloor. Margolies ate shredded wheat biscuits and milk, Rodney Cathcart ate a steak, and Margo took on the end of her fork a few pieces of a lobsterpatty.

"A blighter needs a drink after that," grumbled Rodney Cathcart, pushing back his plate after polishing off the last fried potato.

Margolies raised two fingers. "Here it is forbidden. . . . How silly we are in this country! . . . How silly they are!" He rolled his eyes toward Margo. She caught a wink in time to make it just a twitch of the eyelid and gave him that slow stopped smile he'd made such a fuss over at Palm Springs.

Margolies got to his feet. "Come, Margo darling . . . I have something to show you." As she and Rodney Cathcart followed him out across the red carpet, she could feel ripples of excitement go through the people in the restaurant the way she'd felt it when she went places in Miami after Charley Anderson had been killed.

Margolies drove them to a big creamcolored apartmenthouse. They went up in an elevator. He opened a door with a latchkey and ushered them in. "This," he said, "is my little bachelor flat."

It was a big dark room with a balcony at the end hung with embroideries. The walls were covered with all kinds of oilpaintings, each lit by a little overhead light of its own. There were Oriental rugs piled on the other on the floor and couches round the walls covered with zebra and lion skins.

"Oh, what a wonderful place!" said Margo.

Margolies turned to her smiling. "A bit baronial, eh? The sort of thing you're accustomed to see in the castle of a Castilian grandee."

"Absolutely," said Margo.

Rodney Cathcart lay down full length on one of the couches. "Say, Sam, old top," he said, "have you got any of that good Canadian ale? 'Ow about a little Guinness in it?"

Margolies went out into a pantry and the swinging door closed behind him. Margo roamed around looking at the brightcolored pictures and the shelves of wriggling Chinese figures. It made her feel spooky.

"Oh, I say," Rodney Cathcart called from the couch. "Come over here, Margo. . . . I like you. . . . You've got to call me Si. . . . My friends call me that. It's more American."

"All right by me," said Margo, sauntering toward the couch.

Rodney Cathcart put out his hand. "Put it there, pal," he said. When she put her hand in his, he grabbed it and tried to pull her toward him on the couch. "Wouldn't you like to kiss me, Margo?" He had a terrific grip. She could feel how strong he was.

Margolies came back with a tray with bottles and glasses and set it on an ebony stand near the couch. "This is where I do my work," he said. "Genius is helpless without the proper environment. . . . Sit there." He pointed to the couch where Cathcart was lying. "I shot that lion myself. . . . Excuse me a moment." He went up the stairs to the balcony and a light went on up there. Then a door closed and the light was cut off. The only light in the room was over the pictures.

Rodney Cathcart sat up on the edge of the couch. "For crissake, sister, drink something. . . ."

Margo started to titter. "All right, Si, you can give me a spot of gin," she said, and sat down beside him on the couch.

He was attractive. She found herself letting him kiss her, but right away his hand was working up her leg and she had to get up and walk over to the other side of the room to look at the pictures again. "Oh, don't be silly," he sighed, letting himself drop back on the couch.

There was no sound from upstairs. Margo began to get the jeebies wondering what Margolies was doing up there. She went back to the couch to get herself another spot of gin and Rodney Cathcart jumped up all of a sudden and put his arms around her from behind and bit her ear.

"Quit that caveman stuff," she said, standing still. She didn't want to wrestle with him for fear he'd muss her dress.

"That's me," he whispered in her ear. "I find you most exciting."

Margolies was standing in front of them with some papers in his hand. Margo wondered how long he'd been there. Rodney Cathcart let himself drop back to the couch and closed his eyes.

"Now sit down, Margo darling," Margolies was saying in an even voice. "I want to tell you a story. See if it awakens anything in you." Margo felt herself flushing. Behind her Rodney Cathcart was giving long deep breaths as if he were asleep.

"You are tired of the giddy whirl of the European capitals," Margolies was saying. "You are the daughter of an old armyofficer. Your mother is dead. You go everywhere, dances, dinners, affairs. Proposals are made for your hand. Your father is a French or perhaps a Spanish general. His country calls him. He is to be sent to Africa to repel the barbarous Moors. He wants to leave you in a convent, but you insist on going with him. You are following this?"

"Oh, yes," said Margo eagerly. "She'd stow away on the ship to go with him to the war."

"On the same boat there's a young American collegeboy who has run away to join the Foreign Legion. We'll get the reason later. That'll be your friend Si. You meet. . . . Everything is lovely between you. Your father is very ill. By this time you are in a mud fort besieged by natives, howling bloodthirsty savages. Si breaks through the blockade to get the medicine necessary to save your father's life. . . . On his return he's arrested as a deserter. You rush to Tangier to get the American consul to intervene. Your father's life is saved.

421

You ride back just in time to beat the firingsquad. Si is an American citizen and is decorated. The general kisses him on both cheeks and hands his lovely daughter over into his strong arms. . . . I don't want you to talk about this now. . . . Let it settle deep into your mind. Of course, it's only a rudimentary sketch. The story is nonsense, but it affords the director certain opportunities. I can see you risking all, reputation, life itself, to save the man you love. Now I'll take you home. . . . Look, Si's asleep. He's just an animal, a brute blond beast."

When Margolies put her wrap around her, he let his hands rest for a moment on her shoulders. "There's another thing I want you to let sink into your heart . . . not your intelligence . . . your heart. . . . Don't answer me now. Talk it over with your charming companion. A little later, when we have this picture done, I want you to marry me. I am free. Years ago in another world I had a wife as men have wives, but we agreed to misunderstand and went our ways. Now I shall be too busy. You have no conception of the intense detailed work involved. When I am directing a picture, I can think of nothing else, but when the creative labor is over, in three months' time perhaps, I want you to marry me. . . . Don't reply now."

They didn't say anything as he sat beside her on the way home to Santa Monica driving slowly through the thick white clammy morning mist. When the car drove up to her door, she leaned over and tapped him on the cheek. "Sam," she said, "you've given me the loveliest evening."

Agnes was all of a twitter about where she'd been so late. She was walking around in her dressinggown and had the lights on all over the house. "I had a vague brooding feeling after you'd left, Margie. So I called up Madame Esther to ask her what she thought. She had a message for me from Frank. You know she said last time he was trying to break through unfortunate influences."

"Oh, Agnes, what did it say?"

"It said success is in your grasp, be firm. Oh, Margie, you've just got to marry him. . . . That's what Frank's been trying to tell us."

"Jiminy crickets," said Margo, falling on her bed when she got upstairs, "I'm all in. Be a darling and hang up my clothes for me, Agnes."

Margo was too excited to sleep. The room was too light. She kept seeing the light red through her eyelids. She must get her sleep. She'd look a sight if she didn't get her sleep. She called to Agnes to bring her an aspirin.

Agnes propped her up in bed with one hand and gave her the glass of water to wash the aspirin down with the other; it was like when she'd been a little girl and Agnes used to give her medicine when she was sick. Then suddenly she was dreaming that she was just finishing the *Everybody's Doing It* number and the pink cave of faces was roaring with applause and she ran off into the wings where Frank Mandeville was waiting for her in his black cloak with his arms stretched wide open, and she ran into his arms and the cloak closed about her and she was down with the cloak choking her and he was on top of her clawing at her dress and past his shoulder she could see Tony laughing, Tony all in white with a white béret and a diamond golfclub on his stock jumping up and down and clapping. It must have been her yelling that brought Agnes. No, Agnes was telling her something. She sat up in bed shuddering.

Agnes was all in a fluster. "Oh, it's dreadful. Tony's down there. He insists on seeing you, Margie. He's been reading in the papers. You know it's all over the papers about how you are starring with Rodney Cathcart in Mr. Margolies' next picture. Tony's wild. He says he's your husband and he ought to attend to your business for you. He says he's got a legal right."

"The little rat," said Margo. "Bring him up here. . . . What time is it?" She jumped out of bed and ran to the dressingtable to fix her face. When she heard them coming up the stairs, she pulled on her pink lace bedjacket and jumped back into bed. She was very sleepy when Tony came in the room. "What's the trouble, Tony?" she said.

"I'm starving and here you are making three thousand a week. . . . Yesterday Max and I had no money for dinner. We are going to be put out of our apartment. By rights everything you make is mine. . . . I've been too soft . . . I've let myself be cheated."

Margo yawned. "We're not in Cuba, dearie." She sat up in bed. "Look here, Tony, let's part friends. The contract isn't signed yet. Suppose when it is, we fix you up a little so that you and your friend can go and start your polo school in Havana. The trouble with you is you're homesick."

"Wouldn't that be wonderful!" chimed in Agnes. "Cuba would be just the place . . . with all the tourists going down there and everything."

Tony drew himself up stiffly. "Margo, we are Christians. We believe. We know that the church forbids divorce. . . . Agnes, she doesn't understand."

423

"I'm a lot better Christian than you are . . . you know that, you . . ." began Agnes shrilly.

"Now, Agnes, we can't argue about religion before breakfast." Margo sat up and drew her knees up to her chin underneath the covers. "Agnes and I believe that Mary Baker Eddy taught the truth, see, Tony. Sit down here, Tony. . . . You're getting too fat, Tony, the boys won't like you if you lose your girlish figure. . . . Look here, you and me we've seen each other through some tough times." He sat on the bed and lit a cigarette. She stroked the spiky black hair off his forehead. "You're not going to try to gum the game when I've got the biggest break I ever had in my life."

"I been a louse. I'm no good," Tony said. "How about a thousand a month? That's only a third of what you make. You'll just waste it. Women don't need money."

"Like hell they don't. You know it costs money to make money in this business."

"All right . . . make it five hundred. I don't understand the figures, you know that. You know I'm only a child."

"Well, I don't either. You and Agnes go downstairs and

talk it over while I get a bath and get dressed. I've got a dressmaker coming and I've got to have my hair done. I've got about a hundred appointments this afternoon. . . . Good boy, Tony." She patted him on the cheek and he went away with Agnes meek as a lamb.

When Agnes came upstairs again after Margo had had her bath, she said crossly, "Margie, we ought to have divorced Tony long ago. This German who's got hold of him is a bad egg. You know how Mr. Hays feels about scandals."

"I know I've been a damn fool."

"I've got to ask Frank about this. I've got an appointment with Madame Esther this afternoon. Frank might tell us the name of a reliable lawyer."

"We can't go to Vardaman. He's Mr. Hardbein's lawyer and Sam's lawyer too. A girl sure is a fool ever to put anything in writing."

The phone rang. It was Mr. Hardbein calling up about the contract. Margo sent Agnes down to the office to talk to him. All afternoon, standing there in front of the long pierglass while the dressmaker fussed around her with her mouth full of pins, she was worrying about what to do. When Sam came around at five to see the new dresses, her hair was still in the dryer.

"How attractive you look with your head in that thing," Sam said, "and the lacy négligée and the little triangle of Brussels lace between your knees. . . . I shall remember it. I have total recall. I never forget anything I've seen. That is the secret of visual imagination."

When Agnes came back for her in the Rolls, she had trouble getting away from Sam. He wanted to take them wherever they were going in his own car. "You must have no secrets from me, Margo darling," he said gently. "You will see I understand everything . . . everything. . . . I know you better than you know yourself. That's why I know I can direct you. I have studied every plane of your face and of your beautiful little girlish soul so full of desire. . . . Nothing you do can surprise or shock me."

"That's good," said Margo.

He went away sore.

"Oh, Margie, you oughtn't to treat Mr. Margolies like that," whined Agnes.

"I can do without him better than he can do without me," said Margo. "He's got to have a new star. They say he's pretty near on the skids, anyway."

"Mr. Hardbein says that's just because he's fired his publicityman," said Agnes.

It was late when they got started. Madame Esther's house was way downtown in a dilapidated part of Los Angeles. They had the chauffeur let them out two blocks from the house and walked to it down an alley between dusty bungalow courts like the places they'd lived in when they first came out to the Coast years ago.

Margo nudged Agnes. "Remind you of anything?"

Agnes turned to her, frowning. "We must only remember the pleasant beautiful things, Margie."

Madame Esther's house was a big old frame house with wide porches and cracked shingle roofs. The blinds were drawn on all the grimy windows. Agnes knocked at a little groundglass door in back. A thin spinsterish woman with gray bobbed hair opened it immediately. "You are late," she whispered. "Madame's in a state. They don't like to be kept waiting. It'll be difficult to break the chain."

"Has she had anything from Frank?" whispered Agnes.

"He's very angry. I'm afraid he won't answer again. . . . Give me your hand."

The woman took Agnes's hand and Agnes took Margo's hand and they went in single file down a dark passageway that had only a small red bulb burning in it, and through a door into a completely dark room that was full of people breathing and shuffling.

"I thought it was going to be private," whispered Margo.

"Shush," hissed Agnes in her ear.

When her eyes got accustomed to the darkness she could see Madame Esther's big puffy face swaying across a huge round table and faint blurs of other faces around it. They made way for Agnes and Margo and Margo found herself sitting down with somebody's wet damp hand clasped in hers. On the table in front of Madame Esther were a lot of little pads of white paper. Everything was quiet except for Agnes's heavy breathing next to her.

It seemed hours before anything happened. Then Margo saw that Madame Esther's eyes were open, but all she could see was the whites. A deep baritone voice was coming out of her lips talking a language she didn't understand. Somebody in the ring answered in the same language, evidently putting questions.

"That's Sidi Hassan the Hindu," whispered Agnes. "He's given some splendid tips on the stockmarket."

"Silence!" yelled Madame Esther in a shrill woman's voice that almost scared Margo out of her wits. "Frank is waiting. No, he has been called away. He left a message that all would be well. He left a message that tomorrow he would impart the information the parties desired and that his little girl must on no account take any step without consulting her darling Agnes."

Agnes burst into hysterical sobs and a hand tapped Margo

426

on the shoulder. The same grayhaired woman led them to the back door again. She had some smellingsalts that she made Agnes sniff. Before she opened the groundglass door she said, "That'll be fifty dollars, please. Twenty-five dollars each. . . . And Madame says that the beautiful girl must not come any more, it might be dangerous for her, we are surrounded by hostile influences. But Mrs. Mandeville must come and get the messages. Nothing can harm her, Madame says, because she has the heart of a child."

As they stepped out into the dark alley to find that it was already night and the lights were on everywhere, Margo pulled her fur up round her face so that nobody could recognize her.

"You see, Margie," Agnes said as they settled back into the deep seat of the old Rolls, "everything is going to be all right, with dear Frank watching over us. He means that you must go ahead and marry Mr. Margolies right away."

"Well, I suppose it's no worse than signing a threeyear contract," said Margo. She told the chauffeur to drive as fast as he could because Sam was taking her to an opening at Grauman's that night.

When they drove up round the drive to the door, the first thing they saw was Tony and Max Hirsch sitting on the marble bench in the garden.

"I'll talk to them," said Agnes.

Margo rushed upstairs and started to dress. She was sitting looking at herself in the glass in her stepins when Tony rushed into the room. When he got into the light over the dressingtable, she noticed that he had a black eye. "Taking up the gentle art, eh, Tony?" she said, without turning around.

Tony talked breathlessly. "Max blacked my eye because I did not want to come. Margo, he will kill me if you don't give me one thousand dollars. We will not leave the house till you give us a check and we got to have some cash, too, because Max is giving a party tonight and the bootlegger will not deliver the liquor until he's paid cash. Max says you are getting a divorce. How can you? There is no divorce under the church. It's a sin that I will not have on my soul. You cannot get a divorce."

Margo got up and turned around to face him. "Hand me my négligée on the bed there . . . no use catching my death of cold. . . . Say, Tony, do you think I'm getting too fat? I gained two pounds last week. . . . Look here, Tony, that squarehead's going to be the ruination of you. You better cut him out and go away for another cure somewhere. I'd hate to

427

have the federal dicks get hold of you on a narcotic charge. They made a big raid in San Pedro only yesterday."

Tony burst into tears. "You've got to give it to me. He'll break every bone in my body."

Margo looked at her wristwatch that lay on the dressing-table beside the big powderbox. Eight o'clock. Sam would be coming by any minute now.

"All right," she said, "but next time this house is going to be guarded by detectives. . . . Get that," she said. "And any monkeybusiness and you birds land in jail. If you think Sam Margolies can't keep it out of the papers, you've got another think coming. Go downstairs and tell Agnes to make you out a check and give you any cash she has in the house." Margo went back to her dressing.

A few minutes later, Agnes came up crying. "What shall we do? I gave them the check and two hundred dollars. . . . Oh, it's awful. Why didn't Frank warn us? I know he's watching over us, but he might have told us what to do about that dreadful man."

Margo went into her dresscloset and slipped into a brand-new eveninggown. "What we'll do is stop that check first thing in the morning. You call up the homeprotection office and get two detectives out here on day and night duty right away. I'm through, that's all."

Margo was mad, she was striding up and down the room in her new white spangly dress with a trimming of ostrich feathers. She caught sight of herself in the big triple mirror standing between the beds. She went over and stood in front of it. She looked at the three views of herself in the white spangly dress. Her eyes were flashing blue and her cheeks were flushed. Agnes came up behind her bringing her the rhinestone band she was going to wear in her hair. "Oh, Margie," she cried, "you never looked so stunning."

The maid came up to say that Mr. Margolies was waiting. Margo kissed Agnes and said, "You won't be scared with the detectives, will you, dearie?" Margo pulled the ermine wrap that they'd sent up on approval that afternoon round her shoulders and walked out to the car. Rodney Cathcart was there lolling in the back seat in his dressclothes. A set of perfect teeth shone in his long brown face when he smiled at her.

Sam had got out to help her in. "Margo darling, you take our breaths away, I knew that was the right dress," he said. His eyes were brighter than usual. "Tonight's a very important night. It is the edict of the stars. I'll tell you about it later. I've had our horoscopes cast."

In the crowded throbbing vestibule, Margo and Rodney Cathcart had to stop at the microphone to say a few words about their new picture and their association with Sam Margolies as they went in through the beating glare of lights and eyes to the lobby. When the master of ceremonies tried to get Margolies to speak, he turned his back angrily and walked into the theater as if it was empty, not looking to the right or the left. After the show they went to a restaurant and sat at a table for a while. Rodney Cathcart ordered kidneychops.

"You mustn't eat too much, Si," said Margolies. "The pièce de résistance is at my flat."

Sure enough, there was a big table set out with cold salmon and lobstersalad and a Filipino butler opening champagne for just the three of them when they went back there after the restaurant had started to thin out. This time Margo tore loose and ate and drank all she could hold. Rodney Cathcart put away almost the whole salmon, muttering that it was topping, and even Sam, saying he was sure it would kill him, ate a plate of lobstersalad.

Margo was dizzygiggly drunk when she found that the Filipino and Sam Margolies had disappeared and that she and Si were sitting together on the couch that had the lionskin on it.

"So you're going to marry Sam," said Si, gulping down a glass of champagne. She nodded. "Good girl." Si took off his coat and vest and hung them carefully on a chair. "Hate clothes," he said. "You must come to my ranch. . . . Hot stuff."

"But you wear them so beautifully," said Margo.

"Correct," said Si.

He reached over and lifted her onto his knee.

"But, Si, we oughtn't to, not on Sam's lionskin."

Si put his mouth to hers and kissed her. "You find me exciting? You ought to see me stripped."

"Don't, don't," said Margo. She couldn't help it, he was too strong, his hands were all over her under her dress.

"Oh, hell, I don't give a damn," she said. He went over and got her another glass of champagne. For himself he filled a bowl that had held cracked ice earlier in the evening.

"As for that lion it's bloody rot. Sam shot it, but the blighter shot it in a zoo. They were sellin' off some old ones at one of the bloody lionfarms and they had a shoot. Couldn't miss 'em. It was a bloody crime." He drank down the champagne and suddenly jumped at her. She fell on the couch with his arms crushing her.

She was dizzy. She walked up and down the room trying to catch her breath. "Goodnight, hot sketch," Si said and carefully put on his coat and vest again and was gone out the door. She was dizzy.

Sam was back and was showing her a lot of calculations on a piece of paper. His eyes bulged shiny into her face as she tried to read. His hands were shaking. "It's tonight," he kept saying, "it's tonight that our lifelines cross. . . . We are married, whether we wish it or not. I don't believe in free will. Do you, darling Margo?"

Margo was dizzy. She couldn't say anything. "Come, dear child, you are tired." Margolies' voice burred soothingly in her ears. She let him lead her into the bedroom and carefully take her clothes off and lay her between the black silk sheets of the big poster bed.

It was broad daylight when Sam drove her back to the house. The detective outside touched his hat as they turned into the drive. It made her feel good to see the man's big pugface as he stood there guarding her house. Agnes was up and walking up and down in a padded flowered dressinggown in the living room with a newspaper in her hand.

430

"Where have you been?" she cried. "Oh, Margie, you'll ruin your looks if you go on like this and you're just getting a start too. . . . Look at this . . . now don't be shocked . . . remember it's all for the best."

She handed the *Times* to Margo, pointing out a headline with the sharp pink manicured nail of her forefinger. "Didn't I tell you Frank was watching over us?"

HOLLYWOOD EXTRA SLAIN AT PARTY
NOTED POLO PLAYER DISAPPEARS
SAILORS HELD

Two enlisted men in uniform, George Cook and Fred Costello, from the battleship *Kenesaw* were held for questioning when they were found stupefied with liquor or narcotics in the basement of an apartmenthouse at 2234 Higueras Drive, San Pedro, where residents allege a drunken party had been in progress all night. Near them was found the body of a young man whose skull had been fractured by a blow from a blunt instrument who was identified as a Cuban, Antonio Garrido, erstwhile extra on several prominent studio lots. He was still breathing when the police broke in in response to telephoned complaints from the neighbors. The fourth member of the party, a German citizen named Max Hirsch, supposed by some to be an Austrian nobleman, who shared an apartment at Mimosa in a fashionable bungalow court with the handsome young Cuban, had fled before police reached the scene of the tragedy. At an early hour this morning he had not yet been located by the police.

Margo felt the room swinging in great circles around her head. "Oh, my God!" she said. Going upstairs she had to hold tight to the baluster to keep from falling. She tore off her clothes and ran herself a hot bath and lay back in it with her eyes closed.

"Oh, Margie," wailed Agnes from the other room, "your lovely new gown is a wreck."

Margo and Sam Margolies flew to Tucson to be married. Nobody was present except Agnes and Rodney Cathcart. After the ceremony Margolies handed the justice of the peace a new hundreddollar bill. The going was pretty bumpy on the way back and the big rattly Ford trimotor gave them quite a shakingup crossing the desert. Margolies' face was all colors under his white béret, but he said it was delightful. Rodney

Cathcart and Agnes vomited frankly into their cardboard containers. Margo felt her pretty smile tightening into a desperate grin, but she managed to keep the wedding breakfast down. When the plane came to rest at the airport at last, they kept the cameramen waiting half an hour before they could trust themselves to come down the gangplank flushed

and smiling into a rain of streamers and confetti thrown by the attendants and the whir of the motionpicture cameras. Rodney Cathcart had to drink most of a pint of Scotch before he could get his legs not to buckle under him. Margo wore her smile over a mass of yellow orchids that had been waiting for her in the refrigerator at the airport, and Agnes looked tickled to death because Sam had bought her orchids too, lavender ones, and insisted that she stride down the gangplank into the cameras with the rest of them.

It was a relief after the glare of the desert and the lurching of the plane in the airpockets to get back to the quiet dressingroom at the lot. By three o'clock they were in their makeup. In a small room in the groundfloor Margolies went right back to work taking closeups of Margo and Rodney Cathcart in a clinch against the background of a corner of a mud fort. Si was stripped to the waist with two cartridgebelts crossed over his chest and a canvas legionnaire's képi on his head and Margo was in a white eveningdress with highheeled satin slippers. They were having trouble with the clinch on account of the cartridgebelts. Margolies with his porcelain-handled cane thrashing in front of him kept strutting back and forth from the little box he stood on behind the camera into the glare of the klieg light where Margo and Si clinched and unclinched a dozen times before they hit a position that suited him.

"My dear Si," he was saying, "you must make them feel it. Every ripple of your muscles must make them feel passion . . . you are stiff like a wooden doll. They all love her, a piece of fragile beautiful palpitant womanhood ready to give all for the man she loves. . . . Margo, darling, you faint, you let yourself go in his arms. If his strong arms weren't there to catch you, you would fall to the ground. Si, my dear fellow, you are not an athletic instructor teaching a young lady to swim, you are a desperate lover facing death. . . . They all feel they are you, you are loving her for them, the millions who want love and beauty and excitement, but forget them, loosen up, my dear fellow, forget that I'm here and the cam-

era's here, you are alone together snatching a desperate moment, you are alone except for your two beating hearts, you and the most beautiful girl in the world, the nation's newest sweetheart. . . . All right . . . hold it. . . . Camera."

Newsreel LXIII

but a few minutes later this false land disappeared as quickly and as mysteriously as it had come and I found before me the long stretch of the silent sea with not a single sign of life in sight

Whippoorwills call
And evening is nigh
I hurry to . . . my blue heaven

LINDBERGH IN PERIL AS WAVE TRAPS HIM IN CRUISER'S BOW

Down in the Tennessee mountains
Away from the sins of the world
Old Dan Kelly's son there he leaned on his gun
Athinkin' of Zeb Turney's girl

ACCLAIMED BY HUGE CROWDS IN THE STREETS

SNAPS PICTURES FROM DIZZY YARDARM

Dan was a hotblooded youngster
His Dad raised him up sturdy an' right

ENTHRALLED BY DARING DEED CITY CHEERS FROM DEPTHS OF ITS HEART

FLYER SPORTS IN AIR

His heart in a whirl with his love for the girl
He loaded his doublebarreled gun

LEADERS OF PUBLIC LIFE BREAK INTO UPROAR AT SIGHT OF FLYER

AVIATOR NEARLY HURLED FROM AUTO AS IT
LEAPS FORWARD THROUGH GAP IN CROWD

Over the mountains he wandered
This son of a Tennessee man
With fire in his eye and his gun by his side
Alooking for Zeb Turney's clan

SHRINERS PARADE IN DELUGE OF RAIN

PAPER BLIZZARD CHOKES BROADWAY

Shots ringin' out through the mountain
Shots ringin' out through the breeze

LINDY TO HEAD BIG AIRLINE

The story of Dan Kelly's moonshine
Is spread far and wide o'er the world
How Dan killed the clan shot them down to a man
And brought back old Zeb Turney's girl

a short, partly bald man, his face set in tense emotion,
ran out from a mass of people where he had been con-
cealed and climbed quickly into the plane as if afraid he
might be stopped. He had on ordinary clothes and a
leather vest instead of a coat. He was bareheaded. He
crowded down beside Chamberlin, looking neither at the
crowd nor at his own wife who stood a little in front of
the plane and at one side, her eyes big with wonder. The
motor roared and the plane started down the runway,
stopped and came back again and then took off perfectly

Architect

A muggy day in late spring in eighteen-eightyseven a tall
youngster of eighteen, with fine eyes and a handsome arrogant way of carrying his head, arrived in Chicago with seven
dollars left in his pocket from buying his ticket from Madi-

son with some cash he'd got by pawning Plutarch's *Lives*, a Gibbon's *Decline and Fall of the Roman Empire*, and an old furcollared coat.

Before leaving home to make himself a career in an architect's office (there was no architecture course at Wisconsin to clutter his mind with stale Beaux-Arts drawings), the youngster had seen the dome of the new State Capitol in Madison collapse on account of bad rubblework in the piers, some thieving contractors' skimping materials to save the politicians their rakeoff, and perhaps a trifling but deadly error in the architect's plans;

he never forgot the roar of burst masonry, the flying plaster, the soaring dustcloud, the mashed bodies of the dead and dying being carried out, set faces livid with plasterdust.

Walking round downtown Chicago, crossing and recrossing the bridges over the Chicago River in the jingle and clatter of traffic, the rattle of vans and loaded wagons and the stamping of big drayhorses and the hooting of towboats with barges and the rumbling whistle of lakesteamers waiting for the draw,

he thought of the great continent stretching a thousand miles east and south and north, three thousand miles west, and everywhere, at mineheads, on the shores of newlydredged harbors, along watercourses, at the intersections of railroads, sprouting

shacks roundhouses tipples grainelevators stores warehouses tenements, great houses for the wealthy set in broad treeshaded lawns, domed statehouses on hills, hotels churches operahouses auditoriums.

He walked with long eager steps

toward the untrammeled future opening in every direction for a young man who'd kept his hands to his work and his wits sharp to invent.

The same day he landed a job in an architect's office.

Frank Lloyd Wright was the grandson of a Welsh hatter and preacher who'd settled in a rich Wisconsin valley, Spring Valley, and raised a big family of farmers and preachers and schoolteachers there. Wright's father was a preacher too, a restless illadjusted New Englander who studied medicine, preached in a Baptist church in Weymouth, Massachusetts, and then as a Unitarian in the Middle West, taught music, read Sanskrit and finally walked out on his family.

Young Wright was born on his grandfather's farm, went to school in Weymouth and Madison, worked summers on a farm of his uncle's in Wisconsin.

His training in architecture was the reading of Viollet le

437

Duc, the apostle of the thirteenth century and of the pure structural mathematics of Gothic stonemasonry, and the seven years he worked with Louis Sullivan in the office of Adler and Sullivan in Chicago. (It was Louis Sullivan who, after Richardson, invented whatever was invented in nineteenthcentury architecture in America.)

When Frank Lloyd Wright left Sullivan, he had already launched a distinctive style, prairie architecture. In Oak Park he built broad suburban dwellings for rich men that were the first buildings to break the hold on American builders' minds of centuries of pastward routine, of the wornout capital and plinth and pediment dragged through the centuries from the Acropolis, and the jaded traditional stencils of Roman masonry, the halfobliterated Palladian copybooks.

Frank Lloyd Wright was cutting out a new avenue that led toward the swift constructions in glassbricks and steel
foreshadowed today.

Delightedly he reached out for the new materials, steel in tension, glass, concrete, the million new metals and alloys.

The son and grandson of preachers, he became a preacher in blueprints,
projecting constructions in the American future instead of the European past.

Inventor of plans,
plotter of tomorrow's girderwork phrases,
he preaches to the young men coming of age in the time of oppression, cooped up by the plasterboard partitions of finance routine, their lives and plans made poor by feudal levies of parasite money standing astride every process to shake down progress for the cutting of coupons:

The properly citified citizen has become a broker, dealing chiefly in human frailties or the ideas and inventions of others, a puller of levers, a presser of buttons of vicarious power, his by way of machine craft . . . and over beside him and beneath him, even in his heart as he sleeps, is the taximeter of rent, in some form to goad this anxious consumer's unceasing struggle for or against more or less merciful or merciless money increment.

To the young men who spend their days and nights drafting the plans for new *rented aggregates of rented cells upended on hard pavements,*
he preaches
the horizons of his boyhood,
a future that is not the rise of a few points in a hundred

438

selected stocks, or an increase in carloadings, or a multiplication of credit in the bank or a rise in the rate on callmoney,

but a new clean construction, from the ground up, based on uses and needs,

toward the American future instead of toward the painsmeared past of Europe and Asia. Usonia he calls the broad teeming band of this new nation across the enormous continent between Atlantic and Pacific. He preaches a project for Usonia:

It is easy to realize how the complexity of crude utilitarian construction in the mechanical infancy of our growth, like the crude scaffolding for some noble building, did violence to the landscape. . . . The crude purpose of pioneering days has been accomplished. The scaffolding may be taken down and the true work, the culture of a civilization, may appear.

Like the life of many a preacher, prophet, exhorter, Frank Lloyd Wright's life has been stormy. He has raised children, had rows with wives, overstepped boundaries, got into difficulties with the law, divorcecourts, bankruptcy, always the yellow press yapping at his heels, his misfortunes yelled out in headlines in the evening papers: affairs with women, the nightmare horror of the burning of his house in Wisconsin.

By a curious irony

the building that is most completely his is the Imperial Hotel in Tokyo that was one of the few structures to come unharmed through the earthquake of 1923 (the day the cable came telling him that the building had stood saving so many hundreds of lives he writes was one of his happiest days)

and it was reading in German that most Americans first learned of his work.

His life has been full of arrogant projects unaccomplished. (How often does the preacher hear his voice echo back hollow from the empty hall, the draftsman watch the dust fuzz over the carefullycontrived plans, the architect see the rolledup blueprints curl yellowing and brittle in the filingcabinet.)

Twice he's rebuilt the house where he works in his grandfather's valley in Wisconsin after fires and disasters that would have smashed most men forever.

He works in Wisconsin,

an erect spare whitehaired man, his sons are architects, apprentices from all over the world come to work with him,

drafting the new city (he calls it Broadacre City).

Near and Far are beaten (to imagine the new city you must blot out every ingrained habit of the past, build a nation from the ground up with the new tools). For the architect there are only uses:

the incredible multiplication of functions, strength and tension in metal,

the dynamo, the electric coil, radio, the photoelectric cell, the internalcombustion motor,

glass

concrete;

and needs. (Tell us, doctors of philosophy, what are the needs of a man. At least a man needs to be notjailed notafraid nothungry notcold not without love, not a worker for a power he has never seen

that cares nothing for the uses and needs of a man or a woman or a child.)

Building a building is building the lives of the workers and dwellers in the building.

The buildings determine civilization as the cells in the honeycomb the functions of bees.

Perhaps in spite of himself the arrogant draftsman, the dilettante in concrete, the bohemian artist for wealthy ladies desiring to pay for prominence with the startling elaboration of their homes has been forced by the logic of uses and needs, by the lifelong struggle against the dragging undertow of money in mortmain,

to draft plans that demand for their fulfillment a new life;

only in freedom can we build the Usonian city. His plans are coming to life. His blueprints, as once Walt Whitman's words, stir the young men:—

Frank Lloyd Wright,

patriarch of the new building,

not without honor except in his own country.

Newsreel LXIV

WEIRD FISH DRAWN FROM SARGASSO SEA

by night when the rest of the plant was still dim figures ugly in gasmasks worked in the long low building back of the research laboratory

RUM RING LINKS NATION

All around the water tank
Waitin' for a train

WOMAN SLAIN MATE HELD

BUSINESS MEN NOT ALARMED OVER COMING ELECTION

GRAVE FOREBODING UNSETTLES MOSCOW

LABOR CHIEFS RULED OUT OF PULPITS

imagination boggles at the reports from Moscow. These murderers have put themselves beyond the pale. They have shown themselves to be the mad dogs of the world

WALLSTREET EMPLOYERS BANISH CHRISTMAS WORRIES AS BONUSES ROLL IN

Left my girl in the mountains
Left her standin' in the rain

OUR AIR SUPREMACY ACCLAIMED

LAND SO MOUNTAINOUS IT STANDS ON END

441

Got myself in trouble
An' shot a county sheriff down

In the stealth of the night have you heard padded feet creeping toward you?

TROTSKY OPENS ATTACK ON STALIN

STRANGLED MAN DEAD IN STREET

Moanin' low . . .
My sweet man's gonna go

HUNT HATCHET WOMAN WHO ATTACKED
SOCIETY MATRON

CLASPS HANDS OF HEROES

GIRL DYING IN MYSTERY PLUNGE

He's the kind of man that needs the kind of woman like
me

COMPLETELY LOST IN FOG OVER MEXICO

ASSERT RUSSIA RISING

For I'm dancin' with tears in my eyes
'Cause the girl in my arms isn't you

SIX HUNDRED PUT TO DEATH AT ONCE
IN CANTON

SEE BOOM YEAR AHEAD

this checking we do for you in our investors consulting service, we analyze every individual security you own and give you an impartial report and rating thereon. Periodically through the year we keep you posted on important developments. If danger signals suddenly develop, we advise you promptly

The Camera Eye (49)

walking from Plymouth to North Plymouth through the raw air of Massachusetts Bay at each step in a small cold squudge through the sole of one shoe

looking out past the gray frame houses under the robin'segg April sky across the white dories anchored in the bottleclear shallows across the yellow sandbars and the slaty bay ruffling to blue to the eastward

this is where the immigrants landed the roundheads the sackers of castles the kingkillers haters of oppression this is where they stood in a cluster after landing from the crowded ship that stank of bilge   on the beach that belonged to no one   between the ocean that belonged to no one and the enormous forest that belonged to no one that stretched over the hills where the deertracks were up the green rivervalleys where the redskins grew their tall corn in patches forever into the incredible west

for threehundred years the immigrants toiled into the west

and now today

walking from Plymouth to North Plymouth suddenly round a bend in the road beyond a little pond and yellowtwigged willows hazy with green you see the Cordage   huge sheds and buildings companyhouses all the same size all grimed the same color a great square chimney long roofs sharp ranked squares and oblongs cutting off the sea the Plymouth Cordage   this is where another immigrant worked hater of oppression who wanted a world unfenced   when they fired him from the cordage he peddled fish   the immigrants in the dark framehouses knew him   bought his fish listened to his talk following his cart around from door to door   you ask them   What was he like?   why are they scared to talk of Bart scared because they knew him scared eyes narrowing black with fright?   a barber the man in the little grocerystore the woman he boarded with   in scared voices they ask Why won't they believe?   We knew him   We seen him every day why won't they believe that day we buy the eels?

only the boy isn't scared

pencil scrawls in my notebook the scraps of recollection the broken halfphrases the effort to intersect word with word to dovetail clause with clause to rebuild out of mangled memories unshakably (Old Pontius Pilate) the truth

the boy walks shyly browneyed beside me to the station talks about how Bart helped him with his homework wants to get ahead   why should it hurt him to have known Bart?   wants to go to Boston University we shake hands   don't let them scare you

accustomed the smokingcar   accustomed the jumble of faces rumble cozily homelike toward Boston through the gathering dark   how can I make them feel how our fathers our uncles haters of oppression came to this coast   how say   Don't let them scare you make them feel who are your oppressors America

rebuild the ruined words worn slimy in the mouths of lawyers   district-attorneys   collegepresidents Judges without the old words the immigrants haters of oppression brought to Plymouth how can you know who are your betrayers America

or that this fishpeddler you have in Charlestown Jail is one of your founders Massachusetts?

Newsreel LXV

STORM TIES UP SUBWAY; FLOODS AND LIGHTNING
DARKEN CITY

Love oh love oh careless love
Like a thief comes in the night

ONLOOKERS CRY HALLELUJAH AS PEACE DOVE
LIGHTS; SAID TO HAVE SPLIT A HUNDRED
THOUSAND DOLLARS

CRASH UPSETS EXCHANGE

CHICAGO NIPPLE SLUMP HITS TRADING ON CURB

Bring me a pillow for my poor head
A hammer for to knock out my brains
For the whiskey has ruined this body of mine
And the red lights have run me insane

FAITH PLACED IN RUBBER BOATS

But I'll love my baby till the sea runs dry

This great new searchlight sunburns you two miles away

Till the rocks all dissolve by the sun
Oh ain't it hard?

Smythe according to the petition was employed testing
the viscosity of lubricating oil in the Okmulgee plant of
the company on July 12, 1924. One of his duties was to
pour benzol on a hot vat where it was boiled down so
that the residue could be examined. Day after day he
breathed the not unpleasant fumes from the vat.

One morning about a year later Smythe cut his face while shaving and noticed that the blood flowed for hours in copious quantities from the tiny wound. His teeth also began to bleed when he brushed them and when the flow failed to stop after several days he consulted a doctor. The diagnosis was that the benzol fumes had broken down the walls of his blood vessels.

After eighteen months in bed, during which he slept only under the effect of opiates, Smythe's spleen and tonsils were removed. Meanwhile the periodic blood transfusions were resorted to in an effort to keep his blood supply near normal.

In all more than thirty-six pints of blood were infused through his arms until when the veins had been destroyed it was necessary to cut into his body to open other veins. During the whole time up to eight hours before his death, the complaint recited, he was conscious and in pain.

Mary French

The first job Mary French got in New York she got through one of Ada's friends. It was sitting all day in an art-gallery on Eighth Street where there was an exposition of sculpture and answering the questions of ladies in flowing batiks who came in in the afternoons to be seen appreciating art. After two weeks of that, the girl she was replacing came back and Mary, who kept telling herself she wanted to be connected with something real, went and got herself a job in the ladies' and misses' clothing department at Bloomingdale's. When the summer layoff came, she was dropped, but she went home and wrote an article about departmentstore workers for *The Freeman* and on the strength of it got herself a job doing research on wages, livingcosts, and the spread between wholesale and retail prices in the dress industry for the International Ladies' Garment Workers. She liked the long hours digging out statistics, the talk with the organizers, the wisecracking radicals, the workingmen and girls who came into the crowded dingy office she shared with two or three other researchworkers. At last she felt what she was doing was real.

Ada had gone to Michigan with her family and had left Mary in the apartment on Madison Avenue. Mary was relieved to have her gone; she was still fond of her, but their

interests were so different and they had silly arguments about the relative importance of art and social justice that left them tired and cross at each other so that sometimes they wouldn't speak for several days; and then they hated each other's friends. Still, Mary couldn't help being fond of Ada. They were such old friends and Ada forked out so generously for the strikers' defense committees, legal-aid funds and everything that Mary suggested; she was a very openhanded girl, but her point of view was hopelessly rich, she had no social consciousness. The apartment got on Mary French's nerves, too, with its pastelcolored knickknacks and the real Whistler and the toothick rugs and the toosoft boxsprings on the bed and the horrid little satin tassels on everything; but Mary was making so little money that not paying rent was a great help.

Ada's apartment came in very handy the night of the big meeting in Madison Square Garden to welcome the classwar prisoners released from Atlanta. Mary French, who had been asked to sit on the platform, overheard some members of the committee saying that they had no place to put up Ben Compton. They were looking for a quiet hideout where he could have a rest and shake the D. J. operatives who'd been following him around everywhere since he'd gotten to New York. Mary went up to them and in a whisper suggested her place. So after the meeting she waited in a yellow taxicab at the corner of Twentyninth and Madison until a tall pale man with a checked cap pulled way down over his face got in and sat down shakily beside her.

When the cab started, he put his steelrimmed glasses back on.

"Look back and see if a gray sedan's following us," he said.

"I don't see anything," said Mary.

"Oh, you wouldn't know it if you saw it," he grumbled.

To be on the safe side they left the cab at the Grand Central Station and walked without speaking a way up Park Avenue and then west on a cross-street and down Madison again. Mary plucked his sleeve to stop him in front of the door. Once in the apartment he made Mary shoot the bolt and let himself drop into a chair without taking off his cap or his overcoat.

He didn't say anything. His shoulders were shaking. Mary didn't like to stare at him. She didn't know what to do. She puttered around the livingroom, lit the gaslogs, smoked a cigarette, and then she went into the kitchenette to make coffee. When she got back he'd taken off his things and was warming his bigknuckled hands at the gaslogs.

"You must excuse me, comrade," he said in a dry hoarse voice. "I'm all in."

"Oh, don't mind me," said Mary. "I thought you might want some coffee."

"No coffee . . . hot milk," he said hurriedly. His teeth were chattering as if he were cold. She came back with a cup of hot milk. "Could I have some sugar in it?" he said, and almost smiled.

"Of course," she said. "You made a magnificent speech, so restrained and kind of fiery. . . . It was the best in the whole meeting."

"You didn't think I seemed agitated? I was afraid I'd go to pieces and not be able to finish. . . . You're sure nobody knows this address, or the phone number? You're sure we weren't followed?"

"I'm sure nobody'll find you here on Madison Avenue. . . . It's the last place they'd look."

"I know they are trailing me," he said with a shudder and dropped into a chair again.

They were silent for a long time. Mary could hear the gaslogs and the little sucking sips he drank the hot milk with. Then she said: "It must have been terrible."

He got to his feet and shook his head as if he didn't want to talk about it. He was a young man lankilybuilt, but he walked up and down in front of the gaslogs with a strangely elderly dragging walk. His face was white as a mushroom, with sags of brownish skin under his eyes.

"You see," he said, "it's like people who've been sick and have to learn to walk all over again . . . don't pay any attention."

He drank several cups of hot milk and then he went to bed. She went into the other bedroom and closed the door and lay down on the bed with a pile of books and pamphlets. She had some legal details to look up.

She had just gotten sleepy and crawled under the covers herself when a knocking woke her. She snatched at her bathrobe and jumped up and opened the door. Ben Compton stood there trembling wearing a long unionsuit. He'd taken off his glasses and they'd left a red band across the bridge of his nose. His hair was rumpled and his knobby feet were bare.

"Comrade," he stammered, "d'you mind if I . . . d'you mind if I . . . d'you mind if I lie on the bed beside you? I can't sleep. I can't stay alone."

"You poor boy. . . . Get into bed, you are shivering," she said. She lay down beside him, still wearing her bathrobe and slippers.

"Shall I put out the light?" He nodded. "Would you like some aspirin?" He shook his head. She pulled the covers up under his chin as if he were a child. He lay there on his back staring with wideopen black eyes at the ceiling. His teeth were clenched. She put her hand on his forehead as she would on a child's to see if he was feverish. He shuddered and drew away. "Don't touch me," he said.

Mary put out the light and tried to compose herself to sleep on the bed beside him. After a while he grabbed her hand and held it tight. They lay there in the dark side by side staring up at the ceiling. Then she felt his grip on her hand loosen; he was dropping off to sleep. She lay there beside him with her eyes open. She was afraid the slightest stir might wake him. Every time she fell asleep, she dreamed that detectives were breaking in the door and woke up with a shuddering start.

Next morning when she went out to go to the office, he

449

was still asleep. She left a latchkey for him and a note explaining that there was food and coffee in the icebox. When she got home that afternoon, her heart beat fast as she went up in the elevator.

Her first thought after she'd opened the door was that he'd gone. The bedroom was empty. Then she noticed that the bathroom door was closed and that a sound of humming came from there.

She tapped. "That you, Comrade Compton?" she said.

"Be right out." His voice sounded firmer, more like the deep rich voice he'd addressed the meeting in. He came out smiling, long pale legs bristling with black hairs sticking oddly out from under Mary's lavender bathrobe.

"Hello, I've been taking a hot bath. This is the third I've taken. Doctor said they were a good thing. . . . You know, relax. . . ." He pulled out a pinkleather edition of Oscar Wilde's *Dorian Gray* from under his arm and shook it in front of her. "Reading this tripe. . . . I feel better. . . . Say, comrade, whose apartment is this, anyway?"

"A friend of mine who's a violinist. . . . She's away till fall."

"I wish she was here to play for us. I'd love to hear some good music. . . . Maybe you're musical." Mary shook her head.

"Could you eat some supper? I've brought some in."

"I'll try . . . nothing too rich . . . I've gotten very dyspeptic. . . . So you thought I spoke all right?"

"I thought it was wonderful," she said.

"After supper I'll look at the papers you brought in. . . . If the kept press only wouldn't always garble what we say."

She heated some peasoup and made toast and bacon and eggs and he ate up everything she gave him. While they were eating, they had a nice cozy talk about the movement. She told him about her experiences in the great steelstrike. She could see he was beginning to take an interest in her. They'd hardly finished eating before he began to turn white. He went to the bathroom and threw up.

"Ben, you poor kid," she said, when he came back looking haggard and shaky. "It's awful."

"Funny," he said in a weak voice. "When I was in the Bergen County jail over there in Jersey I came out feeling fine . . . but this time it's hit me."

"Did they treat you badly?"

His teeth clenched and the muscles of his jaw stiffened, but he shook his head. Suddenly he grabbed her hand and his eyes filled with tears. "Mary French, you're being too good to me," he said. Mary couldn't help throwing her arms around

450

him and hugging him. "You don't know what it means to find a . . . to find a sweet girl comrade," he said, pushing her gently away. "Now let me see what the papers did to what I said."

After Ben had been hiding out in the apartment for about a week, the two of them decided one Saturday night that they loved each other. Mary was happier than she'd ever been in her life. They romped around like kids all Sunday and went out walking in the park to hear the band play in the evening. They threw sponges at each other in the bathroom and teased each other while they were getting undressed; they slept tightly clasped in each other's arms.

In spite of never going out except at night, in the next few days Ben's cheeks began to have a little color in them and his step began to get some spring into it.

"You've made me feel like a man again, Mary," he'd tell her a dozen times a day. "Now I'm beginning to feel like I could do something again. After all, the revolutionary labor movement's just beginning in this country. The tide's going to turn, you watch. It's begun with Lenin and Trotsky's victories in Russia." There was something moving to Mary in the way he pronounced those three words: Lenin, Trotsky, Russia.

After a couple of weeks he began to go to conferences with radical leaders. She never knew if she'd find him in or not when she got home from work. Sometimes it was three or four in the morning before he came in tired and haggard. Always his pockets bulged with literature and leaflets. Ada's fancy livingroom gradually filled up with badlyprinted newspapers and pamphlets and mimeographed sheets. On the mantelpiece among Ada's Dresdenchina figures playing musical instruments were stacked the three volumes of *Capital* with places marked in them with pencils. In the evening he'd read Mary pieces of a pamphlet he was working on, modeled on Lenin's *What's to Be Done?* and ask her with knitted brows if he was clear, if simple workers would understand what he meant.

One Sunday in August he made her go with him to Coney Island where he'd made an appointment to meet his folks; he'd figured it would be easier to see them in a crowded place. He didn't want the dicks to trail him home and then be bothering the old people or his sister who had a good job as secretary to a prominent businessman. When they met, it was some time before the Comptons noticed Mary at all. They sat at a big round table at Stauch's and drank nearbeer. Mary found it hard to sit still in her chair when the Comptons all turned their eyes on her at once. The old people were very polite with gentle manners, but she could see that they wished she hadn't come. Ben's sister Gladys gave her one hard mean stare and then paid no attention to her. Ben's brother Sam, a stout prosperouslooking Jew who Ben had said had a small business, a sweatshop probably, was polite and oily. Only Izzy, the youngest brother, looked anything like a workingman and he was more likely a gangster. He treated her with kidding familiarity; she could see he thought of her as Ben's moll. They all admired Ben, she could see; he was the bright boy, the scholar, but they felt sorry about his radicalism as if it was an unfortunate sickness he had contracted. Still his name in the paper, the applause in Madison Square Garden, the speeches calling him a workingclass hero, had impressed them.

After Ben and Mary had left the Comptons and were going into the subwaystation, Ben said bitterly in her ear, "Well, that's the Jewish family. . . . What do you think of it? Some straitjacket. . . . It 'ud be the same if I killed a man or ran a string of whorehouses . . . even in the movement you can't break away from them."

"But, Ben, it's got its good side . . . they'd do anything in the world for you . . . my mother and me, we really hate each other."

Ben needed clothes and so did Mary; she never had any of the money from the job left over from week to week, so for the first time in her life she wrote her mother asking for five hundred dollars. Her mother sent back a check with a rather nice letter saying that she'd been made Republican State Committeewoman and that she admired Mary's independence because she'd always believed women had just as much right as men to earn their own living and maybe women in politics would have a better influence than she'd once thought, and certainly Mary was showing grit in carving out a career for herself, but she did hope she'd soon come around to seeing that she could have just as interesting a career if she'd come back to Colorado Springs and occupy the social position her mother's situation entitled her to. Ben was so delighted when he saw the check, he didn't ask what Mary had got the money for.

"Five hundred bucks is just what I needed," he said. "I hadn't wanted to tell you, but they want me to lead a strike over in Bayonne . . . rayonworkers . . . you know the old munitionplants made over to make artificial silk. . . . It's a tough town and the workers are so poor they can't pay their union dues . . . but they've got a fine radical union over there. It's important to get a foothold in the new industries . . . that's where the old sellout organizations of the A.F. of

L. are failing. . . . Five hundred bucks'll take care of the printing bill."

"Oh, Ben, you are not rested yet. I'm so afraid they'll arrest you again."

He kissed her. "Nothing to worry about."

"But, Ben, I wanted you to get some clothes."

"This is a fine suit. What's the matter with this suit? Didn't Uncle Sam give me this suit himself? . . . Once we get things going, we'll get you over to do publicity for us . . . enlarge your knowledge of the clothing industry. Oh, Mary, you're a wonderful girl to have raised that money."

That fall, when Ada came back, Mary moved out and got herself a couple of small rooms on West Fourth Street in the Village, so that Ben could have some place to go when he came over to New York. That winter she worked tremendously hard, still handling her old job and at the same time doing publicity for the strikes Ben led in several Jersey towns. "That's nothing to how hard we'll have to work when we have soviets in America," Ben would say when she'd ask him didn't he think they'd do better work if they didn't always try to do so many things at once.

She never knew when Ben was going to turn up. Sometimes he'd be there every night for a week and sometimes he would be away for a month and she'd only hear from him through newsreleases about meetings, picketlines broken up, injunctions fought in the courts. Once they decided they'd get married and have a baby, but the comrades were calling for Ben to come and organize the towns around Passaic and he said it would distract him from his work and that they were young and that there'd be plenty of time for that sort of thing after the revolution. Now was the time to fight. Of course she could have the baby if she wanted to, but it would spoil her usefulness in the struggle for several months and he didn't think this was the time for it. It was the first time they'd quarreled. She said he was heartless. He said they had to sacrifice their personal feelings for the workingclass, and stormed out of the house in a temper. In the end she had an abortion, but she had to write her mother again for money to pay for it.

She threw herself into her work for the strikecommittee harder than ever. Sometimes for weeks she slept only four or five hours a night. She took to smoking a great deal. There was always a cigarette resting on a corner of her typewriter. The fine ash dropped into the pages as they came from the multigraph machine. Whenever she could be spared from the office, she went around collecting money from wealthy women, inducing prominent liberals to come and get arrested

on the picketline, coaxing articles out of newspapermen, traveling around the country to find charitable people to go on bailbonds. The strikers, the men and women and children on picketlines, in soupkitchens, being interviewed in the dreary front parlors of their homes stripped of furniture they hadn't been able to make the last payment on, the buses full of scabs, the cops and deputies with sawedoff shotguns guarding the tall palings of the silent enormouslyextended oblongs of the blackwindowed millbuildings, passed in a sort of dreamy haze before her, like a show on the stage, in the middle of the continuous typing and multigraphing, the writing of letters and workingup of petitions, the long grind of officework that took up her days and nights.

She and Ben had no life together at all any more. She thrilled to him the way the workers did at meetings when he'd come to the platform in a tumult of stamping and applause and talk to them with flushed cheeks and shining eyes, talking clearly directly to each man and woman, encouraging them, warning them, explaining the economic setup to them. The millgirls were all crazy about him. In spite of herself Mary French would get a sick feeling in the pit of her stomach at the way they looked at him and at the way some big buxom freshlooking woman would stop him sometimes in the hall outside the office and put her hand on his arm and make him pay attention to her. Mary working away at her desk, with her tongue bitter and her mouth dry from too much smoking, would look at her yellowstained fingers and push her untidy uncurled hair off her forehead and feel badly-dressed and faded and unattractive. If he'd give her one smile just for her before he bawled her out before the whole office because the leaflets weren't ready, she'd feel happy all day. But mostly he seemed to have forgotten that they'd ever been lovers.

After the A.F. of L. officials from Washington, in expensive overcoats and silk mufflers who smoked twentyfivecent cigars and spat on the floor of the office, had taken the strike out of Ben's hands and settled it, he came back to the room on Fourth Street late one night just as Mary was going to bed. His eyes were redrimmed from lack of sleep and his cheeks were sunken and gray. "Oh, Ben," she said and burst out crying. He was cold and bitter and desperate. He sat for hours on the edge of her bed telling her in a sharp monotonous voice about the sellout and the wrangles between the leftwingers and the oldline Socialists and laborleaders, and how now that it was all over here was his trial for contempt of court coming up.

"I feel so bad about spending the workers' money on my defense. . . . I'd as soon go to jail as not . . . but it's the precedent. . . . We've got to fight every case and it's the one way we can use the liberal lawyers, the lousy fakers. . . . And it costs so much and the union's broke and I don't like to have them spend the money on me . . . but they say that if we win my case, then the cases against the other boys will all be dropped. . . ."

"The thing to do," she said, smoothing his hair off his forehead, "is to relax a little."

"You should be telling me?" he said and started to unlace his shoes.

It was a long time before she could get him to get into bed. He sat there halfundressed in the dark shivering and talking about the errors that had been committed in the strike. When at last he'd taken his clothes off and stood up to lay them on a chair, he looked like a skeleton in the broad swath of gray glare that cut across the room from the streetlight outside her window. She burst out crying all over again at the sunken look of his chest and the deep hollows inside his collarbone.

"What's the matter, girl?" Ben said gruffly. "You crying because you haven't got a Valentino to go to bed with you?"

"Nonsense, Ben, I was just thinking you needed fattening up . . . you poor kid, you work so hard."

"You'll be going off with a goodlooking young bondsalesman one of these days, like you were used to back in Colorado Springs. . . . I know what to expect . . . I don't give a damn . . . I can make the fight alone."

"Oh, Ben, don't talk like that . . . you know I'm heart and soul . . ." She drew him to her. Suddenly he kissed her.

Next morning they quarreled bitterly while they were dressing, about the value of her researchwork. She said that after all he couldn't talk; the strike hadn't been such a wild success. He went out without eating his breakfast. She went uptown in a clenched fury of misery, threw up her job, and a few days later went down to Boston to work on the Sacco-Vanzetti case with the new committee that had just been formed.

She'd never been in Boston before. The town these sunny winter days had a redbrick oldtime steelengraving look that pleased her. She got herself a little room on the edge of the slums back of Beacon Hill and decided that when the case was won, she'd write a novel about Boston. She bought some school copybooks in a little musty stationers' shop and started right away taking notes for the novel. The smell of the new copybook with its faint blue lines made her feel fresh and new. After this she'd observe life. She'd never fall for a man again. Her mother had sent her a check for Christmas. With that she bought herself some new clothes and quite a becoming hat. She started to curl her hair again.

Her job was keeping in touch with newspapermen and trying to get favorable items into the press. It was uphill work. Although most of the newspapermen who had any connection with the case thought the two had been wrongly convicted, they tended to say that they were just two wop anarchists, so what the hell! After she'd been out to Dedham jail to talk to Sacco and to Charlestown to talk to Vanzetti, she tried to tell the U.P. man what she felt about them one Saturday night when he was taking her out to dinner at an Italian restaurant on Hanover Street.

He was the only one of the newspapermen she got really friendly with. He was an awful drunk, but he'd seen a great deal and he had a gentle detached manner that she liked. He liked her for some reason, though he kidded her unmercifully about what he called her youthful fanaticism. When he'd ask her to dinner and make her drink a lot of red wine, she'd tell herself that it wasn't really a waste of time, that it was important for her to keep in touch with the press services. His name was Jerry Burnham.

"But, Jerry, how can you stand it? If the State of Massachusetts can kill those two innocent men in the face of the protest of the whole world, it'll mean that there never will be any justice in America ever again."

"When was there any to begin with?" he said with a mirthless giggle, leaning over to fill up her glass. "Ever heard of Tom Mooney?" The curly white of his hair gave a strangely youthful look to his puffy red face.

"But there's something so peaceful, so honest about them; you get such a feeling of greatness out of them. Honestly they are great men."

"Everything you say makes it more remarkable that they weren't executed years ago."

"But the workingpeople, the common people, they won't allow it."

"It's the common people who get most fun out of the torture and execution of great men. . . . If it's not going too far back, I'd like to know who it was demanded the execution of our friend Jesus H. Christ?"

It was Jerry Burnham who taught her to drink. He lived himself in a daily alcoholic haze carrying his drinks carefully and circumspectly like an acrobat walking across a tight wire with a tableful of dishes balanced on his head. He was so used to working his twentyfourhour newsservice that he attended to his wires and the business of his office as casually as he'd pay the check in one speakeasy before walking around the corner to another. His kidneys were shot and he was on the winewagon he said, but she often noticed whiskey on his breath when she went into his office. He was so exasperating that she'd swear to herself each time she went out

458

with him it was the last. No more wasting time when every minute was precious. But the next time he'd ask her out, she'd crumple up at once and smile and say yes and waste another evening drinking wine and listening to him ramble on. "It'll all end in blindness and sudden death," he said one night as he left her in a taxi at the corner of her street. "But who cares? Who in hell cares . . . Who on the bloody louse-infested globe gives one little small microscopic vestigial hoot?"

As courtdecision after courtdecision was lost and the rancid Boston spring warmed into summer and the governor's commission reported adversely and no hope remained but a pardon from the governor himself, Mary worked more and more desperately hard. She wrote articles, she talked to politicians and ministers and argued with editors, she made speeches in unionhalls. She wrote her mother pitiful humiliating letters to get money out of her on all sorts of pretexts. Every cent she could scrape up went into the work of her committee. There were always stationery and stamps and telegrams and phonecalls to pay for. She spent long evenings trying to coax communists, socialists, anarchists, liberals into working together. Hurrying along the stonepaved streets, she'd be whispering to herself, "They've got to be saved, they've got to be saved." When at last she got to bed, her dreams were full of impossible tasks; she was trying to glue a broken teapot together and as soon as she got one side of it mended the other side would come to pieces again; she was trying to mend a rent in her skirt and by the time the bottom was sewed the top had come undone again; she was trying to put together pieces of a torn typewritten sheet, the telegram was of the greatest importance, she couldn't see, it was all a blur before her eyes; it was the evidence that would force a new trial, her eyes were too bad, when she had spelled out one word from the swollen throbbing letters she'd forgotten the last one; she was climbing a shaky hillside among black guttedlooking houses pitching at crazy angles where steel-workers lived, at each step she slid back, it was too steep, she was crying for help, yelling, sliding back. Then warm reassuring voices like Ben Compton's when he was feeling well were telling her that Public Opinion wouldn't allow it, that after all Americans had a sense of Justice and Fair Play, that the Workingclass would rise; she'd see crowded meetings, slogans, banners, glary billboards with letters pitching into perspective saying: *Workers of the World Unite*, she'd be marching in the middle of crowds in parades of protest. They Shall Not Die.

She'd wake up with a start, bathe and dress hurriedly, and

rush down to the office of the committee, snatching up a glass of orangejuice and a cup of coffee on the way. She was always the first there; if she slackened her work for a moment, she'd see their faces, the shoemaker's sharplymodeled pale face with the flashing eyes and the fishpeddler's philosophical mustaches and his musing unscared eyes. She'd see behind them the electric chair as clear as if it were standing in front of her desk in the stuffy crowded office.

July went by all too fast. August came. A growing crowd of all sorts of people began pouring through the office: old friends, wobblies who'd hitchhiked from the Coast, politicians interested in the Italian vote, lawyers with suggestions for the defense, writers, outofwork newspapermen, cranks and phonies of all kinds attracted by rumors of an enormous defensefund. She came back one afternoon from speaking in a unionhall in Pawtucket and found G. H. Barrow sitting at her desk. He had written a great pile of personal telegrams to senators, congressmen, ministers, laborleaders, demanding that they join in the protest in the name of justice and civilization and the workingclass, long telegrams and cables at top rates. She figured out the cost as she checked them off. She didn't know how the committee could pay for them, but she handed them to the messengerboy waiting outside. She could hardly believe that those words had made her veins tingle only a few weeks before. It shocked her to think how meaningless they seemed to her now like the little cards you get from a onecent fortunetelling machine. For six months now she'd been reading and writing the same words every day.

Mary didn't have time to be embarrassed meeting George Barrow. They went out together to get a plate of soup at a cafeteria talking about nothing but the case as if they'd never known each other before. Picketing the State House had begun again, and as they came out of the restaurant Mary turned to him and said, "Well, George, how about going up and getting arrested. . . . There's still time to make the afternoon papers. Your name would give us back the front page."

He flushed red, and stood there in front of the restaurant in the noontime crowd looking tall and nervous and popeyed in his natty lightgray suit. "But, my dear g-g-girl, I . . . if I thought it would do the slightest good I would . . . I'd get myself arrested or run over by a truck . . . but I think it would rob me of whatever usefulness I might have."

Mary French looked him straight in the eye, her face white with fury. "I didn't think you'd take the risk," she said, clipping each word off and spitting it in his face. She turned her back on him and hurried to the office.

It was a sort of relief when she was arrested herself. She'd planned to keep out of sight of the cops, as she had been told her work was too valuable to lose, but she'd had to run up the Hill with a set of placards for a new batch of picketers who had gone off without them. There was nobody in the office she could send. She was just crossing Beacon Street when two large polite cops suddenly appeared, one on each side of her. One of them said, "Sorry, Miss, please come quietly," and she found herself sitting in the dark patrolwagon. Driving to the policestation, she had a soothing sense of helplessness and irresponsibility. It was the first time in weeks she had felt herself relax. At the Joy Street Station they booked her, but they didn't put her in a cell. She sat on a bench opposite the window with two Jewish garmentworkers and a welldressed woman in a flowered summer dress with a string of pearls round her neck and watched the men picketers pouring through into the cells. The cops were polite, everybody was jolly; it seemed like a kind of game, it was hard to believe anything real was at stake.

In a crowd that had just been unloaded from the wagon on the steep street outside the policestation, she caught sight of a tall man she recognized as Donald Stevens from his picture in *The Daily*. A redfaced cop held on to each of his arms. His shirt was torn open at the neck and his necktie had a stringy look as if somebody had been yanking on it. The first thing Mary thought was how handsomely he held himself. He had steelgray hair and a brown outdoorlooking skin and luminous gray eyes over high cheekbones. When he was led away from the desk, she followed his broad shoulders with her eyes into the gloom of the cells. The woman next to her whispered in an awed voice that he was being held for inciting to riot instead of sauntering and loitering like the rest. Five thousand dollars bail. He had tried to hold a meeting on Boston Common.

Mary had been there about a halfhour when little Mr. Feinstein from the office came round with a tall fashionably-dressed man in a linen suit who put up the bail for her. At the same time Donald Stevens was bailed out. The four of them walked down the hill from the policestation together. At the corner the man in the linen suit said, "You two were too useful to leave in there all day. . . . Perhaps we'll see you at the Bellevue. . . . suite D, second floor." Then he waved his hand and left them. Mary was so anxious to talk to Donald Stevens she didn't think to ask the man's name. Events were going past her faster than she could focus her mind on them.

Mary plucked at Donald Stevens's sleeve, she and Mr. Feinstein both had to hurry to keep up with his long stride.

"I'm Mary French," she said. "What can we do? . . . We've got to do something."

He turned to her with a broad smile as if he'd seen her for the first time. "I've heard of you," he said. "You're a plucky little girl . . . you've been putting up a real fight in spite of your liberal committee."

"But they've done the best they could," she said.

"We've got to get the entire workingclass of Boston out on the streets," said Stevens in his deep rattling voice.

"We've gotten out the garmentworkers, but that's all."

He struck his open palm with his fist. "What about the Italians? What about the North End? Where's your office?

Look what we did in New York. Why can't you do it here?" He leaned over toward her with a caressing confidential manner. Right away the feeling of being tired and harassed left her, without thinking she put her hand on his arm. "We'll go and talk to your committee; then we'll talk to the Italian committee. Then we'll shake up the unions."

"But, Don, we've only got thirty hours," said Mr. Feinstein in a dry tired voice. "I have more confidence in political pressure being applied to the governor. You know he has presidential aspirations. I think the governor's going to commute the sentences."

At the office Mary found Jerry Burnham waiting for her. "Well, Joan of Arc," he said, "I was just going down to bail you out. But I see they've turned you loose."

Jerry and Donald Stevens had evidently known each other before. "Well, Jerry," said Donald Stevens savagely, "doesn't this shake you out of your cynical pose a little?"

"I don't see why it should. It's nothing new to me that collegepresidents are skunks."

Donald Stevens drew off against the wall as if he were holding himself back from giving Jerry a punch in the jaw. "I can't see how any man who has any manhood left can help getting red . . . even a pettybourgeois journalist."

"My dear Don, you ought to know by this time that we hocked our manhood for a brass check about the time of the First World War . . . that is if we had any . . . I suppose there'd be various opinions about that."

Donald Stevens had already swung on into the inner office. Mary found herself looking into Jerry's reddening face, not knowing what to say. "Well, Mary, if you have a need for a pickup during the day . . . I should think you would need it . . . I'll be at the old stand."

"Oh, I won't have time," Mary said coldly. She could hear Donald Stevens's deep voice from the inner office. She hurried on after him.

The lawyers had failed. Talking, wrangling, arguing about how a lastminute protest could be organized, Mary could feel the hours ebbing, the hours of these men's lives. She felt the minutes dripping away as actually as if they were bleeding from her own wrists. She felt weak and sick. She couldn't think of anything. It was a relief to be out in the street trotting to keep up with Donald Stevens's big stride. They made a round of the committees. It was nearly noon, nothing was done.

Down on Hanover Street a palefaced Italian in a shaggy Ford sedan hailed them. Stevens opened the door of the car.

"Comrade French, this is Comrade Strozzi . . . he's going to drive us around."

"Are you a citizen?" she asked with an anxious frown.

Strozzi shook his head and smiled a thinlipped smile. "Maybe they give me a free trip back to Italy," he said.

Mary never remembered what they did the rest of the day. They drove all over the poorer Boston suburbs. Often the men they were looking for were out. A great deal of the time she spent in phonebooths calling wrong numbers. She couldn't seem to do anything right. She looked with numb staring eyes out of eyelids that felt like sandpaper at the men and women crowding into the office. Stevens had lost the irritated stinging manner he'd had at first. He argued with tradeunion officials, socialists, ministers, lawyers, with an aloof sarcastic coolness. "After all, they are brave men. It doesn't matter whether they are saved or not any more, it's the power of the workingclass that's got to be saved," he'd say. Everywhere there was the same opinion. A demonstration will mean violence, will spoil the chance that the governor will commute at the last moment. Mary had lost all her initiative. Suddenly she'd become Donald Stevens's secretary. She was least unhappy when she was running small errands for him.

Late that night she went through all the Italian restaurants on Hanover Street looking for an anarchist Stevens wanted to see. Every place was empty. There was a hush over everything. Deathwatch. People kept away from each other as if to avoid some contagion. At the back of a room in a little upstairs speakeasy she saw Jerry Burnham sitting alone at a table with a jigger of whiskey and a bottle of gingerale in front of him. His face was white as a napkin and he was teetering gently in his chair. He stared at her without seeing her. The waiter was bending over him shaking him. He was hopelessly drunk.

It was a relief to run back to the office where Stevens was still trying to line up a general strike. He gave her a searching look when she came in. "Failed again," she said bitterly. He put down the telephone receiver, got to his feet, strode over to the line of hooks on the grimy yellow wall and got down his hat and coat. "Mary French, you're deadtired. I'm going to take you home."

They had to walk around several blocks to avoid the cordon of police guarding the State House.

"Ever played tug of war?" Don was saying. "You pull with all your might, but the other guys are heavier and you feel yourself being dragged their way. You're being pulled forward faster than you're pulling back. . . . Don't let me talk like a defeatist. . . . We're not a couple of goddamned liberals," he said, and burst into a dry laugh. "Don't you hate lawyers?"

They were standing in front of the bowfronted brick house where she had her room.

"Goodnight, Don," she said.

"Goodnight, Mary, try and sleep."

Monday was like another Sunday. She woke late. It was an agony getting out of bed. It was a fight to put on her clothes, to go down to the office and face the defeated eyes. The people she met on the street seemed to look away from her when she passed them. Deathwatch. The streets were quiet, even the traffic seemed muffled as if the whole city were under the terror of dying that night. The day passed in a monotonous mumble of words, columns in newspapers, telephone calls. Deathwatch. That night she had a moment of fierce excitement when she and Don started for Charlestown to join the protest parade. She hadn't expected they'd be so many. Gusts of singing, scattered bars of the *International*, burst and faded above the packed heads between the blank windows of the dingy houses. Deathwatch. On one side of her was a little man with eyeglasses who said he was a musicteacher, on the other a Jewish girl, a member of the Ladies' Fullfashioned

Hosiery Workers. They linked arms. Don was in the front rank, a little ahead. They were crossing the bridge. They were walking on cobbles on a badlylighted street under an elevated structure. Trains roared overhead. "Only a few blocks from Chalestown jail," a voice yelled.

This time the cops were using their clubs. There was the clatter of the horses' hoofs on the cobbles and the whack thud whack thud of the clubs. And way off the jangle jangle of patrolwagons. Mary was terribly scared. A big truck was bearing down on her. She jumped to one side out of the way behind one of the girder supports. Two cops had hold of her. She clung to the grimy girder. A cop was cracking her on the hand with his club. She wasn't much hurt, she was in a patrolwagon, she'd lost her hat and her hair had come down. She caught herself thinking that she ought to have her hair bobbed if she was going to do much of this sort of thing.

"Anybody know where Don Stevens is?"

Don's voice came a little shakily from the blackness in front. "That you, Mary?"

"How are you, Don?"

"O.K. Sure. A little battered round the head an' ears."

"He's bleedin' terrible," came another man's voice.

"Comrades, let's sing," Don's voice shouted.

Mary forgot everything as her voice joined his voice, all their voices, the voices of the crowds being driven back across the bridge in singing:

Arise, ye prisoners of starvation . . .

Newsreel LXVI

HOLMES DENIES STAY

A better world's in birth

Tiny wasps imported from Korea in battle to death with Asiatic beetle

BOY CARRIED MILE DOWN SEWER; SHOT OUT ALIVE

CHICAGO BARS MEETINGS

For justice thunders condemnation

WASHINGTON KEEPS EYE ON RADICALS

Arise rejected of the earth

PARIS BRUSSELS MOSCOW GENEVA ADD THEIR VOICES

*It is the final conflict
Let each stand in his place*

GEOLOGIST LOST IN CAVE SIX DAYS

The International Party

SACCO AND VANZETTI MUST DIE

Shall be the human race.

Much I thought of you when I was lying in the death house—the singing, the kind tender voices of the children

467

from the playground where there was all the life and the joy of liberty—just one step from the wall that contains the buried agony of three buried souls. It would remind me so often of you and your sister and I wish I could see you every moment, but I feel better that you will not come to the death house so that you could not see the horrible picture of three living in agony waiting to be electrocuted.

The Camera Eye (50)

they have clubbed us off the streets   they are stronger   they are rich   they hire and fire the politicians the newspapereditors the old judges the small men with reputations the collegepresidents the wardheelers (listen businessmen collegepresidents judges   America will not forget her betrayers) they hire the men with guns   the uniforms the policecars the patrolwagons

all right you have won   you will kill the brave men our friends tonight

there is nothing left to do   we are beaten   we the beaten crowd together in these old dingy schoolrooms on Salem Street   shuffle up and down the gritty creaking stairs sit hunched with bowed heads on benches and hear the old words of the haters of oppression   made new in sweat and agony tonight

our work is over   the scribbled phrases   the nights typing releases the smell of the printshop the sharp reek of newprinted leaflets the rush for Western Union stringing words into wires the search for stinging words to make you feel who are your oppressors America

America our nation has been beaten by strangers who have turned our language inside out who have taken the clean words our fathers spoke and made them slimy and foul

their hired men sit on the judge's bench they sit back with their feet on the tables under the dome of the State House they are ignorant of our beliefs they have the dollars the guns the armed forces the powerplants

they have built the electricchair and hired the executioner to throw the switch all right we are two nations

America our nation has been beaten by strangers who have bought the laws and fenced off the meadows and cut down the woods for pulp and turned our pleasant cities into slums and sweated the wealth out of our people and when they want to they hire the executioner to throw the switch

but do they know that the old words of the immigrants are being renewed in blood and agony tonight do they know that the old American speech of the haters of oppression is new tonight in the mouth of an old woman from Pittsburgh of a husky boilermaker from Frisco who hopped freights clear from the Coast to come here in the mouth of a Back Bay socialworker in the mouth of an Italian printer of a hobo from Arkansas   the language of the beaten nation is not forgotten in our ears tonight

the men in the deathhouse made the old words new before they died

If it had not been for these things, I might have lived out my life talking at streetcorners to scorning men. I might have died unknown, unmarked, a failure. This is our career and our triumph. Never in our full life can we hope to do such work for tolerance, for justice, for man's understanding of man as now we do by an accident.

now their work is over   the immigrants haters of oppression lie quiet in black suits in the little undertaking parlor in the North End   the city is quiet   the men of the conquering nation are not to be seen on the streets

they have won why are they scared to be seen on the streets?   on the streets you see only the downcast faces of the beaten   the streets belong to the beaten nation all the way to the cemetery where the bodies of the immigrants are to be burned   we line the curbs in the drizzling rain we crowd the wet sidewalks elbow to elbow silent pale looking with scared eyes at the coffins

we stand defeated America

Newsreel LXVII

when things are upset, there's always chaos, said Mr. Ford. Work can accomplish wonders and overcome chaotic conditions. When the Russian masses will learn to want more than they have, when they will want white collars, soap, better clothes, better shoes, better housing, better living conditions

> *I lift up my finger and I say tweet tweet*
> > *slush   slush*
> > > *now now*
> > > > *come come*

REPUBLIC-TRUMBULL STEEL MERGER VOTED

> *There along the dreamy Amazon*
> *We met upon the shore*
> *Tho' the love I knew is ever gone*

WHEAT OVERSOLD REACHES NEW HIGH

> *Dreams linger on*

the first thing the volunteer firefighters did was to open the windows to let the smoke out. This created a draft and the fire with a good thirty mile wind right from the ocean did the rest

RECORD TURNOVER IN INSURANCE SHARES AS TRADING PROGRESSES

outside the scene was a veritable bedlam. Well-dressed women walked up and down wringing their hands, helpless to save their belongings, while from the windows of the upper stories there rained a shower of trunks, suitcases and clothing hurled out indiscriminately. Jewelry and bricabrac valued at thousands was picked up by the spectators from the lawn, who thrust the objects under their coats and disappeared

BROKERS LOANS HIT NEW HIGH

Change all of your gray skies
Turn them into gay skies
And keep sweeping the cobwebs off the moon

MARKETS OPTIMISTIC

learn new uses for cement. How to develop profitable concrete business. How to judge materials. How to figure jobs. How to reinforce concrete. How to build forms, roads, sidewalks, floors, foundations, culverts, cellars

And even tho' the Irish and the Dutch
Say it don't amount to much
Fifty million Frenchmen can't be wrong

STAR-SPANGLED BANDIT GANG ROBS DINERS

MURDER DARES QUAKER STATE FANTASIES

POKER SLAYER PRAISED

Poor little Hollywood Rose
so all alone
No one in Hollywood knows
how sad she's grown

FIVE HUNDRED MILLIONS IN BANK DEAL

Sure I love the dear silver that shines in your hair
And the brow that's all furrowed
And wrinkled with care
I kiss the dear fingers so toil worn for me

CARBONIC BUYS IN DRY ICE

the broad advertising of the bull markets, the wide extension of the ticker services, the equipping of branch brokerage offices with tickers, transparent, magnified translux stockquotation rolls have had the natural result of stirring up nation-wide interest in the stockmarket

Poor Little Rich Boy

William Randolph Hearst was an only son, the only chick in the richlyfeathered nest of George and Phebe Hearst.

In eighteen-fifty George Hearst had left his folks and the farm in Franklin County, Missouri, and driven a team of oxen out to California. (In fortynine the sudden enormous flare of gold had filled the West;

the young men couldn't keep their minds on their plowing, on feeding the swill to the pigs, on threshing the wheat

when the fires of gold were sweeping the Pacific Slope. Cholera followed in the ruts of the oxcarts, they died of cholera round the campfires, in hastilybuilt chinchinfested cabins, they were picked off by hostile Indians, they blew each other's heads off in brawls.)

George Hearst was one of the few that made it;

he developed a knack for placermining;

as a prospector he had an accurate eye for picking a goldbearing vein of quartz;

after seven years in El Dorado County he was a millionaire, Anaconda was beginning, he owned onesixth of the Ophir Mine, he was in on Comstock Lode.

In sixtyone he went back home to Missouri with his pockets full of nuggets and married Phebe Anderson and took her back by boat and across Panama to San Francisco the new hilly capital of the millionaire miners and bought a mansion for her beside the Golden Gate on the huge fogbound coast of the Pacific.

He owned vast ranges and ranches, raised cattle, ran racehorses, prospected in Mexico, employed five thousand men in his mines, on his estates, lost and won fortunes in mining deals, played poker at a century a chip, never went out without a bag of clinkers to hand out to old friends down on their uppers,

and died in Washington

a senator,

a rough diamond, a lusty beloved whitebearded old man with the big beak and sparrowhawk eyes of a breaker of trails, the beetling brows under the black slouch hat of an oldtimer.

Mrs. Hearst's boy was born in sixtythree.
Nothing too good for the only son.
The Hearsts doted on their boy;
the big lanky youngster grew up solemneyed and selfwilled among servants and hired men, factotums, overseers, hangerson, old pensioners; his grandparents spoiled him; he always did everything he wanted. Mrs. Hearst's boy must have everything of the best.
No lack of gold nuggets, twentydollar goldpieces, big silver cartwheels.
The boy had few playmates; he was too rich to get along with the others in the roughandtumble democracy of the boys growing up in San Francisco in those days. He was too timid and too arrogant; he wasn't liked.
His mother could always rent playmates with icecream, imported candies, expensive toys, ponies, fireworks always ready to set off. The ones he could buy he despised, he hankered always after the others.
He was great on practical jokes and pulling the leg of the grownups; when the new Palace Hotel was opened with a reception for General Grant he and a friend had themselves a time throwing down handfuls of birdshot on the glass roof of the court to the consternation of the bigwigs and stuffedshirts below.

Wherever they went royally the Hearsts could buy their way,
up and down the California coast, through ranches and miningtowns
in Nevada and in Mexico,
in the palace of Porfirio Diaz;
the old man had lived in the world, had rubbed shoulders with rich and poor, had knocked around in miners' hells, pushed his way through unblazed trails with a packmule. All his life Mrs. Hearst's boy was to hanker after that world
hidden from him by a mist of millions;
the boy had a brain, appetites, an imperious will,
but he could never break away from the gilded apronstrings;
adventure became slumming.
He was sent to boardingschool at Saint Paul's, in Concord,

New Hampshire. His pranks kept the school in an uproar. He was fired.

He tutored and went to Harvard

where he cut quite a swath as businessmanager of the *Lampoon*, a brilliant entertainer; he didn't drink much himself, he was softspoken and silent; he got the other boys drunk and paid the bills, bought the fireworks to celebrate Cleveland's election, hired the brassbands,

bought the creampies to throw at the actors from the box at the Old Howard,

the cannon crackers to blow out the lamps of herdic cabs with,

the champagne for the chorines.

He was rusticated and finally fired from Harvard, so the story goes, for sending to each of a number of professors a chamberpot with the professor's portrait tastefully engraved on it.

He went to New York. He was crazy about newspapers. Already he'd been hanging around the Boston newspaperoffices. In New York he was taken by Pulitzer's newfangled journalism. He didn't want to write; he wanted to be a newspaperman. (Newspapermen were part of that sharpcontoured world he wanted to see clear, the reallife world he saw distorted by a haze of millions, the ungraded lowlifeworld of American Democracy.)

Mrs. Hearst's boy would be a newspaperman and a Democrat. (Newspapermen saw heard ate drank touched horsed kidded rubbed shoulders with real men, whored; that was life.)

He arrived home in California, a silent soft smiling solemn-eyed young man

dressed in the height of the London fashion.

When his father asked him what he wanted to do with his life,

he said he wanted to run the *Examiner* which was a moribund sheet in San Francisco which his father had taken over for a bad debt. It didn't seem much to ask. The old man couldn't imagine why Willie wanted the old rag instead of a mine or a ranch, but Mrs. Hearst's boy always had his way.

Young Hearst went down to the *Examiner* one day and turned the office topsyturvy. He had a knack for finding and using bright young men, he had a knack for using his own prurient hanker after the lusts and envies of plain unmonied lowlife men and women (the slummer sees only the streetwalkers, the dopeparlors, the strip acts and goes back

474

uptown saying he knows the workingclass districts); the lowest common denominator;

manure to grow a career in,

the rot of democracy. Out of it grew rankly an empire of print. (Perhaps he liked to think of himself as the young Caius Julius flinging his millions away, tearing down emblems and traditions, making faces at togaed privilege, monopoly, stuffedshirts in office;

Caesar's life like his was a millionaire prank. Perhaps W. R. had read of republics ruined before;

Alcibiades, too, was a practical joker.)

The San Francisco *Examiner* grew in circulation, tickled the prurient hankers of the moneyless man

became *The Monarch of the Dailies.*

When the old man died, Mrs. Hearst sold out of Anaconda for seven and a half millions of dollars. W. R. got the money from her to enter the New York field; he bought the *Morning Journal*

and started his race with the Pulitzers

as to who should cash in most

on the geewhizz emotion.

In politics he was the people's Democrat; he came out for Bryan in ninetysix; on the Coast he fought the Southern Pacific and the utilities and the railroad lawyers who were grabbing the state of California away from the first settlers; on election day in ninetysix his three papers in New York put out between them more than a million and half copies, a record

that forced the *World* to cut its price to a penny.

When there's no news make news.

"You furnish the pictures and I'll furnish the war," he's supposed to have wired Remington in Havana. The trouble in Cuba was a goldmine for circulation when Mark Hanna had settled national politics by planting McKinley in the White House.

Hearst had one of his bright young men engineer a jailbreak for Evangelina Cisneros, a fair Cuban revolutionist shoved into a dungeon by Weyler, and put on a big reception for her in Madison Square.

Remember the "Maine."

When McKinley was forced to declare war on Spain W. R. had his plans all made to buy and sink a Britishsteamer in the Suez Canal

but the Spanish fleet didn't take that route.

He hired the *Sylvia* and the *Buccaneer* and went down to Cuba himself with a portable press and a fleet of tugs and brandishing a sixshooter went in with the longboat through the surf and captured twentysix unarmed half-drowned Spanish sailors on the beach and forced them to kneel and kiss the American flag

in front of the camera.

Manila Bay raised the circulation of the *Morning Journal* to one million six hundred thousand.

When the Spaniards were licked, there was nobody left to heckle but the Mormons. Polygamy titillated the straphangers, and the sexlife of the rich, and penandink drawings of women in underclothes and prehistoric monsters in four colors. He discovered the sobsister: Annie Laurie, Dorothy Dix, Beatrice Fairfax. He splurged on comics, the Katzenjammer Kids, Buster Brown, Krazy Kat. Get excited when the public is excited;

his editorials hammered at malefactors of great wealth, trusts, the G.O.P., Mark Hanna and McKinley so shrilly that when McKinley was assassinated most Republicans in some way considered Hearst responsible for his death.

Hearst retorted by renaming the *Morning Journal* the *American*

and stepping into the limelight

wearing a black frockcoat and a tengallon hat, presidential timber,

the millionaire candidate of the common man.

Bryan made him president of the National Association of Democratic Clubs and advised him to start a paper in Chicago.

After Bryan's second defeat Hearst lined up with Charles F. Murphy in New York and was elevated to Congress.

His headquarters were at the Holland House; the night of his election he gave a big free show of fireworks in Madison Square Garden; a mortar exploded and killed or wounded something like a hundred people; that was one piece of news the Hearst men made that wasn't spread on the front pages of the Hearst papers.

In the House of Representatives he was unpopular; it was schooldays over again. The limp handshake, the solemn eyes set close to the long nose, the small flabby scornful smile were out of place among the Washington backslappers. He was ill at ease without his hired gang around him.

He was happier entertaining firstnighters and footlight favorites at the Holland House. In those years, when Broadway still stopped at Fortysecond Street,

Millicent Willson was a dancer in *The Girl from Paris;* she

and her sister did a sister act together; she won a popularity
contest in the *Morning Telegraph*
and the hand of
William Randolph Hearst.

In nineteen-four he spent a lot of money putting his name
up in electric lights at the Chicago Convention to land the
Democratic nomination, but Judge Parker and Wall Street got
it away from him.
In nineteen-five he ran for Mayor of New York on a
municipalownership ticket.
In nineteen-six he very nearly got the governorship away
from the solemnwhiskered Hughes. There were Hearst for
President clubs all over the country. He was making his way
in politics spending millions to the tune of *Waltz Me Around
Again, Willie.*
He managed to get his competitor James Gordon Bennett
up in court for running indecent ads in the New York *Herald*
and fined twentyfive thousand dollars, a feat which hardly
contributed to his popularity in certain quarters.
In nineteen-eight he was running revelations about Standard Oil, the Archbold letters that proved that the trusts were
greasing the palms of the politicians in a big way. He was the
candidate of the Independence Party, made up almost exclu-
sively, so his enemies claimed, of Hearst employees.
(His fellowmillionaires felt he was a traitor to his class but
when he was taxed with his treason he answered:
*You know I believe in property, and you know where I
stand on personal fortunes, but isn't it better that I should represent in this country the dissatisfied than have somebody else
do it who might not have the same real property relations that
I may have?*)
By nineteen-fourteen, although he was the greatest newspa-
perowner in the country, the proprietor of hundreds of square
miles of ranching and mining country in California and Mexico,
his affairs were in such a scramble he had trouble borrowing a million dollars,
and politically he was ratpoison.

All the millions he signed away
all his skill at putting his own thoughts
into the skull of the straphanger
failed to bridge the tiny Rubicon between amateur and
professional politics (perhaps he could too easily forget a dis-
appointment buying a firstrate writer or an embroidered slip-

per attributed to Charlemagne or the gilded bed a king's mistress was supposed to have slept in).

Sometimes he was high enough above the battle to see clear. He threw all the powers of his papers, all his brilliance as a publisher into an effort to keep the country sane and neutral during the first world war;

he opposed loans to the Allies, seconded Bryan in his lonely fight to keep the interests of the United States as a whole paramount over the interests of the Morgan banks and the anglophile businessmen of the East;

for his pains he was razzed as a pro-German,

and when war was declared had detectives placed among his butlers,

secret-service-agents ransacking his private papers, gumshoeing round his diningroom on Riverside Drive to investigate rumors of strange colored lights seen in his windows.

He opposed the Peace of Versailles and the league of victorious nations

and ended by proving that he was as patriotic as anybody

by coming out for conscription

and printing his papers with red white and blue borders and with little American flags at either end of the dateline and continually trying to stir up trouble across the Rio Grande

and inflating the Yankee Doodle bogey,

the biggest navy in the world.

The people of New York City backed him up by electing Hearst's candidate for Mayor, Honest John Hylan,

but Al Smith while he was still the sidewalks' hero rapped Hearst's knuckles when he tried to climb back onto the Democratic soundtruck.

In spite of enormous expenditures on forged documents he failed to bring about war with Mexico.

In spite of spraying hundreds of thousands of dollars into moviestudios he failed to put over his favorite moviestar as America's sweetheart.

And more and more the emperor of newsprint retired to his fief of San Simeon on the Pacific Coast, where he assembled a zoo, continued to dabble in movingpictures, collected warehouses full of tapestries, Mexican saddles, bricabrac, china, brocade, embroidery, old chests of drawers, tables and chairs, the loot of dead Europe,

built an Andalusian palace and a Moorish banquethall and there spends his last years amid the relaxing adulations of screenstars, admen, screenwriters, publicitymen, columnists, millionaire editors,

a monarch of that new El Dorado
where the warmedover daydreams of all the ghettos
are churned into an opiate haze
more scarily blinding to the moneyless man
more fruitful of millions
than all the clinking multitude of double eagles
the older Hearst minted out of El Dorado County in the old
days (the empire of the printed word continues powerful by
the inertia of bigness; but this power over the dreams
of the adolescents of the world
grows and poisons like a cancer),
and out of the westcoast haze comes now and then an old
man's querulous voice
advocating the salestax,
hissing dirty names at the defenders of civil liberties for the
workingman;
jail the reds,
praising the comforts of Baden-Baden under the blood and
bludgeon rule of Handsome Adolph (Hearst's own loved invention, the lowest common denominator come to power
out of the rot of democracy)
complaining about the California incometaxes,
shrilling about the dangers of thought in the colleges.
Deport; jail.
Until he dies
the magnificent endlesslyrolling presses will pour out print
for him, the whirring everywhere projectors will spit images
for him,
a spent Caesar grown old with spending
never man enough to cross the Rubicon.

Richard Ellsworth Savage

Dick Savage walked down Lexington to the office in the
Graybar Building. The December morning was sharp as steel,
bright glints cut into his eyes, splintering from storewindows,
from the glasses of people he passed on the street, from the
chromium rims of the headlights of automobiles. He wasn't
quite sure whether he had a hangover or not. In a jeweler's
window he caught sight of his face in the glass against the
black velvet backing, there was a puffy boiled look under the
eyes like in the photographs of the Prince of Wales. He felt
sour and gone in the middle like a rotten pear. He stepped into
a drugstore and ordered a bromoseltzer. At the sodafountain
he stood looking at himself in the mirror behind the glass

shelf with the gingeralebottles on it; his new darkblue broadcloth coat looked well, anyway.

The black eyes of the sodajerker were seeking his eyes out. "A heavy evening, eh?" Dick nodded and grinned. The sodajerker passed a thin redknuckled hand over his patentleather hair. "I didn't get off till onethirty an' it takes me an hour to get home on the subway. A whale of a chance I got to . . ."

"I'm late at the office now," said Dick and paid and walked out, belching a little, into the sparkling morning street. He walked fast, taking deep breaths. By the time he was standing in the elevator with a sprinkling of stoutish fortyish welldressed men, executives like himself getting to their offices late, he had a definite sharp headache.

He'd hardly stretched his legs out under his desk when the interoffice phone clicked. It was Miss Williams's voice: "Good morning, Mr. Savage. We've been waiting for you . . . Mr. Moorehouse says please step into his office, he wants to speak with you a minute before the staff conference."

Dick got up and stood a second with his lips pursed, rocking on the balls of his feet looking out the window over the ashcolored blocks that stretched in a series of castiron molds east to the chimneys of powerplants, the bridge, the streak of river flashing back steel at the steelblue sky. Riveters shrilly clattered in the new huge construction that was jutting up girder by girder at the corner of Fortysecond. They all seemed inside his head like a dentist's drill. He shuddered, belched, and hurried along the corridor into the large corner office.

J. W. was staring at the ceiling with his big jowly face as expressionless as a cow's. He turned his pale eyes on Dick without a smile. "Do you realize there are seventyfive million people in this country unwilling or unable to go to a physician in time of sickness?" Dick twisted his face into a look of lively interest. He's been talking to Ed Griscolm, he said to himself. "Those are the people the Bingham products have got to serve. He's touched only the fringes of this great potential market."

"His business would be to make them feel they're smarter than the bigbugs who go to Battle Creek," said Dick.

J. W. frowned thoughtfully.

Ed Griscolm had come in. He was a sallow long man with an enthusiastic flash in his eye that flickered on and off like an electriclight sign. He had a way of carrying his arms like a cheerleader about to lead a college yell.

Dick said "Hello" without warmth.

"Top of the morning, Dick . . . a bit overhung I see. . . . Too bad, old man, too bad."

"I was just saying, Ed," J. W. went on in his slow even

480

voice, "that our talking points should be, first, that they haven't scratched the top of their potential market of seventy-five million people and, second, that a properlyconducted campaign can eradicate the prejudice many people feel against proprietary medicines and substitute a feeling of pride in their use."

"It's smart to be thrifty . . . that sort of thing," shouted Ed.

"Selfmedication," said Dick. "Tell them the average soda-jerker knows more about medicine today than the family physician did twentyfive years ago."

"They think there's something hick about patent medicines," yelled Ed Griscolm. "We got to put patent medicines on Park Avenue."

"Proprietary medicines," said J. W. reprovingly.

Dick managed to wipe the smile off his face. "We've got to break the whole idea," he said, "into its component parts."

"Exactly." J. W. picked up a carvedivory papercutter and looked at it in different angles in front of his face. The office was so silent they could hear the traffic roaring outside and the wind whistling between the steel window frame and the steel window. Dick and Ed Griscolm held their breath. J. W. began to talk. "The American public has become sophisticated . . . when I was a boy in Pittsburgh, all we thought of was display advertising, the appeal to the eye. Now with the growth of sophistication we must think of the other types of appeal, and the eradication of prejudice. . . . Bingo . . . the name is out of date, it's all wrong. A man would be ashamed to lunch at the Metropolitan Club with a bottle of Bingo at his table . . . that must be the talkingpoint. . . . Yesterday Mr. Bingham seemed inclined to go ahead. He was balking a little at the cost of the campaign. . . ."

"Never mind," screeched Ed Griscolm, "we'll nail the old buzzard's feet down yet."

"I guess he has to be brought around gently, just as you were saying last night, J. W.," said Dick in a low bland voice. "They tell me Halsey of Halsey O'Connor's gone to bed with a nervous breakdown tryin' to get old Bingham to make up his mind."

Ed Griscolm broke into a tittering laugh.

J. W. got to his feet with a faint smile. When J. W. smiled, Dick smiled too. "I think he can be brought to appreciate the advantages connected with the name . . . dignity . . . . established connections. . . ." Still talking, J. W. led the way down the hall into the large room with a long oval mahogany table in the middle of it where the whole office was gathered. J. W. went first with his considerable belly waggling a little from side to side as he walked, and Dick and Ed Griscolm, each with an armful of typewritten projects in paleblue covers, followed a step behind him. Just as they were settling down after a certain amount of coughing and honking and J. W. was beginning about how there were seventyfive million people, Ed Griscolm ran out and came back with a neatly-drawn chart in blue and red and yellow lettering showing the layout of the proposed campaign. An admiring murmur ran round the table.

Dick caught a triumphant glance in his direction from Ed Griscolm. He looked at J. W. out of the corner of his eye. J. W. was looking at the chart with an expressionless face. Dick walked over to Ed Griscolm and patted him on the shoulder "A swell job, Ed, old man," he whispered. Ed Griscolm's tense lips loosened into a smile. "Well, gentlemen, what I'd like now is a snappy discussion," said J. W. with a mean twinkle in his paleblue eyes that matched for a second the twinkle of the small diamonds in his cufflinks.

While the others talked, Dick sat staring at J. W.'s hands spread out on the sheaf of typewritten papers on the table in front of him. Oldfashioned starched cuffs protruded from the sleeves of the perfectlyfitting doublebreasted gray jacket and out of them hung two pudgy strangely hicklooking hands with liverspots on them. All through the discussion Dick stared at the hands, all the time writing down phrases on his scratchpad and scratching them out. He couldn't think of anything. His brains felt boiled. He went on scratching away with his pencil at phrases that made no sense at all. On the fritz at the Ritz . . . Bingham's products cure the fits.

It was after one before the conference broke up. Everybody was congratulating Ed Griscolm on his layout. Dick heard his own voice saying it was wonderful, but it needed a slightly different slant.

"All right," said J. W. "How about finding that slightly different slant over the weekend? That's the idea I want to leave with every man here. I'm lunching with Mr. Bingham Monday noon. I must have a perfected project to present."

Dick Savage went back to his office and signed a pile of letters his secretary had left for him. Then he suddenly remembered he'd told Reggie Talbot he'd meet him for lunch at "63" to meet the girlfriend, and ran out, adjusting his blue muffler as he went down in the elevator. He caught sight of them at a table with their heads leaning together in the crinkled cigarettesmoke in the back of the crowded Saturdayafternoon speakeasy.

"Oh, Dick, hello," said Reggie, jumping to his feet with his mild smile, grabbing Dick's hand and drawing him toward the table. "I didn't wait for you at the office because I had to meet this one. . . . Jo, this is Mr. Savage. The only man in New York who doesn't give a damn. . . . What'll you have to drink?"

The girl certainly was a knockout. When Dick let himself drop on the redleather settee beside her, facing Reggie's slender ashblond head and his big inquiring lightbrown eyes, he felt boozy and tired.

"Oh, Mr. Savage, what's happened about the Bingham account? I'm so excited about it. Reggie can't talk about anything else. I know it's indiscreet to ask." She looked earnestly in his face out of longlashed black eyes. They certainly made a pretty couple.

"Telling tales out of school, eh?" said Dick, picking up a breadstick and snapping it into his mouth.

"But you know, Dick, Jo and me . . . we talk about everything . . . it never goes any further. . . . And honestly, all the younger guys in the office think it's a damn shame J. W. didn't use your first layout. . . . Griscolm is going to lose the account for us if he isn't careful . . . it just don't click. . . . I think the old man's getting softening of the brain."

"You know I've thought several times recently that J. W. wasn't in very good health. . . . Too bad. He's the most brilliant figure in the publicrelations field." Dick heard an oily note come into his voice and felt ashamed in front of the youngsters and shut up suddenly. "Say, Tony," he called peevishly to the waiter. "How about some cocktails? Give me a bacardi with a little absinthe in it, you know, my special. . . . Gosh, I feel a hundred years old."

"Been burning the candle at both ends?" asked Reggie.

Dick twisted his face into a smirk. "Oh, that candle," he said. "It gives me a lot of trouble." They all blushed. Dick chuckled. "By God, I don't think there are three other people in the city that have a blush left in them."

They ordered more cocktails. While they were drinking, Dick felt the girl's eyes serious and dark fixed on his face. She lifted her glass to him. "Reggie says you've been awfully sweet to him at the office. . . . He says he'd have been fired if it wasn't for you."

"Who could help being sweet to Reggie? Look at him." Reggie got red as a beet.

"The lad's got looks," said the girl. "But has he any brains?"

Dick began to feel better with the onionsoup and the third cocktail. He began to tell them how he envied them being kids and getting married. He promised he'd be bestman. When they asked him why he didn't get married himself, he confusedly had some more drinks and said his life was a sham-

bles. He made fifteen thousand a year, but he never had any money. He knew a dozen beautiful women, but he never had a girl when he needed her. All the time he was talking, he was planning in the back of his head a release on the need for freedom of selfmedication. He couldn't stop thinking about that damned Bingham account.

It was beginning to get dark when they came out of "63." A feeling of envy stung him as he put the young people into a taxi. He felt affectionate and amorous and nicely buoyed up by the radiating warmth of food and alcohol in his belly. He stood for a minute on the corner of Madison Avenue watching the lively before-Christmas crowd pour along the sidewalk against the bright showwindows, all kinds of faces flushed and healthylooking for once in the sharp cold evening in the slanting lights. Then he took a taxi down to Twelfth Street.

The colored maid who let him in was wearing a pretty lace apron. "Hello, Cynthia." "How do you do, Mr. Dick." Dick could feel the impatient blood pounding in his temples as he walked up and down the old uneven parquet floor waiting. Eveline was smiling when she came out from the back room.

She'd put too much powder on her face in too much of a hurry and it brought out the drawn lines between her nostrils and her mouth and gave her nose a floury look.

Her voice still had a lovely swing to it. "Dick, I thought you'd given me up."

"I've been working like a dog. . . . I've gotten so my brain won't work. I thought it would do me good to see you." She handed him a Chinese porcelain box with cigarettes in it. They sat down side by side on a rickety oldfashioned horsehair sofa. "How's Jeremy?" asked Dick in a cheerful tone.

Her voice went flat. "He's gone out West with Paul for Christmas."

"You must miss him . . . I'm disappointed myself. I love the brat."

"Paul and I have finally decided to get a divorce . . . in a friendly way."

"Eveline, I'm sorry."

"Why?"

"I dunno. . . . It does seem silly. . . . But I always liked Paul."

"It all got just too tiresome. . . . This way it'll be much better for him."

There was something coolly bitter about her as she sat beside him in her a little too frizzy afternoondress. He felt as if he was meeting her for the first time. He picked up her long blueveined hand and put it on the little table in front of them and patted it. "I like you better . . . anyway." It sounded phony in his ears, like something he'd say to a client. He jumped to his feet. "Say, Eveline, suppose I call up Settignano and get some gin around? I've got to have a drink. . . . I can't get the office out of my head."

"If you go back to the icebox you'll find some perfectly lovely cocktails all mixed. I just made them. There are some people coming in later."

"How much later?"

"About seven o'clock . . . why?" Her eyes followed him teasingly as he went back through the glass doors.

In the pantry the colored girl was putting on her hat. "Cynthia, Mrs. Johnson alleges there are cocktails out here."

"Yes, Mr. Dick, I'll get you some glasses."

"Is this your afternoon out?"

"Yessir, I'm goin' to church."

"On Saturday afternoon?"

"Yessir, our church we have services every Saturday afternoon . . . lots of folks don't get Sunday off nowadays."

"It's gotten so I don't get any day off at all."

"It shoa is too bad, Mr. Dick."

486

He went back into the front room shakily, carrying the tray with the shaker jiggling on it. The two glasses clinked.

"Oh, Dick, I'm going to have to reform you. Your hands are shaking like an old graybeard's."

"Well, I am an old graybeard. I'm worrying myself to death about whether the bastardly patentmedicine king will sign on the dotted line Monday."

"Don't talk about it. . . . It sounds just too awful. I've been working myself . . . I'm trying to put on a play."

"Eveline, that's swell! Who's it by?"

"Charles Edward Holden. . . . It's a magnificent piece of work. I'm terribly excited about it. I think I know how to do it. . . . I don't suppose you want to put a couple of thousand dollars in, do you, Dick?"

"Eveline, I'm flat broke. . . . They've got my salary garnisheed and Mother has to be supported in the style to which she is accustomed and then there's Brother Henry's ranch in Arizona . . . he's all balled up with a mortgage. . . . I thought Charles Edward Holden was just a columnist."

"This is a side of him that's never come out. . . . I think he's the real poet of modern New York . . . you wait and see."

Dick poured himself another cocktail. "Let's talk about just us for a minute. . . . I feel so frazzled. . . . Oh, Eveline, you know what I mean. . . . We've been pretty good friends." She let him hold her hand, but she did not return the squeeze he gave it. "You know we always said we were just physically attractive to each other . . . why isn't that the swellest thing in the world?" He moved up close to her on the couch, gave her a little kiss on the cheek, tried to twist her face around. "Don't you like this miserable sinner a little bit?"

"Dick, I can't." She got to her feet. Her lips were twitching and she looked as if she was going to burst into tears. "There's somebody I like very much . . . very, very much. I've decided to make some sense out of my life."

"Who? That damn columnist?"

"Never mind who."

Dick buried his face in his hands. When he took his hands away, he was laughing. "Well, if that isn't my luck. . . . Just Johnny on the spot and me full of speakeasy Saturday afternoon amorosity."

"Well, Dick, I'm sure you won't lack for partners."

"I do today. . . . I feel lonely and hellish. My life is a shambles."

"What a literary phrase!"

"I thought it was pretty good myself, but honestly I feel

every whichway. . . . Something funny happened to me last night. I'll tell you about it someday when you like me better."

"Dick, why don't you go to Eleanor's? She's giving a party for all the boyars."

"Is she really going to marry that horrid little prince?" Eveline nodded with that same cold bitter look in her eyes. "I suppose a title is the last word in the decorating business. . . . Why won't Eleanor put up some money?"

"I don't want to ask her. She's filthy with money, though, she's had a very successful fall. I guess we're all getting grasping in our old age. . . . What does poor Moorehouse think about the prince?"

"I wish I knew what he thought about anything. I've been working for him for years now and I don't know whether he's a genius or a stuffed shirt. . . . I wonder if he's going to be at Eleanor's. I want to get hold of him this evening for a moment. . . . That's a very good idea. . . . Eveline, you always do me good one way or another."

"You'd better not go without phoning. . . . She's perfectly capable of not letting you in if you come uninvited and particularly with a houseful of émigrée Russians in tiaras."

Dick went to the phone and called up. He had to wait a long time for Eleanor to come. Her voice sounded shrill and rasping. At first she said why didn't he come to dinner next week instead.

Dick's voice got very coaxing. "Please let me see the famous prince, Eleanor. . . . And I've got something very important to ask you about. . . . After all, you've always been my guardian angel, Eleanor. If I can't come to you when I'm in trouble, who can I come to?"

At last she loosened up and said he could come, but he mustn't stay long. "You can talk to poor J. Ward . . . he looks a little forlorn." Her voice ended in a screechy laugh that made the receiver jangle and hurt his ear.

When he went back to the sofa, Eveline was lying back against the pillows soundlessly laughing. "Dick," she said, "you're a master of blarney." Dick made a face at her, kissed her on the forehead and left the house.

Eleanor's place was glittering with chandeliers and cutglass. When she met him at the drawingroom door, her small narrow face looked smooth and breakable as a piece of porcelain under her carefullycurled hair and above a big rhinestone brooch that held a lace collar together. From behind her came the boom and the high piping of Russian men's and women's voices and a smell of tea and charcoal. "Well, Richard, here you are," she said in a rapid hissing whisper. "Don't forget to kiss the grandduchess's hand . . . she's had such a

488

dreadful life. You'd like to do any little thing that would please her, wouldn't you? . . . And, Richard, I'm worried about Ward . . . he looks so terribly tired . . . I hope he isn't beginning to break up. He's the type you know that goes off like that. . . . You know these big shortnecked blonds."

There was a tall silver samovar on the Buhl table in front of the marble fireplace and beside it sat a large oldish woman in a tinsel shawl with her hair in a pompadour and the powder flaking off a tired blotchy face. She was very gracious and had quite a twinkle in her eye and she was piling caviar out of a heaped cutglass bowl onto a slice of blackbread and laughing with her mouth full. Around her were grouped Russians in all stages of age and decay, some in tunics and some in cheap business suits and some frowsylooking young women and a pair of young men with slick hair and choirboy faces. They were all drinking tea or little glasses of vodka. Everybody was ladling out caviar. Dick was introduced to the prince, who was an olivefaced young man with black brows and a little pointed black mustache who wore a black tunic and black soft leather boots and had a prodigiously small waist. They were all merry as crickets chirping and roaring in Russian, French, and English. Eleanor sure is putting out, Dick caught himself thinking, as he dug into the mass of big graygrained caviar.

J. W. looking pale and fagged was standing in the corner of the room with his back to an icon that had three candles burning in front of it. Dick distinctly remembered having seen the icon in Eleanor's window some weeks before, against a piece of purple brocade. J. W. was talking to an ecclesiastic in a black cassock with purple trimmings, who when Dick went up to them turned out to have a rich Irish brogue.

"Meet the Archimandrite O'Donnell, Dick," said J. W. "Did I get it right?" The Archimandrite grinned and nodded. "He's been telling me about the monasteries in Greece."

"You mean where they haul you up in a basket?" said Dick.

The Archimandrite jiggled his grinning, looseliped face up and down. "I'm goin' to have the honorr and pleasurr of introducin' dear Eleanor into the mysteries of the true church. I was tellin' Mr. Moorehouse the story of my conversion." Dick found an impudent rolling eye looking him over. "Perhaps you'd be carin' to come someday, Mr. Savage, to hear our choir. Unbelief dissolves in music like a lump of sugar in a glass of hot tay."

"Yes, I like the Russian choir," said J. W.

"Don't you think that our dear Eleanor looks happier and younger for it?" The Archimandrite was beaming into the

489

crowded room. J. W. nodded doubtfully. "Och, a lovely graceful little thing she is, clever too. . . . Perhaps, Mr. Moorehouse and Mr. Savage, you'd come to the service and to lunch with me afterwards. . . . I have some ideas about a little book on my experiences at Mount Athos . . . We could make a little parrty of it."

Dick was amazed to find the Archimandrite's fingers pinching him in the seat and hastily moved away a step, but not before he'd caught from the Archimandrite's left eye a slow vigorous wink.

The big room was full of clinking and toasting, and there was the occasional crash of a broken glass. A group of younger Russians were singing in deep roaring voices that made the crystal chandelier tinkle over their heads. The caviar was all gone, but two uniformed maids were bringing in a table set with horsd'oeuvres in the middle of which was a large boiled salmon.

J. W. nudged Dick. "I think we might go someplace where we can talk."

"I was just waiting for you, J. W. I think I've got a new slant. I think it'll click this time."

They'd just managed to make their way through the crush to the door when a Russian girl in black with fine black eyes and arched brows came running after them. "Oh, you mustn't go. Leocadia Pavlovna likes you so much. She likes it here, it is informal . . . the bohème. That is what we like about Leonora Ivanovna. She is bohème and we are bohème. We luff her."

"I'm afraid we have a business appointment," said J. W. solemnly.

The Russian girl snapped her fingers with, "Oh, business, it is disgusting. . . . America would be so nice without the business."

When they got out on the street, J. W. sighed. "Poor Eleanor, I'm afraid she's in for something. . . . Those Russians will eat her out of house and home. Do you suppose she really will marry this Prince Mingraziali? I've made inquiries about him. . . . He's all that he says he is. But heavens!"

"With crowns and everything," said Dick; "the date's all set."

"After all, Eleanor knows her own business. She's been very successful, you know."

J. W.'s car was at the door. The chauffeur got out with a laprobe over his arm and was just about to close the door on J. W. when Dick said, "J. W., have you a few minutes to talk about this Bingham account?"

"Of course, I was forgetting," said J. W. in a tired voice. "Come on out to supper at Great Neck. . . . I'm alone out there except for the children." Smiling, Dick jumped in and the chauffeur closed the door of the big black towncar behind him.

It was pretty lugubrious eating in the diningroom with its painted Italian panels at the Moorehouses' with the butler and the secondman moving around silently in the dim light and only Dick and J. W. and Miss Simpson, the children's so very refined longfaced governess, at the long candlelit table. Afterwards, when they went into J. W.'s little white den to smoke and talk about the Bingham account, Dick thanked his stars when the old butler appeared with a bottle of Scotch and ice and glasses.

"Where did you find that, Thompson?" asked J. W.

"Been in the cellar since before the war, sir . . . those cases Mrs. Moorehouse bought in Scotland. . . . I knew Mr. Savage liked a bit of a spot."

Dick laughed. "That's the advantage of having a bad name," he said.

J. W. drawled solemnly, "It's the best to be had, I know that. . . . Do you know I never could get much out of drinking, so I gave it up, even before prohibition."

J. W. had lit himself a cigar. Suddenly he threw it in the fire. "I don't think I'll smoke tonight. The doctor says three cigars a day won't hurt me . . . but I've been feeling seedy all week. . . . I ought to get out of the stockmarket. . . . I hope you keep out of it, Dick."

"My creditors don't leave me enough to buy a ticket to a raffle with."

J. W. took a couple of steps across the small room lined with unscratched sets of the leading authors in morocco, and then stood with his back to the Florentine fireplace with his hands behind him. "I feel chilly all the time. I don't think my circulation's very good. . . . Perhaps it was going to see Gertrude. . . . The doctors have finally admitted her case is hopeless. It was a great shock to me."

Dick got to his feet and put down his glass. "I'm sorry, J. W. . . . Still, there have been surprising cures in brain troubles."

J. W. was standing with his lips in a thin tight line, his big jowl trembling a little. "Not in schizophrenia. . . . I've managed to do pretty well in everything except that. . . . I'm a lonely man," he said. "And to think once upon a time I was planning to be a songwriter." He smiled.

Dick smiled too and held out his hand. "Shake hands, J. W.," he said, "with the ruins of a minor poet."

"Anyway," said J. W., "the children will have the advantages I never had. . . . Would it bore you, before we get down to business, to go up and say goodnight to them? I'd like to have you see them."

"Of course not, I love kids," said Dick. "In fact, I've never yet quite managed to grow up myself."

At the head of the stairs Miss Simpson met them with her finger to her lips. "Little Gertrude's asleep." They tiptoed down the allwhite hall. The children were in bed, each in a small hospitallike room cold from an open window, on each pillow was a head of pale strawcolored hair.

"Staple's the oldest . . . he's twelve," whispered J. W. "Then Gertrude, then Johnny."

Staple said goodnight politely. Gertrude didn't wake up when they turned the light on. Johnny sat up in a nightmare with his bright blue eyes open wide, crying, "No, no," in a tiny frightened voice.

J. W. sat on the edge of the bed petting him for a moment until he fell asleep again. "Goodnight, Miss Simpson," and they were tiptoeing down the stairs. "What do you think of them?" J. W. turned beaming to Dick.

"They sure are a pretty sight. . . . I envy you," said Dick.

"I'm glad I brought you out . . . I'd have been lonely without you . . . I must entertain more," said J. W.

They settled back into their chairs by the fire and started to go over the layout to be presented to Bingham Products. When the clock struck ten, J. W. began to yawn.

Dick got to his feet. "J. W., do you want my honest opinion?"

493

"Go ahead, boy, you know you can say anything you like to me."

"Well, here it is." Dick tossed off the last warm weak remnant of his Scotch. "I think we can't see the woods for the trees . . . we're balled up in a mass of petty detail. You say the old gentleman's pretty pigheaded . . . one of these from newsboy to president characters. . . . Well, I don't think that this stuff really sets in high enough relief the campaign you outlined to us a month ago . . ."

"I'm not very well satisfied with it, to tell the truth."

"Is there a typewriter in the house?"

"I guess Thompson or Morton can scrape one up somewhere."

"Well, I think that I might be able to bring your fundamental idea out a little more. To my mind it's one of the biggest ideas ever presented in the business world."

"Of course it's the work of the whole office."

"Let me see if I can take this to pieces and put it together again over the weekend. After all, there'll be nothing lost. . . . We've got to blow that old gent clean out of the water or else Halsey'll get him."

"They're around him every minute like a pack of wolves," said J. W., getting up yawning. "Well, I leave it in your hands." When he got to the door J. W. paused and turned. "Of course, those Russian aristocrats are socially the top. It's a big thing for Eleanor that way. . . . But I wish she wouldn't do it. . . . You know, Dick, Eleanor and I have had a very beautiful relationship. . . . That little woman's advice and sympathy have meant a great deal to me. . . . I wish she wasn't going to do it. . . . Well, I'm going to bed."

Dick went up to the big bedroom hung with English huntingscenes. Thompson brought him up a new noiseless typewriter and the bottle of whiskey. Dick sat there working all night in his pajamas and bathrobe smoking and drinking the whiskey. He was still at it when the windows began to get blue with day and he began to make out between the heavy curtains black lacy masses of sleetladen trees grouped round a sodden lawn. His mouth was sour from too many cigarettes. He went into the bathroom frescoed with dolphins and began to whistle as he let the hot water pour into the tub. He felt bleary and dizzy, but he had a new layout.

Next day at noon when J. W. came back from church with the children, Dick was dressed and shaved and walking up and down the flagged terrace in the raw air. Dick's eyes felt hollow and his head throbbed, but J. W. was delighted with the work.

"Of course selfservice, independence, individualism is the

word I gave the boys in the beginning. This is going to be more than a publicity campaign, it's going to be a campaign for Americanism. . . . After lunch I'll send the car over for Miss Williams to get her to take some dictation. There's more meat in this yet, Dick."

"Of course," said Dick, reddening. "All I've done is restore your original conception, J. W."

At lunch the children sat up at the table and Dick had a good time with them, making them talk to him and telling them stories about the bunnies he'd raised when he was a little boy in Jersey. J. W. was beaming. After lunch Dick played pingpong in the billiardroom in the basement with Miss Simpson and Staple and little Gertrude while Johnny picked up the balls for them. J. W. retired to his den to take a nap.

Later they arranged the prospectus for Miss Williams to type. The three of them were working there happily in front of the fire when Thompson appeared in the door and asked reverently if Mr. Moorehouse cared to take a phonecall from Mr. Griscolm. "All right, give it to me on this phone here," said J. W.

Dick froze in his chair. He could hear the voice at the other end of the line twanging excitedly. "Ed, don't you worry," J. W. was drawling. "You take a good rest, my boy, and be fresh as a daisy in the morning so that you can pick holes in the final draft that Miss Williams and I were working over all last night. A few changes occurred to me in the night. . . . You know sleep brings council. . . . How about a little handball this afternoon? A sweat's a great thing for a man, you know. If it wasn't so wet I'd be putting in eighteen holes of golf myself. All right, see you in the morning, Ed." J. W. put down the receiver. "Do you know, Dick," he said, "I think Ed Griscolm ought to take a couple of weeks off in Nassau or some place like that. He's losing his grip a little. . . . I think I'll suggest it to him. He's been a very valuable fellow in the office, you know."

"One of the brightest men in the publicrelations field," said Dick flatly. They went back to work.

Next morning Dick drove in with J. W., but stopped off on Fiftyseventh to run round to his mother's apartment on Fiftysixth to change his shirt. When he got to the office, the switchboard operator in the lobby gave him a broad grin. Everything was humming with the Bingham account. In the vestibule he ran into the inevitable Miss Williams. Her sour lined oldmaidish face was twisted into a sugary smile. "Mr. Savage, Mr. Moorehouse says would you mind meeting him and Mr. Bingham at the Plaza at twelvethirty when he takes Mr. Bingham to lunch?"

He spent the morning on routine work. Round eleven, Eveline Johnson called him up and said she wanted to see him. He said how about toward the end of the week. "But I'm right in the building," she said in a hurt voice.

"Oh, come on up, but I'm pretty busy. . . . You know Mondays."

Eveline had a look of strain in the bright hard light that poured in the window from the overcast sky. She had on a gray coat with a furcollar that looked a little shabby and a prickly gray straw hat that fitted her head tight and had a kind of a lastyear's look. The lines from the flanges of her nose to the ends of her mouth looked deeper and harder than ever.

Dick got up and took both her hands. "Eveline, you look tired."

"I think I'm coming down with the grippe." She talked fast. "I just came in to see a friendly face. I have an appointment to see J. W. at eleven-fifteen. . . . Do you think he'll come across? If I can raise ten thousand, the Shuberts will raise the rest. But it's got to be right away because somebody has some kind of an option on it that expires tomorrow. . . . Oh, I'm so sick of not doing anything. . . . Holden has wonderful ideas about the production and he's letting me do the sets and costumes . . . and if some Broadway producer does it he'll ruin it. . . . Dick, I know it's a great play."

Dick frowned. "This isn't such a very good time . . . we're all pretty preoccupied this morning."

"Well, I won't disturb you any more." They were standing in the window. "How can you stand those riveters going all the time?"

"Why, Eveline, those riveters are music to our ears, they make us sing like canaries in a thunderstorm. They mean business. . . . If J. W. takes my advice, that's where we're going to have our new office."

"Well, goodbye." She put her hand in its worn gray glove in his. "I know you'll put in a word for me. . . . You're the whitehaired boy around here."

She went out leaving a little frail familiar scent of cologne and furs in the office. Dick walked up and down in front of his desk frowning. He suddenly felt nervous and jumpy. He decided he'd run out to get a breath of air and maybe a small drink before he went to lunch. "If anybody calls," he said to his secretary, "tell them to call me after three. I have an errand and then an appointment with Mr. Moorehouse."

In the elevator there was J. W. just going down in a new

overcoat with a big furcollar and a new gray fedora. "Dick," he said, "if you're late at the Plaza, I'll wring your neck. . . . You're slated for the blind bowboy."

"To shoot Bingham in the heart?" Dick's ears hummed as the elevator dropped.

J. W. nodded, smiling. "By the way, in strict confidence what do you think of Mrs. Johnson's project to put on the play? . . . Of course, she's a very lovely woman. . . . She used to be a great friend of Eleanor's. . . . Dick, my boy, why don't you marry?"

"Who? Eveline? She's married already."

"I was thinking aloud, don't pay any attention to it." They came out of the elevator and walked across the Grand Central together in the swirl of the noontime crowd. The sun had come out and sent long slanting motefilled rays across under the great blue ceiling overhead. "But what do you think of this play venture? You see I'm pretty well tied up in the market. . . . I suppose I could borrow the money at the bank."

"The theater's always risky," said Dick. "Eveline's a great girl and all that and full of talent, but I don't know how much of a head she has for business. Putting on a play's a risky business."

"I like to help old friends out . . . but it occurred to me that if the Shuberts thought there was money in it they'd be putting it in themselves. . . . Of course Mrs. Johnson's very artistic."

"Of course," said Dick.

At twelve-thirty he was waiting for J. W. in the lobby of the Plaza chewing sensen to take the smell of the three whiskies he'd swallowed at Tony's on the way up off his breath. At twelve-fortyfive he saw coming from the checkroom J. W.'s large pearshaped figure with the paleblue eyes and the sleek strawgray hair, and beside him a tall gaunt man with untidy white hair curling into ducktails over his ears. The minute they stepped into the lobby, Dick began to hear a rasping opinionated boom from the tall man.

" . . . never one of those who could hold my peace while injustice ruled in the marketplace. It has been a long struggle and one which from the vantage of those threescore and ten years that the prophets of old promised to man upon this earth I can admit to have been largely crowned with material and spiritual success. Perhaps it was my early training for the pulpit, but I have always felt, and that feeling, Mr. Moorehouse, is not rare among the prominent businessmen in this country, that material success is not the only thing . . . there is the attainment of the spirit of service. That is why I say to you frankly that I have been grieved and wounded by this dark conspiracy. Who steals my purse steals trash, but who would . . . what is it? . . . my memory's not what it was . . . my good name . . . Ah, yes, how do you do, Mr. Savage?"

Dick was surprised by the wrench the handshake gave his arm. He found himself standing in front of a gaunt loose-jointed old man with a shock of white hair and a big prognathous skull from which the sunburned skin hung in folds like the jowls of a birddog. J. W. seemed small and meek beside him.

"I'm very glad to meet you, sir," E. R. Bingham said. "I have often said to my girls that had I grown up in your generation I would have found happy and useful work in the field of publicrelations. But alas, in my day the path was harder for a young man entering life with nothing but the excellent tradition of moral fervor and natural religion I absorbed if I may say so with my mother's milk. We had to put our shoulders to the wheel in those days and it was the wheel

of an old muddy wagon drawn by mules, not the wheel of a luxurious motorcar."

E. R. Bingham boomed his way into the diningroom. A covy of palefaced waiters gathered round, pulling out chairs, setting the table, bringing menucards.

"Boy, it is no use handing me the bill of fare," E. R. Bingham addressed the headwaiter. "I live by Nature's law. I eat only a few nuts and vegetables and drink raw milk. . . . Bring me some cooked spinach, a plate of grated carrots and a glass of unpasteurized milk. . . . As a result, gentlemen, when I went a few days ago to a great physician at the request of one of the great lifeinsurance companies in this city he was dumbfounded when he examined me. He could hardly believe that I was not telling a whopper when I told him I was seventyone. 'Mr. Bingham,' he said, 'you have the magnificent physique of a healthy athlete of fortyfive' . . . Feel that, young man." E. R. Bingham flexed his arm under Dick's nose.

Dick gave the muscle a prod with two fingers. "A sledgehammer," Dick said, nodding his head.

E. R. Bingham was already talking again: "You see I practice what I preach, Mr. Moorehouse . . . and I expect others to do the same. . . . I may add that in the entire list of remedies and proprietary medicines controlled by Bingham Products and the Rugged Health Corporation, there is not a single one that contains a mineral, a drug, or any other harmful ingredient. I have sacrificed time and time again hundreds of thousands of dollars to strike from my list a concoction deemed injurious or habitforming by Doctor Gorman and the rest of the splendid men and women who make up our research department. Our medicines and our systems of diet and cure are Nature's remedies, herbs and simples culled in the wilderness in the four corners of the globe according to the tradition of wise men and the findings of sound medical science."

"Would you have coffee now, Mr. Bingham, or later?"

"Coffee, sir, is a deadly poison, as are alcohol, tea, and tobacco. If the shorthaired women and the longhaired men and the wildeyed cranks from the medical schools, who are trying to restrict the liberties of the American people to seek health and wellbeing, would restrict their activities to the elimination of these dangerous poisons that are sapping the virility of our young men and the fertility of our lovely American womanhood, I would have no quarrel with them. In fact, I would do everything I could to aid and abet them. Someday I shall put my entire fortune at the disposal of such a campaign. I know that the plain people of this country feel as I do because I'm one of them, born and raised on the farm of plain Godfearing farming folk. The American people need to be protected from cranks."

"That, Mr. Bingham," said J. W., "will be the keynote of the campaign we have been outlining." The fingerbowls had arrived. "Well, Mr. Bingham," said J. W., getting to his feet, "this has been indeed a pleasure. I unfortunately shall have to leave you to go downtown to a rather important directors' meeting, but Mr. Savage here has everything right at his fingertips and can, I know, answer any further questions. I believe we are meeting with your sales department at five."

As soon as they were alone, E. R. Bingham leaned over the table to Dick and said: "Young man, I very much need a little relaxation this afternoon. Perhaps you could come to some entertainment as my guest. . . . All work and no play . . . you know the adage. Chicago has always been my headquarters and whenever I've been in New York I've been too busy to get around. . . . Perhaps you could suggest some sort of show or musical extravaganza. I belong to the plain people, let's go where the plain people go."

Dick nodded understandingly. "Let's see, Monday afternoon . . . I'll have to call up the office. . . . There ought to be vaudeville. . . . I can't think of anything but a burlesque show."

"That's the sort of thing, music and young women. . . . I have high regard for the human body. My daughters, thank God, are magnificent physical specimens. . . . The sight of beautiful female bodies is relaxing and soothing. Come along you are my guest. It will help me to make up my mind about this matter. . . . Between you and me Mr. Moorehouse is a very extraordinary man. I think he can lend the necessary dignity. . . . But we must not forget that we are talking to the plain people."

"But the plain people aren't so plain as they were, Mr Bingham. They like things a little ritzy now," said Dick, following E. R. Bingham's rapid stride to the checkroom.

"I never wear hat or coat, only that muffler, young lady," E. R. Bingham was booming.

"Have you any children of your own, Mr. Savage?" asked E. R. Bingham when they were settled in the taxicab.

"No, I'm not married at the moment," said Dick shakily and lit himself a cigarette.

"Will you forgive a man old enough to be your father for pointing something out to you?" E. R. Bingham took Dick' cigarette between two long knobbed fingers and dropped it out of the window of the cab. "My friend, you are poisoning yourself with narcotics and destroying your virility. When

500

was around forty years old, I was in the midst of a severe economic struggle. All my great organization was still in its infancy. I was a physical wreck. I was a slave to alcohol and tobacco. I had parted with my first wife and had I had a wife I wouldn't have been able to . . . behave with her as a man should. Well, one day I said to myself: 'Doc Bingham'—my friends called me Doc in those days—'like Christian of old you are bound for the City of Destruction, and when you're gone, you'll have neither chick nor child to drop a tear for you.' I began to interest myself in the proper culture of the body . . . my spirit, I may say, was already developed by familiarity with the classics in my youth and a memory that many have called prodigious. . . . The result has been success in every line of endeavor. . . . Someday you shall meet my family and see what sweetness and beauty there can be in a healthy American home."

E. R. Bingham was still talking when they went down the aisle to seats beside the gangplank at a burlesque show. Before he could say Jack Robinson, Dick found himself looking up a series of bare jiggling female legs spotted from an occasional vaccination. The band crashed and blared, the girls wiggled and sang and stripped in a smell of dust and armpits and powder and greasepaint in the glare of the moving spot that kept lighting up E. R. Bingham's white head. E. R. Bingham was particularly delighted when one of the girls stooped

501

and cooed, "Why, look at Grandpa," and sang into his face and wiggled her geestring at him. E. R. Bingham nudged Dick and whispered, "Get her telephone number." After she'd moved on he kept exclaiming, "I feel like a boy again."

In the intermission Dick managed to call Miss Williams at the office and to tell her to suggest to people not to smoke at the conference. "Tell J. W. the old buzzard thinks cigarettes are coffinnails," he said.

"Oh, Mr. Savage," said Miss Williams reprovingly.

At five Dick tried to get him out, but he insisted on staying till the end of the show. "They'll wait for me, don't worry," he said.

When they were back in a taxi on the way to the office, E. R. Bingham chuckled. "By gad, I always enjoy a good legshow, the human form divine. . . . Perhaps we might, my friend, keep the story of our afternoon under our hats." He gave Dick's knee a tremendous slap. "It's great to play hookey."

At the conference Bingham Products signed on the dotted line. Mr. Bingham agreed to anything and paid no attention to what went on. Halfway through, he said he was tired and was going home to bed and left yawning, leaving Mr. Goldmark and a representative of the J. Winthrop Hudson Company that did the advertising for Bingham Products to go over the details of the project. Dick couldn't help admiring the quiet domineering way J. W. had with them. After the conference Dick got drunk and tried to make a girl he knew in a taxicab, but nothing came of it, and he went home to the empty apartment feeling frightful.

The next morning Dick overslept. The telephone woke him. It was Miss Williams calling from the office. Would Mr. Savage get himself a bag packed and have it sent down to the station so as to be ready to accompany Mr. Moorehouse to Washington on the Congressional. "And, Mr. Savage," she added, "excuse me for saying so, but we all feel at the office that you were responsible for nailing the Bingham account. Mr. Moorehouse was saying you must have hypnotized them."

"That's very nice of you, Miss Williams," said Dick in his sweetest voice.

Dick and J. W. took a drawingroom on the train. Miss Williams came, too, and they worked all the way down. Dick was crazy for a drink all afternoon, but he didn't dare take one, although he had a bottle of Scotch in his bag, because Miss Williams would be sure to spot him getting out the bottle and say something about it in that vague acid apologetic way she had, and he knew J. W. felt he drank too much. He felt so nervous he smoked cigarettes until his tongue began to dry up in his mouth and then took to chewing chiclets.

Dick kept J. W. busy with new slants until J. W. lay down to take a nap, saying he felt a little seedy; then Dick took Miss Williams to the diner to have a cup of tea and told her funny stories that kept her in a gale. By the time they reached the smoky Baltimore tunnels, he felt about ready for a padded cell. He'd have been telling people he was Napoleon before he got to Washington if he hadn't been able to get a good gulp of Scotch while Miss Williams was in the ladies' room and J. W. was deep in a bundle of letters E. R. Bingham had given him between Bingham Products and their Washington lobbyist Colonel Judson on the threat of puretood legislation.

When Dick finally escaped to his room in the corner suite J. W. always took at the Shoreham, he poured out a good drink to take quietly by himself, with soda and ice, while he prepared a comic telegram to send the girl he had a date for dinner with that night at the Colony Club. He'd barely sipped the drink when the phone rang. It was E. R. Bingham's secretary calling up from the Willard to see if Dick would dine with Mr. and Mrs. Bingham and the Misses Bingham.

"By all means go," said J. W. when Dick inquired if he'd need him. "First thing you know, I'll be completing the transaction by marrying you off to one of the lovely Bingham girls."

The Bingham girls were three strapping young women named Hygeia, Althea, and Myra, and Mrs. Bingham was a fat faded flatfaced blonde who wore round steel spectacles. The only one of the family who didn't wear glasses and have buckteeth was Myra, who seemed to take more after her father. She certainly talked a blue streak. She was the youngest, too, and E. R. Bingham, who was striding around in oldfashioned carpetslippers with his shirt open at the neck and a piece of red flannel undershirt showing across his chest, introduced her as the artistic member of the family. She giggled a great deal about how she was going to New York to study painting. She told Dick he looked as if he had the artistic temperament.

They ate in some confusion because Mr. Bingham kept sending back the dishes, and flew into a towering passion because the cabbage was overcooked and the raw carrots weren't ripe, and cursed and swore at the waiters and finally sent for the manager. About all they'd had was potatosoup and boiled onions sprinkled with hazelnuts and peanutbutter spread on wholewheat bread, all washed down with Coca-Cola, when two young men appeared with a microphone

503

from N.B.C. for E. R. Bingham to broadcast his eighto'clock health talk. He was suddenly smiling and hearty again and Mrs. Bingham reappeared from the bedroom to which she'd retreated crying, with her hands over her ears not to hear the old man's foul language. She came back with her eyes red and a little bottle of smellingsalts in her hand, just in time to be chased out of the room again. E. R. Bingham roared that women distracted his attention from the mike, but he made Dick stay and listen to his broadcast on health and diet and exercise hints and to the announcement of the annual cross-country hike from Washington to Louisville sponsored by *Rugged Health,* the Bingham Products houseorgan, which he was going to lead in person for the first three days, just to set the pace for the youngsters, he said.

After the broadcast Mrs. Bingham and the girls came in all rouged and powdered up, wearing diamond earrings and pearl necklaces and chinchilla coats. They invited Dick and the radio young men to go to Keith's with them, but Dick explained that he had work to do. Before Mrs. Bingham left, she made Dick promise to come to visit them at their home in Eureka.

504

"You come and spend a month, young feller," boomed E. R. Bingham, interrupting her. "We'll make a man out of you there. The first week orangejuice and high irrigations, massage, rest. . . . After that we build you up with crackedwheat and plenty of milk and cream, a little boxing or trackwork, plenty of hiking out in the sun without a lot of stifling clothes on, and you'll come back a man, Nature's richest handiwork, the paragon of animals . . . you know the lines of the immortal bard . . . and you'll have forgotten all about that unhealthy New York life that's poisoning your system. You come out, young man. . . . Well, goodnight. By the time I've done my deep breathing it'll be my bedtime. When I'm in Washington I get up at six every morning and break the ice in the Basin. . . . How about coming down for a little dip tomorrow? Pathé Newsreel is going to be there. . . . It would be worth your while in your business."

Dick excused himself hastily, saying, "Another time, Mr. Bingham."

At the Shoreham he found J. W. finishing dinner with Senator Planet and Colonel Judson, a smooth pink toadfaced man with a caressingly amiable manner.

The senator got to his feet and squeezed Dick's hand warmly. "Why, boy, we expected to see you come back wearin' a tigerskin. . . . Did the old boy show you his chestexpansion?" J. W. was frowning.

"Not this time, senator," said Dick quietly.

"But, senator," J. W. said with some impatience, evidently picking up a speech where it had been broken off, "it's the principle of the thing. Once government interference in business is established as a precedent, it means the end of liberty and private initiative in this country."

"It means the beginning of red Russian bolshevistic tyranny," added Colonel Judson, with angry emphasis.

Senator Planet laughed. "Aren't those rather harsh words, Joel?"

"What this bill purports to do is to take the right of selfmedication from the American people. A set of lazy government employees and remittancemen will be able to tell you what laxative you may take and what not. Like all such things, it'll be in the hands of cranks and busybodies. Surely the American people have the right to choose what products they want to buy. It's an insult to the intelligence of our citizens."

The senator tipped up an afterdinner coffeecup to get the last dregs of it. Dick noticed that they were drinking brandy out of big balloonglasses. "Well," said the senator slowly, "what you say may be true, but the bill has a good deal of

505

popular support and you gentlemen mustn't forget that I am not entirely a free agent in this matter. I have to consult the wishes of my constituents . . ."

"As I look at it," interrupted Colonel Judson, "all these so-called pure food and drug bills are class legislation in favor of the medical profession. Naturally the doctors want us to consult them before we buy a toothbrush or a package of licorice powder."

J. W. picked up where he left off: "The tendency of the growth of scientificallyprepared proprietary medicine has been to make the layman free and selfsufficient, able to treat many minor ills without consulting a physician."

The senator finished his brandy without answering.

"Bowie," said Colonel Judson, reaching for the bottle and pouring out some more, "you know as well as I do that the plain people of your state don't want their freedom of choice curtailed by any Washington snoopers and busybodies. . . . And we've got the money and the organization to be of great assistance in your campaign. Mr. Moorehouse is about to launch one of the biggest educational drives the country has ever seen to let the people know the truth about proprietary medicines, both in the metropolitan and the rural districts. He will roll up a great tidal wave of opinion that Congress will have to pay attention to. I've seen him do it before."

"Excellent brandy," said the senator. "Fine Armagnac has been my favorite for years." He cleared his throat and took a cigar from a box in the middle of the table and lit it in a leisurely fashion. "I've been much criticized of late, by irresponsible people, of course, for what they term my reactionary association with big business. You know the demagogic appeal."

"It is particularly at a time like this that an intelligentlyrun organization can be of most use to a man in public life," said Colonel Judson earnestly.

Senator Planet's black eyes twinkled and he passed a hand over the patch of spiky black hair that had fallen over his low forehead, leaving a segment of the top of his head bald. "I guess it comes down to how much assistance will be forthcoming," he said, getting to his feet. "The parallelogram of forces."

The other men got to their feet too. The senator flicked the ash from his cigar.

"The force of public opinion, senator," said J. W. portentously. "That is what we have to offer."

"Well, Mr. Moorehouse, you must excuse me, I have some speeches to prepare. . . . This has been most delightful. . . . Dick, you must come to dinner while you're in Washington. We've been missing you at our little dinners. . . . Goodnight, Joel, see you tomorrow." J. W.'s valet was holding the senator's furlined overcoat for him.

"Mr. Bingham," said J. W., "is a very publicspirited man, senator; he's willing to spend a very considerable sum of money."

"He'll have to," said the senator.

After the door had closed on Senator Planet, the rest of them sat silent a moment. Dick poured himself a glass of the Armagnac.

"Well, Mr. Bingham don't need to worry," said Colonel Judson. "But it's going to cost him money. Bowie an' his friends are just trying to raise the ante. You know I can read 'em like a book. . . . After all, I been around this town for fifteen years."

"It's humiliating and absurd that legitimate business should have to stoop to such methods," said J. W.

"Sure, J. W., you took the words right out of my mouth. . . . If you want my opinion, what we need is a strong man in this country to send all these politicians packing. . . . Don't think I don't know 'em. . . . But this little dinnerparty has been very valuable. You are a new element in the situation. . . . A valuable air of dignity, you know. . . . Well, goodnight."

J. W. was already standing with his hand outstretched, his face white as paper.

"Well, I'll be running along," said Colonel Judson. "You can assure your client that that bill will never pass. . . . Take a good night's rest, Mr. Moorehouse. . . . Goodnight, Captain Savage. . . ." Colonel Judson patted both J. W. and Dick affectionately on the shoulder with his two hands in the same gesture. Chewing his cigar he eased out of the door leaving a broad smile behind him and a puff of rank blue smoke.

Dick turned to J. W. who had sunk down in a red plush chair. "Are you sure you're feeling all right, J. W.?"

"It's just a little indigestion," J. W. said in a weak voice, his face twisted with pain, gripping the arms of the chair with both hands.

"Well, I guess we'd better all turn in," said Dick. "But J. W., how about getting a doctor in to take a look at you in the morning?"

"We'll see, goodnight," said J. W., talking with difficulty with his eyes closed.

Dick had just got to sleep when a knocking on his door woke him with a start. He went to the door in his bare feet. It was Morton, J. W.'s elderly cockney valet. "Beg pardon, sir, for waking you, sir," he said. "I'm worried about Mr. Moorehouse, sir. Doctor Gleason's with him . . . I'm afraid it's a heart attack. He's in pain something awful, sir."

Dick put on his purple silk bathrobe and his slippers and ran into the drawingroom of the suite where he met the doctor. "This is Mr. Savage, sir," said the valet. The doctor was a grayhaired man with a gray mustache and a portentous manner. He looked Dick fiercely in the eye as he spoke: "Mr. Moorehouse must be absolutely quiet for some days. It's a very light angina pectoris . . . not serious this time, but a thorough rest for a few months is indicated. He ought to have a thorough physical examination . . . talk him into it in the morning. I believe you are Mr. Moorehouse's business partner, aren't you, Mr. Savage?"

Dick blushed. "I'm one of Mr. Moorehouse's collaborators."

"Take as much off his shoulders as you can."

Dick nodded. He went back to his room and lay on his bed the rest of the night without being able to sleep.

In the morning when Dick went in to see him, J. W. was sitting up in bed propped up with pillows. His face was a rumpled white and he had violet shadows under his eyes. "Dick, I certainly gave myself a scare." J. W.'s voice was

508

weak and shaking; it made Dick feel almost tearful to hear it.

"Well, what about the rest of us?"

"Well, Dick, I'm afraid I'm going to have to dump E. R. Bingham and a number of other matters on your shoulders. . . . And I've been thinking that perhaps I ought to change the whole capital structure of the firm. What would you think of Moorehouse, Griscolm and Savage?"

"I think it would be a mistake to change the name, J. W. After all, J. Ward Moorehouse is a national institution."

J. W.'s voice quavered up a little stronger. He kept having to clear his throat. "I guess you're right, Dick," he said. "I'd like to hold on long enough to give my boys a start in life."

"What do you want to bet you wear a silk hat at my funeral, J. W.? In the first place, it may have been an attack of acute indigestion just as you thought. We can't go on merely one doctor's opinion. What would you think of a little trip to the Mayo clinic? All you need's a little overhauling, valves ground, carburetor adjusted, that sort of thing. . . . By the way, J. W., we wouldn't want Mr. Bingham to discover that a mere fifteenthousand a year man was handling his sacred proprietary medicines, would we?"

J. W. laughed weakly. "Well, we'll see about that. . . . I think you'd better go on down to New York this morning and take charge of the office. Miss Williams and I will hold the fort here. . . . She's sour as a pickle, but a treasure, I tell you."

"Hadn't I better stick around until we've had a specialist look you over?"

"Doctor Gleason filled me up with dope of some kind so that I'm pretty comfortable. I've wired my sister, Hazel, she teaches school over in Wilmington, she's the only one of the family I've seen much of since the old people died. . . . She'll be over this afternoon. It's her Christmas vacation."

"Did Morton get you the opening quotations?"

"Skyrocketing. . . . Never saw anything like it. . . . But do you know, Dick, I'm going to sell out and lay on my oars for a while. . . . It's funny how an experience like this takes the heart out of you."

"You and Paul Warburg," said Dick.

"Maybe it's old age," said J. W., and closed his eyes for a minute. His face seemed to be collapsing into a mass of gray and violet wrinkles as Dick looked.

"Well, take it easy, J. W.," said Dick and tiptoed out of the room.

He caught the eleveno'clock train and got to the office in time to straighten things out. He told everybody that J. W. had a light touch of grippe and would be in bed for a few days. There was so much work piled up that he gave Miss Hilles his secretary a dollar for her supper and asked her to come back at eight. For himself he had some sandwiches and a carton of coffee sent up from a delicatessen. It was midnight before he got through. In the empty halls of the dim building he met two rusty old women coming with pails and scrubbingbrushes to clean the office. The night elevatorman was old and pastyfaced. Snow had fallen and turned to slush and gave Lexington Avenue a black gutted look like a street in an abandoned village. A raw wind whipped his face and ears as he turned uptown. He thought of the apartment on Fiftysixth Street full of his mother's furniture, the gilt chairs in the front room, all the dreary objects he'd known as a small boy, the *Stag at Bay* and the engravings of the Forum Romanorum in his room, the bird'seyemaple beds; he could see it all sharply as if he was there as he turned into the wind. Bad enough when his mother was there, but when she was in St. Augustine, frightful. "God damn it, it's time I was making enough money to reorganize my life," he said to himself.

He jumped into the first taxi he came to and went to "63." It was warm and cozy in "63." As she helped him off with his coat and muffler, the platinumhaired checkgirl carried on an elaborate kidding that had been going on all winter about how he was going to take her to Miami and make her fortune at the races at Hialeah. Then he stood a second peering through the doorway into the low room full of wellgroomed heads, tables, glasses, cigarettesmoke spiraling in front of the pink lights. He caught sight of Pat Doolittle's black bang. There she was sitting in the alcove with Reggie and Jo.

The Italian waiter ran up, rubbing his hands. "Good evening, Mr. Savage, we've been missing you."

"I've been in Washington."

"Cold down there?"

"Oh, kind of medium," said Dick and slipped into the redleather settee opposite Pat.

"Well, look who we have with us," she said. "I thought you were busy poisoning the American public under the dome of the Capitol."

"Wouldn't be so bad if we poisoned some of those western legislators," said Dick.

Reggie held out his hand. "Well, put it there, Alec Borgia. . . . I reckon you're on the bourbon if you've been mingling with the conscript fathers."

"Sure, I'll drink bourbon . . . kids, I'm tired . . . I'm going to eat something. I didn't have any supper. I just left the office."

Reggie looked pretty tight; so did Pat. Jo was evidently sober and sore. I must fix this up, thought Dick, and put his arm round Pat's waist. "Say, did you get my 'gram?"

"Laughed myself sick over it," said Pat. "Gosh, Dick, it's nice to have you back among the drinking classes."

"Say, Dick," said Reggie, "is there anything in the rumor that old doughface toppled over?"

"Mr. Moorehouse had a little attack of acute indigestion . . . he was better when I left," said Dick in a voice that sounded a little too solemn in his ears.

"Not drinking gets 'em in the end," said Reggie. The girls laughed. Dick put down three bourbons in rapid succession, but he wasn't getting any lift from them. He just felt hungry and frazzled. He had his head twisted around trying to flag the waiter to find out what the devil had happened to his filet-mignon when he heard Reggie drawling, "After all J. Ward Moorehouse isn't a man . . . it's a name. . . . You can't feel sorry when a name gets sick."

Dick felt a rush of anger flush his head: "He's one of the sixty most important men in this country," he said. "After all, Reggie, you're taking his money . . ."

"Good God!" cried Reggie. "The man on the high horse."

Pat turned to Dick, laughing. "They seem to be getting mighty holy down there in Washington."

"No, you know I like to kid as well as anybody. . . . But when a man like J. W., who's perhaps done more than any one living man, whether you like what he does or not, to form the public mind in this country, is taken ill, I think sophomore wisecracks are in damn bad taste."

Reggie was drunk. He was talking in phony Southern dialect. "Wha, brudder, Ah didn't know as you was Mista Moahouse in pussen. Ah thunked you was juss a lowdown wage-slave like the rest of us pickaninnies."

Dick wanted to shut up, but he couldn't. "Whether you like it or not, the molding of the public mind is one of the most important things that goes on in this country. If it wasn't for that, American business would be in a pretty pickle. . . . Now we may like the way American business does things or we may not like it, but it's a historical fact like the Himalaya Mountains and no amount of kidding's going to change it. It's only through publicrelations work that business is protected from wildeyed cranks and demagogues who are always ready to throw a monkeywrench into the industrial machine."

"Hear, hear," cried Pat.

"Well, you'll be the first to holler when they cut the income from your old man's firstmortgage bonds," said Dick snappishly.

"Senator," intoned Reggie, strengthened by another old-fashioned, "allow me to congrat'late you . . . ma soul 'n body, senator, 'low me to congrat'late you . . . upon your val'able services to this great commonwealth that stretches from the great Atlantical Ocean to the great and glorious Pacifical."

"Shut up, Reggie," said Jo. "Let him eat his steak in peace."

"Well, you certainly made the eagle scream, Dick," said Pat, "but seriously, I guess you're right."

"We've got to be realists," said Dick.

"I believe," said Pat Doolittle, throwing back her head and laughing, "that he's come across with that raise."

Dick couldn't help grinning and nodding. He felt better since he'd eaten. He ordered another round of drinks and began to talk about going up to Harlem to dance at Small's Paradise. He said he couldn't go to bed, he was too tired, he had to have some relaxation. Pat Doolittle said she loved it in Harlem, but that she hadn't brought any money.

"My party," said Dick. "I've got plenty of cash on me."

They went up with a flask of whiskey in each of the girls' handbags and in Dick's and Reggie's back pockets. Reggie and Pat sang *The Fireship* in the taxi. Dick drank a good deal in the taxi to catch up with the others. Going down the steps to Small's was like going underwater into a warm thicklygrown pool. The air was dense with musky smells of mulatto powder and perfume and lipstick and dresses and throbbed like flesh with the smoothly balanced chugging of the band. Dick and Pat danced right away, holding each other very close. Their dancing seemed smooth as cream. Dick found her lips under his and kissed them. She kissed back. When the music stopped, they were reeling a little. They walked back to their table with drunken dignity. When the band started again, Dick danced with Jo. He kissed her too.

She pushed him off a little. "Dick, you oughtn't to."

"Reggie won't mind. It's all in the family. . . ." They were dancing next to Reggie and Pat hemmed in by a swaying blur of couples. Dick dropped Jo's hand and put his hand on Reggie's shoulder. "Reggie, you don't mind if I kiss your future wife for you just once."

"Go as far as you like, senator," said Reggie. His voice was thick. Pat was having trouble keeping him on his feet. Jo gave Dick a waspish look and kept her face turned away for the rest of the dance. As soon as they got back to the table, she told Reggie that it was after two and she'd have to go home, she for one had to work in the morning.

When they were alone and Dick was just starting to make love to Pat, she turned to him and said, "Oh, Dick, do take me someplace low . . . nobody'll ever take me any place really low."

"I should think this would be quite low enough for a juniorleaguer," he said.

"But this is more respectable than Broadway, and I'm not a juniorleaguer . . . I'm the new woman."

Dick burst out laughing. They both laughed and had a drink on it and felt fond of each other again and Dick suddenly asked her why couldn't they be together always.

"I think you're mean. This isn't any place to propose to a girl. Imagine remembering all your life that you'd got engaged in Harlem. . . . I want to see life."

"All right, young lady, we'll go . . . but don't blame me if it's too rough for you."

"I'm not a sissy," said Pat angrily. "I know it wasn't the stork."

Dick paid and they finished up one of the pints. Outside it was snowing. Streets and stoops and pavements were white, innocent, quiet, glittering under the streetlights with freshfallen snow. Dick asked the whiteeyed black doorman about a dump he'd heard of and the doorman gave the taximan the address.

Dick began to feel good. "Gosh, Pat, isn't this lovely," he kept crying.

"Those kids can't take it. Takes us grownups to take it. . . . Say, Reggie's getting too fresh, do you know it?" Pat held his hand tight. Her cheeks were flushed and her face had a taut look. "Isn't it exciting?" she said. The taxi stopped in front of an unpainted basement door with one electriclightbulb haloed with snowflakes above it.

They had a hard time getting in. There were no white people there at all. It was a furnaceroom set around with plain kitchen tables and chairs. The steampipes overhead were hung with colored paper streamers. A big brown woman in a pink dress, big eyes rolling loose in their dark sockets and twitching lips, led them to a table. She seemed to take a shine to Pat. "Come right on in, darlin'," she said. "Where's you been all my life?"

Their whiskey was gone, so they drank gin. Things got to whirling round in Dick's head. He couldn't get off the subject of how sore he was at that little squirt Reggie. Here Dick had been nursing him along in the office for a year and now he goes smartaleck on him. The little twirp.

The only music was a piano where a slimwaisted black man was tickling the ivories. Dick and Pat danced and danced and he whirled her around until the sealskin browns and the highyallers cheered and clapped. Then Dick slipped and dropped her. She went spinning into a table where some girls were sitting. Dark heads went back, pink rubber lips stretched, mouths opened. Gold teeth and ivories let out a roar.

Pat was dancing with a pale pretty mulatto girl in a yellow dress. Dick was dancing with a softhanded brown boy in a tightfitting suit the color of his skin. The boy was whispering in Dick's ear that his name was Gloria Swanson. Dick suddenly broke away from him and went over to Pat and pulled her away from the girl. Then he ordered drinks all around that changed sullen looks into smiles again. He had trouble getting Pat into her coat. The fat woman was very helpful. "Sure, honey," she said, "you don't want to go on drinkin' tonight, spoil your lovely looks." Dick hugged her and gave her a tendollar bill.

In the taxi Pat had hysterics and punched and bit at him when he held her tight to try to keep her from opening the door and jumping out into the snow.

"You spoil everything. . . . You can't think of anybody except yourself," she yelled. "You'll never go through with anything."

"But, Pat, honestly," he was whining, "I thought it was time to draw the line."

By the time the taxi drew up in front of the big square apartmenthouse on Park Avenue where she lived, she was sobbing quietly on his shoulder. He took her into the elevator and kissed her for a long time in the upstairs hall before he'd let her put the key in the lock of the door. They stood there tottering clinging to each other, rubbing up against each other through their clothes, until Dick heard the swish of the rising elevator and opened her door for her and pushed her in.

When he got outside the door he found the taxi waiting for him. He'd forgotten to pay the driver. He couldn't stand to go home. He didn't feel drunk, he felt immensely venturesome and cool and innocently excited. Patricia Doolittle he hated more than anybody in the world. "The bitch," he kept saying aloud. He wondered how it would be to go back to the dump and see what happened and there he was being kissed by the fat woman who wiggled her breasts as she hugged him and called him her own lovin' chile, with a bottle of gin in his hand pouring drinks for everybody and dancing cheek to

cheek with Gloria Swanson who was humming in his ear: Do I get it now . . . or must I he . . . esitate.

It was morning. Dick was shouting the party couldn't break up, they must all come to breakfast with him. Everybody was gone and he was getting into a taxicab with Gloria and a strapping black buck he said was his girlfriend Florence. He had a terrible time getting his key in the lock. He tripped and fell toward the paleblue light seeping through his mother's lace curtains in the windows. Something very soft tapped him across the back of the head.

He woke up undressed in his own bed. It was broad daylight. The phone was ringing. He let it ring. He sat up. He felt lightheaded, but not sick. He put his hand to his ear and it came away all bloody. It must have been a stocking full of sand that hit him. He got to his feet. He felt tottery, but he could walk. His head began to ache like thunder. He reached for the place on the table he usually left his watch. No watch. His clothes were neatly hung on a chair. He found the wallet in its usual place, but the roll of bills was gone. He sat down on the edge of the bed. Of all the damn fools. Never never never take a risk like that again. Now they knew his name, his address, his phonenumber. Blackmail, oh Christ. How would it be when Mother came home from Florida to find her son earning twentyfive thousand a year, junior partner of J. Ward Moorehouse, being blackmailed by two nigger whores, male prostitutes receiving males? Christ. And Pat Doolittle and the Bingham girls. It would ruin his life. For a second he thought of going into the kitchenette and turning on the gas.

He pulled himself together and took a bath. Then he dressed carefully and put on his hat and coat and went out. It was only nine o'clock. He saw the time in a jeweler's window on Lexington. There was a mirror in the same window. He looked at his face. Didn't look so bad, would look worse later, but he needed a shave and had to do something about the clotted blood on his ear.

He didn't have any money, but he had his checkbook. He walked to a Turkish bath near the Grand Central. The attendants kidded him about what a fight he'd been in. He began to get over his scare a little and to talk big about what he'd done to the other guy. They took his check all right and he even was able to buy a drink to have before his breakfast. When he got to the office, his head was still splitting, but he felt in fair shape. He had to keep his hands in his pockets so that Miss Hilles shouldn't see how they shook. Thank God, he didn't have to sign any letters till afternoon.

Ed Griscolm came in and sat on his desk and talked about J. W.'s condition and the Bingham account and Dick was sweet as sugar to him. Ed Griscolm talked big about an offer he'd had from Halsey, but Dick said, of course, he couldn't advise him, but that as for him the one place in the country he wanted to be was right here, especially now as there were bigger things in sight than there had ever been before, he and J. W. had had a long talk going down on the train.

"I guess you're right," said Ed. "I guess it was sour grapes a little."

Dick got to his feet. "Honestly, Ed, old man, you mustn't think for a minute J. W. doesn't appreciate your work. He even let drop something about a raise."

"Well, it was nice of you to put in a word for me, old man," said Ed, and they shook hands warmly.

As Ed was leaving the office he turned and said, "Say, Dick, I wish you'd give that youngster Talbot a talking to. . . . I know he's a friend of yours, so I don't like to do it, but, Jesus Christ, he's gone and called up again saying he's in bed with the grippe. That's the third time this month."

Dick wrinkled up his brows. "I don't know what to do about him, Ed. He's a nice kid all right, but if he won't knuckle down to serious work . . . I guess we'll have to let him go. We certainly can't let drinking acquaintance stand in the way of the efficiency of the office. These kids all drink too much, anyway."

After Ed had gone, Dick found on his desk a big lavender envelope marked Personal. A whiff of strong perfume came out when he opened it. It was an invitation from Myra Bingham to come to the housewarming of her studio on Central Park South.

He was still reading it when Miss Hilles's voice came out

of the interoffice phone. "There's Mr. Henry B. Furness of the Furness Corporation says he must speak to Mr. Moorehouse at once."

"Put him on my phone, Miss Hilles. I'll talk to him . . . and, by the way, put a social engagement on my engagement pad . . . January fifteenth at five o'clock . . . reception Miss Myra Bingham, 36 Central Park South."

Newsreel LXVIII

WALL STREET STUNNED

This is not Thirtyeight but it's old Ninetyseven
You must put her in Center on time

MARKET SURE TO RECOVER FROM SLUMP

DECLINE IN CONTRACTS

POLICE TURN MACHINE GUNS ON COLORADO
MINE STRIKERS KILL 5 WOUND 40

sympathizers appeared on the scene just as thousands
of office workers were pouring out of the buildings at the
lunch hour. As they raised their placard high and started
an indefinite march from one side to the other, they were
jeered and hooted not only by the office workers but also
by workmen on a building under construction

NEW METHODS OF SELLING SEEN

RESCUE CREWS TRY TO UPEND ILL-FATED CRAFT
WHILE WAITING FOR PONTOONS

He looked 'round an' said to his black greasy fireman
Jus' shovel in a little more coal
And when we cross that White Oak Mountain
You can watch your Ninety-seven roll

I find your column interesting and need advice. I have
saved four thousand dollars which I want to invest for a
better income. Do you think I might buy stocks?

POLICE KILLER FLICKS CIGARETTE AS HE GOES
TREMBLING TO DOOM

PLAY AGENCIES IN RING OF SLAVE GIRL MARTS

MAKER OF LOVE DISBARRED AS LAWYER

Oh the right wing clothesmakers
And the Socialist fakers
They make by the workers . . .
Double cross

They preach Social-ism
But practice Fasc-ism
To keep capitalism
By the boss

MOSCOW CONGRESS OUSTS OPPOSITION

It's a mighty rough road from Lynchburg to Danville
An' a line on a three mile grade
It was on that grade he lost his average
An' you see what a jump he made

MILL THUGS IN MURDER RAID

here is the most dangerous example of how at the deci-
sive moment the bourgeois ideology liquidates class solidarity and turns a friend of the workingclass of yesterday
into a most miserable propagandist for imperialism today

RED PICKETS FINED FOR PROTESTS HERE

We leave our home in the morning
We kiss our children goodbye

OFFICIALS STILL HOPE FOR RESCUE OF MEN

He was goin' downgrade makin' ninety miles an hour
When his whistle broke into a scream
He was found in the wreck with his hand on the throttle
An' was scalded to death with the steam

RADICALS FIGHT WITH CHAIRS AT UNITY MEETING

PATROLMEN PROTECT REDS

U.S. CHAMBER OF COMMERCE URGES CONFIDENCE

REAL VALUES UNHARMED

While we slave for the bosses
Our children scream an' cry
But when we draw our money
Our grocery bills to pay

PRESIDENT SEES PROSPERITY NEAR

Not a cent to spend for clothing
Not a cent to lay away

STEAMROLLER IN ACTION AGAINST MILITANTS

MINERS BATTLE SCABS

But we cannot buy for our children
Our wages are too low
Now listen to me you workers
Both you women and men
Let us win for them the victory
I'm sure it ain't no sin

CARILLON PEALS IN SINGING TOWER

the President declared it was impossible to view the increased advantages for the many without smiling at those
who a short time ago expressed so much fear lest our
country might come under the control of a few individu-
als of great wealth.

HAPPY CROWDS THRONG CEREMONY

on a tiny island nestling like a green jewel in the lake
that mirrors the singing tower, the President today partic-
ipated in the dedication of a bird sanctuary and its peal-
ing carillon, fulfilling the dream of an immigrant boy

521

The Camera Eye (51)

at the head of the valley in the dark of the hills on the broken floor of a lurchedover cabin a man halfsits halflies propped up by an old woman two wrinkled girls that might be young   chunks of coal flare in the hearth flicker in his face white and sagging as dough   blacken the cavedin mouth the taut throat the belly swelled enormous with the wound he got working on the minetipple

the barefoot girl brings him a tincup of water   the woman wipes sweat off his streaming face with a dirty denim sleeve   the firelight flares in his eyes stretched big with fever in the women's scared eyes and in the blanched faces of the foreigners

without help in the valley hemmed by dark strikesilent hills the man will die (my father died we know what it is like to see a man die) the women will lay him out on the rickety cot the miners will bury him

in the jail it's light too hot the steamheat hisses we talk through the greenpainted iron bars to a tall white mustachioed old man some smiling miners in shirtsleeves a boy   faces white from mining have already the tallowy look of jailfaces

foreigners what can we say to the dead?   foreigners what can we say to the jailed?   the representative of the political party talks fast through the bars join up with us and no other union we'll send you tobacco candy solidarity our lawyers will write briefs speakers will shout your names at meetings they'll carry your names on cardboards on picketlines   the men in jail shrug their shoulders smile thinly our eyes look in their eyes through the bars   what can I say?

(in another continent I have seen the faces looking out through the barred basement windows behind the ragged sentry's boots I have seen before day the straggling footsore prisoners herded through the streets limping between bayonets   heard the volley

I have seen the dead lying out in those distant deeper valleys) what can we say to the jailed?

in the law's office we stand against the wall the law is a big man with eyes angry in a big pumpkinface   who sits and stares at us meddling foreigners through the door the deputies crane with their guns   they stand guard at the mines   they blockade the miners' soupkitchens

they've cut off the road up the valley   the hiredmen with guns stand ready to shoot (they have made us foreigners in the land where we were born they are the conquering army that has filtered into the country unnoticed they have taken the hilltops by stealth they levy toll they stand at the minehead   they stand at the polls

they stand by when the bailiffs carry the furniture of the family evicted from the city tenement out on the sidewalk they are there when the bankers foreclose on a farm they are ambushed and ready to shoot down the strikers marching behind the flag up the switchback road to the mine   those that the guns spare they jail)

the law stares across the desk out of angry eyes his face reddens in splotches like a gobbler's neck with the strut of the power of submachineguns sawedoffshotguns teargas and vomitinggas the power that can feed you or leave you to starve

sits easy at his desk his back is covered he feels strong behind him he feels the prosecutingattorney the judge an owner himself the political boss the minesuperintendent the board of directors   the president of the utility the manipulator of the holdingcompany

he lifts his hand towards the telephone

the deputies crowd in the door

we have only words against

Power Superpower

In eighteen-eighty when Thomas Edison's agent was hooking up the first telephone in London, he put an ad in the paper for a secretary and stenographer. The eager young cockney with sprouting muttonchop whiskers who answered it

had recently lost his job as officeboy. In his spare time he had been learning shorthand and bookkeeping and taking dictation from the editor of the English *Vanity Fair* at night and jotting down the speeches in Parliament for the papers. He came of temperance small shopkeeper stock; already he was butting his bullethead against the harsh structure of caste that doomed boys of his class to a life of alpaca jackets, penmanship, subordination. To get a job with an American firm was to put a foot on the rung of a ladder that led up into the blue.

He did his best to make himself indispensable; they let him operate the switchboard for the first halfhour when the telephone service was opened. Edison noticed his weekly reports on the electrical situation in England

and sent for him to be his personal secretary.

Samuel Insull landed in America on a raw March day in eightyone. Immediately he was taken out to Menlo Park, shown about the little group of laboratories, saw the strings of electriclightbulbs shining at intervals across the snowy lots, all lit from the world's first central electric station. Edison put him right to work and he wasn't through till midnight. Next morning at six he was on the job; Edison had no use for any nonsense about hours or vacations. Insull worked from that time on until he was seventy without a break; no nonsense about hours or vacations. Electric power turned the ladder into an elevator.

Young Insull made himself indispensable to Edison and took more and more charge of Edison's business deals. He was tireless, ruthless, reliable as the tides, Edison used to say, and fiercely determined to rise.

In ninetytwo he induced Edison to send him to Chicago and put him in as president of the Chicago Edison Company. Now he was on his own. *My engineering,* he said once in a speech, when he was sufficiently czar of Chicago to allow himself the luxury of plain speaking, *has been largely concerned with engineering all I could out of the dollar.*

He was a stiffly arrogant redfaced man with a closecropped mustache; he lived on Lake Shore Drive and was at the office at 7:10 every morning. It took him fifteen years to merge the five electrical companies into the Commonwealth Edison Company. *Very early I discovered that the first essential, as in other public utility business, was that it should be operated as a monopoly.*

When his power was firm in electricity he captured gas, spread out into the surrounding townships in northern Illinois. When politicians got in his way, he bought them, when laborleaders got in his way he bought them. Incredibly his power grew. He was scornful of bankers, lawyers were his hired men. He put his own lawyer in as corporation counsel and through him ran Chicago. When he found to his amazement that there were men (even a couple of young lawyers,

Richberg and Ickes) in Chicago that he couldn't buy, he decided he'd better put on a show for the public;

Big Bill Thompson, the Builder:
punch King George in the nose,
the hunt for the treeclimbing fish,
the Chicago Opera.

It was too easy; the public had money, there was one of them born every minute, with the founding of Middlewest Utilities in nineteen twelve Insull began to use the public's money to spread his empire. His companies began to have open stockholders' meetings, to ballyhoo service, the small investor could sit there all day hearing the bigwigs talk. It's fun to be fooled. Companyunions hypnotized his employees; everybody had to buy stock in his companies, employees had to go out and sell stock, officeboys, linemen, trolleyconductors. Even Owen D. Young was afraid of him. *My experience is that the greatest aid in the efficiency of labor is a long line of men waiting at the gate.*

War shut up the progressives (no more nonsense about trustbusting, controlling monopoly, the public good) and raised Samuel Insull to the peak.

He was head of the Illinois State Council of Defense. *Now,* he said delightedly, *I can do anything I like.* With it came the perpetual spotlight, the purple taste of empire. If anybody didn't like what Samuel Insull did he was a traitor. Chicago damn well kept its mouth shut.

The Insull companies spread and merged put competitors out of business until Samuel Insull and his stooge brother Martin controlled through the leverage of holdingcompanies and directorates and blocks of minority stock

light and power, coalmines and tractioncompanies

in Illinois, Michigan, the Dakotas, Nebraska, Arkansas, Oklahoma, Missouri, Maine, Kansas, Wisconsin, Virginia, Ohio, North Carolina, Indiana, New York, New Jersey, Texas, in Canada, in Louisiana, in Georgia, in Florida and Alabama.

(It has been figured out that one dollar in Middle West Utilities controlled seventeen hundred and fifty dollars invested by the public in the subsidiary companies that actually did the work of producing electricity. With the delicate lever of a voting trust controlling the stock of the two top holdingcompanies he controlled a twelfth of the power output of America.)

Samuel Insull began to think he owned all that the way a man owns the roll of bills in his back pocket.

Always he'd been scornful of bankers. He owned quite a few in Chicago. But the New York bankers were laying for him; they felt he was a bounder, whispered that this financial structure was unsound. Fingers itched to grasp the lever that so delicately moved this enormous power over lives,

superpower, Insull liked to call it.

A certain Cyrus S. Eaton of Cleveland, an ex-Baptistminister, was the David that brought down this Goliath. Whether it was so or not he made Insull believe that Wall Street was behind him.

He started buying stock in the three Chicago utilities. Insull in a panic for fear he'd lose his control went into the market to buy against him. Finally the Reverend Eaton let himself be bought out, shaking down the old man for a profit of twenty million dollars.

The stockmarket crash.

Paper values were slipping. Insull's companies were intertwined in a tangle that no bookkeeper has ever been able to unravel.

The gas hissed out of the torn balloon. Insull threw away his imperial pride and went on his knees to the bankers.

The bankers had him where they wanted him. To save the face of the tottering czar he was made a receiver of his own concerns. But the old man couldn't get out of his head the illusion that the money was all his. When it was discovered that he was using the stockholders' funds to pay off his brothers' brokerage accounts it was too thick even for a federal judge. Insull was forced to resign.

He held directorates in eightyfive companies, he was chairman of sixtyfive, president of eleven: it took him three hours to sign his resignations.

As a reward for his services to monopoly his companies chipped in on a pension of eighteen thousand a year. But the public was shouting for criminal prosecution. When the handouts stopped newspapers and politicians turned on him. Revolt against the moneymanipulators was in the air. Samuel Insull got the wind up and ran off to Canada with his wife.

Extradition proceedings. He fled to Paris. When the authorities began to close in on him there he slipped away to Italy, took a plane to Tirana, another to Saloniki and then the train to Athens. There the old fox went to earth. Money talked as sweetly in Athens as it had in Chicago in the old days.

The American ambassador tried to extradite him. Insull hired a chorus of Hellenic lawyers and politicos and sat drinking coffee in the lobby of the Grande Bretagne, while they proceeded to tie up the ambassador in a snarl of chicanery as complicated as the bookkeeping of his holdingcompanies. The successors of Demosthenes were delighted. The ancestral itch in many a Hellenic path was temporarily assuaged. Samuel Insull settled down cozily in Athens, was stirred by the sight of the Parthenon, watched the goats feeding on the Pentelic slopes, visited the Areopagus, admired marble fragments ascribed to Phidias, talked with the local bankers about reorganizing the public utilities of Greece, was said to be promoting Macedonian lignite. He was the toast of the Athenians; Madame Kouryoumdjouglou, the vivacious wife of a Baghdad datemerchant, devoted herself to his comfort. When the first effort at extradition failed, the old gentleman declared in the courtroom, as he struggled out from the embraces of his four lawyers: *Greece is a small but great country*.

The idyll was interrupted when the Roosevelt Administration began to put the heat on the Greek Foreign Office. Government lawyers in Chicago were accumulating truckloads of evidence and chalking up more and more drastic indictments.

Finally after many a postponement (he had hired physicians as well as lawyers, they cried to high heaven that it would kill him to leave the genial climate of the Attic plain),

he was ordered to leave Greece as an undesirable alien, to the great indignation of Balkan society and of Madame Kouryoumdjouglou.

He hired the *Maiotis* a small and grubby Greek freighter and panicked the foreignnews services by slipping off for an unknown destination.

It was rumored that the new Odysseus was bound for Aden, for the islands of the South Seas, that he'd been invited to Persia. After a few days he turned up rather seasick in the Bosporus on his way, it was said, to Rumania where Madame Kouryoumdjouglou had advised him to put himself under the protection of her friend la Lupescu.

At the request of the American ambassador the Turks were delighted to drag him off the Greek freighter and place him in a not at all comfortable jail. Again money had been mysteriously wafted from England, the healing balm began to flow, lawyers were hired, interpreters expostulated, doctors made diagnoses;

but Angora was boss

and Insull was shipped off to Smyrna to be turned over to the assistant federal districtattorney who had come all that way to arrest him.

The Turks wouldn't even let Madame Kouryoumdjouglou, on her way back from making arrangements in Bucharest, go ashore to speak to him. In a scuffle with the officials on the steamboat the poor lady was pushed overboard

and with difficulty fished out of the Bosporus.

Once he was cornered the old man let himself tamely be taken home on the *Exilona,* started writing his memoirs, made himself agreeable to his fellow passengers, was taken off at Sandy Hook and rushed to Chicago to be arraigned.

In Chicago the government spitefully kept him a couple of nights in jail; men he'd never known, so the newspapers said, stepped forward to go on his twohundred-andfiftythousanddollar bail. He was moved to a hospital that he himself had endowed. Solidarity. The leading businessmen in Chicago were photographed visiting him there. Henry Ford paid a call.

The trial was very beautiful. The prosecution got bogged in finance technicalities. The judge was not unfriendly. The Insulls stole the show.

They were folks, they smiled at reporters, they posed for photographers, they went down to the courtroom by bus. Investors might have been ruined but so, they allowed it to be known, were the Insulls; the captain had gone down with the ship.

Old Samuel Insull rambled amiably on the stand, told his lifestory: from officeboy to powermagnate, his struggle to make good, his love for his home and the kiddies. He didn't deny he'd made mistakes; who hadn't, but they were honest errors. Samuel Insull wept. Brother Martin wept. The lawyers wept. With voices choked with emotion headliners of Chicago business told from the witnessstand how much Insull had done for business in Chicago. There wasn't a dry eye in the jury.

Finally driven to the wall by the prosecutingattorney Samuel Insull blurted out that yes, he had made an error of some ten million dollars in accounting but that it had been an honest error.

Verdict: Not Guilty.

Smiling through their tears the happy Insulls went to their towncar amid the cheers of the crowd. Thousands of ruined investors, at least so the newspapers said, who had lost their life savings sat crying over the home editions at the thought of how Mr. Insull had suffered. The bankers were happy, the bankers had moved in on the properties.

In an odor of sanctity the deposed monarch of superpower, the officeboy who made good, enjoys his declining years spending the pension of twentyone thousand a year that the directors of his old companies dutifully restored to him. *After fifty years of work,* he said, *my job is gone.*

Mary French

Mary French had to stay late at the office and couldn't get to the hall until the meeting was almost over. There were no seats left, so she stood in the back. So many people were standing in front of her that she couldn't see Don, she could only hear his ringing harsh voice and feel the tense attention in the silence during his pauses. When a roar of applause answered his last words and the hall filled suddenly with voices and the scrape and shuffle of feet, she ran out ahead of the crowd and up the alley to the back door. Don was just coming out of the black sheetiron door talking over his shoulder as he came to two of the miners' delegates. He stopped a second to hold the door open for them with a long arm. His face had the flushed smile, there was the shine in his eye he often had after speaking, the look, Mary used to tell herself, of a man who had just come from a date with his best girl. It was some time before Don saw her in the group that gathered round him in the alley. Without looking at her, he swept her along with the men he was talking to and walked them fast toward the corner of the street. Eyes looked after them as they went from the groups of furworkers and garmentworkers that dotted the pavement in front of the hall. Mary tingled with the feeling of warm ownership in the looks of the workers as their eyes followed Don Stevens down the street.

It wasn't until they were seated in a small lunchroom under the El that Don turned to Mary and squeezed her hand. "Tired?"

She nodded. "Aren't you, Don?"

He laughed and drawled, "No, I'm not tired. I'm hungry."

"Comrade French, I thought we'd detailed you to see that Comrade Stevens ate regular," said Rudy Goldfarb with a flash of teeth out of a dark Italianlooking face.

"He won't ever eat anything when he's going to speak," Mary said.

"I make up for it afterwards," said Don. "Say, Mary, I hope you have some change. I don't think I've got a cent on me."

Mary nodded, smiling. "Mother came across again," she whispered.

"Money," broke in Steve Mestrovich. "We got to have money or else we're licked."

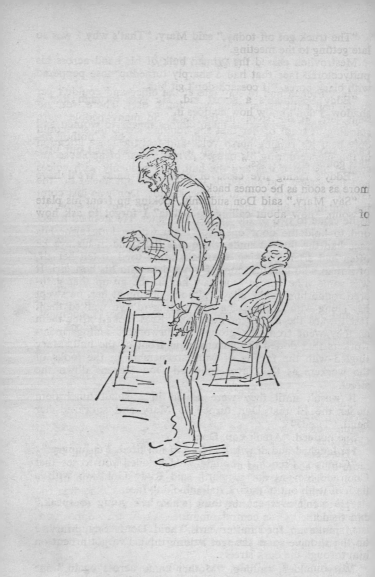

"The truck got off today," said Mary. "That's why I was so late getting to the meeting."

Mestrovitch passed the grimed bulk of his hand across his puttycolored face that had a sharply turnedup nose peppered with black pores. "If cossack don't git him."

"Eddy Spellman's a smart kid. He gets through like a shadow. I don't know how he does it."

"You don't know what them clothes means to women and kids and . . . listen, Miss French, don't hold back nothin' because too raggedy. Ain't nothin' so ragged like what our little kids got on their backs."

"Eddy's taking five cases of condensed milk. We'll have more as soon as he comes back."

"Say, Mary," said Don suddenly, looking up from his plate of soup, "how about calling up Sylvia? I forgot to ask how much we collected at the meeting."

Young Goldfarb got to his feet. "I'll call. You look tired, Comrade French. . . . Anybody got a nickel?"

"Here, I got nickel," said Mestrovich. He threw back his head and laughed. "Damn funny . . . miner with nickel. Down our way miner got nickel put in frame sent Meester Carnegie Museum . . . very rare." He got up roaring laughter and put on his black longvisored miner's cap. "Goodnight, comrade, I walk Brooklyn. Reliefcommittee nine o'clock . . . right, Miss French?"

As he strode out of the lunchroom the heavy tread of his black boots made the sugarbowls jingle on the tables. "Oh, Lord," said Mary, with tears suddenly coming to her eyes, "That was his last nickel."

Goldfarb came back saying that the collection hadn't been so good. Sixtynine dollars and some pledges. "Christmas time coming on . . . you know. Everybody's always broke at Christmas."

"Henderson made a lousy speech," grumbled Don. "He's more of a socialfascist every day."

Mary sat there feeling the tiredness in every bone of her body waiting until Don got ready to go home. She was too sleepy to follow what they were talking about, but every now and then the words centralcommittee, expulsions, oppositionists, splitters, rasped in her ears. Then Don was tapping her on the shoulder and she was waking up and walking beside him through the dark streets.

"It's funny, Don," she was saying, "I always go to sleep when you talk about party discipline. I guess it's because I don't want to hear about it."

"No use being sentimental about it," said Don savagely.

"But is it sentimental to be more interested in saving the

531

miners' unions?" she said, suddenly feeling wide awake again.

"Of course that's what we all believe, but we have to follow the party line. A lot of those boys . . . Goldfarb's one of them . . . Ben Compton's another . . . think this is a debatingsociety. If they're not very careful indeed they'll find themselves out on their ear. . . . You just watch."

Once they'd staggered up the five flights to their dingy little apartment where Mary had always planned to put up curtains but had never had time, Don suddenly caved in with fatigue and threw himself on the couch and fell asleep without taking off his clothes. Mary tried to rouse him, but gave it up. She unlaced his shoes for him and threw a blanket over him and got into bed herself and tried to sleep.

She was staring wide awake, she was counting old pairs of trousers, torn suits of woolly underwear, old armyshirts with the sleeves cut off, socks with holes in them that didn't match. She was seeing the rickety children with puffy bellies showing through their rags, the scrawny women with uncombed hair and hands distorted with work, the boys with their heads battered and bleeding from the clubs of the Coal and Iron Police, the photograph of a miner's body shot through with machinegun bullets. She got up and took two or three swigs from a bottle of gin she kept in the medicine closet in the bathroom. The gin burned her throat. Coughing she went back to bed and went off into a hot dreamlesssleep.

Toward morning Don woke her getting into the bed. He kissed her. "Darling, I've set the alarm for seven. . . . Be sure to get me up. I've got a very important committeemeeting. . . . Be sure and do it." He went off to sleep again right away like a child. She lay beside his bigboned lanky body, listening to his regular breathing, feeling happy and safe there in the bed with him.

Eddy Spellman got through with his truck again and distributed his stuff to several striking locals U.M.W. in the Pittsburgh district, although he had a narrow squeak when the deputies tried to ambush him near Greensburg. They'd have nabbed him if a guy he knew who was a bootlegger hadn't tipped him off. The same bootlegger helped him out when he skidded into a snowdrift on the hill going down into Johnstown on the way back. He was laughing about it as he helped Mary pack up the new shipment.

"He wanted to give me some liquor. . . . He's a good feller, do you know it, Miss Mary? . . . Tough kinder . . . that racket hardens a feller up . . . but a prince when you know him. . . . 'Hell, no, Ed,' his name's Eddy too, I says to him when he tries to slip me a pint, 'I ain't goin' to take a drink until after the revolution and then I'll be ridin' so high I won't need to.'"

Mary laughed. "I guess we all ought to do that, Eddy. . . . But I feel so tired and discouraged at night sometimes."

"Sure," said Eddy, turning serious. "It gits you down thinkin' how they got all the guns an' all the money an' we ain't got nothin'."

"One thing you're going to have, Comrade Spellman, is a pair of warm gloves and a good overcoat before you make the next trip."

His freckled face turned red to the roots of his red hair. "Honest, Miss Mary, I don't git cold. To tell the truth the motor heats up so much in that old pile of junk it keeps me warm in the coldest weather. . . . After the next trip we got to put a new clutch in her and that'll take more jack than we kin spare from the milk. . . . I toll you things are bad up there in the coalfields this winter."

"But those miners have got such wonderful spirit," said Mary.

"The trouble is, Miss Mary, you kin only keep your spirit up a certain length of time on an empty stumick."

That evening Don came by to the office to get Mary for supper. He was very cheerful and his gaunt bony faco had more color in it than usual. "Well, little girl, what would you think of moving up to Pittsburgh? After the plenum I may go out to do some organizing in western Pennsylvania and Ohio. Mestrovich says they need somebody to pep 'em up a little."

Eddy Spellman looked up from the bale of clothes he was tying up. "Take it from me, Comrade Stevens, they sure do."

Mary felt a chill go through her. Don must have noticed the pallor spreading over her face. "We won't take any risks," he added hurriedly. "Those miners take good care of a feller, don't they, Eddy?"

"They sure do. . . . Wherever the locals is strong you'll be safer than you are right here in New York."

"Anyway," said Mary, her throat tight and dry, "if you've got to go, you've got to go."

"You two go out an' eat," said Eddy. "I'll finish up . . . I'm bunkin' here anyway. Saves the price of a flop.. . . You feed Miss Mary up good, Comrade Stevens. We don't want her gettin' sick. . . . If all the real partymembers worked like she does, we'd have . . . hell, we'd have the finest kind of a revolution by the spring of the year."

They went out laughing, and walked down to Bleecker Street and settled happily at a table in an Italian restaurant and ordered up the seventyfivecent dinner and a bottle of wine. "You've got a great admirer in Eddy," Don said, smiling at her across the table.

A couple of weeks later Mary came home one icy winter evening to find Don busy packing his grip. She couldn't help letting out a cry, her nerves were getting harder and harder to control. "Oh, Don, it's not Pittsburgh yet?" Don shook his head and went on packing.

When he had closed up his wicker suitcase, he came over to her and put his arm round her shoulder. "I've got to go across to the other side with . . . you know who . . . essential party business."

"Oh, Don, I'd love to go, too. I've never been to Russia or anywhere."

"I'll only be gone a month. We're sailing at midnight . . . and Mary darling . . . if anybody asks after me I'm in Pittsburgh, see?"

Mary started to cry. "I'll have to say I don't know where you are . . . I know I can't ever get away with a lie."

"Mary dear, it'll just be a few days . . . don't be a little silly."

Mary smiled through her tears. "But I am . . . I'm an awful little silly."

He kissed her and patted her gently on the back. Then he picked up his suitcase and hurried out of the room with a big checked cap pulled down over his eyes.

Mary walked up and down the narrow room with her lips twitching, fighting to keep down the hysterical sobs. To give herself something to do, she began to plan how she could fix up the apartment so that it wouldn't look so dreary when Don came back. She pulled out the couch and pushed it across the window like a windowseat. Then she pulled the table out in front of it and grouped the chairs round the table. She made up her mind she'd paint the woodwork white and get turkeyred for the curtains.

Next morning she was in the middle of drinking her coffee out of a cracked cup without a saucer, feeling bitterly lonely in the empty apartment when the telephone rang. At first she didn't recognize whose voice it was. She was confused and kept stammering, "Who is it, please?" into the receiver.

"But, Mary," the voice was saying in an exasperated tone, "you must know who I am. It's Ben Compton . . . bee ee enn . . . Ben. I've got to see you about something. Where could I meet you? Not at your place."

Mary tried to keep her voice from sounding stiff and chilly. "I've got to be uptown today. I've got to have lunch with a woman who may give some money to the miners. It's a horrible waste of time, but I can't help it. She won't give a cent unless I listen to her sad story. How about meeting me in front of the Public Library at twothirty?"

"Better say inside. . . . It's about zero out today. I just got up out of bed from the flu."

Mary hardly knew Ben, he looked so much older. There was gray in the hair spilling out untidily from under his cap. He stooped and peered into her face querulously through his thick glasses. He didn't shake hands.

"Well, I might as well tell you . . . you'll know it soon enough if you don't know it already . . . I've been expelled from the party . . . oppositionist . . . exceptionalism . . . a lot of nonsense. Well, that doesn't matter. I'm still a revolutionist . . . I'll continue to work outside of the party."

"Oh, Ben, I'm so sorry," was all Mary could find to say. "You know I don't know anything except what I read in the *Daily*. It all seems too terrible to me."

"Let's go out, that guard's watching us."

Outside Ben began to shiver from the cold. His wrists stuck out red from his frayed green overcoat with sleeves much too short for his long arms.

"Oh, where can we go?" Mary kept saying.

Finally they went down into a basement automat and sat talking in low voices over a cup of coffee. "I didn't want to go to your place because I didn't want to meet Stevens. . . . Stevens and me have never been friends, you know that. . . . Now he's in with the comintern crowd. He'll make the centralcommittee when they've cleaned out all the brains."

"But, Ben, people can have differences of opinion and still . . ."

"A party of yesmen . . . that'll be great. . . . But, Mary, I had to see you . . . I feel so lonely suddenly . . . you know, cut off from everything. . . . You know if we hadn't been fools we'd have had that baby that time . . . we'd still love each other. . . . Mary, you were very lovely to me when I first got out of jail. . . . Say, where's your friend Ada, the musician who had that fancy apartment?"

"Oh, she's as silly as ever . . . running around with some fool violinist or other."

"I've always liked music. . . . I ought to have kept you, Mary."

"A lot of water's run under the bridge since then," said Mary coldly.

"Are you happy with Stevens? I haven't any right to ask."

"But, Ben, what's the use of raking all this old stuff up?"

"You see, often a young guy thinks, I'll sacrifice everything, and then, when he has cut off all that side of his life, he's not as good as he was, do you see? For the first time in

535

my life I have no contact. I thought maybe you could get me in on reliefwork somehow. The discipline isn't so strict in the relief organizations."

"I don't think they want any disrupting influences in the I.L.D.," said Mary.

"So I'm a disrupter to you too. . . . All right, in the end the workingclass will judge between us."

"Let's not talk about it, Ben."

"I'd like you to put it up to Stevens and ask him to sound out the proper quarters . . . that's not much to ask, is it?"

"But Don's not here at present." Before she could catch herself she'd blurted it out.

Ben looked her in the eye with a sudden sharp look.

"He hasn't by any chance sailed for Moscow with certain other comrades?"

"He's gone to Pittsburgh on secret partywork and, for God's sake, shut up about it. You just got hold of me to pump me." She got to her feet, her face flaming. "Well, goodbye, Mr. Compton. . . . You don't happen to be a stoolpigeon as well as a disrupter, do you?"

Ben Compton's face broke in pieces suddenly the way a child's face does when it is just going to bawl. He sat there staring at her, senselessly scraping the spoon round and round in the empty coffeemug. She was halfway up the stairs when on an impulse she went back and stood for a second looking down at his bowed head. "Ben," she said in a gentler voice, "I shouldn't have said that . . . without proof. . . . I don't believe it." Ben Compton didn't look up. She went up the stairs again out into the stinging wind and hurried down Fortysecond Street in the afternoon crowd and took the subway down to Union Square.

The last day of the year Mary French got a telegram at the office from Ada Cohn.

> PLEASE PLEASE COMMUNICATE YOUR MOTHER IN
> TOWN AT PLAZA SAILING SOON WANTS TO SEE YOU
> DOESN'T KNOW ADDRESS WHAT SHALL I TELL HER.

Newyear'sday there wasn't much doing at the office. Mary was the only one who had turned up, so in the middle of the morning she called up the Plaza and asked for Mrs. French. No such party staying there. Next she called up Ada. Ada talked and talked about how Mary's mother had married again, a Judge Blake, a very prominent man, a retired federal circuit judge, such an attractive man with a white Vandyke beard, and Ada had to see Mary and Mrs. Blake had been so sweet to her and Ada asked her to dinner at the Plaza and wanted to know all about Mary and that she'd had to admit that she never saw her, although she was her best friend and she'd been to a Newyear'seve party and had such a headache she couldn't practice and she'd invited some lovely people in that afternoon and wouldn't Mary come, she'd be sure to like them.

Mary almost hung up on her, Ada sounded so silly, but she said she'd call her back right away after she'd talked to her mother. It ended by her going home and getting her best dress on and going uptown to the Plaza to see Judge and Mrs. Blake. She tried to find some place she could get her hair curled, because she knew the first thing her mother would say was that she looked a fright, but everything was closed on account of its being Newyear'sday.

Judge and Mrs. Blake were getting ready to have lunch in a big private drawingroom on the corner looking out over the humped snowy hills of the park bristly with bare branches and interwoven with fastmoving shining streams of traffic. Mary's mother didn't look as if she'd aged a day; she was dressed in darkgreen and really looked stunning with a little white ruffle round her neck sitting there so at her ease, with rings on her fingers that sparkled in the gray winter light that came in through the big windows. The judge had a soft caressing voice. He talked elaborately about the prodigal daughter and the fatted calf until her mother broke in to say that they were going to Europe on a spree; they'd both of them made big killings on the stockexchange on the same day and they felt they owed themselves a little rest and relaxation. And she went on about how worried she'd been because all her letters had been returned from Mary's last address, and that she'd written Ada again and again and Ada had always said Mary was in Pittsburgh or Fall River or some horrible place doing social work and that she felt it was about time she gave up doing everything for the poor and unfortunate and devoted a little attention to her own kith and kin.

"I hear you are a very dreadful young lady, Mary, my dear," said the judge, blandly, ladling some creamofcelery soup into her plate. "I hope you didn't bring any bombs with you." They both seemed to think that that was a splendid joke and laughed and laughed. "But to be serious," went on the judge, "I know that social inequality is a very dreadful thing and a blot on the fair name of American democracy. But as we get older, my dear, we learn to live and let live, that we have to take the bad with the good a little."

"Mary dear, why don't you go abroad with Ada Cohn and have a nice rest? . . . I'll find the money for the trip. I know it'll do you good. . . . You know I've never approved of

537

your friendship with Ada Cohn. Out home we are probably a little oldfashioned about those things. Here she seems to be accepted everywhere. In fact, she seems to know all the prominent musical people. Of course how good a musician she is herself I'm not in a position to judge."

"Hilda, dear," said the judge, "Ada Cohn has a heart of gold. I find her a very sweet girl. Her father was a very distinguished lawyer. You know we decided we'd lay aside our prejudices a little . . . didn't we, dear?"

"The judge is reforming me," laughed Mary's mother coyly.

Mary was so nervous she felt she was going to scream. The heavy buttery food, the suave attentions of the waiter and the fatherly genialty of the judge made her almost gag.

"Look, Mother," she said, "if you really have a little money to spare, you might let me have something for our milkfund. After all, miners' children aren't guilty of anything."

"My dear, I've already made substantial contributions to the Red Cross. . . . After all, we've had a miners' strike out in Colorado on our hands much worse than in Pennsylvania. . . . I've always felt, Mary dear, that if you were interested in labor conditions the place for you was home in Colorado Springs. If you must study that sort of thing there was never any need to come East for it."

"Even the I.W.W. has reared its ugly head again," said the judge.

"I don't happen to approve of the tactics of the I.W.W." said Mary stiffly.

"I should hope not," said her mother.

"But, Mother, don't you think you could let me have a couple of hundred dollars?"

"To spend on these dreadful agitators; they may not be I Won't Works, but they're just as bad."

"I'll promise that every cent goes into milk for the babies."

"But that's just handing the miners over to these miserable Russian agitators. Naturally, if they can give milk to the children it makes them popular, puts them in a position where they can mislead these poor miserable foreigners worse than ever."

The judge leaned forward across the table and put his blueveined hand in its white starched cuff on Mary's mother's hand. "It's not that we lack sympathy with the plight of the miners' women and children, or that we don't understand the dreadful conditions of the whole mining industry . . . we know altogether too much about that, don't we, Hilda? But . . ."

Mary suddenly found that she'd folded her napkin and gotten trembling to her feet. "I don't see any reason for further prolonging this interview, that must be painful to you, Mother, as it is to me . . ."

"Perhaps I can arbitrate," said the judge, smiling, getting to his feet with his napkin in his hand.

Mary felt a desperate tight feeling like a metal ring round her head. "I've got to go, Mother . . . I don't feel very well today. Have a nice trip. . . . I don't want to argue." Before they could stop her, she was off down the hall and on her way down in the elevator.

Mary felt so upset she had to talk to somebody, so she went to a telephone booth and called up Ada. Ada's voice was full of sobs, she said something dreadful had happened and that she'd called off her party and that Mary must come up to see her immediately. Even before Ada opened the door of the apartment on Madison Avenue, Mary got a whiff of the Forêt Vierge perfume Ada had taken to using when she first came to New York. Ada opened the door wearing a green and pink flowered silk wrapper with all sorts of little tassels hanging from it. She fell on Mary's neck. Her eyes were red and she sniffed as she talked.

"Why, what's the matter, Ada?" asked Mary coolly.

"Darling, I've just had the most dreadful row with Hjalmar. We have parted forever. . . . Of course I had to call off the party because I was giving it for him."

"Who's Hjalmar?"

"He's somebody very beautiful . . . and very hateful. . . . But let's talk about you, Mary darling . . . I do hope you've made it up with your mother and Judge Blake."

"I just walked out. . . . What's the use of arguing? They're on one side of the barricades and I'm on the other."

Ada strode up and down the room. "Oh, I hate talk like that. . . . It makes me feel awful. . . . At least you'll have a drink. . . . I've got to drink, I've been too nervous to practice all day"

Mary stayed all afternoon at Ada's drinking ginrickeys and eating the sandwiches and little cakes that had been laid out in the kitchenette for the party and talking about old times and Ada's unhappy loveaffair. Ada made Mary read all his letters and Mary said he was a damn fool and good riddance. Then Ada cried and Mary told her she ought to be ashamed of herself, she didn't know what real misery was. Ada was very meek about it and went to her desk and wrote out a check in a shaky hand for a hundred dollars for the miners' milkfund. Ada had some supper sent up for them from the uptown Longchamps and declared she'd spent the happiest afternoon in years. She made Mary promise to come to her concert in the small hall at the Aeolian the following week. When Mary was going, Ada made her take a couple of dollars for a taxi. They were both reeling a little in the hall waiting for the elevator. "We've just gotten to be a pair of old topers," said Ada gaily. It was a good thing Mary had decided to take a taxi because she found it hard to stand on her feet.

That winter the situation of the miners in the Pittsburgh district got worse and worse. Evictions began. Families with little children were living in tents and in brokendown unheated tarpaper barracks. Mary lived in a feeling of nightmare, writing letters, mimeographing appeals, making speeches at meetings of clothing and fur workers, canvassing wealthy liberals. The money that came in was never enough. She took no salary for her work, so she had to get Ada to lend her money to pay her rent. She was thin and haggard and coughed all the time. Too many cigarettes, she'd explain. Eddy Spellman and Rudy Goldfarb worried about her. She could see they'd decided she wasn't eating enough because she was all the time finding on the corner of her desk a paper bag of sandwiches or a carton of coffee that one of them had brought in. Once Eddy brought her a big package of smearcase that his mother had made up home near Scranton. She couldn't eat it; she felt guilty every time she saw it sprouting green mold in the icebox that had no ice in it because she'd given up cooking, now that Don was away.

One evening Rudy came into the office with smiles all over his face. Eddy was leaning over packing the old clothes into bales as usual for his next trip. Rudy gave him a light kick in the seat of the pants.

"Hey you Trotskyite," said Eddy, jumping at him and pulling out his necktie.

"Smile when you say that," said Rudy, pummeling him.

They were all laughing. Mary felt like an oldmaid schoolteacher watching the boys roughhousing in front of her desk. "Meeting comes to order," she said.

"They tried to hang it on me, but they couldn't," said Rudy, panting, straightening his necktie and his mussed hair. "But what I was going to say, Comrade French, was that I thought you might like to know that a certain comrade is getting in on the *Aquitania* tomorrow . . . tourist class."

"Rudy, are you sure?"

"Saw the cable."

Mary got to the dock too early and had to wait two hours. She tried to read the afternoon papers, but her eyes wouldn't follow the print. It was too hot in the receptionroom and too cold outside. She fidgeted around miserably until at last she saw the enormous black sheetiron wall sliding with its rows of lighted portholes past the openings in the wharfbuilding. Her hands and feet were icy. Her whole body ached to feel his arms around her, for the rasp of his deep voice in her ears. All the time a vague worry flitted in the back of her head, because she hadn't had a letter from him while he'd been away.

Suddenly there he was coming down the gangplank alone, with the old wicker suitcase in his hand. He had on a new belted German raincoat, but the same checked cap. She was face to face with him. He gave her a little hug but he didn't kiss her. There was something odd in his voice.

"Hello, Mary . . . I didn't expect to find you here. . . . I don't want to be noticed, you know." His voice had a low furtive sound in her ears. He was nervously changing his suitcase from one hand to the other. "See you in a few days. . . . I'm going to be pretty busy."

She turned without a word and ran down the wharf. She hurried breathless along the crosstown street to the Ninth Avenue El. When she opened her door, the new turkeyred curtains were like a blow from a whip in her face.

She couldn't go back to the office. She couldn't bear the thought of facing the boys and the people she knew, the people who had known them together. She called up and said she had a bad case of grippe and would have to stay in bed a couple of days. She stayed all day in the blank misery of the narrow rooms. Toward evening she dozed off to sleep on the couch. She woke up with a start thinking she heard a step in the hall outside. It wasn't Don, the steps went on up the next flight. After that she didn't sleep any more.

The next morning the phone woke her just when she settled herself in bed to drowse a little. It was Sylvia Goldstein saying she was sorry Mary had the grippe and asking if there was anything she could do. Oh, no, she was fine, she was just going to stay in bed all day, Mary answered in a dead voice.

"Well, I suppose you knew all the time about Comrade Stevens and Comrade Lichfield . . . you two were always so close . . . they were married in Moscow . . . she's an English comrade . . . she spoke at the big meeting at the Bronx Casino last night . . . she's got a great shock of red hair . . . stunning, but some of the girls think it's dyed. Lots of comrades didn't know you and Comrade Stevens had broken up . . . isn't it sad things like that have to happen in the movement?"

"Oh, that was a long time ago. . . . Goodbye, Sylvia," said Mary harshly, and hung up. She called up a bootlegger she knew and told him to send her up a bottle of gin.

The next afternoon there was a light rap on the door and when Mary opened it a crack there was Ada wreathed in silver fox and breathing out a great gust of Forêt Vierge. "Oh, Mary darling, I knew something was the matter. . . . You know sometimes I'm quite psychic. And when you didn't come to my concert, first I was mad, but then I said to myself I know the poor darling's sick. So I just went right down to your office. There was the handsomest boy there and I just made him tell me where you lived. He said you were sick with the grippe and so I came right over. My dear, why aren't you in bed? You look a sight."

"I'm all right," mumbled Mary numbly, pushing the stringy hair off her face. "I been . . . making plans . . . about how we can handle this relief situation better."

"Well, you're just coming up right away to my spare bedroom and let me pet you up a little. . . . I don't believe it's grippe, I think it's overwork. . . . If you're not careful you'll be having a nervous breakdown."

"Maybe sumpen like that." Mary couldn't articulate her words. She didn't seem to have any will of her own any more; she did everything Ada told her. When she was settled in Ada's clean lavendersmelling spare bed, they sent out for some barbital and it put her to sleep. Mary stayed there several days eating the meals Ada's maid brought her, drinking all the drinks Ada would give her, listening to the continual scrape of violin practice that came from the other room all morning. But at night she couldn't sleep without filling herself up with dope. She didn't seem to have any will left. It would take her half an hour to decide to get up to go to the toilet.

After she'd been at Ada's a week, she began to feel she

ought to go home. She began to be impatient of Ada's sly references to unhappy loveaffairs and broken hearts and the beauty of abnegation and would snap Ada's head off whenever she started it.

"That's fine," Ada would say. "You are getting your meanness back."

For some time Ada had been bringing up the subject of somebody she knew who'd been crazy about Mary for years and who was dying to see her again. Finally Mary gave in and said she would go to a cocktail party at Eveline Johnson's where Ada said she knew he'd be. "And Eveline gives the most wonderful parties. I don't know how she does it because she never has any money, but all the most interesting people in New York will be there. They always are. Radicals too, you know. Eveline can't live without her little group of reds."

Mary wore one of Ada's dresses that didn't fit her very well and went out in the morning to have her hair curled at Sak's where Ada always had hers curled. They had some cocktails at Ada's place before they went. At the last minute Mary said she wouldn't go because she'd finally got it out of

544

Ada that it was George Barrow who was going to be at the party. Ada made Mary drink another cocktail and a reckless feeling came over her and she said all right, let's get a move on.

There was a smiling colored maid in a fancy lace cap and apron at the door of the house who took them down the hall to a bedroom full of coats and furs where they were to take off their wraps.

As Ada was doing her face at the dressingtable, Mary whispered in her ear, "Just think what our reliefcommittee could do with the money that woman wastes on senseless entertaining."

"But she's a darling," Ada whispered back excitedly. "Honestly, you'll like her."

The door had opened behind their backs letting in a racketing gust of voices, laughs, tinkle of glasses, a whiff of perfume and toast and cigarettesmoke and gin.

"Oh, Ada," came a ringing voice.

"Eveline darling, how lovely you look! . . . This is Mary French, you know I said I'd bring her. . . . She's my oldest friend." Mary found herself shaking hands with a tall slender woman in a pearlgray dress. Her face was very white and her lips were very red and her long large eyes were exaggerated with mascara.

"So nice of you to come," Eveline Johnson said and sat down suddenly among the furs and wraps on the bed.

"It sounds like a lovely party," cried Ada.

"I hate parties. I don't know why I give them," said Eveline Johnson. "Well, I guess I've got to go back to the menagerie. . . . Oh, Ada, I'm so tired."

Mary found herself studying the harsh desperate lines under the makeup round Mrs. Johnson's mouth and the strained tenseness of the cords of her neck. Their silly life tells on them, she was saying to herself.

"What about the play?" Ada was asking. "I was so excited when I heard about it."

"Oh, that's ancient history now," said Eveline Johnson sharply. "I'm working on a plan to bring over the ballet . . . turn it into something American. . . . I'll tell you about it sometime."

"Oh, Eveline, did the screenstar come?" asked Ada, giggling.

"Oh, yes, they always come." Eveline Johnson sighed. "She's beautiful. . . . You must see her."

"Of course, anybody in the world would come to your parties, Eveline."

"I don't know why they should . . . they seem just too boring to me."

Eveline Johnson was ushering them through some sliding doors into a highceilinged room dusky from shaded lights and cigarettesmoke where they were swallowed up in a jam of welldressed people talking and making faces and tossing their heads over cocktail glasses. There seemed no place to stand, so Mary sat down at the end of a couch beside a little marbletopped table. The other people on the couch were jabbering away among themselves and paid no attention to her. Ada and the hostess had disappeared behind a wall of men's suits and afternoongowns.

Mary had had time to smoke an entire cigarette before Ada came back followed by George Barrow, whose thin face looked flushed and whose adam'sapple stuck out further than ever over his collar. He had a cocktail in each hand.

"Well well well, little Mary French, after all these years," he was saying with a kind of forced jollity. "If you knew the trouble we'd had getting these through the crush."

"Hello, George," said Mary casually. She took the cocktail he handed her and drank it off. After the other drinks she'd had, it made her head spin. Somehow George and Ada managed to squeeze themselves in on the couch on either side of Mary.

"I want to hear all about the coalstrike," George was saying, knitting his brows. "Too bad the insurgent locals had to choose a moment when a strike played right into the operators' hands."

Mary got angry. "That's just the sort of remark I'd expect from a man of your sort. If we waited for a favorable moment there wouldn't be any strikes. . . . There never is any favorable moment for the workers."

"What sort of a man is a man of my sort?" said George Barrow with fake humility, so Mary thought. "That's what I often ask myself."

"Oh, I don't want to argue . . . I'm sick and tired of arguing. . . . Get me another cocktail, George."

He got up obediently and started threading his way across the room. "Now, Mary, don't row with poor George. . . . He's so sweet. . . . Do you know, Margo Dowling really is here . . . and her husband and Rodney Cathcart . . . they're always together. They're on their way to the Riviera," Ada talked into her ear in a loud stage whisper.

"I'm sick of seeing movie actors on the screen," said Mary, "I don't want to see them in real life."

Ada had slipped away. George was back with two more

546

cocktails and a plate of cold salmon and cucumbers. She wouldn't eat anything.

"Don't you think you'd better, with all the drinks?" She shook her head. "Well, I'll eat it myself. . . . You know, Mary," he went on, "I often wonder these days if I wouldn't have been a happier man if I'd just stayed all my life an expressagent in South Chicago and married some nice workinggirl and had a flock of kids. . . . I'd be a wealthier and a happier man today if I'd gone into business even."

"Well, you don't look so badly off," said Mary.

"You know it hurts me to be attacked as a laborfaker by you reds. . . . I may believe in compromise, but I've gained some very substantial dollarsandcents victories. . . . What you communists won't see is that there are sometimes two sides to a case."

"I'm not a partymember," said Mary.

"I know . . . but you work with them. . . . Why should you think you know better what's good for the miners than their own tried and true leaders?"

"If the miners ever had a chance to vote in their unions you'd find out how much they trust your sellout crowd."

George Barrow shook his head. "Mary, Mary . . . just the same headstrong warmhearted girl."

"Rubbish, I haven't any feelings at all any more. I've seen how it works in the field. . . . It doesn't take a good heart to know which end of a riotgun's pointed at you."

"Mary, I'm a very unhappy man."

"Get me another cocktail, George."

547

Mary had time to smoke two cigarettes before George came back. The nodding jabbering faces, the dresses, the gestures with hands floated in a smoky haze before her eyes.

The crowd was beginning to thin a little when George came back all flushed and smiling. "Well, I had the pleasure of exchanging a few words with Miss Dowling, she was most charming. . . . But do you know what Red Haines tells me? I wonder if it's true. . . . It seems she's through; it seems that she's no good for talkingpictures . . . voice sounds like the croaking of an old crow over the loudspeaker," he giggled a little drunkenly. "There she is now, she's just leaving."

A hush had fallen over the room. Through the dizzy swirl of cigarettesmoke Mary saw a small woman with blue eyelids and features regular as those of a porcelain doll under a mass of paleblond hair turn for a second to smile at somebody before she went out through the sliding doors. She had on a

yellow dress and a lot of big sapphires. A tall bronzefaced actor and a bowlegged sallowfaced little man followed her out, and Eveline Johnson talking and talking in her breathless hectic way swept after them.

Mary was looking at it all through a humming haze like seeing a play from way up in a smoky balcony.

Ada came and stood in front of her rolling her eyes and opening her mouth wide when she talked. "Oh, isn't it a wonderful party. . . . I met her. She had the loveliest manners . . . I don't know why, I expected her to be kinda tough. They say she came from the gutter."

"Not at all," said George. "Her people were Spaniards of noble birth who lived in Cuba."

"Ada, I want to go home," said Mary.

"Just a minute . . . I haven't had a chance to talk to dear Eveline. . . . She looks awfully tired and nervous today, poor dear."

A lilypale young man brushed past them laughing over his shoulder at an older woman covered with silver lamé who followed him, her scrawny neck, wattled under the powder, thrust out and her hooknose quivering and eyes bulging over illconcealed pouches.

"Ada, I want to go home."

"I thought you and I and George might have dinner together."

Mary was seeing blurred faces getting big as they came towards her; changing shape as they went past, fading into the gloom like fish opening and closing their mouths in an aquarium.

"How about it? Miss Cohn, have you seen Charles Edward Holden around? He's usually quite a feature of Eveline's parties." Mary hated George Barrow's doggy popeyed look when he talked. "Now there's a sound intelligent fellow for you. I can talk to him all night."

Ada narrowed her eyes as she leaned over and whispered shrilly in George Barrow's ear. "He's engaged to be married to somebody else. Eveline's cut up about it. She's just living on her nerve."

"George, if we've got to stay . . ." Mary said, "get me another cocktail."

A broadfaced woman in spangles with very red cheeks who was sitting on the couch beside Mary leaned across and said in a stage whisper, "Isn't it dreadful? . . . You know I think it's most ungrateful of Holdy after all Eveline's done for him . . . in a social way . . . since she took him up . . . now he's accepted everywhere. I know the girl . . . a little bitch if there ever was one . . . not even wealthy."

"Shush," said Ada. "Here's Eveline now. . . . Well, Eveline dear, the captains and the kings depart. Soon there'll be nothing but us smallfry left."

"She didn't seem awful bright to me," said Eveline, dropping into a chair beside them.

"Let me get you a drink, Eveline, dear," said Ada. Eveline shook her head.

"What you need, Eveline, my dear," said the broadfaced woman, leaning across the couch again, ". . . is a good trip abroad. New York's impossible after January . . . I shan't attempt to stay. . . . It would just mean a nervous breakdown if I did."

"I thought maybe I might go to Morocco sometime if I could scrape up the cash," said Eveline.

"Try Tunis, my dear. Tunis is divine."

After she'd drunk the cocktail Barrow brought, Mary sat there seeing faces, hearing voices in a blank hateful haze. It took all her attention not to teeter on the edge of the couch. "I really must go." She had hold of George's arm crossing the room. She could walk very well, but she couldn't talk very well. In the bedroom Ada was helping her on with her coat.

Eveline Johnson was there with her big hazel eyes and her teasing singsong voice. "Oh, Ada, it was sweet of you to come, I'm afraid it was just too boring. . . . Oh, Miss French, I so wanted to talk to you about the miners . . . I never get a chance to talk about things I'm really interested in any more. Do you know, Ada, I don't think I'll ever do this again. . . . It's just too boring." She put her long hand to her temple and rubbed the fingers slowly across her forehead. "Oh, Ada, I hope they go home soon. . . . I've got such a headache."

"Oughtn't you to take something for it?"

"I will. I've got a wonderful painkiller. Ask me up next time you play Bach, Ada . . . I'd like that. You know it does seem too silly to spend your life filling up rooms with illassorted people who really hate each other." Eveline Johnson followed them all the way down the hall to the front door as if she didn't want to let them go. She stood in her thin dress in the gust of cold wind that came from the open door while George went to the corner to get a cab.

"Eveline, go back in, you'll catch your death," said Ada.

"Well, goodbye . . . you were darlings to come." As the door closed slowly behind her, Mary watched Eveline Johnson's narrow shoulders. She was shivering as she walked back down the hall.

Mary reeled, suddenly feeling drunk in the cold air and

550

Ada put her arm round her to steady her. "Oh, Mary," Ada said in her ear, "I wish everybody wasn't so unhappy."

"It's the waste," Mary cried out savagely, suddenly able to articulate. Ada and George Barrow were helping her into the cab. "The food they waste and the money they waste while our people starve in tarpaper barracks."

"The contradictions of capitalism," said George Barrow with a knowing leer. "How about a bite to eat?"

"Take me home first. No, not to Ada's," Mary almost yelled. "I'm sick of this parasite life. I'm going back to the office tomorrow. . . . I've got to call up tonight to see if they got in all right with that load of condensed milk. . . ." She picked up Ada's hand, suddenly feeling like old times again, and squeezed it. "Ada, you've been sweet, honestly you've saved my life."

"Ada's the perfect cure for hysterical people like us," said George Barrow. The taxi had stopped beside the row of garbagecans in front of the house where Mary lived.

"No, I can walk up alone," she said harshly and angrily again. "It's just that being tiredout a drink makes me feel funny. Goodnight. I'll get my bag at your place tomorrow."

Ada and Barrow went off in the taxicab with their heads together chatting and laughing. They've forgotten me already, thought Mary as she made her way up the stairs. She made the stairs all right, but had some trouble getting the key in the lock. When the door finally would open, she went straight to the couch in the front room and lay down and fell heavily asleep.

In the morning she felt more rested than she had in years. She got up early and ate a big breakfast with bacon and eggs at Childs on the way to the office. Rudy Goldfarb was already there, sitting at her desk.

He got up and stared at her without speaking for a moment. His eyes were red and bloodshot and his usually sleek black hair was all over his forehead. "What's the matter, Rudy?"

"Comrade French, they got Eddy."

"You mean they arrested him."

"Arrested him, nothing, they shot him."

"They killed him." Mary felt a wave of nausea rising in her. The room started to spin around. She clenched her fists and the room fell into place again. Rudy was telling her how some miners had found the truck wrecked in a ditch. At first they thought that it had been an accident, but when they picked up Eddy Spellman he had a bullethole through his temple.

"We've got to have a protest meeting . . . do they know about it over at the Party?"

"Sure, they're trying to get Madison Square Garden. But, Comrade French, he was one hell of a swell kid." Mary was shaking all over. The phone rang. Rudy answered it. "Comrade French, they want you over there right away. They want you to be secretary of the committee for the protest meeting."

Mary let herself drop into the chair at her desk for a moment and began noting down the names of organizations to be notified. Suddenly she looked up and looked Rudy straight in the eye. "Do you know what we've got to do . . . we've got to move the reliefcommittee to Pittsburgh. I knew all along we ought to have been in Pittsburgh."

"Risky business."

"We ought to have been in Pittsburgh all along," Mary said firmly and quietly.

The phone rang again.

"It's somebody for you, Comrade French."

As soon as the receiver touched Mary's ear, there was Ada talking and talking. At first Mary couldn't make out what it was about. "But, Mary darling, haven't you read the papers?"

"No, I said, I hadn't. You mean about Eddy Spellman?"

"No, darling, it's too awful; you remember we were just there yesterday for a cocktail party . . . you must remember Eveline Johnson, it's so awful. I've sent out and got all the papers. Of course the tabloids all say it's suicide."

"Ada, I don't understand."

"But, Mary, I'm trying to tell you . . . I'm so upset I can't talk . . . she was such a lovely woman, so talented, an artist really . . . Well, when the maid got there this morning she found her dead in her bed and we were just there twelve hours before. It gives me the horrors. Some of the papers say it was an overdose of a sleeping medicine. She couldn't have meant to do it. If we'd only known, we might have been able to do something, you know she said she had a headache. Don't you think you could come up, I can't stay here alone I feel so terrible."

"Ada, I can't. . . . Something very serious has happened in Pennsylvania. I have a great deal of work to do organizing a protest. Goodbye, Ada." Mary hung up, frowning.

"Say, Rudy, if Ada Cohn calls up again, tell her I'm out of the office. . . . I have too much to do to spend my time taking care of hysterical women a day like this." She put on her hat, collected her papers, and hurried over to the meeting of the committee.

Vag

The young man waits at the edge of the concrete, with one hand he grips a rubbed suitcase of phony leather, the other hand almost making a fist, thumb up

that moves in ever so slight an arc when a car slithers past, a truck roars, clatters; the wind of cars passing ruffles his hair, slaps grit in his face.

Head swims, hunger has twisted the belly tight,

he has skinned a heel through the torn sock, feet ache in the broken shoes, under the threadbare suit carefully brushed off with the hand, the torn drawers have a crummy feel, the feel of having slept in your clothes; in the nostrils lingers the

staleness of discouraged carcasses crowded into a transient camp, the carbolic stench of the jail, on the taut cheeks the shamed flush from the boring eyes of cops and deputies, rail-roadbulls (they eat three squares a day, they are buttoned into wellmade clothes, they have wives to sleep with, kids to play with after supper, they work for the big men who buy their way, they stick their chests out with the sureness of power behind their backs). Git the hell out, scram! Know what's good for you, you'll make yourself scarce. Gittin' tough, eh? Think you kin take it, eh?

The punch in the jaw, the slam on the head with the night-stick, the wrist grabbed and twisted behind the back, the big knee brought up sharp into the crotch,

the walk out of town with sore feet to stand and wait at the edge of the hissing speeding string of cars where the reek of ether and lead and gas melts into the silent grassy smell of the earth.

Eyes black with want seek out the eyes of the drivers, a hitch, a hundred miles down the road.

Overhead in the blue a plane drones. Eyes follow the silver

Douglas that flashes once in the sun and bores its smooth way out of sight into the blue.

(The transcontinental passengers sit pretty, big men with bankaccounts, highly paid jobs, who are saluted by doormen; telephonegirls say goodmorning to them. Last night after a fine dinner, drinks with friends, they left Newark. Roar of climbing motors slanting up into the inky haze. Lights drop away. An hour staring along a silvery wing at a big lonesome moon hurrying west through curdling scum. Beacons flash in a line across Ohio.

At Cleveland the plane drops banking in a smooth spiral, the string of lights along the lake swings in a circle. Climbing roar of the motors again; slumped in the soft seat drowsing through the flat moonlight night.

Chi. A glimpse of the dipper. Another spiral swoop from cool into hot air thick with dust and the reek of burnt prairies.

Beyond the Mississippi dawn creeps up behind through the murk over the great plains. Puddles of mist go white in the Iowa hills, farms, fences, silos, steel glint from a river. The blinking eyes of the beacons reddening into day. Watercourses vein the eroded hills.

Omaha. Great cumulus clouds, from coppery churning to creamy to silvery white, trail brown skirts of rain over the hot plains. Red and yellow badlands, tiny horned shapes of cattle.

Cheyenne. The cool high air smells of sweetgrass.

The tightbaled clouds to westward burst and scatter in tatters over the strawcolored hills. Indigo mountains jut rimrock. The plane breasts a huge crumbling cloudbank and toboggans over bumpy air across green and crimson slopes into the sunny dazzle of Salt Lake.

The transcontinental passenger thinks contracts, profits, vacationtrips, mighty continent between Atlantic and Pacific, power, wires humming dollars, cities jammed, hills empty, the indiantrail leading into the wagonroad, the macadamed pike, the concrete skyway; trains, planes: history the billiondollar speedup,

and in the bumpy air over the desert ranges towards Las Vegas

sickens and vomits into the carton container the steak and mushrooms he ate in New York. No matter, silver in the pocket, greenbacks in the wallet, drafts, certified checks, plenty restaurants in L. A.)

The young man waits on the side of the road; the plane has gone; thumb moves in a small arc when a car tears hissing past. Eyes seek the driver's eyes. A hundred miles down the road. Head swims, belly tightens, wants crawl over his skin like ants:

went to school, books said opportunity, ads promised speed, own your home, shine bigger than your neighbor, the radiocrooner whispered girls, ghosts of platinum girls coaxed from the screen, millions in winnings were chalked up on the boards in the offices, paychecks were for hands willing to work, the cleared desk of an executive with three telephones on it;

waits with swimming head, needs knot the belly, idle hands numb, beside the speeding traffic.

A hundred miles down the road.

SELECTED BIBLIOGRAPHY

by John Dos Passos

One Man's Initiation—1917, 1920
Three Soldiers, 1921
Streets of Night, 1923
Manhattan Transfer, 1925
The 42nd Parallel, 1930
  (Signet Classic 0451-524578)
1919, 1932 (Signet Classic 0451-522486)
The Big Money, 1932
  (Signet Classic 0451-524012)
The Grand Design, 1949
Midcentury, 1961
Occasions and Protests, 1946
The Best Times, 1967
The Fourteenth Chronicle: Letters and Diaries of John Dos Passos, 1973

Selected Biography and Criticism

Belkind, Allen, ed. *Dos Passos, the Critics, and the Writer's Intention.* Pref. Harry T. Moore. Introd. Allen Belkind, Carbondale and Edwardsville: Southern Illinois Univ. Press, 1971.

Cowley, Malcolm. "Dos Passos: The Learned Poggius." *The Southern Review,* 9, No. 1 (1973), pp. 3–17. *In A Second Flowering: Works and Days of the Lost Generation.* New York: Viking Press, 1973, pp. 74–89.

———. "John Dos Passos: Poet Against the World." In *After the Genteel Tradition.* New York: W. W. Norton and Co., Inc., 1937, pp. 134–46.

Diggins, John P. "Visions of Chaos and Visions of Order: Dos Passos as Historian." *American Literature,* 46 (1974), pp. 329–46.

Geismar, Maxwell. *Writers in Crisis.* Boston: Houghton Mifflin Co., 1942.

Gurko, Leo. "John Dos Passos' 'U.S.A.': A 1930's Spectacular." In *Proletarian Writers of the Thirties.* Ed. David Madden. Carbondale and Edwardsville: Southern Illinois Univ. Press, 1968, pp. 46–63.

Hoffman, Frederick. *The Twenties.* New York: The Free Press, 1965.

Hook, Andrew, ed. *Dos Passos: A Collection of Critical Essays.* Englewood Cliffs, N.J.: Prentice-Hall, Inc., 1974.

Kazin, Alfred. *On Native Grounds.* New York: Harcourt, Brace and World, Inc., 1942.

Leavis, F. R. "A Serious Artist." *Scrutiny,* 1 (1932), pp. 173–79. Rpt. in *Don Passos: A Collection of Critical Essays,* pp. 70–75.

McLuhan, Herbert Marshall. "John Dos Passos: Technique Vs. Sensibility." In *Fifty Years of the American Novel: A Christian Appraisal*. Ed. Harold Charles Gardiner. New York: Charles Scribner's Sons, 1951, pp. 151–64. Rpt. in *Dos Passos, the Critics, and the Writer's Intention*, pp. 227–241.

Millgate, Michael. "John Dos Passos." In *American Social Fiction: James to Cozzens*. New York: Barnes and Noble, 1964, pp. 128–41.

Morse, Jonathan. "Dos Passos' *U.S.A.* and the Illusion of Memory." *Modern Fiction Studies*, 23 (1977-78), pp. 543–55.

Sanders, David. "John Dos Passos: An Interview." In *Writers at Work: The Paris Review Interviews: Fourth Series*. Ed. George Plimpton. Introd. Wilfrid Sheed. New York: Viking Press, 1976, pp. 67–89.

Sartre, Jean-Paul. "John Dos Passos and *1919*." In *Literary and Philosophical Essays*. Trans. Annette Michelson. New York: Philosophical Library, 1957, pp. 86–96. Rpt. in *Dos Passos, the Critics, and the Writer's Intention*, pp. 70–80.

Trilling, Lionel. "The America of John Dos Passos." *Partisan Review*, 4 (1938), pp. 26–32. Rpt. in *Dos Passos, the Critics, and the Writer's Intention*, pp. 35–43.

Walcutt, C. C. *The Divided Stream*. Minneapolis: Univ. of Minnesota Press, 1956.

Whipple, T. K. *Study Out the Land*. Berkeley: Univ. of California Press, 1943.

SIGNET CLASSICS for Your Library

☐ **EVELINA by Fanny Burney.** Introduction by Katherine M. Rogers.
(525604—$6.95)

☐ **EMMA by Jane Austen.** Afterword by Graham Hough.   (523067—$3.50)

☐ **MANSFIELD PARK by Jane Austen.** Afterword by Marvin Mudrick.
(525019—$4.95)

☒ **PERSUASION by Jane Austen.** Afterword by Marvin Murdick. (522893—$3.95)

☒ **SENSE AND SENSIBILITY by Jane Austen.** Afterword by Caroline G. Mercer
(524195—$3.50)

☐ **JANE EYRE by Charlotte Brontë.** Afterword by Arthur Ziegler. (523326—$3.95)

☐ **WUTHERING HEIGHTS by Emily Brontë.** Foreword by Goeffrey Moore.
(523385—$3.95)

☐ **FRANKENSTEIN or THE MODERN PROMETHEUS by Mary Shelley.** Afterword by
Harold Bloom.   (523369—$2.50)

☐ **THE AWAKENING and SELECTED SHORT STORIES by Kath Chopin.** Edited by Barbara Solomon.   (524489 $4.95)

☐ **MIDDLEMARCH by George Eliot.** Afterword by Frank Kermode. (517504—$5.95)

☐ **THE MILL ON THE FLOSS by George Eliot.** Afterword by Morton Berman.
(523962—$5.95)

☐ **SILAS MARNER by George Eliot.** Afterword by Walter Allen. (524276—$2.95)

Prices slightly higher in Canada.

STIRRING CLASSICS

☐ **WUTHERING HEIGHTS by Emily Bronte. With a New Introduction by Susan Fromberg Schaeffer.** Here is the story of a savage, tormented foundling, Heathcliff, who falls wildly in love with Catherine Earnshaw, and of the violence and misery that result from their thwarted longing for each other. Filled with the raw beauty of the moors and an uncanny understanding of the terrible truths about men and women. (523385—$3.95)

☐ **MY ÁNTONIA by Willa Cather. With an Introduction by Sharon O'Brien.** A moving story of a pioneer woman. Willa Cather's lush descriptions of the rolling Nebraska grasslands interweave with the warmly human tale of a woman coming of age in the early days of the century to become an epic tale and a chronicle of America's past. One of those rare, highly-prized works of great literature. (525795—$4.95)

☐ **CHRIST IN CONCRETE by Pietro di Donato.** Vibrant with the rich ethnicity of the city neighborhood, sonorous with a prose that recalls the speaker's Italian origins, and impassioned in its outrage at prejudice and exploitation, this genuine American classic is a powerful social document and a rare, deeply moving human story about the immigrant experience. Throbbing with reality, harsh, beautiful, and uncompromising! (525752—$5.95)

Prices slightly higher in Canada.

Buy them at your local bookstore or use this convenient coupon for ordering.

PENGUIN USA
P.O. Box 999 — Dept. #17109
Bergenfield, New Jersey 07621

Please send me the books I have checked above.
I am enclosing $_____ (please add $2.00 to cover postage and handling). Send check or money order (no cash or C.O.D.'s) or charge by Mastercard or VISA (with a $15.00 minimum). Prices and numbers are subject to change without notice.

Card #_____ Exp. Date _____
Signature_____
Name_____
Address_____
City _____ State _____ Zip Code _____

For faster service when ordering by credit card call **1-800-253-6476**

Allow a minimum of 4-6 weeks for delivery. This offer is subject to change without notice.